HOOLIGAN

Robert A Chesney

Man's inhumanity to man makes countless thousands morn.

Robert Burns

ing1

CHAPTER 1: As Drunk As A Lord

Cold and grey as the gloom beneath the forest oaks a coven of wraiths trudged sap-slowly through a deeply cut and dank bridleway. Breaking ground was a youth who carried a sleeping toddler on his shoulders while two other children well beyond tears clung to his clothing, lolling in exhaustion as they were dragged along. At a too great and lengthening distance to the rear halted Nancy, the family's mother, who carried her new baby. Entering a sudden clearing, Percy found the air agreeably warmer and the day advanced by a full hour over that within the woods; he also found a gibbet on which hung the putrescent remains of a man a woman and two children of perhaps eight or nine years of age. The low-hanging limbs of the adults had been ripped away to the knees by boars or wolves while what remained was alive with maggots and the stench unbearable. He turned urgently, the children protesting unconsciously; intent on ensuring that his mother not witness this bleak manifestation of English Justice. 'Mayhap the poor man had slaughtered a sheep on which his starving family had also fed and thus been found by the wig to be as guilty as he.'

Without a word the youth guided his dear parent into the undergrowth on the unpolluted side of the track where the family persevered until he was certain that the repugnant sight and strangling odour were well behind them.

''Percy''

The unspeakable torment in his mother's voice was an icicle through the lad's heart for it surely meant that his baby sister had died as they had feared she would for Nancy had no milk to give. Lifting his little brothers into a wet but grassed bank he hurried to her to hold and comfort her as best he could. Coaxing that loving soul to where the nippers now slept, he eased the distraught woman down beside them and there she lay, sobbing, till at last exhaustion and misery overcame her and she slept. In the pre-dawn mirage, having ascertained that everyone was deeply asleep he crept away through the horribly cold and dripping undergrowth to find a kindly place where his little sister could rest undisturbed, a place which he would be able to locate even after absences which would likely be measured in years. Thankfully the bush soon relented; abruptly revealing the pastured shoulder of a tall scarp whose impressive elevation looked down upon a broad starlit vista so lovely as to infer a land where injustice, starvation, eviction and misery could not possibly hold sway. Dominating the ribbonlike plateau, a majestic pine, bare of branches to a great height declared itself a headstone without equal. He went sadly to it, pheasants and hares bursting from cover at his approach to tear at his threadbare nerves. With infinite care he chose the very best place; one which offered shade from the hot summer sun and shelter from winter's snow and there he began to dig. With nothing but bits of sticks as tools and his ruined claw-like hands as shovels the task took an age; or so it seemed, for making a grave for your own baby sister is the saddest task, bar none. He lined the poor crib with such buds and leaves as he could find, then of necessity took a moment to rest, deeply moved the while by emerging vistas which he fondly believed would please his elfin sister also. On that broad valley floor beneath him the pale pastel pallet of a dry summer was becoming evident all of the way to the colourless and receding horizon while among the folds, dips and shady places of that discarded plaid an elegance of sika-dear retreated to the safety of the daytime woods, boars rooted conscientiously, and domestic cattle loitered insentient.

'Venison and milk; ana day too late, thank you god you slut.' The exhausted mourner did not have sufficient energy to waste any of it by verbalising the profanity.

'If you're so sodding clever then you knows wot 'I' bloody fink of 'you.'' Humming a familiar tune so as not to terrify his family with his return, he found everyone still asleep, the children foundering on a reef of dreams too cruel for innocence to contend, Nancy's cheeks, pale and damp. Aching to the very marrow of his bones to lie down, to hug the little-ones and to sleep beside them Percy doggedly remained standing, the dangers both animal and human being too great to disregard.

A mansion was now visible ahead; in whose still-dark windows dozens of candles were being lit, each one worth more than a field-hand earned in a month. The thought had his ever-present anger roiling in his empty guts.

''We'll ave yous wun o' these days.'' He muttered. Some filthy, lucky sod appeared at a high window of that arrogant bastion of man's inhumanity to man, and clambering out, descended rapidly with the aid of an invasion of ivy which had somehow vanquished the roof's overhang of thatch and was advancing on a wide front towards the ridge itself.

'With any luck the stuff will smuvver the place and strangle the filth inside.'

Percy was himself strangled; by his need for revenge on that avaricious tribe who claimed ownership the land, the rivers and everything that moved; even rabbits and birds.

A ragged crescent of night sky was lightening imperceptibly beyond the eyes of the windows under their brows of thatch.

"You must 'go,' Mikey," the beauty insisted; her voice in keeping with her body, deeply moved by the events of the night, even as her traitorous hips arched extravagantly in order to assist him in his pretence of a search for treasures whose hiding place he was intimately acquainted with. Ruth Montague's conveniently deaf lover maintained his gently controlling hold of her body, pressing his lips to her perfectly formed abdomen with insincere devotion, and remained there, utterly incommunicative, if not silent, clasping her in his embrace for what seemed to the prisoner to be an eternity and more; deeply pleasurable though it was.

"Mikey, if they wake, I'm ruined." Ruth Montague eldest daughter of the bishop Montague despised herself for adopting a tone with the yet to-be-housebroken fool, but his behaviour was frighteningly unpredictable, and she feared that he might alarm the house just for the sheer madness of it and to the devil with herself and her reputation. Such unthinkable badness amused the rudderless hulk no end. Despite-all however he was a perfect lover and understood her woman's body and her deepest longings with an intuition that was utterly to her adventurous taste in every point and for that, she could forgive him almost anything. That forgiveness fell just short of allowing herself to be discovered, gloriously spread beneath a famous whoremaster. She filled her hands with his over-long hair and was about to remind him painfully of her predicament, when the fool popped up like a genie, recently escaped from the bottle.

"No more Witch. I'm not at stud you know."

"You preposterous child. If only you were gifted so. Go away. 'Now.'" The sated nymph pushed the grinning-idiot source of her bliss from its intimate association with her body.

Deeply wounded by this rebuff, Michael Astor freed himself from his woman's still-reluctant thighs; clambered from her bed and grumbling like a spoiled child dressed himself after a fashion, careful to tread only on those floorboards which would not betray him while the nymph watched his every sinful movement assiduously. He was 'The Boy David,' come to life. Michelangelo's depiction naturally, it was too horrible even to consider Donatello's unnatural offering. Ruth wondered a moment, as she had previously about what the Don was suggesting by such a girly representation of a giant-killer soon to be king. 'She would,' she resolved, 'discover the truth of the matter.'

"I'll see myself out." The remark was predictable, causing her to hate him fleetingly for this corrosive flaw in his otherwise worshipful persona. With his shirt open to the navel while his coat clung by its arms around his waist Astor negotiated the high windowsill with practised technique, contorting his huge frame in order to squeeze through the narrow space. Twixt the heaven within, and hellfire without, he fixed her with a killing stare.

"Tell me you love me, Montague," he demanded; adopting the basso-profundo tone which often accompanied his more outrageous performances, "or I go to meet my maker."

"Oh goodie." Ruth lunged naked from her damp and odoriferous bed and dashing at the rogue attempted to assist him in his avowed intent.

"Go and repent," she laughed. "To the devil with you; you despoiler of virgins." He was too quick for her. His arm was around her, and he held her prisoner.

"Ha, 'virgin,' is it?" You never knew an hour in that condition. You were a halfpenny harlot from day one."

"Swine. Go on Mikey, jump. Lucifer will catch you. I'd wager your life on it."

"Tell me you love me, trollop, or I'm a gonner."

"Satan doesn't want you any more than I do. Jump! Go on; do it!"

"Too cruel." The poor thespian threw himself in to the grey void. In that same instant Ruth's heart faltered; even as her tormentor grabbed the oaken window-frame and saved himself. She had died; only to be instantly reborn. The swine, curse him, was wallowing in her torment. Clasping him to her in an agony of the heart she recovered at the mockery in his brutal laugh and punched him as girls do, a love-pat which he barely felt.

"You stupid boy, I love only Sebastian, your one-eyed friend," she caressed that rigidly attentive gentleman even as she denied her crushing burden of adoration.

"Get thee behind me, public woman," Lord Michael Astor, drunkard, womaniser and wastrel rejoiced in the sublime creature's unquenchable need for him but unable to stay one minute longer he crushed her desperately tightly, kissed her as though wishing to meld into one with her; liberated her and began his descent of the ivy-cloaked rampart. His affectionate farewells accompanying him,

"Floozy… trollop… hussy… jezebel."

Supremely ravaged; ravaged beyond the telling of it, and exhausted; Ruth searched out a dry place in her bed and collapsed into it; recalled the champagne bottle in a paroxysm of near-hysterical fright and snatching-up that magnum of guilt, skipped quickly to the window where she dropped it, aiming for her darling's beautiful head.

"Take your vinegar bottle with you."

Her intended victim cheated death with the panache which he exhibited in all things; took a one-handed catch, blew her a kiss and was gone. Insufficiently drunk, tired-to-death and irked by his expulsion; his 'premature withdrawal,' as he chose to think of it, Astor shambled away through the grounds to find his horse while the very thought of that murderous beast restored much of his habitual good humor. A fresh source of excitement was in the air for Cossack was as fast as a burning borzoi and could leap anything smaller than a cottage. It was a toss-up whether it was best to have a woman or the horse beneath him. In the case of Montague's offspring of course, the girl won hands-down, she rutted with a maddening need, swam into paradise in a torrent of her own manufacture and glory of glories, was not acquainted with the word 'no,' or of beastly inhibition; best of all she actually understood when she was not ovulating and would urge him to take that most exquisite of liberties with her which of course he had been well-pleased to do. Often. Clearly, not-so the voluptuous Lady Montague herself, whom he just 'had to boff,' one of these fine days; that scrumptious tart must also have jumped a fence or two in her time because there was no way in hell that the malodorous orangutan of a Bishop could have fathered such a girl as Ruth. His lordship considered dropping that thought into impolite conversation one of these fine days. He could hear it now, 'Ruth Montague? Do I 'know,' her? Doesn't everyone? Have you ever wondered whom the father might be?' What a hoot that would be.' To keep his boots from the muck of a cabbage patch, he was dawdling along by a stone wall through margins of long, wet grass bound together in sheaths of silvered webs when he was wrenched from his reverie by the presentiment that he was not alone. Looking up sharply, he discovered that he shared the paddock with a dozen or so individuals of the 'smelly peasant,' species, many of them dressed almost as well as scarecrows, leaning on agricultural implements, and staring at himself; a lord of the land, in the rudest fashion imaginable and neither a doffed-hat, tug of forelock nor a 'by your leave,' between them. They were Montague's clodhoppers obviously, whom it would seem, had arrived only moments earlier for the express purpose of 'leaning on agricultural implements.'

"Mornin' yur majity, sor." It was the nearest of the thicket, an ancient, mucky old stick who was the proprietor of a tooth. Quite properly the relic tried for a bow but crumpled into the dirt mid-genuflection. Scrambling hurriedly to his feet; 'an age-long process,' 'Tusker,' then took to pointing with the grace of a weathervane towards the cops where Cossack was tethered; much to the annoyance of his tribe.

''E can see the bloody thing you old fool.''

''You'll be suckin is dick next?''

Feeling enormously virtuous due to his own forbearance Astor nodded his condescension as he passed. 'How drunk would one have to be,' he mused, 'to forget where one had tethered a fucking great horse?'

"A man e would a-wooin gew." The voice was male, tuneless and obviously speaking a second language; christ all bleeding mighty he had known dirty bloody blacks who could better articulate the mother-tongue. Mockery! He, a lord of this land was being mocked! Mocked by an unwashed, *maggot-minded surf; one disenchanted with living obviously. The malcontent, soon to be a 'dead malcontent,' was posturing like a drab cockerel before his fellow shit-kickers, amusing them greatly at the expense of himself, 'Lord Michael Astor,' of all people, an expert with all manner of weapons, a formidable swordsman, marksman, and pugilist. The filthy little weasel didn't have a clue what it was dealing with. In one slick move Astor smashed the all-but-empty magnum against the wall and hurled the remnants with gratifying accuracy at the druid's Easter Island face. With infuriating composure, the irritant considered the missile's flight in the manner of a veteran infantryman, stepping neatly aside a mere breath before catching it in his teeth; thereby condemning to death the grisly creature who stood behind him, a shapeless mustachioed old mare whose empty dugs hung down to her bellies. *Omar Khyyam Rubayiat

''She even flings loik a gurrul.'' The self-satisfied impresario was oblivious even to the ogre's agonised hysterics as her lifeblood gushed from her throat through the neck and shoulders of the magnum. What joy it was to see her 'decant and serve' her red wine all at once. The fast-emptying carcass crumpled slowly to the ground as though sitting down intentionally in the dirt while the hoi polloi crowded helplessly around in a welter of futility, all grunting at once, like pigs at a trough.

'Voyeurs the lot of them.' His lordship continued in his line of march, consumed by rage but ill-prepared to sacrifice his dignity through labouring around in the filth teaching new tricks to dogs. A criminally ugly sow with a piglet slobbering at its distended udders slumped against the wall adjacent to a hand barrow in which Astor then discovered to his enormous gratification, the enemy's provisions. 'There was a god after all.' Three huge earthenware jugs of their gut-rot, apples, loaves, lumps of cheese and a kettle of recently regurgitated puke; all of it even more enticing than syphilis.

Without so much as a ''by your leave,'' the sow had the gall, 'the utter gall,' to address him! Jabbering some unintelligible rubbish at himself, and loudly too, by which affront Astor was forced to conclude that every straw-sucker in the land had 'taken of the insane root' and the world was now standing on its arse. Ignoring the hideous beast imperiously he halted; as did the singing, the thing's infernal yakking, the expressions of concern for the injured moustaches, and even she quit gargling as though in sympathy with the rest. Choosing his moment with care he bent over his find; paused for dramatic effect, then straightened to face the enemy with a jug in each extended arm. The herd lowed. Exhibiting the perfect timing of a well-rehearsed thespian full to the brim with malice, he smashed the things together in a glorious shower of golden liquid and shards of pottery. The tang of the stuff, instantly rank in his cultured olfactory organ

''We was in jest only.'' Above the predictable cacophony of dismay, wailing and cursing there were unbelievably, threats. Threats directly against his person from the

ing9

composer and soloist who could be identified signing away his life in his uncontrollable rage.

But! The sneaky sow had meanwhile scrambled to her feet and was making off with her piglet and the surviving jug. Grabbing a handful of the mewling runt Astor squeezed the thing, hard; giving it something to squeal 'about,' causing the sow to capitulate instantly and drop the piss as he knew she would. With clods of dirt, stones and strangely, a wimble-knife now being hurled at him, 'hanging offences all,' some of them finding their mark and painfully at that, he snatched-up the last of their falling-down water and hurled it against the wall to spectacular effect.

Delighted with the success of his offensive he then drove-home his gains by upturning the barrow and at the expense of his footwear stamping every lump of their vomitous mealies into the sticky paspalum, exaggerating his action for theatrical effect and mocking his tormentors with a beatific smile,

''As am I.'' He chortled. ''As am I.'' The peasantries' aim was improving. Certain elements of their grapeshot now struck him with such stinging force that he was very much tempted to resort to gunfire or swordplay but damn it all, such as these were mere flies landing on his skin; he had done himself more insult shaving, so laughing not at them but at what he was going to have done to them, to their families, to their friends and to their so-called homes, he goaded them for a while, side-stepping their artillery with arms akimbo. Insurrection was on the rise across the land and he, Lord Michael Astor would have none of it. On behalf of his class, he would play his part by ridding the mother country of this nest of filthy ingrates. 'Every last one of them.'

His army of bush-bashing slaves in Jamaica would have the best of times with this lot; 'the swine will think that they've been fucked by a herd of elephants, it would be better to die, 'broken on the wheel.' His lordship departed the field of battle, bloodied and sore; victorious and vengeful.

''God all sodding mighty,'' Yet another of the stinkers was messing with Cossack. As he drew closer to the scruffy bitch he sucked-in breath like a bellows and was on the very cusp of bawling at her to remove her diseased self from contiguity with his horse and empty her thieving sack too when she turned and looked straight into his eyes; even having the temerity to hold his gaze though he closed on her as would a grizzly on an injured deer.

It was not possible for a woman to be as beautiful; as perfect, as she. Astor's exalted self was instantly effaced. He was deflated, estranged from everything that he was or had ever been. Her perfection traduced him; rebirthed him as a naked, superstitious aboriginal who had crept timidly into the womb-house intent on being at-one with his god, only then to realise the utter futility of such an errand, acknowledging that the highest state that man can achieve lies merely in loving a woman.

His soul lay in rubble at her feet. Looking at her made his eyes bleed. He must have her. Own her. Be loved by her. Keep her from every other man alive. He was utterly consumed, defeated, enfiladed and enslaved by her glance.

No sooner had the delightful landscape of Astor's carefree world been drenched in this sewer of filthy adoration for something so transient, ephemeral even, worthless at bottom and ultimately indefinable; than masculine arrogance, savage and battle-scarred, came galloping to his rescue aboard an ugly piebald, the bit between its teeth, foaming and sweat-soaked, a head like a hammer and the gait of a camel. Girding his loins, he cursed himself foully for entertaining such maudlin thoughts; fabrications utterly inimical to those of which the fortress of his ego was constructed. Not for him endless weeks spent with just one woman with all of that bowing to her will; castrated by her cursed 'feelings' and flayed by her limitless damned 'emotions.'

He emerged in high dudgeon from the breathless nightmare, eagerly adopting his well-polished seduction persona which of course was second nature to him. He would enslave this one as he had the legions who preceded her, which was to say, until she bored him and when that moment arrived, he would get rid. The world was chocca with women and it was his certified moral duty to do every last one of them.

> 'Was the hope drunk
>
> In which you dressed yourself.'

'Aphrodite she was. But in rags?' It was intolerable to him that perfection should be so demeaned. Part of Lord Michael Astor searched assiduously for the guilty party in this insult to the numinous. The symphony's coverings had obviously been handed-down via several of her older brothers being largely male and fitting only where they touched; she sported a hob-nailed coal-barge on each foot and a coat large enough for herself and several of her afore-mentioned relatives.

"Goo-mornin' sor. Them meant no 'arm, Oi'm sure. Just a bit o' a lark. Were it you as urt that'un?" Heaven's favourite contrived to admonish him, seemingly unaware of the social chasm which lay bottomless and wide between them. Indeed, her manner; incredibly, exhibited no deference whatsoever, and almost implied that he and she were equals and good friends into the bargain. 'What the fuck happened to 'obsequious?' He weighed the contesting forces of 'rape,' and 'seduction,' in the balance.

''Wot's wrong wi er then?'' the nubile insisted, irritating him with her persistence and casting her concerned yet worshipful glance in the direction of the dying bawd.

''Too much of the bottle I'll be bound,'' He snorted, well pleased with his own wit while making his voice deep and caring as befits matters of seduction. His traitorous bloody Arab meanwhile ignored his master roundly and nuzzled its new favourite's oh-so-perfect cheek.

'''E' is bootful sor,'' the girl drooled, fondling the turncoat's slobbering face. ''Wot's is name?'' Her ingenuous state and innocence of her own desirability was so complete that his lust, so recently reined-in had returned in full force. Had she been his own, rather than Montague's he would have shagged her on the spot. 'Actually, if he said true; he didn't care a tinker's toss that she was not his own property; he simply couldn't stuff her with half of the county's ditch-diggers looking on.'

"I call him Co… I call him Condor," he lied, in what was now pointless obfuscation.

"Ca-an-door," the Nilotic princess repeated, drawing out the word to a full octave in length in the most seductive accent that ever entered the ears of man.

"Wot be wun o they then, sor?" Michael tightened the cinch and climbed, erect, into the swimming saddle. With a glance at the child's loathsome associates and wondering which; if any of them was the husband, he leaned right down to boot-top level and kissed her cheek, 'gentle and lingering,' in imitation of Cossack while taking great care to allow his moustaches to caress the pink petals of those full, slightly parted lips.

"It is a great bird," he whispered, taking-in all-of-her at once, "which flies to wherever the darling is more beautiful than the rose in her hair."

The huge and splendidly clear, green-flecked eyes flew wide,

"Oh sir," she breathed, opening like a dawn rose before his less-than-oblique advances. Her teeth were clean, white and even. If ever a wench was born to be kissed, it was she. To his lordship's great satisfaction, one of the tenors had stepped forward with an oath, only to be quickly restrained by what, 'judging by their girth,' had to be the bass section. 'So, that was how the wind blew.' Precarious in the saddle he leaned yet further, threw an arm around the nubile's slender form and lifting her from the ground to hold her against his chest assaulted her most intimate self with his hand under the ragged skirt, kissing her long and passionately as her body quivered in his arms like that of a captured songbird. To his deep satisfaction the lass returned his kiss with a fervour that astounded him; even going so far as to throw a wonderfully well-turned limb over the horse and settle astride his thighs in order to aid him in his ministrations.

When the hero of the hour released the child, recently returned from an unrestrained paradise which must have woken half of the county he told her gently,

"Auf wiedersehen liefling, I will find you again soon or die of a broken heart."

''A man must fust ave a eart for a gel to breck.'' Was the pleasingly breathless and unexpectedly tangential response. Astor urged Cossack homeward singing loudly.

"A man e would a-wooin gew." It was with intense satisfaction that he located the much put-out hopeful, who was now stamping off towards the other end of the paddock smashing his pet rake repeatedly into the dirt. Accordingly, the victor selected a fresh target for his parting volley by addressing the choir.

"Come on you dogs," he bellowed, "where's your fucking chorus now?"

Regaining the homeward bridleway, he discovered that his conquest had not moved; the 'wild rose,' was watching him still, with an expression in which conflicting emotions were evident. He knew with certainty, then and there, that if he crooked a finger, that beauty would run to him through fire. He waved farewell to her and just for the fun of it waved to the great-unwashed also; pleased as could be when they turned their seething, impotent backs on him.

The temptation to take that utterly divine child home to The Granary and pound her insensible persisted, 'those eyes that mouth.' He wondered in parting what her body was like beneath those rags. She would have to be soaked in hot-soapy water for a week or two and then in champers for a further week naturally; one could grow potatoes between the toes of these people. Touching Cossack with the spurs he promised himself; 'Soon but not now,' he was utterly shagged-out and his wedding-tackle was hors-de-combat.

On so foul and fair a morning, drunk and all but finished, Astor was content to let Cossack find his own way home along the lanes; he had a girl and a kiss to dream about. A girl with a rose in her hair, a kiss that was softer than summer and eyes in which drowning would be bliss. Soon, the sun came up, warming him, he began to doze, then slept. Initially, Astor's dreams that morning were very pleasant, providing him a brief respite from the rigours and responsibilities of his arduous life, his atrocious memories, and unsolicited imaginings.

A cottager gave voice to her release.

"Good on yer our Enry." Applauded a fieldhand who was passing-by beneath the eves of the lady's house.

"Filthy lucky bitch." The man's wife traduced her uncomprehending dolt of a husband with both tone and glance. Doors were flung open and slammed shut as people rushed to and from the bushes at the end of their gardens. Thin grey twists of smoke issued from cold cottage chimneys and hooves echoed reassuringly between the walls as ploughmen and their teams returned home in order to break their fast having been in the field since four; dogs stretched extravagantly yawning loudly and cocks crowed in annoyance at the usurpers.

 Within a confusion of elderberry that crouched in a seldom-frequented corner of the lane, Coward luxuriated in idleness. He and several others had been hired to search for and capture a dangerous one-eyed criminal who went by the name of Hooligan, but Coward had no intention of searching for any bastard, because success would hurl him back on to the starving road. Thusly he was being paid to idle-away the day. The sly outcast approved wholeheartedly of this searching game because it was nothing whatsoever to do with barrows, shovels, scythes and hard labour and his ardent hope was that should the murderous Hooligan ever 'be' captured, He Coward would be nowhere in the vicinity of those doings. The Irishman's propensity for violence being common knowledge.

Beyond the adjacent garden-wall a pretty woman dashed to the bushes gathered her skirt and squatted to pee. Breaking cover he announced with an arrogant 'hail fellow well met,' tone,

"Oi fawt oi recinised yer smile gel. You aint got that one-eyed Irish prick up there ave yer?" Shocked and deeply offended, the maid dropped her skirt, calling urgently to her husband.

"Henry? Quick."

Coward's bombast deflated instantly, an experience with which he was well acquainted when "Henry," emerged from his cottage in the manner of the main attraction at a bear baiting. Taking in the situation instantly, the outraged husband went for the tramp at the double march.

"That-un reckons eel foind a Irishman up my skirt."

"What he'll find is my fist down his throat."

In unalloyed terror Coward fled; at the very edge of panic when on looking back he saw 'Henry the hairy horror' vault the wall. Out of sight of his pursuer for a moment he seized his opportunity and dashed into a chicken house, breathing hard and peeking through the slats in a sweat of foul-tasting fear while praying for deliverance to a non-existent deity. Rickets, an imbecilic member of the gang, presently searching a nearby pigpen, watched these proceedings with huge satisfaction because he loathed Coward who bullied him mercilessly.

"Not so bloody ard 'now' is we?" he shouted, but not sufficiently loudly for Coward to hear him. At this point the cretin dropped his apple in pig muck, bent quickly to retrieve it and in so doing smashed his face excruciatingly into the top of a fencepost. Collapsing within reach of his apple and similarly besmirched he lay moaning in great distress, eventually coming to his senses due to a cockerel perching on his head and piercing his scalp agonisingly in a dozen places. Poor Rickets then discovered a one-eyed giant corpse partially submerged in the lake of stinking slurry which oozed beneath the fence.

"It's 'im. It's bloody ooligan." The terrified frail leapt to his feet and dashed-away several paces before daringly returning to retrieve his apple and dashing-away again.

"It's 'im. It's 'im," the fugitive croaked, repeating this apparent declaration of the second coming until the others turned up, bludgeons at the ready and hopeful of the chance to thrash Hooligan senseless in a four against one contest from which they would emerge unscathed. Coward watched-on, still trying to summon-up the courage to abandon his hiding place when a soft, pink hand entered the hutch through a flap; selected an egg and withdrew. This operation was repeated a second or two later. Coward dashed to the little access, ripped down his draws and thrust his groin into the space.

"Aagh! Ooh you filfy. I'll get my usbin onto yoo." The elephantine owner of the soft hands trundled away, her obesity swaying uncontrolled from side to side; paused thoughtfully; then returned with hope and no small quantity of excitement in her expression.

"Gareth it's you intit. You bad boy." she whispered. "Oim marrid now." The hand crept in again, found Coward's now very hard erection and soon broke for him his ages-long drought, surprising the lady with his alacrity.

"Gord that were quick Gasa, you've come all over me 'ands."

"They's a broffel in Brisle."

His helpful suggestions were drowned by the lady's scream.

"You filfy! You wait!"

"Us'n could make fortunes wiv 'ands loik…"

"I'll ave my usbin on tu you. Horatio, Horatio. Come quick. I'm   ad a uge dick shoved in me…." At this unfortunate juncture the full-figured woman's breath betrayed her; enabling Coward to make what was almost an intelligent and even humorous repost.

''That's a bloody lie.'' He snorted, all indignation, a state of mind of which he knew precious little.

''Ands,'' the princess concluded.

Peering through the flap, Coward's vision was seared by the impossible corpulence of the wanton and now irate woman whose manner of perambulation was not unlike that of an elephant seal assaulting a steep beach of pebbles. His enjoyment of this abomination was multiplied ten-fold when the vaunted Horatio appeared. The pathetic, scared and unwilling fellow had less fat on him than a boiled egg. He resembled a cadaver recently succumbed to starvation. Coward 'fled the coup,' concerned that he had been in hiding too long and that his employer, the hated and feared Macbeth and the three idiots would by now be well on their way to the killing-ground dragging Hooligan with them. Such a contingency could cost him his day's pay, to say nothing of missing the chance to carve-up the swine. 'Ears, nose, tongue; Coward really enjoyed that part of the job.

The exhausted, shivering and painfully hungry Percy considered his several options as the sleeping toff approached, but as each of those bloody paths led directly to the gallows, he resolved instead to play the Good Samaritan and see what advantage came of it. Torn by leaving his family either defenceless or starving or both, he got to his feet and went stiff-legged and with all manner of hurt to meet the magnificent horse which never faltered in its regal progress. Breathless as he eased the reins from the rider's fingers, he noticed a cowardly little pistol in a sleeve. With infinite care he activated the spring-mechanism which held the weapon at the ready and caught it without waking its owner who strangely enough bled a bit here and there. He breathed again and walked away beside the animal with many a backward glance. The tall horse gave the gallows of earlier that morning a wide berth, rolling its eyes and shivering at the spectacle and its stink as they passed by, but otherwise retained its composure. When approaching an innocuous humpback bridge however just a field or two further on it flung its great head around and pawed at the ground, refusing to advance so much as another step even though the rider berated it in his sleep. Percy released the reins and mounted the steep little incline, his complacency evaporating at the instant in which he discovered the robber lying in the track on the reverse. The filth got clumsily to its feet, dropping and retrieving its weapon, and approached him in the clumsiest manner imaginable. She was fifty if she was a minute, awkward, slow, clumsy and well-passed such work. Percy raised his pistol straight-armed and pointed the thing at the blue scars between the cataract-dimmed eyes.

''I'll do it.'' He assured her, calm as the dead.

''Tosser.'' the frustrated murderer retreated sufficiently to deposit her fat arse on the low parapet while Percy, returning to his work, gathered up the reins and led horse and rider safely passed the threat. When, a minute later he checked his rear; the slut was once again lying-in-ambush on the track.

''I've no need of a wetnurse whatsoever, so hand me that pistol and fuck off.'' Michael Astor had already encountered a sufficiency of the hoi-polloi for one day and was in no mood to mince words with another.

''Fanks,' woo'nt urt.'' Percy was in full control of the unfolding events.

''I'll give you 'fanks,' if I dismount; now hand me my reins and that piece; I'm sick to death of you already. 'And' your delicate perfume.''

''Youd'a bin 'acked' ta def if it wunt fer me.'' In his counterfeit anger Percy glanced back significantly at the bridge, causing the 'perfumed prick' to twist in the saddle.

''Well, I'll be a donkey's dick, that 'is' a 'woman.' isn't it?''

''Used to be. Pit gell. Em gose down a woman but them comes-up men. Tha'sa adze wot she've got there. It digs lumps outa oak.'' Astor was not impressed. The thought of catching such a weapon with his face was not a pleasant one. With the early sun now pleasantly warm on him, glorious mischief in the air and a target for his pent-up anger presenting itself wonderfully well, he chose not to restrain his lordly impetuosity.

"It would seem that I am indebted to you boy. What will be your reward? My arse is out of the question."

"Don't get yer opes up.   Grub.   Wee's starvin. Me mam an' the nippers. Gie us some bleedin grub." How vile those words; how sickening this capitulation.

The owner of everything and everyone for miles around, considered the stunted, round-shouldered, sunken-chested little lump of filth intently. It was composed of one part 'survival at any cost,' one part 'animal cunning' and one part 'iron-hard resolve.' He liked it enormously. It would have taken rare qualities and balls the size of mangos for a mere stripling to embark on this adventure with no guarantee of reward and every chance of coming to grief.

"I am Michael Astor, Lord Michael Astor actually, of The Granary."

"King Percy. Shit Street acchully." The youth proffered a filthy, ruined hand which the rider ignored pointedly while resisting the urge to thrash its insolence with the crop.

"Tell me King Percy." Astor was glowering at his would-be nemesis.

"Were you in my employ at this very moment; what would you advise?" In the knowledge acquired by long acquaintance with scum of all sorts Percy handed-back the reins, checked the loading of the pistol and pausing sufficiently to divine the big bastard's commitment to his veiled invitation to do murder and judging him ardent, trudged away, swaying in exhaustion, heart labouring, toward the bridge and its stinking occupant.

"Ha! Kicked yer scrawny little arse outonit dinte?" The gallows-bait clambered to her feet as Percy approached.

"I'll ave them boots. Gerrum off." Utterly contemptuous of her, Percy limped straight through the loathsome slut only to be grabbed predictably by the hair as the adze was flung upwards. Smashing his weapon into the pox-blistered mouth Percy squeezed the trigger and heard the hammer's empty boast.

. Recovering instantly, he 'nutted,' her; hurling his forehead into her hate-riven features with every drop of energy left in him, revelling in the crushing impact and the destruction of her ugly beak. She dropped all but unconscious like a sack of shit to the sets, blood and filth mixing in the sunken pits of her almost blind eyes.

Dragging the impossibly heavy carcass into the cover of the long weeds, a task which all but finished him, Percy made sure that the crim on the horse was watching, rolled the thing onto its back so that she could see what was coming and drove the adze into her screaming gob. Getting the blade out of there was a task for a smith; the thing had wedged-tight in the bones. Blood sprayed into the air, blinding him as he caught it in the throat on the second blow even as he shoved his boot into its now separated jaw to stop it cawing so fucking loudly. There were people only a field away and guilt rides a fast horse in hell. Wearing the colours of his trade and with a hay-wain approaching through ten acres of stubble Percy the murderer negotiated the treacherous streambank clinging for safety to the rough stonework of the arch and submerged himself; his tears seeming to pollute every drop of the veritable oceans that had flowed beneath that bridge.

"Well-played your majesty," Astor enthused, accepting the wet and bloody pistol. "You have a certain style about your, 'execution,' shall we say." His gratified Lordship exchanged a few coins; one of them gold, and a silver button which he had cut from his coat, for the faulty weapon which he fiddled with irritably.

"Get yourself some lodging and report to Hastings at The Granary. The tradesman's gates. Give him that button. The house is on the Great South Road. Over there. If you keep your nose clean and obey, in all things, no matter what; you need never go hungry again." Percy was not listening; he was polishing the gold piece.

"Gord luvs you marster." He lied.

"Now you're pushing shit uphill with a warm fork," observed the much-mollified

Astor.

"Go on damn you. Cast off."

CHAPTER 2: Ignorance Is Not Bliss

Deep in the forest, the killing-ground sweltered in the midday heat, loud with a cacophony of insects and birds. The stocks and pillories were bloodstained but empty. Hanging from the scaffold was a shapeless lump of something which might once have been human wearing a coat of iridescent blue which it flung off occasionally only to put it back on moments later.

The tartan individual who rode into this tribute to the character of English law was unmistakeably a soldier to his marrow. His hugely arrogant posture in the saddle was upright, his glance direct and his manner belligerent. Indeed, his acquaintances knew this man to be the living embodiment of his clan's motto. "Nemo me impune lacessit. No man provokes me without consequences."

The warlike creature was inordinately hairy; his black locks hung to his shoulders while little of his face could be seen due to briar of a beard which had ever looked askance at shears. Close cousins of the facial growth escaped at both the neck and cuffs of his shirt of brilliant white, while the ambitious bind-stems had overrun the backs of his hands and established outposts on each of his broken knuckles.

Stumbling at the end of a rope in the rear of this soldier of fortune, came a creature who may well have been of another species; one composed of deprivation, hunger, a love of the bottle, homelessness, ignorance and violence. From his plastered-down hair to his brimming boots he dripped liquid pig shit while his limping gate and limited use of his limbs proclaimed that he had been beaten mercilessly. Such of the prisoner's wounds as were visible would have put an end to many a lesser soul or robbed him of spirit; but this individual was not reduced by all that he had suffered. The man oozed malevolence.

The horse which had dragged him by the neck since dawn, halted. The rope dropped to the ground and Lliam Shaun Hooligan hobbled into shade where he collapsed in the weeds, gasping in the pain that resulted. Worse by far than the Irishman's desperate wounds was his thirst. Even when ordered by the horseman to give him water the bastards had denied him that fundamental decency. As he lost consciousness, he glimpsed the scaffold and his worst fears for what they had in store for him were confirmed.

The rider turned on the two hirelings who had managed to keep pace with his horse.

''Savage,'' he snarled. ''Where's that bloody drunken fool, Rickets? If that man is as good as ye could find, ye didnae look tae hard. He's nae guid tae me, so get rid o' the bastart. Hang the wee swine. Do it the minute ye lay eyes on him. I'll nae be telling ye agen. I want tae see him up there when I get back.'' The Scot indicated the scaffold with a dip of his bison head.

Savage, from whose aquiline nose and wet mouth blood still occasionally dribbled in bright crimson, peered back down the lane hoping to catch sight of the two men missing in action but only one could be seen; in the far distance Coward was stumbling about in the dust.

"He be along thoon, Mithta Macbeth." Savage was incomprehensible due to the injuries which Hooligan had inflicted on him.

"Get rid o im. Today! Pairmanently! He's nae bloody good tae me."

''Yethor.'' The ruffian acquiesced hurriedly as he wilted under the mountain's crushing belligerence; his pride expunged his masculinity reduced to a trail of slime.

''I'll be back in a couple of hours.'' The rider's departure was concealed by a cloud of floury dust. Exhausted by the march infantry eased their insulted bodies to the ground in solid shade; well away from the stinking Irishman and made gestures of a perverted nature at their employer's receding back. Two became three when they were joined in silent misery by the exhausted Coward.

"Wather, ya bathds!''

"Pith off."

''Die, fuck you.''

Savage tugged open his waistcoat and considered the aching purple bruise in the centre of his chest.

"My turn'll come you slug." Hooligan dry-reached noisily   .

"I 'ope for his thake that Wickets duth a wunna… I' aint lookin' forwud to doin' im in," claimed Lawless.

''Bollox; you can't wait,'' Savage did not like Lawless.

The desperately ill Lliam Shaun Hooligan of the County Mayo Hooligans escaped nightmare only to find himself in Hell. He had been woken by the unmistakeable sounds of frantic combat. Struggling up on to an elbow he could see that the herd of swine who had thrashed him were fighting at the base of the gallows. Three of them were trying to hang another. A rope was thrown. Vicious kicking, biting and gouging. The rope coming up tight; the vermin hauled up on his toes and strangling. Dangling by his neck and twitching, toes scrabbling at the ground. Squealing like a sow with its throat slit, Rickets grabbed hold of the rope above his head and gasped one last time before his strength deserted him. All three of the bastards now pulling on the rope but unable to lift the little sod clear of the deck because the fools had it over a square beam. One of them darting in and heaving the bastard off the ground.

 Purple face, huge swollen tongue protruding. Writhing. Flailing.

Hooligan crossed himself in the abstract, going gently into the darkness.

When murderous, wuthering, consciousness once again imposed its unwelcome presence on his thirst-tortured remains he was being imprisoned in a pillory. Blood had scabbed painfully inside his single eye, blinding him.

''Wader! Fug you.'

''What were that? I din catch it. Is it watter yu want?'' Coward cupped his hand to his ear to the amusement of the others. Turning sour quicker than a saucer of milk in the sun the sadist kicked Hooligan's legs away so that the prisoner hung terrifyingly by his neck as he struggled to get his feet back under him. His audience laughed without mirth. Coward emptied the dregs his canteen into the dust at Hooligan's feet, his rancid breath revolting even to a dying man.

''You're going to die. Takes a day or two useally. Me on the uvver 'and. I'm orff to the rivu for a long cold drink and a cool cool swim,''

''Wodder.''

Coward punched Hooligan hard in the face in farewell and the three unnatural creatures shambled away sniggering in a futility of male bonding. Single-file, well-spaced and predatory they headed for the wide body of water which flowed passed within sight of the furniture-of-attitude-adjustment. Shunning such animal tracks as there were and staying deep in the undergrowth, they soon came across a clearing so close to the river that the surrounding trees rippled with dappled light, salt on the breeze. A caravan, green and pretty stood beneath an oak, washing decorated bushes and tethered goats had cropped the grass down to the dirt. Horses stood around disinterested. Breathless with lethal intent, they waited. Soon bored, and about to rush the place they heard a brief call in the distance. The voice was young, the sound truncated. Intuitively, in the manner of a pack of wild dogs they hurried towards that sound, initially as an arrowhead; in the reverse when closing on the prey. A gypo and his woman sat in the riverside sand eating meat which they were roasting over a driftwood fire. Indecipherable speech and the tantalizing aroma of food carried freely to where three syphilitic minds convulsed and seethed. The loving couple knew nothing of Coward's approach until the gypsy's blood spewed from his throat to hiss and steam in the fire. In that same instant, the horrified woman, who was lighting her pipe with a flaming brand rammed the scarlet point deeply into the murderer's eye. Screaming like a hare torn by hounds, and clutching at his face, Coward fell forward into the blaze, a fireiron emerging through his upper back, flesh and cloth decorating its intricate extrusions. He screamed again. And again. Drenched in her lover's blood the woman was on the murderer with catlike agility and was driving Coward's own blade into his head when she was rendered senseless by the enthusiastic swing of a club. Dropping the bludgeon, Savage fell on the raven-haired beauty and throwing up her skirt he drove himself painfully in to her, almost tearing his dick in his determination to make ejaculation a part of his revenge on bitches everywhere and cursing the slut for his pain.

"C'mon. Urry it up. I wants my go fuck you," Lawless clutched his erection; hopping from one foot to the other in his urgency. Regaining an element of consciousness, the tormented woman ripped at the eyes of the wild beast that was rutting in her, cursing it to hell and biting at any part of it within reach. Savage shuddered, moaning loudly and was dragged violently off his victim by Lawless who was on the woman in an instant, punching her viciously and forcing himself into her but ejaculating too soon.

"Fuckin twat." He drew his blade deeply through the beauty's flawless throat wallowing in the fountain of her blood and laughing so hard that he almost choked on it.

"You prick. We coulda ad anuver go."

"You   still   can." Lawless was convulsed with breathless joy.

"Ony this time   she won't   gi you a bloody   good iding." He could barely hear himself speak because of the noisy bitch gasping and choking. Grabbing a handful of her hair he stuffed her gob with sand. That put an end to her moaning, but not her convulsions. The stupid cow looked like she was fucking fresh air. Shambling to the water, stuffing the last of the gypo's too-hot delicious meat into his mouth and cursing the roasting-alive Coward for a 'noisy prick,' as he went Lawless waded hip-deep into the river's welcome chill, toppled forward contentedly and submerged.

Moments later he surfaced and less incarnadine peered out happily across the wide sunlight-planished surface of the water.

"Well now, wot ave we got ere ven?"

A stone's-throw further out in the river, a girl-child trod water.

Lord Fotheringhay, Earl of Dorset, Order of the Garter, Kings Councillor, abolitionist and owner of vast swathes of southern England and the population thereof was today attired in silk of French-Marine with startlingly white lace at cuffs and collar, tall black riding boots and a wide-brimmed hat adorned with ostrich feathers. His sartorial splendour was complimented by black-leather gloves and a crop, heavy with silver. A jovial score or so of the nobility still bubbling with the excitement of discovering 'a massacre of all things' rode in a drug and alcohol induced stupor at the rear while by the great-one's right-hand rode Macbeth whose very posture proclaimed a deep unhappiness if not poorly concealed disgust. Returning with his employer to the killing ground, this outing of powdered and painted misanthropes had been deeply insulting to the murdered gypsy family to a degree that had turned his stomach. In his mind these spineless dogs were on apar morally with the diseased creatures responsible for the rape and slaughter.

"I can freely understand a man wishing to boff one of those gypsy tarts," Fotheringhay was saying, "all that smooth, brown skin and pitch-black hair, but why slit her throat when one's done with her? It's beyond me." Macbeth was not listening; he looked back with loathing at Coward's now-distant form; more than content to leave the bleating swine to cook; his urgent concern was Hooligan's present condition. It had taken him a month to capture the man and now the signs were that the Irishman no longer needed to be guarded. Infuriated, he touched his horse with the spurs causing the half-wild creature to drop on its haunches and go off at the charge.

"Is he awive? With the Scot-bastard and the big-wig Fotheringhay likely to turn up at any moment, Savage was all-concern for Hooligan's wellbeing. Lawless listened intently for any evidence of life with his ear to the Irishman's open mouth.

"If e aint I'm doin a runna."

"Calm down, fuck you, this bastard ain't killable. We best get im outa ere though.

Between them Satan's acolytes heaved upwards the beam of the pillory allowing the receptacle of suffering to collapse amusingly face-first to the baked-hard ground. About to give him water and thereby save themselves both shuddered, galvanized with fear by the murderous timpani of a galloping charger. Macbeth was back.

It was too late to desert; the tartan fury emerged from the forest at a full gallop his furious blood-congealing battle cry seizing them. Shaping to run for their lives the criminals collided face to face and collapsed on top of the Irishman. Dragging his horse to a halt the warrior leapt from the saddle at the run and kicked Savage in the groin with every ounce of venom in his giant frame. Hoist momentarily clear of the ground by the impact the agonised victim collapsed, vomiting in excruciating pain. Lawless meanwhile had run for the woods. Having lost his already tenuous grasp on those mores, norms and customs which govern human behaviour the crazed warrior dashed to his horse, freed his war-axe and balling at his newly arrived infantry to,

"Get the fuck out of ma way," hurled the weapon of twin crescent blades at the fast-receding back which is cowardice.

The strike was a thing of rare beauty. At incredible speed the weapon's glittering perfection scribed a barely perceptible parabolic arc. Rotating only twice, the harbinger of death settled blades-foremost at the apex of its flight and in the fascinated hush which followed, closed the remaining distance javelin-like smashing into the fugitive's spine to the accompaniment of a mass expulsion of breath from the hypnotized lordlings. Charging in pursuit of his axe even as it flew, the crazed clansman was on the broken vermin in an instant, hacking, slashing and stabbing through its clothing until he was certain that he had separated it from its manhood. At which point he paused, breathless, his need for justice merely whetted.

Savage who witnessed this frenzy of violence in unsupportable agony and horror now knew what was about to happen to himself. His tortured ejaculations were supplanted by the bleating of abject terror.

Having regained a modicum of self-control due to the small pleasures in which he had so recently indulged Macbeth now operated in a more considered fashion, carving away methodically at the noisy misanthrope's private parts but dissatisfied with a sentence of such leniency he blinded it, removed its ears, its nose and its lips and at last in an inspired moment its scalp.

Content with his work and in blatant defiance of his employer's orders to 'silence the swine,' he then left his victims to caw and hurried to comfort his horse; the poor creature being much unsettled by the stink of blood.

''Into the shade with him. 'Now,' damn your eyes. Water. Water, water.'' The signs were that Fotheringhay was about to exorcise his frustrations on some poor sod of an infantryman chosen at random so gasping for breath the sweat-soaked ruffians set to work energetically while 'little-boy-blue,' lashed out with his stick at the nearest of their number, eager as any martyr is for paradise to acquaint himself with a soon-to-be convert to the abolitionist cause.

"Ye gods and little fishes, but he's a big lad. Look at the size of that head; not unlike my left testicle, eh, eh what do you say? Come here Macbeth?" Fotheringhay was ebullient.

"Orter," croaked Hooligan. Someone kicked him in the ribs and breathed gin into his face. Gin and something else.

"Waa du."

"Good christ, this man is half dead. Look at that wound. His head's cut in half. Why the devil did you do this to a man whom we need. Have you lost your mind? I should have your balls in a jug for this." Fotheringhay was now incandescent.

"Orter."

"I sent thay two tae find this thing and this is what they did to."

"Was it not 'you' Macbeth who did the sending?"

"Wada. WADA." Hooligan wailed in purgatory.

"Aye, it was sur."

"I give you fair warning, Haggis Hunter, if this thing isn't up to the job; you will do it your sheep-shagging self."

"Order."

"We had tae knock him arou—"

"Silence! Damn your eyes!" Boy Blue struck The Scot in the chest with his crop. You forget yourself Sir; how dare you speak while I'm interrupting. It was I who raised you from the gutter, and with one word I can cast you back down amongst the sodomites and Glaswegians where you belong. Is that to your liking?"

"Waadour."

"Not at all, sur."

"Get him up. Get him sorted and give him a drink. I want to speak to him."

Hooligan was vaguely aware of being lifted, dragged, then thrown down painfully like a sack of offal against the bowl of a tree by people who would rather witness his demise than his resuscitation. He hung on grimly to life, then, 'holy of holies,' cold, blessed, water was poured over his head and into his broken mouth. He gagged and choked, unable to swallow until the desiccated tissue of his throat was repaired by the magical stuff. Croaking incomprehensibly to he knew not whom he demanded more until at last the canteen was thrust with a curse into his desperate hands and he drank until his belly was distended and the container was empty. He would live.

"What is your name?"

Lliam Shaun Hooligan, all but dead footpad, robber, arsonist and cattle thief, opened his single eye as widely as the tightly stretched skin around it would allow, and discovered that he was being appraised by a brace of spalpeens. One was Macbeth, the malignant skirt-wearing ear-chewing bitch who had damn near killed him. The other had to be Fotheringhay, 'the master' that the English lickspittles were so bloody proud of; he was decked-out like a sodding king after all. Hooligan knew cruelty when he saw it and the perfumed bitch in blue had distilled the very essence of the stuff and wore the mess as a face. The man from County Mayo bridled. Cruelty and injustice were the two things he hated most in this life.

"Ask your eejit." He stared unblinking at Macbeth, then noticed the newly dead who now decorated the woodwork.

"Jasus. There 'is' a god."

A nod from Fotheringhay caused one of the roughnecks to mangle the prisoner's broken hand. Hooligan screeched in the torment of the damned.

"Your name." The words were spoken quietly with the composure of an individual who invariably got what he wanted while the victim of his impatience gasped for breath; his chest heaving and water running from his eye.

"Hooligan! Hooligan, ya lousy bastard."

"Indeed? Of the poteen-guzzling Hooligans of the peat bogs of Sligo. That Hooligan?" Lliam Shaun Hooligan of the County Mayo Hooligans almost smiled as he envisioned tearing this swine apart between a couple of horses; the ropes attached around the middle of the fucker.

"Don't take umbrage with your betters, Bastard. That would never do. Well?"

"Yes, Oi said. Arr you fookin deaf?" The answer was snarled in a tone composed of nothing 'but' umbrage.

"You come highly recommended which is to say, that you are the scum of the earth. You are a cattle thief, a robber, a poacher a smuggler and an arsonist."

"Arsist? Me? It's the wrong man you have Sunshoine." The physical effort involved in making conversation brought Hooligan almost to the loss of consciousness, but even so, his gaze swept the flower garden of bewigged, rouged-cheeked dandies with loathing. He raked his throat extravagantly and spat at them; gutted when the viscous filth clung to his badly used mouth and mated with his beard. A reluctant smile had formed on the granite-outcrop features of the inquisitor while among the colourful entourage general merriment had broken out as those at the back were being informed of this bilge-rat's utterly exceptional faux pas.

"There is a shipyard, by the river, at Minster about fifteen miles downstream from here. Do you know the place, Mr Hooligan of the Sligo Hooligans? Hooligan emitted a sound more suited to a dog about to bite.

"The owners are a devil called Bismark Astor, and his malignant whelp Michael by name. They build ships there which they employ in their filthy trade in human flesh. The slave-trade. Are you acquainted with the slave trade? The God-cursed buying and selling of His likeness. They tear black men, women and children from their homes, and whip them in chains to these ships, in the holds of which they bury these poor people alive, in conditions too appalling even to contemplate. Those who survive the voyage to the Americas are sold into slavery. Well?"

''Oim fookin starvin.'' Despite the expression of sublime disinterest on the ruined features before him, Fotheringhay continued doggedly.

"I have made it my life's work to destroy this obscenity and am hereby enlisting 'your,' services.''

The desperately ill prisoner did not have a clue what this eedjit was blabbing about. Not one word of it did he understand. In fact, he even thought that 'black people' were in there somewhere. The only things that he 'did' understand were 'pain and hunger.' He'd had enough and more of this filthy stinking world and couldn't wait to leave it. Between the two of them, his torn-off ear and the open wound that joined the thing to his one good eye were killing him sure; his neck was sawed right through, his poor hand was deadly, thanks to this poo pusher, and everything else was in smithereens.

"Me?" he snarled. ''Sure, Oi can't help me fookin self.''

"Your dole will improve very definitely for the better at the very instant in which you sincerely throw in your lot with the anti-slavery movement, and my oath on it," the big-wig threw his pearl-barley before swine.

"Is that roight?"

"It most certainly is." Fotheringhay's manner changed subtly. Discarding his pig shit fouled gloves he approached and sat on a fallen tree, still carefully out of range of the prisoner's refined perfume.

"Sure, moi luck changed when I met your pals before." The sick man greeted his captor, as the wig dusted the bark; silver between unread parchments, with a virginal kerchief prior to shimmying his bony arse down like a clucky hen on an egg.

"Good as gold oi was.   Look at me   now. Lame   bloind but for all the saints.''

"An arsonist," intoned Fotheringhay as though to a child, ''is someone who burns buildings.''

''Is that roight?''

The King's Councillor stiffened at the sarcasm, white in the painted and powdered face while his supremely articulate eyebrow promised, 'Any more in that vein and you'll die here, now.'

The herd lowed.

''Oi meant, 'Tanks your majesty.'''

"Please," a bloodless, blemish-free palm was displayed for Hooligan's inspection.

"Don't elevate me to the throne prematurely. My instruction to you is this. 'Burn that cursed yard Hooligan.''' The pagan eyes which reflected no light, considered the prisoner for such a long moment that Hooligan thought that there was worse to come. Unable to lift his one good hand, he was making the sign of the cross in the dust when Fotheringhay seemed to arrive at the resolution to some weighty problem or other and nodded at Macbeth in consequence of this.

Fishing around in his saddlebag the Scot found what he was searching for and threw it underhand so that it landed in the dust between Hooligan's feet.

'A purse!' The newly christened abolitionist was perplexed. Sure, he had never at all got his wages 'before,' he had worked his arse off, atall, atall.

"You will find me to be a generous employer. However, should you speak my name to a living soul; I include in that number your sodomite confessor, your gin-soaked friends, and whore of a mother, in conjunction with this business, or fail me," at this point the aquiline profile turned towards the gibbet and considered the putrefaction and its new neighbours now suspended agonisingly there.

"That rotten thing took my purse then failed to deliver the goods. Didn't hang him. That would have been far too sentimental; the lesson would not have been learned by others of his ilk, You! For instance! No! We sawed off his nose, his ears, ripped out his tongue, and then we tied him in a clove-hitch and hung him up in the pillory like that, in order to teach him a lesson. He lasted for several days I believe. Died a ''swine'' of a death." This observation brought an appreciative swelling of amusement from the silken cavalry as though they shared some esoteric knowledge.

"Thirsty too, I imagine. You know about 'thirst' don't you?"

"No. Oi fuckin don't."

It occurred to Hooligan that this eedjit who avowed such deep concern for poor ignorant 'black' folk, was none too picky about what he did to the Irish, or any other poor sod who crossed him.

"Macbeth here will watch out for you as you go about the business and approach you when it's done." Fotheringhay went on, indicating the heap of tartan with a hoick of his thumb, as though his victim would not have recognised the swine just by his stink.

"Should you prove to be so inept as to be apprehended in the execution of your task, simply hold your diseased tongue until my people set you free which they 'will,' do, by hook or by crook. Remember this though you weevil in a ship's biscuit; let them rip out that tongue rather than speak my name, because if they don't, I most assuredly shall. You will be well rewarded for success, never fear."

With the interview concluded, Fotheringhay had himself thrown aboard his majestic mount and gathering the reins pulled the animal's head around cruelly.

"Hoi." Little Boy Blue turned in the saddle, resting a manicured hand on his mount's rump,

"What is it?" Easing his arse free of the ground Hooligan tried for a fart but failed miserably.

"Would ye be havin a lump of bread and a drop o' grog about ye? Me fookin troat's slit so it is." From the crowd of dandies and lickspittles there came an audible intake of breath at the insane risk-taking of the battered tramp, but Fotheringhay's scar of a mouth merely softened somewhat, becoming an open wound in the process.

"Naturally,"

Throwing back his flesh-free scull in amusement the latter-day Caligula rode away, followed by his adoring cavalry still enjoying the filth's undeniable chutzpah. The infantry trotted in the rear, though not before hurling stones viciously into the invalid from no distance at all; two of which sucked the very breath out of him. Agonised and dying Lliam Shaun Hooligan crawled into the deepest shade and was soon whimpering in his sleep, the purse lying where it fell so that when they came sneaking back to get it, they would have little excuse for finishing him.

The theropoden monster came in the night; a primeval creature standing four feet tall at the shoulders; drawn inexorably by the scent of the sows in Hooligan's stench. Travelling silently though quickly on its neat, cloven hooves the ravenous, lusting creature closed to within sight of what had drawn it there, hesitating in deep cover while it sought out danger. Finding none it sped across the open ground and bit greedily. Hooligan was wrenched from sleep screaming in agony and terror as the remnants of his tattered ear were ripped from his skull, startling the awful spectre so that it broke off its attack and rushed away. Thoughtless in his extremity of his broken hand the tortured individual leaped for the limb of oak above his head and in an effort which lasted through aeons of fear at the thought of his legs being savaged, pulled himself up to safety. Unmanned as any eunuch, he clambered, crying out in extremis, along the branch into the massive juncture of trunk and limbs, murderous pain dispelling all other human considerations and there he crouched shivering, gasping and occasionally crying like a child, nearer death than life. The remainder of the endless day all but put an end to him, while darkness heaped insult on top of outrage. Tortured, starving, friendless and alone, hopeless and scared of death, sickened by the sounds of the boars tearing at the screaming feast and weary of life to the very marrow of his bones he clung on to life while praying for death.

In the pre-dawn cold the nauseating cacophony diminished and came at last to an end. Hooligan's miserable existence had been reduced beyond anything that he had thought possible. The Slough of Despond in which he was perennially mired was a sunlit upland when compared to these fires of hell and he cursed the catholic church, the brits, and those damnable priests who had lied their much-abused arses off about god's fucking love.

If he was to survive, he had to get away from this place and find a quack but desperate though he was to avoid the clutches of the grim reaper, he would not abandon the security of the tree while the gloom persisted. Another age and a day had to drag passed before sunlight at last speared through the leaves and he could see well enough to discover any ravenous monsters that might be waiting in hiding. Scouring the forest floor all around; holding his breath while straining to detect the smallest sound, and as certain as it was possible to be that the hideous creatures had gone, he dropped to the ground, shuddering at the agony which the impact caused. Crouching down arthritically like an ancient beggar under *sacks he pocketed the purse, grabbed a stone that filled his good hand and equating for no good reason the appalling constructions of stocks and gibbet with a degree of safety he limped across the open arena at the best speed he could muster, drenched in the sweat of the terror which racked him. The thought of such creatures coming at him in a herd unmanned him altogether.   * Dulci et decorum est. Wilfred Owen

Hanging barely above the ground the murdered things had been consumed almost to the groin; bones and all while Rickets' little dick peered down unhappily at the churned up bloody mess beneath. 'You dirty bastards... Oi couldn't do better meself.' His thoughts were dense with satisfaction yet still made redundant by his discovery of 'Rickets' quality leather belt with a knife, and a pannikin of brass-bound leather. 'What,' he wondered, 'was a starving village idiot doing with quality stuff like this about him; a midget who earned his pittance by thrashing innocent Irishmen with a stick? And why had Savage and his filth not had it away with these valuable items?' He hesitated superstitiously as he tested the weight of his discovery. The thing was full.

"Please God," he groaned. Three parts full, and so beautiful it was in its brass and leather. With hope burgeoning, he tore out the cork, held the container to his nose, and sniffed deeply. Yes! Rum! Unbelievably, it was rum. Jesus, Joseph and Mary and all the saints. Rum. Almost four pints of the falling-down water. Guzzling like a mill-race; revelling in the glorious sensation of the fiery liquids burning progress down to his empty belly he choked and damn near lost his life by drowning.

"That's enough, sure," he gasped, wiping his dribbling mouth sympathetically with the back of his hand but causing the blood to flow all over again. Rigidly suppressing his urge to hve more, he replaced the cork and tapped it back in with his elbow.

"You liddle darlin'."

Heartened by this endless succession of good fortune, the cripple went in search of boots, and found some with feet still inside. The leather had been well-chewed as the beasts tried to get at the meat inside them, but they were still a thousand times better than the tatters which hung around his own poor ankles. With unjust, infuriating difficulty, because of the blood, the pig's slobber, and the unspeakable state of his hand, he undid the straps and removing the feet limped back to the gallows where he left them beneath the dripping corpses, not really knowing why. Slug-slowly but with the resolve of the persecuted he started for the river and the sea, happy as hell that the bastards who had crucified him went out the hard way. Eaten alive? For 'chrise sake?'

There was not room enough in Ruth Montague's heart to contain her jealousy, her love, disappointment, feelings of abandonment and rejection. Every great house in the county had received invitations to Michael's coming of age. Every great house but her own. Her friends, all of whom she loathed with a passion were invited but not herself. There were difficulties naturally. An invitation solely for the daughter of the house would clearly cause a bow-wave or two while one which included her parents would be no less suspicious; but if Michael truly loved her, he would have found a way. It had been weeks since he had gentled her from sleep in one of his truly imaginative ways and she missed him and his touch desperately. She needed to be 'used' and that particularly lewd hunger intensified hour after hour, day after day; she was possessed by it and her poor attempts at self-gratification were a dismal and ultimately disgusting affair. From beneath the rim of her bonnet she took-in again the wonderfully pretty gardener boy who was so lean and hard and quite possibly innocent if his shyness and reticence were genuine. What if she were to teach him 'everything,' everything that there is to know in just one night? She rejected the thought with a brief quiver of revulsion. Ruth Montague was trapped in love with Michael Astor, and she was horribly aware of the fact.

"If I can't have him," she concluded, "nobody can."

"Jasus Joseph and Mary and all the saints." Hooligan stood among the horror of the riverside massacre; enraged, endlessly sorry for the gypsy couple, and starving. The rabbit bones had been well cleaned but he had managed to get a bit of gristle off here and there. Coward moaned, cried like a girl and twitched. Wisps of grey smoke escaped from beneath him as he squirmed. Wanting to piss, Hooligan rolled the tortured thing onto its back, dropped his draws and aimed a torrent of bloody urine with satisfying accuracy into its open gob hoping it would drown; but the thirst-tortured Coward choked and gasped and swallowed like a sluice. Meat! There was meat in the embers where Coward had lain. Snatching it up and burning his hand in the process he sat his arse down on the bastard's fat gut, thereby eliciting welcome exclamations of excruciating torment and bit greedily into a lump of delicious meat. He ate with a sort of reverence, revelling in every bight, every swallow; until the awful moment when he noticed what appeared to be another corpse. The body lay separated from the others by a far stretch of sand. Unbearably, it appeared to be the body of a child. Flooded by legions of agonising emotions every one of the bastards clawing at his soul; savaging his poor heart and about to blind his poor with its outrage

he staggered towards that which he loathed to confront, falling twice as he hurried to the scene, falling on a third occasions only to crawl onwards in his desperation and confusion. Sure enough, it was a little girl, barely nubescent obviously, They had raped her and killed her. The diseased English slugs had slit her darling throat. Sobbing now; tear-blinded he placed the poor thing's skinny little legs together, rearranging what clothing there was in order to preserve the child's modesty, hoping devoutly the while that the malignant scum who had done this had suffered for a long, long time as the boars had inflicted their unique attentions on them. ''Is dere no *dethp that English scum will not sink to?''

''Oi swear by all the foockin saints,'' he declared, confronted and inexplicably contaminated by this barbarism, "that from here on in, Oi'll do the roight ting and O'ill murder every fooker Oi meet what does shoite loike this. It's fookin war!"

With the poor family covered in sand; an endless task which used up the very last dregs of his strength and much of the day Hooligan turned his attention to Coward who still groaned, smoked and blubbered.

"Not so fookin hard now," he observed laconically, even permitting himself a painful smile as Coward belched one of his agonised ejaculations. Hooligan placed more dry twigs in the hot embers; blew them into life then dragged Coward back to the flames, arranging him carefully so that it was his crotch that now benefitted from the refined torment that is burning. Pleased with his inventiveness but sorely hurt physically and flayed emotionally by the fate of the gypsy family he trudged away to the south. Passing the place where the little girl lay, he paused momentarily, lamenting burying her so far from her parents and was wondering whether he could find the strength to move her, when his father's voice shocked him.

"Was that it?

After what yer man did to ye?

Have ye forgot the wee one? A innocent little colleen ya fuckin spalpeen.

Get back there and have the balls off the bastard."

Deeply affected by the stentorian indictment Hooligan returned, as full of hates he had ever been, to where Coward lay croaking and twitching. The remaining-fire iron stood alone, clearly lacking purpose in life. He drew it from the sand, snarling; insane.

"This is going to hurt you a lot. Grasping the arrow-sharp steel in his good hand and applying his bodyweight straight-armed, he thrust the thing into the beast's thigh; careful to avoid the artery.

"Sure, we don't want yer man to bleed to death, do we now?" His good intentions were shouted down by the thing that screamed and thrashed like a hound-ripped hare as the spike mined its flesh till with a sudden rush it exited in a seepage of purple blood.

''When a man arks for water,'' the revenant raged. Breathless.

''Give the fucker.''

Screeching and blubbering in turn, Coward was still singing when the reborn individual paused for a breather downstream.

''Die you English bastard and make less noise about it.''

Sod the lot of them; he would get himself sorted and then he would take himself off miles and miles away from here to some place where they would never find him. Away from lunatics like that Scotsman and his princess Fartinghay with his stocks and his painted fairies and his chopping off noses and hangin' people for nuthin atall. Sure, while the fiend was breakin' his bleeding heart about 'black' men, the English and the Irish were starvin' and white men all over the shop were getting hung for snaring a rabbit.

"Black men; what a pail of puke."

A sandy backwater blessed with large, still pools of clean salt water presented him with an excuse to rest. Now, at last, he might find something to eat, a fish trapped by the receding tide, a crab or a shell or two, and even if he didn't, he could at least wash off the pig-shit and cool the awful hurts that were destroying him. He let fall his greasy rags and stood naked in a pattern of blue-green bruises, rusty cuts and brown smears of blood. Kicking his stuff and his squelching footwear into a pool of their own he armed himself with a fistful of weed, crouched down hyperventilating and shivering in a horribly cold bath and began to wash himself, gently. He had undertaken a particularly refined torture, knowing in advance that the salt water would bite him in every graze and cut. Even so he watched with a sense of satisfaction as his skin mellowed from a deep, grey to a pinky-white sort of a thing, like the face of a priest. Scrubbed all over until he could take no more he crawled to a virgin pond, and contriving to roll himself into it, took a deep breath and submerged completely, staying under the surface for as long as he could until the lice and fleas, to which he played perennial host, were all drowned. Abandoning this badly used pool for his third choice he cleaned every protesting inch of his skin again with sand and lovely dark-green slimy seaweed, until he felt as clean and shiny as that Scottish eedjit Macbeth appeared to be. Some of the drowned maggots, flaccid and white, still hung-on in his wounds and he took to splashing them gently in revulsion until the salty, biting water washed them all clean away, unaware that the maggots ate only his rotting flesh and not the healthy meat. The cold had, thank Christ, eased just a faggot of the raging fire.

The poisonous truth which coiled behind his protracted ablutions, was fear. Naked dismal fear. Many a man abandoned ship because of filthy wounds being left to putrefy, and Lliam Shaun Hooligan was having none of that, but salvation necessarily meant the poring of the hard stuff into his cuts. The salt-water had caused him the burning of the damned in purgatory itself, and he well knew that the agony associated with the rum could well kill him stone dead. Downing a good gutful from his canteen to ease what was coming he slithered in to yet another uncontaminated bath and girding his loins poured a small quantity of the precious red-gold spirits into his palm. Gritting his teeth, he applied the cursed cure firmly though hesitantly, cupping his hand to the hanging tatters where his ear used to be.

He had teemed white-hot liquid-iron straight from the Pudlers' Hearth into his butchered flesh. Screaming with each successive application, water flowing unbidden from his eye, his chest heaving like a bellows, he persisted, time after shrieking time because there was nothing else for it. He collapsed.

Much later, with just his legs left to murder he was shivering uncontrollably and as the business went further still, so the intervals between agonies grew longer, despite his self-contempt. His torture all but complete he looked up instinctively and was shocked to see a rider approaching, 'from the south strangely.' It was that motherless Scott bitch that had done this to him. His shivering good hand sought the knife. Creeping to where his rags were soaking, he trod filth out of them to pass the time until the bastard got near enough to gut. The Scott had a second saddlehorse with him.

'Now there's a ting! Could that bugger be for me?'

Changing to an underhand grip on his weapon the vengeful one watched unblinking. The swine rode well for a man who wore a skirt; relaxed in the saddle, long stirrups, allowing his mount to find its own way around the fallen trees, rocky outcrops and deeper pools. Despite his sworn intention of kicking the shit out of the bastard at the first opportunity, Hooligan found himself envying the arrogant pig; even admiring the bastard. They were alike as peas in a pea-thingy in some ways, himself and that ball-sack, and yet, so different. Today, Macbeth was dressed in a suit of tweed. Himself was stamping ten years of filth, sweat and blood out of a heap of rags. The Scot rode a dappled charger with his handsome hunter for Sunday best, Himself was on Shank's pony. Judging by the size of the sod the hardman was the best-nourished citizen for miles around while his own belly was rubbing up against his backbone. Christ almighty, he could not wait to ram this knife into the fucker's guts. He wanted those horses as much as he needed his next breath.

"So, the pigs didnae eat ye after all," the Scot bawled at a distance of five feet, "they just kicked the stuffin out of ye."

''Drop dead.''

"Well done, laddie. I'll be twenty guineas and this horse better-off because of it." Macbeth slapped the charger affectionately, a blow which would have killed many an Englishmen.

"Odd, what ye did wi' they feet though." The horseman hurled a bundle of cloth at Hooligan's face.

"Dress yersel laddie," he ordered,

"I'm starving and I cannae eat with that wee wullie o' yoors winkin at me." Suddenly defensive and exasperated, his murderous intention relegated, Hooligan protested vehemently.

"Sure, Oi've bin freezin' moi arse off this fookin day past in oice as cold as... cold stuff," he bleated; angry with his shrivelled dick and his hibernating balls for bringing such humiliation upon him, but such considerations were swept aside by the flood of genuine gratitude that the clothes engendered in him. The huge bundle of warm, clean, sweet-smelling cloth felt unutterably good in his arms. Since the very day that he had acquired them, his own rags had never parted company with his filthy spotty back. He cut the twine that held the impossible treasure and struggled to dress his still-damp body before the hairy pig could change its mind; luxuriating in the unimaginable caress of the silk shirt, the fit of the tweed trousers and coat, so much better than homespun which was often more holes than cloth. *There were boots. Real cobbler-made boots.* His first ever in this life.

It was all too much for a man to grapple with. Knee high black leather riding boots which had never been worn before. The smell of the leather was so good, and the soles! There was not a mark was on them. Smooth polished hide they were as thick as the rind on a leg of ham, with the white stitching deep and safe in its grooves, and the knots, happy as rich people in their thimbles of tough yellow resin. Like...... ''floies in amber,'' they were. The delighted soul hastily brushed the sand from his feet and stood on the remains of his jerkin as he tugged them on, falling over in the process, then completing the process while prostrate in the sand.

"My wurrd, look at you laddie, they things fit ye well. They wur made for ma brother-in-law o'coorse. He was a dwarf tae. Come and eat. Ye must be a wee bit peckish the noo."

''FUCK OFF YOU SHOITE.''

It was all too recent for Hooligan to come to heel like a well-thrashed dog when the master called, but the cunning bastard had put down a groundsheet with enough food for Enniskillen. Despite his rage and his need to kill this prick as dead as mutton Hooligan crawled quickly to the feast.

''Suit yersell.'' Unconcerned, by the Irishman's pathetic little temper tantrum Macbeth selected a thick cut of beef, smeared it with relish and bit ravenously. Bereft of every shred of pride the starving invalid advanced on the banquet like a badly mauled detachment of infantry and for the next hour, found no difficulty in utterly ignoring the sarcasm, insults and derogatory insinuations thrown at him. He was, however, sufficiently cognisant of his surroundings to nod his head to the beer when asked on several occasions whether he would prefer more beer, tea or whisky.

"Mother of God," seriously discomfited by his inability to get under the stinking bogtrotter's skin and recalling how he had recently sunk his teeth into the Irishman's ear in order to hold him still, Macbeth inquired facetiously.

"What happened tae yer ear?" Hooligan palmed another lump of chicken and his fifth Cornish pasty, and with his mouth overflowing, snorted,

''Pig.'' Macbeth was disgusted by what he was looking at.

"My wurrd! That's awful," he declared.

"Ye shouldnae speak with yer mooth full. It looks wurse than yer face."

Hooligan laughed like a drain for the first time in many a long day; choked on almost a whole foul and suffered a backslapping from Macbeth which bordered on serious physical assault, before the offending carcass was dislodged.

"Ye'd best get yersel tae a surgeon wi' that." The burst mattress resumed his seat on the opposite side of the canvas groundsheet and nodding at the remnants of Hooligan's ear declared,

"There's an excellent fellow where yer going. Beam by name, lives in a wee place called Bramley, three or four mile this side o' Minster. Dinnae let on a wurrd to the nosey old bastart but. If he or any other buddy wur to get wind o' our wee bit business, it could well go the wurse fer ye." Hooligan chewed open-mouthed on a boiled potato with butter and parsley dressing.

"And what would the loikes of me be paying a quack wit?" he enquired obnoxiously and over-loudly, the potato, egg yolk and parsley, well to the fore,

"My arse?"

Macbeth's steel-blue eyes glittered with naked revulsion and malevolence in their hairy home. With disgust dripping from every word, he declared,

"It's clear to me the noo, Sur, that you Sur, are faar too busy talking filth Sur, wi' yer mooth full, to count yer purse, Sur."

Every 'Sur' was thrust like a blade between Hooligan's ribs, but the seemingly oblivious Irishman continued to feed in a fashion not dissimilar to that favoured by starving wolves. He soon refrained however from adding to the disgusting volume of well-masticated food which his mouth was struggling but failing to contain. He swallowed hugely, drained his beer mug, rolled over and crawled on all fours to where his few belongings, belt, sheath, rum and purse, lay in the sand, keen to discover whatever good fortune might be contained within. Pausing a while as he prepared himself for the inevitable disappointment, he sat on his arse, tore open the pretty suede bag and poured out the contents in a long stream on to the remains of Rickets' jacket. Such was the unleavened nature of Hooligan's decade-long poverty, so few were his expectations, and so deep was his conviction that the labourer was 'not' worthy of his hire, that for the very smallest part of measurable time he saw pennies; detestable, virtually worthless copper coins, sufficient to sustain him for only one or two more days. Then, magically, just as the trees turn to gold at sunup every copper coin became silver.

"Silver!" This was not possible, yet he was seeing it. He was rich. Silver! Lliam Shaun Hooligan of the County Mayo Hooligans had never seen so much money in one place, and miraculously, that one blessed place was the inside of his own purse.

"Holy mother of shoite."

"Just one o' they will be enough fer surgeon Beam and a decent horse in tae the bargain, I'm thinking," observed Macbeth caustically. Hooligan was suddenly and inexplicably rich. Rich! Cramming the coins back into their little home he lashed the treasure securely to his belt and secreting it inside his trousers where he could feel it resting against his belly, he undertook the arduous journey to where the Scot now sat atop a boulder, gazing out over the river while smoking a long clay pipe in which he was clearly burning dead flesh.

"Thank you, Macbeth," the words issued of their own volition so that incredibly, the mannerly gesture cost the Irishman nothing; nothing at all.

"Don't thank me, laddie. It's Fartinghay paying ye. Ye'll earn every penny mind, and there will be more when ye get yer wee job done."

"The cloves. You didn't need." The Scot removed the pipe from his camouflaged mouth and considered his employee's expression for a long moment.

"Is it just you, Sur?" he demanded insultingly,

"Or do all you Irish donkeys say, 'thanks' with a face like the Gordian fucking knot?" Lliam Hooligan's expression did not alter by one flicker, he wouldn't have known 'Gordon' from a lump of cheese, but he caught this big bastard's gist well enough. His response matched the Scot's, in candour.

"I'm glad for the cloves Macbeth," he said bluntly, but thanks to you, Oi'm pissing blood. Oim digging maggots out of every hole but my arse, and you bit my fucking ear off. You could have told me the story in that village; but no; you had to crucify me altogether.

If it's 'smiles' you're after, you have the wrong man. I'll be after kickin' shit out of you before this divilment's done."

"ENOUGH!" Utterly exasperated, Macbeth slithered from his perch, dropping to the sand, furious and threatening.

"I am yer employer man,'' he insisted.

''Dinnae 'ever' threaten 'me' sur or I'll feed ye tae thae fish oot there." His right hand jerked violently as though throwing off a gauntlet, and by some trickery he was instantly holding a long blade.

"Ye're armed bog trotter so what's it to be?" Lliam Hooligan had never in his life feared another man. He had fought so many battles with fists and boots that he had come to think of violence as life's currency, but he had never fought with a knife, a sword, or a gun in his fist as a matter of choice. He sensed that at this moment he had arrived at a critical juncture; he stood on a mountaintop looking down at a new land where there was food, drink, warmth and even friendship. In his refractory glance at the bearded clansman, he saw beyond the giant with the knife, he saw the promise of more purses full of silver and imagined again that smallholding with a cottage newly thatched, a milk cow, his own horse, a vegetable patch and even a kitchen orchard. Thinking to surrender his own knife, he drew it.

All too late he saw his mistake. At incredible speed the Scot dropped into the fighting stance and closed for the kill.

'He was dead.'

In that same instant Hooligan's legs had been kicked from under him and the Scotsman's fast blade had burned his chest painfully as he fell on his arse. Defenceless on his back he thrust his hands skyward in submission.

''No! Ya stupid bast.''

The animal-like fury held-up its murderous dance; seemed to debate whether to finish the business despite the surrender, slid his blade back into its hiding place and became calm. Hooligan could breathe again.

"That's yer answer?" With a nod of his head, Macbeth indicated Hooligan's knife leaning in the sand.

"I was trowin' the fucking ting!" Incensed at being forced into this worst of shame, this ball-crushing, intestine-grinding, eye-watering capitulation Hooligan was about to do murder, yet he hesitated, a previously unknown behaviour. He was, he realised; about to kill the very thing that he desperately wanted to be. The pride-filled bastard who had brought all this pain on him and worse still had just-now shamed him at the hard-stuff, was standing there like the king of the fucking castle with his darling horses, his mountain of grub, darlin clothes and a sporran full of gold. Not known for thinking things through, he understood and accepted, then and there that from here on in, no matter what it was that Macbeth told him to do, he would do it without hesitation. He liked this eating game, this clean new clothes world this horse-riding easy life.

"But I'm your man, right enough," he said, knowing that he had been bought. His conscience, completely untroubled.

"And another thing," the Scot relaxed slightly,

"Fartinghay likes tae know that his people can take it as well as dish it oot. It was a wee bit test, ye ken."

"A wee bit test, ye ken." mocked the convert in a fair imitation of Macbeth's brogue.

"Will Oi be keepin company with your pals, swingin on a rope when this divilment is done?" The question was rhetorical; the seriously ill and bewildered tramp was verbalising the last dregs of his disbelief. To Hooligan's unplumbed surprise, the hairy loon suddenly roared with inexplicable amusement, breaking the long stem of his recently retrieved pipe in his agitation.

"Oh, ye of little faith," the bear gasped, and advanced on the Irishman preparatory to applying one of his trademark constrictions but the object of his affections backed-off, maintaining a safe distance between himself and the bloody cannibalistic Scottish goat.

"Ye do know that you're an idiot, do ye not?" the Scot inquired with no intention whatsoever of being rude.

"Wash yer filthy Irish face. There's enough food in yer beard te feed a fambly* fer a week, ya durty pig."   *family

Lliam Hooligan the rich was finding that the swine's ability to change the subject and the direction of his attack had him chasing his own tale. To hide his intense irritation and his sudden hot surprise at the man's disgust with his eating habits, he went off to the river's edge, ostensibly to wash when there were clean pools all around. Passing by on that silver highway was the strangest craft imaginable. Interested, he appreciated that effortless relocation of the huge boat, adjusting his vision to the water-reflected light and shading his eyes in order to catch the minutiae of the goings-on, so far out.

"The filth is busy, laddie." Macbeth appeared at Hooligan's shoulder, and master and man stood side by side; a thousand miles apart.

"Bye-the-bye; that wurrm Rickets that they three did for, was in the pay of Astor, or some other buddy, as well as us.'' Lliam Hooligan was no politician, but he had the guile to recognise this confidence for what it was; the outreach of a brother in arms and he rejoiced inwardly accordingly. Having once again put his well-booted foot in his own mouth, he was keen to change the subject.

"That's the ugliest boat on earth," he declared. The craft had only three feet of freeboard, and virtually no superstructure other than a couple of cabins which were so square as to utterly defeat what he understood to be the fundamental notions of boat building. Its sails were both too far forrard and too far aft and strangest of all, there were cooking fires burning on the deck. A woman was working at one of them. At the stern, a gypsy-seeming character struggled with what appeared to be a gigantic steering pole. Macbeth contained the impulse to point out that the object wasn't actually 'on earth,' concluding that the jest would not be understood.

"It's a raft laddie, two tae be precise. Logs being floated down tae the Astor's yard, the one you're goin tae torch. The durty swine."

"Why is that then?" Hooligan had absorbed not-a-word, of what he had been told on the previous day and was still trying to make sense of what he had got in to.

"Did ye no hear Fartinghay? He's a slaver, laddie; fer all his fine ways, a durrty bloody-handed slaver, and a king's man intae the bargain. Ye cannae get wurse than that." Now that the craft were further downstream it became clear to the pressganged abolitionist that sure enough, he had been looking at two rafts sailing close, and not just one boat. The cabins were mere tents and the sails were jury-rigged repurposed sheets of canvas.

"Is it because Astor's a slave that yer ganger-man wants to burn him out?" Angered and shamed by his own ignorance, Hooligan refrained from meeting the Scot's glance and asked the question of the river, the rafts, and the far-off shoreline. There followed a long pause during which Macbeth turned slightly scrutinising this poor battered, lonely individual who had clearly never in his miserable life experienced a day of ease or plenty, and whose ignorance of the world was unequalled. What he saw was a starving child on the streets of Peebles, its mother lying dead beside him as passers-by stepped over the corpse, some of them none too carefully. He cleared his throat, one hairy fist to his mouth.

"Astor's a slaver, not a slave. Do ye not know what slavery is?" Hooligan could suffer no more

"Just tell me, for the love of Chroist. Oi'm igorant, not bloody stupid," he railed.

"I'm aboot to, laddie. Calum yersell, calum yersell." The Scotsman pronounced the 'Ls.' " Now. The ships that Astor builds at Minster," he began, "sail frae England, that's here," he jabbed a map which he was drawing in the wet sand,

"south to the west coast of Africa, 'here,' where it's very hot. Twice as hot as this summer has been. So hot that the people are black with it." Lliam Shaun Hooligan, man of means, drew breath hugely; about to ridicule the stupid ballsack for a simpleton when he remembered the knife that was hidden up the man's sleeve. He relented.

"For a handful of glass beads, he can purchase a human being, man woman or child. It takes about four hunnerd o them tae fill a big ship. Then he sails tae the new lands, Haiti, Jamaica, Cuba, the colonies, where he sells these people as slaves fer the growing of baccy, sugar, spices, rum. He brings a cargo of tobacco or sugar, rum any o' them, back here. Then it's aff tae the white man's grave again. The whole thing makes so much profit that they call it the Golden Triangle. This is England, where we are now. Here is Africa, the White Man's Grave, the Ivory Coast, home to killer animals the likes of which you could never imagine in a hunnerd years. Poisonous snakes, spiders, disease, and men as black as yer hat. It's cawd 'the fever coast as well.''

"They'd be white at the start but?"

"What?" Macbeth straightened up from his drawing.

"When they're whelped. They'd be white. Am I roight?"

The teacher stared intently into his student's face in order to discover whether he was being mocked. He was not.

"No, they are born black." The inquisitor could see what the ignoramus was thinking but had changed his mind about the advisability of starting the man's education at this juncture.

"You're talkin' shoite," Hooligan laughed, inviting Macbeth to laugh with him.

"How so?" demanded the irascible Scot shortly. Hooligan was still seeking collusion.

" Well, the sun can't bake a man in his mammy's oven?" Macbeth all but rolled his eyes. This was like talking to a four-year-old.

"Do you look like yer parents. Is yer father's beard red? Do ye look like ye grandfaither?

"I do, and it is," Hooligan would have smiled at the obvious truth, but was unable without a dire increase in discomfort. Macbeth simply raised the jungle of bind-stems which passed for his eyebrows.

"Ooooh." The sick man shuddered. Taking the agonised man's arm over his shoulder, the Scot assisted his unlikely hireling back to the groundsheet where he lowered him considerately to the canvas and fed him rum. The spasm passed sufficiently for the ignoramus to require a full understanding of what was being said.

"Where is Oireland?"

Shaking his head in despair, Macbeth obliged and drew a new map with that country carefully located.

"That dog Astor, and his poisonous pup, are in the business of human misery, and me and you are in the business of putting an end tae them. Kill them both dead if ye ever get the chance. Farthinghay gets through fortunes year after year, trying tae outlaw the thing in parrlument and doing any damn thing that he can think of tae wreck the business itself. If you do a good job wi' your wee bit work, there'll be three less slave ships fer us tae sink."

"And he can't build more of the buggers without a yard," Hooligan observed with a hint of insight that provided Macbeth a grain of pleasure amid a bushel of surprise. He wanted to say no more about slavery.

"You see they gypos out there," Macbeth's pagan glance stabbed the distant rafts; "that tribe of animals have been swimmin the swine's timber down tae Minster fer twenty years or more. They're loyal as dogs to those two and they can slice a man more ways than you'd like tae know, keeping him alive fer days on end while they're about it. Dinnae let yersel fall into their haunds, laddie. Put an end to yersel rather than let that happen.

"Twenty years? He must be out of trees." Hooligan's tone declared his astonishment.

''Jeez-oh, laddie. The man has thirty thousand acres up there alone, and that wee bokle*, Michael, o' his has as much or more just along the coast." Macbeth glanced reluctantly in the direction of the enemy.

"Not only that; for every tree he cuts down, he plants ten more. Astor's a bastard, but he's a clever bastard." The floating evidence of his sworn-enemy's industrial juggernaut had sobered the big Scotsman greatly, his manner changed, he became businesslike and walked his ailing soldier to where the horses stood.

''This is merlin,'' he declared, forgetting that Hooligan was well acquainted with the animal's arse if not the rest of it as it had dragged him through a seven-hour stint in hell.

*A weak ineffective man.

"He's my own horse so ye can give him back later. The bastard will kill you if he gets a chance so look out for him. Get the job done as soon as you're healed and remember, if they take ye; keep yer mooth shut. It'll not be for long. There will be men watching out fer ye every minute o' the day." A natural pause in the conversation culminated with Lliam Hooligan bleating loudly,

"You can't get four hunnered men in a ship." It was more a plea for knowledge and understanding thus far denied him than an expression of disbelief. He desperately needed both. He wanted to rage also that you can't burn a man till he was black without killing him as dead as mutton but was afraid that somehow it might be true, and Macbeth would jeer at his ignorance again; or stab him. Much to the surprise of the all-but-perfect ignoramus, the Scot barely reacted at all. Instead, he again retrieved a stick from amid the detritus of the high-water mark and began to draw in the wet sand. With a few simple strokes, he created the instantly recognisable plan-view of a ship, replete with keel. At right angles to the keel, he drew stick people, several of them.

"At the very bottom, juist above the bilges, they chain down the first layer of people," he began, "wee'uns, children up front so as not tae waste space, then, only a yard above the faces of these poor bastarts, they lay in a temporary deck." He used his impossibly thick, simian forearm to suggest the deck just a yard above the sand,

"On this level, they chain down another hundred or more, and so on till the boat cannae hold even one maire but what it would roll over, or founder in the furrst big wave."

"But…" Lliam Shaun Hooligan was incredulous. Anticipating the next question, Macbeth went on.

"Ye can smell a slaver ten miles downwind, laddie. They shit, piss, vomit, die and rot where they lay, for a journey that may take months. They poor buggers at the bottom sometimes drown in it. Now and then, the crew will drag out the dead ones and heave them over the side for the sharks. Ye can see their fins a yard high, monster fish as big as a horse, wi' mouths like a mantrap full of tooth that are longer than that wee wullie o' yoors." Hooligan was staring into what little was visible of Macbeth's face as the man spoke.

"Mother of Christ, you were there. Your man has seen it wit yer own oiyes." Macbeth did not reply, but he did whirl the stick far away in disgust, as though discarding his past. Lliam Hooligan was silenced; embarrassed by the knowledge which had passed between himself and his benefactor. He gathered his few worldly goods and allowed the Scot to help him as he struggled into the saddle, more purposeful than he thought possible, troubled by his new-found knowledge, in pain from his stamped-on feet up to his shredded ear, and impatient to find Astor's shipyard and plan its demise. Almost dismissive of his injuries now that he was mounted, he wanted to get away. To start his new life. To discover the extraordinary and perilous business that he was about to undertake.

The conspirators shook hands firmly in determination if not camaraderie and bid each other 'good hunting;' Macbeth perturbed briefly by memories of his days aboard slavers, Hooligan, physically distressed, hopeful in spirit, and aware of the fact that he was already in above his head.

'Nothing had changed there then.'

Inured to such minor discomforts as the stinging sleet lashing his exposed flesh, a drenched cabin boy raced barefoot along the crowded dock, dodging between the bayonets of the marine guards and the stones being flung by shipwrights at a column of filthy dejected prisoners. Struggling to mount the crowded gangplank of the 'Bird,' the lad had almost reached the deck when the grey afternoon exploded in light and thunder and the spire of St Thomas Aquinas close-by collapsed in a rockfall of red-hot granite. This extraordinary event barely registered with him for he had located his hero and object of his search, Captain Wynnychuk of the Restless, the man who had brought the filthy American pirates of the Bird to justice. The great man and his hellish boatswain were standing on the deck, watching everything and missing nothing. Noticing the lad's approach the captain squatted down so that he could hear whatever would be bawled into his ear. Understanding at the first telling he straightened energetically, shoving the shivering lad towards the warmth of the galley.

''Get below and stay there boy. Mister Symes. Fling this filth back where you got it; the shed's full.''

''Eye eye Sir,'' Symes lashed out at the nearest deckhand with his monkeyfist.

"You 'eard the capn," he raged; a fatuous claim, "get that scum back below."

As Wynnychuk disembarked, he confronted the first of the returning prisoners. Disgusted, and overcome by loathing of these murderous abolitionists he grabbed the hopeless creature and launched him bawling into the closing space between the ship and the dock. Deaf to both the man's screams and his shipmate's horrified exclamations he strode on alone and empty-handed through the enemy in what was a calculated challenge and insult, interrogating every face which held his gaze. His search for the Bird had consumed almost two years of his life and looking back at her now he resented the fact and wondered why it was that he had bothered. She was just a ship after all. Sleek, fast, valuable but still just a ship. His morale withered within him as he searched desperately for vindication which came to him with the reality of his distinct physical discomfort now that he was as wet as a herring and cold to the bone. Moments earlier he had killed without hesitation or so much as a second of introspection or regret. The thing that he had expunged however was not a human being it was vermin; a creature which had not only released dirty black animals but murdered the white Christian men who owned them. His vindication resurgent he hurried onward to bring the news of his success to his friends and to his country.

The organisation of the yard had changed greatly during his odyssey causing him to meander fruitlessly through a maze composed of spars and planks, coiled ropes, breweries of barrels, jungles of grotesque tree roots, roles of canvas, heaps of glistening pitch and the stink of piss towards the red-brick building which sat in clear view Buddha-like at the top of the slope. Head down against the rain he all but collided with a detachment of marines who advanced at the slow march due to the device encumbering their naked prisoner. Wynnychuk had purloined the idea from the Chinese many years earlier; it consisted of a thick wooden disk two feet in diameter which attached around the neck; agony to wear and immobilising. The captain grabbed the timber and forced the shivering skeleton to its knees all but breaking his victim's neck with the violence of it.

"Make the bastard crawl there," he ordered, kicking the bloody-handed captive viciously for the deep satisfaction and revenge that was in it."

Lord Michael Astor's drawing office was a warm haven of light where delicious food, cold German wine, and the music of the child prodigy Amadeus, could be enjoyed. His lordliness was at his drawing board surrounded by a litter of his remarkable detail-drawings; more art than engineering, some were of ships' componentry, others of a great house; 'Jamaica Place.' The tall, muscular young man would break-off from his work occasionally in order to conduct his string quartet who studiously ignored their employer's assistance, while Veronica the singer who sat with the musicians would not so much as look at 'the white demon.' She was as black as night, a slave and Nilotic queen of ravishing beauty. Metronome-like in a substantial rocking chair built to his specific requirements Hastings an enormous bodyguard was toasting himself at one of three blazes. He was bored and consequently very dangerous. Bristling with pent-up energy he was polishing an ivory dagger; an artistic masterpiece fashioned by a long-dead craftsman of Zanzibar. His intense appreciation of the weapon bordered on worship so that his latent ferocity and affection for the blade transmitted itself and scared the servants, Mammaluke uniforms or not. Smacking the wig from the head of the flunky who was engaged in polishing his boots, Hastings shaved a path through the fuzz on the man's pate then stood on the poor fellow's fingers as he tried to retrieve the headpiece.

"Leave off Hasty," the draughtsman drawled without so much as looking up from his preoccupation.

"He's not yours."

"Right-you-are my" A thunderous kicking at the door caused Astor to reach instantly for the pistol which lay close to hand and for the pent-up Hastings to charge into this opportunity for gratuitous violence. Drawing the bolt and ripping open the weighty mass of oak-and-iron the man of action admitted the fury of the storm and a more furious robber.

Smashing Hastings aside using the door as a weapon, Wynnychuk took aim at Astor's pretty face and bawled,

"Hand over your cash."

"You're robbing the wrong people you egg," advised Hastings, much happier now and wearing a wonderful grin.

"Shut yer hole else I'll make you a new one," the intruder glanced only momentarily at the equally massive guard, but on turning back to the younger man found a double-barrelled pistol aimed at his suddenly uncomfortable crotch. Astor was already using a servant as a human shield.

"A quick prayer perhaps," quipped the youth and the robber felt Hastings' blade, cold and skin-deep on his throat.

"Dogs' bollox." He lamented, "Can't a man ever win with you two sluts?"

"Wynny?"

"Wynnychuk is it you?"

It was at this moment that the ancient servant whom Michael had by the throat chose to drop to the floor as dead as a nail.

"You can't get good people anywhere today." Astor's handsome face was a blank canvas.

"Mickey, you've doubled in size. When I departed these shores, you were just a soft penis and a long streak of piss," Wynnychuk cast off his cloak confirming his identity and the three huge men came together in a welter of backslapping and hand-crushing as servants rushed to remove the inconsiderate bounder who had displayed the worst possible form by expiring while on duty. Veronica fainted, collapsing on top of her seated violinist;

thereby contriving to smash his Stradivarius to matchwood. He in turn lost consciousness at this catastrophe and fell to the floor also where he lay with his face firmly lodged in the lady's crotch; an arrangement which was appreciated greatly by the licentious onlookers in a silence broken by Astor who remarked sang-froid.

"He's wanted to do that ever since he set eyes on her. What the hell are you doing here Wynn; I'm told that the Bird still floats?"

"You've never been right in your life child, and you're wrong again." Wynnychuk proceeded portentously to the windows followed closely by his newly expectant friends, from which vantage point he could see his naked prisoner below and the superstructure of the Bird in the distance.

"I have the Bird. I have her crew and I have her bloody-handed captain. That's him down there. The one in the wooden suit.

CHAPTER 3: A Close Call

Lord Michael Astor horseman supreme, entered the Great South Road just minutes from home by leaping Cossack over a five-barred gate without so much as the need to ask the question. Unusually the ribbon of holes, puddles and ruts was devoid of travellers but for a lone horseman of remarkable proportions just a stone's-throw ahead. Tall, in the saddle the lean individual was well-dressed. His midnight boots were superb with blood-red lapels and silver spurs of rising sun design; all topped off with in an acre or two of Harris Tweed which, along with Glenfiddich and the road to England, were the only good things to come out of that fastness of barbarism to the north; Scotland. Intent on overtaking the low-flying haggis without the need for civilities or worse still, conversation, Astor spurred Cossack onwards as the big fellow, clearly weary of this life, pitched from the saddle and struck the road, neck first, like a poleaxed ox.

'Jesus bloody Christ, another fifty yards and I would have known bugger all about this.' His lordship was not pleased. Hauling back on the reins he brought the utterly insane Cossack to a halt hard-by the clearly unwanted horse his knowing eye declaring the creature flawless, a perfect specimen. The die was cast, he would adopt it.

''This business might be very fortuitous after all.'' he declared aloud then reprimanded himself for talking in the absence of an audience; doing so phonetically. Peering down belatedly from his lofty station he addressed the apparently dead nuisance instead.

''Are you alive?'' he laughed. The bounder's face was the remains of a lion's meal, and at the point where an ear should have resided was a mess not unlike the crotch of a freshly castrated nigger. As no reply was forthcoming, his lordship dismounted and tapped the thing with his boot; Polyphemus groaned.

"Shit," said Astor.

''Mornin moi lord.'' Said a bunch of cretins.

If the presence of dead bodies littering the gates of his home were not insult enough, three buffoons, probably gardeners or woodcutters or some such oafish thing, in total disregard for his rules, had appeared through the gates of the Granary, mumbling sickening protestations about how he could safely leave this business in their capable unwashed hands et-fucking-cetera. Had his pistol been ship-shape he would have shot all three of them in the face. Gathering up the reins of his latest equine acquisition he mounted and rode through the gates of home.

"Wot shall we do wiv im marsta?"

"Chuck him in a ditch."

Disdaining the portico and his wide and lofty doors of iron-studded oak the tired and happy man rode around to the furthest extremities of his home where lay the subterranean domain of the incomparable Mrs Crabtree; thirty stones of culinary genius.

"Mrs Crabtree, remove your bloomers, I have come to ravish you," he announced, bursting through the kitchen door like a spring gale.

"You there, take my horses to the stables. Ring for my butler. I want that tailor's-dummy down here yesterday. My mistake, as I recall you wear no bloomers, you little strumpet. Where the hell are you woman?" The re-energised home-comer received the plaudits of the dozen or so kitchen staff in the fashion of an Italian tenor, firstly with deep bows, then with arms thrown asunder, as though to beg 'more, more.'

"Promises, promises." The accents of Devon emanated from the pantry at the far end of the glistening white room, warm as Mandalay, where a vast white arm, dewlap swinging, had been extended, and several members of the well-nourished kitchen staff were engaged in freeing the enormous softness of the queen-of-the-kitchens piecemeal from her own Aladdin's cave where all manner of riches were hiding despite their olfactory fascinations declaring their presence to anyone with a nose.

"You rang, sir?"

It was Michael Astor's considered opinion that Delavier, his butler, was the very best of fellows in the whole world, but for some perverse reason; which, for the life of him he could not fully comprehend; he found it necessary to treat the man like dirt. And worse. Had the man been born a horse Michael would have gelded him by now; or at the very least thrown a saddle on him and introduced him to the joys of spurs.

"Don't you ever sleep, Man?" He complained, while examining in detail his servant's sartorial presentation, which despite the ungodly hour, was perfectly exquisite.

"Indeed, I do sir, deeply and serenely; thank you for your enquiry. One feels that it is the duty of this gentleman's gentleman to take his rest when not required by."

"Yes, yes for the love of Clitoris Delavier, I asked you whether you. Must I be lectured at every turn by a dribbling servant? Here am I, about to expire of hunger; dry as a nun's…"

"Mr Michael, sir!" The horrified tones of the venerable Mrs Crabtree, recently liberated from her incarceration in the pantry were quite sufficient to put an end to Michael's bogus tantrum, but the silver salver resting on her elephantine stomach settled the matter completely. The centrepiece comprised of two roasted chickens smelling of heaven and exquisite in the colours of a crucifixion by Durer, due to the many segments of orange, cupolas of bright yellow mustard, green leaves, scarlet strawberries and peach sauce in which they were dressed.

"Mrs Crabtree, if I could find the right wrinkle I'd do you this instant," declared the delighted home-comer, his irritation forgotten, as he ripped a leg from one of the fouls.

"How on earth did you know to do all…?"

"One took the liberty" Delavier intoned, "to divine your lordship's wishes should he return this morning."

"Did you really?'' How he loved to employ heavy sarcasm.

''Then why am I perishing of thirst at this very…?" Michael's pitcher of enjoyment at baiting his perfect servant failed in the decanting as the much-abused butler placed a tall flute of white wine on the virginal perfection which was the cloth of Polish lace.

"Warm as piss, I'll wager," the master countered, not to seem pleased at any cost, but drinking like a monk he found the nectar to be as cold as a mountain stream, which was just how he liked it. He relented enthusiastically.

"Ye gods, that's passable. How on earth did you get it so cold?" he proffered his empty glass, and the butler obliged him.

"I had a case suspended in our deepest well, Mr Michael Sir, and ordered that it be brought indoors at the instant of your return."

"You did 'well," choked his lordliness, through a mouth which was full of chicken.

''Do you see? 'You did 'Well.' It's a jest.''

His adoring audience being tickled-to-death, the thespian changed tack yet again and surrendering unconditionally, said with certainty,

"You have drawn my bath, haven't you?'' The pomaded head inclined.

"It is filling as we speak, my lord."

"My bed is freshly made in silk, is it not?"

A further inclination confirmed that all was ready in the bedroom.

"Egyptian cotton today my lord the morning being a trifle cooler"

"Cossack the murderer is well taken care of?"

Delavier refilled his master's flute a second time.

"Particularly well, sir. The stables report that both animals are uninjured and in fine fettle." His lordship accosted his greasy chin with a staysail of a napkin.

"Delavier," he began, portentously, "we will soon remove to Jamaica Place, once the furniture, and paintings and objet d'art and whatnot are installed, that is. When we do, would you sooner dwell in-house as you do here, or in a home of your own with a garden for your brood. You do have a brood, don't you?" Against his bidding, sudden tears welled up in the butler's eyes and meandered downwards until they fell from his smoothly shaven chin, plump as tiny cherubs, to leave a constellation of dying stars on the flags.

"May God bless you ever further sir," the man croaked.

"I shall take your bleating to be a 'yes,'" snorted Michael.

"You and your lady wife will drive over to Jamaica Place this very day to select a plot for your home. Take a carriage. A hamper Mrs Crabtree, a hamper of nothing but the best for Delavier and his lady to top the whole thing off, if you would be so kind." Then for the consumption of the staff, all of whom were now listening intently, smiling and weeping by turns, declared,

"I would advise you not to select a possie directly in front of my home, lest I have to shoot you for the second-rate servant that you are." Delavier opened a second bottle of wine with a flourish, dipping his head in acquiescence, his pleasant, normally imperturbable expression wreathed in damp smiles.

"I am speechless with happiness, my lord," he sobbed.

"So, all I have to do in order to vanquish your endless prattling is to give you a house. Is that what you're implying?" Michael was enjoying his own performance deeply.

"I'm quite sure that one such gift will secure my unfailing reticence, Master. On the matter of Jamaica Place my lord I greatly regret to.'

"Get to the curs-ed point!"

"Your gardener, Sir, Mr Brown sir, Mr Capability Brown; Jamaica place being all but complete has taken up residence there; himself and his underlings." Absolute silence greeted this devastating news so that the dripping of fat from a spitted carcass of beef punctuated the space phonetically. Lord Michael Astor absorbed this unimaginable, poisonous intelligence the way a swamp absorbs the unwary, there was the slightest ripple on the surface and then the event might never have occurred. The staff were painfully aware that the magnificent new mansion was the master's magnum opus the greatest creation of his inordinately creative life. The House and the vast fortune being expended on its construction had been the talk of the country for a twelvemonth. Following several years of planning, drawing and building, the superb concept was now receiving its final artistic touches prior to Lord Michael taking up residence on his twenty first birthday just days away. There would be blood. That was a certainty.

''I will not think on it directly. You must now postpone your excursion,''

''Naturally Sir. I gave instructions that your guest; the injured gentleman, be lodged in the blue Caravaggio room of the west wing and sent for your surgeon with all haste to attend to your lordship's wounds and his. I do hope that these arrangements meet with your approval." Delavier had abandoned the source of his employer's discomfiture with supreme professionalism.

"The cyclops is not my guest. I have never previously set an eye on the beast. Get him doctored quick-sharp' tie him on his horse and get rid. Today preferably. Belay that, keep his horse. Put him on an old nag if one can be found and while you're about it get rid of those idiots who brought him inside.''

"As you say, sir. Also, your father Lord Bismark Astor, and certain peers-of-the-realm are in residence."

"The House of Lords has set up shop under my roof? At whose expense, might I ask?"

"Your father, Lord Bismark Astor and his party have been most appreciative of your unequalled hospitality, sir," declared Delavier diplomatically,

"Your father, Lord Bismark Astor begs a moment of your time at your convenience; as do the Marques Cornwallis and the Generals Howe and Carlton.''

"I can't talk to that lot till I've bathed and had several hundred snoozeywinks. It's up to you to keep the old boy at bay until, shall we say luncheon on the terrace at one. No! Luncheon in the green summerhouse at two. It's cooler. To my bath we go, bring some wine. Mrs Crabtree, you are a goddess among cooks. Several goddesses in fact. An entire convocation." Mrs Crabtree melted like butter in a hot pan as her much loved master bowed over her hand.

The bathroom was Michael's own invention. He had learned somewhere or other that King Henry VIII had enjoyed piped water, both hot and cold, and would bathe on a very regular basis, enjoying the sensation of a body free of sticky perspiration, accumulated foot and under-arm. His lordship was henceforth a convert to cleanliness. There was nothing sweeter in this world, he had concluded, on the first occasion of bathing in its tiled opulence, than to wash one's women and one's perspiration of the day from one's-self in hot fragrant water, prior to falling into one's bed; preferably on top of yet another woman. He had designed it himself naturally, down to such details as the shell pattern with which the golden taps, soap dishes and a frieze or two of the floor-tiles were decorated. That idea had been purloined from Botticelli's, 'The Birth of Venus,' seeming thusly to his lordship, eminently fitting for such a watery backdrop. Arriving at his bedroom door he had beaten the footman to the gilded handle when the thing was opened from within by a spring-day of a housemaid who, startled at coming face to face so unexpectedly with her distant and revered employer stood blushing and stammering her apologies for nothing at all. Hoisting the flustered angel from the floor to hold her against his chest Astor entered, closing the door behind him with his heel.

"Delavier, you may go," he bawled through two inches of dense, highly polished oak. One second later, he reappeared; relieved Delavier who had not moved, of the wine with the adjunct,

"I'll have that," and disappeared a second time, only to open the door yet again to say,

"Send Hastings to me, Delavier. If I'm asleep, he must wake me." With that, he slammed the door in his servant's face for the third and last time. When a while later,

Hastings knocked and entered the bathroom, Astor was on his back in his tiled sarcophagus tormenting the nubile who was astride him; bringing her to the very gates of heaven before disappointing her tantalisingly, only to repeat his ministrations a moment later. Ignoring the girl's presence, her utterly divine form and her delirium tremens completely, Hastings greeted his employer, eyes averted, and stood in motionless silence waiting to receive his orders.

"Hastings, are you aware that certain rats have taken up residence in Jamaica Place? My Jamaica Place. The greatest achievement of my life. No, don't answer. If you did not know, then I for one would like to know, why?

If you 'did' know, then I would have expected you to have done something about it. So you can't win." Between passages of cool attentions, during which Michael ensured that the girl remained frantic with her need to climax yet again, he went on to outline the steps that he wished Hastings to take in respect of this unprecedented crime as it was as clear as day that Hastings was not sufficiently interested in his master's welfare to initiate a suitable revenge; or just too idle to get off his arse. The civilities dispensed with, and the girl's needs now relegated, the master went on to relate the events of earlier that morning, concerning the uppity choir, with particular mention of the soloist with the scars in his brows.

''Rebellion is on the increase Hasty. It must be eradicated, root and branch. Have your people deal severely with any individuals so inclined wherever they travel. Do give these matters some thought, won't you? There's a good man."

"Certainly, my lord," replied Hastings with the hint of a bow; raising his voice in order to be heard above the delight of the girl, who, unable to delay a second longer, had returned to paradise by virtue of her own energetic reciprocation. Hastings' bow was followed by a click of his heels, and he was gone.

CHAPTER 3: The Maelstrom

He must have died a second time in a matter of days, because it was beyond dispute that he was now in heaven itself. Everything but the birds and the posh music was hushed. There were white clouds of sweet-smelling softness for his head while clean sweet smelling peach skins shrouded his naked state, all cool to the touch and gentle. Cherubs hovered in the sky above, smiling down on him from their frescoed clouds in pleasure at his very presence. Glistening rosewood furniture upholstered in silk of the softest blue stood all around as though revelling in its own perfection while beyond the open French doors and the Capulet terrace, sublimely colourful and seemingly endless congregations of trees and flowers, made a delight of the late afternoon while sweetening the air so thoroughly that it was a joy evident even to *his* olfactory ruins.

"Good day sir, I do hope that you slept well." Lliam Shaun Hooligan found a painted-child arse-bandit in a pink coat and a white wig; his hands folded neatly in front of his crotch, standing by his bed like a virgin defending her most precious possession. It occurred to Hooligan to ask the self-satisfied little runt what business it was of his whether a man slept well or not, but he was overcome by the strangest sense of wellbeing and affection for all men which mollified him greatly.

"Sure, oi slept better than a babby on the gin," he declared generously, and wondered what it was about himself that was different, and why the sudden frown on the leprechaun's painted face.

"Let me help you to dress, sir. Your injuries will obviously be causing you such difficulty."

That was it! The pain! The pain was gone! Hooligan put his hand to where raw meat had supplanted an ear and found it bandaged and incredibly, no longer agonizing to the touch. Sure, he was swaddled in the stuff, like the baby Jesus his self all bandages and flowery-smelling purple muck which had to be some class of balm or other.

"The stitches are causing you no concern, sir?" With a dip of his wig the flunky indicated a huge gilt-framed mirror. Hooligan descended from the plateau of his lofty couch and approached the thing as though the creature inside it might leap out to bite him. To his astonishment the desperate wound to the side of his face had been pulled shut and tied with black horsehair. Incredibly, the stuff had been stitched through his living flesh. 'Stitched' loik a sack of spuds.'

"Jasus, Joseph and Mary, and all the saints," he breathed, "and oi never felt a ting." The hand he raised to explore his ear, his broken and agonized hand, was bandaged and splinted, and not so much as a squeak.

"Sure, oi can't feel nuthin atall."

"Of course not, sir."

Hooligan concentrated his enlarged but not limitless tolerance on the mincing excuse for a man as though it had lost its wits, only for the fellow to respond by indicating with the very slightest inclination of the head and the facial expression of a cherub, two medicine bottles standing on half of a round table which was sticking out of the wall hard by.

"The laudanum, sir. Doctor Reynolds is Lord Bismark Astor's personal surgeon. Lord Michael's also, of late. The gentleman is very highly skilled, very well thought of in all of the best circles. He works miracles with opium, laudanum and half a dozen concoctions which are all very hush-hush."

Hooligan was astounded and troublingly confused, 'Lord Astor!' The dwarf said, 'Lord Astor.' His sedative-affected mind struggled to cope with this suddenly threatening situation.

"Lord Astor!" he blurted, his guilty conscience almost betraying him. He was on the cusp of quoting Macbeth's; 'he's a bastard, but he's a clever bastard,' but saved himself just in time.

"This is The Granary sir, the home of Mister 'Michael' Astor, of course, Lord Astor the younger," explained the poodle, misunderstanding the Irishman's response. From an adjoining room he had retrieved a wheeled rack bearing Hooligan's clothes and was suggestively holding up the silk shirt, freshly laundered.

Lliam Shaun Hooligan recognized the 'bum's rush' when it was foist upon him.

"Any chance of a lump o' bread an' a dram afore Oi piss off sunshoine?" Obviously startled by this further use of the language of the gutter from one whom his master clearly presumed to be a gentleman and had therefore brought into his home, the flunky was momentarily speechless, but recovering his equanimity replied,

"Absolutely sir. Mister Michael wishes me to relay his regrets that you are unable to remain with us longer and has asked me to inform you that he is presently playing host to the General Staff and requires every room. I'll arrange a repast while you dress." He bowed,

"If you will excuse me."

Hooligan knew right away that he had blown his cover. The bastard whose house he was now in must have seen the class of his clothes and the beast he was riding and taken it for granted that yer man was one of the filthy few. At the instant in which the door closed behind the little puff, Hooligan scrambled into his clothes like a lover, about to be discovered by the cuckolded husband. Stamping his feet into his lovely boots, he damn-near smashed his toes to smithereens, his poor, innocent toes, on the wooden feet that some maleficent swine had put in them. Unbelievably, his purse, still weighing about right, was in his coat pocket. He rushed to the door, turned on an afterthought, dived full length across the bed, grabbed the two bottles of magic medicine, and charged out into a mile-long road which went to both the front and the arse of this bloody castle. Hopping to the southern window, the one which glittered in sunlight, he peered out

Beyond a puddle of a lake, resplendent in their girly uniforms, were tribes of soldier-boys all pissed as farts, outdoing each other with their strutting and posing while dozens of others were galloping up and back sticking lances into perfectly innocent fruit. He wondered smartly which of them would be the Astor's, concluding that it would likely be the two big bastards, the only ones out of uniform.

Just as he had suspected; across the vast acreage of deep green clover, hurried the girly lickspittle, the tail of his pretty white wig wagging and his little silver buckles glimmering in the light, going as fast as his skinny wee legs would carry him while preserving his dignity. In a panic he galloped to the other side of the house, hurtling past startled maids and flunkies as he leapt down endless flights of stairs, and after a dozen cul-de-sacs and as many terrifying wrong turns, dashed out into the sunlight. A gardener crawling around in an herbaceous border doffed his cap with the alacrity of a guardsman saluting Georgie Porgy; startled out of his wits by a half-undressed troglodyte exploding through the door.

"Stables," demanded the escapee, and the tremulous fellow indicated a distant village of mansions arranged in a sentimental bower within a great expanse of grass, cut short as the nap on the seat of his pants.

"The stables, oi said. Are ye fookin deaf?" Hooligan enquired snottily, but to the thoroughly scared escapee's consternation, the man gave the same response. Having no option, he charged away, seeming in his agitated condition to travel at half his best speed due to the bloody knee-deep pebbles around the house clutching 'loik the divil hisself,' at his shiny new boots while with every step his backbone spasmed in dread at the thought of a lead ball smashing it to jelly. Miraculously, as he neared the artistic sand-colored homes with the rust–tinted Roman-tiled roofs and latticed windows, the old gardener was proven correct. Each of the superbly appointed residences was home to a magnificent horse; his beautiful big hunter, Merlin, instantly recognizable in one of the half-doors. The luck of the Irish, sure. Several stablemen noticing the gentleman's haste; left off with their work and rushed to provide whatever assistance was required and in less time than he could have got his mount out of its palace and climbed onto its bare back he was mounted with saddle bridle, the lot, and wished, 'good hunting,' into the bargain.

"The coast?" the pirouetting equestrian demanded of his equally excited assistants, and three arms rose as one, to point in three exclusive directions; two of these being diametrically opposed. Hooligan dug his heels into his mount's ribs and the great beast went off at a dead run in a direction of its own choosing. He had long forgotten the inexplicable thrill of having a galloping thoroughbred beneath him; letting the creature have its head and surrendering his soul to death or glory. Having escaped what could have become hell, he had been boosted directly into heaven. He was filled from his toes to the top of his head with ecstasy so that this entirely novel experience, unable to be contained, burst forth in loud ejaculations of glee. He was aboard an exceptional horse, well fed and watered; clothed in the very best, with a purse full of promise. 'AND' he was pain-free with bottles in his pocket which would perpetuate that happy condition.

For several heart-pounding miles he clung joyously to Merlin's back as the magnificent creature exultant in its own speed leaped majestically over fences and ditches; frightening to death the occasional pheasant, peasant, and flocks of sheep, human and otherwise.

Sensing his mount beginning to labor, he considerately brought Merlin down to a walk, a task which required another quarter of a mile to affect and on coming across a place where the soil had been pugged by cattle the ebullient escapee veered off his line of flight using the churned-up soil to disguise his tracks. Doubling back at the walk he allowed his new friend to carry him to water and with their thirsts quenched the happy couple travelled on to an elevated place just north of the house which he had fled and from there he watched as the pursuit set off. Macbeth had been right enough when he had said, 'Make no mistake lad, this is war.'

Field Marshall Charles Cornwallis was a very poor loser; the worst in fact, and it was due to this feature of the man's repulsive character that Bismarck Ludwig Astor, politician, landowner, industrialist, farmer, slave trader and Lord of the realm derived his pleasure in humiliating the man, rather than in the size of the pot, which after all was a mere few hundred guineas. If the charmless drone would only lay the seven then he, 'Bisy' as he was known to his friends, would carry the day and he was at this moment employing every ounce of his cerebral faculties in willing the Field Marshal to do just that. 'Lay the seven. Lay the seven.'

Cornwallis glowered at his traitorous, insubordinate cards for a week or so as was his style when overrun by the enemy, sipped at his champagne, nibbled at his bred with mutton and mustard and even flicked his handkerchief at an imaginary fly before accepting the inevitable. Mournful as though going down on one knee at Breda, the field marshal reached out and lay his card on the baize, 'face down.'

General Howe, instantly outraged by this breach in etiquette, was about to protest, and drew in breath like a sucking chest wound preparatory to launching a frontal assault, but before the outraged general could give vent to his displeasure, the Marques came to his senses and surrendered, flipping the card face-up revealing nothing other than the seven of clubs. 'The seven,' Astor's joy was worth ten times more than the gold itself for this was a war of egos and in his book this self-satisfied, pompous oaf of a soldier who had the unmitigated gall to flaunt what was merely inherited wealth in the face of better men and was never required to risk a hair of his bewigged head, needed taking down like a hore's draws. With all eyes on him, and the suspense so thick that it could be cut with a gun carriage, Bismarck Ludwig Wolfgang Astor delayed with perfect timing and control, holding off until the very second at which the field marshal's restraint deserted him.

"For the love of God, Bisy..." the man expostulated, only for the ebullient one to lay down his winning hand with the disdain that he would the bone of a well-chewed chop.

"My game I believe, Charles," Astor drawled, and drew the bagatelle that was the heap of gold carelessly to him across the baize.

"Guy? General Howe?"

Guy Carlton, the First Baron Dorchester, and General Howe understood perfectly well what had just taken place and in their measured style merely smiled and refrained from comment. Both men knew that Cornwallis would be smarting as things stood but it was not in their nature to kick a man when he was down, even though such behaviour had become the fashion of late.

"It is indeed, Bisy," agreed Carlton, breaking off as the low growl of the thousand men bivouacked in the orchards of The Granary and the park adjacent ceased. All four cardplayers rushed out of the cool of the summerhouse into the broiling glare of the sun to investigate this unusual occurrence, pursued by a pink and blue tail of frantic aides-de-camp, butlers, footmen and secretaries. Beyond the ornamental lake, the regiment were staring, every man-jack of them at the great house as though Helen of Troy beckoned, while at the French-windows of one of the third-floor bedrooms a bearded giant of a man had appeared, naked as the day he was born but for a black eye-patch and more bandages than are to be found at Chelsea Military Infirmary, all of which endowed the fellow with something of a piratical air. The strapping individual seemed, even at a distance, to be unsteady on his feet and somewhat bewildered to the point of being completely unaware of his considerable audience. Releasing his necessary grip on the doors, the nude advanced as far as the low, decorative parapet which surrounded the terrace and to the accompaniment of premature laughter from those incredibly few soldiers who could boast the wit to foresee what was about to happen, pissed blood freehand like a dray-horse in a considerable and seemingly endless stream, over the parapet. This performance met with general acclaim from the throats of every ranker present, while the camp-followers, who covered their eyes with their hands, peeked between their fingers. Drummers seized their sticks and rapped out an accompaniment. Muskets were fired into the air. The comedians in the ranks bawled observations regarding length and circumference and felt compelled to liken the thing to a baby's arm holding an orange in its hand. Comparisons were made with creatures of the four-legged persuasion, thoroughbred and otherwise, and even volumes and duration of flow were accorded scientific explanation. All of which caused great amusement among the bored. Shading his eye from the glare of the sun, the hero of the hour belatedly discovered the extent of his celebrity, and supremely unabashed, continued to completion with the draining of his abused bladder. Deeming such an appreciative audience to be worthy of some form of recognition, the shameless person's finale was to shake in a wildly exaggerated fashion, and as the delighted soldiers applauded rapturously, he then raised both arms in the fashion of a Caesar recognising the adoration of the plebs. This extravagant behaviour proved to be too much for him in his weakened condition; his arms flopping unbidden to his sides. He staggered and for a moment seemed about to topple to his death but saving himself with a snort of amusement the offender against decency pulled himself erect, saluting meanwhile with the wrong hand; the unbandaged one. His ablutions complete, the pirate turned and retreated to his room as unsteadily as he had come, leaving behind him an atmosphere noticeably more joyful than that which had previously prevailed and the punishable salutes of a regiment. Still smarting from his defeat at cards and exigent for a scapegoat, Charles Cornwallis called out in his unfortunately high-pitched voice that the men who had fired their weapons should be rewarded with ten strokes of the cane and a week's-worth of bread and water, then stalked into the shade of the trees, a very disgruntled Field Marshall indeed.

"I say Bisy," yelled Howe above the reports of imagined cannon-fire and at a range of four feet, "isn't that your aide-de-camp Michael approaching our left wing?" General Howe had not seen action for almost two years but affected being permanently at war. Turning hopefully; mainly because his belly felt as though his throat had been slit, Bismark discovered his son, pushing his way rudely through the crowd of pen-pushers and servants whom Cornwallis seemed to find indispensable when he was in the field. A head taller and a foot broader in the shoulders than most, the boy had filled out even in the few months since Bisy had seen him last, and in his upsurge of pride he charged headlong into Howe's ambush.

"It is indeed, General," he rejoiced, "now we can eat."

"Well set up sort of a horse; handsome even, are you sure that you're the father?" Bismark Astor was deeply insulted and before he could achieve mastery of his emotions, he was challenging Howe to a dual.

'I cannot pass that remark,' was what he intended saying, but what he uttered was "I cannot pass… another minute without sustenance." After all, General Howe and his chums had the government's purse strings where the troubles in the colonies were concerned, and Astor was lusting after a million of those pounds at the very least. It was to this end that he had suggested that 'Cornwallis Own' regiment of foot take advantage of a few rest days here at The Granary; Michael's home. This, and a further few days at Windward Palace, one of his own country places, prior to the final legs of the regiment's footslog to the port of Weymouth. He could not risk losing that windfall simply for the pleasure of killing a man who had insulted his late wife. No, that would never do.

"Michael, my boy," carolled the father offering his hand, "It's wonderful to see you. You know my colleagues of course." The son almost wrenched the father's arm from its socket with the vigor of his greeting and glowered past him at the three peacocks.

"Indeed, I do," he drawled, grinning with the sincerity of a salt-water crock and shaking with insulting brevity the hands of the generals in order of seniority he announced.

"Business can wait. I could scoff a rancid rat, and quaff a spittoon so come and eat." To everyone's surprise, including that of his master Delavier led the party through the cold depths of the extensive summer house exiting soon in a wonderfully shady bower which enjoyed a cool and fragrant breeze and was further enhanced by a view of the ornamental lake. On that silver and blue mirror, swans tacked and luffed effortlessly in white, while beyond its verdant borders, the scarlet and black of the regiment moved among the pastel shades of the orchards. Here, a table had been set, blindingly white in its cloth of Venetian lace worked with threads of both silver and gold where liveried servants in pink and azure-blue drew back the scarlet chairs as the nobility approached and magician-like, whipped away the covers to reveal plate and cutlery of gold, Bohemian glassware, and Waterford crystal containing a feast of cold meats, cheeses, grapes, vegetables and fruits all wonderfully suited to the heat of the day. No one remarked on the fact, naturally enough; that would not be the 'done thing,' but every man present was beginning to understand that in keeping with his sire, the younger Astor was fast becoming a man to be reckoned with. The swine's love for and appreciation of the numinous was evident in every aspect of his life. A surprising condition for a filthy slaver.

"Marques Cornwallis, if you would be so kind," intoned Delavier, and seated the Field Marshal at the head of the table, with Lord Bismark Astor facing the soldier at a stone's-throw distant.

"Gentlemen, please don't stand on ceremony," he urged, and the others, their mouths watering at the sight of the extraordinarily appetizing feast before them, took the man at his word. Had any of the great personages present expected to be fawned over and regaled with witty small-talk by their youthful, upstart, arrogant host they would have been disappointed. Michael Astor ate and drank as though it were his sworn duty to clear the table of food and drink with or without assistance from the other men, and he did so interminably and rudely, apparently deaf to their bonhomie. Once he had consumed a sufficiency however, he was a curiously different and deeply irate creature.

"I'm reasonably certain that as I left the house earlier, I heard muskets fired," he declared loudly, spreading the blame like grape shot.

"Can't be having that; scares my horses, damn it. My Arabs, highly strung, every one of 'em." He worried his wide mouth with a snowy napkin then threw the thing down gauntlet-like in a general challenge.

This forthright approach had two results. One was a flanking-manoeuvre by Cornwallis, a man whose family motto could well have been, 'Never Apologize,' and the second was the knowledge that his unwanted houseguest had recovered sufficiently to piss publicly down the side of the house, this being the cause belli. Michael's fury on the receipt of this slap in the face was of course enjoyed root and branch by his guests, who were thoroughly put-out by their host's earlier reticence and his failure to exhibit the deference which they felt was their due. He had shown no interest at all in any of their adventures on behalf of king and country, or even the wounds which they had suffered in the course of those hostilities.

The arrival of an over-excited, under-sized servant at Michael's table set in motion a veritable epidemic of whispering. The childlike individual whispered in the ear of Delavier, who in turn whispered in the ear of his master. Lord Michael then whispered to his father, who listened with beetling brows beckoning a couple of his bare-knuckle retainers urgently to his side as he processed the poisonous information. Bismark then whispered into the cauliflower which served Scylla as an ear and the bodyguard whispered to his collaborator Charybdis in a language of their own. The enormous twins set off in the footsteps of the little servant in the fashion of two well-nourished rottweilers intent on setting a miniature poodle.

"Preserve the bastard's jaw," their employer called, "I want to question him." He was then himself questioned by the military men. The result of all this whispering was to pique the curiosity of every waking man on the property, so that when the gladiatorial twins returned disappointingly empty handed, in excess of a hundred soldiers sensing an adventure in the air, had drifted towards the picket-lines, some going so far as to saddle their mounts. Incandescent at being denied the opportunity to beat answers out of the vulgar swine who had inveigled his way into The Granary through lies and deceit, Michael hurled his monogram-engraved, gold-piped wine glass into the lake, and set off for the stables at what was intended to be a brisk pace and direct route, but which was rendered both pedestrian and serpentine by his full load of wine. His vanguard was comprised of Astor senior, Cornwallis, Carlton and Howe, and the inebriated officer cadre of Cornwallis Own; with Lord Astor's heavies, Wynychuk and Michael's man Hastings, just two paces behind, with sundry servants and soldiers bringing up the rear; in short, every man who owned a horse and was still capable of riding it.

The offended one was ill-prepared for the information which he was about to receive. He and his expeditionary force had barely entered the stable area proper which comprised four or five acres, when they met an ancient blacksmith who greeted his employer with the words,

"Art'noon Mister Mikle, sor. Oi just 'membered where I seed that feller's 'oss. 'Im what's just rid off afore; it blong to that heathen fella as wears a frock, an' all covered in air, E must've kilt 'im to get that 'oss." This explained a great deal. Michael was aware that the hirsute individual who ran certain estates neighboring his own, was in the pay of the abolitionists. It followed that the tweedy, one-eared one-eyed rogue whom he had, through the kindness of his heart brought into his home; was also one of *them*.

The company was overjoyed by this unexpected improvement to what promised to be yet another humdrum day on their march to the ocean because the hunt was on, and not for some mangy old fox; the quarry was a man; better still; the bounder was mounted on a good horse, so the chase would be worthy of the name. Who knew, one might even get the opportunity to draw blood; it was all just too good for words. Several individuals, all deeply the worse for wear considered it their prerogative to take command, at which assertion serious arguments broke out about dates of commission, experience or lack of it in this or that type of exercise, choice of mount, tactics, and a dozen other irrelevant topics, until Lord Michael, intent on gaining control of the situation, leapt theatrically onto a barrel-end. Unfortunately for his lordship the rotten wood gave way under his considerable weight, and he dropped ingloriously with one leg inside the deadly affair, and one not.

Though, as he hastened to assure his suddenly hushed audience that the family jewels had not been crushed, it was, when all was said and done, a very painful accident and in consideration of this, his appeal for calm when once again capable of speech, was conceded. It was agreed that on setting off from The Granary, the twenty men of the pursuit detachment would, as soon as feasible, form up in a skirmish line and advance southwards, towards the coast, each man visible to those on either side of him. They would proceed at a canter as the quarry 'being a plebeian' by all reports, would inevitably hag-rid his horse and soon be overtaken by the more measured approach of the professionals. Three shots fired in the air would indicate the capture of the interloper, at which everyone would form up and return to The Granary for dinner after which there would be an inquisition; courts-martial would be convened and the bounder would be hung or flogged or put in the stocks, and all of the enemy's plans would be extracted from him by fair or foul, as the prevailing mood ordained. A junior officer in his cups pointed out, with some difficulty it must be said, that little information would be got from the spy after he had been hung, therefore the inquisition had better take place prior to that. The general feeling of the assembly was that this made a lot of sense, and thus the motion was carried unanimously, and the pursuit was on. As the afternoon tired and the miscreant had not been apprehended, the group's canter slowed to a very pleasant walk while the distance between the senior officers at the center of the line shrank to nothing at all with the result that Bismark Astor and the general officers, now almost sober, fell into animated conversation. It was a conversation to which Michael Astor contributed nothing at all, other than to be a very good listener indeed. All four of the participants were members of the House of Lords, and what passed between them as they rode would have done justice; and more besides, to that institution's reputation for venality, parsimony, conspiracy, blackmail, vulgarity, intrigue, half-truths, damned lies and slander. The ridiculous Cornwallis maintained that what Britain was faced with in the colonies, was nothing more than a passing discontent with certain officials employed in the collection of taxes. A discontent which had merely simmered during the previous eighteen months and would blow over within the next six.

'And this while the *discontent* had been growing exponentially for a decade, and the fool was marching his Own Regiment of Foot to the coast prior to embarkation for Boston where a major battle was raging as he spoke.' Michael's scorn plumbed previously inconceivable depths. Carlton and Howe, schoolboys both, were outdoing each other in promoting the unlimited intensification of hostilities between the mother country and her colonies for no better reasons than that they relished a fight and nursed a congenital loathing of what they referred to as 'malcontents.' This definition it seemed, embraced those inferior type who worked for a living, foreigners, niggers, natives, Jews, Catholics fuzzy wuzzies whirling Dervishes and those persons unfortunate enough to have received their education elsewhere than Eton, prior to their introduction to society politics and lechery otherwise than at Oxford or Cambridge. It was Michael Astor's considered opinion that were he to shoot all three of the retarded buffoons at this very minute, he would be performing a great service to both the King and his dominions. He and his father were making fortunes year on year by selling-at-auction slaves from the fever coast, in ports up and down the eastern seaboard of America and he was furiously aware that the war between Britain and the colonists; if it worsened still further would have adverse effects on that trade, possibly for many years to come. It might even bring the business to a permanent halt should the British Navy find it necessary to blockade those ports against the importations to the colonists, and the export of their mutinous Orinoco.

Michael reserved his most damning judgment however for his father. The old fool had just as much to lose as himself as they were partners in the trade just as they were in a score of other enterprises, yet the mouthy old goat was more adamant than the other three put together that to intensify the present sanguinary hostilities to a war of attrition was the only way to stem the ambitions of the naughty Americans. In response to Cornwallis' assertion that the colonists were merely fishermen, farmers, carpenters and plantation owners. Astor senior had observed that they were fishermen, farmers and carpenters, every one of whom was joined at the hip to a musket and could shoot the eyes out of a squirrel at forty paces. He had pointed out that the eastern seaboard was two thousand miles long if it was an inch, and that the minute men, excellent horsemen that they were, would be creating havoc in every one of those miles except the one where a British regiment happened to be stationed. It followed, therefore, that massive military intervention was needed. Cavalry, infantry, sappers, artillery, marines the lot; and this prior to the bloody French coming in on the side of the enemy which he would wager 'a pound to a pinch of shit,' was a certainty.

"Worst of all," he had ranted, "ideas such as this *freedom* notion being promulgated by these rebels were contagious, and if the devils in the colonies got away with it then the great-unwashed of Britain would surely follow suit. Did we really want our grooms and woodcutters murdering our families, mounting our wives and daughters, and so forth?" The military men generally had found themselves quite unable to pass this line of questioning and had suffered an infectious cough at the mention of plebeians mounting their wives; an affliction which had the desired effect of bringing Astor to heel. Cough though they might; the buffoon had scored a hit, and the off-color remark was the cause of the single moment of serious reflection in the whole gin-fueled quarrel.

"Gentlemen," Bismark announced as a sullied ocean came in to view beyond a smokey village smugly nestled in a hollow.

"I recognize this place. We are much closer to Windward Palace than to The Granary, so I hope that you will do me the honor of accepting my hospitality."

With the pursuit now a distant memory, the dry horror taking its toll, and the dismal prospect of a further three hungry and sober hours in the saddle being the only other option, this offer was accepted with alacrity. The party picked up the pace and rode on to Windward Palace in no time at all, forgetting intentionally about the junior officers involved in the pursuit, and leaving them to their own devices.

In point-of-fact, the junior officers had long since recognized that the game was up and had ridden off to find lodgings for the night. The rankers at either end of the line; on the other hand; had absconded each with a small fortune in horse flesh under him. Those men understood perfectly well that once aboard that ship to the colonies, they would never see their families again; furthermore, should they be unlucky enough to upset the Americans, they would, in all probability, never see anything, ever again.

The following morning, Michael Astor who was incensed by his father's treacherous and damnably insulting actions in pursuing an agenda with outsiders before discussing it with himself barged into the traitor's office where he found the fool as always, scratching away at a ledger with one of his pretentious quills. The abomination was worked in gold leaf and rubies and was so large that were it able to take to the air again, would have carried-off Bismark with it.

"What the hell do you think you were up to?" he snarled incorporating as much insult as he could muster short of gutting the man.

"And a very good morning to you also, Michael. I trust you slept well under my roof?"

"Christ man; you were doing your damndest to get our buyers slaughtered, God knows why; but I'm bloody sure that I don't. Total war in the eastern seaboard will completely bugger our trade and cost us millions. More to the point still, I had to discover your filthy intentions second-hand, by overhearing the puke you were spewing at Cornwallis and his arse-lickers. What sort of partnership is that, damn your bleeding eyes?"

"Michael, Michael."

"I'll thank you not to patronize me, Pater," the son snapped, unable to resist a play on words even in his anger,

"I want some categorical answers not platitudes, so do me the kindness of speaking man to man." With slow deliberation Lord Astor lay down his quill and rolled his work with the pink and gold blotter, by which device he gained time enough to compose both himself and his speech.

"Total War in the colonies was inevitable, Michael… in fact, as you know it has become the real thing during the last twelvemonth after puttering along for ages. We're hammering them in New York as we speak; Boston too. Cornwallis and his clowns are simply as thick as shit in a bottle." he began and would have explained his reasoning but was shouted down.

"Only because you and the rest of the fools of the British East India Company are determined to swindle the colonies out of the tax on tea, which by-the-by the government; 'of which you are obviously a 'sleeping' partner has already paid you to forgo."

Annoyed by this pertinent observation Bismark stood abruptly and came from behind his desk, wide as the deck of a coaster,

"I'm not certain that I enjoy being called a fool, Michael," he hissed, his manner on the very edge of physical threat.

"Then you'll have a miserable time ahead if you push on with this thing because the peasant population of both this country and that will be calling you a fool, and much worse." Aware that he had asked for much of what he had just got, the senior man ever the pragmatist, changed tack easily.

"Walls have ears," he observed. "Let's walk in the grounds where we can't be overheard. What I have to say is for your ears alone."

"That's a first." far from mollified, Michael stalked out of the house alone because he could not stand at that moment to walk alongside the three-faced fool. He was waiting impatiently on the terrace looking at, but not seeing the delightful panoramas boasted by the wonderfully well situated but otherwise unexceptional Windward Palace, when the gremlin emerged through some French doors, shading his bleary old eyes from the low sunlight. Father and son met at the top of wide steps and descended in acrimonious silence two meters apart to the vivid pallet and fragrant atmosphere of the formal gardens. Only when he was certain that they were alone and could not be overheard did Bismarck address his son even then doing so in hushed tones.

He began by apologizing for the complete breakdown in communications between them as trustworthy partners, but true to form, scuppered the gesture with an aside to the effect that communicating with a man who very rarely spent even two successive nights in the same bed, was the work of the devil himself.

"You will discern Michael, that when something is inevitable, it is best to accept the new reality and profit from it as well as is possible. The fire that's burning so furiously under the homespun shirts of our unwashed American cousins is very little to do with minor irritations such as the tax on tea. That is merely 'the last straw,' as our Bedouin friends would say. It is their appetite for freedom. To be out from under the thumb of every conceivable form of oppression, and in many cases, even of mild authority. Every one of them is determined to be his own master. Determined. Think of it. Most of them risked the Atlantic in something rather less seaworthy than a horse trough in order to escape persecution right here in England, and to live in 'Freedom.' Those who didn't drown, have fought every conceivable enemy just to stay alive. Naughty natives, starvation, freezing winters, wolves, disease, broken bones, you name it. They are as tough as teak. They live in a country of their own making. Their farms are their own. They hacked every single field out of the forests. They plough the earth two thousand miles from London and see no good reason why they should bend the knee to the crown, or to anyone else. As for the King? Why, the man doesn't even enter their thoughts. To them, if the English are weak-minded enough to let one unelected German turnip rule over them, and be taxed outrageously for the privilege, then more fool they. They will fight to the end of this filthy business mark my word, and they will win because on every corner they see a redcoat, a symbol of British rule. Every Sabbath they are subjected to some loyalist Church of England parson telling them to know their place under God and the King. Every document they sign is written on paper imprinted with the royal coat of arms, and thusly carries an associated tax which supports the English privileged class. They've had it up to here.'' He tapped the top of his head. ''And they enjoy not a word of representation. Worse still; hear me well boy. My people assure me that the bastards have a crew in France persuading the bloody frogs to come in and help them. Revolution spreads like wildfire Michael, the French love it. And if it should spread to these shores and infect our own drones, 'we,' will be the worse for it.

Therefore, I say the following. Finish them; and finish them cruelly and permanently. When push comes to shove, the first step that the Admiralty will take is to blockade the eastern seaboard against the importation of war-materials to the rebels and the export of their tobacco and the rest, thereby bringing our nigger trade, along with everything else, to an impecunious halt. In the thirteen colonies, that is. The islands, Cuba, Haiti, Jamaica and the southern continent will perhaps continue unscathed. In place of slaves, we should be prepared and ready to make ten times the profit, twenty; a hundred times the profit; by supplying the materials of war to our army out there. Think of this Michael, capturing the entire market. We are ideally positioned. Our foundries, mines, arsenals, potteries, mills, glassmakers, shipyards. Our farms, fishing fleets, forests, timber mills, its endless. And then there's the transports for the thousands of soldiers who will be involved over the duration of hostilities. Carrying the reinforcements out and bringing the sick-and-dying back. Such a conflagration properly mismanaged may last for five years; perhaps even ten. When I, 'eventually' shake off this mortal coil, you sir, on that far distant day, will be the richest man in all of Britain."

"Shuffle," noted Michael, who had listened intently to his father's diatribe without once attempting to interrupt, even though none of it was new to him. The company was involved in all-of those opportunities that Bismark had enumerated and more besides.

"Pardon me?"

"When you 'shuffle' off. What would you say to supplying 'both' sides?" An ironic smirk had replaced the irritation in Michael's expression.

"What a wheeze that would be. By judicious control of ammunition and food shipments, winter clothing and so forth, we could extend hostilities for bloody ages. Even have the fools competing on price for every cargo. The possibilities are endless." Bismark Astor studied his son's cruelly handsome features, unable for a moment to compose a reply. The puppy's concept was so daring, so utterly unthinkable, the rewards for success, and the consequences of failure immeasurable. The little snake had stunned him yet again.

"That's an incredible notion," he enthused, wishing that he were his son's age once more.

"I shall need some time to think those ideas through. On the face of it, it's a winner; but the risks must be weighed, don'cha think?"

"Aaahh. I have it!" Michael had already improved on his initial plan.

"We import the materials for the English army through the major ports, Boston, New York, Charleston, which Britain will of course control, the British Navy being what it is. With the stuff for the rebels however, we will stand off at deserted beaches, there are thousands of miles of them; and float it ashore under cover of darkness on sacrificial old hulks. Just beach them and run. Flying a flag of convenience naturally, using frog vessels of course, and at a very long arms-length from ourselves so that nothing can come back to you and me. What do you think?" Astor was appalled by the audacity of it, incredulous, a convert,

"It's brilliant Michael, brilliant. By the by, what do we own over there in the way of land and houses? Just in case the colonists win the day, so to speak, or we somehow get caught with our hand in the coffers."

"Actually, a hell of a lot. We've got half a dozen plantations on the James River and more on the Rappahannock and the York, all of them are growing tobacco and more importantly for future profitability, breeding huge niggers. There's a fleet of dredgers on the Chesapeake, oysters and fish don'cha know, shipbuilders, printing presses, banks. Yes, a very considerable portfolio. I've put managers in the tobacco plantations whose pay is tied to the overall profitability of the plantation, not just the simple calculation of income versus expenditure on the tobacco. Seems to be working well. Our private houses, hotels and businesses are, for the most part in Boston and New York, but you can say goodbye to them. The British Army will have flattened them by now. But as you know, the climate is best in the Chesapeake and further south still. Should we ever need to take up residence the southern way of life would be delightful, their women are… But Venice has always been more to your taste. You would go insane with only yokels to converse with." Bismark Astor almost stammered, so keen was he to demand a detailed explanation of what had just been disclosed to him.

"What's this 'overall profitability' notion that you mentioned," he asked, "and 'breeding'?" unable and unwilling to guess at his son's latest infamy. Michael sprawled on a cast-iron bench, oblivious to its wetness, and contemplated where to begin with a subject that boasted no natural starting point.

"I'm bloody starving," he began, "so I'll keep this short. We are breeding slaves father, mostly for size and strength, and training them for specific purposes such as tree-felling, pit-sawing, shipbuilding, plowing, bare knuckling, bridge-building, coopering, you name it. We sell them and hire them out,' at hugely inflated prices. That's where the big money lies. Selling 'em." Bismark sat down at the opposite end of the cast iron bench because he suddenly felt the need.

"Breeding? Like dogs? Putting a dog to a bitch, sort of thing?" There followed a very long pause before the son responded to the father's evinced incredulity.

"More like horses. Don't look so dam shocked, man." Michael laughed superciliously at both his play on words and the expression of bafflement which showed briefly in his father's face.

"We are talking about creatures whom you and I have enslaved. Rutting isn't the worst thing that we make the blacks do. Not by a long chalk."

"But you will sell their children away?"

"Jesus, what a bloody hypocrite. You've stolen a million of them away from everything that they ever knew in your time. Don't find fault with me for selling-off their litters." Michael rose suddenly and strode off, still incandescent at his father's betrayal.

"Let me know your thoughts about playing both ends against the middle. I'm keen to get started… if you are," he added sarcastically.   Two minutes later the irate one returned and found that his father had not moved.

"And another thing," he began, as though there had been no hiatus.

"It is vomit making in the extreme to hear you desperately trying to sell our services to that bloody drawing-room ninny Cornwallis, like a fishmonger at a street market. That's not the way it's done. Only days ago, Cornwallis' favorite niece, the Lady Margaret, unable to tolerate the treasonable utterances of those ungrateful rebels one minute longer, arrived home to Portsmouth in our ship, *Senator*, at no charge. Today she will drive to her place in Buckinghamshire in a landau which I was thoughtful enough to provide, along with the protection of half a dozen of my ruffians. Let the soldier boy know *that*, and he will be falling over himself to buy our goods and transport his armies in *our* ships. Furthermore, you have obviously forgotten her existence, but *Glorious* sits a stone's throw from here at Minster. Brand spanking new she is. Perfect in every detail. Ready for her maiden voyage 'cept for officer selection; provisioning and the like. To say nothing of twenty guns. Get the pompous ass aboard her and let him find out for himself how bloody well he and his armies will cross the pond in real ships. Ships designed and built by Michael Astor. She smells of timber and resin and fresh paint; not cack and rats. And best of all, the grand cabin is so bloody tall that even Cornwallis; long streak of piss that he is, could stand up straight in it. That's how it's done today. You are not still a market trader in some dung heap of a town in darkest Shropshire. You are probably the 'second,' richest, most powerful man in England. I'd greatly appreciate your acting like it. Particularly in the company of inbred sodomites." With that, Michael turned on his heel and strode away a second time.

"Don't hold back so, 'Bastard.' Tell me what you really fucking think. And it's 'Astor and Son," you bloody ingrate. On later reflection, Bismark became even more deeply enraged by the sod's criticism, and more so by the manner of its delivery, which was fundamentally an accusation of incompetence. He had taught the puppy everything it knew and was now obliged to listen to its yapping. He scuttled to his library snarling at the servants as he went, slammed the door of his cave behind him and attempted to continue with the task that he was engaged in prior to the little shite-hawk's frontal assault. It was a futile waste of time. Despite half an hour of conscientious effort he had achieved precisely nothing, having drafted no less than five letters, each of them tarred with the brush of his anger, torn them up and thrown them into the fire

"I'll kill the mutinous rat," he snorted, dragging himself out of his seat and setting off to find the know-all little shipworm. He was well on the way to the breakfast room when he recalled his son's 'tasteless' habit of taking breakfast in the kitchens. With the staff! A detour of a hundred paces was therefore required, adding further to the depths of his irritation.

"Out! Out! All of you, get out," his lordship hollered from the doorway; while fixing the blackguard with a glare of hostility, which to his consternation, merely caused it to roll its eyes in mockery,

"So! Incompetent, am I?" Astor approached and seizing a much-needed chair dropped into it as the staff fled past him though the saucy minx sitting on the mongrel's lap from where she was feeding him his breakfast, was, he observed, on the verge of mutiny.

"Fishmonger at a street market, am I?" He resolved to get rid of that disloyal little bitch before the end of the day. Michael shoved the wench unceremoniously from his knee, causing her to fall on her bottom, pick herself up and run from the room in tears. Michael chewed pleasurably on the last of his eggs, drank off a full glass of white wine and waited for the last of the staff to get out of the line of fire.

"You must be famished old man," he observed dryly, approaching the range from which he returned a moment later with a generous serving of food which he placed in front of his now livid parent.

"Spanish omelet," he crooned, "you'll love it." Michael poured two glasses of white wine, sat back and waited. Despite his righteous anger, Lord Bismark Astor picked up an utterly divine, superbly balanced fork by De Beers and began to eat, tasting ambrosia the likes of which he had never known.

"This is marvelous," he enthused, relishing the new dish which was such an improvement on porridge.

"I suppose that woman of yours …"

"Mrs. Crabtree."

"…Mrs. Crabtree invented it."

"Indeed, she did. Chopped ham, toasted onion with carrot, potato and garlic, all in a brandy sauce and a dozen eggs flavored with half a dozen of those spices which Astor and Son; that's you and me by the by, are importing from the Spice Islands. All fried in olive oil. Your white wines are the perfect complement, don't you think?"

"Thank you, Michael. Yes, I've got an excellent fellow in charge of my cellars now." Much ameliorated, Bismark shoveled another heap of the sublime Spanish omelet into his mouth.

"You have come in expectation of an apology, and I freely and willingly give it," said Michael, striking while the omelet was hot.

"Omniscience coupled with out-of-place magnanimity in one so young is very trying," responded Bismark sarcastically, his hauteur significantly reduced by a mouthful of partially masticated ambrosia. He swallowed hurriedly and thus, painfully in his urgency to return fire.

"I came to inform you; that as you consider me to be an unfit business partner, I hereby free you provisionally of all obligations of that nature. My lawyers will call on your own and take care of the minutiae in the very near future." Dropping his fork simply for effect Bismark instantly regretted the minor sacrilege. As he got to his feet, he touched his lips with the napkin which he then threw down histrionically, as he had seen Michael do at The Granary recognizing an infuriating second too late the implied compliment to the little sod.

"I'll bid you good day, sir."

Michael was on his feet in an instant his chair clattering to the flags.

"What 'is' this shit?" he snarled. "Stay right there, dog breath!"

"You have a short memory for 'fishmongers' you mongrel; 'market traders and dung heaps', I believe it went."

"For Christ's sake, is that all that this little tantrum is about? Bloody well grow up. So I speak my mind. Is that so surprising? At fifteen, you had me captaining a slaver! Heaving diseased corpses to the sharks was my daily bread. 'SIT,' At seventeen thanks to your loving guidance, I was four hundred miles up the Rima. It's a tributary of the Niger in case you've never visited; where; by the bloody way, I had no option but to slit the throats; before they slit mine, of four murderous Arab bastards as they slept. I attend that tea-party every fucking night of my life."

"I didn't," Bismark stuttered. "Why did you not---?"

"Shut your porridge chute and listen damn you. On that picnic as I recall, I loaded *Prometheus* with so many niggers that she had barely an inch of freeboard left, but I made us a fortune on the block at Jamestown and bought us three plantations on the north shore of the James, one on the York and one on the Rappahannock. Not that you ever noticed. You were too busy licking dick in parliament. Every single man of the crews you supplied me with father dear, was a murdering, backstabbing fucking Moslem, who felt it his bounden duty to kill Christians so it's hardly surprising, is it, that I learned to call a spade, a nigger. It's a bit bloody late to get all precious with 'me' sir. Now finish your breakfast and give me peace."

With the air thus cleared and being somewhat deflated by this defence-in-depth he was well pleased to do just that, even going to the range to help himself to more of the exquisite, Missus Whatzit concoction. He had worked the Africa trade himself in a previous life, when he had started out in the business, and knew it intimately, so he was cognisant of the horrors that he had caused his son to live through.

"What if I were to give those stuffed uniforms a slap-up dinner aboard the *Glorious* one of these fine evenings?" he beamed, in a sly nod to his son's earlier advice, returning to the table with a full plate.

"That would have them using our fleets, would it not?"

"Now you're talking, and don't forget to mention our generosity to Lady Margaret the harlot either. She left me for dead the dirty filthy bitch. She sucks like a Newcomen Pump. You'll have old Corncob eating out of your hand while we pig-out on the contents of His Majesty's purse."

''Please Michael; I'm eating.'' Such was the spirit of bonhomie which developed in the kitchens of Windward Palace that morning that Bismark was able to beg a loan of the redoubtable Mrs. Crabtree for his proposed festivities, with no compunction whatsoever, and Michael able to acquiesce with not a shred of reservation, a previously unthinkable state of play. When father and son parted that morning, they did so in the knowledge that their partnership had been strengthened, and growing dissatisfactions had been uprooted; thus they went their separate ways intent on giving their all to their latest perfidy; the promotion of full-scale, total warfare between Britain and the colonies of America and the prospect of making vast fortunes by turning traitor and providing both sides of the conflict with everything that they bloody-well needed. At a huge markup naturally.

Lord Bismark Astor was never again squeamish about taking breakfast in the kitchen, while his son recalled that on more than one occasion during the adventures he had just now related his goose would have been burned to a cinder were it not for the intervention of the ever-faithful Hastings, and his roughnecks. It would be fitting to thank those staunch men and purchase their never-ending loyalty simultaneously with a small expression of appreciation. 'Homes of their own perhaps.' That was the story! He would design and build a village for them with an acre of soil around each house.

CHAPTER 4: Salt Of The Earth

Far to the south-west amid the farthest glories of the great forest, beyond the reach of the longest arm of the law, ignorant of madding crowds and modern inventions lies the unremarkable hamlet of Thorpe, which grows organically out of the fertile soil at the foot of an endless scarp. This steepest of slopes does to the land, as a breeze might do to a cloak of green wool. The geological events which created this exceptional feature of the country's topography also exposed a layer of impermeable clay, which in turn caused countless springs of the coldest, purest water to leap forth at points all along the valley where the trees give way to pasture, and for this reason; the fertile nature of the soil, and the bounty of the forests, there has always been a human presence in this place.

The people hereabouts are a taciturn lot, independent and distrustful of 'furriners,' which is to say, anyone not born and bred amid these steep slopes and wide flat valleys. They attach the sobriquet 'newcomer' to the name of anyone with less than a quarter of a century of residence with no 'side' whatsoever. Such pride as these agrarian peasants can boast resides in their Christian Englishness though unbeknown to them, their ancestors mated enthusiastically with Roman soldiers, Normans, Vikings, Engels, and Saxons and with anyone else who happened by. As what passes for education in these parts hovers between 'loose' and 'non-existent' however, the denizens are blissfully innocent even of the fact that the word 'Thorpe' or 'Thrupe' is derived from the language of a minor German tribe and means simply 'place'. They call their fields by such names as Danesholme, and Shakle Oder; never wondering why, and as for their Christian protestations, they protect every hayrick, cottage and barn, from fire, flood, evil-spirits and all manners of assault from the elements, gods, devils and men, with an icon of straw; a Pagan icon.

Although it lay at a bull's roar from Thorpe, the field known as Danesholme was the most popular of all with the cottagers for it had the distinction of being the only stretch of soil hereabouts still in the ownership of the families who cleared the land of forest hundreds of years earlier, the rest having been appropriated by force, murder, trickery and deceit, by the now 'great houses' of the county. Concealed by a coat of moss and leaf detritus, a forgotten stone lies near the outhouse known as the parish church of this unremarkable outpost of ignorance and poverty. On its face the plinth records, how it was that on that spot only one hundred years earlier, forty-seven strip-farmers were killed in battle against the well-armed mercenaries of the 'great houses.' Clearly visible from that spot is a vastly impressive mansion still inhabited by the descendants of those murderous thieves while all but for Danesholme the land for miles around is held in the avaricious grip of those people. Naturally, human nature being what it is, Danesholme produced more food than any five of the fields owned by the lords, in which the cottagers were obliged to toil endlessly in order to rent a cold, leaking, infested, one-room cottage without water or sanitation of any kind.

A piece of cloth tied beneath her chin shaded the crown of Dora Huffer's head where her black hair was beginning to grey; her exposed skin was the colour of tanned doe, and little creases were evident between her brows, and at the corners of her wide mouth which when it smiled, exposed inexplicably, a full complement of perfect teeth.

Dora's gentle eyes of cyan blue were reduced to mere slits in swollen flesh as she had been reduced to tears on several occasions as the day progressed and the terrible thing which she had to do came closer. Almost blinded, she employed her hoe, in a completely democratic fashion and was thus guilty of the murder of as many beets as she was of weeds. From time to time, she would raise her head and peer towards the far end of the field where her deeply loathed, esstranged husband, Tansley Huffer, was loitering on another of the family's five strips. Whenever she did this, an expression of insupportable grief would mar the loving mother's features further and she would utter an ancient incantation beneath her breath. This ritual was followed without exception by the quick confirmation that her beautiful daughter, Angelique, had not ambled off and was still safely working just a couple of strips away. Only when she had done this, could she relent and go back to her work. Evening's shadows had barely begun to reclaim the soil for the night when Tansley Huffer cripple, nair-do-well and incestuous father downed tools and limped away in the company of Kane Seed an outcast criminal of fearsome reputation, one of the few people who would afford the cripple so much as the time of day. In recent years, Tansley would always down tools before anyone else; he who used to set such a high standard in Thorpe. Witnessing this seemingly insignificant occurrence, something tore in the threadbare fabric of Dora's mind, she dropped her hoe, rushed to the nearest scarecrow, snatched the little figure of straw set there to protect it and holding the thing up in the direction of Tansley's receding back shrieked,

"Tansley Huffer, loathed by the Gods," ritualistically tearing off one of the icon's legs. "Tansley Huffer, 'neath the sods." The remaining leg was disposed of similarly.

"Mother!" It was Angelique's horrified voice, and the tone of it seemed to effect Dora deeply, as though she had suddenly recalled something awful but long forgotten. Her arms dropped to her sides, as she considered the straw remnants in consternation at what she had just done. She had summoned the Grim Reaper to take a life, her husband's life. Restrained by the unwritten prohibition on setting foot on someone else's strip, Angelique had a long way to run to reach her mother, but run she did, and coming up on the distraught woman she took that slender, much-loved figure in a great hug as though to forestall any further breach of the peace and held her till at last she was herself again.

"Come mam," the girl gentled, when at last her dear parent's trembling lessened,

"we'd best go home-along," and she led the unresisting woman from the field, the hoes over her shoulder and an arm around her mother's waist.

"Witch." The dreaded appellation chased mother and daughter through the trees, and though no sane body still believed in witches Angelique recognised that there would unquestionably be no going straight home for them now.

"Mam," she announced firmly, "on second thoughts, we must best go up to the god-botherers' first and put that 'witch' stuff to bed with a bit of grovelling. There's always them as would do a body harm, aint there?"

The tormented woman barely hesitated as she realised that this course of action suited her purpose well for it would delay for a little while longer the terrible thing that she had to do. She acquiesced with a nod and was once again on the verge of tears.

"What is it, mam?" young Angelique settled both hoes more comfortably on her shoulder; the baskets hanging from them at her back and mother and daughter directed their march towards Thorpe.

"You've been upset all day."

"Yes, my lovely, but it be best if we waits till we gets up over by there," Dora indicated by a slight lift of her brow the ugly Saxon tower of the despised parish church which showed above the trees.

"We ain't going inside daughter." The lych-gate squeaked behind them as the couple went to kneel in the shadows; settling on a spot where they would be clearly visible to passers-by as the whole purpose of the exercise was to proclaim their saintly natures, and thereby their detestation of witchcraft in all its forms. Kneeling side by side in the attitude of prayer, the conspirators set about the impossible task of maintaining expressions of deep and abiding piety while each tried to make the other laugh with whispered blasphemy. In a curious twist; as the sun fell to earth, mother and daughter found that their initially shaded eyes were once again subject to its squint-causing rays, so with their knees and lower backs aching, and convinced that they had performed sufficient public penitence to throw the keenest witch-hunter off the scent, they exited the churchyard and seated themselves on a convenient bench into which the carpenter had carved the words, 'Rest and be thankful'. Caused to confront just how little she had to be thankful for; the thing that Dora had so dreaded doing, occurred unbidden.

"I can't hold it in, my sweetheart," she sobbed, grasping for her daughter's hand.

"You must go from home this very day, my darling. It's not safe."

"What? No, mam. No." the nubile was horrified. Her small safe world reduced to ashes in an instant.

"Why, mam? Don't send me." The two women threw themselves into each other's arms and cried till they had no option but to address the matter at hand. Angelique was the first to compose herself, and holding her dear mother at arms-length, asked in despair.

"Why send me away, mam? I love you, mam." At that moment, the pain and desperation in her daughter's voice almost broke Dora's will, and she came as close as it is possible to be to begging her lovely child to stay and never leave, but despite this, she heard herself saying.

"It's your father, darling girl mine. There is things wot you are too young to… Your sisters had to run." Angelique silenced her mother, gently placing a hand over the distraught woman's mouth.

"Mother dearest," she said, "I am not a baby. I know how father used our darling Petra and Noelle; everybody knows and everybody has took a great deal of pleasure in telling me bout it; for ever it seems now."

"Oh, my poor girl. You poor, poor little thing. But sweetheart it's you what the devil is lookin at now? You must get clean away from him. You must go to your Auntie Maud's in Gratton. I have sent word for her to spec you."

"Mam I am not going to leave you simply cause father is cursed. He has been looking at me for half a year or more, but I keep myself safe. Long as I stay where there is other bodies they's nowt he can do. I aint afeart of him mam."

"Oh chile, don't you think that Petra and Noelle telt me the same, but he had them both, for months it seems, telling them that if all was knowed it would be they what got the blame for leading him into sin. He is the very devil." Angelique paused, studying her mother's dear, care-worn face as though considering a tremendously serious course of action, then with the strength of her convictions which she was always apt to display, she drew back the sleeve of her smock, revealing a sheathed blade bound to her inner forearm.

"I don't fear him, mother," she repeated simply. Dora's shock and dismay crushed her. She could not cope with what she was seeing and hearing. She drew down that sleeve in a single swift movement, concealing the awful thing as she heard an expostulation at the lych-gate behind her.

"Never interrupt me again. I hope that I make myself clear," carried in sanctimonious tones to where the miserable women were sitting, followed directly by the unappetising appearance of the noisome vicar Penny and his wife who, having negotiated the gate, came their way.

"Ain't it sod's law?" breathed Angelique, in a stew of exasperation, and with her head almost inside her basket, took to excavating all manner of objects from it in the search for none of them while Dora's undivided attention became glued to a very ordinary horse grazing in the paddock to the rear. The women's efforts to avoid a meeting with the poisonous bigots were in vain, and the couples collided in a welter of insincerity, all four individuals attempting unsuccessfully to hide their true feelings behind painful smiles which leaked a variety of emotions not one of which was even distantly related to Christian charity.

"Sisters," the 'Penny-Halfpenny' slowed to a halt, though their earnest desire to 'pass by on the other side,' was evident in every pore.

"I observed you at prayer in the lord's garden. I hope that you will enter his house when next you visit so that we might worship him together and beg forgiveness for our sins." As he enunciated his poorly disguised orders, the vicar's eyes seldom left Angelique's generous bosom while on those few occasions when he managed to drag his glance away he obsessed with her mouth in an extraordinarily obvious fashion which angered that flower, almost to the point of leaping at the loathsome creature and scratching his lecherous eyes out.

The Halfpenny, the vicar's wife, so called because the comparison of her size with that of her husband almost exactly replicated that of the coinage; seemed quite unaware of the man's deplorable behaviour, directing her adoring gaze vertically at the lecher's white, waxy features; 'probably,' Angelique hoped, 'at the cost of a cricked neck.'

"You are out of your way this evening, sisters…"

Penny slyly left the gaping chasm for one or other of the Huffers to topple into, and before Angelique could restrain her, Dora obliged.

"Angie's goin to rest up a mite at my sister's place," she confessed, turning to Angelique with an expression that begged forgiveness for her weakness, even as she displayed it.

"Just for a while." Angelique took the reins.

"Then I shall probly go to a town. I want to see the real world." She placed the emphasis on 'real' in order to deflate the pompous windbag, if ever so little and remind him that he was nothing more than an ineffective nonentity in a starving parish, lost in the English woods. Penny threw back his damp-porcelain face; eyes closed and raised his calloused palms in horror as though creating a physical barrier against such an ill-advised course of action.

"I won't hear of it," he decreed, "far too young. Far too innocent of this world." The man of god was obliged to adopt his preaching volume due to the rumbling of approaching wagons and a regiment of heavily shod feet; not all of them equine.

"Every cloud has a silver lining, child," he shouted grandly, addressing his remarks to the thatched roofs and stone chimneys.

"At this very moment, I have a vacancy at the rectory which I am prepared to."

"No, Mister Penny, my mind is made up." Angelique intentionally denied Penny his title.

"Don't be foolish child; the reverend Penny knows better than a chit of a girl such as yourself where you would be best suited." The halfpenny was at her condescending best, eager to take up the cudgels on behalf of her adored and feared lord and master.

"You must come to us this very evening. I won't take 'no' for an answer." A rowdy army of field hands, their wagons and horses, on their way home from work, had entered the highroad and were soon trudging past only yards from the intense little cameo. As usual, many of the younger ones had consumed far more ale than was good for themselves or for anyone else and were on the lookout for mischief and figures of fun. Some of the young women in the mob interpreted the scene with knowledge born of experience and were of a mind to come to the aid of the oppressed at the expense of the oppressor.

"Don' do it chile, dawn till dusk and endless tongue-lashing."

"On yer knees, gel" bawled another. "Oooh. Aaaah."

"'Memba to lock yer door, gal."

"Tongue lashing? Lashings of tongue, you mean." The handsome young blackguard who was responsible for this indecency, but who barely understood the implications of his own remark, was set upon delightedly by a bevy of girls, ostensibly for cutting too close to the bone but in truth because the criminal was so very, very pretty.

"He works in mysterious ways does that one."

"It'll be our little secret lass."

This last brought a roar of insulting laughter from the victorious army, at whom the Penny-Halfpenny had at the outset nodded condescendingly, fully expecting that any remarks the hoi polloi might make would be of an obsequious nature, as custom demanded. Outraged by this unprecedented turn in events, the black-draped couple gave up the ghost in fury and with a brief "Good day," and frozen countenance, continued their locomotion in the direction of their fashionable little gig, which stood in the shade of an oak on the village green. The inelegantly tall Penny loping along in the ungainly fashion which identified him with certainty even from great distances, while his wife, displaying no evidence of perambulation seemed to race on castors beside him. This reaction caused great rejoicing among the field-hands, so much so that they could still be heard laughing and calling out as they were lost to sight behind the church and the high stone walls which served to buttress that corner of the graveyard. Mother and daughter were quite taken-out of themselves by the infectious mood of the home-comers, and their spirits revived in their relief at escaping the Penny-Halfpenny inquisition. Before she spoke again, Angelique had experienced a great shift in outlook. She had resolved to go, to leave home. What she had feared and hated, she now welcomed. This, she realised, was her opportunity to embark on a life full of things other than hoeing turnips in the snow, digging up potatoes and wearing her one poor dress on what the god botherers called 'holy' days. She wanted to see a city, an ocean, houses which had an upstairs and more than one room. She wanted to ride in a coach, visit what were called 'emporiums' in which wooden dolls as tall as herself wore dresses, shoes and hats, that a person could buy. She had been told that it was possible to sit at a little round table for two which would be covered with a brilliant-white cloth, and have a person bring her a pot of tea, which she would drink from a delicate white cup with its own saucer, all hand-painted and beautiful beyond the telling of it. She did not completely believe that this story could be true, but if it turned out to be so, then she would love to give it a go. Not for her, Auntie Maud's place, where chickens strutted through the house, the sky showed through the thatch and winter's snow drifted inside as far as the cold midnight hearth. Worst of all Uncle Thomas, who worked as a tanner stumbled about the place in a miasma of rotting flesh. The man was less use than tits on a bull. After ten years of broken promises, he had still not got around to digging a proper stool pit, so the bushes beyond the garden had to suffice, snow or rain, winter or summer, night or day.

Angelique longed to see the world and find her sisters. Mayhap even find the man of her dreams. And her brother! 'Oh,' how awful. She had almost forgot him, the poor thing.'

"Alex," she sobbed, "where are you?" Driven out of the house for daring to stand between his sisters and Tansley's sick obsession, he could be anywhere; always supposing that he had not already perished, alone, hungry and cold.

"Mam, I 'will' go. I think you are right, and I've made up my mind to do it now." The announcement squeezed more water from Dora's swollen eyes.

"Give me that horrible thing then, my Angie, it can only bring you 'arm." Dora reached for the knife with something of her old authority, but Angelique drew away with no hesitation.

"Not at all Mam I cannot stay at Auntie Maud's. It's too close. He will find me there. I shall go to the sea. I hear tell there are towns there with herds of people and paid work. But till I feel safe, I will keep it with me."

"Oh my, I din't mean for you to go far off and leave me my lovely." Dora's cheeks became little saltwater deltas.

"I'll never zee you agen. I'll be on my own." Angelique smothered her dear mother in a loving hug.

"Of-course you will see me, mam," she crooned.

"I ain't goin' to 'leave' you; I'm goin' so as to find our Petra and Noelle, and our poor Alexander an bring em ome.''

"Oh my lovely." Dora smiled painfully,

"What a girl you are. You're a Hooligan to the marrow. Now, you will bide at Auntie Maud's this night o' course. It's gettin late."

"I will mam, but I must go this minute, or I'll be trudging the lanes in the dark. Come with me, there's nowt to hold you here now."

"Oh, my lovely, I's too old. Old and scared. Never in my life have I strayed furver than the mill at Danby. I would be just a burden to you."

"Never."

"There's something else though daughter mine, that I will tell you now. The cottage," Dora paused briefly as though Angelique would require a moment to recognise the dwelling where she had lived her whole life,

"It is my own entire. I owns it. Them can't be victin us. Your father owns not one stone of it or a blade of grass. The house and land will all be yours. Not his."

"Don't say like that, our mam, I shall be home before you know it, with the others too."

"I've put everything that I can in the basket for you my lovely, and there's some coppers that I put away tied in that-there bit o cloth."

"Oh Mam, I love you heaps, you know."

Mother and daughter embraced again briefly and despairingly, then the younger woman turned and strode away, not looking back as the older watched her from a particularly deep place in the vale-of-tears that her life had become. At the moment in which her dear mother's form was lost to view the child lately become adult had the strength to alter her plans radically. She hurried back to the despised church where she moved silently and breathless through the cloying stink of the place and climbed the almost vertical helix of steps of the tower. Accessing the flat roof, she stood on tiptoes and peered between the battlements and the waving leaves of the oaks and the beech trees and right away uttered a choked cry.

"Mam," she cried as she glimpsed the far distant figure of her poor deserted mother trudging along the pathway to insupportable loneliness.

It is one thing to say, 'I shall walk to the sea our Mam.' It is quite another thing to do it. The newly liberated one had decided to spend the night in her little eerie and catch a lift on one of the carts leaving for town early in the mornings. She would stay awake, she resolved, so as not to miss them.

She woke in darkness.

A sound! A mere exhalation. 'Just a beast grazing nearby as like as not.' The thought did little to calm the child's fraying nerves. Again! a gasp, then a gasp? A plosive, another which almost contained a word. She rose slowly, camouflaged the paleness of her face with her hood and peered down timorously as her eyes adjusted to the thicker darkness of the churchyard, surrounded as it was by trees and bushes. Nothing moved. Barely a voal stirred. Time dragged passed laden with horrible superstition till at last her indomitable spirit roused itself and fought back. Approaching the tower's castellations a second time she stilled, watching. A clink of metal, shockingly. Barely daring to breathe, terrified, she moved towards the source of that sound, searching now from the western side of the tower and all but screamed as something moved directly below her. She flung herself back. Two hunched figures were labouring to drag a body from its grave, the face of the dead man shining almost as brightly as a full moon.

Angelique fled; stooping falcon-like down the cliff of steps, raced to the door and from there to the traitorous gate which squealed a warning for the dead to hear. Racing headlong now down the slope, grey between black, the sharp point of panic pricking less painfully; beginning to believe that she was safely away, then a dark figure dropping from the overgrown bank into the road directly in front of her.

Fear, ugly, odoriferous and carrion, stole her breath; beat loudly on the drum of her heart, then spoke.

"Don't be afeart gel, it's only me." Angelique's father crept towards her, stalking her, gentling her, steeped in such naked lust that she felt she must vomit in disgust and fear. Retreating, unblinking before her father's sickening advance, never taking her eyes from him as he came on, intense as any hunter cornering his prey. A glance behind her and she shrieked; a tall figure, dark but terribly familiar; stood threateningly still in the bushes, the distance between herself and it, shrinking with every step. She reached for her knife, knowing full well that she must make the first move and attack one or the other, rather than hesitate and let both come at her at once. Frantic with terror she ran at the cripple, the smaller of the two, brandishing her blessed weapon with real intent. Something was coming. A pale shape. Now two of them, bobbing in that unmistakeably charming way, and as the perverted individual crabbed across her path, arms outstretched, the shapes resolved themselves into the feathering of draught horses. 'A team of shires. Adorable shires'

"Help." The shriek seemed torn from her throat. With the blade always between herself and the deranged 'thing,' which was once her parent, she flew past untouched to the wagon which floated like an island of safety in the gloaming. Drawn upwards as though weightless into the tall vehicle she crouched shivering on the wide seat, dimly aware of the driver climbing down, whip in hand. In his shapeless mess of a hat and voluminous moleskin coat, the man seemed cumbersome and even clumsy, but he travelled faster than a rumour as he disappeared energetically into the gloom. A second or two later, there came the unmistakable sound of a horse whip used with intent, followed instantly by shrieks of terrible agony.

Someone was coming. Out of the darkness, a dark horror, a shapeless being was approaching. She 'knew,' that it was the carter and yet terror vanquished the evidence of her own eyes. Her heart raced, tripping painfully, stumbling over outcrops of fear which multiplied until in the most loving fashion the spectre paused to gentle the horses. That simple gesture restored her.

The whip hand climbed aboard, rocking the wagon and its occupant.

"Are you hurt, lass?" the baritone asked gently, and when Angelique signified that she was not, and succumbed to tears, he let her be, spoke reassuringly to his team, and the wagon moved on.

Despite all that had occurred in the past; her father's exile of her brother, his despicable treachery towards her sisters and herself and his betrayal of his wife, Angelique's pity for the poor crippled creature when she heard that awful scream was more than she could bare.

She searched assiduously for the injured little man as she was carried her away. Black blood had run the full length of her blade to contaminate her hand.

The sun came up as the fields and woods passed slowly by at a plod, but still the very large carter sitting next to her did not speak; it seemed that he would refrain until doomsday yet it did not occur to her to break the silence.

"Were you setting off late yesterday or early today?" the composed one inquired at last, and Angelique could not help but be amused.

"I was waiting for you," she declared, surprising herself and laughing aloud at the sheer brazenness of it.

"For me? Should I be afraid or flattered? You're not going to take advantage of me I hope; though I'd prefer that, to whatever you intend to do with that little toy you have up your sleeve. What on earth are you thinking about, having such a thing as that about you?"

"That man back there is my father," she said simply.

"I've had to keep myself safe from him these months past." Her face was burning.

"The Scotsman got wind of it, and he was searching for father. He was going to. I asked him; Mr Macbeth, that is, to please not hurt father and he agreed, thank goodness, so long as I carried this thing and promised to use it if need arose."

"Whoaaa." The carter drew rein, turned and studied the girl's face candidly for a long moment then seeming to have arrived at a conclusion asked,

"Where shall we take you?"

"Are we passed Gratton?

"My word yes, but it's no bother to put you down there when we come home-along in a few days. Always supposing that you're happy to travel with us until then?"

"Us?" The carter nodded at his team as though the answer were evident.

"Oh, I'd love to. To ride along with you I mean. I am going off from home to find my brother and my sisters, and I don't have a clue where to start, so if you'll put me down anywhere you like, that would be lovely. Thank you." There was no response for a moment, the driver simply nodded his head, secured the reins to the break, then climbed down.

"I tend to go wherever Dolly takes me. What did you mean; 'find your brother and sisters?'"

"They ran off cause of father."

'"Dolly?"' Her new friend nodded at his team a second time.

"My lead hoss," he smiled.

"Her with the white socks."

"You have no idea what this means to me," Angelique declared, suddenly shy, exceedingly happy and unable to look at the quietly spoken stranger.

''Then we won't mention it ever again." The very last thing that Angelique wanted to do at that moment was to break the spell, but she was tormented by worry; she had to know.

"What did you do to him? My father."

"I took the whip to him."

"He screamed so?" Angelique the daughter gulped back her sobs in great distress.

"Had I known then, what I know now, I would have given him much worse, and then delivered him to the Macbeth. Such as he don't deserve to breathe. Father or no. Come on, we've got cheese to load and I'm promoting you to cheese loader. A very important job is cheese loader." They had drawn up at a farm gate, adjacent to which was a little house on stilts. Behind its unlocked door sat round cheeses, each bigger than a shire's hoof and richly yellow which between them the couple heaved into the wagon and stacked securely just behind their seat for easy retrieval. As they stood there in the new dawn, their breathing accelerated by their exertions, the carter held out his hand for the second time to his exquisite passenger and said,

"I am Andrew Carnegie."

"Angelique Huffer," the nubile responded doing likewise, and felt firstly her hand being engulfed, then her arm being shaken, but oh so gently. Carnegie took a small notebook and a crayon from his pocket and recorded the cheese collection.

"Oh, you can write," the ingenue gushed, and right away felt foolish and unsophisticated.

"I can read also. In fact, there is no end to my talents. I can talk to horses, lift cheese and all manner of things." In that instant, her new friend's easy self-deprecation demolished any last barriers of reserve which she maintained, and she felt that she could hug him tightly and give him a big kiss, so grateful was she for everything; for saving her, for his openness, and for his easy friendship, and most of all because in his company, she felt so very safe. She would very much have liked to give him a big kiss.

The new friends drove on in companionable silence and as the sun rose, warming them, the young adventuress began to feel very tired indeed.

The sky above was a decidedly cobalt blue, and she was admiring it from the softest bed that she had ever known, 'the slight depression of a bird's nest,' atop a mountain of wool bales. Andrew must have lifted her as she slept and placed her here. She blushed at the very thought of it. Herself fast asleep and probably snoring and looking a wreck, and he, carrying her in his arms. She had not previously entertained such thoughts about a man as she did that day about this capable, forthright and oh so handsome and smelly individual. He had chosen a lovely place for his camp. It was out of sight of the road at a place where there were huge sheltering rocks, ferns and a stream. Sheep had cropped the grass giving the place a garden-like appearance. Everything was still and peaceful and there was a pretty patchwork of fields beyond the low hills. The horses were grazing contentedly round about, and birds and insects were celebrating fit to wake the dead. There was no sign of her rescuer. He would be sleeping nearby having driven who knows how far. Two ponies were tethered further down the clearing, and what had been an empty wagon was now this huge load, and her, like an eagle in its eyrie, safe atop it. She snuggled happily back down, seduced by the beauty of the place and the unaccustomed comfort of the carter's protection but had barely closed her eyes but what she was up again, and making her way on hands and knees towards the front of the load. Sleeping-in late, like the lady of the manor, was hardly the way to thank Mr Carnegie for everything he had done for her. Angelique Huffer had been brought-up far better than that. Terrified of falling from the dizzy and swaying height, she navigated the length of the schooner on one intake of breath, gripping tightly to the twine bindings which secured the overhanging load, as she went. Reaching the front of the wagon safely, she took a deep breath, then descended slowly and carefully into the seat, holding on much too tightly to the cords and hurting her hands. It was an easy matter from there to the ground.

Andrew Carnegie was lying on his back on the baize beneath the wagon, his breathing measured, and deep. He was still fully dressed in his voluminous coat and shapeless hat and his obviously heavy, hob-nailed boots, which, Angelique noticed, had turned his ankles out to what appeared to be the most uncomfortable degree. Why had he not removed the awful things she wondered, or made up a bed for himself instead of simply collapsing on the ground? Men were such indecipherable creatures. Looking at him lying there on the short grass, Angelique was overcome with the desire to repay him for everything he had done for her. But where to begin?

'First things first,' her mother always said. Angelique was the only woman present in this camp and therefore this was her camp; she was its mistress and it followed that it was her duty to make it the most comfortable camp ever. So went her thinking; and she was free to go about her work; the threat which her father represented now being a mere memory and all due to this lovely man. Beneath the driver's seat, in the huge coffin of a box which extended the full width of the wagon, she found food, spare clothing, tools, lashings, nosebags, horseshoes and dozens of other things all thrown together in a horrible mess. It was a labour of Herculean proportions to obtain the things that she needed but obtain them she did though it meant climbing up and down on the spokes of the wheel a dozen exhausting times or more. Only when the fire was going beneath the bread, the porridge, and a pan of cabbage, while potatoes baked in the ashes and the tea-water bubbled in the billy, did she go off to take care of her toilet. Returning scrubbed and combed with an armful of sticks and a canvas bucket of water, she found her new friend sitting in his shirt-sleeves, his back against a wheel, looking particularly pleased with life, and so much younger without the hat and coat.

"Good day, Miss Huffer," he called, embracing her with one of his lovely smiles.

"I've been stirring the porridge in case it burned, and I drained the cabbage as it was cooked to perfection. Good, aint I?"

"Good day, Andrew," she responded gently, her residual emotions of the dark hours dispelling any discomfort which she may have experienced about this situation. She was startled to discover that her saviour was little more than a youth, certainly a very large, handsome, exceedingly dirty and smelly youth, but a youth nevertheless. He could surely not be much beyond his maturity. He approached the fire and was about to sit down to eat when she said without meaning to,

"The bread and potatoes will be a little while yet. You will just have time to take your bath and change your clothes. Your fresh ones are here by the fire, they were a bit damp." Andrew Carnegie eyed the porridge, the potatoes baking in the ashes, the determined look in the heaven that was the little girl's eyes, and lastly his own filthy condition.

"It has begun." he announced in stentorian tones,

"The tyranny of women is upon us. Angelique Huffer, mistress of all she surveys commands me, 'wash or starve,' and me in my own camp." Getting to his feet and becoming enormous in the process, he squashed his new mistress in a great bear hug, which both embarrassed and amused her, then without further protest, gathered up his fresh clothes and went off to the stream to rid himself of the accumulated dirt of weeks.

"Leave your dirty stuff to soak," she called after him. Suddenly happy beyond her experience and composed as she had ever been, Angelique returned to her ministrations without a care in the world, singing snippets of songs from home as she sliced the ham, brewed the tea, and rinsed Andrew's horribly greasy pewter-ware with boiling water.

CHAPTER 5: Bad Pennies

'The game was up.' Snarling a string of vile oaths, the reverend Penny, terrified for his life now that all was known loped back through the bushes into the open space of the graveyard, snatched up a long-handled spade and as the screaming Huffer staggered blindly towards him, one eye hanging by a thread, swung with murderous force. The edge of the thing bit deeply into pleb's face, almost cutting his head in half, 'like topping a boiled egg,' and stuck there. The screaming halted as the mortally wounded daughter-fucker crumpled to the ground wrenching the spade from Penny's grasp. Inconsiderately the thing was still alive and twitching like something run over by a wagon, so that he was obliged to step in the bloody mess in order to pull the thing free. He struck a second delicious blow, blood spattering him like warm rain, but still the swine gargled. Throwing down his imperfect weapon in disgust the fisher-of-men cast around for something heavy with which to give wings to this infuriating member of his flock; wrenched a child's gravestone from the dirt and standing astride the twitching thing, smashed the boulder into the unrecognisable mess.

Carved poorly into the bloody stone was a small cross, its outline softened by the years, by lichen, and by bloody, human brains. Only then was his rage vanquished by fear and like a child, desperate to escape the scene of his crime and who can conjure nothing other than to run home and hide, he turned his back on the murder, the barking dogs and the rush flares which now moved among the cottages. In a sickening panic, he ran for the false security of the vicarage his throat soon painful due to the unaccustomed exercise. He ran through fields populated by terrifying bulls, which would appear without warning out of the darkness; absurd walls which would do justice to Jericho, and ditches like chasms, every one of which was disgustingly full of cow shit. An aeon slunk passed before the roof of home came into sight against a sky in which light thickened, his racing heart slowed a little and he began to think rationally again. He need only get indoors and remove his guilty clothing for burning later, wash away the evidence against him then sneak back to his bedroom before that mouthy bitch of a maid Betty woke. For the first time ever he was praying sincerely, and what he was praying for was deliverance; his own. Kicking-off his filthy shoes at the servants' door and holding them at a distance he stepped quietly inside. Beyond the kitchen, in a narrow passage leading to the scullery was a deep walk-in cave of a cupboard, once used as a pantry but now as a convenient hiding place for gardening things, old clothes, stacks of unfashionable objects, kindling and the work clothes of a murderer. He made his way there cautiously, in the gloom, careful not to collide with the wooden furniture and thus wake the house. Ripping off his bloodied garments, he made a bundle of the loathsome thing as he stuffed them into an old tea chest then hurried naked down the horrid gangplank of a passageway to the scullery where he washed thoroughly paying particular attention to those parts of him which were exposed to the splash of blood. The stuff had dried hard on his skin and in his hair, and the task dragged on for ever. Not trusting to cloth, he dashed the excess water from his body with his hands as he negotiated the return journey, the ancient cobbles hurting his feet. Crossing the kitchen as a murderer he climbed the servants' stairs to his prison-cell room.

Abbigail's wondrous invitation of black glistening hair on his pillow surprised and aroused him instantly, despite his torment.

"Get out, it's late," he told her even though he was desperate to have her; his all-consuming lust for the girl tormenting him. The beautiful somnambulist rolled out of the bed warm and fragrant to float naked across the room. The filthy crime was already exacting an incomprehensible price. Hating Tansley Huffer in death as much as he had despised the little worm in life, Penny dropped on to the edge of his bed, mocked by the so called good book, which lay like an indictment on the table. He grabbed the thing, loathing it for its slippery coldness and its silent judgement of him, and hurled it petulantly against the wall, pleased that the spine broke so that it lay like the crippled Huffer, broken open on the ground. Unable to sit-still he dressed again and prowled around aimlessly, a prisoner of terror. The corpse! Why had he left it there? If there was no body then there was no murder, and he would not swing. Jesus bleeding Christ, why had he been so stupid. Why had he gone there in the first place, when the thing was being done? Greed of course. He'd been unable to stay away in case that disordered little swine, may he burn in hell, had cheated him out of some of his share. For a few silver coins he had risked it all. If the body was not discovered today, he would have to go back there tonight and bury the disgusting thing, but if someone stumbled across it, he was done-for. Cold, oily fear filled his belly to bursting, and the urge to vomit became almost uncontrollable.

The thought of such a nauseating task as burying the thing was terrible to him beyond belief. To help the others had been revolting enough, but to be alone in the darkness with a 'corpse?' It was too disgusting to think of. Worse still, were those cursed bulls. To get there he would have to cross field after field of the huge terrifying beasts. Bad enough in daylight, but he simply couldn't do that in the dark. There had to be some other way. By midmorning Penny could bear the 'real' purgatory no longer. No one had come breaking down his door gabbling about a gruesome murder, so it stood to reason that the thing had still not been discovered. But it also stood to reason that sooner or later, some two-faced snotnose peasant would come mewling and sobbing around the graves of people despised in life, but much loved in death, and step on the damned thing. He desperately needed to bury it but he daren't go back there in daylight to do it. As things stood now, it would be just another murder done by lord knows whom … No! That cursed girl. She would have known him even in the darkness; he stood a foot taller than any of the stunted denizens of this outpost of aridity. She had seen him at the church, hours before dawn; if the killing came to light, whom would she aim her unwashed digit at? Himself! He had come full-circle and was back to shifting the corpse. To be completely safe of course, he had to risk waiting till dark. That was what he would do. He was resolved. He would contain himself till night and then he would sneak out and bury the thing in the hole where he and Huffer had dug up that John Smith fellow; for which he would not get a farthing, by the by. Penny's unshakable resolve disintegrated within minutes. Unable to contain himself for yet another second, he hurried from the house and scuttled, famished, to the stinking outhouse of a church along little-used paths that circumvented the village, his legs weak, mouth dry, palms greasy with cold sweat. He did not take the trap because it would advertise his presence there, and as like as not, he would have some fool blundering into the graves talking drivel, and tripping all over the revoltingly dead daughter fucker.

In her attic quarters beneath the shingles of the rectory's roof, Betty, the maid of all work, was pulling her hated, sweat-stinking uniform over her head in preparation for yet another endless day of thankless scrubbing when she saw with a fright, a dark shape clambering over the wall at the top of the garden. It dropped clumsily to the ground and moved rapidly in a long-striding, loping run, toward the house, almost as though it were being pursued; seeming to know the garden well enough to step around obstacles, and duck below bean poles perfectly positioned to blind the unwary. As the man came nearer, Betty's suspicions were confirmed. Without a shadow of doubt, she was watching her employer and one-time user of her body, the not at all reverend Penny; sneaking home at the crack of dawn after who knows what. Betty's tired face broke into one of its least common expressions, a smile. Her first thought was to drop her washbowl and confound him by waking the Halfpenny, but she held off, guessing slyly that there was something in this wind which was much more promising than mere filth. Crouching in the darkness beneath her ladder-like stairs, she listened intently to the lecher's progress around the house, mapping his movements by sound alone.

Silently, on bare feet now across the kitchen to the passageway. The old pantry by the sound of it. Doing something in the old pantry, hiding something? Now to the scullery of all places. Working the pump. Washing? Washing in the scullery? Washing what? What on earth needs washing at four o'clock in the bleeding morning? Why? Coming this way up the back stairs; there's guilt for you, God preserve me. He was too proud ever to climb the back stairs. Her heart about to burst, wide eyes unblinking, Betty held her breath and watched trembling as Penny's form emerged through the gloom. Naked! Not a stitch on him. Though he had mounted her in every room in the house, in every conceivable fashion, she had never seen his body completely unclothed. It was a shocking sight. He was white, so big, heavy in the muscles. He passed so close to her that for a fleeting moment she felt the warmth of him enfilading her, his huge thingy hanging. She recalled the delicious pain of it. He had liked to hurt her with it. There had been none of that since miss, butter-wouldn't-melt, Abigail had washed up at the back door begging for food. Betty cursed the source of her frustrations with vicious intent for the thousandth time for her pretty face and her figure which men could not look away from. A door opened and a moment later, closed with theatrical care. Opened and closed a second time. He was coming back. No. It was only Abi-bleeding-gail, ambling along half asleep. The dirty slut. With any luck the stuck-up bitch would fall pregnant. Why would the bloody charlatan hide his clothes? As the door to Abigail's room, 'which used to be her own,' closed behind the bleeding cuckoo, Betty side-stepped hurriedly down the stairs to the old pantry. Searching the smelly darkness silently now, barely breathing in the fear of she knew not what. Yes! Here they were. Warm. Damp to the touch. That smell? Damp and sticky. Blood? Her nerve failing her. Frightened by this discovery, but strangely gleeful also while not knowing why, she retreated to the safety of the kitchen and lit a lamp then blew the red-hot embers in to life. With the kettle set to boil she hurried back to what obsessed her, lighting several candles despite daily admonitions to be frugal.

'She' didn't have to sneak around. 'She,' Betty; maid of all work; was 'supposed' to be up and about before dawn. She welcomed the light; 'not like some she could mention.'

'Blood.' There was blood on her hands brown in the light of the lamp. Quickly, back to the pantry before the bitch came through. Her breathing accelerated she snatched up one of the smaller articles of the dirty sod's guilty clothing and scurried silently outside where the light was better. Out there in the dawn, any doubt in her mind that the wetness on the cloth was blood was quickly dispelled. Blood on his clothes? What had he done? She ran to the garden wall and dropped the thing; a waistcoat, over the top then raced back inside. About to begin sweeping she found herself humming happily 'because she was free!' *"Abby is a filthy slut, Penny's for the gallows."* she sang, and continued singing and composing new and pertinent verses as Abigail flounced into the kitchen, late as always.

"What's that you're saying?" demanded the raven-haired beauty,

"Nothing at all for you to know bitch." In that moment the cathartic understanding dawned on Betty that she really 'was' free. ''FREE.'' she threw the brush at the hated beauty and started for her room.

''Get on wi it,'' she bawled.

"Abby is a filthy slut, Penny's for the gallows.

Dum de dum de dum de dah..."

''I'm goin to tell on you.'' There was no confidence in Abigail's riposte.

''Oh no!'' joyfully from Betty.

CHAPTER 6: Persuasion

The good lord's facilitator, tax-collector and enforcer in this nothing of a hamlet lost in a forest, abandoned the track at a place where there was no hedge or wall and hid his conveyance in a deserted, uncultivated spot where it would not be discovered. Stuffing his vestments under the seat he hurried away, advancing carefully between the brambles and boulders, carrying his steel-handled walking stick like a weapon in his fist.

'I hope to Christ the bastard is home.' He started down the overgrown slope to the distant hovel, its rotting roof almost concealed by creepers. His foul mood not improved by the need to stalk through a martyrdom of gorse thorns, convolvulus and stinking tobacco weed, and to retrace his steps a dozen times having got into yet another dead-end of impenetrable growth. The murderer entered the clearing ready to do violence again. Breaking into the open, he leapt back in terror as a frenzied animal crashed into his chest, its jaws clashing shut only a stinking slavering breath from his face. As the incensed creatures collapsed in a torture of gorse the two-legged animal lashed at his distant cousin's head with the viciously curved handle of his walking stick, happily bursting one of its eyes in a shower of warm liquid. The hunter became the hunted. The slavering beast, screaming horribly; agonized and whining, broke off its attack and tried desperately to disengage from the melee of arms and legs, but Penny was not finished with it yet by any means. As the defeated creature tried to turn away on pads which were pierced right through with thorns, he renewed his attack, thrashing it about the eyes and mouth with the awful weapon. The blinded animal absorbed more punishment as it tried unsuccessfully to get free from its prison of needles, then all too late, made its escape and scuttled lamely behind the shack with its tail between its ugly bent legs. It whined in much the same way that Huffer thing had whined, providing the victor in the engagement with a deep sense of satisfaction. Now for the big dog. His true nature now ascendant, the sadist jumped into the clearing and loping to the door of the shack, hammered on it with the stick.

"You bastard. You'll pay for that." Kane Seed had come around the corner of the building and ran at Penny in the manner of one accustomed to physical confrontation, his white-knuckled fists balled. Penny let the attacker come on; his weapon concealed behind his body, and in the instant that Seed struck, thrashed him murderously in the face with the stick. So vicious was the blow that it stopped Seed's forward-momentum instantly, and with a grunt of surprise and pain, the man went down like a god-cursed Moslem at prayer. Penny stood over the pig as it knelt in the dirt.

"Your dear friend. That cripple. Huffer. He is lying dead in my churchyard, stinking up the lord's house with his putrefaction, I know that you murdered the swine so get rid of him. Now. Today. Or I'll see to it that you'll swing for murder and grave robbing, and my word on it. Answer me. Do you hear?" Seed tried to stand but made no coherent sounds, so Penny thrashed him in the face again.

"Do you understand me?" he raged. The barely conscious Seed tried to nod his head.

"Yeth," he lisped and lay down in the dirt, drops of his blood coagulating freely with the dust to make tiny flowers of exquisite beauty. That night, Penny buried his bloodied clothes deeply in his vegetable patch and the following morning, the remains of the miserable cripple were gone from the graveyard. Relief washed over him, welcome as a cool breeze on a summer's day. He was saved. He would live. His elation was immeasurable, his confidence burgeoned. He was once again able to pause among the graves, pretending to meditate as he searched for any tell-tale evidence of violence around the murder site. There was none. Now there was only the girl to take care of. Or was there? The little bitch knew him to be a grave robber; she had seen himself and her 'loving' father doing just that very thing, but she did not know him for a murderer. With no body, there was no murder. For all she or anybody else knew, that ne'er-do-well… cripple had simply gone off to parts unknown. If she opened those wonderfully soft lips of hers, it would be her word against his, and who would believe her? A strip-farming, turnip digger, and a girl at that, against a supposedly ordained minister of the church.

The same applied with that goat, Seed. It had taken only the threat of the hangman to bend the swine to his will. The filthy outcast would stay schtum from now till doomsday. Penny's frown of intense concentration was replaced by something approaching a smile.

CHAPTER 7: Dora

'How she loved this soil. She had always loved it; so rich and dark that the spade sank in deeply, almost on its own, full of worms it was and not a stone in sight, and so friable that with just a shake it fell cleanly from the roots of the weeds. It was a joy to work with.'

"Leave off with that digging, woman, and get me some food before oi perish." Even as she turned, Dora was saying his name; her eyes were flooding with joy and relief. "Lliam," she cried, and ran to her young brother's open arms. Her delight at seeing him again as he crushed her to him and lifted her off her feet already cloying with consternation as she registered his smashed nose, his single eye hugely purple and almost closed, and the great wound to his face, incredibly seeming to be tied closed in knots like a roast of lamb.

"Oh Lliam, what have they 'done' to you?" she wept, horrified by it all. Hurrying to relieve the obviously ill man of his bundle she helped him into the cottage.

"We will put you on my bed and I shall have Angie's place; be careful now in case the old thing won't hold up under you." Guiding the lad to the marriage bed which was little more than a raft of logs and planks tied together she helped him out of most of his outer garments.

"This won't please that wee boele of a husband of yours," he groaned happily.

"He sleeps with the firewood." Dora said shortly,

"I'll get you some good food and do for your horse. She hurried away.

"Dora," Hooligan called to her, "water, quickly. Get me one of the bottles in me pack." Dora hurried to comply and watched fascinated as her darling long-lost-brother tipped a drop from a bottle into the water and drank off the mixture. The effect on him was almost immediate and inexplicable. All the tension of his pain eased from his limbs as though the spirits had interceded for him. Sighing in relief, he fell back, and with no more mention of food was asleep, snoring loudly. Easing the medicine bottle and the mug from the boy's implacable grip she placed them in the corner for safety then pulled off his beautiful boots before lugging his huge legs onto the bed.

Once positive that he would not roll off and add to his injuries, and that the ancient relic of a bed would not collapse beneath his great weight, she went to the barrel-end to prepare the large quantities of food which she knew she would be needing. As the day progressed into evening, she returned often, and creeping silently up to him, would inspect and bathe his open wounds with suffusions of herbs from the hedgerows; the swollen, almost closed eye, the side of his face tied together with horsehair in what appeared to be a torture in-itself and his poor ear totally shrouded in white stuff, through which blood and lymph were seeping. One of his hands appeared to be broken but splinted and from the state of his poor bandaged neck it looked for all the world as though they had tried to hang him. She would whisper his name under her breath and go back to her work, her tears running freely; great sobs shaking her.

Despite his sister's mild protests, Hooligan dragged himself outside the very next morning, and sat by the cottage wall, enjoying the cool drizzle and taking advantage of the warmth given back by the stonework. He seemed content, for the moment at least, to rest and watch Dora cultivating the run-down garden, pass the occasional remark or a jest, and to fill his stomach with roast lamb, baked potato, cabbage with butter and salt, home-made bread still warm from the pan, cheese and cider; lots of cider, and anything else she brought to him.

He ate so much with no evidence of having consumed a sufficiency, that she grew concerned that she might have to feed him the chickens which she was preparing for the following day. Her little brother was now rich beyond the telling of it and she was happily free to buy whatever he fancied. As she feared and suspected would be the case there was no 'middle time,' a period of rest and gentle walks, conversations amid shared meals and memories. Lliam, her much loved little brother was not that sort of man. He fretted and resisted his physical limitations and cursed foully but quietly at every disappointment. Something big, she knew, was in the wind.

The day that Dora had dreaded arrived soon enough. The little devil planted a big kiss on her forehead one morning then walked away without a word. She would not ask him where he was going for if he wanted her to know he would have told her.

''Yer too bloody kind for your own good sis.'' He called back. The words brought a smile to her caring face. He had always been her favorite and she his. At nightfall, Lliam had not returned, neither had Tansley and in spite-of-everything, Dora was concerned for the pathetic excuse for a man, thinking that he may have suffered an accident and be lying somewhere, alone and in pain. Lliam she knew, was man enough to look after himself. She slept little that night, kept her fire going just a mite to keep off the chill, and before dawn of the following day, there being no sign of either man, had left the cottage and was on her way to Danesholme with an extra bit of sacking over her shoulders against the early chill.

Despite trudging around the perimeter of the huge, still deserted field, Dora could find no sign of her estranged husband though she called out his name as she went along. Leaving off with it reluctantly because of the faint possibility that she might have overlooked him, she walked on to Shakle Oder where she had no more success than before, though again she called out to him until she was hoarse and inquired of the early birds as they arrived at their strips whether they had seen anything of him.

At last, with no prospect of a satisfactory resolution imaginable, she was forced to face the fact that she had been delaying going to the lair of the criminal Seed a terrifying individual, believed to be responsible for violent crimes all over the county, and at whose property Tansley was rumored to spend considerable time. But no one in their right mind would approach the lair of that creature. Even the criminal people gave it a wide berth. Seed and Tansley, she had heard, drank and gambled in each-others unlikely company. She had always wondered where the deviant would acquire the money for drinking and gambling, while the family was forced to live so close to the bone. About to drive the reckless idea from her mind she thought of her infamously violent brother and her heart swelled. No one; not even Seed would hurt her while Lliam Shaun Hooligan was looking out for her. She would tell Mister Seed, should he offer her harm, of her brother's presence in the village. Her decision made, the newly determined little woman stepped out smartly with a new sense of security and resolve. It did not last. The awful criminal lived but a couple of miles from Thorpe, in a hovel which was lost in a jungle of gorse and bramble, and as she picked her way through that malignant growth there being no obvious path, she became more and more concerned that at any moment, Seed might leap out and inflict violence on her. Exhausted and drenched in the cold sweat of fear, she emerged at a clearing in which squatted a decaying shack. The space was all baked-hard dirt and not a blade of grass grew there; its lifelessness seeming to infect the old hovel whose dark windows stared rudely at her as though considering what her fate should be.

"Mister S" The words caught in her throat causing her to start again.

"Mister Seed, are you home?"

"I am."

Scared beyond her experience and trembling. Dora discovered Seed in the clearing with her, standing at no distance at all, standing somehow threateningly still.

"I can't find my husband, Mister Seed," Dora managed.

"He's not here Mrs." Seed mumbled,

"You come the ard way. Keep to the tree line as you go back." There was blood! Blood trickled from the corner of the man's mouth and most of his face resembled a dish of raw tripe. He wiped away the rubies absentmindedly with his sleeve, grimacing slightly.

"Thank you, Mister Seed." Dora tried to smile her thanks, but it was too much for her. As she struggled away from the squalor of the place and its awful guardian her breathing was far too fast, her heart was trying to escape from her chest and her skin crawled in expectation of a commotion in the gorse behind her, followed immediately by hellish agony as some bloodthirsty animal ripped her to shreds. She had heard that the man owned terrible mastiffs which attacked for no reason. It took an age to negotiate the tree line, but at last she arrived in what was familiar territory near the churchyard but just as she began to feel a little safer, her legs failed her; she sank to the ground within 'cooey,' of Jessie Cumberpatch's cupboard.

CHAPTER 8: Copplestone

In deep cover on a half-naked hill overlooking Astor and Son, Shipwrights, at Minster, Lliam Shaun Hooligan closed his telescope and replaced it in its leather case, the intense and completely novel feeling of legal ownership of the superb instrument strong upon him. At this point, he had seen all that could be seen from outside of the yard, but it was insufficient; he needed to somehow get inside the place in order to discover how to best spread his intended inferno quickly enough to defeat any efforts that were made to quench it. No matter how unappealing the prospect was, he was committed to breaking-in, because recurring visions of the rotting thing on Fotheringhay's gallows still unsettled him, as did the prospect of missing out on a second purse full of silver.

Having silver in your purse he had discovered was akin to owning a magic wand, and there were a million spells that Lliam Shaun Hooligan had yet to cast. He had arrived in Minster late in the afternoon as an unpaying passenger on the post-gig having simply sat his arse on the luggage rack at the rear when the contraption halted for a paying passenger.

Acutely aware of the dangers which attended upsetting either slavers or anti-slavers he allowed himself to be carried well past the object of his interest before alighting to saunter back to the shipyard arriving just as the great doors were heaved open to allow a torrent of shipbuilders to pour out of the yard, tired but happy. The gates had remained open for a considerable length of time on that occasion as evidenced by the fact that during his reconnaissance, as he recalled later, the church bells had rung twice. He had therefore been able to study the place surreptitiously from several vantage points; the first being a public bench directly opposite the gates, where he had relaxed holding a broadsheet of which he understood very little. An even more comfortable seat in a chophouse had provided a second perspective through its open windows, and lastly, there was the graveside where he had paid his respects to victims of the plague who had passed away in excess of a century earlier. From that spot, he got a clear view of a ship whose name he was told later was *Glorious*, which appeared from this vantage point at least, to be ready for the sea. What a shame it would be if some bad man were to torch that lovely new boat. The last of the stragglers to leave the yard had hauled the great doors shut and swung the locking bar into place, then applied a padlock as big as a new moon. Thinking that there was nothing left to see, Hooligan was about to forsake the grave of his dear departed, when someone emerged through a Judas door which had gone unnoticed. The lock with which the dapper little fellow secured the thing was a mere toy compared to its cousin. He could tear-out its fixings with his teeth if required.

By circuitous means, avoiding footpaths, taking cover behind hedgerows, haystacks, herds of cattle and even dirtying his lovely new boots by wading along damp ditches, he had so far as he knew achieved this vantage point atop a hill without being seen. The night, when it arrived, was almost as bright as day due to an overcast of cirrus so that he was able to establish that no matter how little the Astors paid their night-watchmen; it was too bloody much. The lazy old buggers sat outside in the fresh air where they passed the time talking, and drinking but never, he noticed, lighting a pipe. Occasionally, one or other would go for a walk and even mount the gangplank to the deck of one of the ships moored at the quay. Interestingly, the old boys hadn't shown-up at the yard until dark; clearly, their unimaginative employers were of a mind that no evil could befall their incalculable investment other than under the cover of night. How very short-sighted of them. But that was fine with Lliam Hooligan, because burning the yard was one thing; murdering a gang of poor old men in order to do it was another.

Well before sunup his hide was far behind him while a good understanding of the organization of Astor and Son Shipbuilders was firmly planted in his mind. He was heading for home. ''Home,'' How good that thought was after all these years of doing it rough. He picked up the pace in his enthusiasm for that much-loved cottage and his little sister's cooking and went generally eastwards, taking the field-way rather than retracing his steps to the Great North Road and bringing attention to himself as an unlikely tramp by following that. As dawn approached, he struck a track which he trod for a while on its more-or-less northward course, until he was fortunate enough to be given a ride to a pleasant little village of which he had faint memories. Memories of the drink, girls, haymaking, a married woman, and one monumental scrap against a brace of soldiers who had left him for dead in a ditch. There he was able to get his bearings from the locals and after another exhausting march, followed by a pleasant ride on the back of a hay wagon, he found himself in the outskirts of Alsop, a town he knew well, it lay only a few miles from home. The place was as busy as an ants' nest due to it being market-day in the high street with people milling around aimlessly at the stalls, laughing about the least thing, and roaring at friends who were only an arm's length distant. By the look of things, eating and drinking seemed to be the major preoccupation hereabouts. The pie-stalls must have been doing a sterling trade because everybody had a 'sore fist' of hot beef pie, cold pork pie, or Cornish pasty. Not for Lliam Shaun Hooligan Esquire a handful of hot pie; he was, for the moment, a man of means and intended seeing something of the other side of life while the chance lasted. He wanted to stroll through the front doors of establishments to which he had previously been denied entry even at the kitchen door; to enjoy hot meals cooked just for him; not devour the left-over scraps which were colder than the charity which had thrown them at him. He sauntered happily, a novel emotion, through the crowds until he arrived opposite The George Inn, a famously respectable hostelry which, prior to his rebirth, he had avoided scrupulously; the exception being one freezing night when forced by starvation to beg for food at the kitchen door. Scraps from the plates of diners was what they had given to him and he was grateful. 'What a waste of a life.' He mused sadly.

The visage of the George was arrogance personified, each of its three tiers advancing one pace further forward than the one beneath. The front doors were wider than a barn, and its face was all black lines and white patches which blinded a man for sure. Outside, where the horses waited was a tall sign with a picture of a fat man in a wig, and taking everything into consideration, the building was the grandest in the town, sitting at the middle of a long row of fine buildings, like the king himself in a mess of hangers-on. With all those white-plastered panels and thick black beams, and the tiny diamond windows shaped in lead, it was a minor bastion of English privilege.

Once inside the place, he discovered that he was as well-dressed as anyone else, despite being crumpled by his night on the hillside, but his injuries and the state of his boots clearly brought attention that he could have done without. Desperately hungry, he had followed a gentleman farmer and his wife into a large room, much quieter than the riotous pot-room opposite, discovering heaps of clean, well-dressed people sitting at stupidly small tables, conversing in whispers as they ate their lunch.

"This is the life, Lliam me boy,'' he rejoiced. This lion among sheep had barely made himself uncomfortable on a tall, ebony settle so narrow in its seat that his arse would not fit but from where he could observe the proper form, when a maid hastily approached him and enquired with a smile what it was that he would like to eat. 'They had,' she assured him, 'cheese, beef, mutton, fish, game and venison, and it would be her pleasure to bring his selection to him. And would he like beer or wine with that?' Lliam returned the girl's smile with one of his own; an expression that would curdle milk, and briefly heard Macbeth's voice lecturing him on his abysmal eating habits. For the next hour, he was on his best behavior, copying the other patrons in his use of knife and fork, and even going so far as to kiss the napkin on occasion just for fun. With the inner man thus restored and glad to rid himself of the insufficiently discreet scrutiny to which he had been subjected by his fellow diners, he rejoined the happy throng of commoners in the street and set about making purchases from a list which he carried in his head. A clothing stall for men drew his attention and he headed straight for it in the pleasing knowledge that he would not need to steal a thing because he could now afford to buy the whole damned lot. Seeing him approach the insane foul-mouthed ancient who owned the business informed the crowd that such a man as he would likely have a cock to rival a horse. Not content with this observation the crazed granny went on to describe loudly and in lurid detail the activities which she would willingly undertake with such a man if only he could last her pace. Halting in indecision at a good ten paces from this escapee from Bedlam he was about to run for his life when he woke to the fact that this behavior was a popular part of the diversions on market days and the crowd were all enjoying themselves immensely at his expense and waiting in the hope of seeing him play the devil's advocate Grasping the nettle; he approached and began the business by treating himself to some work clothes as these which Macbeth had given him were far too good to ruin through the sort of stuff that he was about. Having had his inside leg and his private parts measured, weighed and attested to being ''simla to that fuckin bull over in Evenoe Quarter,'' he decided to go the full hog because the massive and expanding gathering had gone into raptures at the wonderful fashion in which he had contributed to the day's entertainment. For his finale he would change into his new togs right here he declared causing paroxysms of glee among his audience. With the depraved crone holding up a piece of cloth in order to preserve the innocence of the fair sex in the crowd he dropped his trousers and seemingly oblivious to the uproar that his thick thighs and barely concealed bits and pieces caused, stepped into his new workaday duds. About her own moral wellbeing 'Maddy,' clearly cared not a jot, for at strategic moments she would drop her arms, claiming to be unable to hold them up a second longer, and stare shamelessly, declaring loudly her expert opinion of the penis, testicles and thick thighs with which she was presently in love. And all of this despite her outraged customer loudly declaring her 'a dirty little strumpet' and 'a filty stop out.'

When it came time to pay, Hooligan observed for the benefit of his adoring audience that it was *she* who owed *him* for the morning's excitement and was called 'a cheeky little bogger' for his trouble. He moved on, shoving his way through his appreciative admirers, his finer sensibilities badly bruised.

The livestock sales, he discovered, were situated behind the emporiums and businesses which faced The George from across the high street, and it was to this place that the extravagantly happy man gravitated next by way of a narrow alley between two buildings. Having been swept by the crowds into this virtual tunnel; 'the buildings either side leaning out to kiss high above,' and been followed in his turn by throngs of locals, there was no escape when progress along the right-of-way unexpectedly slowed to a crawl. It soon transpired that an obscenely fat individual, moving at a snail's pace, was choking the flow of both the uphill and the downhill tribes to the point where Hooligan concluded, that it would have been quicker to tramp to the end of the street and go around. By the time it came for Himself, 'master of finance, frequenter of fine-dining institutions, and soon-to-be owner of a horse,' to take his turn at squeezing past the rolling obstruction he found himself deeply aggrieved by the bloody nuisance. Spotting a wide entranceway in the wall just ahead of the snail he concluded that remedial action was not only advisable it was obligatory. Dropping his shoulder, he flung himself into the task of stuffing the great mountain of slop into the portal until the fellow was wedged tight and mooing like a cow giving birth. This was clearly the sort of rough and ready justice that was appreciated by the good people of Alsop, who cheered the man of action universally and added their own weight to his task. He, at whom, they had once thrown stones and 'booed,' in chorus.

In contrast to the joyous mood of the high street, the atmosphere of the livestock auctions was all business, and though much of the stock had obviously been sold and driven away, there were still so many horses for sale that he remained confident of finding one which he liked. Thinking it best to have a glance at everything on offer and intending to lap the field to achieve this, he stepped out energetically but had not gone far when he fixated on an incredible beast which he recognized immediately as the little darling that he was looking for. The dejected owner, a soldier, had chosen to stand on a slight rise apart from the body of commerce, almost implying by his detachment that the animal was not for sale. Hooligan approached, beginning meanwhile to feel a deep sympathy for the man whom he suspected would be selling his friend through dire necessity only. With memories of his own immeasurable gratitude to Macbeth for the clothes which the Scotsman had given him, and the loan of a mount in addition, he approached the sergeant who clearly saw the prospective buyer coming and turned his back, as though this might make the unwelcome interest evaporate.

"Lliam Hooligan," announced the now-reluctant purchaser, smiling and offering his good hand.

"Are you selling him?" The soldier shook hands readily enough.

"I am selling him, but I doubt that you have his price."

'Shortarse,' hoist one eloquent eyebrow as he inspected Hooligan's workaday clothes while playing irritatingly with his moustaches.

"Let me be the judge of that," retorted the Irishman whose sympathy evaporated with remarkable ease,

"I've given you my name, is yer own a big fat secret?"

"I am Sergeant Trewin Copplestone," responded the soldier, as though that was an end to the matter, and therefore Lliam Hooligan should take himself off and look into the mouths of horses more suited to his pocket.

"Hear me well, Couple o bones," growled Lliam, suddenly angry and sticking his jaw out at the man.

"Your sergeanting days are over by the look of you, and your arm will be broke afore ye get that toy out, so take yer fuckin fist off it." The soldier's hand stayed right where it was, on the hilt of his scabbard.

"I'm starving," the sergeant responded in calm, measured and distinctly dangerous tones,

"and it's been a while since I had 'pork' on a 'spit,' so may I suggest that you annoy me no further. Show me the color of your money Fooligan or go to the other place." Copplestone stared up challengingly into Hooligan's eye, not backing off so much as one inch.

''Right ye are Private Parts!'' Desperate not to be thought poor now that he had money, the would-be buyer delved deeply into the front of his new granny-stitched corduroys ignoring the soldier's unoriginal reference to 'pigs' and 'spits,' and brought out his pleasingly heavy purse, from which he decanted a couple of silver coins into his bandaged palm.

"His name is Bengal," said the much-deflated vendor, seemingly hypnotized by the silver coins, as though they were the eyes of a cobra.

''However, I wouldn't let 'you,' come near him in a thousand years.

''Oh, is that the way of it?''

''I say what I mean and I mean what I say. Are you deaf, stupid or both?

Lliam Shaun Hooligan of the County Mayo Hooligans, in keeping with all men of his roots, loved horses. He could boast no scientific knowledge of what constituted a good animal but when he saw quality, he knew it instinctively. The grey owned a noble head, a powerful chest and stood sixteen hands at the withers. Surveying its short back and small round hooves he was transported. Even so, despite the insults and the acrimony, the thought of divorcing the man from his friend was no longer part of his thinking. He tried a new tack.

"He's a beauty. What breed would he be?"

"Barb. African."

"Oh, from the jungle," he was hoping to impress with his new knowledge of the world, but the dragoon rolled his eyes in silent mockery at this response much to Hooligan's surprise, to which was added his annoyance and uncertainty.

''So; it's deaf no, stupid yes.'' The soldier had clearly suffered enough.

"Oh, it's 'stupid,' is it?" determined to uphold those new standards to which he now held himself, the purchaser was curbing his ire with a very tight rein; not being 'absolutely certain' of his ground.

"I happen to know from people who have *been* there, that Africa is full of jungle, and snakes and bloody big aminals and black people. Yes, 'black' people." Copplestone turned in order to scrutinize this inexplicable ignoramus who wanted to own his beloved Bengal concluding that the man was probably a prize-fighter who had come into his fortune by robbery, theft, and beating men to death with his fists; a savage who would treat Bengal in much the same way as he treated any fool desperate enough to toe his line.

'How is it possible,' he wondered, 'for a grown man to be so utterly ignorant of ''everything,'' in this fast-paced world where knowledge was free for the taking and science and advancement were all around?'

"It makes no sense to say that you have *been* to Africa," he snorted rudely, turning his back once again and looking away with no appetite for the conversation. The beautiful irritant persisted.

"Are you saying there is no jungle in Africa?" The question was couched rhetorically and pugnaciously because Hooligan was in new territory and had not previously had his genius tested.

"Or black people?"

The soldier's answer was a long time coming.

"There *are* jungles in Africa. And black people also, just as there are deserts of sand bigger than whole countries, snow-topped mountains, swamps big enough to lose... Ireland, hopefully, with room to spare, grasslands that roll on and on forever it seems, and there are brown people, and people like you and me. Then again, there are some tribes much taller even than you, and reed thin, and others who even when they are fully grown, are no taller than an English child. Africa is endless. I ask you 'Droolagain', could a horse like this run through dense jungle? No. But on bare dirt, baked to stone by the sun, he is faster than a slingshot." As he spoke, the dragoon appraised his mount lovingly. Poor ignorant Hooligan was positively elated, inspired and fascinated that any man could be a repository of such seemingly inexhaustible, stupefyingly rich seams of knowledge. Never in his life had he met anyone so capable of articulating his thoughts or with such powers of recall. It was as though he had sought shelter from the world in a cave and discovered the hoard of gems beyond price which is 'Education and Knowledge.'

"Tell me this then, Mister Seargent Trewin Copplestone," he requested, transformed instantly from marauding lout to fascinated inquirer after truth; and creaking cautiously down in real discomfort on one knee, he drew in the dust, the map, accurately and in detail, which Macbeth had drawn in the river-sand,

"What is this? I've got to know for sure." Mimicking the colossus, the soldier dropped down next to him, bemused and charmed by the chameleon-like transformation which he had just witnessed.

"Why, this is the Golden Triangle," he began; surprised that this troglodyte would know of such a thing let alone be able to draw it from memory. Hooligan gasped audibly at the confirmation.

"So it is," He gushed, utterly astounded that such as this was common knowledge. He had supposed that these gems were privy to Macbeth and himself and perhaps a few of the better-educated sorts. "Carry on, Mister Sergeant, oi won't interrupt ye again, oi promise."

"This is the south coast of England, where you and I are at this moment. Ships sail from here, let's say Portsmouth, southward to this part of Africa here, 'the white man's grave.'" The mentor indicated a stretch of the African continent's coast.

"All along this south-facing region, which is known as The Fever Coast, The Ivory Coast and The Slave Coast, they trade all manner of rubbish, mirrors, glass beads, knives, cloth, in exchange for living human beings, black human beings as you said, and yes, this area is covered in heavy forest and impenetrable jungle, thousands of miles of it. They sail from there with a cargo of people chained or caged below, in conditions in which you would not keep a rat, along this line, across the Atlantic to the Americas, and sell the poor devils there; those who have survived the journey, that is. In the islands and Brazil, these poor people are used as slaves for the growing of sugar and coffee while up here," he pointed to where Virginia might lie, "it's tobacco for the most part. Then they sail back across the Atlantic to England with a cargo of tobacco, rum, sugar, molasses, spices, which is snapped up in London, Bristol, Southampton, Glasgow, you name it. Then it's off to Africa again to repeat the trip."

"It's a cruel business?" asked the student getting to the point of his interrogation of the soldier.

"If you consider burning alive, branding with red hot irons, crucifixion, multiple rape, castration, the selling of family members, cruel, then yes, it is. There is no limit to the cruelty that those people will resort to. When the poor devils are suffering with the shits, the sellers stuff knotted rope up their backsides to conceal the fact. They are well-aware that the victim, man or woman, will die a horrifying death. But they will have made the sale by then and that is all that matters to them. The ones who can't be sold are left to wander and starve to death. When they catch a runaway slave, they are just as likely to chop off half of the man's foot as a little reminder to him not to run away again, or maybe his testicles to take some of the spirit out of him. Nothing is too horrible for slavers to inflict. In the sugarcane fields and jungle-bashing in Brazil and Jamaica, the poor devils last only months, a year at most. Sometimes a year or two longer at tobacco in the colonies."

"How long is it since you had some grub, Trewin Copplestone?" enquired academia's freshman having very definitely come to a favorable conclusion about the man.

ing139

His defences irreparably breached the soldier merely shrugged his shoulders and looked away.

"What if you could do a bit of work for me? For cash. And keep your pal. Would you let me buy you a meal?"

"This work; is it legal?"

"It is!" Hooligan's joyful surprise at this declaration was manifest.

"Bengal could do with some oats."

"He'll have them." The delighted Hooligan patted the animal affectionately and in a momentous release of tension, the two men shook hands energetically, scowling so as not to commit the offence of smiling, then with the posturing, breast beating, and territory-marking amicably resolved with not so much as a drop of blood spilt or of urine sprayed, they set off at Hooligan's suggestion to The George, which of course 'Captain of Industry Hooligan' could recommend. Any observer; no matter how dull-witted, watching the two men that day, would have seen that the unlikely couple were soon totally absorbed in each other's company, and an eavesdropper would have discovered that their conversation fell quickly into a very distinct pattern, with the Irish giant continually asking questions; some of them outlandish, of the little soldier, who, to his credit, exhibited endless patience; proffering answers couched in simplistic terms which he threw carelessly into the chasm, wide and deep, where his new acquaintance's knowledge of the world should have been.

With Bengal unsaddled and feeding on corn, hay and dark beer in his own loose box, courtesy of The George's stables, the ill-matched duo repaired to the dining room where Hooligan was unable to resist, despite having dined well just a couple or three hours earlier, a platter of various cold meats, boiled eggs, onion, mustard, and pickles with bread, and beer; while he watched Copplestone making hard work of game soup, herring, beef with potatoes and vegetables, stewed apple with fresh cream; then finishing up with cheese, which the soldier was most particular in choosing from a tray laden with a selection of the things, some of which had obviously lain there so long that they were blue with mold and stank of feet.

 The soldier's table-manners were fascinating to the man opposite. Although the little tough had not seen food for a couple of days, he ate as though every morsel would choke the living daylights out of him; he cut his meat into little pieces which he introduced reluctantly to his mouth one at time, even putting down his knife and fork in-between morsels, then dabbing the corners of his lips with his napkin before beginning all over again. He behaved just like an English version of Macbeth. 'Sure they were all as mad as hatters these foreigners.' Hooligan gave thanks that he was the son of a civilized nation.

The host's most enjoyable moment of the productive detente arrived when Copplestone picked of all things, the moldy cheese from the dozen on offer and ate every morsel of it with hard biscuits and white wine as though it were ambrosia. Hooligan for his part was inordinately proud of himself for neither laughing at, nor mocking the charming fellow for his stupidity.

Despite the vast quantity of food that the hungry soldier put away, and his natural preoccupation with it after days of going without; as their repast lasted a good couple of hours, Hooligan was able to discover from this veritable library of information, that India, where the little bugger had done a lot of soldiering for the British East India Company, was not a place in Africa. It was a huge country, vastly bigger than England and was home to a hundred times more people. Brown people. The brown people were made to grow tea on bushes, and the bushes in turn were grown on farms as big as Armagh, created from vast tracts of jungle which had been cleared for growing stuff and 'John Company' whoever *he* might be, made lots of money growing the brew for next to nothing, and selling it all over the world.

For his part, Trewin Copplestone found the mountainous object sitting across the table from him to be a complete enigma. The man clearly knew 'nothing.' A substantive, *nothing*. He could, in all probability, neither read nor write and yet he was obviously known to and popular with the staff at this perfectly respectable inn. He was wearing working man's clothing, clean, and even new by the look of them, but working mans' at bottom, yet carried a purse which held a small fortune in silver, in addition to a bundle of clothing of the very highest quality; Harris Tweed by the looks of it and riding boots of the very best manufacture. 'General Officer Class.' Then there were the atrocious wounds which he had suffered recently, some of which had clearly been stitched by a surgeon who knew his stuff and would have charged the earth for his services. The blow which had almost cost Hooligan his sight had clearly been delivered from the side and rear with a reverse upward cut, and though it had obviously been made with a club, not a blade, the force of it had been so great as to slice open the flesh. It was the sort of attack that a thugee of the Thug Behran cult of the Hyderbad region would deliver, sufficient to render the victim unconscious, if not dead, and thus unable to later identify the man who had robbed him. Strangest of all, was the fact that though his wounds had been bandaged by an expert with the correct surgical material, manufactured specifically for the purpose, the dressings had not been changed and were now filthy and weeping. That was a contingency which he would have to attend to in short order. He did not want this generous and enormously likeable man to lose his life to something as eminently preventable as infection.

By unspoken agreement, the acquaintances brought their repast to a close and repaired in order to enjoy what Copplestone called with a gay laugh, their ''postprandial.''

"Some new treads is what 'you' need sunshoine; you stick out loike dog's balls in that shit," declared the ignoramus once more able to employ his own tongue, with no intention whatsoever of being rude. The unlikely couple were thusly sailing in the direction of the stall owned by the octogenarian lunatic through crowds which opened wondrously before them, as though they were one of the fair's attractions, when Hooligan announced,

"You'll have to look-out for yourself mind, or this one will have your virginity. She's a hooer of the first watter." Lliam had spoken loudly, and the old crone heard this last comment as she was intended to.

"Don't bother your head about the pretty soldier, Narcissitus," she retorted acerbically. "You are the only virgin hereabouts, you soft penis."

"Less of the flattery you young hussy and fit up my son here wit some work clothes loike moine, and it had better be half the price because as you can see, he's only half the man. And be quick about it if ye don't mind. We've tings to attend to before we take the road." The novice entertainer's stage-whispers amused the crowds for yards around. Before he could establish a defensive position, poor Copplestone found his inside-leg being measured mischievously, and his private parts fondled lasciviously and quite 'unnecessarily,' as that gentleman pointed out to his new admirer. As a piece of string was an indication of the ancient's accuracy in such matters, and because the clothes which she sold fitted only where they touched the soldier thereafter worked by eye while an ever-growing crowd joined with Hooligan in egging the stallholder on to even more disgusting excesses, much to his friend's chagrin.

"That's the one sheriff, the big one, attacked me he did. Tried to rob me, but I held him off."

The 'big one,' in question had barely recognized that it was himself that the high-pitched, whining voice was referring to when he was grabbed from behind by rough hands which he threw off energetically wearing a scowl of annoyance which would have been warning enough for anyone with some awareness of human behaviour. Unfortunately, the lawman involved stood well outside of that small circle.

"I ham har-restin you," announced the public servant, addressing Hooligan's crotch as he concentrated, not on the business at hand, but on verbalizing his memorized arrest speech,

"for bodil-ily assaultin' the body of the perso." Incisive as a scalpel, Copplestone leapt to his friend's rescue.

"This is clearly a case of mistaken identity ocifer," he announced grandly, drawing attention to his sword by waggling it about freely.

"You are addressing Major Mishap of the Camel Corp of India. 'Rearguard.' I can assure you, my good fellow that this gentleman has been at my side all morning, just as he was in doing battle on England's behalf against the Fuzzy Wuzzy, the Whirling Dervishes and the Dung Beetles. I would advise you sir, to go no further with this charade, lest you find yourself at the center of courts martial followed instantaneously by a firing squad." With that, the comrades turned their backs and marched away, deaf to all successive appeals to return.

"What exactly did ye say to yer man back there?" enquired Hooligan.

"Wouldn't have a clue," declared Copplestone.

The next port of call that the sartorially identical twins sailed in to was a builder's yard where Hooligan's estimation of the soldier scaled even greater heights than those previously established. He was in the process of obtaining a price for the removal and rebuilding of the roof of Dora's cottage when Copplestone touched his arm and drew him aside, out of earshot of the builder, a larcenist who was beginning to think that Christmas had come early.

"It's your money, Lliam," he observed "but if we can't slide straw off a roof and rebuild it for a quarter of the price that this highwayman will charge you, then I'm a Dutchie. This fellow will get his wood from the woodyard, his straw from any flour mill and charge you four times what he pays for it. Let's canter round there and buy our own." The fledgling entrepreneur took no persuading at all; sure, hadn't he built the bloody cottage from scratch, way back when? Ten minutes later, he was prowling among huge stacks of filleted timber which stood drying in the sun at the premises of the town's only timber dealer, Bowman and Son, explaining to the owner, one Isambard Bowman, the job to be done. Trewin Copplestone meanwhile took himself off and was browsing around seemingly interested in everything; the various types, grades, lengths and widths of wood on sale, the way the saws were fashioned and the intricate designs of their businesslike teeth. Even the way in which each successive tooth leant left then right of perpendicular in order to give width to the cut and so let the saw pass easily through the timber in a manufacturing technique known as 'relief.'

"Now sir, as we don't have the benefit of measurements, this here is how I would go on if I were you," Isambard advised the overpowering stranger.

"The cottage is of solid stone in good condition, but as for the roof, straw and timber both, them's had their day; correct?"

"Correct," enthused the customer who was enjoying the novelty of being legally inside a builder's yard.

"And the building is an 'L' in shape; and you estimate about five yards long on the longer sides and the gables be about three, maybe four?"

"Could ye draw what that is fer me so's Oi get it roight?" enquired the awful head and the woodman, guessing correctly what the problem was, drew on a newly sawn plank the outline of the cottage as he understood it.

"That's the one. The very one." Hooligan was greatly impressed by Bowman's grasp of the situation. Continuing with his use of the drawing for ease of explanation, the woodman went on.

"You believe these sides to be five yards long, so we will choose beams of about six yards long. You can always cut them but it's not advisable to extend them. That would make the remainder of the roof just two yards at its shortest, and up to three and a half yards at its longest, so we'll do you a range between the two and a half, and four yards, in order to cover all possy-bilities. With any left-over timber, you can easily lay in a half-floor at wall height. To give an extra bed or storage."

"That's a good idea. Dora would like tha…"

"Lliam." It was Trewin calling him from down the yard. "Come and have a look at these." The student of the world at large had discovered a stack of flat, wafer-thin sheets of grey stone, each with a small hole drilled near one side.

"Slates," he said. "They work out at the same price as thatch because you don't need to pay a thatcher, but they will last forever, won't rot, won't catch fire and roast you in your drunken stupor, won't leak either. What do you think?" The friends turned their attention to the lad who stood close by, a youthful version of Isambard Bowman, interrogating him in silence.

"They're the coming thing alright." confident on his home ground, the youth waxed positively,

"All of the well-to-do buildins in town are avin um now, as you can see sir." He nodded in the direction of Main Street not far off, where sure enough, the roofs were a patchwork; some still wearing thatch and some of them re-covered in slates.

"Also, if you buys a ouse-lot, I'll drive over home with you and give you a 'and layin' 'em into the bargain. It's no matter cos I'll be havin' to drive our wagon over home with you anyways."

"Done," said Lliam decisively. "Trewin, dear boy would you be a pal and go with this man and work out a price for everything." He indicated the senior Bowman and handed Trewin some silver. Lliam's never-ending discomfort soon amplified to the point where he was forced to take another guzzle of his magical medicine, with the result that when the men returned, they found the big fellow lying barely conscious on the ground, his open rucksack and a medicine bottle sitting precariously on the edge of his newly purchased stack of slates. Copplestone wrenched the stopper from the bottle and waved it under his nose, sniffing suspiciously.

"Opium." he nodded reassuringly to the concerned Bowmans.

"For pain. He'll be alright."

As darkness fell, the little caravan passed through the outskirts of Alsop; in the lead was the young woodman, Philip Bowman, driving the six-in-hand schooner; a massive vehicle drawn by six Cleveland Bays, laden with the wood required for the new roof, a cast-iron cooking range all black and shining and half of the slates. He was followed by Copplestone driving a smaller cart containing the remainder of the slates, tools, and assorted odds and ends, the oddest and biggest being Hooligan, slumped in his seat, neither use nor ornament. With possibly five miles still to go to the village of Thorpe, greatly concerned by his big friend's declining interest in all material things, Copplestone declared it best for Lliam that they make camp and a brew, and let the big man get some sleep, as he was clearly exhausted due to his poor state of health. Knowing the district well, Philip was soon steering his team off the road at a spot where grass, water and firewood were all in good supply, and the three men passed a pleasant evening under the stars, drinking rum and gazing into the fire. In the morning they broke camp late; proceeding with things at a pace more suited to the patient and arrived at Dora's unhinged gate towards noon.

* * *

Dora woke beneath a ceiling of canvas. She was in her own bed, but unbelievably, she and it were outside under what appeared to be a tent with only two sides.

"About time too, my girl." Her little brother was holding her hand for goodness knew what reason.

"Scaring the living daylights out of me you were." The tiny woman could barely hear what young Lliam was saying because of the banging and shouting that was going on. 'Her cottage had no roof!'

"It's alright. It's alright," she was assured.

"You're getting a new roof this very day." Dora sat up and swung her legs over the side of the bed, feeling as well as ever.

"I must have fainted, Lliam," she offered; embarrassed and not knowing why.

"And why are my bits and pieces outside?"

"Well, as you can see sis, the inside is outside. Sure, if we didn't move it, we'd have men tripping all over it and God knows what. It was that Mrs Cumberpatch woman who sells the poteen that found ye. Lying in the reeds like Moses you were. I've got her doin' some cooking on yer new range for these fellas, seeing as how you'd rather sleep, ya wee floozy. Did that shit of a husband of yours turn up?"

"Let me see. Let me see." Dora was concerned that her hot-headed brother might be destroying her home in his desire to improve things for her.

"I went a-lookin for him, brother, but not a sign. It wouldn't susprise me if he has tooken hisself off out of it. He is not poplar in the village no more." Dora took hold of the boy's arm, and brother and sister embarked on a tour of inspection of the property, which was as rewarding to the bear as it was enchanting to the doll. Dora wanted to look firstly at her house, and once inside, she saw that not only had the men removed the rotten old thatch; they were demolishing the rickety wooden framework which supported it and replacing that with sturdy lengths of freshly cut aromatic timber. She shook her head in happy appreciation.

"Oh my word, Lliam, I can hardly believe it," she laughed.

"Only the other day, I was worrying myself sick about the state of the place, and now, all this. Mrs Cumberpatch is cooking on a what?" she asked and was led proudly to where that lady was sweating over half a dozen pans, two ovens, and a barrel of her own infamous brew which squatted on a handbarrow like a poisonous toad on a lily pad.

"Mrs Cumberpatch. Jessie," smiled Dora, and the two women hugged briefly but warmly.

"Thank you so much for caring for me and bringing me home-along. You're a little sweetie, is what you are. Can I give you a hand? You looks run off your feet."

"It crossed me mind to leave you in the grass, but you was scaring-off me customers," laughed the flustered cook.

"Only if you're up to it m'dear, it's all much easier on this thing. There be pink in them cheeks already, I see." Mrs Cumberpatch wiped her forehead with the back of her arm and flung a silver lance of perspiration into the grass. The pans were sitting on top of a huge, black contraption as long as Dora's kitchen. On its front were pretty doors piped in gold with handles of thick, silver wire in the shape of a fir-cone and though a prodigious heat was radiating from the thing, Mrs Cumberpatch employed these handles with no discomfort at all. With not so much as a bit of cloth in her hand! Looking at the beautiful shiny object, Dora was quite overcome by a proprietary jealousy and wanted to usurp Jessie immediately but restrained herself knowing that soon; possibly even today, the men would have installed this marvelous invention in her newly roofed home, and she could cook on it to her heart's content.

"I'll have a look around, and then I'll come back and lend a hand," Dora promised and hardly able to drag her eyes away from her new possession she allowed the wonderful adventure to continue.

"I think you'll be likin' this next bit," her little brother declared, proudly dragging her to the far end of the property where a cow now grazed in the kitchen-orchard behind a new fence which seemed to be growing out of the ground at the insistence of Mister Salter, the man who had made the bench at the church and given it free to one and all. She was delighted to see that Lliam had chosen a beautiful Jersey for her; they were the very best milkers and had a lovely gentle disposition. The animal's tan coat positively shone with health.

"Now all that grass won't go to waste, and you'll have milk every day into the bargain." The prodigal was enjoying himself immensely, clearly expecting some sort of agreeable remark from her and hearing none he turned to find Dora's face in her hands and her skinny little shoulders shuddering in distress. Instant anger flooded through him.

"What in the name of chroist is it woman?" He demanded so loudly that everybody paused to look their way, only to have Dora dismiss him with an irritated little gesture of her hand. 'Men were such fools at bottom,' it said.

As a direct result of this misunderstanding, Hooligan spent the next hour stamping around the property glowering at work that was being performed in a perfectly professional and energetic manner, with every intention of bawling his head off at any man who so much as held his glance. Luckily, for the preservation of peace, it was then that the women called everyone to come and eat, and as though with the wave of a magic wand, everything was once again as right as rain. In order to work on his burgeoning business skills Hooligan ate his lunch sitting with his new advisor in the shade of a wagon,

"How much did that builder want to rob me all up?" he asked without preamble. Surprised by Lliam's choice of topic for a lunchtime conversation, the soldier gave the price to the penny.

"And how much did we pay at the wood yard?" Copplestone again had the information in his recollection.

"So how much did I save on the deal?" The soldier-come-financial adviser did not need to calculate how much hard cash he had saved his friend by his intervention. He had already done that at the time and gained great satisfaction from his input. He drank deeply from his jug of wonderfully cold cider.

"You saved a ransom, your holiness," the accountant smiled, and wiped his mouth and his wet neck with a stained kerchief, happy to have been the author of his friend's good fortune and stated the figure down to the penny.

"So, Mister Clever Clogs, work out what is half of my savings, if you would be so kind." This was meat and drink to Copplestone, and he gave the answer to this seemingly fruitless request with no apparent effort. Placing his meal on the grass beside him, Hooligan stuffed his now almost pain-free hand into his money bag and withdrawing a messy wad of banknotes and coins set it in the grass at Trewin's side with the words.

''Be so kind Private Parts as to take half of that lot, out of this lot, and put it in your lot."

CHAPTER 9: Trader Huffer

Carnegie and his adorable companion had unloaded the wool bales at an ugly, red brick building which propped up a tall, square chimney held together by large black devices in the shape of the letter S which adorned much of its surface. Then they had dispensed with the cheese at the property of a cheese maker, of all places, before Angelique got up the courage to ask Andrew what his plans were for the two ponies that he had acquired.

"I got them at a very reasonable price from someone who just wanted rid, so I'll probably wait for an offer. Keep them with me and wait for an offer. Won't take long, always in high demand, ponies."

"What will you get for them?" With the merest trace of a smile the trader scrutinized the angel shrewdly.

"Are you making me an offer, Angelique Huffer? A prospective purchaser, are we?" Carnegie smiled his perfectly adorable smile; behaviour which the child considered very unfair when she was trying so hard to be businesslike.

"If you tell me your price, you will find out," the incipient businesswoman intoned, mortified meanwhile by the thought that Andrew might find rude this bluntness on her part, but pleased also at how ruthless she had sounded.

"I see," he responded, and what sweet relief she felt to find that he was not in the least offended.

"They may not look it Angelique, all covered in mud and so skinny, but they are quality animals you know, so I'll be holding out for a guinea each. Some deep-pocket or other will snap them up for his little ones and no bother. 'Come up, hoss.'"

"I will pay you one pound for each animal and not a penny more," the ingenue stated her position with a firmness that was all play-acting, almost breathless at making that huge financial leap.

"Done." Andrew thrust that farm implement of a hand at her, and Angelique found herself sealing her first business venture by being gently shaken from head to foot. What a wonderful feeling filled her, she sat up straighter in her seat looking away so that Andrew could not see her victorious smile as she glowed all over in her commercial victory over him.

"*W-e-ll?*" Andrew was looking askance at her and had drawn the word out to three times its natural length. She returned his look, vacantly.

"It's generally accepted that this is when you pay me my two pounds."

"Oh, I haven't got it right now," the incipient businesswoman stammered, but in a manner which implied that any carter worth his salt would have understood this to be the case. Then of necessity she had to explain the clever plan that she had conceived.

"I thought that if you could wait until I sold them, I could pay you then." She appraised him with an expression which begged for kindness; her businesswoman ego utterly deflated.

"Ha!" shot Carnegie, "Trader Huffer wants her cake *and* to eat it too. She won't meet my price, yet wants time to pay, and with the cheek of old Nick wants possession of my goods into the bargain. I really don't know what we are going to do with the girl." Realizing what she had done, she blushed fit to combust.

"Oh, I'm so 'sorry' Andrew," she began, but he silenced her by flinging an arm around her shoulder and crushing her bones in the friendliest manner imaginable.

"Don't you be bothered, Angie," he assured her.

"You shall have them at a pound each, and you can pay me when you sell them."

"Really? Oh, thank you," the words seeming so inadequate. She took her mother's cloth-wrapped treasure from her pocket and proffered it.

"I have three shillings and five pence ha'penny which I can pay you now," she said proudly.

Turning momentarily from the business of driving his six-in-hand, then closing her fingers gently around the coins, the handsome young man appraised her lovingly and declared.

"You are well-named, Angelique."

His words and the expression in his grey eyes, made her heart beat too quickly. Thus began a brief holiday-time in her life as the young friends followed Dolly and the rest of the shires aimlessly around the countryside, buying and selling and occasionally transporting goods for cash payment; cheeses to market towns, and wool bales to the factory, one of the few places that she recognized in those early days. Whenever they made camp, the grateful girl would find ways of improving her skills in order to lessen the hardships of her friend's life and in addition, improve her ponies' condition in expectation of the day of sale. On her twelfth day, at the end of a long, slow climb which had the horses leaning into the traces, the wagon breasted an endless slope and began the descent with the drag kicking up dust behind and there laid out before her was yet another perfectly wonderful scene. A wide valley contained by steep green walls, and so flat that its river meandered through silvered mirrors, as a bracelet would through charms. The full width and breadth of it, all of the way to the mirage of the horizon presented as an immaculate garden, bordered and at places interspersed with forest. It seemed to Angelique that she recognized this scene or that they had possibly passed through it on a different road in the past few days, but the solution to the question evaded her until Andrew asked,

"Aren't you glad to be home, Trader Huffer?"

"Oh, you horrible man," she cried and wrapping her arms around his neck, kissed him on the cheek as they continued in their measured pace towards the village of Thorpe just five miles ahead. Unnoticed in their rear the skies darkened to a deep purple-and-blue as the long, hot spell was dismissed by a cold wind which caught up with them, shoving maliciously at the tall load and tugging at their clothing. Angelique began to shiver uncomfortably. Pulling the brake on hard and lifting the seat, Andrew rummaged in the box, eventually dragging out his oilskin and a parcel which he handed to her with a smile. Quickly unwrapping it while taking care to preserve the brown paper, Angelique found a new oilskin coat identical to Andrew's own, but one third of the size complemented by a leather hat with a brim as wide as her shoulders.

"Put them on, Angie," he said, "you're going to need them any moment now." He was as good as his word. Within minutes, the rain struck with the malice of a flight of javelins, only to be repelled by the hard track in a manner which frightened the horses causing Andrew to harangue them constantly, shouting support and love over the roar of the storm, so that his voice took precedence in their minds over the assault of nature. By the time that their huge ship of trade hove-to at Angelique's gate, the summer downpour had undergone a metamorphosis, it had become a malevolent force which stung exposed skin, blinded the careless eye and forced the travelers to sit bent-over to protect their faces, though smugly dry in their wet-weather coats.

"Would you like to say hello to your mother as we pass?" roared Andrew pulling up the team in expectation of an answer in the affirmative.

"I shall be here with my girls in case your father has had the gall to show his face. Macbeth will know what to do with him." Leaning into the wind, Angelique meandered in approximations of the direct route to the cottage door which was opened early by strangers who pulled her through it despite her protestations into an atmosphere which was so warm and dry, noisy and cheerful, that for one moment, she believed that she might have entered the wrong cottage. She was hugged and kissed by her mother who would not release her hand, smothered by a terrifying giant who might have been her Uncle Lliam, almost fainted in the miasma of Mrs Cumberpatch's halitosis, felt her wet hand being kissed by a tough-looking individual of soldierly bearing whose blond moustaches tickled her, then found herself gawking upwards at a tall young man. He was speaking to her while her mother interrupted annoyingly to assure her that her father had not been seen in days. She could not have cared less because the stranger's eyes were those of an angel. The divine being had stopped talking and was looking at her almost as though he expected a reply, but Angelique had never spoken to an angel before, so she had nothing at all to say. 'Anyway' she told herself huffily, 'if he was really an angel, he would know that her heart had stopped working and that she was thus incapable of speech.'

She was required to look down at a black something which cooked meals *and* warmed the house all at the same time, then up at the roof which did something to the rain and heard herself ooh'ing and aah'ing in what may have been the right places. Then she was outside in the rain because of the poor horses, and soon she would be driving on, when all that she really wanted to do was to look at the angel and listen to his voice.

"Andrew," she had to shout to be heard above the storm.

"I won't be a moment. You get aboard." Running back into the cottage, she drew her mother aside, intent on what she had to say, yet distracted by her search for just one face. Breathlessly, she told Dora about the horrible events of a week earlier; on the night on which she should have walked to Auntie Maud's in Gratton, how she had delayed and as a result Tansley had come across her. How Andrew Carnegie had saved her and injured

Tansley in the process, and lastly, of how she intended to travel with Andrew till she found her brother and her sisters. All too soon, she was outside again and climbing on to the wagon, leaving her mother in tears of guilt but in good company. So good that it included the man she would marry Philip Bowman, angel, and dealer in fine timber.

Lliam Hooligan paused in his work to peek beneath Merlin's bulk at Copplestone who was currying Bengal.

"There's something I'd like you to do for me, general Nuisance," he announced.

"Just put a name to it Lavender," Copplestone replied without pausing in his vigorous brushing, "and if it's legal, for a change, I'll do it."

"Could you drive the wagon back to the timber yard at Alsop? That would be good. Now, there is a fellow…" Lliam glanced over at Angelique who was kneeling while she polished the hooves of one of her newly acquired ponies, and lowered his voice to a shout, though he was reasonably sure that his niece was out of earshot,

"There is a highland goat goes by the name of Macbeth. Dora tells me that he is a very big shot for miles around. Hairy sort of a bastard. This horse is his. Would you take it back to him? Mind and tell him thanks from me."

"That's two things, but yes of course I can do that for you. One, two, three. Now you try it." The soldier repeated himself slowly, holding up the requisite number of fingers as he spoke, as though for the instruction of an infant,

"One, twooo, threeeee." Hooligan would have rolled his eyes at the fool.

''Corporal punishment; you're an idiot.''

"No bother at all. Bengal could do with a run."

"Can that thing run?"

"Though I'll have to curry your nag into the bargain, once you give-over going against the grain."

"What goes against the grain, is listening to Englishmen running off at the mout," observed Lliam to his friend's obvious amusement.

"I'd take care of it moiself, but I have to go off for a couple of days. Something I've got to do." Lliam's muffled voice came from behind the horse.

"So why don't we do it together, all in a wunner? Many hands make light work, my child." Once again, Hooligan checked that his niece was not listening.

"I'd like nothin' better, but this work will be a bit rough for a wee girl with soft little hands."

"Listen!" hissed Trewin, cupping his ear,

"I just heard a goose farting in the fog. Oh, I'm so sorry; you don't have ears to cup, do you? How thoughtless of me.

"Hooligan pulled a wry face which expressed his deep pity for the fool.

"I wish you'd go with him, Trey." Angelique had come to stand at the soldier's side, and together they watched Lliam shoulder his pack, hug Dora then stride away, almost his old self but not quite.

"I volunteered Angie, but he wouldn't hear of it. Reckoned that what he was going to do was too rough for a man of my gentle disposition and refined manner." Trewin resumed his work with Bengal.

"Still, he's in better shape now to cope with whatever slings and arrows come his way. It's incredible what ordinary salt water, a handful of maggots and some bulbs of garlic can do for a soul, and that's the truth."

"He's a new man, thanks to you. Did you learn all that medicine stuff in the army? You should have seen uncle's face when you opened the box of maggots." Angelique smiled happily at the memory.

"Mostly."

"Trewin," she said, "I've been wanting to ask your advice about my ponies."

"Ask away then, my dear."

"I've agreed to pay Andrew a pound each for them, and I wondered if I'd done a silly thing, and what I would get back on them once they've put on a bit more condition." The soldier secured his brush between the topping stones of the wall.

"Did you indeed? Then you have a better eye than most for horseflesh, and a better one still for a bargain; they are fine animals."

"Are they?" Angelique's smile appeared like the sun from behind clouds.

"Oh yes, these are Austrian Warmbloods, a cavalry horse. I wouldn't be surprised if you realized ten pounds each for them."

"But there's not that much money in the whole world."

"You would think not, wouldn't you lass. You could buy this village for a hundred pounds and yet, there are those who would pay that sum for a bottle of wine or a pair of slippers and think nothing of it."

"Never!"

"There are more things in heaven and earth my dear." Twiddling his moustaches as was his habit, Trewin was suddenly businesslike.

"You get to pay him only when you sell them?"

"Yes, that's it."

"Aren't you the clever one? You know," he began, "you could take a quick profit, and a healthy one at that, an exceptionally healthy one or you could do the other thing and possibly become very rich indeed, in a matter of a few years." Angelique looked first at her ponies and then back at Trewin in incredulity.

"Get rich?"

"You could breed them," the horseman stated bluntly; not restrained by the conventions.

"They are as good as I've seen, and believe me, I've seen a few. You could stand these two beauties at stud all over the county and make a fortune; and still own your animals into the bargain." He ran a knowing hand down the fetlock of one.

"What with Bengal here and your Uncle Hooligan's mount, which is the best of all, you could make a fortune." At the mention of Merlin, Angelique's concern for her uncle resurfaced again, stronger than ever.

"Trey? Why has Uncle Lliam gone off on foot when he has Merlin here?" her face was in her hands.

"There, there lass," crooned the soldier, suddenly out of his depth and hesitating to comfort the beautiful girl by putting his arms around her as he desperately wanted to do,

"There could be a dozen innocent reasons. Not the least of which is that Merlin belongs to a Mister Macbeth, not to your Uncle Lliam. He's only got the borrowing of him, you know. I've to take the horses back, Merlin, and the team from the wood yard yonder, both." At the mention of the wood yard, Angelique's vision of her angel, which, since her meeting with him the day before, was never far from the surface of her mind, immediately came into sharper focus and she blushed guiltily so that she had to turn away and resume her grooming.

"And where would that be, Trey?" she asked, almost choking on the inquiry.

"I wouldn't have a clue where Macbeth stays; I shall have to ask around," laughed Trewin, "but the wood yard is over in Alsop. Do you know it?"

"I've barely been beyond our strips at Danelaw in all of my life," confessed the smitten one with a helping of perverse pride, uncaring of the tears on her cheeks,

"But now that I am travelling with Andrew, that is changing fast. I'm going to find them, Trewin, all three of them."

"Your brother and your sisters," confirmed the little soldier, who had heard snippets of the family's unfortunate history.

"I'm sure of it, lass," he said sincerely. "There's Andrew now." Over Angelique's shoulder, Andrew was drawing rein beyond the gate.

"Oh my word, I must run." Angelique kissed the soldier on the cheek, her concerns instantly forgotten."

"Before you go, I'd like to put a business proposition to you, Trader Huffer."

"Ha. That's what Andrew calls me." she laughed.

"What if I pay off your debt to Andrew, and you and I go into business together, breeding quality horses? War is raging, as sure as eggs are boiled, in the thirteen colonies. The army is already buying quality mounts, and the demand will rise and rise. Will you consider it?"

"I will have to talk to mother and Uncle Lliam," Angelique responded well out of her depth. "And Andrew," she added as a guilty afterthought.

"Of course, you must. Have a good trip, and a prosperous one. Take this so that you can conclude the business whenever you feel right about it." Copplestone handed Angelique the two pounds which would clear her debt. He pressed the money into the nubile's palm and closed her fingers around it to somehow indicate its great value, and the imperative that she must not lose it.

"Please excuse my atrocious manners," he said, with just the hint of a bow, meaning the business of handing money to a lady, but discerned from Angelique's expression that the delightful maiden did not comprehend the subtlety.

"Thank you, Trey," she smiled, and ran to the cottage where, like Lliam before her, she received a week's supply of food from her mother, exchanging it for a loving hug, and drove off waving, laughing and carefree as she went.

CHAPTER 10: Unrequited

Day after day of heavy weather kept Copplestone close to home, where he passed the hours by gathering firewood, repairing stone walls, and partially damming the stream to make a fine bathing place, but when the sun shone again, he put the woodyard team to the schooner, hitched Merlin behind, and with Bengal saddled and walking free, drew up at the cottage to let Dora know that he would be back by nightfall. That wonderfully kind and thoughtful woman surprised him by handing him a reed basket heavy with food sufficient to feed a regiment for the day and expressed the hope that it would 'tide him over' until he returned. Trewin, unable to do otherwise, squeezed her as though she were mother, sister and best friend, leaving her blushing, stammering and turning away as coy as a young girl and hers was such an effusive reaction that he grew serious and wondered about it for a spell. As he drove along, he found himself reflecting happily on how life had changed for him in the space of a few days. Fate had put a roof over his head, friends in his heart, and dispelled with a vengeance his lifelong exile. Inexplicably he suddenly laughed aloud rejoicing in the cool breeze, the sunlight and the beauty of his native land.

He was as pleasant as a soldier knows how, when Bowman the younger approached to relieve him of the wagon and thank him for his business. Also, to ask after news of Miss Angelique Huffer, and would Trewin be so kind as to relay his compliments to that young lady. For a moment, the smitten Copplestone experienced an intense jealousy of the tall youth, who by the look of him could be only five years younger than himself in years, but a lifetime in experience, hardship and deprivation. He felt more like an elder than the lad's contemporary. It had never struck the taciturn soldier to say something to the beautiful Angelique because he felt more like a father figure to her than a lover. Nevertheless, he agreed to do as Bowman requested and relay the boy's compliments.

Putting frivolity behind him, he decided that while he was in Alsop, he would seize the opportunity to buy a couple of changes of clothing, and as those which he had purchased from the ancient harridan who kept the market stall had proven to be particularly well-made, marched from Bowman's along the high street to give her his business once again. The scandalous old crone watched the trim and muscular individual approach with naked lust, and loud proclamations of the obscenities that she would perform with him given half a chance. Despite the mortifying embarrassment of this public outrage, the customer went through with his intention of giving the madwoman his business but denied her the opportunity to measure any of his limbs, most notably, his inside leg, satisfying himself as to size by holding up his chosen garments against himself. He emerged from this public humiliation relatively unscathed.

Finding Macbeth's residence was not difficult. Everybody, it seemed, knew the man, or wanted to know him, and the closer the rider got to that worthy's home, the more detailed and meaningful the directions he received from the populace. The sublime reality of the Scotsman's smallholding confirmed for the soldier that his long-cherished dream of a place of his own could, after all, take solid form for such as himself. Every aspect of the place spoke of peace, security, reciprocated love, and a sense of pride of place; from its tawny, stylized thatch and the eyebrow windows of the upper story, to the porch with the port-wine bougainvillea and the glistening oak door replete with shining brasses. Trewin Copplestone fondly fashioned a narrative in his imagination, of a man who likely had risen from nothing, and by hard work, dedication and adherence to sound principles had carved this paradise out of the wilderness; he therefore approached and applied the heavy brass knocker, wearing his heart on his sleeve.

When Macbeth's wife opened the door and stood before him, an angel of loveliness, with flour up to her elbows, he knew for a certainty that he had found his love, and lost her, all in an instant. At the angel's knee was another, much smaller angel dressed similarly. He bowed to the little one and returned the child's perplexed expression with a warm smile.

"Mrs Macbeth?" he enquired of the woman, praying fervently meanwhile for a reply in the negative.

"I am indeed." The beauty's voice, was the essence of honey, as was her enchanting complexion.

"Mister Macbeth is behind the house."

"Daddy is… daddy is bidding a gwait big wall," added the miniature angel, with a deeply troubled expression as though building "gwait big walls" was something which one should stay well clear of. When she put her tiny hands to her cherubic face, in concern about daddy's present occupation, Trewin saw that the child too, had been baking.

Melting. Copplestone knelt so that he could answer the divinity as a friend.

"Then I shall go to help your daddy," he replied in a soft voice which he did not recognize. The child nodded very seriously at this intelligence and inquired,

"Do you like my, my, dwess? It's i… it's ided'cal to mummy's.''

"It is beautiful," the strange voice said, "and so are you."

Only Macbeth's movement eventually betrayed the hirsute one's presence. Copplestone could not find him anywhere in the kitchen-orchard; the man's plaid had camouflaged his lower half, while his hair shirt did likewise with the upper. The irascible Scot was repairing a wall which had clearly slumped in the foundations, and eventually collapsed through the passage of time. Unaware of Trewin's presence, the monster stood over a boulder of a size too big for one man to contemplate lifting but contemplate it he clearly did. He understood at once what the warrior was about. The boulder had one flat side to it which, if he guessed correctly, would, when in its intended home, complement the face of the wall, while the shape of the thing was such that it would fill perfectly, the space awaiting it. All that was left for the Scot to do was to raise the thing above waist height. With the air of one who simply did not contemplate failure, he shuffled around the object, getting his feet as close as possible, and settling for a stance which would require no adjustment once lifted, or require any steps to be taken with the weight in his arms. Squatting down straight-backed, the Scot wrapped his arms around the thing, and by trial and error, got a satisfactory grip. At that moment, the watcher realized that far from feeling threatened by the task, the man was enjoying himself. This was merely an exercise in confirming his strength. Slowly, the tartan draped legs straightened and the boulder, held very close, rose inexorably up the shins, over the knees to where it was supported on the thighs, while the gorilla sucked in air. Easier now, leaning back with belly thrust forward, counterbalancing the monstrous weight. shuffling closer to the wall with the slightest lean forward to let the existing structure take some of the weight. Resting now, sucking in breath like a drowning man reaching the bank. From there, it was a simple matter of easing the thing backwards into position. Unaware still of being watched, the colossus stood back and began to recover his breath, appearing like nothing so much as a victorious clansman who might at any moment beat his chest in confirmation of his invincibility.

"Well done," called the soldier, and saw within the space of a heartbeat, the reaction of a man whose instinct is to fight, instantly giving way to that of a gentleman farmer.

"Good day. I imagine that you have brought Merlin," gasped the Scot with no inflexion whatsoever.

"I have," blurted Trewin, appalled by the man's prescience.

"So, his majesty the lord Hooligan is too important now tae return in person, a horse lent tae him by his employer? When I lend a man a horse I expect that man tae return him tae me. Nae some stranger who could well ride off to fuckin' Wales wi' him or some other godforsaken corner." The strangest thing was happening to the Scotsman's torso. The massive effort which he had recently engaged in, had caused his blood to flow into his muscles, and the unnatural things were expanding, fit to burst as Trewin watched. Thick blue veins snaked beneath the tight skin.

"You've rehearsed your lines prettily, but they would be more properly addressed to Lliam Hooligan, so I would be obliged if you would spare me your bleating." Trewin would have liked nothing more at that moment than a little blood-letting.

"He'll be lyin' drunk somewheres, I suppose."

"You're seldom right and you're wrong again. He had to go about some business, and he had to go on foot," Copplestone was making an unmistakable effort to get under the fur coat of the irate bear. He did not take kindly to being spoken to with profanity. Neither did he appreciate the suggestion that he was a potential thief.

"As to your lack of etiquette Macbeth; since I have returned your horse to you, it follows that your observation is not only redundant it's insulting, and so I shall be obliged to bleed you a little and release those nasty vapours." Copplestone's threats were punctuated by the tinkling of a delicate bell.

"Mister Macbeth." It was the angel calling.

"Mitha Mabeth." And the little angel.

"That'll be refreshments," the savage observed very civilly, as though the soldier had not spoken one acrimonious word, and clearly oblivious to his threats. He retrieved a shirt which he had discarded in the grass.

"We'll go up tae the hoose."

Trewin was not thrown by this strange behaviour. Listening to his chum ramble on about this loon, he had long since concluded that the Scot was probably socially inept, unbalanced, or worse and therefore he let matters slide for the present. It was far more important to him to glimpse the beautiful woman again than to satisfy his anger. Disappointingly, Macbeth shepherded him not to the house but to the roadside where the horses were tethered at a trough. The cavalryman in him was pleased to observe the real appreciation that the giant displayed for both animals.

"Where's yer pal off tae then?" the question was posed casually while the man inspected Bengal's mouth as though the answer to his own question was to be found in the animal's dentistry.

"Can't be far." frowned Trewin, his vague concern returning.

"Two or three days. On foot. Said it was too rough for one of my gentle disposition." He smiled at the memory.

"Aye yer right; cannae be much," the Scot dismissed too easily an issue which he himself had raised as he unsaddled Merlin and freed him into a paddock of long, silvered greenery.

"Lemonade?" he inquired, hefting the saddle and tack easily in one hand.

"Thank you, no. I'll be on my way." Trewin would have traded his soul for one more glimpse of the ravishing Mrs. Macbeth, but could not, on reconsidering, so much as contemplate being in the company of both man and wife at one time. The Scot did not press his offer home. The soldier mounted and rode away. At an elevation slightly higher than the Macbeth homestead he found a suitable place in which to conceal himself and nudging Bengal off the path into good cover he settled down to watch the smallholding while he considered the question of why it was that a man such as Macbeth; well set up and able to spend his days at home, would loan a hundred pounds worth of horseflesh to an unlettered, homeless, drunken individual such as Lliam Hooligan. It was not long before a youngster exited the property at the gallop, and moments later passed directly in front of where Trewin sat, urging his horse on with bare heels; quite unafraid and thinking himself invincible. The sleuth followed the child at a distance by sound, dust, and the occasional distant glimmer of the lad's white shirt and was led within a couple of miles to a place where several rock-breakers were road making. One of the laboring hammer men, on hearing the boy's approach, left off work and was lost to sight for a while, reappearing mounted on a decent seeming horse. By this time, the investigator was wondering most seriously about Lliam Hooligan's adventures and just what the big fellow had got himself into.

'Since when could a common rock-breaker afford a horse?' The world was standing on its ear. When the boy and the ruffian parted, Copplestone chose to follow the boy, because, surprisingly, the little warrior went onwards, rather than turning for home. It soon became clear that the brave little aide-de-camp was heading for a scattering of cottages which nestled in a wide flat valley given over to the immaculate patchwork of English agriculture. Trewin went there cross-country, giving Bengal his head in order to arrive before the child and was sitting on a bench by the village pump when he arrived, sneakily entering the village at a walk to disguise the urgency of his errand, which happily had its conclusion directly over the road from the pump, the bench, and its occupant.

A disreputable seeming inn which seemed to have emerged from a steep hillside, stood nearby, its lowest window presenting itself high above the grassy slope. The lad, who had clearly done this ride before, walked his horse hard up against the wall, stood on his saddle, reached up to the window and spoke to someone inside. Trewin stayed with the 'someone inside' and was rewarded an hour or so later when the stone breaker and the gentleman from the inn; another well-mounted ruffian, met on the high road travelling toward Minster, at a gentle canter. Irritated by the constant need for secrecy, Copplestone allowed himself to be persuaded that the conspirators were indeed heading to that little market town and nowhere else. Abandoning the track for the appeals of pasture he rode to Minster at his leisure, enjoying the ride now that he was not restrained; confident that in a small town such as it was, he would find both Hooligan, and Macbeth's heavies. Renting a pleasant room above a chop house for a couple of nights lodging, the sleuth set about acquainting himself with the town as he scoured it for that best of men.

'What would? What ''could'' Lliam Hooligan be doing here in this sleepy backwater?' On the face of it, apart from being home to a shipyard which seemed to be the major employer in the district, Minster appeared to be the embodiment of the typical English country town, servicing the agricultural requirements of the county through a host of businesses which sold everything that went into the fields while buying and financing everything which came out of them. He proved methodical enough but seriously lacking in the suspicious nature inherent in the effective investigator. Beginning at the riverside, he sloped around the docks in the manner of the denizens of that disreputable area, which is to say, slowly, aimlessly, in drink, and lacking any sense of endeavor. Having listened uninvited to many a conversation and afterwards wishing that he hadn't, nothing had been added to the sum of his knowledge, and neither had he seen anything of Hooligan or Macbeth's grunts. He moved on; his frame of mind improving with every step he took, as he ascended the gentle slope which led to the more respectable areas of town. Lliam Hooligan, he ruminated, would not however be found among the whitewashed walls and well-tended flower gardens which stood in serried ranks that seemed to the pedestrian to go on forever. He returned to his lodgings, washed under the pump and retired for the night. The following days were as thankless as the first, so that one afternoon, he took a seat at his open window from where he could let the town come to him rather than vice versa as he drank coffee at his leisure, with his booted feet crossed on the sill.

CHAPTER 11: The Raft

At the conclusion of a long, tiring and eventually bloody-annoying search, undertaken on foot, Lliam Hooligan located the sack of spew known as Kane Seed a nair-do-well with a reputation worse than his own in a crowded down-at-heel tavern which lay miles from anywhere. He bided his time until Seed was alone, standing at a window sucking on an empty pipe and at the dregs of his mug while peering out through a hole which he had rubbed in the filth of the oiled paper. He approached obliquely.

"They tell me that you go by the name of Seed," he began.

"Do they?" the badly scarred criminal grunted sarcastically, trying to walk away but finding himself detained by a hand which enclosed his upper arm, his knife arm, and squeezed so hard that he winced.

"Don't annoy me Seed, oim not in the fuckin mood."

"What do you bloody want?" Seed demanded, trying manfully to mask his discomfort but failing. Hooligan muscled his new friend to a settle which benefitted from a handy barrel-top; doing so with no outward sign of violence whatsoever, almost in the fashion in which a man might assist a lady, so that none of the many criminal element present would suspect a thing.

"Have a seat," he ordered, forcing Seed down effortlessly on to the settle and positioning himself opposite the man in order to keep his own back to the wall. He poured himself a large brandy from a jug as he appraised the recent wounds to the man's face.

"You're looking well," he observed.

Seed lifted his greedy, bloodshot eyes from Hooligan's hypnotizing jug of spirits and scrutinized the interesting physiognomy that was far too near for comfort; it was one of a kind. One of the bastard's eyes must have been ripped out by an eagle. The nose had been altered beyond recognition and there was a killing trench across the side of the face that was decorated with a pattern of small marks, as though it had been tied shut at some point. They were like lace-holes at the throat of a smock. The purple swelling of it had almost closed the beauty's solitary good eye.

"Thanks," he said levelly, "but you'll take 'best cabbage in show,' hands down. What do you fucking well want? And no, I won't suck your dick."

"I have a couple or three days work for you."

"What's the pay?"

Hooligan lifted one edge of his chipped mug to reveal a glimpse of a silver coin. Seed's eyes spoke first.

"You're on." A dirty paw slowly crossed the table and stealthily retrieved the coin, which Hooligan in his turn, allowed it to do.

"I have only one of those with me," he warned," so stabbing me in the back will just get you hung. Nothing more. My people know that it's you I've come to find."

"You have a winning way about you," volunteered Seed. "Your mother must be very proud."

"That'll do!" warned Hooligan and called for food.

"What's the job then?" the well-paid individual was wearing an eloquent sneer which inferred that he would have to earn every penny of his huge salary by murdering half of the population of England and laying waste to whole counties.

"There's a place up the river from here, where they drop trees and float them down to the yard at Minster."

"They is. I knows it well." Seed played with an empty mug he had found.

''I done many a raft when I were a lad." He belched, loud and smelly, in Hooligan's face.

"So I heard. I want you to help me bring a raft down. They tell me that it's a two-man job."

"And?"

"And nothing. As well as my silver, you can have whatever they pay for the rafting, all of it, and be on yer way. Free and clear."

"I smell shit but I don't see any flies." Seed leaned back on his creaking settle as though to distance himself from what was coming.

"The only risk to you is bein' seen alongside o' me; if I'm spotted by the owners, that is. But there's no chance of that. I hear tell that the Astors don't have to dirty their hands for a crust."

"The Astors? You've upset the Astors? Aren't you a turn up? What did you do, smile at one of them, did ye?" Hooligan let slide this insulting reference to his less than handsome looks as two vast platters of hot food and wooden forks were dumped unceremoniously in the poisonous divide by a woman who stank like a latrine.

"Dig in," invited the host, his sleeve over his nose. Seed shoved the wooden fork onto the floor, took a knife from his boot and skewered a chop.

"Is that bleeder empty?" he inquired rudely, eyeing the large jug of the hard stuff at his host's elbow. The Irishman re-filled his own mug to the brim; paused significantly, then did likewise for his dear friend. 'It was best to establish the pecking-order when dealing with slime like this.'

"Oi'll be hoiding meself away in there if Oi get the chance. You must go on by yerself. Get our pay and clear off. You can keep yer mouth shut they tell me."

"They tell you right," snuffled Seed proudly, speaking through a mouth full of mutton and gravy. The Englishman ate with his mouth open, conjuring feelings in the new abolitionist which equated with Macbeth's disgust at his own eating habits.

"That's good to hear because oi don't want to come lookin' for ye again." Seed patted the back of Hooligan's hand with a grubby paw, the way a mother might do with a naughty boy.

"There, there," he whispered, all consolation, "don't upset yourself. It'll stunt yer growth. What in God's name is worth nickin' from a shipyard?"

"None of your business."

"Fuck you then."

Both men ate until they could not swallow another mouthful and drank sufficiently to anaesthetize them through the long tramp ahead, then with reciprocal nods, they rose and left, squeezing through the rowdy mass of bodies that was pressed into the room. The doorway, a narrow, dark place much like the entrance to a mine, was stiff with surly-looking dullards who saw no reason to give way to any man, and these very hard boys shoved back at the ugly stranger with great enthusiasm; refusing to let him pass. They were determined to know from Seed's own mouth if the crim was alright, and was leaving of his own accord, and as the odds were five or more to one; six if Seed joined them; Lliam had his hand on his concealed peacemaker before Seed could put the criminal fraternity at their ease.

"He's alright boys," he bellowed over the growling of the pack, "we'se just away to do a bit of mischief." This declaration brought the Irishman rotten-toothed grins and instant acceptance, expressed by thumps on his back, with wishes for a profitable doins, and many a request to 'give her one for me.'

Both men filled their canteens from the cold spring flowing into the horse trough and without a word set off; tramping hard right from the start in order to come across their destination in daylight. To the abolitionist's satisfaction, his recruit settled in well, and went at a good clip as though trying to sweat-out his cargo of beer and brandy. Best of all, he trekked in silence, an unusual quality in an Englishman, with not a word out of him. The poor collaborators rested only once on the journey. In mid-afternoon they brewed some tea and boiled a few potatoes which they ate on the march, juggling with the painfully hot food to protect their hands and laughing at each other's antics. The food being consumed without serious injury silence was restored and another two or three miles were put behind them before Seed suggested that they divert slightly to the top of a hill, from which, he claimed, they would get a distant view of their destination. He was as good as his word. The crest of the slope provided an unhindered, though distant, view of their objective, and the conspirators lay in the grass studying the embarkation point in safety from prying eyes. Hooligan's luck was in. Sure enough, there was a huge raft of logs secured at the riverbank, and what appeared to be a tent already erected.

"That's no good," observed Seed.

"They's gypos on there a'ready. We shall have to take 'vasive action, I'm a thinkin'. They'll 'ave ter go." Hooligan drew his telescope from his knapsack and extended it to Seed's obvious fascination. Not only was the tent up but the steering pole was already in place and some firewood was heaped midships.

"They've very kindly got our boat ready for us," he announced happily, having paid scant attention to Seed's murderous intentions. He passed his telescope to the enthusiastic Englishman, who put it to his eye and gasped at its efficacy.

"Fuckin oath," it's sovrin."

"What are they doing? Can you see anyone?" asked Hooligan and waited impatiently as the man studied the wide-open space at the bank of the river where long, straight trunks were crawling along, drawn by teams of twenty or more oxen.

"Aah, here we go. They're heading off home in a wagon. Well, I never did. There was never no wagon in my day; when I worked for a crust, a man walked it or slept on the job, and that was that."

"You never worked a day in your life." The Irishman drew the instrument slowly, but insistently, from Seed's covetous grasp.

"That's good news," he continued, "I want to make camp on the far side so that they tink we've come from up-river. We's off to the coast to ship out, if anyone asks."

"Yea, I know," said Seed irritably, deeply protective of his professional reputation. Less than an hour later, they were stealthily approaching the vicinity of the raft, while exhibiting the bushcraft of a regiment of artillery; the twigs underfoot being dry as a priest's sole crackling loudly underfoot. More cautious even than the Irishman the English barbarian proposed that they settle down in the undergrowth and give it an hour. If they saw no one in that time, he said, then they could risk a crossing of the open ground; a huge circle of white dust with tracks radiating from it into the forests like spokes in a broken wagon wheel.

It was so pleasant there in the shade, resting with their boots off after their trek, gorging on the delicious bread and roast beef that Dora had provided, and guzzling rum, that they overstayed till dusk. Seed was holding forth on the treatment meted out to both himself and Buttercup by the vicar of Thorpe no less, and the plans he had laid for his upcoming revenge when he paused in mid-flow and became perfectly still. Hooligan turned slowly and following Seed's gaze discovered a tall youth, thin as a reed, standing on the raft directly opposite the door of the tent. The bronzed gypsy wore a blood-red kilt around his middle from which protruded the yellow handle of a knife. His only other article of clothing was a leather waistcoat which left his excessively long arms free. There were no shoes on his feet but interestingly despite every indication of poverty, gold glittered in both ears and on his wide, flat chest. As he stood there, the wild creature scoured the countryside with the serious intent of a carnivore, sniffing the air almost in the fashion of an animal while suddenly snapping his head around this way and that as though to catch out any unwary spy. Seemingly satisfied, the man loped a few paces further from the tent, lifted his kilt urinated then went back inside.

"That's not good. Oi 'need' that raft. Would they bugger off for a shillin do you tink?''

''Do 'I' tink? 'You' tink about it about it you stoopid sod." Seed's anger, preposterously, was righteous.

"If you do that; they'll finger you to the Astors an wen we gets to Minster, they'll be a mob waitin wi a rope, and we'll swing for sure. Get your clothes off, and bring that peacemaker wot you've got down yer pants leg. That thing *is* your stick, isn't it?" Seed snorted down his nose, as his own jest caught him by surprise and Hooligan who was about to murder Seed a mere second earlier, saved the situation by seizing the lightening mood.

"It is not; but it *is* a woody,'' he laughed, and for a moment, there passed between these allies-of-convenience the merest breath of warmth.

"We can't do him in, man." Hooligan protested pathetically, repulsed on two fronts as he was confronted by Seed's pimply arse and the man's full meaning.

"I'm no bloody murderer."

"Wait a couple of mumfs for the next raft then. It aint murder to drown a bloody rat of a gypo? The bastards live by killin,' doin' away wi' nippers, thievin', burnin' and God knows what-all. Send 'em all back to Roman Eayah or wherever, says I." Chilled by a momentary but terribly clear vision of the thing hanging on the gibbet next to Rickets, Hooligan heard again Basset's oblique threat. 'Took my purse, then failed to deliver.' He shrugged out of his clothes and naked as the damned in purgatory followed Seed to the water. Silent as death in a desert, the committed killers negotiated the open space of the riverbank on their bellies slithering into the flow like a couple of deadly albino otters. Swimming clumsily due to the weapons in their fists, and staying in the cover of the logs, they struggled to the offshore side of the raft, then turned and labored upstream against the considerable current until it was adjudged that they were at the rear of the tent. Getting the Englishman's attention by hosing river water at the back of his head Hooligan signed that he was about to risk a look. Receiving a nod in reply he eased himself inch by inch out of the river and with only his eye above the rough bark he scanned the huge expanse of the wooden island. 'No one.' Giving the thumbs-up, he took the lead, pressing on for another ten or eleven yards, which he believed would position him directly behind the enemy's go-down. With infinite care the assassins hoist their torsos slowly out of the river and onto the deck, letting the water run quietly from their bodies. Desultory conversation confirming that only two of the enemy were inside. Getting to his knees Hooligan was momentarily fascinated by the log's ability to grow a stiletto which had appeared in the timber between his hands, vibrating shrilly with the force of its delivery. As he looked up there was a sudden rush, his water-blurred vision filled with a charging man wild and snarling and a murderous blade tugged at his beard, missing his throat by what could have been his last breath. The ensuing collision drove him backwards into the river, his club lost but replaced by a firm grip on the wrist that held the knife. Driven under the surface but with a lung-full of air, he wrapped his legs around the wild individual, thin as a girl, crushing the resistance out of the weakling and wrenching the knife-arm in a direction denied it by physiology, cruelly intent on ripping the shoulder. In unbearable torment the savage emptied his lungs, writhing like a mating snake as he was held beneath the surface. Hooligan had only to wait. Barely a breath later, the gypsy's desperate struggles lessened then ceased as great balloons of air escaped his tortured mouth. Grabbing the bearded chin, the killer wrenched it around viciously and the horror of it was over. The wiry body became limp, and he kicked it away in revulsion at what he had done. Surfacing on the edge of panic Hooligan found himself a long swim downstream of his reward for the act of murder and ploughed strongly through the considerable current in case he had to kill again. Two combatants were still engaged in a macabre dance, close enough to touch without being touched. With the distance to the logs halved he came across the dead man's cork-handled weapon, floating just below the surface; it would do to cover the loss of his club. Snatching it gratefully he drove onwards and hauled himself aboard just as his strength was waning. Through the cascade of water caused by broaching like a whale, he saw that Seed was still on his feet not an arm's length from the twin brother of the individual whom he had just now fed to the fish. Both men seemed to be looking and waiting. Looking and waiting. Stepping back a pace in order to better enjoy the spectacle Seed revealed the cause of the hiatus. Both combatants were fascinated by the handle of a knife, the blade of which was buried up to the hilt at the place where the Romany's ribs met. The youth's knees gave-way and he knelt silently like a monk at evensong. Struggling aboard the raft Hooligan raced to the tent; slit the canvas and stepped inside, knife at the ready, all in one movement.

'No one.' The deceased's few belongings lay scattered around.

Grabbing up everything that he could hold he raced outside to discover Seed dragging the dead body to the edge of the raft.

"Get rid of this," the bloody fighter ordered and racing the length of the raft dived at a full run, entering the water six or seven yards out barely disturbing the surface, leaving his collaborator incredulous at the refinement of skill involved. He had disposed of the body as he had been instructed and was wrestling unsuccessfully with his conscience when Seed's far distant shape reappeared still swimming strongly and so naturally. The creature seamed made for it. When at last he dragged himself wearily aboard the man gasped,

"You… must be… bloody… mad," and opening his hand displayed gold chains and earrings replete the ears in which they hung.

"That's a year's… grub… that is," the Caligula and cannibal was ecstatic with the profitability of his day's work while apparently unaffected by the murders involved. Moments later, the last of the evidence that the two gypsies had ever lived was disappearing beneath the surface of the river downstream, only to reappear at the forefront of Hooligan's mind. With the blood washed from the logs and their breathing returning to normal, Seed said accusingly,

"There's blood on you, are you cut?"

"On you, too," the chastened Irishman responded, and both men plunged back into the current, to scrub away the remaining evidence against them. A couple of hundred yards or so upstream from the scene of their recent handiwork, the exhausted conspirators found an excellent campsite that had firewood in good supply and there they threw themselves down to rest. They fed well from the vast store of food that Dora had provided but not even the comforting nourishment, the campfire and hot strong tea could ease the Irishman's state of mind and he remained silent, even as the night betrayed him by turning witness for the prosecution. Seed never parted from his equanimity. Though the man was well-aware of the gypsy love of gold it was the quantity of it that had surprised and pleased him. He poured the small fortune from hand to hand continuously; seeming never to tire of the captivating fashion in which gold chain runs like precious water.

Watching the odious individual surreptitiously Lliam Shaun Hooligan, spearpoint of the abolitionist cause realized that as Seed was now in-funds he would certainly desert. He lay back against a sun-warmed boulder with the fire between him and the ever more detested individual and fell to wondering about the form the man's revenge on the vicar Penny would take and recalled with loathing the expression of satisfaction on Seed's face as the gypsy youth died at his feet.

He slept very little that night, and then only in error, made sure that Seed didn't do a runner; stoked the fire and drank like sand. By dawn his mood was murderous as he spied on the arduous labor being undertaken at this outpost of Astor's industry when the mongrel woke and came quietly to join him.

"I could eat a scabby rat," were the first words out of the Englishman's mouth, and in that moment, Hooligan loathed the man as much as he had ever loathed anyone.

"What's happening?"

Certain that if he were to reply, his accomplice would detect the murderous intention in his voice, the Irishman held his council and merely nodded at a distant gang of woodsmen now standing by a bullock team so numerous that the beasts at the rear still faced the river, whilst those at the front had begun their return journey to the forests. The signs were that there was friction down there. The ganger man would be wanting and not getting, volunteers to float the raft to the yard. Shoving Seed out of his way Hooligan hurried to gather a handful greenery which he threw on to the fire, encouraged when thick clouds of dark foul-smelling smoke billow up around him He poured tea, broke out bread, mutton and boiled potatoes, and relaxing on a convenient hummock began breakfast. Seed needed no invitation and both men were silently enjoying their food when the bushes were parted and the strangest individual imaginable overran the campsite in the style of one who owns everything in sight.

The ganger man clearly suffered from a serious identity crisis, his coverings being representative of no fewer than six distinct individuals. 'An officer of French cavalry, an English gentleman farmer, an Apache, a Zulu, a Scottish clansman, and a Maori warrior,'' were among the crowd

"You can put that out." The English Gentleman Farmer stabbed a finger at the campfire as though it were a cat which had just now voided its bowels on his rug.

"We will that, gaffer," responded Hooligan getting to his feet respectfully.

"We mun't be goin round burning down the country wi' our half-pie ways."

"Good morning to you too," Seed remarked sarcastically without so much as a glance at the strangers; only to be ignored for his trouble by all of them.

"That's right, you can't. How'd you know me to be the gaffer?" the farmer tried for a compliment just as the French officer of cavalry wrenched off his shako in order to wipe away sweat with his forearm thereby revealing a Pawnee whose head was bald but for a ridge of hair which stood up vertically like a fence, dividing his white skull in half. The fence was decorated with feathers and strings of beads, which had given up the ghost years earlier, unlike the Maori warrior's *moko which made a threatening killer of the strangers' face.

"Whoi sor, she sticks out loike a sore tumb when a man has that way aboutim. Autority. That's what tis, autority, sor."

Frustrated by the dirth of resistance, the 'united nations,' tried a new tack.

"All this is private proppity. Yous two is treadpassin' on 'ere." The war party made an energetic little upward motion with both fists as though the land was *so* private, that the 'treadpassers' should relieve the soil of their unwelcome weight by jumping up into the air. One of those fists clutched a Maori chief's patu, a superb war-club fashioned from greenstone.

Hooligan of the tortured conscience had already reached the limit of his tolerance for bastards like this lot and was giving serious consideration to throttling the next one of them who opened his gob when he heard himself say.

"Ah, now us bein' simple folk, sor, us was ig'orant of that fact sor. Us be on the good queen's chain god bless her, and all those who shag her which it be every man's roight. We'll be on us ways to the sea directly, sor." Hooligan could not have been more obliging had he been paid in gold.

''To foind work you see sor.''

"You'se aint shy of a bit of work then, the both of you?" the gang was drawing it out to the last.

"Not usn, sor," volunteered Hooligan the downtrodden with the enthusiasm of one who, for a bowl of gruel, would move a mountain with a toothpick.

"It just so 'appens as I 'ave a stick or two of wood as wants floatin' down to Minster. What would you two say to floatin' down wif it? 'Bout a couple of days south.

Cash on delivery." He made it sound as though the wood guided itself down the river and gave free rides to the more fortunate travelers.

"We're your men, gaffer," Hooligan poured the dregs of his tea into the fire as though to christen the union of labor and capital.

"We'd sooner swim than tramp."

"Done. Come bye as soon as you've packed away and got the fire out. I'll be aboard. The sooner you start, the sooner you harrive. How do they call you?"

"I'm Mick, and that there is Richard the Turd," said Hooligan indicating the recumbent Seed with loathing.

"We will be there soon as our bellies is full.

"You will," confirmed the Zulu, giving his ankle-rattles a shake, in order to have the last word, and because the Zulu spoke little English.

"What's the pay?" demanded Seed evilly, again refusing to recognize the stranger with a look, and concentrating on the bread which he was now toasting.

"What's the pay?" There was communal astonishment at such ingratitude, everyone clearly resenting the notion that persons offered the privilege of laboring in the name of Astor should exhibit any interest whatsoever in their remuneration.

"It's two days sitting on your arse for starters, and two days nearer't sea," observed the clansman who was as careful with Astor's cash as he was with his own. Abandoning confrontation in favor of condescension, for reasons known only to himself, Farmer Brown added,

"You can have coin if you wish it; or a goat or two, or tatties, the choice is yours when you works for Lord Astor."

"By crikey sor, we will bless the day we met all of yous," Hooligan hid his sarcasm behind his beauteous smile.

"There you go then," concluded the less aggressive faction in accent-less English determined to have the last word, and they all strode away well pleased with themselves, the decorative ribbons of the shako, the breechclout and Pui Pui* catching the breeze very prettily.

In the gang's wake the incensed Irishman snapped to attention saluting smartly.

"Thank you very much, Captain Sor. Sure Oi'd love to sail under you, on a raft, on a river, yards from the nearest land. Whip me again should it please ye sir."

"Taking a napple from a child," said the newly christened Richard the Turd, shaking his head in unstinting admiration.

"Well done, Dave my boy."

"Thank you, Richard, Things is starting to take shape. Let's get over there before more gypos turn up and nick our magic carpet."

True to their word, the representatives of the family of nations in this neck of the woods were impatiently awaiting their arrival when the crew jumped aboard the vessel. One of the ferocious individuals had tied a bit of rag to a stick and referred to the product of his ingenuity as a flag, an innovation of which the collaborators were inordinately proud. The new deckhands had not so much as dumped their belongings but what the French cavalryman was instructing them on how to deploy this vital piece of equipment. Apparently, it was of the utmost importance that on coming within sight of the shipyard which lay a couple of days downstream on this side of the river, they must 'Halloo' at the top of their lungs and wave the flag in the fashion

*A maori warrior's kilt of beaten flax strands.

demonstrated; namely by scribing vast arcs of a complete and 'perfic.' semicircle, until such times as they received a reciprocal signal. Otherwise, they would float right passed the mole and disappear into the wastes of the 'Lanic never to be seed again,' to die of thirst, or to pitch up on some strand in darkest Africa and be cooked and eaten by cannybulls. One man had to be at the tiller day and night to keep the vessel in midstream, and woe-betide the unfortunate that failed in this duty. Seed felt obliged to inquire as to how many unfortunates had sailed off into the 'lanic,' over the years and suffered the awful fate of beaching in Jersey or worse still, 'Brest,' only to be ignored a second time that day for his disbelieving nature, presumptuous lack of respect, and surly manner. With everything shipshape and the technical instructions clearly misunderstood and vouched for, it was time to launch the great expedition; the ropes were cast off and between them the raft-builders and the immeasurable power of the river, impelled the vast acreage of timber away from the bank, and the Raft Of The *Medusa began her journey southward.

Hooligan quickly claimed the tiller in order to have some fun getting to grips with the steering of the craft but Seed; true to form; snatched up the flag and took to practicing his waving technique in a ludicrously exaggerated fashion, as though he had lost his mind. For the one and only time in the two days that followed, Hooligan was glad to be holding on to that clumsy lump of wood, otherwise he would have fallen overboard so hard did he laugh at the man's ridiculous antics. Seed's mentors on the other hand, were not at all amused. Incensed beyond reason by this mockery, the warlike personalities on shore; the Zulu, the Scottish clansman the Red Indians, and the Maori, pursued the raft in a frenzy; charging along the bank, hurling oaths and stones in an uncontrollable rage, while Seed, dropping his flag, cupped his hands to his mouth and 'hallooooed' at the top of his lungs.

"You're all mad, you bastards," at which the objects of his mockery ripped off their buckskin shirt and Patu-in-fist raced along the bank from where they hurled the priceless artifact in an excess of fury.

*See the work by Theodore Gericault.

Even before the club struck the deck the war party had dived into the river intent on revenge. Witnessing this performance with great amusement the escapees waited for the fool to surface so that they could mock him some more. The moment when the war party had to either surface or drown came and went with no sign so Hooligan followed Seed to the side of the raft where they waited for the opportunity to slap the enemy silly should any of them try to come aboard. Clearly the poor madmen were never going to surface again. The absurdity of the incident struck the raft's crew as the funniest thing imaginable, and they laughed in that vulgar fashion which is limited only by the volume of air which one is capable of inhaling. And they laughed until it hurt.

When once again able to catch his breath Seed crossed the strip-farmed landscape and recovered the patu; a superbly well fashioned implement in stone of a deep green hue, polished until it was as smooth as an uncut diamond. Overcome by the beauty and artistry of it and sensing instinctively that ownership of such a piece could bring him wealth the likes of which he had never known he feigned disinterest and showed it to Hooligan in a deprecating manner. One glance was sufficient for the man, causing Seed to rejoice inwardly.

As evening approached on that first day afloat, Hooligan was once again at the tiller when Seed, returning from his meanderings was reaching out to relieve his crewmate of the tedious job when the seemingly somnolent Irishman erupted with shocking violence. Grabbing the smaller man by the throat and the hair and sweeping his legs from under him he smashed Seed to the deck dropping on top of him to drive the wind from his victim's lungs. Hunting for breath and with his arms pinioned never to work again the victim could do nothing but wait in choking terror for the knife. What an inexpressible relief it was to the captive to find himself being searched and not stabbed; searched so thoroughly that he was robbed of all three of his hidden weapons, his gold and the superb green-stone and then released; thrown across the deck like so much offal.

Terror was instantly replaced by rage which Seed expressed in a flood of the foulest language known to man which vomited forth until his impressive vocabulary failed him. Unimpressed and smiling broadly Hooligan reassured his victim, whom he held at bay with one of his own knives that what he had just done was simply to ensure that Seed did not abandon ship and swim ashore under cover of darkness.

"You will get your shit back once we're insoide that yard," he concluded.

"Until then, if you come within ten yards of me in the night, when you think Oive gone by-byes I'll drown you like a rat." On hearing this reassuring news Seed calmed down appreciably and seemed to harbour no grudge at all, even going so far as to infer that he trusted his companion's word that his valuables would be restored to him and that were their roles reversed he would have employed the same tactic.

"Now," said Admiral Hooligan portentously, "get a hold of this stick and get us back on course, while I go and dangle me poor feet in the watter."

As he stepped over the bulwark of the cutter which brought him ashore Hooligan was well pleased at the prospect of parting company with his execrable crewman. Kane Seed was the worst sort of creature imaginable. If the Englishman's own words were to be believed, he was guilty of the filthiest of crimes; in addition to which the man's persona exhibited not one saving grace. The dog's pastime had been to brag about the myriad insults to humanity that he had committed, telling and retelling every sordid detail and wallowing in the unbelievable cruelty of them. Out of his own mouth, he stood convicted of stealing children, horses, cattle and anything else that wasn't nailed down. Grave robbing, arson, blackmail, and murder, the latter of which Hooligan had witnessed but not imitated because it was 'he,' Hooligan who had been attacked.

The prevailing mood of the daily battle for survival which is modern industry was that of a clog dance clog with herds of men; each one an island to himself going about their unique tasks with a concentration that clearly excluded everyone and everything else. No one so much as glanced at the two strangers.

"I see the very place," Hooligan nodded at a horizontal forest of drying-timber resembling nothing more than a little Russian village, the hundred or so 'houses,' resting peacefully deserted amid this island of turbulance.

"Here's your purse," he shoved the canvas sack at Seed as he would a dagger.

''Me club, give it.'' The tormented creature demanded, reaching without conviction. Wallowing in the minor cruelly Hooligan did not so much as respond to this unreasonable claim of ownership.

''Oi'll make as if Oi'm taking a piss by them stacks and when you give me the all-clear, I'll nip in between them. If anyone is watchin', let me know and I'll wait to make me move when the coast is clear. Have you got that?"

"Of 'course,' I've got it, Gimme my fucking club." Were he armed, Seed would have shot Hooligan in the face in order to reverse this barefaced robbery.

"You did well friend. I'll be in touch whenever I need a steady hand.'' Hooligan lied.

''My fucking club you bastard.''

Squeezing into the narrow space between two tall cottages, Hooligan pretended to be urinating.

''It's not your club.''

"All clear," lied Seed.

Lliam Shaun Hooligan's next step carried him across the invisible boundary between the safety of the innocent worker and the killing ground of the guilty saboteur. Safely out of sight, he shouldered his pack and started into the depths of the wooden canyons, struggling along until he judged himself to be somewhere near the middle of the horizontal forest and thusly susceptible to discovery only by those who had mastered the art of flight. He was getting himself comfortable to await nightfall when an agonized screeching straight from the maw of hell itself shocked him horribly out of his conceit. Satan relented while he took a breather and Hooligan was thanking every saint whose name he could recall, when the torture was applied again, and yet again. Ripping one of his shirtsleeves he stuffed a little bit of cloth into his ear and angered beyond reason, went with murder in his soul in search of the tortured beast intent on putting an end to its big gob and it.. Travelling between the ends of the timbers was considerably easier than it was between their sides, there being no fillets waiting to skewer a man with their vicious foot-long splinters and he made good progress, soon coming up against a high canvas wall which stretched away in both directions as far as he was able to see. 'Obviously, the thing was chained up inside.' Whipping the dead gypo's impossibly sharp knife from his belt, he gashed the heavy canvas, twisted the blade in the wound, then risking his one good eye peeked through. The Harpy's corrosive breath caught in his throat, and he gagged. Its lair was a glimpse of hell itself where the naked damned, their flayed bodies running sweat, toiled mindlessly in the sulfuric yellow fog of its poisonous exhalations. Never still the demented crew threw themselves around with astounding energy, racing to keep pace with the relentless cadence of the *Dearg Due's* pounding drum. At some distance from him, giant iron wheels bigger even than those of a water mill, rimmed with enormous square teeth, tessellated one with the other in the cleverest fashion imaginable, the great gravestone maulers of each biting cleanly as could be between those of the other.

They were *turning*. '*Both*' of them and not so much as a cross word spoken. Like the fingers of children playing, *Here is the church, and here is the steeple,* so they were. Hooligan was astonished, astounded, disbelieving, even though he could see it happening right there in front of him. Sure, dis was cleverness as close to magic as 'bugger' is to 'off.' Huge arms of iron joined in the show with magic of their own. Forward and back, forward and back they went, quicker and quicker, like the arse of a priest on top of the mother superior, then not ten steps from where he watched, a gigantic silver saw blade armed with a score of barbaric scimitar teeth began to move. Faster and faster, up and down it went, until those teeth became a blur and then, the whole trunk of a giant tree charged like a battering ram into his limited view, slowed of its own accord and moved sedately, straight at the blur which had been the saw blade. At the instant in which the two came together, the shrieking of hell itself occurred again as bits of wood were ripped out and hurled around the place, hitting him in the face with stinging force. The whole length of the tree passed slowly in front of his fascinated eye, and as 'God was his witless,' a great plank of timber fell from its side as sweetly as a slice from a roast of beef on a plate at the George. Lliam Shaun Hooligan, spearpoint of the abolitionist movement, conspirator, infiltrator, killer and employer of killers in pursuit of freedom, trustee of powerful men, friend of the people, arch enemy of the Aristocracy and rich as plum pudding could not have been more pleased with his discovery. He had not the least understanding of the sorcery that could do such things, but he would have bet good money that it had cost the Astor tribe plenty. His curiosity satisfied, he turned his back happily and retreated to his little den where he curled up on the floor and pulled his coat over his head. 'Sure, the silence of the grave would be the best place ever for that noisy *Dearg Due* bastard.'

CHAPTER 12: Astor Senior

With a sword at his side and a loaded pistol in his boot, Bismark Astor assisted by grooms mounted Maximus his most malignant horse among a whole stable of malignant horses from a tall platform accessed via a set of steps and set out for Minster and the well-regarded *Glorious.* Of his senior bodyguards there was irritatingly no sign, but he proceeded regardless; the unsettling spirit which had driven him to rebel against the assaults of age still strong upon him. The frank exchange of views with his son had affected him deeply for in every point of comparison he had come off a very poor second indeed. He had been forced to confront the truth that his work in The House, or more sensibly his dalliance in the parks and coffee shops with the other lords of the land, talking philosophy, poetry, rumor, slander and the likes, although enjoyable, was distinctly unprofitable and had distracted him from business, thus leaving the boy to shoulder the burden. Why, he didn't have a clue that vessels of the Astor partnership were engaged in bringing home loyal Englishmen from the traitorous colonies, or that Herculean slaves were being bred like horses in his name. Neither did he know that the partnership had engaged in the spice trade. He had even forgotten that a massive investment such as the *Glorious* was sitting idle at Minster, a mere hour from Windward Palace. The facet of that illuminating and frank exchange that had really shocked his lordliness however, was just how energetic, ruthless, and businesslike Michael had appeared, in comparison with himself. He was, he realized, letting himself grow old and soft without so much as a whimper he who had once herded niggers by the thousand to the barracoons. No more. Astor and Son were a partnership once again and he, Bismark Ludwig Astor was back.

His shipyard at minster was a thoroughly masculine world, a world which he loved, one of industry, noise, energy, danger, and the stink of timber, tar, paint, turpentine, sweat and piss. A world where fundamentally, the workforce of a whole town slaved in order to make one man rich; himself; 'two' actually; what could be more beautiful than that? The yard manager, whose name he could not remember for the life of him, came swaying up the slope from the river, red in the face and sweating profusely. Spying his employer, the harassed individual approached seemingly on the verge of collapse and wheezing.

"M'lord. What a bloody day.'' The young fellow was too fatigued to talk normally. "I've just been down to… the *Glorious*, Lord Astor… The soldiers have… arrived… for tonight's honor… guard and the… orchestra is sorting itself out on… deck." His shortage of breath punctuating his words in the most amusing fashion imaginable.

"There's a Mrs some-it or tother; cook, huge fat bitch, army of people… from Mister Michael's…   … doing some-it in… the galley. Shall I come back… down with… you… my lord?"

"Not at all." replied Astor.

"Go about your business as though I wasn't here. I came to look at how things are going, production, stock-levels. That sort of thing; not just at the *Glorious*." The concern that this statement caused the manager registered in the man's face, while Astor gloated cruelly behind the innocent expression he wore. He was aware that, terrified of losing his job, the man would stretch every sinew to breaking point for the benefit of Astor and Son over the coming months and drive production to record heights.

"Firstly however, I want to use your office; I have need of parchment and quill and three of your lads who can ride without falling off. Have those soldiers keep everyone well away from that damned black outside; he kicks and bites; and set a sly child to watching the pale moustaches in the pie shop thonder." He nodded in the direction of 'Henry's.'

"Without being twigged, if you please. Follow him when he leaves the place. See what he's up to.'' he concluded. In the rank and dusty office, surrounded by drawings of every part of a ship he found quill and ink, and quickly wrote three letters which he sealed with scarlet wax and imprinted with his coat of arms by virtue of the gold ring on the first finger of his left hand. One of these missives, he addressed to Captain Anderson of the *Senator*, now at anchor in Portsmouth, ordering him to make his ship ready with great urgency for a return crossing of the North Atlantic carrying an unknown number of soldiers; possibly as many as three hundred, and to be ready to proceed to Minster, if required. The other two were addressed to Michael; one to Windward Palace, while the other was dispatched to The Granary. He had covered all eventualities. The *Glorious* he discovered was aptly named; a masterpiece of design and craftsmanship which begged with every enchanting curve of her body for the freedom of the ocean and a fair wind. With her raked masts and thrusting bowsprit, she was all speed, and Astor's reservations, such as they were, evaporated with his first glance. The blood-red wound of her plimsoll line contrasted wonderfully well with the massive black hull below and the blindingly white superstructure above. The flag of union, big as the front of a townhouse hung somnolently from her jack staff, far too tired to be woken by a mere breeze. Workmen were attaching decorative bunting to her rigging while those of Cornwallis' Own Regiment of Foot were applying blanco to their webbing belts, and polishing their muskets, bayonets and brasses. On speaking to the officer in charge, he discovered that unbeknown to Cornwallis, 'and himself,' these men were to form an honor-guard at the upcoming celebration. Some enterprising individual had established a superb table for a hundred or so on the deck between the main-masts, and high above it, fashioned an ingenious ceiling of canvas. An orchestra was making itself at home in a corner and the redoubtable Crabtree woman was on deck where she was inspecting a delivery of produce. Astor was well pleased; everything seemed to be proceeding according to plan without his raising a finger. Delegation was a wonderful skill, he reflected smugly, as was his forethought in siring an evil genius of a son. The great cabin was magnificent beyond belief, resembling as it did in so many ways, a gentleman's study. The place was airy and light with almost continuous windows on three sides. It was as large as a respectable drawing-room, and so high that; as Michael had claimed, even Cornwallis; long streak of piss that he was, would be able to stand upright in it without braining himself. Its glimmering hardwood deck was a work of art and Turkish rugs of many bright and contrasting colours reduced any tendency for sound to echo. Bulkheads done in ivory, added to the wonderfully fresh atmosphere and prompted the massive teak furniture to glisten while reflecting the numerous brass instruments and fittings in a most complementary fashion.

On the master-table he discovered charts. Charts of such accuracy and detail as he had never seen before. Fascinated; he poured over them and discovered that a new center-of-gravity was present in the preparation, printing and compilation of these scientific works. There was no mention of dragons on any one of them. Neither were there depictions of happy whales spouting water all over the place, simply the most informative and beautifully drawn and colored representations of the known world. It was possible to claim on studying these works that 'fact' had replaced 'guesswork' where navigation was concerned. Astor would not have believed, was he not seeing it with his own eyes, that so much information was now available to the commander of an ocean-going vessel. These obviously expensive and beautifully manufactured works must have been drawn by the highest authority and placed here specifically for the purposes of the evening's business. 'This ship has Michael's hand all over it,' Bismark noted.   Reluctantly.

There came a commotion beyond the double doors, and a moment later, these were flung open admitting a dozen or so individuals, who were all-haste and irritatingly full-to-the-brim of their own importance. It stood to reason that the buggers knew him to be their employer, yet they paid him no more homage than they would have had he been a stick of furniture, they took instead to adorning the tables and benches with humidors, candelabra, bowls of fruit, bowls of nuts, coffee services, exquisite flowers and, it would seem, every intoxicating beverage known to man. Those bearing flowers had clearly been blessed with senses previously the domain only of bats, because they carried before them jungles of greenery and brilliantly colored blooms, which certainly obscured their vision in all directions but to the rear. Even so, they made their way unerringly around the cabin, depositing vast shrubberies in locations of their educated choosing, before returning to fuss and dither around ad nauseam with each of them, then having achieved, from Astor's point of view, absolutely nothing at all, went reluctantly away with many a backward glance as though being dragged bodily from their firstborn. This unpleasant illness was clearly contagious because it afflicted the whole tribe of 'interior decorators,' or whatever they were, so that before Astor's very eyes, one of them, who may have been a man, shifted a bundle of spills by a trifling amount, stood back to properly appreciate his own genius, then repeated the sequence no less than eleven times. The fool would not be satisfied until the much-travelled spills had completed a circumnavigation and returned safely to their home port. By the time these simpletons forsook the scene of their crimes, Astor was thoroughly exhausted. Vacating the great cabin to continue his inspection, he consulted the barometer on the bulkhead as he passed, noting with satisfaction that the superb instrument predicted that the fine weather would persist for the foreseeable future. It was a good omen.

The gun-deck was shocking; it was as dark, threatening and warlike, as the cabins, galley and wardrooms were light, welcoming and attractive. Here, he found to his satisfaction, that Michael had specified root-wood at every junction of deck and hull; that enormously strong part of the tree where trunk becomes root; the twisting fibers of the wood at that juncture providing enormous rigidity and toughness to the vessel. The hull, he discovered, by a close inspection of one of the open gun ports, was constructed with a vertical scantling of live oak; that incredibly tough American timber, sandwiched between two walls of pit-sawn planks of English oak, and fully a foot and a half thick. The design of the *Glorious* clearly employed the principles which underlay the building of the American 'Ironsides.' With such good bones as these she was well-nigh impervious even to a full broadside. To his great surprise, each of the monstrous bronze guns was already supplied with both iron and wooden shot, which stood in the prescribed pyramidal formation, 'as though she was about to go into battle.'

With his curiosity piqued the proud owner of this magnificent vessel reached up and tipped the cleverly hung powder-horn suspended above one of the breeches. It was full, and powder in excellent condition, dry as dust, small grained and of regular size with a good nose to boot, flowed like salt at a banquet.

Assuming correctly that the magazines would lie directly below the cannon and be easily accessible even when the vessel was fully laden with cargo, he restricted his search to the strip of deck closest to the hull, and soon located the access tunnel. Removing the covering plate, he discarded his coat and squeezed himself down into a space built for striplings, not grown men, crawling quickly along the narrow warren. Just a few steps from the opening, it became as dark as faith, obliging him to advance by touch alone. Brought to his knees by the lowering roof he completed the journey at the crawl with his shoulders being scraped uncomfortably as he proceeded, occasionally reaching out in front so as not to advance face-first into the magazine. A few more yards and he had reached it; the hugely timbered structure that isolated the massive store of powder from the flames of battle. He struggled through the semi-turnstile door, Michael's invention; and working by touch alone in stygian darkness located the sliding trap to one of the powder chutes and pulled it upwards. The door resisted. Cursing, he wrenched at it only to have the damned thing suddenly free itself and travel to the very end of its guides. Rushing powder filled his shoe and its pepper filled his nostrils. What was the meaning of it all, he wondered? *Glorious* was no warship, yet Michael had gone to great lengths and expense in equipping her with firepower sufficient to fight her way through seriously sticky situations. Had that scheming son of a bitch whelp of his known all along about the state of play in the colonies, he wondered. What was it that the puppy knew and he, the big dog, did not? His anger and suspicion jousted.

 On the now crowded and resplendent deck the preparations were well advanced, even on the mayhem of a couple of hours earlier, while those who were contributing to the fine show were watching something on the port bow. Piqued; Bismark leapt on to the bulwark 'not entirely convincingly' and climbed until he had a clear view of what it was that had captured the communal interest. Directly ahead, stretching back a considerable distance upstream floated an acre and more of timber which had just now arrived from his forests upstream. To Astor, it was a common enough sight and held no interest whatsoever. The workforce had placed the raft well and she would come sweetly into the shallows behind the mole, built specifically for the purpose. Taking no chances however, the crew of a longboat were attaching hawsers, which at a signal from the raft, would be brought into play by capstans ashore and the vast mass of timber would be secured. A red-bearded giant strode to the near side of the floating island, yanked down his draws and oblivious to the finer feelings of his audience, dangled his thing, which rightly belonged on a four-legged creature and pissed rosewater into the river. Freehand. With many a backward glance, the ladies dragged themselves away from the awful spectacle, murmuring hollow-sounding protestations which had their men folk squirming inwardly about certain points of comparison. With evening fast approaching, Astor disembarked with a last proprietary scrutiny of the preparations. His exertions below decks had given him the appearance of an overgrown powder monkey, and he needed to see the inside of his bathroom and get dressed before returning in time to greet the first of his guests. He would return to Windward Palace forthwith to take care of these matters, get a quick bite to eat and most importantly, a peek at his correspondence, without which he felt like a fish out of water, but first he would have to talk to Walker. 'Ha, the manager's name was Walker.'

He was making his way through the yard, interested in everything that he came across, when he noticed the underdog in a saw pit; the devil was black. Approaching the station he stood at the edge looking down at the naked African while wondering where his predecessor was working now. The fellow was composed of fine sawdust. Though he had no intention whatsoever of being rude to the pitman the creature took great offence at being watched. Having tolerated Astor's scrutiny for several seconds the man relinquished his loathed grip on the saw, adopted a posture identical to Astor's own; namely feet wide apart with hands on hips, and in clear English announced,

"Last thing I seen standin' like that be a two-bit whore."

Scylla and Charybdis who had arrived minutes earlier dropped into the pit before Bismark's fury could find voice, causing the hugely muscled sawyer to square up to their attack with enthusiasm, a snake moving in the dust around his ankles.

"Wait," called Astor, forestalling certain violence, "what's that at your feet?" The underdog obligingly displayed his pink soles, lifting them alternately out of the ankle-deep sawdust in which he stood. The man's legs were tied to a post with rope. Scylla and Charybdis examined their own feet also but found nothing.

"It's a damn rope, 'case a barenaked black man 'scapes out of this shit bucket." This was more than the pugilists could stand and they looked up appealingly at their master.

"He's from the *Bird*, Mu Lord." Walker had appeared at Astor's shoulder. "American ablutionists. We got heaps of 'em prisoner here in one of the sheds, and there be 'bout twice as many on that boat out there."

"Explain," hissed Astor, beckoning his guards from the pit and continuing his progress in the direction of the main gate where his dreaded mount waited, drawing Walker, with him.

"Well," said the habitually harassed individual, "it seems as there is them around wot don't old wiv slavery. They's taken to catching slave ships and freein the blacks on Jamaicy and, Cooba, is it? And Africar its elf, dependin' on where the ship was took, I s'pose."

"Get to the point, Walker. How did he and his mates end up here?" Clearly, the story which the manager was about to impart amused the young man greatly, because he snorted mirthfully in the most immature manner as he recalled it.

"Well," he began, "it were Mister Michael really speakin, he filled this here slaver ship wiv marines and them ablution fellers fell for it. Them marines give 'em a bloody good hidin' and took 'em prisoner; ship an' all. They be goin' up to Brissle soon for hangin. After the trial like. That's the *Bird* out there in the roads. Their ship." Walker turned and nodded southwards at a sleek craft lying in midstream.

"Excellent," spat Bismark; utterly disgusted that an employee was privy to knowledge of this import whilst he was not.

"Secure, are they, the ones that you've got in there?"

"That they are, m'lord. That there's the old joiners shed, as was. Stone flagged floor and oak built. Them won't be gettin' out o' there in a urry."

"Glad to hear it. See to it that you send the workforce home at five o'clock. I don't want any of them on the property when my guests arrive. And let the soldiers know that they must take up their positions at the gates by six. Any news yet, about the pie shop moustaches?"

The manager paused momentarily, flicking urgently through the rooms of his memory palace in a second or less and with his fear receding replied.

"The boy ain't back yet m'lord, but soon as he is, I'll get a message to you 'bout anyfing wots appening."

"Do that."

His Lordship returned to Windward Palace on a civilized horse hired from the local stable, excusing his own timidity by way of needing to think, convincing himself that he could not do both the thinking and the control of the bloody bad-tempered Magnus at one and the same time. He was in much the same frame of mind on return as that in which he had ventured out which is to say that somewhere in its shady depths writhed a matter of the greatest moment which obstinately refused to reveal itself.

CHAPTER 13: Adversaries

Of a certainty, not one of Capability Brown's Barbary apes nor the vagabond himself would escape from Jamaica Place that day, for while it was still dark, a veritable army of gamekeepers, woodcutters, grooms, gardeners and retainers from all over the Astor estates, farms, factories and fisheries had surrounded the superb house forming a ragged cordon at fifty yards from its mellow walls. All was thus in readiness when Michael Astor's carriage drew up adjacent to the main entrance of his magnificent new home shortly after dawn. Around the great one's vehicle were one small army of scarlet-clad footmen, and another of mounted roughnecks; men who despite their respectable great-coats bowler-hats and cravats seemed even at a mere glance, anything but housebroken.

Scylla and Charybdis; 'borrowed for the occasion from Bismark,' disembarked from their seat at the rear followed shortly by Delavier, who sat with the whip hand. These three men mounted the wide steps to the mansion and passed through the splendidly majestic doors so high and wide that they could admit a fully laden hay-wagon. After a while, Michael Astor and Philip Bowman, of Bowman and Son, stepped down from the landau; Bowman from the luggage rack at the rear, and strolled at their leisure in the rapidly improving formal gardens, admiring Jamaica's magnificent facade, all eighty-two yards of it, while Michael proudly pointed out the finer elements of design to the enthusiastic and appreciative young man.

The destroyers returned barely ten minutes later, driving before them with sticks as though he were a bullock, the portly figure of Capability Brown, landscaper to the nobility and welcome guest in many of the great houses of England, wearing nothing but his nightshirt, crying like a child, and protesting volubly. The universally recognized horticulturist was driven to stand before his present employer like an insolent pupil before the headmaster where his protests were shouted down in a barrage of profanity which brought flecks of foam to the corners of Michael Astor's mouth.

"You jumped up, pompous, social-climbing, fat windbag," Michael began; occasionally glancing at Hastings and Wynnychuk for inspiration but finding none.

"What thoughts could possibly have invaded your thick head to make you believe that you; a mere tradesman; a bloody 'shit kicker' of all things should install himself and his scum in *my* home? What was wrong with your rooms at the Granary? Is my present residence not up to your very high standards? No! Don't! Open your mouth and by the lord Harry, I'll cut out your gangrenous tongue. Get off my land and never show your ugly face to me again. GO!"

Brown was hustled capably from the property, barefoot, into the wide world; his reputation and popularity nationwide saving him from a horrible fate. The first part of the operation having gone smoothly, the terrors went indoors again, this time accompanied by ten very hard men, each of whom carried with him his weapon of choice. During the next twenty minutes these people returned, sometimes singly, sometimes together with various others, but always dragging, driving or beating, dependent on the degree of resistance exhibited, one or other of Brown's lickspittles. The intruder's dollies were removed via the servants' doors, searched much more intimately and enthusiastically than was entirely necessary by almost everyone though it was quite impossible to conceal architectural fitments in some of the places explored, then with their services properly appreciated were sent on their way.

Capability Brown's henchmen, there were eight of them, battered, agonized, bleeding and fearful, were made to stand in front of the young Bowman, the timber dealer, who, without hesitation, picked out the guilty party who had sold timber to him during the summer.

"This is the man, Lord Astor," Bowman declared confidently, doing so, loudly enough, for all to hear.

"Sold one hundred and seventy cubes in total this summer, to Bowman and Son." The young businessman waved several pieces of paper, which were presumed by all present to be the proof of the pudding. Michael took back control quickly, not appreciating one bit the acquisitive Bowman's appropriation of the limelight.

"'You,' have been selling 'my' timber," he declared, stepping forward and prodding the captive's chest with a gloved finger; at which point the accused foolishly began to protest his innocence. He had barely begun when Astor punched him viciously in the solar plexus. Gasping in pain and terror and collapsing as his breath failed him the accused knelt in the pebbles in a most fortuitous manner. Michael kicked the man savagely in the face, hurling him on to his back as the others groaned at the brutality of it. Hoist to his feet by a couple of fun-loving ruffians, the thief was supported once again in front of his interrogator.

"Where is my money?" asked Michael conversationally, and not wanting more of the same, the troubled fellow managed to indicate that the product of his criminality was inside Jamaica Place.

"Take him inside and get it," Michael ordered, and the thief was hurried back with much low-level kicking slapping and punching from whence he had come, to surrender the money from his bedroll hiding place; an exercise which obviously required a modicum of attitude adjustment, for when he was dragged back outside some ten minutes later, he was bleeding from various wounds to the face and head. Clearly the roughnecks had found cause to use him as a punching bag of the heavier weight division.

"Get rid of your army Hastings, thank you," bellowed Michael, at which the giant responded by tapping his forehead with the silver skull which adorned his stick. Turning to face his motley legions he waved them away to the purgatory of the wage slave from whence they came. Those poor people had never known such excitement and had wanted desperately to witness the climax of it and extend this brief holiday. Their disappointment was manifest.

"Count it, Delavier," Astor snorted, and Delavier immediately gave the amount to the penny, having foreseen this requirement on his master's part. Michael already knew of course, exactly how much the thief had made on the sale of the stolen timber, having met with young Bowman and Bowman senior, to study the receipts. He was pleased to discover that most of the money was accounted for. He stood face to face with the prisoner a second time.

"Do you know what our Muslim friends do to larcenist swine such as you?" he enquired very civilly of the now scared and trembling criminal.

"They give them the chop." Incredulity, terror, and infuriatingly to Michael's way of thinking; a mere trace of arrogant denial, registered on the doomed individual's face, as he realized what was being implied.

"No," Sweat burst through the man's pores despite the dawn chill.

"Yes," countered Michael happily.

"Which one will it be?"

With a theatrical flourish Astor drew his sword and indicated the eight-foot-tall rim of steel-shod oak at the rear of the landau with a flick of the glittering, murderously sharp blade.

''Grip that wheel.'' He commanded.

Suddenly incensed by the thief's hesitancy, his face contorting in loathing, judge, jury and executioner raged at the shivering thing whose previous arrogance had stemmed from the belief that no Englishman would commit such an atrocity.

"Do it now, or it'll be both of them." An expectant, knowing and fascinated silence fell over the watching roughnecks. Blubbering and praying all at once, the thief grasped the iron felloe of the tall wheel with his left hand, the one least valuable to him, screwing his eyes shut in submission, fury, and dread of the agony to come. With no hesitation whatsoever, Astor swung expertly and removed the thief's right arm, just below the elbow. The forearm dropped to the ground, the fingers gripping then releasing as though attempting to catch the dark arterial blood which splashed it. For a full two seconds the condemned was unaware that his punishment had been inflicted. Then the pain struck. Screaming uncontrollably above the great upwelling of sound from the watching crowd, the agonized man grasped his truncated member, trying desperately to stop the awful intermittent rushing of blood and save himself; but an Astor victory never once occurred on a field of grace and mercy. The badly wounded man's preoccupation was interrupted and foiled completely by a noose being thrown around him, and he was dragged away behind a horse, thrashed every step of the way with knotted ropes, to the trees; one of which was to be his gallows. Or worse. Lord Astor had, it's true, mentioned, 'tenterhooks,' during his preparations for this jaunt.

"Do you need a hand?" the swordsman bawled, laughing at his victim's departing figure, and pointing with his blade at the unpleasant thing now clutching at the pebbles of the driveway. Delavier, Michael noticed, with some irritation, was vomiting in volumes which rivaled the Trevi Fountain. Despite his annoyance at this slack-twisted behavior he decided graciously to give his servant a moment.

"Hastings," he called loudly, looking around for his chief bailiff who had momentarily abandoned station, locating that gentleman as he disengaged himself from a crowd of his ruffians. The jovial fellow approached hippo-like behind a couple of mastiffs which he kept on a single leash. The dogs, Michael noted were prettier by far than their master, but the young lord liked Hastings immensely; always had, he was the sort of friend who inspired confidence. Instructed to chop an infant in two and give half to each of the claimant mothers; Hastings would have asked,

"Shall I slice lengthways or across, master?" In appearance, he was the embodiment of the known universe all in one individual. His perfectly spherical torso was the planet earth of course, above which sat the sun of his polished dome, all shiny and round. His ridiculously swollen calves were the inner planets as were his monstrously muscled thighs, which were presently performing parabolic oscillations with an energy of their own, and lastly, the fellows swollen testicles, of which Hastings was inordinately proud, bouncing from thigh to thigh as he advanced; filling the fellows knickerbockers with their roundness which the unashamedly lusty, lecherous and amoral Hastings liked to believe sent the ladies into a tizzy. He should be so lucky. The bailiff, bodyguard and blood-brother, halted at a respectful five paces distant from his master and waited. He did not speak, he merely waited for the orders which he had been summoned to receive, and there lay another reason why Michael liked the man. Though the two of them had been friends since childhood, Hastings had developed in to one of those chaps who understood the notion of *place*. He was one of the few who had taken in with his mother's gin, the irrefutable knowledge, the immutable truth; that the hoi polloi, have nothing whatever to say that is of any interest at all to the aristocracy.

"Well done, Hasty," Michael began.

"Ride over there and tell your men that they can beat him to a sticky consistency before they tenterhook the bastard. Over there, beyond Jacob's Ladder* will do. I don't want my visitors to see him. Or hear him. Now, to business. The watchmen who allowed this outrage to occur. Punish them. Punish them, severely. Dismiss them and chuck them out of their cottages. Replace them with ruffians. The furniture will be arriving any day now and I don't want to have it purloined. Secondly, I want every trace of this obscenity obliterated, removed, destroyed. Every room, wall, floor, you name it, that is marked or stained, I want the very air those bastards breathed, out of my house so that not a thing on this earth reminds me of their disgusting existence. You will take your direction from Delavier, as it's an inside job." Michael looked around for his man and found that his butler was much recovered, pale but functioning.

"Be sure to use men who have a bit of backbone and are capable of resisting all authority except mine, on pain of; let's say, 'being cut down to size.' Now, as to your reward, Hastings, for a job well done." His Lordliness stepped forward, well inside his man's personal space, and tucked a considerable sum of cash from the recovered loot into the pocket of Hastings' marigold waistcoat.

Scowling over his friend's wide shoulder at the remaining prisoners, he announced,

"I declare that we have found some volunteers for our whaling fleet." Poking the severed limb with the toe of one highly polished boot he observed.

"This can go in the hole with chummy over there naturally; and your lads can play the gauntlet with our new deckhands here. That should help square the ledger somewhat, but bear in mind Hasty, they're no good to a whaling ship if they're crippled or blinded."

"Aye, aye sir," Hastings nodded, and bashed his own skull with the silver one on his stick.

''Beat them to a paste.'' He roared and the army of roughnecks instantly laid into those unfortunates who would spend the rest of their short lives suffering bitter cold, disgusting food, damp hammocks, brutal treatment, hellish danger and not a sou in wages aboard a whaler in the South Atlantic. Until death.

"Delavier, go indoors and search for stains, spillage, vomit, marks in the parquet, that sort of thing." Astor had to shout above the groans and cries of the men being thrashed while Delavier who was revolted by what was happening to the prisoners went quickly and willingly.

"Be rigorous. Replace anything whatsoever that requires it; no matter what the cost," bawled Michael.

"As you say, sir."

"And Delavier, have a word with my curators and discover whether those dogs had access to anything movable. We will send the bill to the late-lamented Brown and discover whether he is 'capable' of that. And don't pay his fee." Soon becoming bored with the poor spectacle of Capability Brown's people undergoing softening-up prior to embarking on their novel-naval careers, he chose a good-looking horse and rode away anticipating the total absorption that tenterhooking always provides. Curiously, everything was still reasonably quiet there among the trees but a forge of industry nevertheless. Possibly half of his army of roughnecks had been drawn to the pornographic business, he noted. The chosen-one was already prostrated face down in the grass, spread-eagled and gagged imaginatively with a blade secured behind his head; it had cut the poor sod's face in half. Interestingly the thief was about to be cauterized to prevent him from dying too soon, and his lordship had arrived just in time to enjoy the spectacle. The blazing iron was approaching amid great reverence and applause from its home in the brazier at that very moment.

"Morning your majity," the unusually short roughneck looked familiar.

"We been waiting for you." Michael rifled through his memories as the lad grinned at him expectantly.

"It's me sir, King Percy of Shit Street."

Astor's pleasure was the real thing. Dismounting he grasped the lad by the shoulders and shook him in affection.

"So, you passed muster King Percy. Are you glad that you joined?"

"That I am your majity. Muvver sends her love. She 'as a cottage now and good vittles. Fanks to you sir," The boy gasped; turning away as his emotions overwhelmed him. Remembering his Place despite his emotional predicament King Percy once again turned to face his employer, bowed and retreated concealing his tears, his new mates conciliatory and even affectionate. Astor waited a moment in order to catch the eye of the now recovered lad and having done so, nodded his approval and with that small and utterly cynical gesture bought the boy's loyalty for life.

Everything was ready. Four tall poles from which the hooks hung, marked the corners of a square and teams had been allotted to each of these, but the sheer joy of the day had been thoughtfully delayed until his arrival. Several men had found it necessary to stand on the chosen one as the red iron was applied to the truncated member, the sizzling sound of which operation would have turned the gut of a hardened gladiator as the victim thrashed about and feinted clean away only to be reinvigorated by freezing water.

"After you Sir," beamed Hastings, formal in the presence of the troops; as the army crowded around for the ceremony; gleeful as their generous employer selected a vicious hook that filled his palm. Standing over the agonized, now mindless criminal whose eyes protruded to an extraordinary degree Astor played to the crowd for a while bringing his hook ever closer to that agonised organ which stared blindly into a far distance. The crowd groaned, the victim hyperventilating. But no! The nape-of-the-neck perhaps? No! It was time. The tension palpable. Relocating to the region of the man's arse Astor crouched and without further play-acting drove his hook as deeply as it would go into the flesh of the perineum; that nerve-filled space between anus and scrotum. The applause was uproarious while Matey gyrated as though stung by a jellyfish, his eyes all but bursting; his shrieks of unsupportable agony denied by the bloody steel which enlarged his mouth.

Removing to the rear of the crowd Astor was pleased to mount his horse and await the 'flying,' while the rest of the hooks were imaginatively implanted to the accompaniment of much roaring, laughing and mock discomfort. The army turned to himself. Expectant. Standing dramatically in the stirrups, he paused theatrically for a long moment then threw his arms high and wide in an extravagant mimicry of flight.

The chosen one hurtled upwards, a naked condor of agony, unbearable, inhumane; white-hot mercury racing through every artery, vein, and capillary. The agony and the ecstasy, poorly distributed. Well pleased with his day's work Astor rode away at the walk, considerately leaving his men to enjoy themselves however they may with no authoritative impediment.

CHAPTER 14: Kissing Cousins

No longer caring a toss about going absent-without-leave but making a great show of innocently collecting rabbit food, Betty, Maid of all Work, sidled her way into the cover of the garden wall where she could not be seen from her loathsome prison then went quickly to where the waistcoat would be lying. For an awful moment, she could not locate it and her chagrin choked her. Even so, nothing in this world could upset her at this moment. Before escaping the 'bawdy house' by another name,' she had ripped to pieces the hated black clothes which the halfpenny forced her to wear and in an inspired moment had defecated in the bed. She went on with her pretence of picking broad leaves, methodically shoving aside the long grass with her shoe, then, quite suddenly, there it was, just where she had thrown it. Thrusting the treasure into her basket, she covered it with grass and slyly ambled away in no hurry at all.

Her excitement at the prospect of getting revenge was short-lived, for now that opportunity had presented its-self she was finding herself nowhere near as brave as she had believed. The very thought of talking to the likes of that giant hairy Scotty man what wore a skirt, or any of the bigwigs for that matter and showing her evidence to such as they, let alone accusing Penny of murder, was simply beyond her comprehension; why, she wouldn't even dare look at him. 'Macbeff! That were is name.'

Nothing if not resourceful, vengeful and bitter however, and true to the adage concerning scorned women, she quickly developed a plan. Determined and confident she set off with her head held high, throwing back the occasional vindictive glance at the scene of her year-long mélange of domestic drudgery, poverty, loneliness and sexual slavery imposed by a man whom she had lusted after but who cared less for her than he did for the house cat. Seeing its prison windows gleaming due solely to her own exertions with chamois and white vinegar she flitted back to the gate, grabbed a handful of pebbles and flung and flung until at last with a terrifying but hugely pleasing tinkle, one of the little diamonds shattered. Betty ran.

Walking at a rate which was almost running, as do all people who envisage something intensely pleasurable at the conclusion of their journey, the escaped prisoner made her way directly through the village, pausing at various cottages to purchase some cheese, a loaf, tomatoes and cider, then feeling very pleased with her forethought, hurried on towards the home of her much loved uncle. Her disappointment was as chilling as a winter wash in a frozen horse trough when she discovered Kane's absence from home; so eager was she to tell her tale and show him the damning evidence of Penny's guilt. Entering by the broken door she remembered to step across the rotting bit of floor just inside and having called-out and peeked into the other room she set about poking the banked-up fire for a cup of tea. The dross was cold to the touch and with that discovery, her spirits sank still further because there was no knowing with Kaney how long he might be away; sometimes it was days on end. No matter, she would make herself comfortable because she was here to stay. As usual, the old place was a mess, so throwing off her cloak and bonnet, Betty set-to. She lit the fire and got her kettle on for tea, but only after she'd taken out six buckets of ash, and once the water was set to boil, she cleared the coffin lid table and took all of the dirty pots outside to Kaney's pride and joy; the pump in the yard. Kane always used every one of his bits of spoons and plates and mugs before he would bother to wash them. Singing to herself she was cutting bread for cheese and tomato wedges when a huge dog dragged itself inside and, ignoring her, flopped down against the wall whining pitifully.

"Buttercup," cried Betty at seeing the animal's horrific wounds, and went to stroke her old friend but was repulsed by the stench of the suffering creature's rotting flesh.

"Outside boy," she said kindly.

"You can't be in here like that, you stink Buttercup," and despite its extreme condition, the animal got to its feet and staggered away, yelping at the worst of the excruciating pains which it was suffering. Betty grasped the superb double-barreled shotgun standing in the corner and broke it, finding both barrels loaded. Nervous and unsure but with growing determination the capable girl was about to step outside just as her Uncle Seed stepped in, as though over a large puddle.

"Uncle Kaney! Oh your face!'' she ran into his arms.

''Wot ave they 'done' to you?''

"Betty!" Seed squeezed her tightly.

"It's another ten years afore your day off; has that bastard Penny gorn soft in the ed? Its nuffin, it don't 'urt much no more really speaking.'' Betty shoved the heavy weapon into her uncle's hand as she touched those awful wounds.

"You got to go take care of Buttercup.''

Without a word, Seed gripped the weapon and went out again to do what he had been reluctant to do, even though his dog was in constant torment. Once Kane had been lost to sight in the undergrowth Betty too went outside, she undressed completely and washed herself at the pump, taking the greatest care in brushing out her damp hair, so that it would look its best when it dried.

Taking the bloodied waistcoat from her basket she hung it over the back of a chair. This was, she felt, the prelude to the most momentous events that would happen if she lived to be a hundred. An age dragged passed before she heard the report of Kaney's shotgun, but that was to be expected; she knew that the loving man would certainly dig Buttercup's grave first so that he could bury his friend quickly, once he had done what was needful. He loved that dog.

"Did you say a word over him?" she asked, all gentleness and consideration, as Seed threw the superb weapon carelessly into the corner and dropped into a seat at the coffin, troubled at heart and showing no interest in the food whatsoever.

"I did, lass but it weren't no bloody prayer. That's twice in a bleedin week. I should mayhap take up burying pu-fessional like. That bastard Penny 'as murdered two good friends of mine in about as many days. First Tans, and now Butter." Shocked by the news, Betty almost dropped the teapot. She sagged into the chair opposite her bereaved uncle and rested her arms on her lap to steady herself. The blood on that waistcoat she realized, was the lifeblood of Tansley Huffer. Penny had murdered that deviant, spineless, cripple.

"What is it, lass?" Kane was all concern as he came to comfort the girl, all thought of his loss thrust aside.

"That waistcoat there, Kaney?" she gasped.

"It's his. It's Penny's. And that muck, that's blood. It must be Tansley's."

"Fuck me dead!"

"He come sneakin' home smornin all wet with it, an' I nicked it cos he's a swine."

"I knew it, our Bett." Seed had stepped over to the garment with its brown stains showing in the spatter that blood always makes on you, no matter what you do. He scrutinized the material and the stuff on it but refrained from touching it, as though afraid that Penny's guilt might somehow rub off on him with the blood.

"He turned up here coosin me of doin' Tansley in. I knowed right away that if Tans were a gonner right enough, then it were Penny wot done for the poor little bugger. Made me do the burying he did. Said the bloody bench would take his word afore mine. And they would."

"Why would…?"

"Body burglin'. Him and Tans ave bin at if for long and weary. The mash musta gone sour. They were a open grave right there, as near to poor old Tans as I am to you Bett. I got old matey into it and covered him up." Seed had opened a drawer in a chest of drawers; a superb article of furniture quite as out of place in his hovel as a lion in a herd of goats and retrieved from it a cottage-made leather belt, which he held up, straight-armed, for Betty's scrutiny as though it were a live snake.

"This be old Tansley's, our Bett. I kep it wen I laid him to rest, poor sod. God, he were a mess. The bastard had used that shovel on him. Same one I had to use to bury him wiv. I tell you this, lass, wot is gospel; with your bit an' my bit, we'se got that swine Penny in our fist."

"What we goin' to do?"

Seed sat down at the table and began to eat ravenously, his appetite which had deserted him due to the business with Buttercup, having returned.

"We shall have to give it a bit of thought, our lass," said Seed, speaking through a mouth which exhibited bread, cheese, and tomato.

"Usn don't want to be leapin' out of the fire into the pan. Give us a cup o' tea, Bett. You bain't goin' back there, o' course. You's stayin' wi' me from ere on in, gal." At that point, the relatives fell into a companionable silence, each engrossed in his or her own thoughts, until the criminal broke the silence with an exclamation of such joy, that one would have thought he had found a nugget of gold amid the pile of food on his plate.

"Got it, Bett," he declared. "I appen to know a few of the souls as deals in stiffs and the likes. What I'll do, I'll have words and make sure that Penny, swings. He'll strangle by the neck when we's done wiv him."

Betty grinned maliciously. "I know'd you could do it you lovely man. Tell you wot.''

''Wots that then?''

''Afore I left, I shit in the bed,''

Kane almost choked in amusement at the news; speechless with joy. The girl would not admit it even to herself, but it was not because Penny was a murderer that she relished seeing him swing; it was because the swine had thrown her over for that skinny bitch, Abigail.

Kane, for his part, would barely admit to himself, let alone to Betty, that he wanted his revenge not for Tansley, or even for himself but for Buttercup. With his meal devoured, and with plenty of beer and some of Betty's cider to wash it down nicely, Kane threw himself down in the ruin of a chair which he found so very comfortable, and was about to light a pipe, when Betty came quickly to him and sat down on his lap, with an arm around his shoulders in a fashion which was intensely evocative to him, and his excitement was immediately visible to his niece.

"Would you like something sweet after that, you handsome man?" She touched him fleetingly.

"No no my dear, we can't be doin' that," Kane was well aware of the utter lack of conviction in his voice.

"Why is that then?" the girl asked, letting her full breast accidentally touch his face.

"Big Kaney loves to bounce on little Betty for hours and hours."

"Wot if you get up the duff, Beth? It'll have five arms." His words lacked even so much as a shred of resistance.

"I'll make it wash the bloody pots," Betty announced triumphantly, and gripping Seed's very hard penis, lead the happy man to the sour unmade bed.

To his knowing eye the cool drizzle of dawn would last all day, so Seed struggled in to his wet-weather gear and was about to go outside to feed Buttercup, when he was confronted by the cold knowledge that he had been robbed of the untrammeled love of that great friend. He would never again exchange greetings with the steadfast creature. His resolve hardened.

"I'm going to kill you dead as mutton, Penny," he said to himself, and with that, he went to the unusually tidy fireplace and threw together a large breakfast of black pudding, eggs, ham, mushrooms, lamb chops and potato, all of which he fried over the fire in tasty dripping.

As he left the house, Betty lay very attractive with her hair in disarray, and with her face turned to one side lit by such an expression of wanton carnality that his arousal was instant, and he came as near as his left was to his right to mounting her as she slept. She loved to be waked-up that way, did Betty. On an afterthought, he left on the table, the money which he had got when he sold the goats and potatoes that the shipyard paid him. He had considered leaving Hooligan's silver also but had come to his senses just in time. It was, after all, sheer folly for a man to give a female person more cash than she absolutely needed. Retrieving a bit of charcoal from the fire, he wrote on the bare wood adjacent to the coins:

'meet bred luv kan xx', then went out to deliver justice. "Not likely," he told himself. "Get me own back."

His intended destination, the busy and fast-growing seaport of Poole lay at a hell of a walk, and that would be in good weather, along a decent road, all of which *this* journey would not be. Once through Alsop and Minster, he would be forced to take to the pretty-way and stay clear of the roads because the nearer a lone traveler came to the coast of late, the greater the chance of his being snatched by the press gangs, and Kane Seed was having none of that. The drizzle persisted all the way to Alsop, whose outposts of orchards and occasional grey-stone cottages, water mill and proper stone-built bridges, Seed enfiladed around mid-morning having been unfortunate enough not to benefit from a ride of so much as a yard on the back of a cart on the way. In the town's commercial heart where the stalls, the eating places banks and the stock-sales were located, he found the place all but deserted probably due to the inclement weather; a state of affairs which suited his purpose well enough, because it was like taking an apple from a child to select the best rake from those on display at the door of the hardware seller, and walk off with it over his shoulder as soon as no one was looking. Just around the corner he came to another place which sold rakes that were obviously made by the same man. Kane barged right in with a show of 'devil may care.'

"Not the best day for it I see," declared the proprietor, who had clearly mastered the art of stating the obvious.

"What can we be doing you for today?" The little fellow rubbed his soft hands together at the prospect of larceny.

"It's me new-bought rake," Seed announced sorrowfully.

"I'm only just recent bought him and never yet had the pleasure of workin' wi' such as him an' father's gone an' sold up and usn is off to distant lands. So, I's 'bliged to return him for cash." The man's hands ceased washing each other, his face fell with a down-turning at the corners of his wet mouth and a great slumping of the shoulders in sympathy with the other parts, and just as Seed began to think that the subsidence was complete, the fellows chirpy voice descended several octaves to subterranean depths in as sad a lament as the thief had ever heard.

"I have a wet-weather-coat which you can have in its stead? You'll need it for the voyage. It's not a lot dearer…?"

"I cannot," said Seed forcibly. "Father telt me, cash, and nuthin' but cash, an' don' come back here without it, or else." The mere thought that 'father's' anger might be deflected from this ruffian onto himself, was quite sufficient to change the little man's mind on the business of a refund, and he reluctantly handed over the price of the rake, which he counted out from the leather bag suspended around his pendulous tummy. Such was his distaste for the vulgar individual that he received the implement handed to him as though he were Herod and the customer Moses.

Seed tucked the coins away in his purse and went on down the road looking for his next opportunity to do business, but was to be disappointed, as many of the stallholders and traders in all manner of stuff for the farm and cottage, were closed-up tight. There was no way on this earth that a bit of rain which had stopped now in any event, could be the reason behind this odd state-of-affairs. He picked up the pace, irritated that such a long journey might pay very little in return, outside of revenge on Penny, the bastard. The explanation for the deserted state of the road from home to Alsop, became abundantly clear on leaving the little market town, and taking the road to Minster. With each mile that passed, the one-way traffic flowing towards that center of commerce and industry grew more and more numerous. Before long, he found the opportunity to ask a carter travelling alone with a seat to spare, why it was that this great mass of humanity was deserting the fields and the barns and their cottage piecework, to flock like headless chickens to that unexceptional town.

"Why, can you not sniff it on the breeze, neighbour?" demanded the carter. "Some fine lad have 'stracted 'vengency on that disciple of Satan, Mucky Mickey Astor," the carter paused at that point to spit on Michael Astor's shadow, "and burned his sweatshop to ash, and us is all agoin' over for a good gloat and to damp the cinders down with our own tears, now that we is without work. Or put out o' business as the case may be, an' about to starve, either way. Git up here an' sit like a Christian.

"No!'' Seed felt the noose coming up tight around his neck. 'So this is what that rare beauty Lliam Hooligan was about.'

''Why did I not think of it?'' He was now going to swing for something which he did *not* do, after a life of getting away with the things he *did* do. Sure as eggs was eggs, the Astors would dig into this business like foxes into a chicken run, and they would find out soon enough everything that there was to be finded out; plus more besides. Then again, there was just a chance that this was a coincidence. What he had to do was to get to the truth of the matter before those Astor swine did, and if necessary, ship out in a hurry.

"Maybe it was just a accident. Baccy from a pipe?" He said lamely.

"Them things don' fire off broadsides and sail away in a fist full of ships m'dear," said the carter. "There be no question of it bein' no haccident."

Seed fell into a morose thoughtful silence, and the carter, being a more perceptive sort than one might have imagined, let the tramp get on with it. With still a mile to go before the outskirts of Minster-proper had been reached, the pedestrian progress on the road came to a halt altogether, and Seed leapt down without a word of thanks or farewell to proceed on foot among the bovine masses eventually finding it necessary to get off the road and walk through the fields, until at last he merged with the onlookers, standing six deep along the boundary of a field of dirty snow which was all that remained of the Astor's shipyard. Keeping his ears open and his mouth shut, he soon judged the mood of the crowd to be virulently opposed to the Astors and everything that those greedy satanists touched while showing great empathy with the 'mericans, whomever *they* might be even though many of the crowd had earned their living in the yard. Queueing to buy a hot pasty at a stall set up on the very edge of the great field of cinders, he was able to earwig on endless opinions about the recent events here, their causes, likely repercussions and much else. It transpired that this shipyard was the biggest employer of men this side of a place called Constance Tinpole, which lay a week's walk away, over by Portsmouth, there being almost four hunnered men working inside its gates and naturally all of these men and their famblies were now without a coin and would likely starve to death as their vegetable plots could not possibly provide in sufficient quantity. That stood to reason. There was more to come. Some of the aggrieved members of the crowd were those who supplied the yard with the miles of cordage, acres of canvas, rivers of paint and forests of spars, ironwork and masts that go into every vessel built, and these people it seemed, had manufactured at great expense to themselves, tons of what they called 'stock,' which they would now be unable to sell. All of this, however, was mere gossip to a realist the likes of Seed, and with a criminal's intuition, he departed the scene in search of real insight into these events and the depth of this filthy mire in which he now found himself, due to Lliam bloody Hooligan, bless him. The riverside and its docks were where the poor, the sick, the habitually drunk, the crippled and the unscrupulous congregated, and there he soon found what he was looking for. High on a muddy bank with her soot-black stern still swimming, a waterlogged coaster, her rotting, mildewed planking sporting a festive coat of emerald moss and variegated marsh flowers had been winched almost out of the river and was now in use as a tavern. Above the hole in her hull which was the door, hung a badly painted swan with some badly written words badly spelled beneath, while around the black and ominous cave hung a ragged crowd of penniless vagabonds, waiting there endlessly in the hope that a miracle would occur and the admission fee; the price of a pot of ale, would fall from the sky and avail them the happiness of this their second home. He made to enter, his hands thrust deeply into his pockets but a grey skinned lout who breathed loudly through his mouth blocked him and grabbed at his throat only to instantly release his grip and double in pained surprise as Seed's unseen dagger pricked his groin horribly close to his penis. Wordless, Seed entered buying himself a cup of rum after asking piteously of the mountain of white flesh who served him, how much this would cost, he then counted out that figure in halfpence. This he did in order to ensure the watchers, of whom there were plenty that he was not worth robbing. He passed over the coin as though it was his last and watched in mild amusement as beer which had been spilled at one end of the plank, slowly ran the length of the thing and dribbled off the other, the place and its poor furniture lying noticeably out of true. Within minutes of washing up at the Swan, Seed was rewarded for his forward-thinking with the truth, straight from the horse's mouth, of the catastrophic fire. At the barrel-top next to the one on which he rested his pot, sat an old, dry husk of a man with wet eyes and toothless pink gums, whom it transpired, worked as a night watchman for Astor and Son, Shipwrights. He was telling his tale for the hundredth time, being well served with free drinks for his trouble.

"Anyways," sighed the old fellow, "as Thomas thought to go orff for a stroll, an' me not feelin' particular' up to it, what did I do but sneak int-ter rope stack wheres a man could earwig on them 'merica fellas. Now, I must've dropped off like…"

"Never. Not you, young Albert Folley."

Albert Folley ignored this remark imperiously.

"Anyow, I is a-wokened by a near riot goin' on aboard *Glorious*, cos hold and below, them drunk lords is now bein' carted home away, arter that there public fornication an' wot not. I could not look. Not I. Then, as God be my witless, there be a stranger wot I never afore set heyes on happear. As near to me as you is now, Sam Collins; only twice as igh and put together like Simpson's bull ower in Evenhoe Quarter."

"Hung like a bull, eh Albert. And just how, might I ask, is you privy to that?"

"He be saying to em that he be goin' to set em free so's they can help him set fire to Astor's erection."

"Wichis ow eight o them vestalls come to dishappear," volunteered another old timer who had endured the story eight times. "*Glorious, Coromandel…*"

"Now!" bawled Folley, with surprising volume, casting a filthy glance at the interloper,

"We come to the himportant bit. Plain as day, the big feller, he sez to the prisoners, them 'mericans, he sez, 'My name…' he ses, he ses, 'My name is Hoo Logan, and I as come to burn out the filfy slavers, Astor and Son, Shipwrights. Curse them.'"

"Bollocks. There bain't be a 'Ooo Logan' this side o' Brissle, an' I should know cos I been traipsin' all over in me line o' work fer forty year'n more."

"Wot line o' work would that'n be then, 'enry 'orrocks? avin' it away wiv uver folks aminals," Insisted a huge red face, adorned with ginger sideboards as it winked conspiratorially at a quiet gang of watchful thugs.

"It's twue, wight 'nough," belched a drunken lad.

"Farver spake to this big work at fella. Black fella. Black as yer at. An' e said as they was fightin;' im an his mates agen' the pern... persh... per-ni-sush sellin' of ooman beans."

"I run down a lookin' for Thomas." yelled Albert Folley.

"But he were nowheres to be found by man or beast, even when the sky went afire."

"You 'run' down, did you Albert?" enquired a listener who was of similar vintage to the storyteller.

"I barely got out of it cooked right through," declared Albert with the skill of a practiced drinker of other person's liquor.

"But Thomas; well, he din't come home this mornin' so him must've bin cinderated, cos I spake to 'is old lady. Anyhow, them musta seed me cos them fired a broadside straight at my corporal bein."

"I woonta come home niver if I were wed to that'n," said the red face.

"It would be you as them 'mericans were arter then Albert." someone concluded mischievously.

"But ten cannon wunt up to that job, eh lad? Us stood on the mole earlier alookin' at the deverstations, an' what should be floatin' there but a bleedin' gypo wiv more oles in him than a sieve, an' my word on it. I tell you one an' all; there be somethin' goin' on here." Seed had heard more than enough. He drank up and left; the crowd outside giving him safe passage, and made his way between cottages, reduced to ruin by the conflagration. He had abandoned his plan of walking to Poole because he was now deeply preoccupied with the matter of how he could benefit from the immense good fortune of Lliam bloody Hooligan. 'A fist full of ships!' The man was suddenly rich beyond the telling of it. It was time for Kane Seed to renew his acquaintance with his great friend and seein' if a bit of that good fortune would rub off on himself and mayhap get his club back. Resorting to the field paths for the homeward leg of his aborted journey, Seed soon met up with a horse which he deemed as lonely as any he had ever met, and out of the goodness of his heart he addressed it kindly. He stroked the creature's neck and muzzle gently till it walked with him across its own field and then through a further two by which time the tired traveler had put his belt around the animal's neck and was resting his knapsack on its back to determine how well disposed it was to being ridden. Well-clear of the site of the theft, he mounted and rode the rest of the way home in style.

"I'm going up in the world, our Betty," he announced, riding out of the tobacco weed, and startling the girl as she hung bits of washing to dry on the bushes. Noticing that his niece had washed a bit of linen for the bed and her petticoats also, he immediately became lewd.

"Have you got something planned, woman?" he asked, glancing suggestively at the stolen cotton.

"You'll just have to wait and see, young Kane," she replied haughtily. And studying the horse said admiringly,

"My word, but he could be your brother." At this remark, Kane lost all self-control as the girl had intended him to. Leaping down, he wrestled her to the ground and thrust his way into the very willing wench, on the spot, concealing exquisite gentleness within his wild assault. Betty was so receptive to this forthright approach; so convulsive under him that he was goaded to a fury which transported them, and in mere moments, both protagonists were freed of their earthly bonds. Separating as energetically as they had come together, in order to get their breath, they lay on their backs in the mud a yard apart, gasping and laughing outrageously at the sheer ecstasy which they had just conjured.

Betty made tea and placed food on the bench where Kane was sitting while telling her about the events of the day and the surprise that had been waiting in store for him. Though his neice was a good listener, and coaxed him on with his tale, and wanted more clarity about various parts of it, he was dimly aware that she was distracted by something or other, and he resolved to ask her considerately whether anything was amiss. As he drained his mug of tea having consumed sufficient bread and mutton, the girl came directly to him, hoist up her skirt and stepping over him, stood astride, wafting her heady scent into his face. Tantalizingly, slowly, she lowered herself, finding him and drawing him in to her with the most seductive undulations of her perfect hips. With a touch that was lighter than a petal, she kept his eager hands at bay; reading his expression intently and reveling in the pleasure that she was giving him. Kane thought no more about fires, other than the furnace in his woman's belly.

CHAPTER 15: Strange Bedfellows

The most magnificent stallion that Trewin Copplestone had ever been privileged to gaze upon pranced in to view and stood, pawing the ground at the shipyard gates white foam descending in quantity from its open mouth. The black-hearted beast must have been torn from a seam of anthracite by Beelzebub himself for such animus to be melded with physical perfection. Composed of sterner stuff than its timorous rider, the creature was well-acquainted with the man's fear. The posturing individual had obviously been driven to challenge himself in this manner for deep-seated reasons which were privy to him alone; why else would he put his life at risk in this manner? The extravagantly decorative scabbard and the pistol secreted in his knee-high riding boots were further testimony to the many and deep flaws in the feint heart's character. Dismounting with poorly concealed signs of relief and tethering his nemesis despite the utmost difficulty, the rider came bandy legged towards the very modest pie shop above which the spy was putting together the many parts of a puzzle.

"It's time for lunch." Copplestone the inquisitive descended to the public room but had not yet reached the foot of the stairs when he realized that it was himself who was already being scrutinized; surreptitiously at that. The man was as sharp as a tack. The sartorially splendid Bismark Astor had been served coffee which he poured into the clever little cup that was the cap of his hip flask; clearly this lord of the land harbored no aversion to rubbing shoulders with the common man, but he drew the line at drinking from his jug. Consuming his beverage thirstily he placed a coin on the table, made a last recce* of the soldier, completing his appraisal with eye-contact sustained just a little too long to be benign and departed.

*reconnaissance

Seargent Trewin Copplestone was now utterly certain that his mad Irish friend had somehow got himself inside that gigantic enterprise across the road. He could not for the life of him imagine why; but whatever the reason, he was prepared to do everything that was required in order to extricate the loon safely. Bar none. Devouring a delicious meal of beef-and-vegetable pie, accompanied by a jug of cider, Copplestone was content to curb his impatience and observe what would eventuate now that the enemy were aware of him. He did not have long to wait. He had barely relinquished his fork when an apprentice-boy came sidling across the street trying ridiculously hard to be inconspicuous only to concentrate attention like the sting of a hornet. The snot-nosed urchin took up a position at the double doors, lent against the post with exaggerated nonchalance and searched assiduously until he found what he was looking for in Trewin's own face. Copplestone allowed his glance to slide over the inept sleuth, and thereafter ignored him; an aim which was easily achieved as the lad's snot had now reached his open mouth. Two coffees later, no less than three more apprentice boys exited the yard, though unlike the pimply individual who preceded them, these three came on at the charge, and headed into town only for two of them to come hurtling passed on horseback ten minutes later, scaring the geese, pigs, sheep, and female pedestrians, and being chased by every dog in the street. Trewin Copplestone simply 'had' to get a better view of what was going on inside that sweatshop. Climbing the stairs he strode to the rear of the rambling old building, climbed out of a tiny knee-high window and dropped to the ground, thereby frightening the life out of a maid who was peeling potatoes in the shade beneath a porch.

"Oh, Lord save me," the girl squealed, as a man crashed out of the sky just a step or two from where she sat; leaping to her feet the lass allowed her tin bowl to clatter to the ground

"I'm not the Lord," the fallen angel assured the flower,

"It's merely a family likeness," and seizing her in his arms, he kissed the pretty thing adoringly on the mouth. A moment later, he was hurrying toward the stables while the lass was hurrying inside, to tell everyone she knew; and a goodly number that she didn't, how she had been thoroughly kissed by a handsome young man who simply could not restrain himself. The sergeant well knew from his earlier reconnaissance of the town, that the best view of the goings-on in the shipyard would be got from a half-forested hill which dominated the site's northern boundary. Striding quickly through the back alleys to the King's Road Stables, he learned there through guarded enquiry that sure enough, the three boys had hired horses on the account of 'Astor and Son, Shipwrights.' Ten minutes later as he considered the barrow from the foot of its steep wooded side, he said to Bengal, who was an excellent listener,

"It wouldn't surprise me if we find that Lliam has spied here before us, old chap." Pleasingly, Bengal nodded vigorously in agreement. He undertook the near-vertical climb on foot and had no sooner reached the point where the very best view would be obtained, than he discovered a bed of dry grasses, discarded apple cores and a fire pit.

"Well, I'll be damned," he remarked happily.

"You never said a truer word." The owner of the Scottish accent was very close behind him. The dragoon turned slowly and found himself looking straight into the boastfully blue eyes of Macbeth though the irritant stood a foot below him. 'This rude impossibly hirsute, and mentally unbalanced individual,' was the husband of the woman he loved.

"You really arr a pain in the arse private."

Copplestone's left hand was on his scabbard.

"I'm delighted to hear it,'' he drawled.

''When we met last, I explained in terms which even a Scot might understand, that as you had insulted me, I would have to demand satisfaction." The sound of furious galloping caused Macbeth to turn, and the interlocutors abandoned their play-acting to watch engrossed as a rider sped away from the foot of the barrow across the open pasture, mounted on no other horse than Bengal.

"The little bastard," Macbeth's rage was volcanic.

"It looks like that big nose o' yoors has cost ye yer horse, soldier boy. That wee bokle Derwent willnae be back now that he's away."

"We shall see," the soldier's eyes were dagger-points in the thief's back. Bengal crossed the open ground at a full gallop urged on by the boy Derwent who clearly did not lack courage. As horse and rider approached an impossibly deep hedge of briar, boulders and gorse, the young fellow gathered his mount, rose in the stirrups and was catapulted out of the saddle as Bengal's legs seemed to break beneath him. A howl of concern issued from a watching gang who now sat their mounts far below. For a long moment, dust all-but-concealed the fates of both horse and rider; then Bengal reappeared, quite uninjured; his supreme musculature shivering beneath his sweating grey hide as he recovered his sense of calm. The gang sounded their relief. With the reins hanging, the beauty trotted back to where his master had left him. 'None of those men who had materialized below had moved a muscle to assist their erstwhile comrade.' It was all beyond Sergeant Trewin Copplestone's comprehension.

"What do ye think you're doing here?" Macbeth demanded as though the incident with horse and rider had not occurred.

"I answer to no man; and that includes those in skirts. If you feel the need to ask questions, why not go and ask your fellow thief why he stole my horse? Always assuming that the fool is still alive" Copplestone was sure that calling the Scotsman a thief would promote the violent response which he sought but he was disappointed.

"You're lookin' fer yer wee pal, are ye not?"

It was as though Trewin hadn't opened his mouth.

"I am. Not that it's any of your damned business."

"And in all of England, you came tae look, frae this wee hill, in this wee toon. How wus that, by the by?" To investigator Copplestone's intense satisfaction, Macbeth's inability to ascertain his motives was clearly choking the oaf. He therefore shook his head in exaggerated sympathy.

"Don't dwell on it 'Muckpile'," he advised, "you'll give yourself a nasty headache." No matter how inventive and amusing his insults he simply could not get Macbeth to draw his sword, or even swing one of those hairy hams.

"I've something tae show ye, 'Cop a feel.'" Macbeth trudged up the remainder of the steep slope, brushing insolently past the smaller man, and disappearing further into the trees at the top of the barrow, only yards from where Lliam had done his spying on the activities of Astor and Son, Shipwrights.

"Come here, man," the kilt snorted, irascible as before and proffering a telescope. Inexplicably, the loon obviously harbored the view that where he went, the rest of humanity should follow. He was beyond belief. Copplestone did as he was bid nevertheless.

"See the big oak on this boundary o' the yard; come round tae ten o'clock and search the timber stacks." With an ill grace, Trewin accepted the instrument, and put it to his eye. He found the oak immediately, and traversed slowly eastward, till he was looking at the wide area of drying timber, stacked roof-beam high; the protruding fillets all clearly visible through the exceptional instrument; so much superior to military issue. Nothing! He continued to do as he was instructed even so, maintaining his vigil patiently, traversing from one end of the area to the other then back, always moving slowly, pedestrian now so as not to. 'What was that?' He had seen something move. He traversed again, finding the place where the bit of movement occurred. Nothing. He had not imagined it. The searcher held steady on that same spot and there, a few minutes later, seemingly close enough to touch, emerged like a giant badger, the big sore face and the one good eye of Lliam Shaun Hooligan, the finest man in Christendom.

With only the top of his head now visible, the big fellow appeared to scan just one point of the compass, then, taking no chances, disappeared, only to turn up five minutes later at a second vantage point to repeat the process. Lliam Hooligan was tucked away in the middle of Astor's boatyard for purposes which were, of course, 'far too rough for one of Copplestone's own gentle disposition.' The soldier almost cried out in the simple pleasure of seeing his great friend, 'Lliam, you mad man, you.' Instead, he turned to the Scots ape,

"What on earth is he doing?" he asked.

"Swing tae nine o'clock," the beard grunted, and when Trewin did as he was ordered, the reason for the instruction was immediately obvious. On the deck of the massive and seemingly brand-new ship, lying in what appeared to be a dry dock, was of all things, a huge table set for dinner; above which was a protective canopy of sorts. The rigging had grown a flower garden of bunting; the 'flag of union,' hung from the jack staff, and redcoats stood on guard at the foot of the gangplank.

"What's he doing in there?" Trewin repeated himself, meaning Lliam Shaun Hooligan

"Time enough for that later, laddy. We've got wurrk tae do. C'mon alang wi' me." Copplestone charged out of control down the side of the barrow in Macbeth's wake, but still the Scotsman made time on him, and was already mounted when Trewin stumbled out of the gorse into the detachment of mounted men waiting there.

"The *Burrd*, we'd better take it sooner rather than later," shouted Macbeth, still incandescent at the recent desertion, and this seemed to mean something to everyone except the soldier. The cavalry moved off at a canter behind the Scottish wild man, while a riderless horse flung around, kicking and bridling and doing its best to bring everyone to grief. Disengaging; Copplestone set off in the tracks of the thief Derwent and having found his stirrup in the grass, did a careful job of re-attaching it, then he went in search of the criminal. Clambering through the mess of briar and wild cherry which formed the hedge, he located the youth just yards away, as he emerged on the other side.

A chill the likes of which he had not suffered since the best-forgotten events of the Khyber Pass, took him so completely by surprise, that he was forced to gird his loins vigorously as though about to charge with a squadron of lancers. The thief was dead. That much was instantly evident. It was the posture of that death which was shocking; it was impossibly ritualistic. 'This was not Afghanistan!' On his knees, head hanging; face concealed by his long, blood-matted hair. An unnatural, not to say, impossible posture for a dead man. The corpse was blood-soaked. The sergeant went quickly to where the carcass knelt; some unimaginable contraption of torture becoming increasingly apparent with every step. Then he had it. A huge set of steel jaws with the triangular, serrated teeth of a white shark had slammed shut with immeasurable impact on the poor devil. Clearly the boy had activated the murderous device as he knelt in the grass, having been thrown from the saddle. He had struggled desperately for his life, but bleeding from so many atrocious wounds, his strength would have deserted him all too soon. Thief or otherwise, Trewin would not leave the young fellow there like that. The least he could do would be to take his remains home. He shrugged out of his leather jerkin, intending to protect his hands with it from those awful spikes as he pulled the jaws apart. Getting down carefully in the grass, he was positioning himself with his boots set against one of the jaws while gripping the other with both hands, when two of Macbeth's toughs appeared above him

"Get away from it! Smartly," ordered one. ''You'll lose yer ands.''

Cognisant of the real concern and dire warning in the fellow's tone, Copplestone hurriedly did as he was told, allowing the smaller of the two men to take his place in the grass and feel for a release trigger beneath the plate. The man clearly knew what he was doing, and easily located what he was looking for. Between them, the three then carefully exerted some mild pressure, and the viciously filed teeth pulled reluctantly out of the victim's still-warm flesh. The jerking moment of release causing a sucking sound that would have turned the stomach of less warlike characters. The body was free.

"I'll take him home," said Trewin.

ing229

"We'll show you the way," the taller of the two men replied, in a tone which would brook no argument, and Trewin understood that whatever the outcome with the would-be horse thief, these two were under orders not to let himself out of their sight. Macbeth knew his business and no mistake.

''So much for comradeship!'' Snapped the soldier.

"He broke ranks. And he disobeyed orders," retorted the big fellow.

"He coulda buggered the whole effort and cost us our."

"He's better off like this." The quieter individual seemed very thoughtful.

"He'd ave paid a 'igh price when Mucbef got a holt on 'im."

About to ask what price it was that could be greater than a man's life, the dragoon thought better of it. He had, after all, a deep and abiding knowledge of the form which that price might take.

"That bastard, Astor. This is wot he does to us. English born and bred. Mantraps for chrissake. Not content wi' torturing black folks. He has to do this to us'n an'all."

"The bastards. They's all the bleedin' same."

"They?" asked Trewin querulously, tilting his head back a fraction.

"The gentry. The landed bloody gentry. Who d'ya bloody fink?" The horseman's words were uttered with some heat, and implied that Trewin should understand such obvious truths.

"The slavers, the bloody drunken lords. The bleedin' aristocracy. Them wot pays a man enough to starve on, an' turfs him on to the road when he's worn-thin."

"But this can't be legal?" Trewin indicated with an inflection the horror before him. "Any child out playing could have stood in this thing."

"Course they could, but that don' matter to our dear friend, his bloody lordship. Oh no. Wot matters to him is that no bastard but him can get a pheasant or a rabbit. An' the bloody frogs call us 'rostbiffs.' Not bloody likely. Where the ell ave you been?"

"It's legal alright. You arks Mucbef. He can do as he bloody well likes. These 'ere bigwigs; them makes laws as suits 'emselves, see." The thoughtful one clearly had a better understanding of his world than one might suspect.

"We ain't got all day, let's get this bleeder home an' catch up or we'll miss the big quid." The tall man clearly had little time for this maudlin introspection.

"We'll put im on my oss. The bugger's bloody bullet proof."

Copplestone surprised his escort by lifting the obscenity, wrestling the bloody murderous contraption through the hedge and securing it with some difficulty behind his own saddle. He had approached the thing with a large stone which he dashed-down full force on to the release plate, causing the jaws to clash together with a violence that shocked him to the soles of his boots. He was not inclined to provide an explanation of his intentions, and neither of his captors 'arksed' for one, though they exchanged significant looks. The manufacturers of the disgusting invention, were so proud of their handywork that they had incorporated their name in its frame; 'Wurm and Son, North Bank, Birmingham.'

The cavalry drew rein in a copse which lay within sight of the Great South Road. Here the Scot left half a dozen of his men with instructions that they should travel to the prearranged meeting point by going through Minster itself, keeping their eyes peeled for any gatherings of the enemy. They were to leave at long intervals and make their way through the town-proper by various streets, and always at the walk attracting no attention at all. The main body crossed the artery unseen, one at a time, then regrouped in a deep gulley through which ran a stream. With the passing of each quarter mile or so of their progress along the banks of that stream, the man in the rear of the file would disengage and make his own way by such farm tracks and bridle ways as he might come across. By this means, the riders took a route which saw them journey in a large and generally semi-circular path around Minster, which culminated in a wooded cwm by the riverside just south of the town. Here they regrouped and after tending to their horses and unsaddling reported to the leader then threw themselves down to rest until the real action of the day commenced.

The appearance of that nosey soldier boy had come as a big surprise to Macbeth. The Scot sat apart from his men as he mulled over the various possibilities that the fellow's presence could conceal. If Trewin Copplestone was a spy, then he was in the best possible company; big Daniel and his reticent friend, Doya by name; either one of those accomplished assassins could finish off the wee soldier before breakfast and wouldn't think twice about it if firm evidence of the man's treachery was discovered. Whoever and whatever he was though, the wee tough had a head on his shoulders. To come to the very place that Lliam Hooligan had come, with not so much as a clue as to the business at hand, he had to be a right sneaky wee bastart, despite his 'holier than thou' ways. Even so, Macbeth liked the wee bokle; just the same as he liked poor, ignorant Hooligan and hoped devoutly that 'Cop A Feel,' was *not* a spy, because he didn't really relish the idea of breaking the snotty little midget's neck. Such an act would end the very promising career of one Lliam Hooligan, who was shaping up brilliantly, but would stick to his wee friend's memory like shit to a blanket. As day became evening; a process which was much accelerated beneath the trees of the cwm, the faint strains of Mozart came to the ears of the men lying there. Those sounds would have emanated from one source only.

"Enjoy it while you can, Astor," someone said cryptically, and those within hearing nodded in stern agreement. The evening passed by and gave way to night; and aboard the *Glorious*, the Mozart gave way to bawdy songs; witty banter became riotous nonsense as satisfying one's appetite for food and drink became gluttony. Alcohol-fueled aggression and lechery ruled the day, all of it audible a mile downstream.

"It's time," announced Macbeth.

"Black yersels" With those few words, the gang stripped naked and began blacking their faces and upper limbs with lumps of charcoal from their saddle bags. Trewin, big Daniel and the quiet man, Doya, chose this moment to ride into camp.

"Can you swim?" a shadowy figure asked, as the three latecomers dismounted. Realizing that it was himself that was being addressed, the soldier replied with a grunt and a barely visible nod; though the ship lying in the river, and which he assumed to be the *Bird*, seemed to be a hell of a long way out.

"Barabas, you will take care of the horses." Macbeth's voice, unusually quiet now, came from among the trees.

"Yus, sur, Mr Mucbeff sur" came the reply. Barabas had the voice of a mere boy.

"We'll go upstream a coupla hunnerd yards. We'll swim oot and agenst the flow. When ye get out level with the *Burrd*, just let the current float ye doon tae her, and we'll go up the anchor chains at the bow.

"'Copp a feel,' black yersell, even in darkness you'l stand oot like dogs' balls. Remember, the Americans are all prisoners below decks. Anybuddy walkin' aboot has tae be dealt tae. Right?" There came a murmur of assent. Macbeth wanted Trewin to answer the question.

"Copplestone! Anybuddy not locked up has to be dealt with, understand?" he insisted.

"I do, Macdeath. I understand English particularly well. Such a pity that you don't speak it," Trewin articulated; quietly but loudly enough for every man present to hear. No one laughed and the ensuing silence warned Copplestone that he was on very thin ice in mocking this man. What was being demanded of him was nothing new to the soldier, and he was not about to fail Lliam, no matter what it took. That mantrap incident had caused in him an anger which raged for revenge on the monkeys who sat on England's shoulders, pissing on everyone else. The black chain gang made their way upstream, slipping and stumbling in the darkness until they were a considerable distance above the place where the *Bird* lay at anchor. There under the trees, they gathered close around their messiah to benefit from his pearls of wisdom.

"Right lads," the creature looked and growled more like a black bear than ever without his clothes, "We've nae bones tae pick wi' oor ain sort, so nae killing if ye can avoid it. Wurrk quietly and strike a blow against slavery this night, and another against the drunken lords. Its here where ye start tae earn the big quid and I'll be watchin. Remember if you are unfortunate this night your people will be well cared fer, a cottage and a wee bit dirt. Swim 'upstream' as well as out, memba. Take good care o' yer comrades."

With that, the men left the concealment of the trees and went down into the black river. Macbeth stood chest-deep in the shallows until every member of the party swam past him, then followed the slow-moving pod, in the fashion of a killer-whale working a shoal of herring. If anybody got into trouble, he would help the unfortunate man before there was any floundering and splashing around, thus warning the sentries on the *Bird* of the coming attack. These were good men however, and he had no real qualms about any of them, though the incident with the Barb horse earlier in the day, still rankled as a great failure of judgment on his part.

'It was just as well for that young Derwent bastard that he had killed himself in the process of disobeying orders.' Macbeth was still irked by the memory of Rickets; and now this! He resolved then and there to be a hell of a sight more careful in his choice of men; even for the most menial tasks, the stakes were too high to permit him these errors of judgment. In midstream, the pod rested and lay perfectly still in the water. They no longer fought the current, allowing it to carry them directly downstream towards the *Bird* and into musket range. Still unseen, as far as anyone could tell, they drifted, almost invisible in their war paint but nervous as kittens and expecting at any moment to hear the explosions of long rifles, and to suffer the agony of the lead shot tearing into their flesh. It seemed to take forever, but at last they came up on her anchor chains undiscovered. Many an impatient individual found other routes up her sides and on to her decks while Macbeth and big Daniel lead the bulk of the party aboard, they swarmed silently over her bows and crouched in deep shadow till the last man had made it.

Unusually, there was not a soul in the rigging. A guard was soon found, deeply asleep in a coil of rope at the bow. He was woken with a hand over his mouth and a dagger at his eyes.

"How many, and where are they?" A naked man with a ploughed field of a back shoved the point of the blade to within an inch of the terrified sailor's eyes.

"Great cabin."

They flew along the open deck and reached their several objectives without meeting a soul. Dropping down the gangway, the murderous individuals paused, regrouping at swing doors from beyond which the sounds of drunken nonsense emanated. With a nod of his head and roaring like a force-twelve gale, Macbeth hurled himself into the cabin, lashing out with his fists at every drunken loathsome face he confronted. This heartening example was followed, with some refinement, by Trewin Copplestone and others whom it transpired, were clearly pugilists of some note; to such great effect that those who came after them found very little to hit that was still standing and had to expend their pent-up aggression by battering and kicking the fallen. It was all over in a few minutes with less blood spilt than would fill a pewter beer mug.

"Keys. Give me the keys," a hugely muscled fighter roared into the face of a man whom he was shaking by the throat, and the terrified sailor's glance rested on an individual who was now trying desperately to look innocent and inconspicuous as he crawled under a table. The gang turned their attention to this disgrace for a man, kicked him unconscious, rolled him onto his back and slashed his wide leather belt on which the keys hung. The sailor, beyond all control of his bodily functions wet his breeches copiously, crying like a child in his induced sleep. In the rear of Macbeth's army those who had thus far been denied the holy grail of extreme violence had heard a girl crying somewhere and charged away in the direction of that intoxicating sound soon smashing through the door of a cabin on the next deck where they found themselves in the disgusting scene that is gang rape. Bawling like cattle they attacked the rapist scum with fists boots and daggers, their weapons used in an incoherent frenzy of hate for these throwbacks to an age without reason. Arterial blood sprayed satisfyingly, and men bathed happily in it. Scalps, testicles, eyes and lumps of flesh were torn away in an orgy of hate that did not cease until the screaming, pleading and gasping had itself ceased and the poor girl was clothed, and her modesty restored. What remained of their victims was dragged on deck and tossed over the side, 'like the filth it was.'

Far below the Bird's waterline, in the certain onset of insanity that is the darkness of the bilges, the sounds of the dead bodies striking the water was clearly audible but of no import whatsoever. None! For the prisoners there were listening horrified, saddened but also relieved by the necessary killing of Kane Dowling, their friend and shipmate by Boatswain Holdsworth. Poor Kane was the most recent among them to part with his senses. He had been biting, kicking, and shit-smearing his shipmates all the while raving obscenities previously unsuspected in the quiet, fiddle-playing, book-reading lad and there was no other way. It was into this miasma of human waste, scurvy, dead bodies and rotting flesh that Macbeth would drop lantern in hand.

"I'm about tae go down in here," he told his men at the entrance to the dungeon.

"Bolt it behind me and dinnae let a soul out till ye hear me say," he paused for a moment,

"Hooligan."

With the pins knocked out and the massive bolts drawn, he wrenched open the trapdoor and stuck his face into the darkness and the stench below.

"I'm a friend," he announced, gagging, "stand aside lads." Without hesitation, he squeezed down through the narrow space vomiting copiously on those below. He had not sunk his feet in the excrement before the trapdoor above him was slammed shut and bolted. In the poor light of his lantern, it was obvious that the Americans were tightly packed and had squeezed back to allow him access. The air was unbreathable, and the stink was damn near as bad as that of a slaver.

"Gie us a wee bit quiet, lads." He roared above the murmur which a naked addition to their number caused.

"Captain, where are ye?" Sixty men answered at one time, and though every one of them was incoherent, Macbeth understood that the Captain of the *Bird* and forty or so of their shipmates, had been taken off to another prison, it being impossible to keep so many sailors all in this and one other space without the death rate soaring to epidemic proportions.

"First mate, here. You speak to me. What's the news, friend?" The speaker was obviously some yards away in the pack and owned an unidentifiable accent.

"The news is that we have taken the ship."

"He's a looney. He's buck nickid and he's locked in, same as we is boys." The foreseeable flash point that Macbeth wanted to avoid, had arrived much sooner than he had anticipated. He had to button that big mouth or he would find himself lynched.

"Who's in charge here, Mister Mate?" he shouted.

"You, or this fool?"

"I am. You be quiet now Gulley. What's the story stranger?"

"We have taken this ship. In a moment you will be free." Sixty voices croaked as one.

"Shut you damn moufs."

"Wot goes fo' Gulley be good fo' ever' damn one o' you."

"We've got the guards tied up in the main cabin, and I intend tae put them ashore unharmed; 'alive anyway,' and send you and the *Burrd* on your way. What they have done tae you, they were ordered tae do. Take it or leave it."

"They done keep us dry as a bone and starvin," said the mate, "an' up to our knees in ow own shit… like niggers," he added, playing for a laugh from his men, which he duly got.

"Take it or leave it, I telt ye," shouted Macbeth angrily.

"You got my word. We won' hurt one hair on theer heads."

"Good. I'll be holding you responsible, Mister Mate." There was an almost perfect hush at this remark; followed by the Mate's.

"You shoo you up to it?"

"I'm up to it, Mister Mate." At the unbelievable confidence of this declaration, utter silence would have reigned again but for the protestations of the fool.

"It's a trick. They'll shoot us fo' tryin' to 'scape." Gulley was obviously one of those men who required regular slapping. His outburst was instantly followed by the sound of a brief scuffle, a blow. Someone grunted.

"What *you* fink, Mister Ben?" It was the mate again.

The mere mention of 'Mister Ben's' name resulted in yet another perfect silence, as the American prisoners strained to hear the man's every word. Macbeth understood that among this hoard, was someone who was no ordinary seaman. In the far darkness, Mister Ben cleared his throat.

"Our new comrade says that he has come to free us and our ship." The voice belonged to a middle-aged educated man, not the sort given to hand-to-hand fighting against slavers.

"Whilst noting that we have everything to gain and not a farthing to lose, I am interested to understand his reasons, because if he says true, and I am sure he does, he has already risked his own life, and certainly his dignity, on our behalf." This observation broke the tension and every man jack roared at it. Macbeth waited impatiently for silence.

"Our understandin' is that you and the *Burrd* are abolitionists. That's all the reason that me and ma people need."

"Well spoken, sir. What do they call you?" A growl of agreement supported Mister Ben's words.

"My name is Macbeth, Mister Ben."

"We owe you our lives, Mister Macbeth. The devils meant to hang every man here, and many more who are not."

"Then we've put an end tae one o' their durrty plans, sur."

Macbeth cupped his hands to his mouth and bawled at the hatch beneath which he was forced to crouch. "Hooligan,'' and every man-jack was electrified by the sound of the bolts being drawn back.

"Get out o' ma damn way. Macbeff fuss, then me." The first mate of the *Bird* had a certain way about him, Macbeth noted. Within minutes of the Americans regaining their freedom, a longboat had been lowered and was ferrying the much subdued, agonised and rapidly sobering English turnkeys to the shore, while sixty American sailors jeered them on their way then promptly dropped into the water, to scrub accumulated human filth from their bodies in the exuberance of freedom and fresh air. The Scot was on deck, deep in conversation with Mister Ben and Holdsworth, the very big and very black first mate of the *Bird*, when the poor girl from below, supported by sailors, emerged on deck in men's attire. Two more bleating would-be rapists were dragged out and seeing the girl took to begging for mercy.

Holdsworth took in the situation and did not hesitate. Grabbing a belaying pin, he beat them both to shrieking agonized blood-spattering death, then heaved the carcasses over the side; no man attempting to assist. His ministrations were watched in a silence that was dense with righteous anger. Most of the men present would have preferred their no-nonsense boatswain to ''hack the balls off the swine.'' As they had done to the others. Content with his work the giant followed his victims over the side.

Upstream of them, the clattering blast of a siege gun ripped apart the cloak of night, liquid fire broke through the earth's crust and the Astor's shipyard was a pyre worthy of Hephaestus.* Innumerable red-hot falcons raced skywards, paused, then stooped vertically to spread the conflagration to places as yet untouched. The surrounding fields, the river and adjacent cottages were all ablaze. Macbeth leapt to the *Bird*'s side staring gleefully upriver.

"Lliam Hooligan, I bloody love ye. 'All hands,''' he bawled. ''Make sail, weigh anchor. Steersman upstream intae they flames. Brek intae the armory, Make ready the boats.'' The badly reduced sailors of the Bird went about their tasks as willingly as any, but it was sad to see them dragging themselves around the decks, so undernourished were they. At this moment Holdsworth and two others clambered aboard dragging lifting and shoving Mr Ben who had jumped into the river to wash but had damn near drowned. As the sails unfurled in the breeze and the anchors broke the surface of the stream, the quiet of the night was shattered. Unbelievably, by further cannon fire. Three shots in all, each one on the heels of the other, their echoes disputing with a pained screeching, as though something inanimate were being tortured.

"More haste, Mister Holdsworth," yelled Macbeth now in an uncontrolled rage, "or my man will cook while you and yer crew pussyfoot around like a gaggle o' fucking weemin." The mate, who had never in his life been likened to a woman, and never expected to be, turned to Macbeth with a face like Satan's well-slapped buttocks and replied in words of one syllable, but he wasted his breath, for a full broadside assaulted the night.

Within the vast and spreading blaze, the cannonade hurled huge flaming projectiles into the sky in a thousand fiery arcs. Even the river and the cottages of Minster were within its orbit, and as the men on the *Bird* watched on fascinated, several more thatched cottages burst into flames.

"I do believe that you indicated 'one man,'" intoned the very naked and very wet Mister Ben in his measured style which nothing, it seemed, had the power to excite.

"It would appear that your most excellent of soldiers in the cause of freedom, has found some little friends to play with Mr Macbeth" Little did the rotund burger know it, but he had just given voice to Macbeth's terrible fear, lately turned hope. It stood to the Scotsman's reasoning that the men whom the hold of the *Bird* could not accommodate, would have been imprisoned in some pit or barn close by, with no consideration of their comfort. Where better or easier, than the Astors' industrial site just upstream. Had Lliam Hooligan not discovered their presence, the poor devils would have been cooked alive for certain. However, all the signs were that he had discovered them; liberated them; and was now operating shoulder to shoulder alongside them. A broadside. Who would have thought of such a thing? "Lliam Hooligan, you are my favorite Irishman on this earth," he shouted gleefully in the direction of that distant stalwart.

"It's moving. The three-master, she's underway."

Every sailor aboard the *Bird* left off what he was doing to stare upstream, riveted by the warning; their fears confirmed.

"She's moving, the three master. We'd better skedaddle."

"Them others too, they're all underway. It's a trap." The observation concentrated the minds and energies of the *Bird's* men as little-else could. The thought of being recaptured was sickening in the extreme.

"I cannae ask ye tae risk the Burd for one man, Mister Holdsworth. Put aboot and run before them, until we can discover who it is that is manning those ships. With any luck, it may be your shipmates and my soldier." Macbeth was almost certain that the three vessels escaping the dreadful conflagration were being crewed by no other than the missing Americans under the orders of the wonderfully dissolute Lliam Hooligan; bless him, but he could not risk the *Bird* and these men for the sake of an hour. The sun would soon reveal the truth. Holdsworth checked his ship's position and the likelihood of coming to grief in the execution of such a manoeuvre and concluding that being a matter of life or death, it was compulsory in either event gave the order to the crew who had heard Macbeth's assessment of the lack of urgency with which they went about their duties, and having pre-empted the order were already at their stations ready to show the 'limey skirt wearing bitch,' what American seamen were made of. The Englishmen could only gawp at the inventiveness of those seriously weakened sailors. With enough malnourished men around it to eat the thing, they heaved the spare anchor from the deck and like a giant centipede moving heel to toe in tiny increments and perfect unison travelled half of the gut-tearing sinew-stretching length of the ship and with the very last dregs of their energy, dropped it over the side. As the massively thick hawser exchanged rigidity for relaxation under its enormous load, jets of water and vulgar complaints spurting from it, the *Bird* halted clumsily, her masts whipping as though she had run aground and swinging around in her own length, all but foundering, she was off and running, making sail by the acre.

CHAPTER 16: A Glorious Dinner Party

With diners to be seated at seven o'clock, Bismark Astor, being by nature a gracious and generous host, rode into Minster High Road around six, having come early as he was intent on greeting every guest personally, whether high or low. He had gone to extraordinary lengths with regards to his appearance and was gratified and a little surprised when the ladies; some of them possibly half-his-age, appraised him admiringly as he passed them at the walk along the high street. He wore a white shirt beneath a coat of privet green, narrow at the waist with wide lapels and a half-belt at the back, piped in black with a double row of gold buttons, as was the fashion with 'out of doors' men. Tight ivory-colored pants and tall black boots completed his ensemble. Once again, he had done without the wig and considered this innovation to be a great step forward, there being none of that abominable itching and scratching and cursed overheating, which went hand in hand with wearing the damnable flea-ridden things. Michael had been correct, he cogitated; a hot bath or two every day was nothing short of a panacea for the modern-man's ills. He was now as clean as a whistle and therefore innocent of perfume, another modification, and was looking forward to the novelty of being able to enjoy the uncontaminated aroma of his dinner.

 At the gates to the yard, the soldiers of Cornwallis' Own regiment; now sparkling in their number-ones, snapped to rigid attention as he passed by, but being hatless, Astor restrained his impulse to return the salute and merely nodded in recognition of their compliment, proceeding along the main thoroughfare of the yard, now resplendent in a deep virgin coat of sawdust, to the gangplank of the *Glorious*.

   "Father!"

Astor's surprise at finding his 'too clever for his own good,' son already aboard was so intense, so genuine that he gained no satisfaction whatsoever from a second salute of marines, or of the honor of being piped aboard by a boatswain, all turned out in white pants, navy jacket and tarred hat. The boy greeted him with a beautific smile, the firmest of handshakes and a flute of too-cold white wine.

"What do you think of her?''

If *Glorious* had been a superb vessel before; she was utterly sublime now. Every inch of her paintwork and varnish shone with a burnished glow, and her brass fittings would have passed for gold. The t'gallants had been shaken-out and the rigging was full of bunting and colorful flags. In addition, an orchestra was playing something divine which he recognized as the work of that child prodigy, Mozart. It was all perfect.

"Our guest of honor, Michael," Bismark began.

"Now, now, father. Enough of that. Everything has been arranged. Everything. If you get to doing that martinet thing of yours, you will ruin the evening, and get indigestion into the bargain. Look, here come the first of your guests."

Astor turned in the direction of the irritatingly clever one's glance, and for a second was utterly beyond words.

"Isn't that the Prime Minister?" he hooted, barely able to believe the welcome evidence of his own eyes.

"It certainly does seem to be the old fart. As I said, everything has been taken care of, so please relax and enjoy yourself for a change. No one deserves this evening more than you."

"I'll do my level best," Astor was quickly half-way down the gangplank in his eagerness to greet his old friend, Lord Frederick North, Prime Minister. The man's carriage leaned precipitously as the enormous politician made for its half door from where it took the combined efforts of his four liveried footmen, two marines and the boatswain to lower his obesity safely to the ground. North, who was unperturbed, took to such a descent no more concerned than a mountain-goat, laughing outrageously at his own indisposition.

"I'd go anywhere for a good meal," he wheezed.

"How are you, Bisy?"

"Couldn't be better, Frederick, come aboard and have a seat."

"I've already got one. Banbury," It was an old, well-worn joke but both men laughed generously, even so.

"I don't understand," began Astor, at a loss to explain the Prime Minister's presence there.

"How could you possibly have known?"

"I'd dearly love to claim prescience old man, but without parliamentary privilege I can't. I was on my way back to Town from Poole, and as we passed through 'Blandford,' is it? Anyhow, to cut a short story shorter, a gang of young Michael's naughty people took me prisoner, and dragged me here, protesting furiously all of the way naturally." In the present circumstances Astor could do no other than relinquish his good intentions and duties as host, and gave himself over to enjoyment, with the result that some of his guests were welcomed by Michael in his stead, others by the boatswain, and others not at all. Cornwallis, the Generals Howe and Carlton, with an arrogance of junior officers; colonels and the like, arrived just as North was taking his seat, and such was their communal surprise and joy at finding their political leader and friend present, that spontaneous combustion occurred, and the party was off to a wonderful start. Even the arrival of Astor's private surgeon with a divine lady young enough to have been his daughter, and whose breasts were utterly magnificent, could not better it. At some point or other, a happily numerous harem of ladies of unknown origin or virtue fluttered aboard ostensibly in the company of a seafaring business acquaintance of Michael's, and with that occurrence all of Astor's hopes of an enjoyable, sober dinner followed by the business coup of the century, went straight down the sluice. Mrs Crabtree and her detachment of assistants had outdone themselves and the food was extraordinarily good, though each sublime course was piped to the table by an individual who obviously harbored a deep loathing of his instrument. There was ham-and-asparagus soup, Scottish salmon, a selection of meats which included Angus beef, lamb, suckling pig, all golden and crisp, chicken, turkey, pheasant and partridge in addition to every vegetable and fruit known to man. Her team had performed miracles with the humble potato, there were tiny new ones drenched in butter and parsley, baked varieties done in the juice of the suckling pigs, mashed potato full of butter, diced onion crisped in garlic and brandy with cottage cheese. There were fritters in an egg batter, and crab and potato patties straight off the grill, all of which were consumed so hot that mouths took days to recover. There were sweets, cheese, grapes and nuts of a dozen breeds while the range of wines, ales and liqueurs was unequalled and more importantly, endless. As the wine took its toll and the meal descended into gluttony; jugglers juggled, knife throwers took incredible risks with the lives of their assistants, acrobats flung themselves around with masochistic intent, and the can-can dancers went to the most extraordinary lengths to prove to the gentlemen that they were wearing absolutely nothing beneath their pretty skirts. Cigars were lit by those still capable of bringing tobacco and flame together in one place; brandy was poured by the gallon, some of it into balloons; and as the 'ladies' forsook their seats to sit astride on the laps of the gentlemen, the revelry exploded in a crescendo of drumming as a tribe of very black, very naked warriors appeared out of the darkness, and charged the length of the deck bearing tall cow-hide shields and armed with assegais; the short stabbing-spears of the Zulu persuasion; causing the ladies to scream in terror, and the hands of the military men present to find the hilts of their swords, so convincing were they.

Clearly, the warriors were terrified when the comfortably upholstered generals reached for their weapons because they abandoned their headlong charge and drawing-up five paces short, gestured, stamped and stabbed the empty air to death, all the while chanting songs in praise of so noble an enemy before retreating in ignominious disorder. The applause stank to high heaven of fear and relief on the part of the uniforms, and unrestrained excitement on the part of the frocks, the naked savages being of the 'almost completely naked,' variety. Carriages were summoned. The dead, and 'qui morituri,' were assisted into them and before two in the morning, the lanterns had been extinguished, and the sole human presence remaining was the brace of exhausted soldiers deeply asleep at the gates of the shipyard.

Peeking out at them as the shipwrights joyfully scurried off home a couple of hours early, Lliam Hooligan knew that his luck was in, and had set about reconnoitering the place prior to sneaking out from between the stacks of timber when he picked up on the most awful sound which was coming so far as he could ascertain from the river or possibly the dry dock at the foot of the slope. Putting on his waistcoat and shrugging into his knapsack, he struggled and squeezed through endless timber canyons, skewering himself a dozen times on lethal splinters. Incredibly the *Glorious* was now done up like a part-time hore. They had dressed the poor bitch in bits of cloth and flags, and she was now flying small canvas though she sat in a dry dock. It was shameful and 'a pain in the arse.' Circus acts were being practiced on her decks, and it looked for all the world as though there were tables presently being concealed by white cloth and gold stuff. The awful sound came again, and 'Macbeth's very far distant cousin appeared in the kilt and the rest of the stupid Scottish get up.

"Sure, only the Irish can play the pipes," he observed snottily. It was as clear as the much-abused nose on his face, that the English persecutors of black men, Irish men, Indian women and undoubtedly anyone else that the swine came across, were flinging a shindig.

"Never you-mind," he warned them, "it'll be the last hooley ye'll be throwing aboard *that* wee boat." During his preparations he had conceived a plan so wicked that the devil himself could not have conjured it up. He was about to earn his silver, and more besides, but first he had to get to the *Glorious* unseen. By the time the piper had discovered a tune which he could play in a recognizable fashion Hooligan had crept, crawled and slithered through a dozen terrifying situations and was hanging spider-like on the massive dry-dock gates beneath the ship's bowsprit. Wary of the casual glance from the celebrations on deck, he crept to the attack in the dead-ground beneath the vast hull, and soon found a convenient forest of trestles with planks between. Climbing laboriously up the wooden scaffold he dived like a rat through a gun port into the business-end of the ship and lay silent but for his accelerated breathing beneath an unbelievably fat cannon. Almost invisible in his dark clothing, with his exposed skin blacked out with muck, he remained under cover until he was certain sure that there were no guards in there with him and that his eye had adjusted to the intense darkness. Taking a handful of wedges from his kit the determined arsonist in the cause of the abolition of slavery and self-preservation made his way to the sharp end, gun by gun, cracking open the ports as he went. It was incredible what a difference those slim shafts of light made to getting around, so that he discovered with great satisfaction that the shipwrights had carried out the first element of his plan for him. The twenty gigantic guns were supplied with shot, wadding, ramrods, and unless he was very much mistaken, powder. He reached up and hefted one of the suspended cones, thanking Beezelebub and all his ministers on finding that sure enough, it was full. Access to the gun deck from above he discovered was through two turnstile doors at the pointy end, one on either side of the ship; if they came at him, it would be from here. He wedged both devices tightly shut with a couple of ramrods. 'There was no sense in giving the enemy a fair go, was there?'

Understanding perfectly well that the measure would not stop a determined kitten for very long he was betting his life on the slim chance that the noise involved in any attackers getting past his little trick would give him half a chance at getting away with his skin in one piece; so far as that was still a possibility. There were several hatches in the deck above his head, but there was nothing he could do about securing them, so he put them out of his mind, determined to think no more about them. At the fat end there was only one turnstile. He had his ramrod in his hand and was about to lodge it in place when the devil himself overtook him altogether. He pushed the gate slowly open. Light burst on him exposing a passageway with double doors, all glass and brass and shining paint the color of blood. His heart was going like it did with a girl when you got to the 'will she, won't she?' bit. He must be mad to be doing this. Macbeth's snotty friend would put him in the stocks and cut off his ear, which was all he had left on his poor head, sure. That's if these people didn't do it for him. In two steps, he was at the doors and peeking in at a coast that was clear, and a feast all set ready and waitin' for Lliam Shaun Hooligan. He was through the doors that instant, into the cabin and into the pastries and the brandy, and very good they were too. Some of them were stuffed with minced beef and some with chicken. He drank his brandy straight from the fancy bottle so as not to leave a clue and was guzzling and gagging in turns when the doors opened of their own volition, held station for a moment then closed with a gentle puff of air. Dumping his spoils in panic he tried to hide and was half-way under the table when he saw beyond it a sort of long box with the lid open. He was across the open ground and into the box, with the lid closing softly above him just as the cabin doors opened again. Easing upwards the roof of his sarcophagus the prisoner peered breathlessly out. It was a 'he' and a 'she' that had entered and there was no, 'will she, won't she?' wit this one; these English tarts bein' filty sluts, every man jack of them. Sure, she was on the flat of her back on the rug in an instant with her petticoats up to her armpits, and her with no drawers on atall atall, and everything she's got winking straight back at himself in the box by the wall.

Now, Irish girls, it is a well-documented fact; do their unmentionable thing, whispering Paternosters, or in a prayerful silence, modestly covered, and with their heels on the floor at a respectable distance apart, with their hands in an attitude of worship; but not these filthy English whooers.

Sure; as your man's skinny ankles appear under the table and he's standin' there admiring what's on offer, herself throws her feet back over her head like the very exciting slut that she is, and her bum is a foot off the floor in her exertions. The purple stockings had no sooner leapt with a holler into that invitation, than Lliam Hooligan, unnoticed, was out of the box, out of the cabin, and out of sorts.

To keep the English and their filthy ways at bay he employed all six of his remaining wedges in barring the door at that end of the ship so that it would never open again and went about his task a very perplexed individual indeed. One hour into putting his sheer genius into action he was beginning to wish that he had not considered himself anywhere near so bloody clever. He had begun with the monstrous dealer-of-death closest to the fat end of the boat, winching the beast's enormous weight further inboard to the loading position, a task usually undertaken by three men judging by the weight of the thing. He got the wadding into the barrel and rammed it home, then rolled the massive iron ball from its pyramid, and in a feat of strength that nearly put an end to him, lifted it chest-high into the muzzle. Ramming everything home 'as tight as a duck's arse;' he finished the job with a second wadding on top, barely able to stand. His hurts were killing him, he was tired to death and sweat was blinding his one good eye; and still there were nine more guns to go. He topped up the breech with a powder bag, keeping his dripping face well clear, set the slow match, and moved on to the next, wishing that he had delayed this shenanigan just a day or two more, till he had got his strength back. When his broadside went off, it would hurl flaming timber all over the shop, and that clever bastard Astor's cruel ships and the yard that made them, would be no more. On and on he worked into the night, the second gun taking longer to serve as his strength inevitably waned. In his exhaustion, he became oblivious to the growing riot above his head, and the awful prospect of capture by people who thought nothing of torturing information out of prisoners, so that the drunken gluttons on deck had long since been dragged to their carriages and driven off to their beds, before he became aware of the silence which they left behind them.

Desperate for rest and a lung-full of fresh air the lone soldier left-off at his debilitating labour, trying to convince himself that he would acquire both by doing an easier task for an hour or so but well-aware that he was a beaten man. Peering out at the night for much longer than his shattered nerves required he descended to the safe ground beneath the ship and began a stealthy journey back to the storage area where the barrels of tar waited obdurately to be upturned. Despair crowded in on him and imminent failure mocked his pride. Creeping from one dark hide to another, crawling on his knees, feeling his way by touch in the darkest corners and at times dragging himself on his belly beneath innumerable obstacles placed there by some malevolent bastard just to thwart him he eventually recognized where he was. He was among the heaps of iron bits, the sails, the spars, and the tent where the screaming monsters lived, but on this occasion the stink of his fear was sickening in the extreme. He was done and he knew it. That bastard Fartinghay would take the knife to him then feed him to the pigs.

'Should he quit now and run?'

Losing his way, he almost crept face-first into the fence and right there almost near enough to touch were a brace of redcoats. They were slumped against the palings, bayonets fixed, but out for the count. He backed away lizard-like, slow as glue and taking the greatest care about where he placed his feet

Desperately afraid of working in a stream of flammable liquid, the now despairing weakling started work on the barrels which stood furthest down the slope; his intention being to progress uphill. At his first attempt the shattered remnant of himself discovered that a barrel of tar weighs about the same as a small house, and it was the devil's own job to tip the thing over. To do it without making a sound was next to impossible, sick as he was. Many of the malevolent bastards around him stood happily hard-up against the slatted side of a barn so he seized the obvious advantage. From long experience of filthy tasks, he knew, that by squeezing between the barrel and the building, he would be able to get purchase enough to heave the things over to their point of balance. Gravity would do the rest. With the heel of his hand, he would then punch the blade of his knife into the cork bungs which would crumble easily, letting the stinking resins, tars and paints glug onto the cobbles, and begin their intensely satisfying journey of destruction downhill. He had squeezed into place ready to begin on his second barrel when he was grabbed impossibly from behind by the bloody barn itself. His hair was being ripped out of his head and he was strangling. When he fought back, his wrists were grabbed, even his ankles. Sure, the bastard had eight arms.

"Tell us true.'' The voice was very close to his single ear, and its breath stank.

''If we even think that you are lying, you will die right here, right now." There was something odd about the voice, but there was nothing odd about the threat. It meant what it said.

"Who are you?"

"Oi, Oi can't breathe, fook you. Lliam.'' The pressure on his throat eased. ''Hooligan."

"Would you burn thirty innocent men to death, Lliam Hooligan?" The arm around Lliam's throat tightened again; damn near strangling him. Another hand got a good grip of his hair and tried to rip it from his skull. Sure, the divil had growed another two arms.

"Not atall, atall. Sure, I had no clue. I've to burn this place, not you. God save me."

"Set fire to it, why is that?"

"Why? I been paid to. That's why. Sure, Oive bin paid."

"Who paid you?"

"He'll cut off moi fookin ear …."

"Listen carefully, Lliam Hooligan. There are thirty of us in here. We are prisoners. The crew of the *Bird*. That's her on the river, the twin master downstream. Get us out and we will help you to destroy this yard, and carry you aboard the *Bird* to safety, anywhere on the globe. You have my word on it."

"Fookin oath." He was released immediately.

"Where's the door?"

"Far end. Hurry."

He barely made a sound as he groped his way around the building and not a sign of the old watchmen allof the way but leaning against the door was a sleeping redcoat who woke with a shock shared by Hooligan. With no room to deploy his musket the startled soldier went for his bayonet just as Hooligan did what came naturally and drove his head into that very scared face. The soldier's head snapped back striking one of the bolts. Aflame with pain the lad drove his knee into Hooligan's groin causing him to double in agony, his teeth meanwhile kindly testing the power of the guard's fist and the two combatants went at it in the knowledge that to lose was to die. The Irishman now had the advantages, size, weight and years of experience in filthy tricks. It was a matter of a minute only before he managed to force the youth face down into a pool of tar and hold him there until the poor bastard sucked-in tar instead of air.

'He was just a boy.' Memories of the poor gypsy child choked him.

The narrow access was secured by three bolts, each one an inch thick and a yard long so that they ran from hinge to jamb. Silent as the grave and clutching his agonized testicles the murderer drew the bolts silently then surprised the americans   by pushing his way inside, keeping the door ajar with his foot, just in case. The discipline of fighting men prevailed there; only the accelerated breathing of the shadow-cloaked army could be heard. These people knew what they were about but Jesus Christ Almighty did they stink?

"Listen boys, Oi'm destroyed so I am. Have ye a Captain?

Someone touched the Irishman's shoulder.

"Here, brother."

Hooligan grabbed the captain's arm, pressing a couple of flints into his hand.

"Burn the place. I'll be on the *Glorious*. They's redcoats at the fence and a dead one outside. Here's luck to all of ye." There was a quiet response charged with the excitement of men given the chance to fight for their lives and their freedom.

"Check for the noight watchmen yous fellas and don't hurt the old boys or Oi'll fuckin hurt you.'' Lliam Shaun Hooligan had just now spoken clearly, concisely and at length for the first time in a decade.

With the sailors peering out on all sides it was soon declared safe for him to leave and opening the door as slowly as night falls Hooligan crept away. Clutching his aching balls didn't help one bit. A worryingly long time later he was wearily charging the third gun of his broadside when he heard a scurrying rat and turned to find the Captain of the *Bird* and a crowd of men, all armed to the teeth with belaying pins, crowbars and mallets, approaching barefoot across the deck.

'Black! One of the buggers was 'black!' Hooligan couldn't believe what he was seeing. He was terrified. 'This could not be roight.'

"Jasus, Joseph and Mary; dat man is black," he protested as the newcomers were clearly unaware of this outrage. The Negro scrutinised his own forearm his face a mask of horror.

"Fuck, wen did 'dat' happen?" he inquired.

"Them guns captain, load em," muttered Hooligan still mesmerized by the apparition. The American gestured and three men, one of whom was the black gent, detached themselves, and went straight to it as though they were born on a gun deck.

"Aint you never see a nigger afore?" grinned the object of the ignoramus's fascination.

"Yo' mowf is open." The African's body shone like burnished timber.

"Of course I... No," Hooligan was greatly impressed that the man spoke Human and gratified to get away from the work at the guns, crossed the deck to the seaward side.

"Captain," he hissed; though he addressed everyone present.

"Get some of these gun barrels over the side and set em ready to blow that wall to get some water under us." The work was instantly under way. The tars had not even waited for their Captain's instruction.

''We're stealing it?'' The master of the bird was delighted.

"You had better rest, Mister Hooligan." he advised sternly, changing tack easily.

"You're unsteady on your feet, and if you should collapse, they'll be hearing it above. In any event, even if they don't, we've enough to do without carrying you around. Never fear, it's you who will give the order to fire." Lliam Hooligan, desperately sore, utterly exhausted and happier than he had ever been but for the state of his poor balls barely nodded in response. Almost collapsing against the mighty bulk of a cannon, he lowered his hateful body thankfully to the deck in the fashion of a very old man. Getting water and food out of his knapsack, he dosed himself with magic medicine and ate ravenously, feeling so much better in the wedding tackle area and with the energy surging back wonderfully into his body. 'Sure this was all great stuff.'

The task of hoisting the massive barrels out of their carriages and through the ports was a task fit for Hercules himself but with ropes around their trunnions, passing through jury rigged pulleys above, they rose like ugly angels from their beds and flew to freedom and all in near perfect silence while Hooligan's loud snoring negated all careful efforts in that regard. He was taking Moira Fay into heaven itself when he was woken by the Captain.

"Wake up mister Mister Hooligan?" hissed the seaman, and the leader of men, waving from his hiding place under a gun clambered to his feet concealing his guilty groin.

"Over here, Captain. How we doin?"

"We're ready to set fire. When the boys emptying the barrels get here, we'll blow the gates. The weight of water coming into this dock will throw her around like a top. If we come through in one piece, we'll give 'em a taste of our gunnery. The other ships are ready to run.

"Send the signal, Captain." The land lubber spoke with so much authority that he might have been leading troops for years.

"Yes sir," the American grinned ironically.

"When the fire-starters get here, we'll be taking the top deck. Are you game for a fight?"

"Oi am," Hooligan lied ruefully, his previously healthy appetite for violence having been somewhat diminished of late, due to being for the most part, on the receiving end of it. The fire was a terrible thing; a scene from hell itself. The deep blue bruises of the night sky were suddenly awash with the crimson breath of eternal damnation which blistered the slope of the yard, igniting everything in its path. The town of Minster, the surrounding countryside and even the river, were illuminated in the searing orange glow, as were the five sailors galloping through the paddocks beyond the tall fence of the yard. Moments later, those same sailors, armed to the teeth, charged up the gangplank of the *Glorious*, as Hooligan and his men attacked simultaneously from below. Disappointingly for those with such awful scores to settle, the ship was theirs in a matter of minutes there being only drunks and night watchmen remaining aboard, all of whom were driven on to the dock and set free with plenty of time to save themselves as best they might. Hooligan hastened at a crawl to the prow of what was now' His' ship and peered over the side. That dam had to be blown; 'Right bloody now.'

'Nuthin. No men, no guns.' Panic and fury seized him, and he charged to the other side, clambering over coiled ropes and hatches, ducking under spars and lines in the manner of a seriously ill octogenarian, shouldering men aside in his rage and concern, bawling blood-curdling oaths as he went, a few of them so foul that even the seamen were impressed. Almost committing suicide in his desperation, he heaved himself bodily on to the bulwark of the bow and would have tipped right over and fallen to his death had not one of those men, appalled and alerted by the Irish giant's ineptitude, leapt on him and held him back.

There was movement directly beneath him.

"Yes!" He coughed, in relief that his instructions had been acted on, much to the amusement of others who, unlike himself had an utter and unshakeable confidence in their shipmates which was yet to develop in 'Admiral' Hooligan as he now thought of himself. In the darkness beneath the huge hull, the three guns now set up there were aimed exclusively at one end of the barrier, each at a different elevation, and packed around with sandbags so that none of their power would be lost. With one end of the dam completely shattered the weight of water would flatten the thing and tear like a tidal wave up the dry dock, floating, but hopefully not damaging the *Glorious* as it went.

He had barely been pulled to safety when he saw the powder trails lit amid a scattering of men.

"Cover." The call was repeated by a chorus of half a dozen others and sailors everywhere threw themselves down behind anything solid, knowing what was coming. Oblivious to almost everything Hooligan watched engrossed, delighted by the pretty silver sparks which hurried up the three trails of powder, ignited the slow match and exploded three enormous charges of gunpowder. The ear-torturing sound and blinding light struck the fool almost as one; followed instantly by the blast of wooden shrapnel which ripped passed him as he ducked all too late. On the heels of this came a great rushing wind that emptied the sails and buffeted exposed men.

Mortally wounded and squealing in agony on an ever-ascending note, the two-foot-thick wall of English oak shuddered, leaned evermore inward and finally crashed to the ground under millions of tons of murderous black water. Cold-hearted malevolence, forty feet deep charged at the *Glorious*, clearly intent on her destruction, and struck in an explosion of bloodied spray which reached out to the masthead. The great ship rocked in her cradles as she was hoist, her superbly modelled prow, strong as the root-wood of English oak could make her, rose higher than the walls of the dock and she rode proudly through the gigantic wave making way rapidly astern as the anchor chains and hawsers came up tight, saving her mere yards from being smashed against the end of her brick-built cell. Her towering masts whipping, the many sailors in the rigging clung on and prayed while more-still raced each other into the clouds where canvas was unfurled and the *Glorious* was making way. Along her sides men rolled barrel into the narrowing space to keep her away from contact with the walls, while every available hand manned the capstans, shortening the anchor chains in step with the great vessel's forward progress towards the channel and the ocean beyond.

"Gunners. To your stations," roared Teach and the call was taken up and repeated from stem to stern while the invalid made his poor best time down the companionway to the gun deck, arriving a poor twentieth to the barefoot ministers of death who already had their hatches open and were laying their aim as he came up on them.

"Your instructions, Mister Hooligan?" The captain's features were a bloody fright in the harsh light of the inferno just beyond the hull.

"Tell them to spread the fire with their shot, if you please," bellowed the invalid thoroughly enjoying experimenting with his newfangled naval tongue; snippets of which he had picked up in Liverpool's docks and always longed to play with.

"That canvas wa ll up there," he pointed at the Dearg Due's lair.

"I see it."

"Knock shit outofit.' With his hands cupped around his mouth, the captain roared his instructions.

"Spread the blaze with your shot. The yellow canvas must go." This instruction caused a great flurry of action with men grabbing their huge crowbars in order to lever their pets around, while others worked at pulleys and wedges as though their lives depended on their efforts, raising or lowering their angle of elevation as the more appealing targets presented themselves.

"Show ready."

One by one in a matter of thirty seconds, which added a full twelve months to Hooligan's age all ten gunners raised burning slow-matches and stepping well to the side of their massive machines of destruction, turned to stare unblinking at their leader.

"Fire!" the man bawled, simultaneously bringing down his arm in a great striking action as though to smash the enemy with his fist. The deck tilted violently under the landlubber's feet throwing him in to collision with two sailors as he toppled backwards in a horrifying world of painful sound, sudden intense heat, and the confusing loss of visibility as the broadside filled the claustrophobic darkness with its acrid breath.

To Hooligan's horror, the enormous guns leapt at him; a full four yards through the air with the ferocity of pit-bull dogs determined to defy the leash. At the limits of massive hawsers, substantial as legs of ham, they crashed to the deck where they were instantly swarmed by their masters as Hooligan thanked all the saints that these gunners were experienced men. To be struck by one of those creatures would mean instant crushing death.

Desperate to witness the destruction of the Astor's empire the avenger staggered through the fog, finding his way topside where he stood transfixed. The inferno was terrible and wonderful to see. The gigantic enterprise, acres of it, was already being consumed by raging flame; the intense heat dragging-in the surrounding air with a furious suction and turning the yard into hell itself. Even some of the thatched roofs of Minster were bursting into flame; there were fires in the fields and hedges, and even on the river where burning timbers drifted slowly towards the ocean.

To his immeasurable satisfaction the efforts of his new comrades had freed the *Glorious*; undamaged, perfectly seaworthy, and unharmed by the fire, a condition which seemed to apply elsewhere for the other two vessels were now making measured headway downstream of him. Aboard all three ships of his little fleet men were cheering and calling out to each other in their exhilaration at their first taste of revenge on the hated Brits. As he stood there in the glare of the destruction that he had wrought, Hooligan wondered vaguely whether Macbeth would be pleased by the extra mile that he had walked. That ruthless soldier's good opinion, always so hard-won, had become tremendously important to him.

"Mister Hooligan," the captain had come running,

"That vessel in midstream, you can just make it out. I'm pretty sure it's my ship; the *Bird*, and there are sixty of my men captive in her bilges. She's running from us." Captain and ship owner hurried to the bows from where sure enough in the approaching dawn, a sleek vessel could be seen cramming on sail.

"Tree tings," enounced Hooligan portentiously.

"Yes sir." the captain responded, fixing Hooligan with his steady gaze.

"First, Captain. What, for the love of clitorus, is yer name?" The American smiled broadly.

"I am Martin Teach," he announced taking Lliam's proffered hand and shaking it energetically, joyfully, and with sincerity.

"And the second?"

"Why, what else, Martin Teach? Can we catch her?"

"In this? Without breaking sweat, Mister Hooligan," said Teach.

"Then kindly make it so, and board them, Captain,"

''And lastly?''

''What happened to yer face Martin? The captain's face resembled an archery target for flaming arrows.

''That swine Astor tried to blind me with a red-hot poker, but I kept squirming till he got bored.'' For a moment Hooligan stood silent, wrestling his emotions.

''I promise you Martin. When I get a grip of that prick, I'll kill the bastard.''

Leaning toward caution on a river which he had not navigated previously, Captain Teach ordered just one more mainsail to be set and advised his crew by use of a speaking trumpet.

"We take back the *Bird*; stand by to grapple and board."

Glorious came up astern of the *Bird* just as the sun topped the horizon, the false dawn was no more and there all but alongside them was their ship, manned not by the hated Brits, but by their own shipmates. Free as a Bird.

"Bring me alongside her, if ye please, Captain Teach," said Hooligan, and when this manoeuvre was accomplished, he found himself looking across a wide torrent at the hairy, possibly smiling face of Macbeth, and not in the least bit surprised by that man's presence. From where he stood on the poop deck the Scot seemed such a long way below him that the very sober Hooligan realized with great satisfaction what a truly gigantic ship he had stolen.

"Top of the morning to ya. What do we do now Macbeth?" he shouted and was transported when the ape replied.

"It's yoor flotilla, Mister Hooligan. While we stand on these decks, we obey yoor orders, sur." Standing next to the hairy Scot was a second grinning monster of a negro, and as Hooligan stood open-mouthed like a grouper, the negro at his own elbow said,

"Fuckin' niggers, send' em all back."

Turning to Teach for advice the temporarily stumped leader of men noticed a lunatic committing suicide right under his eyes. The loon dived into the river from the deck of the *Bird* and struck out for the *Glorious*.

"What do we do now Rosemary?" he inquired of Teach, shamelessly dodging the responsibility bullet yet again.

"We'd best run for a few hours Darling, then put-in somewhere and get fresh water and food, we're starving."

"Make it so," laughed the object of Rosemary's affection, overcome by an inexplicable happiness and was about to abandon the poop deck in order to strut the deck below with his hands crossed at his back as he had seen done by men in pretty uniforms when his arm was grasped, and he found himself looking down at a small, soaking-wet sailor, whose face was the color of night.

"Lliam. Or do I have to call you 'Captain Hooligan,'" his friend laughed.

"Trewin!" Hooligan's delight at this totally unexpected reunion was immeasurable, and the two men took to wrestling and thumping each other on the back like a couple of children.

"We were reconnoitering your position in the wood piles through a telescope," the wet black face announced.

"Macbeth and myself and you kept popping-up like a mole." For some obscure reason, this declaration was the funniest thing that either man had heard in years, and the friends resumed wrestling and punching and laughing like hyenas, till at last they tripped each other and collapsed in a heap on the deck. The watching American's shook their heads in pitying disbelief as they exchanged quizzical looks. 'These were the men to whom every one of them owed his life and his liberty?'

The reunited chums were lying asleep in the scuppers where they had found some canvas when a seaman interrupted their rest with the intelligence that a bay well-suited to their purposes had presented itself and the flotilla was at anchor.

CHAPTER 17: The Devil Comes of Age

Having lost all patience with his fellow man, through the loss of successive hands of cards to the exceedingly drunk, and even more obnoxious Cornwallis, Lord Bismarck Astor stepped out of the Holbein room onto the scented walk which he so enjoyed. He would, he decided, smoke a last cigar compose his thoughts and then retire for the remainder of the night. Who could tell? Perhaps the bur which had been under his saddle since The Granary…

"It's him!" he exclaimed. A picture had formed in his mind of that monstrous barbarian pissing blood from a balcony at Michael's home. He and the individual on the raft at the shipyard, were one and the same. The giant had discarded the eyepatch and the bandages, but it was without doubt the same man. 'The swine was inside the yard.' Tottering unsteadily toward the house he was chilled to the marrow by the clatter of distant cannon-fire and turned in instant agitation; further enraged by the emergence of a great glow behind the Minster horizon. It was as bright as dawn in Zanzibar.

"No!" he asserted, as though to forbid what was already happening. As he stood there watching impotently, mesmerized; a full broadside shattered the night's calm, and the glow was suddenly an inferno. Great masses of flaming debris raced into the sky describing parabolic curves of agonizing beauty to spread the contagion further. Moments later his guests came staggering from the house to watch in awed silence.

"The shipyard," Astor remarked redundantly. At that point, Field Marshall Cornwallis collapsed, vomiting copiously on those near him, rolled through a very smelly pool of his own spew into a mess of roses, and became still, snoring. Astor set off to find his devious son, but then reconsidered and leaving the detested Marques where he lay in the hope that he would choke on his own vomit went off to his rest.

Even at a hundred paces, the residual heat from beneath the blanket of dirty ash was exceedingly uncomfortable. The Astors, father and son, surrounded by guards sat their mounts on the same half-shaven hill from which Lliam Hooligan, Macbeth and Trewin Coppelstone, each in their season, had spied on the workings of the yard. His son's face, Astor noted, was uncommonly pale, and his normally generous mouth was now held tightly and cruelly in the most bitter of expressions. The sly dog was agitated to such a degree that his mount; sensing its master's mood, became similarly affected and would not rest; it stepped and bridled incessantly, unsettling the others. Of the gigantic investment that was the shipyard, there was nothing left but that acreage of dirty snow surrounded at this time by hundreds, perhaps a thousand, gawping peasants like so many cattle fenced off from a paddock of new grass. Astor the younger also contemplated that bovine mass but not with the older man's unruffled calm. To him these ungrateful swine who relied on himself for their very existence clearly had nothing that they would rather do than revel in his misfortunes. Their poorly concealed pleasure in his catastrophic loss was evident in every bovine face. Their guttural exchanges brought their sour malice on the wind.

'That ghastly cyclops; troglodyte pig did this.' The thing which he, Lord Michael Astor had undoubtedly saved from the attentions of the grim reaper. 'That's right, it was on the road to Damascus, and whilst all others had crossed over, He the disciple Michael; exceptional individual that he was had shown pity and come to the aid of the injured beast.'

He would, he resolved, when the opportunity presented itself, relieve that bovine ingrate of his other eye and various body parts which he would make the victim choose from a range of options. 'His enormous package, his toes, fingers, scalp;' the choice was endless, while keeping him alive with the help of surgeons for as long as was humanly possible. White hot, ungovernable rage coursed through his veins as the cattle now jeered and openly rejoiced. What if anything, he wondered, was between their ears? Could they possibly believe that he was obliged to rebuild and then re-employ them?

He 'would' start again, 'in this very location,' there was advantage in all of this. He would build bigger; much bigger, and in doing so, create a process, a 'system,'' of shipbuilding which was ten times more efficient and made far greater profit. He would achieve this by employing the maxim; 'devices, not men.' Devices were the very latest development. By boiling water and making steam, a 'piston' could be forced to move up and down relentlessly in what was called a 'cylinder,' just as a boiling kettle will lift off its own lid. That movement could be harnessed to a whole range of tasks. Devices did not require to be paid and lasted forever once purchased. They did not get sick or drunk nor did they go up in flames, they would function every day of the year, 'day and night,' and not even quibble about working on the Sabbath. His new steam-saws had proven beyond any doubt that he was correct.

Brilliant! Yes, he would rebuild and yes, he would replace those two saws which lay in twisted heaps out there like the bones of long-dead warriors. If there was a device built for tasks presently being done manually, then he would purchase the invention and get rid of the loathsome dullards. He could barely wait to inform the disloyal swine of their fate. That would take the smiles from their pimply unwashed faces. Mother of God! Some… stupid bastard was interrupting his thoughts!

"I simply cannot understand it. It would have required a hundred men to make off with three ships. For my own part, the only clue was that chance sighting which I mentioned to you. That impostor who inveigled himself into your home. For the life of me, I still cannot fathom why he did that. After all, you say that nothing was stolen; nobody was hurt or poisoned, and naturally he was not privy to any conversations abou… "

"For the love of Clit!" Michael erupted, turning like a starving dog whose bone has been snatched; his sudden ferocity making his horse shy.

"If you don't give over bleating like a well thrashed slut, I swear to Christ I'll shoot you in the face like a syphiliti.''

"Bastard!" Bismark snatched at his flintlock, but Michael's man Hastings beat him to the weapon only to be instantly battered to the floor by Charybdis.

Well beyond the restraints imposed by filial bonds and lily-livered observance of other people's sensitivities Michael raged at the filthy peasant upstarts,

''Curse you all. Ungrateful swine. Rebellious dogs. You will pay.'' He was incensed. He was incensed by the loss of his ships and yards, by the affront to his dignity implicit in this despicable arson, and not least, by his father's girly behavior. The old fool was bloody senile.

"I repeat; you heap of afterbirth; one more fucking word, and I'll shoot you where you sit, then I'll burn down your ugly fucking palace and slaughter your stupid fucking thoroughbreds." Michael had lost all control. His handsome face contorted like that of a frenzied mastiff; his eyes seemed impossibly white, and flecks of foam showed at the corners of his mouth. Lord Bismark Astor was no drawing-room dandy. Neither the language nor its intent so much as bothered him even though it was his own son that was issuing the threats, but he was appalled that the ungrateful little bastard harbored, ''unsuspected,'' such virulent feelings against him; there was the rub. He recalled instantly the terrible cruelty which the little swine had exhibited, firstly as a small child, then again after a considerable hiatus, as a youth, committing unbelievable acts of torture on his hounds, his ponies, and then of course, there was that business with the gardener or woodcutter, or whatever he was. The poor man's bones, barely one of them unbroken, lay buried under one of the stables to this day. 'Could the hand-biting fucking mongrel be losing its sanity?' he wondered.

With no resolution to the squabble possible in the prevailing circumstances, and nothing but further abuse in the offing, Astor urged his horse into the descent, travelling only a few yards before hearing the traitorous bastard's voice again. The ingrate was gazing out across the devastation at the inlet where three of his vessels had lain, but he; like them, was oceans away from there. He was talking to himself.   'Mad bastard.'

"It was sheer chance, you old fool. The man's wounds were real enough, and the fall he took from his horse should have killed him. That was no concoction. There was no plot. It was sheer fate that the rogue turned up at my home. He was travelling south. Probably heading for this very place, but he'd taken a hell of a beating and just fell off his horse at the worst possible spot. And it was 'four' ships not three. Stupid old fanny can't even count. There were our three and that American sloop, the *Bird*. That's where he got his crews from. He got into the yard on a raft. You 'saw' him for Christ's sake. You 'SAW' him and did ''nothing.   NOTHING!''

 Inexplicably ashamed of his unintentional eavesdropping on the lunatic's ramblings the enraged Bismark completed the descent and addressed his bodyguards who had come within a breath of killing Hastings.

"From this moment," he told them, "That little bastard up there presents a greater threat to my life than any other man. Accordingly, you must hire more good people as you see fit, and mind my back day and night, from every possible and impossible source. I want you to be aware of poison, arson, drowning, industrial accidents; everything. He is as you know, a very inventive bastard. You shall both have a considerable increase in your retainers, and rooms within the palace if you wish it. Lastly, I want one of your men, if not yourselves between him and me at all times; night and day." Bismarck Astor had no intention of ending his days all too soon, buried beneath the floor of the stables.

"My lawd; if he 'appens to 'ave a real go like, we would 'ave to 'urt 'im bad. Real bad. Him bein' a big lump of a lad like."

"Put your mind at rest about this matter and make it clear to everyone; your first duty is to protect my life. Should you find it necessary to hurt the bleeder to the point of extinguishing him, then so be it; he will have signed his own death warrant. He is surplus to requirements. You'll be well protected, never fear and my oath on it. That's my last word on the matter."

"Yus, my lawd," the bruisers confirmed, and Astor rode on; a safer, angry man.

Saint Michael was in torment. He had been skewered on a spit and was roasting in the flames of Purgatory while devils armed with red hot tridents poked him agonizingly in the arse, no doubt in order to ascertain whether he was cooked through and ready for hell itself. All was ashes. This place, this industrial hub was ash. These milling, bovine and now redundant wage slaves were ash. Not only were the swine redundant; worse still they were disloyal, and for that, they were ash. Three ships of the Astor line were gone, lost at sea and gone to ash. His mother had deserted him, died and gone to ash. Today was the twenty-first anniversary of his birth, yet his girly bitch father was oblivious to it. He too, then, was condemned and gone to ash. Jamaica Place was com… Jamaica Place! The reality of that magnificent construction; his greatest work of art and architecture expunged all other trivial matters, and he was raised up, redeemed, saved from the flames. He, Michael Astor, industrialist, landowner, banker, slaver, homeowner, horseman and whoremaster; he liked the alliteration of that; would abandon this morass, this filth, with its morbid concerns and crawling inhabitants for another day, and repair to Jamaica Place where he would rest and recuperate, and when he was once more himself, then, and only then, would he return to his life's work of molding a sublime future for his class, sustained naturally by the filthy existence which would be the doll of the laboring clay. It was confirmed. Strangely, he did not have the energy to gallop his mount as he would have wished, so he set-off at a walk, tentative as a child on its first pony, followed at a distance, he noticed, by the injured Hastings and his small army of very hard men. God how he loved them. Everywhere from the interior of the dark continent to the Susquehanna and the Rappahannock they had ridden, trudged, eaten, got fucking legless and fought at his side.

Rain then made the world a cold uncomfortable place. As the horse he rode clearly did not have the common sense to get inside out of the weather, he would, he decided, let the beast continue with the journey and get as wet and as painfully cold as himself. He was shivering like a tortured kitten.

"Warm clothes," he protested loudly to a little shit of a beggar cowering beneath a lump of sacking,

"are not at all warm once they become wet." This redundant observation had barely left his lips when good old Hastings appeared alongside and rode with him for a while in companionable silence. 'The village.' He had still not built that village for Hastings and his lovely men.

"I will commence with the village just as soon as I've got the war under way in the colonies," he announced.

"Got you Mike," the mystified, sympathetic Hastings cracked his forehead again as though it were Big Ben. The habit had formed quite a dent in the loyal chap's soaking-wet head.

The trog who had incinerated his shipyard and made off with the *Glorious* and the rest, had pissed blood when he amused the redcoats at The Granary. What did that infer? Of a certainty the swine's health was already in a parlous state when he fell from his horse, yet his clothing showed no sign of his having been involved in a violent attack. Had he robbed a gentleman of his horse and clothing and suffered those wounds in the process. Did the gentleman victim's dog do the well-deserved business with the ear? It was all very perplexing. He would invent a suitable reward for the pond dwelling slime. How if it were to go on living blind, deaf and speechless and without hands in a world of shrieking fear and exquisite pain? Astor suddenly laughed aloud as he imagined the enemy in a state of perpetual drowning.

Several icy millennia later, the newly constructed walls of Jamaica Place, presented themselves to his lordship's grateful self, tall and solid in a pleasant sandy-colored stone, albeit temporarily darkened to a textured-umber by the rain, which transformation, he was pleased to observe, caused no offence to the surrounding nature. That fool Culpability Brown, managed to get 'some' things right.

He joined with a caravan of wagons which were heading for his gates, each load guarded by its gang of toughs, bringing furniture, artworks, carpets, drapes and the rest, from all over the world. The spectacle reminded him of his entrepreneurial brilliance in refusing to take ownership of or pay more than twenty pounds in the hundred for the thousands of individual items which he had personally selected, until these objects were safely installed within Jamaica's walls and had been authenticated by his lovely curators. At the main gates, all very pleasingly completed now with crowds of statuary and wrought iron by the mile; he was deeply satisfied to find that the gatemen were literate beings of all things and were checking the arriving objects against an itinerary before permitting entry. So pleased was he with this discovery that he turned in his painfully wet clothing, and nodded his appreciation to Hastings, who had considerately dropped back and rode with his men a few lengths in the rear. He simply had to get on to that village thing.

Such was the extent of Brown's 'capabilities,' that although the house lay unseen only a few hundred yards from the gates, he had yet to ride two more miles, cross three bridges, each of which would do the Thames proud, skirt a lake where no lake existed before, and which boasted several substantial islands, one replete with marble summer house; and splash through an imitation ford, not one brick of which existed prior to the descent of that mad genius; in order to reach her.

At last! Jamaica Place! Salvation! How magnificent she was. But he had not the strength to dismount from this sodding horse; perhaps if he had someone break its legs it would collapse and thus lower him gently to earth.

The last occurrence which Michael Astor observed that morning was that of a regiment of footmen charging down the prairie-wide steps of his magnificent new home, led by none other than that paragon of virtue Delavier.

He clung tenaciously and spitefully to consciousness until his servant reached him.

"Where the hell were you in my hour of need?" he enquired capriciously and collapsed on the loyal fellow's narrow shoulders. ''Get my men inside.''

Michael woke in stunning form; argumentative as a tribe of baboons, aggressive as a cannon full of chain; and starving. It was evening, he knew it, the ambience of his surroundings, the light, the warmth, and the air itself, so full of the scents and pollens of the day, now that the rain had ceased.

So! He had spent his twenty-first birthday; his first day at home in his sublime Jamaica Place, unconscious. Clearly, immediate corrective action was required. This room in which Delavier had lodged him was so very much to his liking that he lay for a luxurious, self-congratulatory while, appreciating his achievements represented here by the ornate plasterwork overhead, positively littered as it was with the family crest, and if you looked closely; Roman gods doing truly imaginative things to the Sabine Women. Showing to advantage against the pale-ivory decor were manly, neo-classical items of furniture, masterfully worked by Chippendale in dark glistening cherry, on carcasses of mahogany upholstered in Chinese silk. 'His requirements had been very detailed.' The bed was magnificent. Big as a field, and as soft as the lovely tits on the Wild Rose. 'Christ, I'd forgotten about her! It's been days since I so much as thought about her; or her chums.' Disdaining the tapestry option, Michael bellowed Delavier's name instead and the bounder fell instantly into the room with the customary silver tray, on which was a bottle and a tall flute.

"Good evening, my lord. I do hope that you are fully recovered," the man spoke with patent sincerity.

"I couldn't be better," Michael responded, accepting a glass of glacial wine.

"Now, explain to me why you have had the unmitigated gall to abandon your post at The Granary."

"Certainly, sir. As today is that of your lordship's esteemed majority, it occurred to me that Sir may have chosen to celebrate the occasion in the home which."

"Yes, yes, Lavatory, why must you make me regret asking you a question on every occasion that I'm foolish enough to do so? I need a bath, and food. I could eat your testicles and quaff vomit. Where's the bath?"

"It's beyond that door, sir. Chin deep, and at precisely the correct temperature. I took the liberties of drawing it for you and laying out black tie for this evening in the adjoining dressing room. Dinner is set in the 'Gold-on-Silver,' in Lakeside. I required Mrs. Crabtree and a detachment of her people from The Granary to accompany me, my lord and hope that arrangement meets with your approval?" Michael stamped naked into his new bathroom, utterly exasperated by his inability to invent a criticism of his butler which would stand up in court.

"Why the devil should I bother with Black Tie, Delavier?" he demanded, standing knee-deep meanwhile in hot water,

"I don't suppose that anyone but yourself will remember the occasion, and if they bloody do, they won't take the initiative and call on me; they must all observe the God-cursed proprieties et cetera, et bloody cetera. People are such drones, Delavier. There should be a law against them." His lordship hurled a large bar of soap at a gilt-framed mirror, smashing it then feeling only a trifle better, dived full length in the fashion of a retriever entering a pond, causing gallons of water to leap the tiled walls and soak both the floors and Delavier.

Unconcerned, the manservant placed the refreshment tray within his master's easy reach, and as the bather submerged completely in protest at the cruelties of an unjust world, replied in his typically stoic fashion,

"I cannot imagine that your lordship would be condemned to dine alone on this of all nights, sir." From his master's now distorted face, large bubbles of disillusionment rose to perish like dreams on the surface. The better part of an hour later, Michael Astor, resplendent in black tie and tails, emerged from his dressing room, followed closely by his butler and a brace of footmen whose Mamaluke-inspired uniforms, even Michael found faultless; and the party set off for Lakeside, the south-facing great dining room; a trek so arduous that any traveler from this part of the house would be guaranteed a ravenous appetite by the time he arrived. At the first junction of broad corridor and prairie-wide staircase, the butler, recognizing the opportunity presented by a barely perceptible hesitancy on his master's part, cleverly took the lead by staying close to the banisters, and seizing the inside running he negotiated the luxuriously carpeted treads several lengths in the van, particularly well-pleased with himself. It was only fitting, after all, that he announce his master's arrival in the best of form. His satisfaction was short lived.

"I don't need to be led like a horse damn it. I designed this bloody house, and I am quite capable of finding my own way to any one of my own dining rooms. Now get out of my way and cringe two paces behind, as a good muslim wife should." The master had obviously recovered completely from his earlier discomfiture.

"Naturally, sir," Delavier, was clearly heartbroken that he had not been the first to think of that arrangement. On arrival at Lakeside, the lord of all that he surveyed, paused momentarily several paces removed from the doors, tugged gently at his snow-white cuffs, more out of habit than need, came to attention as crisply as an officer of the guards, and eager to view for the first time the glories of this huge room in its completed magnificence, most particularly the Bacchanalia-decorated ceiling which good old bloody-lecherous Guardi had done, nodded to the doormen. Even if he were unjustly friendless, and dined with only the beastly servants for company, he would do so in style. The doors swept gracefully inwards, and Michael beheld the most wonderful sight imaginable, a host of smiling faces. Everyone that he ever knew, it seemed, was here.

"Michael, Michael, Michael," they chanted, their glasses raised, and as he accepted their good wishes, his handsome face creased in pleasure. Lord Beastly Astor himself, stepped forward from the front rank of the revelers, and handing him a glass of champagne and a parchment, which was obviously a deed to something or other, said,

"Congratulations Michael."

"Thank you, Sir." Michael responded, accepting the gift and shaking the man's proffered hand with a smidgeon of sincerity. Turning to his butler he said,

"Go home to your family, Delavier. This instant. Take the month off and, as you go; my roughnecks; they have my permission to enjoy the banquet food and to admire the interior. On no account should they speak to my guests or meet their glance.''

''Absolutely sir.''

Excruciatingly, Bismark had a heavy on each side of him; the arrangement made the old goat look like one skinny volume between two hippo-shaped bookends. Why the devil had he brought Scylla and Charybdis into the house? They were bovine peasants. He may as well have driven a couple of bullocks indoors. Bad form indeed. Michael glanced at the superb parquet flooring to discover whether the monsters' clod hoppers were marking it. Happily, the hardwoods of Malaysia were impervious to cloven hooves.

Absolutely everyone was here; good old Molesworth, fatter than ever, Holland, the drunken fool, what fun the man was, Carlisle, all the way from Boston, 'how on earth did he get out of the place? The Brits were all over it,' scrawny little Walpole, talkative as a woman, Surrey, who owned half of that county, dozens of other sterling fellows and better still, a sweet-smelling flower-garden of utterly delicious women. Christ, he could taste one or two of them now. In his first glance, he detected several wives and a bevy of daughters whom he had known in the biblical sense, and a dozen more whom he would like to. 'This might be a celebration worthy of the name.'

ing274

Rather imaginatively, in order to cope with the entire civilisations present, the tables had been extended beyond the confines of the room through each of the French doors, across the patio and on to the lawns where several of his ship-captains, the younger element of the House of Lords, his lawyers, bankers, and hunting friends, were obviously having a rollicking time. The high command of the British Army was here, along with officers of a score of regiments. Admiral Harding seemed to be posing for a portrait, while other old salts clung like barnacles to the great man's sides. Even dotty old Surgeon Reynolds with that delicious maiden of his were on public view.

'Delavier,' he mused, 'you are a true friend. You must have been planning all of this for a twelvemonth.' Gravitating across the room towards the predominantly male company outside, he pausing only momentarily to greet and be greeted; share a word and a smile with certain of the beauties vying for his attention, but mainly to admire the room and its decoration. One woman, or even two in private was one thing; a herd of them in public was quite another. He was stunned by how wonderfully-well his concept had come together. Guardi had performed a masterpiece with the ceiling by making the vast bacchanalia perfect in every dimension, every curve and shade. The decorative plasterwork was unequalled anywhere in the country, and the paintings which he had selected personally, were so tastefully at home here. He had chosen Pinnotte because of that ruffian's seeming inability to portray anything but the kitchen and assorted items of food, and Tremain for a very different reason. If any artist could divest a maiden of all virtuous notions and leave her naked and ready to be taken in every conceivable fashion; it was he. There was such a close relationship between food and sex, was there not? Crucially, the parquet floor was a masterpiece of the woodworker's art. He had stipulated both teak and mahogany from Burma, and a smattering of English beech to attract the eye, the whole thing to be herringbone-patterned within margins of red Meranti, the famed timber of Malaya, the heartwood of which takes on such a shine. Considering it now in its finished state, perfect in every respect, he somehow envied those simple tradesmen who, in their quiet unassuming way, were capable of such a work of art. The fools worked for a shilling an hour.

"He's twenty-one today, he's twenty-one today,

Ee-I-adio, he's twenty-one..."

Michael's friends were not the sort of men to pass-up the opportunity to mock a fellow drunkard, and predictably they set about the business with gusto as he approached. The object of their affection, however, was one of those individuals who was devoid an embarrassment bone.

"Your taste in music has improved enormously since our last meeting gentlemen," he observed, going on the offensive straight away.

"However, any more of the same and it'll be no dinner and an early bed for the lot of you."

"If your grub is the equal of this cooking champagne, we wouldn't eat it in any event." Holland was clearly in the best of form. The charming fellow draped an enormously heavy arm around his host's shoulders and announced,

"Congratulations my child, from this day forth you may partake of strong drink. They tell me however, that you remain a virgin." Michael was in no hurry to answer and waited until Holland's delighted audience had recovered their breath.

"On that score, you've been misinformed, old boy." he spoke barely above a whisper, so slowly and quietly that the obnoxious gang had to listen intently to his reply.

"Not only have I been relieved of my virginity; I have been used in the most lascivious fashion by as many as four women at one time. All of them using myself and each other, until we all, 'came together,' so to speak. By the way, do give my regards to your mama and your three sisters, Holland, old man." On hearing this rejoinder, Walpole, with the timing of a true thespian, put his hand to his heart and lamented,

"Woe is me, my women have betrayed me with another, and another, and each other." These fusillades set a wonderfully low tone for the evening, which was very much to the taste of the womanizing gathering.

Dinner was a triumph, with the modern, well-equipped kitchens of Jamaica Place situated as they were directly beneath the dining room delivering endless streams of dangerously hot food via half a dozen dumbwaiters to where a regiment of Delavier's people; assisted by the uniforms of Windward Palace, were able to rush it to the tables to the immense satisfaction of the diners. All eighteen courses were exquisite in flavor and presentation and brought general acclaim as they were tasted. To the host's great satisfaction, the Prime Minister was seated a furlong or two distant from himself, an arrangement which suited him down to the ground, because Cornwallis and his acolytes, the Hessian officers, the God-botherers and the political supplicants, all crowded as near to the great man as they could; thereby freeing himself and men of similar appetites to adore longingly the eyes, the shoulders, the shapely arms, and almost completely naked cleavages of an available sorority of lovely women. Free of the presence of bothersome husbands Astor's gang could talk the twaddle that the fair sex loved to hear, while lapping, licking and fingering their food as though it were the very bodies of those delightful creatures. By the time the beef had been consumed, the nubiles had made their selection and communicated this news to the deeply gratified lechers with bold stares, followed by glances at their own cleavage, and much touching of their moist and slightly parted lips with fingers which then found their way inexorable between their heaving breasts. To his utter glee and indescribable, limitless amusement, Michael found himself the chosen-one of a flaxen-haired beauty whose husband, 'or whatever,' a military man by the look of him, sat at her elbow, more interested in the suckling pig he was devouring, than in the utterly perfect swelling of his wife's tits. Michael's response was to gaze adoringly first into her cornflower blue eyes, and then at her bosom until the little honeypot parted company with her composure. It wasn't at all subtle, but subtlety has little place in adultery. The angel had exhibited sufficient modesty to blush and break off her advances when adored so candidly, but when she had recovered sufficiently to look his way again, Michael turned his gaze upward at the Bacchus, particularly at a point where the naked, supine Adonis was being fed grapes by a similarly undressed maiden who writhed in extremis astride the young god's loins. On this occasion, having followed his glance, the young lady's blushes and confusion were such that her husband or grandfather or whatever the old fart was, noticed the harlot's distress and inquired after her health; at which she explained that the spicy sauce had been so hot as to burn her lips. Michael overheard the remark and resolved that, if not actually burned, her lips wherever he 'came across them,' would at least be very warm by the time that he was through with her. With the spadework done, which would hopefully ensure that the rest of the evening went off with a bang, Michael had suffered enough of the dinner table small talk to choke a horse, so he left it, displaying a complete disregard for convention; an idiosyncrasy for which he was infamous. All that god-cursed trivia and drivel that women found necessary to utter whenever they had a captive male around them was threatening to ruin his excellent humour. He had made the necessary approach, so it was now up to the Norse goddess to free herself of her ancient grandfather and put herself in her admirer's line of fire. He would be happy; very happy to do the rest. For a moment or two, Michael dallied with the notion of interrogating Delavier as to why he had invited the old man to the celebrations, only to realize that he had been undressing the reason with his eyes for the previous hour.

This event was not only the celebration of his lordship's coming-of-age, it was his first experience of Jamaica Place in its wondrously complete form and he wanted to wallow in this manifestation of his own brilliance while there was still light. Ignoring the calls from the inebriated individuals staggering around the place, he crossed the divine mosaic of the foyer and passing through the great porch went out into the fresh air where he stood enthralled by the delightful 'Jacob's Ladder,' its liquid-silver cascade so breathtakingly beautiful that it took one's artistic sentiment captive and held it prisoner.

Ron Sismey, a planter, over from the Chesapeake on business, elbowed him in the ribs, breaking the spell cruelly.

"Any news about your ships yet?"

Michael seethed with instant scorn. From the moment he had discovered the piracy, he had tried to accept that his vessels were a dead loss. The oceans were a very big place in which to hide.

"What the hell du ya mean?" he snorted, lapsing into the American vernacular.

"How on earth could there be any news? They were pirated you idiot."

"Yeah, I know, but old Brassert here seems to think there's a good chance of getinum back." The American indicated the gentleman in question with a flicker of his cold grey eyes. Michael grabbed Nathaniel Brassert by the arm, interrupting the man's telling of one of the outrageous lies for which he was famous and had earned him the nickname; Brassballs.

"Brassy, what's this about my ships?" he demanded. The individual so assaulted wrenched his arm free of his host's grasp, excused himself to his friends on the grounds that his advice was required by an imbecile, and gave Michael his complete condescension.

"Don't put your fucking hand on me again friend, if you want to keep the damned thing." The 'advice' was delivered in a whisper, but with deadly intent; it was the American way. Then with the civilities given due diligence, Brassert went on with a faraway look in his tanned, scarred and annoyingly handsome face, strangely, in Michael's opinion, tapping his foot to the delightful strains of a string quartet on the lawn.

"I weren't gonna say nothin' till ah head sompun' ta say Mick."

"Christ; is that it?" Michael's hopes had risen unchecked. Brassballs sucked in a deep breath.

"It's like this, me old son," he began.

"Them thar soldier boys, Marines? I hear tell they done give ma countrymen on the *Bird* a helluva taam. Dun them wus than niggus. I guess thet's down to you. All the way across the 'Lanic; follered baa all them weeks here at Minster, the word goes." Michael bit his tongue and waited. The man would get to the point eventually.

"'Bout a dozen of 'em daad. Scurvy. Open wounds. Kep' in the dark. Knee deep in shit. No call fer it."

"Have you got something to tell me, or are you about to take holy fucking orders? Get to the sodding point, I haven't got all night.''

''Allraght allraght don spit you pacifaar. Just think about it. They be starving,' sick, injured, scurvy. You name it. Top o' which, they aint got no food nor no water on board, leastways not enuff fer a hunnerd men to cross the 'Lanic. Now! Aa'll bet your ass that right this minute, they be searchin' out some quaat lil spot where they can put in and fill they water barrels, git some vittles tagetha, tend to the wounded and the laak. They shoo aint crossin' no pond, state they're in. I'm guessin' that they be no food, nor no water on them ships of yourn what they stole neither, them bein' in fer repair an all that." Brassballs now came to the brilliance of his ruminations.

Incredibly, despite the vital nature of what the man had to say, Michael found himself totally preoccupied with his friend's excruciating bastardization of the English language and was hard put to follow the man's thinking.

"Are you suggesting that all I have to do is search every cove from Land's End to the Thames Estuary to find them?" Michael was by now keeping a very tight rein on his temper.

"Chrise, but you dense at taams."

''The coast of this island o' yourn, all of it, is fished by someone or tother. All of it; and them thar fishmen, they like nothin' better than a good chinwag. If one o' them drowns

ing280

off Ports Mouth on Fraady, they weep in Brigton on Sadurday. I just put it abaat that fowur ships in a bay could mean a hunnered pounds to the man as takes you to 'em."

Michael clapped his old school friend on the shoulder.

"You're a good man, Brassy," he observed.

"If anything at all comes of this, you'll be well looked after."

"Go shit in you drawers, Astor," snorted Brassert.

"Aah don need yow filthy charidy." The antagonists shook hands with the sincerity of highly valued friendship.

The evening was as enjoyable as dinner had been delicious. Michael positively revelled in his superb billiards room, playing cards in exclusively male company. The extensive chamber had filled with men of similar mind who gravitated there inevitably until a hundred of them were growling away happily in a miasma of tobacco smoke, which hung like low cloud over a green baize sea. Well pleased with life Astor went on his way as darkness fell, happy and as deeply at peace as he had ever been since the loss of his virginity. She had been a black whom he had kept on the deck above the grand cabin of 'Ruthless.' The ungrateful savage had contrived to bite off a pound or two of his ear. The pain was bloody awful and 'in his outrage,' he had fed the screaming cannibal to the sharks at the stern. The annoying part of the whole business was that she had been the most sublime, utterly flawless divinity that he or anyone else had ever set eyes on. He would happily have installed her in a mansion on the York River and played mummy and daddy with her whenever he visited.

The last of the upper floor candles were being extinguished as the deeply contented individual sauntered towards Jamaica's glorious portico, elegantly held aloft as it was by Doric columns alternated with caryatids, all of them female and wonderfully undressed. His chest swelled with pride at the beauty of it all as he paused to let his eyes feast. His guests were taking to their beds and only the dirtiest of girls were to be spied loitering abroad and by the lake as he embarked on a casual lap of it in order to reflect, enjoy a cigar and pass a little time.

"Michael." He could not locate her in the darkness, but he recognized, that it was Ruth Montague who was calling and though he was unable to discover her whereabouts the sneaky bitch could obviously see him. How bloody annoying that she had turned-up uninvited. This meeting would probably not go well for the possessive cow. No wonder he could not locate her, she was rowing a bloody boat and handily too. She brought it stern-first to the bank, and he stepped in as she clearly wished. 'Christ almighty she was beautiful.'

"I need you this minute Michael," her whispered declaration was urgent, "we will go to that island." As her coat fell open a trifle it was shockingly apparent that she was damn near naked beneath it. An age and a throbbing millennia later the lusting antagonists arrived in the wonderful solitude of their island refuge where Michael jumped into the shallows eager to tie up, he would take the insistent nuisance to heaven then strangle her there. What could be more considerate? Turning back to lift his stewing prize from the ark he discovered a very businesslike pistol pointing at his heart. Its report, the smoke and the agony of the large lead ball smashing through his chest were the last features of his life as he abandoned his corporeal self in fury that a mere girl had beaten him soundly at his own filthy game.

It was approaching one o'clock when he regained an uncomfortable consciousness. His ribs had taken on a particularly pretty shade of purple and were good for nothing, but his cigar-case; a treasured gift from his adorable never to be forgotten darling Jodie Michelle Fontein which had absorbed the awful strike was now an ashtray. Folding his clothes neatly he swam awkwardly ashore and ambled homeward nodding-to and sharing a knowing laugh and brief explanation with the vigilant roughnecks who apprehended him as they searched for the armed intruder. It pleased him to send them in the wrong direction. His revenge would be personal in the extreme.

It was time to commence with the education of the Nordic tart who thought herself so emancipated. With a new urgency in his stride and a very definite tingling in the supreme groin, he went directly to his office where Delavier, considerate as always of his master's needs, had originated a ledger of the rooms allocated to his guests.

"Well done, dear boy," he murmured as he scanned the page and located the name he was seeking. The goddess would presently be wetting herself in a stew of lust as she waited for him to arrive at her bedside; he would wager good money on it, and only two suites away along the corridor. He took a bath, warm this time, scrubbed himself dry in places, then with the master-key in his hand, strolled naked along the thickly carpeted passageway to her room sending away footmen and the occasional slaves found sleeping at doorways as he went. With his ear against her door, he could hear the old walrus snoring. He unlocked; and astoundingly tumescent; went inside. She was not in the bed. The fat-bellied husband snored alone lying on his back more like a sow than a boar, diagonal in the middle of the four-poster. The all but naked tottie was resting on her belly on a chaise longue, reading a text which lay on the rug beside her. Turning her exquisitely modelled head, she took in his naked form, her eyes settling unashamed and widening on his erect member and its twin friends. She groaned involuntarily and her hips began to undulate unbidden, almost as though she had him inside her already. Closing the door quietly with his heel, he strode quickly to her. She looked away arching her perfect body, lifting her delicious rear slightly in the most provocative invitation for him to take her firstly from behind. Michael dispensed with the diaphanous nothing which barely concealed her adorable bottom and covered her, realizing as their bodies met, why it was that she was so, ready. The book was pornographic and showed a lady being taken from behind by one individual, while she sucked hungrily at the member of another, whose thighs she was clutching. The goddess raised that perfect arse still further, reciprocating as he delved in her wonderfully moist purse, so gently; so very slowly. Tantalizingly. All without a word. Reaching back, she urged him to thrust deeper and harder into her, turning her head away to conceal her expression of utter carnality, as on her rider's violent assault she reached her orgasm, soaking them both with an effusive gush of her secretions. Passing her hand between her perfect thighs, she found him and drove him insane with the tips of her fingers, causing him to come mightily in her, much sooner than he had wished while she gloried in receiving his ejaculation; biting her wrist a second time, in order not to scream.

"We will go to your room," the beauty gasped at last.

When she stood, her diminutive proportions became erotically apparent, her breasts large for her delicate frame. She held his erect member in her hands as she allowed her nipples to brush his belly. Michael slipped an arm around the divine child, drawing her to him, but with a touch which was as gentle as a feather, she rebuked him, then capturing his erection between those breasts, she massaged, kissed and caressed him until he came in her clever hands. She stood on the couch, which he noticed bore the evidence of her release and drew him close. Very close. As they kissed and explored the glories which each held for the other, she eased herself up, her mouth on his, her arms about his neck, and embracing him with her legs around him, she found his hardness with her loins and took him deeply inside her again. The happy couple proceeded from the room as one. The motion of their perambulation proved unendurable for her, and Mirabelle shuddered in extremis again as they proceeded along the passageway. On this occasion, her exaltation was such that she could not endure in silence, and the scream that would have betrayed her was muffled only by her lover's cruel kiss. Michael lay his treasure gently in his bed without ever withdrawing from her warmth; desperate to have her again and to have her completely; indefensibly.

Folding double, the more than willing child, like a delectable omelet he plunged into her with the abandon and ferocity of battle, without any attempt at restraint. She was perfect, and met every thrust with growing need, shared his incoherence, and clasped him to her with unalloyed devotion, goading him to ever more strenuous assault. They came as one in a crescendo which mingled their cries, their sweat, their shuddering oneness, their ejaculations and their rapture.

CHAPTER 18: Pride Goes Before A Fall

Captain Bartholomew Plumly-Horton vomited his breakfast over the side of the *Justice* and wondered as he did so, why it was that during twenty-seven years at sea, he had not managed to overcome this affliction. He blamed his demotion from Captain of a sixty-gun ship of the line, to master of this so-called officer training ship, on this, his only failing. In every other quality, skill, and field of endeavor that could conceivably be required of an officer of the British Navy, he was clearly unequalled. Feeding the fish yet again he coughed up with some difficulty a lump of porridge which had stuck in his throat and reached for his flask.

"Good morning, sir. We have made our offing and with your permission will come to east-south-east along the coast as instructed." It was Carstairs, naturally; the ingratiating little bastard; famously a bumboy of Admiral Gosling, would find every excuse imaginable to kiss the backside of his betters. The captain scrubbed the filth from his face with a handkerchief then washing out his mouth with gin, hosed the odious mixture over the side.

"Make it so," he nodded, concealing his gin-breath from the junior officer by a tactful deployment of the silk. Why this ugly, immature barnacle had to be so infuriatingly happy at every hour that God sent, was totally beyond the good Captain.

"Thank you, sir," beamed Carstairs, and strode off to inform his fellow officer cadets that they now had the captain's permission to break their backs turning a hundred tons of ship. Good Christ, it was all so cursed unfair. Of course, the Admiralty had sugared the medicine and insisted that this was a promotion, and that no other Captain was as well-equipped as he to complete the training of the next brood of fluffy young officers to join the service, et bloody cetera but it was as clear as day to himself however that the vomiting business had cost him his career. 'The *Justice*!' Even the name of this floating kindergarten was an insult. If there were any 'justice' in the world, he would have a leviathan under him with a hundred guns at his disposal, not a mere six plus a stern-chaser, all at the mercy of fifty sons of gentlefolk, unable to find their way out of the Thames Estuary in broad daylight.

'The *Indomitable*,' now there was a name for a ship. Sixty guns and a crew of two hundred and sixty-three. She had been lost off Akimiski Island in the James Bay, the solitary testicle of the Hudson; through no fault of his own of course; crushed by the ice during his search for the North-West Passage. The crew had perished to a man on the dreadful walk out; every single one of the lazy, unwashed, illiterates but to his great and undying credit he had saved every member; 'every member;' of his officer cadre. That singular accomplishment had not gone unnoticed by the Admiralty. Oh no. Indeed, it had been mentioned in awe on several occasions during the inquisition which always follows such events. He could well remember the astonishment on Admiral Trumper's screwed up parchment of a face, as the old seadog enunciated, "So... conditions were so... appalling... that every member of... your crew perished in the snow and... yet you managed to save... the ship's officers to a man?"

It was then, of course, that he, Bartholomew Plumly-Horton, had made his shortest, yet most brilliant remark.

"Not all of the credit is mine, sir." Suitably modest; understated, yet subtly pointing up the magnitude of his achievement.

"I do believe that we have found them, sir." It was that confounded Carstairs again breaking into a man's deliberations, curse him. The leader of men well knew that his powers of concentration were so great that he often spent the whole day philosophically preoccupied and a glance at the sun confirmed that this had occurred yet again; mid-day was upon them.

"The devil, you say."

"Yes, sir. The masthead reports ships at anchor in the bay off the port bow, and better still a small army of them ashore." Carstairs' joy was such that one would think that he had discovered El Dorado, rather than a bunch of colonial farmers attempting to escape British justice. For a moment or two, the brat's beautific visage became distorted as though under water, as Plumly-Horton imagined the man, hands and feet securely bound; drowning; his flesh being ripped piecemeal from his bones by the barnacles as he was keel-hauled beneath this floating playpen. But he digressed. Throwing up his glass with a theatrical flourish, he scoured the enemy's now visible disposition with the professional thoroughness for which he was famous. Just as he had predicted; the poor, ignorant fools had left their vessels unmanned but for a few oafs who were engaged in splashing paint down their sides; the numbers bore out this finding; there had to be seventy or eighty or so of the half-naked philistines roaming the foreshore like the marauders they were.

"It's too late for that, you scoundrels," he bawled, playing to the crowd.

''Plumly-Horton has you on a lee shore." It was then, in a 'eureka' moment of intense excitement, that the good captain saw with utter certainty, his route back to preferment with the powers that be. Soon, 'his' would be the name on the lips of everyone in Whitehall. Everyone who 'mattered,' at least. Indeed, when this business was over, he would be promoted master of a hundred-gun ship of the line, or he was a cheesehead. Morbidly cautious; as old women invariably are, his superior had ordered him only to find the American miscreants and report their position overland to Fastor or Castor or some-such from the nearest port so that the money bags could dispatch a squadron to regain his property. 'Four ships,' the fact that there were only 'three' vessels visible at anchor was a rotten apple in his full barrel of joy, but one that could easily be disposed of. He would capture these three, thusly earning the undying gratitude of the owners, whom he understood were as rich as Croesus; and maroon the filthy nest of rats on the shore; all at a single stroke. With four vessels thusly at his disposal, it would then be a simple matter to take the fourth prize when it returned. Twenty guns or not.

"Brilliant!"

"Brilliant, sir?"

"Fancy a bit of swordplay, Carstairs?" Plumly-Horton inquired, gloating as the perennial smile fell from the idiot's face.

"Put us between the two on the left and ready the boats. 'Doubleday' and your esteemed self will lead the boarding parties. Ten men to a lighter, while I go on to take the three-master. We will then make for Portsmouth through the Solent." Delighted by the prospect of boarding an unguarded ship, Carstairs touched his tricorn to his Captain, then forgetting his dignity, raced away to harangue the boatswain. Before this day was out, he would be famous for taking one '*Bird*' and two others, and his career would be off to a flying start. How proud of him his Mummy and his beloved Nursy would be. He enjoyed a slight stiffening at the very thought of Nursey and the things that she would do to him. She had probably been dismissed by now due to his protracted absence from home poor thing. 'She would take his thingy in her mouth, and oh the wonderment of it as she swallowed so, so, hungrily. Best of all she worked for a shilling a week.

Far below the clifftop eyrie on which he was perched, the row of simple crosses behind the beach encampment had increased by two in number since he last stood here. There were seven of them now. Seven good young men lost. Not in battle, about which he would have no qualms, but by the conditions of their captivity. Macbeth was saddened and angered by this unnecessary and criminal loss of life that Astor's creatures had inflicted on the Americans through their mistreatment of them but had long ago learned to accept that such were the excesses of the class against which he was committed. Life was cheap to them. The pain and suffering of others; was of no consequence to such people. The sides of the infirmary tent had been rolled up to allow a cooling breeze to reach its inhabitants, but the measure would bring them little enough relief. Despite the large quantities of good food now being purchased from the county's farms the lives of several more of the *Bird*'s sailors still hung by threads. The poor sods were so reduced by scurvy and starvation that they could not benefit from this improvement in their situation. Death of scurvy was a slow, ugly affair, and the Scot had seen more than enough of it over the years so that he now found himself incapable of doing anything at all for the dying. He left such things to others and gave the place a wide berth. That girl who had been captive aboard the *Bird* was apparently proving to be an angel to those men. No one, not the foraging parties or the ones sent to buy food, had been able to find a sawbones within ten miles of here; and so there had been no relief at all for their suffering, until that is; Hooligan of all people, had fronted up with a part-bottle of opium. The magical liquid was being used, albeit sparingly in the form of laudanum, but even so, rumor had it that there was only an inch or two of the elixir left in the bottom of the container. At the present rate of consumption, that quantity would last perhaps three more days according to Boatswain Holdsworth, who oversaw such things. Yet-another reason to quit this place at the earliest possible moment. Just how the Irishman could have got his dirty big paws on opium was beyond Macbeth's imagination. 'Sure,' he thought, adopting the madman's expression, 'if the loon fell intae a bucket o' shit, he'd climb out smellin' o' roses.'

Macbeth couldn't help smiling as he recalled wrestling the crazy generous, likeable, ignoramus in a village lane on the first occasion that they bumped heads with one another. The leprechaun 'had-been,' covered in shit on that occasion, but he had certainly not smelled of roses. Fretting at his own enforced inaction he scanned the pale, empty horizon, behind which Hooligan and his new chum Teach were on station in the *Glorious*. During times of quiet such as this it was critical to keep the men on their toes, and for that reason, only an hour or so before negotiating the suicidal goat-track to this lookout, he had conducted a tour of inspection of the *Bird*, and then the *Liverpool* and the *Boston*, as the ships were now known. He had been well pleased with his findings.

After their months of near starvation, the Americans were now devouring mountains of fresh fish, beef, vegetables and fruit, but despite this, the ships' reserves of potatoes, lentils, squash, flour and the like, were building steadily and he had estimated that within a couple of days, three or four at the most they would have supplies enough to make the much-anticipated voyages to Perth in Scotland and Nantes in France. It would be a great relief to get his people off this bloody beach and escape this trap which they had of necessity, made for themselves. 'Nantes.' That thought struck a nerve. Why did that strange old 'Ben' fella want to go there of all places? That business meant several days spent travelling in the opposite direction to Perth. Was it to give Astor's ships more time to find them? Nantes sat ufifty miles inland from the Atlantic; you had to navigate the narrows of the Loire at Saint-Nazaire to get to the place; would there be a nasty surprise waiting for the *Glorious* down there? If that was the case the very furrst thing he'd do would be to strangle the wee snot and dump his carcass over the side. Ben! What sort of a name was that? With every day that passed, Macbeth had grown more suspicious of the pretentious old fart. Lliam Hooligan had sensed it too, so he wasn't just imagining things. He recalled Hooligan's reaction when Ben had absentmindedly claimed the top of the table for himself.

"You're a spy in lawyer's clothing, Benny boy," he murmured. The urgent work of disguising the ships was going ahead satisfactorily. They had been re-named, as Hooligan had required. Those ridiculous baroque figureheads had been chopped away, and the paintwork and rigging were in the process of being altered to make them unrecognizable. From where he stood, he could just make out tiny sailors suspended against their sides, painting as though their lives depended on it, which they probably did.

He had been pleased to find that the three stern-chaser cannons had been professionally installed and ruggedly secured with hawsers as thick as a man's arm; supplied with grape shot, wooden cannonballs, powder, wadding, and American-made ramrods fashioned from English oars. The water barrels had been scrubbed clean and were full to their brims with cold sweet water, the decks had been made shipshape and even holystoned in places and the worn and damaged rigging replaced. At this rate, he would soon be in Perth, thank goodness, where he would make his report to the Laird, receive his new instructions, and then it would be home to his wee angels at the gallop. Or by ship. 'Thank God the wee one takes after her mother and not me.'

What a report this one would be. Three excellent vessels wrenched out of Astor's grubby paws for starters. One of the swine's most productive shipyards burned to the ground and an abolitionist ship set free, along with its crew of four score and more, all committed to the cause. Then of course, there were the issues of Hooligan and Ben. Would Hooligan commit himself and his ships to the cause? Macbeth devoutly hoped so because the Irishman certainly stood out from the crowd in a fight. As for that lying Ben character, the wee man's very presence was like a stone in his shoe. He was a bucket of wurrums that one. Suspicion ran through Macbeth's veins as blood does in other men, so he would not trust that old charlatan as far as he could throw him. The dissembler spoke like an American, but every now and then he would employ a word or phrase or pronounce a word in a way which only the English gentry would do. Also, a spoonful of sincerity would poison the man; he was far too much the politician, and a diplomat come to that to be the genuine article. He had a way of trying to be all things to all men. How convenient it was for the auld fraud that he had been driven thousands of miles by a storm, only to end up safe and sound precisely where the *Burrd* was about to put to sea. A ship with a price on it. He had fooled his American crewmen, but he was not fooling Macbeth, not by a long chalk. And another thing! The man was far too clever to be a merchant or whatever it was that he reckoned to be, you could tell that he understood every damn thing he came across as though he'd invented it. The man was up to his neck in book-learning. Merchants didn't waste time reading books; half o' them were illiterate anyhow and they didn't have to work into their old age either. They were all up to their fat knees in gold.

Far below him; a coaster was making laborious, if not foolhardy headway, climbing huge swells and falling from the top of them into deep troughs, every one of which promised to drive it down-under. It was probably making for the Isle of Wight, by way of Davy Jones' locker, judging by its present course which was fundamentally, 'steering south while being driven east.'

Every day saw shipping of a dozen nations navigate this coast, generally 'on, or just below' the horizon where only their tops'ls showed, though fishing boats close to shore were such a common sight, that the lookouts and guards no longer signaled their approach. There would be no fishing boats today with the ocean as angry as this. He was livid beyond speech at the sentries' slack-twisted behavior in this regard, recognizing it for what it was; the thin end of a wedge which could prize open the doors to catastrophe.

"What was the point of mounting guard if ye didnae sing oot," he fumed. 'Not while I have breath in me.' Macbeth made himself more comfortable in his grassy lookout; he had earned a wee rest after all. There was no way on Beelzebub's well-smacked arse that he would let these good men fall into English hands a second time. They had shown themselves to be the salt of the earth, so he would protect them as though they were his own, even if he had to kill one or two of them to do it. Ben would be first. A stern word or two with Holdsworth about security wouldn't hurt either. The black man was presently on watch at the highest point on this cliff only a couple of hundred yards away, his red pea jacket showing clearly against the grey of the rocks. The fool was looking straight back at him instead of at the sea. And now he had the gall to wave both of his big pink paws. As Macbeth's hackles rose at this childish stupidity, Holdsworth suddenly got to his feet and inexplicably, raised the Alarm flag, waving the thing two-handed above his head.

Startled; and mystified, he turned hastily, scouring the ocean avidly, with and without his glass, but incredibly, there was nothing to be seen. The sea was empty of craft of any persuasion other than the coaster which was stubbornly refusing to founder; it was wallowing like a snail traversing a washboard.

Holdsworth was still signaling, and the four guard stations below; those aboard the ships, and the one on the rocks at the extreme reaches of the sand were now signifying their battle stations. With the alarm raised successfully, the big fellow secured his flag under a stone and sprinted away, moving with surprising speed for such a muscled individual. Risking it all the American hurtled down the steep sward to the maw of the horrible path and a fall of a hundred yards and was lost to sight behind the edge of the cliff. Incredibly, there was still nothing to be seen on the water. Snapping his glass shut and shoving it into his pack, he set out at a lumbering run in Holdsworth's footsteps, cursing the man for not letting-on what was happening. Behind him, someone was hailing from a distance, and he turned. Unbelievably, it was that lying bastard Ben of all people, approaching in obvious distress at the unaccustomed exertion.

"Wait. Wait," the old liar gasped. The fool still had that dead-cat on his head. Macbeth hesitated; behaviour which was completely out of character for him, caught as he now was between this old devil and the deep blue sea; the impulse to action on the one hand, and the anchor of suspicion on the other. The anchor prevailed. Why else would a man of his years risk death, inching his way up that godawful goat track if he wasn't being paid to do it? He fumed inwardly at the delay but resolved to get the truth out of him right this minute or oblige him to jump. One or the other. His pals could like it or lump it.

"Oh it's you… Mister… Macbeth." The old fart was winded when he eventually got within shouting distance.

"Where's… Boatswain Holds…?"

"He's gone below, where I should be if it wusnae fer 'you', sur," Macbeth started as he meant to go on.

"There's an alarm and I'm standin' here gabbin' to *you*." The word 'you' was uttered with such disgust that only a deaf man could have been unaware of its insult. Desperately concerned for the safety of the trapped ships and their crews, Macbeth took out his glass again and scoured the still-innocent water as he waited for the timewaster to stagger the last few yards. Nothing. There was absolutely nothing to be seen, yet it stood to reason that if Holdsworth had spied so much as a smudge on the horizon, it would be showing as a sail by now, so why couldn't he find it?

"He was… he was waving… at… at me… not you." Ben was gasping painfully by the time he made it to where the Scotsman fumed impatiently.

"What?" Macbeth was utterly disbelieving of this outlandish assertion.

"Friend Holdsworth… he was… signal… ling… to me, Macbeth… not to you, respon… ding to *my* signal."

"Wus he, indeed? An' what the hell are you doin' up here in the furrst place?" Macbeth brushed the man's drab lie aside. Utterly exhausted, and not very well, Ben promptly dropped his backside down on a boulder and motioned for the agitated warrior to do likewise. The Scot, in his stew of suspicion of 'the printer,' as the man characterized himself, remained standing and continued to sweep every visible inch of water. Several minutes passed and still there were no ships to be seen, and Macbeth's hopes that Holdsworth had been mistaken seemed to be realized. 'It's an ill wind,' he concluded thankfully, and began to relax just a little. There was nothing lost after all, and it would do the lookouts no harm to suffer a false alarm; it might even waken the wee buggers up a bit. Ben spoke at last, having got his breath back somewhat.

"Boatswain Holdsworth… assigned me to sentry… duty… back there. Behind that hill." Ben nodded briefly to the west, the direction from which he had come,

"From where I… was… standing, I could see right along the coast… Miles and miles. My orders were to… signal to friend Holdsworth should I see anything… so close to shore that they might be …looking for us… as opposed to staying out in the shipping lanes, that is. And I did. And the crafty devil… is about to round our headland over there." Ben nodded at the bay below as though he were expecting visitors for tea, rather than a gun-platform which would smash the fleet to splinters.

"What! Mother of Christ. Are ye bloody mad?" Macbeth gave full vent to his fury. It was all he could do not to grab the bastard by his wrinkly fat throat and the seat of his pantaloons and hurry him over the edge. He ran for the goat track.

"Be still, sir." It was an order. And a contemptuous one at that.

"You are not the *only* man here you know, Macbeth. Show some faith… in Captain Teach, Mister… Hooligan, Boatswain Holdsworth… and the rest. We have a hundred… fighting men and twenty guns at our disposal… One more man will make *little* difference." Ben succeeded wonderfully well in returning the compliment of Macbeth's 'you', with his, 'little.'

"And who the devil are *you* tae take that tone wi' *me*, sur?" Macbeth raged, turning back as though to do murder.

"Any more and I'll be teaching ye how tae fly. It was nae so lang ago that you and yer hunnered hard men were very pleased tae see this 'singular' individual. As I recall, ye were starving in the dark and stondin in shit. As for yer twenty guns it has obviously escaped yer sneaky notice that they're nowhere to be seen. Now sur, before I do something about which 'you' will be more than a wee bittie sorry, tell me who the fuck ye really are, and what you are doin' here, because you, sur, are nae maire a merchant than my fucking arse."

Very much aware of the proximity of the cliff and the murderous mountain's propensity for violence, Ben almost spat-out his reply.

"The truth is, Mister Macbeth, that I am Benjamin Franklin, leader of the United States, Delegation to the court of King Louis the Sixteenth of France," managing it all in just one breath.

"There ye go," the Scotsman bawled into Franklin's face,

"That wusnae so hard, was it? Do yer pals know this, or do ye lie yer arse aff tae them as well as tae the people who saved yer miserable life, and yer ship too? Is that the way it goes?"

"No, they don't. They are unaware. They believe that… I am a… simple merchant trying to… get to France on business. Circumstances are such that I may not… reveal my… identity, even to them."

"Oh, and why might that be?" Macbeth was beginning to believe what he was hearing.

"I must sit down," sobbed Franklin. Realizing that his prisoner was trembling, Macbeth loosened his grip on the old man's coat and allowed him to rest his arse on a boulder, greatly relieved that the American's secret was such an innocuous one. There was silence for a while as the ancient recovered from his earlier exertions and the shock of Macbeth's onslaught. Delving in his pack and bringing out a flask of rum the inquisitor shoved it at the ancient who grasped the container gratefully and seemed to recover somewhat after a few sips.

"I cannot take any risks with my identity and my commission being discovered," he began.

"You see, my primary objective in France is the business of securing French support in our struggle. If I were to fail …"

"And what struggle might that be?" Macbeth sat down facing Franklin, and spoke a little less threateningly, though his tone dripped sarcasm. What Franklin said next, shocked all such conceit out of him.

"Mister Macbeth." Franklin announced portentously then paused as though weighing the likely result of his disclosure,

"You must surely be aware that for some considerable time now, your country and mine have been at war." Macbeth almost fell off his boulder.

"You're mad tae say it," he scoffed, and seizing the flask from Franklin's shaking hand, drank deeply.

"Clearly you don't; or can't read Macbeth. Such a pity. The diplomat suffered a coughing fit due to the liquor and was thus unaware of the Scotsman's burning indignation on hearing this assumption.

"We of the Army of the Continent are few in numbers," he managed, coughing uncomfortably.

"Comparatively speaking that is, and light on supplies. We need French help. English ships of the line are denying our ports to us, and New York is already lost, though we have them trapped at Boston. You declared yourself no loyalist Macbeth. You won't betray me to the…?"

"Dinnae fash yersel, laddie," exclaimed the suddenly ebullient Scot, leaping to his feet as though to join the American struggle immediately,

"I've said it afore an' I'll say it again, Georgie boy's nae king o' mine, an' I'd bet a pound to a pinch of shit that young Hooligan is o' like mind. We'll see ye safe to Nantes, and tae Paris too if ye wish it, always supposing that you're telling me the truth. If not; then you'll just be swimmin' and not flyin.'" Franklin clasped his palms together in a gesture which seemed part-prayer and part-victory celebration breathing a few words which his interrogator did not catch. Wagging a cautionary finger larger than a French sausage the Scot continued,

"Now, I wouldnae want ye to think me a sceptic…"

"Heaven forbid," protested Franklin. With patent sincerity.

"But ye 'wull' be showin' me yer letters of intri-duction afore this day is oot, mind."

"I wull er 'will,'" Franklin affirmed,

"I hid them away aboard the *Burrd*. The '*Bird*', rather, and not even the English found them."

"That's braw."

"What are you going to do about this ship that's coming though?" Franklin was all concern again. The hairy marauder turned to face the sea as though it was his private domain.

"Not a thing," the giant replied phlegmatically

"Her master will plot our position on his charts and in a couple o' days, he'll be back wi' the big guns tae hang the lot of us, but by then, you will be half-way to Nantes, and I will be half-way home."

"Look," said Franklin, utterly convinced by the Scot's authority in such matters, and nodded at the *Bird* lying below where a longboat crammed with saber-wielding American sailors rose and fell against her hull, disgorging several of its occupants each time it crested. Men who scrambled energetically up its sides and toppled over its bulwarks, then raced across the decks into hiding. Holdsworth, recognizable in his red jacket, was already in the rigging. With the air cleared so much to the satisfaction of both the American and the Scot; freedom-fighters both; the two men were then content to sit together in a thoughtful silence which extended to almost an hour, awaiting the inevitable.

It was there; a twin-masted vessel of six guns appeared from the west and rounded the headland, just as Franklin had predicted, but instead of going on her way to report her findings and return with reinforcements, as would be the sensible; 'the only' course of action, the enemy did the unbelievable, she turned hard to port in her own length, and raced under full sail at the anchored merchantmen, lying seemingly deserted and at her mercy.

"That man is mad; or he's aff his heed, one or the other," belched the Scot, jumping up and locating the Englishman with his glass.

"Mother of mine, it's the British Navy. What the devil is he playing at? Surely tae Christ, Astor cannae get the Admiralty tae dae his durrty wurk?" Another sail appeared on the horizon due south of where the two men stood, causing Macbeth to groan aloud. All the signs were that a trap was closing.

"Thank goodness. The *Glorious*," rejoiced Franklin, seemingly quite unconcerned by the approach of the British Navy now that *Glorious*, with her fourteen remaining guns, was entering the fray. Getting arthritically to his feet, he reached for Macbeth's telescope with comradely assurance.

"I hate tae disappoint ye Benjy but that big bastard is nae the *Glorious*." Macbeth relinquished the instrument abstractedly.

"She's hermaphrodite rigged, and black between sea and sky… Can ye really see that far wi' they eyeglasses o' yoors?" Franklin pushed his spectacles up on to his forehead and put the telescope to his eye.

"I certainly can. 'Bifocals' I call them. I can read through one lens and see distances through the other. Try them." Macbeth took the eyeglasses from Franklin's head and was startled by their efficacy.

''My sainted..!''

"It's just a family resemblance,'' Franklin was regaining his composure.

''I invented them for purposes of my printing business and various other occupations. You know what they say."

"No, I don't. What do they say?" Macbeth was intrigued and charmed by this empirical proof of the man's genius, realizing meanwhile why it was that the Bird's crew were so in awe of the wee tub o lard.

"'Necessity is the mother of invention… ' Oh, ye of little faith," Franklin chided the giant standing over him.

"What have we been doing to these ships?" He nodded at the vessels below.
"Disguising them, of course, dear friend. Captain Teach and Mister Hooligan have been doing the same to the *Glorious*. Naturally enough."

"Well I'll be damned." Macbeth swapped the eyeglasses for his telescope.

"Nothing could be more certain."

"Look at the speed of her. They'll drive her unner if they dinnae slacken aff." Franklin reached out to the telescope and gently redirected it so that Macbeth found the English six-gunner again. In a remarkable display of seamanship, the English attackers closed rapidly on Hooligan's prizes, *Liverpool*, *Boston* and the *Bird*. They hove-to as abruptly as if they had beached her, at a spot precisely mid-way between the *Bird* and the *Liverpool*, emptied the wind from her sails, and launched cutters to port and starboard replete with boarding parties, all in one thoroughly practiced and brilliantly executed manoeuvre.

"They know what they are doing," snarled Macbeth grudgingly,

"but they're in for a surprise when they reach the *Burrd*. Admiralty or not. What they are doing is piracy, by the way."

"I'm afraid not," observed Franklin.

The English boarding parties were already pulling like well-whipped galley slaves for both the *Bird* and the *Liverpool*, clearly intent on capturing the unmanned ships, thereby marooning the escapees on the beach. From high above, twice as many American sailors could be seen in ambush as were visible in the *Bird*'s rigging, their numbers now augmented by the three men who had been painting her sides and had supposedly fled in terror. The odds were now twenty-three hardened fighters against a dozen uniformed men of his Britannic Majesty's Royal Navy. Macbeth wondered whether the English would have pulled quite so hard had they known what was waiting for them. Incredibly everyone aboard those lighters seemed to be completely unaware of the approaching gun-platform, probably due to their preoccupation with conquest. The speed of the *Glorious* was remarkable. In moments she had halved the distance between shore and sky, and was continuing with her headlong lunacy, charging straight into what could so easily become self-destruction, under such an acreage of sail that her masts must fail, or she must founder in one of the huge swells into which she was smashing, leap after leap. Captain Teach was risking all with every roller she struck.

"Probably egged on by Hooligan," said the worried Scot, then realized that he had spoken aloud. The thunder of those collisions was so loud that they were now audible on the clifftop. Macbeth put his glass on her again and was not in the least surprised to see; large as life and twice as ugly none other than Lliam Shaun Hooligan Esquire laughing uproariously as he hurtled into the fight. On came *Glorious*, with caution thrown to those same winds from which her perfect trimming was extracting every ounce of advantage; gun ports closed and intent on grappling. Racing like a clipper now, in the smoother waters of the bay. Yet again; Macbeth rejoiced in the day he became acquainted with a drunken Irish tramp.

"Lliam Hooligan," he bawled.

"I bloody love ye."

Franklin smirked superciliously but tactfully refrained from comment. If the English seamanship had been remarkable, that of the Americans aboard *Glorious* was inspired. *Glorious*, now renamed *Liberty*, struck the smaller English vessel in her stern-port-quarter, with an impact which all but capsized the smaller vessel, throwing her crew violently around the decks, and shattered her fore mast, bringing down its upper third, along with miles of rigging and tons of canvas, on the terrified youths below. Clearing a path for herself, like a granite curling-stone, the *Liberty* smashed her way along the Englishman's side, devastating the anchor-points of her remaining rigging and ripping away great swathes of her superstructure. A score of well anchored grapples were thrown, and the *Liberty* shuddered to a halt slewing around with such tremendous momentum that the smaller ship was hoist upwards from the ocean until with a savage splintering of timbers she sank again swaying dangerously close to destruction.

Hooligan had chosen as his personal target, the fat pretentious uniform whom he imagined to be the Captain of the *Justice*, even before the cataclysmic collision of the two ships. The bloodsucker stood out like a spare prick at a wedding, posturing grandly on the poop deck of the six-gun plaything which he commanded.

The avenger had sprinted the length of the *Liberty* and clambered on to the bulwark, shoving other warriors aside in order to claim the most advantageous spot from which to launch his attack. As the grapples came in to play, he allowed himself to be catapulted into the smaller ship's rigging, from where he dropped to the deck within a few yards of the chosen one, just as that individual regained his feet; a yard of shining steel magically appearing in the man's hand. Belatedly realizing that this was not just another scrap in an ale house and avoiding the Englishman's first thrust by the skin of his non-existent belly, Hooligan smashed the steersman in the face and took refuge behind the enormous wheel, just as an over-enthusiastic Plumly-Horton slashed at him in what the now very scared pirate considered to be an act of gratuitous violence. Such was the ferocity of the good Captain's blow that the hardened steel of the naval cutlass bit deeply into the age-toughened mahogany of the wheel and mated with it, seemingly for life. Snarling like a pit-bull-bitch, Plumly-Horton wrenched at his weapon in a fury, while Hooligan, initially astonished that his prayers had been answered; 'this being a first,' saw his hilarious opportunity and spun the oversized edifice of timber and brass enthusiastically. Unwilling and a second later, unable, to relinquish his grip on the cutlass, his hand being trapped in the guard, Plumly-Horton was painfully contorted to the point where his right arm passed over his left shoulder, and he was wrestled inexorably over and down, till he found himself attempting to limbo backwards between the spokes. At the limit of his gymnastic ability, the intrepid swordsman collapsed on his back in the missionary position, enabling his adversary, a one-eyed monster, to drop agonizingly, knees first, onto his chest and pummel his face into a bloody mess.

The naval cutlass is a terrible weapon; long, heavy, and with a razor-sharp blade on one edge only. Its other edge is a thick backbone of steel, which provides sufficient momentum to drive it through clothing as heavy as a naval greatcoat, prior to severing flesh and bone. Seldom is a blow struck with this weapon without the victim being killed or maimed. The English youths who boarded the *Bird*, were novices with this heavy, clumsy death dealer, whilst the Americans who were very well practiced with both it and the naval war axe came at them like berserkers. Within minutes of hostilities beginning, half of the youths in uniform lay dead or nearly so, while the survivors were disarmed and cowed.

The boarding party dispatched to take the *Boston* fared little better, they were barely half-way to their objective when a racing twenty-gunner called *Liberty* filled their field of vision. In a state of panic, they 'came-about,' when to carry on would have been by far the better option, and labored back to the mother ship, reaching its comforting sides just as the enemy struck. The bow of their cutter was driven beneath the waves as the *Justice* rolled on top of it under the impact of Liberty's assault, crushing some of the boys horribly and drowning others, while those in the stern were thrown violently into the air to crash against the ship's side before dropping into the ocean.

On board the Justice the sons-of-gentle-folk were unceremoniously disarmed, herded together and driven up Liberty's precipitous hull, to await their fate on her decks. The sympathy which the American's naturally felt for their surprisingly youthful captives, some of them mere boys, evaporated rapidly when, under the protection of their surrender, the newly christened 'little bastards,' began to bleat about how they never would have gone 'hands up' had they known that they were fighting a gang of uneducated colonials, people who were unable to conjugate their Latin verbs, went barefoot and spoke the mother tongue no better than a bunch of stinking coolies.

Naked but for his hair shirt and tired after a long swim Macbeth clambered aboard and into a free-for-all which had erupted when the English realised that their captors were loath to shoot them. Grabbing a musket from the hands of a seaman the scot fired a shot that got the full attention of the miscreants.

''Shoot the next man that strikes a blow,'' he bawled.

''Either side mind.'' The Americans extricated themselves and muskets were aimed, this time with real intent.

''Get these wee bastarts chained below. Who the hell is in charge here?''

"I am," laughed Teach from the head of the gangway,

"so watch your mouth.' Followed by Hooligan, Teach approached the 'otter in human form,' with arms thrown wide in greeting.

"Whenever we meet you discard your clothes Macbeth. Is there something that you wish to share with me? Bosun some clothing for the gentlemen before I lose all control."

The atmosphere in the grand cabin was that of a war-room for 'The Brass,' as they were now known, Hooligan, Teach Macbeth the captains and the boatswains were hammering out an escape plan. It was a simple affair and in so far as could be ascertained; foolproof. The Liberty under Teach and Hooligan would carry Mister Ben to Nantes and then race for the Firth of Tay in Scotland; to which waterway the slower ships would sail directly in order to report to the Laird Monteith the senior abolitionist and Macbeth's paymaster.

Hooligan, who had never seen France or a French woman, or much of anything at all really, was desperately keen to sail to that country and the sooner the better. For the greater part of his life, he had listened wide-eyed whenever lurid tales of the insatiable sexual appetite of the 'Mademoiselles' were being told, and he very much wanted to investigate the voracity of these claims. He also wanted to discover how his mighty *Liberty* coped with the open ocean and most interestingly; by discovering his present location and that of Nantes on the wonderful pictures that he now owned, he figured that he could learn something of the size and shape of the world, and by extension, discover which countries; their women and their grog, were at last within his reach.

The doors of the grand cabin burst inwards as though struck by a grenade followed by an apparition wearing the uniform of an English naval officer, sword in hand and bloody. Obviously under hot pursuit and fleeing for his life the desperate fugitive shaped to bar the doors behind him then glimpsed the new threat. In one fluid movement, he turned and slashed at the nearest of the enemy. Caught seated and completely off-guard Teach shoved his chair over backwards but he was too late, a thin red line appeared across his belly.

''Bastard!'' witnessing the gutting of his friend, Hooligan who when armed with a sword was as effective as a cow with a gun, had barely managed to draw the thing from its scabbard when the 'bastard,' went for him. Leaping at the Irishman and landing in that 'down on one-knee' pose which soft-headed Englishmen adopt when proposing marriage, the visitor thrust for Hooligan's throat. Horrified; the Irishman's single-eyed gaze transfixed on a ruby at the weapon's tip. Under violent acceleration the gem's liquid heart burst through the purple skein of surface-tension that restrained it and, scarlet now in its freedom, raced downhill toward the hilt clinging ever to that glacial edge where patently there was nothing on which to cling. Hooligan knew that he was dead; but at that fleeting, yet age-long moment, when the lethal point pricked his throat, the Irishman was hurled violently aside; struck it seemed to him, by Thor's hammer from shoulder to hip. As he smashed agonizingly against a wall of oak, he glimpsed Holdsworth tearing into the attack armed with nothing less than a couple of hundredweight of mahogany table which the black fury hurled ferociously, edge first, into the Englishman's narrow chest. The impact made a sound much like that caused when an ox is poleaxed. The Englishman made a sound not dissimilar to that made by the unfortunate ox. He went down backwards to the deck where he was kicked and stamped into oblivion by his enraged pursuers who had piled in a stampede through the doors.

Clearly much aggrieved by the runaway; the angry mob in a display of unalloyed savagery broke those of the Englishman's bones which Holdsworth may have neglected, and clearly intended finishing the man off.

"What's occurred?" roared the resurrected Teach, getting miraculously to his feet and inexplicably throwing men aside in order to keep the enemy alive. The answer came from a dozen throats in a dozen variations but the long and the short of it was that the son of a bitch had snatched up a sword and murdered Harry the cook; *after* the English had surrendered, thrown down their weapons and been granted clemency. This revelation drove the already murderous Holdsworth into a rage, and he laid about him with the back of his skillet fists doing real damage, not to the murderer, but to his crew.

"Cain't you motherless bitches tend a bunch of snot-nosed, limey arse-bandits?" he roared.

"Get that turd topside," Teach was incandescent at his friend's murder. Grabbed by willing hands the Englishman was dragged feet-first up the companionway, his smashed face beating bloodily against the treads. Teach meanwhile bent to aid the winded Hooligan, assisted by an unusually sympathetic Holdsworth.

"Us cain't spec lil whaat boys to do real men's work," the Negro advised the invalid kindly, lifting him to his feet in an exhibition of extraordinary power. Hooligan made no reply as he required every gulp of air that he could drag in simply to remain conscious.

The sight of Harry's dead body effected the captain sorely; the man had been a great favorite aboard the Bird; an atrocious cook but kindly. In his many years fighting slavery, the gentle fellow had never held a weapon, yet now he lay murdered by a wet-behind-the-ears, good-for-nothing lordling. The murderer lay conscious and bleating mere yards from his victim.

''Get that swine out of my sight,'' the captain roared.

''Hang the bastard.''

Carstairs was dragged to the rope pissing in his draws and screaming in pain and terror while his chums were forced to watch at gunpoint. There being no drop the coward was hauled off his feet and left to twitch and die. An outcome which pleased the now blood-thirsty men of the Bird as no other could.

"You sir, are the author of this calamity." The needle point of the captain's sword had swung back From Plumbly–Horton's broken nose to the dead and wounded men who lay on the deck below.

''Don't make any plans for your future.''

''You verminous dog…''

The newly upright Plumly-Horton was punched in his badly cut face for this transgression and collapsed again, his head battering against the deck in the process. Well pleased with this 'the brass' convened another meeting which was brief and productive and very soon Lliam Shaun Hooligan lately the owner of four seagoing vessels approached the rail.

"The prisoners will be shared between our ships," he announced.

''As barginin stuff. This thing," he pointed at the still comatose Horton.

"Chain it below. We are at war against the fookin Brits. We sail on the toide.''

CHAPTER 19: A Double-edged Sword

Seed never made it home. There was no need. Dressed for the road and with their spare clothes in a bundle, Betty was waiting for him, posing in imitation of the Madonna which he had stolen from the manse at Bristol; all legs and breasts and smiling hair, on Mrs. Cumberpatch's cup board. Seed helped the girl to mount, making her laugh with a hand up her skirt and the two set off with seed leading the horse and Betty sitting astride it, reveling in the animal's motion, and happily aware of the effect which the exaggerated fucking action of her hips had on him, and wondering how long Kane could last before he dragged her off this hoss and gave her a good stiff seeing to. She hoped it would not be many minutes.

Good Christ how these vermin stank. Did they never wash? No, of course they didn't. Cleanliness would imply something higher in the order of creatures than that of bovine straw-sucking omnivores. Vicar Penny was beginning to feel better after that terrible Huffer business; his old arrogance was back now that the corpse had disappeared. He had suffered the torment of the damned, thinking that he had been recognized by the toothsome daughter, but apparently not; she hadn't done a thing. As far as anybody knew, Huffer had taken to the road along with the thousands of other useless outcasts who littered them, and no one would ever miss him. He was going to get away with murder.

If he were able to afford incense; he would, he schemed, stride up and down that aisle and choke every one of these smelly moles with an asphyxiating cloud of it. Unfortunately, he could not. He spent far too much on keeping Abigail happy, but the girl was worth every penny of it; she simply never said, 'no'. And there was not one filthy thing in this whole world that she didn't absolutely love doing. Best of all she screamed her beautiful face off; it was a habit which drove him almost insane with lust.

He had not prepared a sermon; it had been ages since he bothered with all of that. What would be the point? These cretins believed that the Red Sea parted in the middle; that good old Noah invited wild animals on to the family boat. 'Come on now little lions, be good and don't bite old Noah, and leave that sheep alone while you're about it, or it will be an early bed and you will get no supper.' Give me strength. Their tuneless bawling had ceased. He would have to say something. He knew what he would do; he would berate them; that was always good for five minutes or so and if there was anything that they really enjoyed, it was being shouted at. 'Did them good.'

That old crow at the back. She's not a regular. But I recognize that face from somewhere or other. Good Christ, it's that bastard Huffer's wife. Mother of God, she's coming this way. Pointing at me. No. Don't say it you bitch. 'Murderer,' the old cow is screaming at me. 'Murderer. Murderer. Murderer.' No, the horror of it competing with his rage at being exposed. Fight or flight. Turmoil. Stand fast or run. Run from this outhouse, from Abigail, run from this easy waste of life? It was the word of a man of the cloth against that of a mere serf. But no, the bitch was holding up something; could it be? No! It was impossible. The old bitch had his waistcoat. His own waistcoat, with Huffer's blood. Huffer's belt. Could that be the cripple's shoe? She had found the body.

Penny ran.

With his very first stride the murderer slipped the dogs of war. The greater part of this sump of ignorant primitives already knew him for a charlatan, a whoremaster and worse and muttered behind their hands about how it was that he retained servants and owned a horse and trap, all on a vicar's dosh. Now they were confronted with the unpalatable truth that they lacked the courage of their own convictions. Accordingly, his flight caused an outburst of pent-up righteous fury. The appalled stillness that followed the Huffer woman's accusation was replaced by the bellowing of a herd of cattle, a stampede of those who knew themselves to be his dupes.

Now that he had, by running, confessed to murder, he could be hung, *for making fools of them.* The mob surged forward trampling on each other and fell in ugly heaps crying out in pain and fear while others bawled furiously in their frustration at being unable to grasp him. Some of the filth near the front straddled the fence to snatch at his clothing as he fled. Sprinting across the flags now, the action coming unnaturally to him as he beat off the grasping claws of the dolts. Out through the tiny door he went, slamming it in their faces; running hard for where his horse stood. Leaping across forgotten graves and fallen headstones he fled, jumping down to the road from the dizzy height of the retaining wall. Tearing off the detested collar, and girly frock he vaulted into the trap, whipped the horse up savagely and raced for the vicarage, on the edge of disaster at every bend and pothole. Thank christ, the trolls were not yet in sight behind him; he would just have time to snatch what he needed most. Charging into the house, he made straight for his study, shoving aside the clutching Abigail and his witch of a wife. There was little enough money in his secret cache. Breathlessly, he grabbed every note and coin, stuffed them into various pockets and bounded up the stairs to his room to pile clothes into a bag, any clothes, then throwing himself down the servant's stairs a flight at a time. Out by the kitchen door. 'Bleating women everywhere else.' A glimpse of his ugly crone of a wife down on her bony knees, jabbering to her God; the only being who could ever love her, or stand to look at her; the hatchet-faced shrew. Leaping aboard he thrashed the horse mercilessly out of the grounds the sexual thrill of the animal's pain driving him to lay it on harder.

"Curse the lot of you," he yelled, laughing as he saw that he would easily escape the exhausted plebs.

Penny's horse died in harness five miles along the road as he flogged its bleeding sides down a horribly steep slope. It collapsed, at an exhausted gallop, the shafts skewering into the ground and catapulting the little chaise and its occupant high into the air. For a moment or two, Penny knew an orgasm of a highly novel ilk; one of physical terror, at the very crescendo of which, was his coming together with the limbs of a huge tree. There was a moment of the most excruciating agony, and nothing more.

The wheels of the little conveyance had only a moment earlier ceased spinning and resorted to the indecisiveness of a pendulum when out of the woods rode two glittering young men in the uniform of Colonel of 'Cornwallis Own Regiment of Foot.'

Utterly lost; and mildly amused by the fact, the twin brothers Pitt-Darcy were in the very best of spirits for only days earlier their dear Papa had on the occasion of their eighteenth birthday purchased their commissions. The evidence of the incident before them could not in any way mar the rosy view of the world which these privileged young people enjoyed, and their reaction to it spoke volumes about their outlook on life. They advanced at their customary walk with not so much as a thought of going to the aid of the injured pleb of a driver. They rode instead, directly to where the dead and obviously maltreated horse lay in the road, and there, on dismounting, they discovered to their fury, the full extent of the torture that the animal had suffered. The poor creature had been whipped till it bled.

"The swine." The utterance came simultaneously from the brothers' throats; an occurrence which was common with them.

"If that bounder still lives," said one, glancing at Penny's crumpled form,

"I'll make him wish that he were dead."

"Capital notion Sir." the other concurred; it was his habit to affect the grammatical patterns of older men, in the belief that it made him seem wise, mature and totally killing to the ladies.

Penny regained a consciousness composed of unbearable agony that peaked with every jolt of the cart in which he was lying face down. Beside him, somebody gasped. Twisting his aching neck slowly around, he discovered a fellow sufferer. It was apparent that he too, had been flogged. His savagely injured back resembled a butcher's bench; it was all trenches and loose bits of flesh as his own had to be. Penny vomited and began to choke as his own agony reached a crescendo. Getting a grip on the side of the cart, he dragged himself up and over and emptied his stomach amid a column of soldiers tramping alongside. The butt of a musket smashed his face. Penny fell back shocked by the violence and lost consciousness as the tattered flesh of his torso touched the boards.

Amid the uproar caused by Dora's accusation and Penny's guilty reaction to it, nobody paid any attention to the old woman who had made the startling denunciation. Wraithlike she made her way beyond the convulsions to the foot of the tower and began to climb. Since the first day of Tansley's disappearance, Dora had known that he was dead and that it was she who had caused his murder. As she mounted the precipitous helix, she recalled her meaningless search of Danesholme, Shakle Oder and Danelaw, which she had known in her spirit-sanctum to be counterfeit even then.

Hadn't she wished him dead? Hadn't she begged the spirits to cleanse this world of his vile presence?

"Tansley Huffer, loathed by the gods, Tansley Huffer, 'neath the sods…" Her guilt was greater than that of the man who had struck the blows. Penny had merely been the instrument by which the 'rulers,' had carried out the deed. With Tansley's poor bits and pieces in her hands, Dora clambered on to the battlements, stood up, proud and straight as a girl for a long moment, spoke her children's names lovingly, then stepped forward.

Approximately half of Cornwallis Own Regiment of Foot, remained ashore on the banks of Poole Harbor, adjacent to the mouth of the Frome, much to the agitation of the local cottagers who kept their daughters locked up indoors and would continue to do so until every man-jack of the criminal wasters had sailed. Bivouacked in the fields and woods, eight hot, dry miles from the flesh pots and grog shops of Poole; their officers had cleverly denied the regiment the diversions of that town by simple distance. This ruse was supported by a screen of Hessians who were flung out across the fields with orders to shoot on sight any man going absent-without-leave, Hessians being soldiers who obey their orders even when it means doing murder.

With every imaginable task completed prior to embarkation, short of polishing the trees, combing the grass, and painting rocks white, Regimental Sergeant Major Jobe, a great believer of the maxim, 'the devil finds work for idle hands to do,' concluded that a small diversion would be in order, and had a runner declare the news of this entertainment throughout the camp. To the enlisted men, non-coms and even certain officers, this news was the cause of great excitement; after all, what could relieve the monotony of camp life more completely than watching Jobe beat some thief to a custard with his boulder-hard fists. To a very few, it was a matter of deep concern and a choice which was no choice at all. You could fight the Goliath or desert. Both were a death-sentence.

When Sergeant Major Jobe as was his wont; declared that he would take on 'all-comers,' what he refrained from saying was that he would personally select the 'volunteers' who would toe-his-line. The older hands were well acquainted with the selection process according to Jobe, and were therefore untroubled, but the thieves, card sharps, bullies, the 'clatty,' which is to say those with a distinct aversion to soap and water, the sodomites, usurers and backstabbers who had continued with their naughty civilian ways even after their acceptance into the hallowed military halls, now cringed at the thought of losing their lives in this grotesque fashion.

The professional soldier's first dancing partner was, so far as anyone knew, presently being stretchered in a state of deep unconsciousness to the land-based sick bay. In truth he had been dumped behind a hedge as the bearers were keen to get back to see the action. He was a loud-mouthed bully and big fish in a small pond, who had 'taken the shilling' on hearing that the regiment was off to kill a bunch of farmers who had insulted England and his majesty. Billy Hutch was his name, and Billy the bully had declared loudly to the recruiting sergeants, and anyone else within a hundred yards, that killing rebels and fucking their sluts was as good a sport as he could imagine. During his brief career in the regiment, Billy had acquired plenty of practice in bending army life to his taste; mostly on the faces and ribs of young English lads whom he had chosen carefully for their inability to fight back. The small, the weak, the young. He made them clean his kit; part with their meals and their pay and stand his guard duty. Yes, life was 'good,' and Billy was glad that he had joined.

It was Jobe's duty as Regimental Sergeant Major to teach Billy Hutch one of life's cruel lessons, namely, 'If you can't take it; don't give it out.' Private Hutch, true to form, had evicted a drummer boy from his place in the front row by the simple expedient of kicking the orphan in the spine. Squatting down cross legged in the hastily vacated spot he intended to wallow in the bloodletting, while having no intention of challenging a colossus the likes of the regimental sergeant major. That had all changed in an instant. Billy's boiled swede of a face had drained of blood when the pugilist had shambled over to him, grabbed a fist full of his hair and dragged him into the center of the ring. It was a situation from which there was no escape. He either declared himself a craven coward, or he toed the line. Either way he was dead. True to form, in a funk of terror, Billy had lashed out at his tormentor before the bell, catching the big man full in the face with a blow which had the lout's full weight behind it. Caught unprepared and off-balance the Sgt Major staggered backwards and fell over his own feet, bleeding at the mouth and Billy, misreading the signs, and contrary to law, stepped across the line to follow-up with his boots. Rolling aside as the steel toecap passed his face much closer than comfort required, Jobe regained his feet courtesy of that momentum and advanced on the walking spitoon with murder in his soul. For the full five minutes of the first round, 'the force of justice' battered Billy the bully with ferocious agonizing blows, which penetrated to the bone, so that in round two, Private Hutch, sadist and loudmouth, could no longer hold up his fists, and let his now autumnally bruised agonized limbs fall uselessly at his sides. Mercilessly, Jobe now went to work on the braggart's torso, with punches of such impact, that they reduced cartilage to jelly, cracked bone and ruptured internal organs. Hutch lost consciousness several times only to be brought back by being doused in cold water. As the bell rang for round three, he was hoist from where he lay crying all but unconscious in the dust and held almost upright by soldiers who wanted to see an end to Billy, the bane of their life, right there. The oak tree finished it. He smashed the bully's nose and broke his cheekbone so badly, that the man's eye seemed to hang out of its socket, unnaturally wide open. Men were detailed to pick the slacker up and this they did with alacrity; they even went the extra mile and continued to hold the swine erect again so that their hero could finish the job. Private Hutch was unconscious before he fell for the last time, so he went down unprotected. His face struck the baked earth with a sickening impact, and his ruined form lay in the dirt, snoring loudly. With wonderful contempt the victor turned and walked away while the body was dragged feet first and intentionally face down, from the ring in the time-honored manner ceded to the world by that elegant contributor to the mores of the modern British army, 'Rome.'

The pugilist's next victim was, in his own fashion, equally detestable with the last. He was a recently pressed man who, according to the newly christened 'baby colonels,' the twins Pitt-Darcy, had 'whipped his horse to death.' To death? The news of this disgusting act had at the time raced through the ranks from private to the moving mountain himself the revered and feared Sergeant Major.

'To death! The bastard!' For that reason alone, the force of justice was intent on administering his unique brand of justice. He could see the sadistic pig now; leaning nonchalantly against a tree as though he was an officer; well away from the men, who would have nothing to do with him. The prick was smoking a pipe and jabbering with a couple of Hessians in order to propound the vulgar goings-on in the ring to be beneath his dignity. Obviously, the square heads were unaware of what the worm had done because the Krauts loved their horses more than they loved their mothers. Jobe wondered for a while whether the lousy German morons 'had' mothers.

Striding to the perimeter on that side of the blood-spattered space the assassin pointed a limb of oak at the horse torturer.

"Him," he growled.

The regiment went into raptures. The next victim was to be the despised sadist, a dolt who thought himself superior to the rest of humanity, to say nothing of flaying one of the most beautiful animals as ever lived. The recently joined upstart was the sort of shit who spoke as though he had a pebble in his mouth and spent his time sucking-up to the brass. Eager to see this one chewing on a knuckle-sandwich, half a dozen men grabbed the tall dilettante soldier, and tearing off his webbing, his red coat and his bayonet, rushed him into the ring. Penny had not resisted this assault upon his person for his presence in the circus was a foregone conclusion. Additionally, he was undismayed by the prospect and considered the unskilled colossus to be easy meat. However, as he was given a farewell shove into the arena one of these enthusiasts for sadistic spectacle gave Penny a vicious kick in the arse to be going on with. Penny twirled in severe pain bawling.

"When I'm through with this one, it's you and me with bayonets."

The roar of derision from the masses who had never witnessed their hero bested or even badly hurt was so loud that it caused yachtsmen racing across the bright water of the harbor to stand-up in their flying craft to understand what had occurred. Those precious-few redcoats with sufficient intuition or understanding of human behavior held their peace; the horse torturer's declaration had been made with such simple, understated confidence and absence of bravado that they knew with certainty that this fight might be worthy of the name. The herd quietened watchfully as Penny removed his shirt, dropping it in the grass without a care in the world; while in the center of the ring, the death dealer dragged his bloodied boot along the ground, making a fresh line against which, according to custom the combatants would position their leading foot. It was the mountain's habit to fight naked but for a pair of long-john pants, from which he had severed the legs with his bayonet. This arrangement provided his overdeveloped torso and Herculean thighs with complete freedom of movement. It also obviated the need for his batman to wash the blood of his victims from his uniform. As he waited impatiently for the snotty git to put his neck on the block, or his toe on the line; it didn't matter which; he felt as fit as a robber's dog. His mild exertions with Billy Hutch had left him sweating lightly and breathing deeply, and he was enjoying the heft of his veined biceps, and the movement of the pectorals of his chest that twitched unbidden with a life of their own. Such was the degree of his muscularity that he seemed positively deformed. His back, chest shoulders arms and legs were the work of a poor sculptor in clay who applied his medium with a trowel. Thick slabs of the stuff clung to his skeleton, jostling, bunching, changing shape and separating; all at the whim and service of malevolence.

Gimlet-eyed, Penny sized up the dolt against which he was pitched and knew without a doubt, that if he was stupid enough to toe that line, he was finished, the bastard would batter him so hard and so long that he would quite literally die as a result of his many injuries. For his own part he could punch that mountain of muscle and bone for a month without troubling the sadistic bastard, any more than would a few flies landing on the man's bare skin. That spawn of Satan, who was waiting for him in a stew of malice, outweighed him by eight stones or more, yet the fool expected him to stand perfectly still and be clubbed to death. What sort of creatures, Penny asked himself, would engage in a fistfight in which the protagonists stood stock still, and disdaining any attempt at defending themselves, simply resorted to trading blows until one or other was dead or simply unable to rise from the dirt. Morons, cretins, and Glaswegians, that's whom. Fighting was about winning and winning was a product of striking without being struck. It was time to strike the noisome bully. What a distinct pleasure this was going to be. Not simply in giving the sadistic dog a great big spoonful of his own medicine, but in humiliating him in front of his acolytes. Physical humiliation would be unbearable to that modern day gladiator. As he sauntered across the open space, the thought of torturing; 'really torturing' this man was very tempting to private Penny who dwelt on the prospect for a while; rejecting it at last because the risks were so great. 'We don't want to end up like that other chap, do we?' From several yards distant Penny advanced quickly, then broke into a charge his fists held high describing elliptical curves through space like planets of cold rock, mesmerising the bovine onlookers but more importantly friend Jobe. Lashing out with his steel-toed boot, he made satisfying contact just below the bastard's knee and predictably the agonized and squealing shit crumpled in the dirt. Penny stood back and let the seriously hurt swine get back to his feet where he now tottered on his one good limb. The option of kicking the pig to death was a very tempting one but penny had an axe to grind. It was this son of Satan who had whipped him near to death and made his back a ploughed field for life. Agonized distracted and unbalanced, Jobe did not even see the dancer's straight left which got through his non-existent guard and drove the knuckles deep into his eye; temporarily blinding it. The crowd erupted yet again.

"Fight fair, you bastard," they roared; conveniently forgetting that not a man present would willingly change places with the object of their anger. Grunting and hobbling in pain and fury, the destroyer lashed-out with both fists in the hope of buying some time until his vision cleared, but he landed what to him were merely glancing hits and succeeded only in losing his balance while causing the horse killer to lose his also. Penny regained his composure first and circled, dancing to the left then to the right, dashing in to smash a fist into the troubled face and out again fully aware that changing his point of attack forced the soldier to move his leg. His probably fractured leg.

Ducking under a haymaker which would have floored him had it made contact, the pugilist went to work on job's floating ribs and kidneys, feasting on the pain he was causing. Tormented beyond endurance the now troubled man broke his own rules and went after a swiftly retreating target. Lifting his mangled limb, he hopped forward on the other. Instantly recognizing the killer opportunity that had presented itself so much sooner than he could have hoped, Penny reacted instinctively. With a sort of clinical detachment that silenced the baying masses, he leapt feet first at the cripple, landing stiff-legged, with every ounce of his eighteen stones of weight on the side of that extended knee, the broken knee. The pugilist's limb crackled like a dry branch as it bent in an anatomically impossible direction and his shrieks of agony were lost in the upwelling of fascinated disbelief at this shocking turn of events. Sickeningly injured; the soldier, unbelievably, got back up on one leg and tried to fight on, wet eyed and keening uncontrollably. The ability to absorb pain was the central pillar of the man's existence. In Jobe's world, such bravery was the only measure of a man. He knew no other and could not relinquish it lest his self-image crumble into dust. Half blinded, crippled and agonized, the battler grabbed at his tormentor as he toppled, and by sheer chance, got a grip on the taller man and dragged him in, prepared to use his great strength in a grappling match that would enable him to strangle or blind the devil by thumbing out his eyes. He was outsmarted. The predictable resistance did not occur; as Jobe pulled his tormentor into a clinch with every ounce of his immeasurable strength, Penny did the unbelievable and adding his own energy to the enemy's hurled his boulder of a head into that hated face. The sergeant's exceptionally wide, badly used and redundant olfactory proboscis was reduced to jelly and a moment later, a curtain of blood flowed down into his eyes from a gash which had opened excruciatingly in his brows. He made to clear his vision with his forearm even as his testicles exploded in agony as Penny's steel toecap lashed into his groin. Hitting out blindly as he went down; grasping protectively at his shattered balls; and desperate for a contact with the enemy so that he would know where to hit he never saw the something that smashed his throat. His breathing failed. Instinctively, he turned his back in panic, clutching at his windpipe, hunting for air, terrified, oblivious to his ribs being broken by those same steel-capped boots designed for that very purpose. Penny stood over the dying man, reveling in his victory and breathing hard; the whole episode had lasted but a few minutes.

The bastard was now choking to death. Noisily. The sound was so very comforting. At a flick of Penny's hand, men rushed into the ring, tripping over each other in their efforts to help their fallen leader but his thrashing around and gagging for air turned to a strangling paroxysm as the fools tried to roll him over and sit him up. One of his acolytes even contriving to trample all over the trailing limb in the process. Spewing blood on his rescuers, the would-be hammer of the enlisted man still gasped, his pagan eyes now mere pools of terror.

It would have been pleasant, Penny mused, to drag out the goliath's humiliation for a dozen or so rounds, but the risk had been far too great. It would have taken only one of those rock smashing blows to find its target to reverse the flow of the battle, and the soldier would have done to himself that which he had done to the fellow presently dying behind the hedge. With his ardor cooling, Penny was already beginning to suffer the effects of his own wounds; both arms were so badly bruised that he could barely contain the torment of them. One of his ears would forever be a cauliflower, and large patches of his torso were turning an ugly blue, leading him to think that he may have sustained damage a great deal worse than a bit of bruising to the serratus anterior. His thoughts soon turned to the gutless bag of slime who had kicked him as he entered the ring. Breathing more easily now, he scrutinized the crowd from under his furrowed and bleeding brows, while the bovine mob cautiously returned his stare. In common with all breeds of cattle, they were chastened by their leader's demise, but they had already abandoned yesterday's man and were on the lookout for a new leader to whom they could kowtow; not one of them believing in himself sufficiently to stand forth and claim the vacant crown. Even a pack of rabid dogs needed a leader however, and for the moment, Penny was content to be that man. What a delicious irony was contained in this rabble's kidnapping of the vicar of Thorpe and stealing him away from his family, 'his hore actually,' his congregation of mouth-breathing, unwashed dolts, and his rights as an Englishman. Without knowing it Cornwallis and his aristocratic arse-kissers were saving him from their own merciless system of justice and its hangman judges. He would have thanked his god if he had one. Naturally, once in America, he would repay the compliment by deserting at the first opportunity. The crowd was becoming wary again; each of these so-called soldiers would now be asking himself; 'was my support of the sarn-major noticed? Will I be the next man in that ring?' With huge disdain, Penny stepped away from the noisy bastard's struggle for life, then with a mere jerk of his thumb caused him to be dragged away to the surgeons. That arrogant gesture and the rankers' immediate obedience, confirming beyond dispute his position as the new top dog of Cornwallis' Own, Regiment of Foot.

The leprous scum who had dragged him into the ring now stood in a deeply concerned huddle noticeably minus the coward who had kicked him. Striding toward them he halted at the front rank of chastened dogs.

"Bayonets," he demanded, and instantly there were three of the weapons thrust his way hilt-first. Wordlessly, he snatched two of them. Sliding one into the frog on his belt and gripping the other in the knife-fight fashion, he addressed the gutless few.

''Go and get him, you've got five minutes.'' He barked.

Turning on his heel Penny strode to the middle of Circus Maximus, dropped the blades, and running to the river, dived in; revelling in the energizing effect of the very cold water. Greatly refreshed and with the blood washed from his skin he returned to the ring while those officers who had watched at a distance which proclaimed their disinterest even as they howled for blood, departed the field. 'To witness the upcoming events would not advance a man's career one jot.'

A commotion in the crowd revealed the arse-kicking coward being manhandled into the ring by his friends who dragged him apologetically to the middle and ran way; unable to look at each other or anyone else. Penny threw a bayonet underhand to land at the trembling individual's feet and pointing his own weapon at an imaginary Ceasar roared 'MORITURI TE SALUTANT '

Instantly shattered by the loud declaration the coward began to tremble like a whipped dog, his face screwed up in abject terror as his tears and piss disgraced a regiment so mean-spirited that not one man would voluntarily defend its honour.

''PICK IT UP'' raged Penny, now blaming this sack of vomit for the loss of his worshipful Abigail as he advanced eager to commit murder a second time. The disgrace stood with feet of clay as might a terrified girl-child unable even to meet the eyes of the enemy while the regiment; convicted in their own eyes, began to slope away in the silence of self-reproach. Several uniforms advanced cautiously, clearly concerned for their own safety and led the broken thing away with patent commiserations; a service which penny in his magnanimity allowed them to perform.

A Sergeant of cavalry forded the river and emerging from the trees on the near bank rode into the circus, careless of pedestrians. Penny wondered whom the fellow was and what it could possibly be that he had come to discuss. Suddenly spurring his mount and clearly intent on riding Penny down, a glistening blade appearing in his left hand, the rider made his intentions clear. Penny stilled, balanced, clear eyed. Lucid in his options and supremely confident of his fighting prowess he waited until the very ground beneath his feet shook to the drumming of hooves and equine malevolence filled his vision. Within the immeasurable part of time when survival and destruction are one, he danced aside; avoiding the blade; the warmth of the beast registering on his skin. Self-congratulations flooded him even as the unseen monkeyfist burst his eyes, made concave his aquiline profile and ripped the incisors from his gums; all of which he understood only as unbearable agony and fear. Fear that he had suffered the death blow.

Dragging his horse down to a painful halt the cavalryman dismounted athletically and utterly contemptuous of the remaining red jackets sauntered to where Penny lay on his back groaning. For several minutes the stranger amused himself by taking his boots to Penny's groin with extreme violence while penny vomited and choked horribly, squealing in unimaginable semi-conscious torment.

Cold, calculated, sadistic malevolence now directed the cavalryman's work. Lifting one of Penny's legs he bent it over the other then bringing his mount to stand alongside, he climbed aboard, stood in the saddle then dropped feet-first on to that vulnerable limb. The thing crackled like a wood-fire while a communal intake of breath punctuated this evidence of the unbridled cruelty which lies at the very core of mankind's nature. The last act of Kane Seed's revenge for his much-loved Buttercup was to hack-off the fingers of Penny's right hand; the hand which had blinded his loving dog.

Not a soul attempting to limit these excesses, the unimpeded, untroubled Seed walked his mount to the river where he washed at his leisure before galloping away. 'The White Gull would sail that day and he would just have time to return the uniform, pay-off his debt and get aboard.'

CHAPTER 20: A Rose By Any Other Name

Something was terribly wrong. Angelique Huffer stood in the strip of grass that was the middle of a little-used cart track, hoping to discover Andrew, her dearly loved Andrew approaching in that energetic walk of his and wearing his silly, big, adorable grin, but a few homeless women and their miserable children were the only people in-sight. In Angelique's hand was a pail of boiled potatoes which she had recently drained, then carried absentmindedly with her to where she now stood, hoping that she would discover her much-loved friend. Deeply worried, and afraid, she returned to camp trying to convince herself that to carry on as usual would be the panacea that would bring Andrew home, aware of, but refusing to accede, what a non-sequitur this was. She drained the vegetables and put everything on the hearthstones to keep warm but delayed eating until Andrew arrived. 'Anything at all could have delayed him,' she told herself, an old chum who wanted to chat, or perhaps a bit of business had cropped up and he had naturally seized the opportunity to pursue it. No matter how vivid and credible the excuses which occurred in her febrile imagination she remained miserable and almost frantic for nothing short of the sight of him all-of-a-piece and uninjured would end her torment. The bitter dregs of an endless day crawled passed only to be supplanted by threatening, fearful night and still he had not come. As the newly dreaded regiments of darkness enfiladed first her camp then her mind and her heart; she consumed a morsel or two, extinguished the fire in case it was seen by any of the numberless ruffians who littered the roads then went off beyond where the horses were grazing to find a place among boulders in which to spend the night. She slept poorly, woke often, and rose before dawn, tired and deeply unhappy. He had not come. She waited for him throughout that unendurably long day but still he did not come. Ill with worry she suffered throughout the next day, eating virtually nothing; not bothering to wash, or cook, or care for the horses till at dusk her misery intensified predictably as fear, guilt and other base emotions polluted it; she crept away to cower through another endless night in her shameful hiding place, heartsick, hungry, unbearably lonely and harried by guilt.

Eventually she began to think the unthinkable that she, a mere girl, could drive on alone in charge of a massive wagon drawn by six enormously powerful horses. Throwing off her blanket she rose, charged with the energy of determination and strode back to the wagon; lit a lantern, then the fire and went to work in their light. The milk had gone off in the churns so she poured the stinking stuff over the side of the wagon, not caring when she got some of it on her clothes, threw away the uneaten food, flung the cooking pots into the box unwashed, gathered up her bedding in a damp heap and flung that behind the seat. Dropping the empty churns to the ground, uncaring about damaging them, she climbed down from the wagon and dragged them, two at a time to the stream, rolling them them in to the torrent where it flowed quickest so that they would wash themselves and save her the bother.

"Andrew," she mourned, her tears flowing as freely as the stream, and kneeling there by the side of that foolishly happy water, she cried until her heart was dry. Never had she so wanted a glimpse of that tawdry little cottage in Thorpe, with her dear mother waiting at the gate.

"Mam," she cried piteously, and the sound would have made stones weep. A hot blast of air found her neck, blowing her hair into her face, and she spun around in fright to find Paula one of her team seeking affection and perhaps an apple.

"Oh, Paula my lovely, you miss him too, don't you? Never mind, we shall go and find him, that's what we'll do," she fondled the huge head, as big as herself. Finding so much comfort in it. From that moment on, Angelique began to get well.

'First things first' was the rule by which she lived on the road, and on that night, which in the future she would remember with a modicum of satisfaction and pride she applied herself to all of her necessary tasks; cleaning the pots which she had put away dirty, scrubbing out the tenaciously stinky churns with sand from the stream bottom, tidying the larder, rearranging the unbalanced load, and lastly, harnessing the team. Harnessing six shires is not an inconsiderable task and what took Andrew half an hour dragged on seemingly for an age leaving her sobbing with exhaustion, but the capable girl learned a little something new as each beauty went in to the traces so that by the time it came to hitch Dolly, the happy last; though tired to the marrow of her bones she was almost as proficient as Andrew, and it all went along as easily as drawing breath. Only when this work was done did she take care of her own person. She rested for a long spell in order to regain some strength, then took a bite to eat before going off for a bath with her bit of cloth, a piece of soap and her silver comb which she had traded for, and which was now her pride and joy. Stepping cautiously into the painfully cold gasp-making stream she hurriedly scrubbed herself pink from head to foot, washed her hair and combed it out right away to stop it going all curly. Shivering, teeth chattering, skin rough with goosebumps, but happy to be clean again the newly resolute young woman had already decided that in the coming dawn she would wear dungarees with an old plum-colored paint-spoiled shirt of Andrew's to complete her disguise, even though it would fit closer if she were triplets. Dressed in men's attire and with her hair gathered up under her leather hat she would certainly be taken for a youth she told herself. Accordingly, she had left these clothes to warm by the fire and was glad of their comforting touch on her chilled skin. Once dressed, she glanced at her reflection in a still pool, and as human beings have a marked propensity for believing whatever suits them best, concluded that her contentions were accurate and under casual perusal she would certainly pass for a male. Her confidence bolstered, the radiantly beautiful youth checked the whole camp to be sure that he was leaving nothing behind, then climbed aboard the schooner, gathered up the familiar weight of the reins, and took Andrew's whip in her hand. Dear Andrew, whatever it was that had befallen him, it was all her fault; it was she who had let the camp run out of flour, then imposed on him to take a stroll to the village over the hill, to buy some if there was any to be had. She had to bite her lip in order to prevent a repeat of her earlier descent into despair.

"I'm coming Andrew," she choked, and clucked to her team.

"Walk on," she requested gently in what she thought of as her most masculine tone. On the day of Andrew's disappearance, the young couple had seen smoke rising from beyond the next hill and assumed that they were nearing yet another unremarkable village. She was appalled to find instead, a midden of mud-and-wattle shacks of the sort flung up by penniless unfortunates, vagabonds, those driven out of the towns because of criminality; the incurably and infectious-sick, and the insane.

'Andrew's dead!' She recognized the horrible truth as she was confronted by this evil-smelling sump. The denizens of this place had done away with him; there could be no other reason for him not to come home to her. Searching frantically, she realized that there was nowhere for her to turn the team. She would have to go straight on and drive right through the length of this foul-smelling cesspit. Sickeningly aware of her vulnerability, she felt for the blade at her wrist and coincidentally obtained some consolation in the fact that none of the scabrous residents were around; just a few unfenced animals which roamed where they wished. On the very edge of panic, she urged her team onward, but as she came into a narrow defile where the leper-dens encroached almost on to the road, noticed with a sickening churning in her stomach a couple of drunken wastrels wrestling ineffectually in the dirt. So engrossed were the tramps in their feud that they seemed not to notice the huge vehicle thus her laboring heart steadied just a little. No sooner had she tempted fate with her premature celebration however than stunted dwarf-like creatures appeared through the bits of sacking that passed as doors, one or two at first, then tribes of them, calling like jackals, skinny, stiff with dirt, and clothed in bits of rag, if at all. They emerged from their slums at first with animal caution, but on discovering a girl, all alone and defenseless they turned gleefully predatory, cackling as they hobbled to the road on rickety legs like packs of starving dogs surrounding a wounded beast. The elders followed their loathsome offspring, the scent of easy prey strong in their nostrils.

"Come up, hoss." Holding down her sickening fear Angelique spoke sternly to her team, flicked the reins hard across their rumps, and watched with dread as a group of what Andrew would call 'knuckle-draggers' went to stand in the middle of the track, barring her way. She was about to vomit in terror but just as she made to draw rein rather than drive over the footpads, she heard Andrew's voice coaching her,

"We never stop, Angie. To draw rein is to draw your last breath. Supposing the swine lay down in the road; we would never stop." One of the footpads; an evil, smirking creature, grey with filth, obviously confident that the lone girl was easy meat, positioned himself where he could take hold of Dolly's harness when the lead horse reached him. It was a fatal mistake. The brazen, insulting arrogance of the move turned Angelique's fear to a fury of which she had never suspected herself capable. As the brigand reached up for the lines, the very tip of Angelique's lash caught him in the face.

"Git up horse," she cried, roughing her voice, and the team jerked forward, badly frightened. She cracked the whip again and her horses began an unaccustomed gallop. The would-be robbers had no chance of escape. The worst of them pilloried when a hoof the size of a dinner plate and weighing a ton squashed his foot; mincing flesh and bone together shrieked like a harpy. The two wastrels directly in front of the giant horses went down under the charge, while the fourth sought to save himself, and ran. Noticing the coward Angelique lashed out again, furious that she had been forced to frighten her darlings. The plaited leather tip, travelling at incredible speed caught the absconder behind the ear and wrapped around his face slashing a thin bone-deep wound. He screamed, tripped in his agony and fell face-first into one of the fires. The massively laden wagon barely swayed as its iron-shod wheels carved their messy way through the screaming torsos of the two outlaws trampled by the horses. Cracking the whip above the hordes of vile, screeching runts, and cursing them as roughly as she was able, Angelique charged on, taking terrified cover in the foot-well from the storm of stones and obscenities which they hurled in their fury at her escape. Urging her team on with every ounce of strength in her young body, the brave child drove away at pace until the awful place lay miles behind her, by which time she ached so badly that she could no longer cope with the weight of the reins.

Thinking it safe to do so, the exhausted horses slowed to a walk and then to their customary plod; an adjustment to which Angelique had no real objection, though for several more miles, she would turn in her seat every so often and scour the road in trepidation. Badly shaken, not least by what she herself had done, she drove on for the remainder of the day, oblivious to hunger and thirst, and careless of direction, steadfastly refusing to let anyone ride beside her, no matter how respectable, or even to hold on to the tailgate and be drawn along, as was the age-old custom. Not even heavily laden women with babes in arms would she aide. Perturbed by guilt at the fate of the criminals who had tried to rob her, or worse; and endlessly fearful of pursuit, Angelique was oblivious to the suffering that she inflicted on her horses as she distanced herself from the scene of her crime. As evening approached, the willing beasts could go no further and stopped of their own volition, exhausted and tortured by thirst in the road, their heads hanging in misery. Realizing what she had done and devastated by the knowledge, she climbed down and went to comfort them.

"Oh, my poor beauties," she lamented, "what have I done to you?"

"I should think so too, you little sod. The man needs horsewhipping that would hag-rid an animal so, such beauties as they are. If you were one of mine, I'd have the skin off you." Angelique turned; incensed by the stranger's rush to judgement. Shockingly the willing whip-hand was a gentleman in appearance if not in manner, who incongruously enough appeared to be directing the efforts of a group of farm laborers in a ploughed field adjacent to the cart-way. Angelique's self-disgust coupled with her chagrin at being thought intentionally cruel, and compounded by the awful events of the morning, all boiled over as uncontrollable anger and she railed at her accuser like any ill-bred harridan.

"Hold your tongue wiseacre," she screeched, her voice breaking infuriatingly,

"Who do you think you are to judge me? I've been set upon by robbers and Andrew is… "She gave way at last, to tears.

"Oh. Oh, my word."

"Tis a lass, Abstemious Fowler."

"I can zee that, Vouchsafe Fowler. I aint blind."

"Water," the tortured girl begged.

"Water for my team?" Forgetting her master plan for a second, Angelique removed her battered hat in order to wipe her tears away with her forearm. The effect on the superior bully and his crony was immeasurable. There was a short, worshipful silence.

"There, there. Please don't take on so, miss. There was no harm intended," said one. Angelique's prosecutor had become council for the defense.

"No, of course not. Just a horsewhipping. Your sort will not tolerate cruelty to an animal, but you'd take a whip to a commoner in an instant." Angelique was not to be won over easily.

"Not likely," hooted one of the field hands, only to be silenced by death-dealing stares from his employers.

"We miss-spoke. We had no idea that   "

"Correct! You had no idea. Perhaps in future you'll reserve your judgment; poor though it may be, until you have some inkling at least of what you are pontificating about." Andrew's verbiage flowed so easily from Angelique's tongue that she barely had to think about what she was saying. Obviously stung, the ludicrously overdressed Vouchsafe Fowler rapped out orders to his laborers, thereby putting an end to their travail. Leading his magnificent saddle horse, he came through the open five-bar and approached the distressed Angelique, doffing his hat as he neared her.

"May I commence our acquaintance again miss… on a more gentlemanly level?" he enquired, and without waiting for a reply went on,

"I am Vouchsafe Fowler, and the vagabond who spoke so roughly to you is my brother, Abstemious."

"Save your mockery, Mister Fowler. It was you, and none other than you who were inclined to lash me. Now, please tell me where I can find water for my animals; then get out of my path." Angelique's nerves were stretched too far for her to respond to this dandy's buffoonery with anything but scorn.

"Of course. Of course. The house lies just opposite," the handsome man positively swam in masculinity and self-confidence and was seemingly oblivious to her rebuff. He indicated a not far-distant property by a slight lift of his thick, black eyebrows.

"If you'll allow me to ride alongside you, you'll have water aplenty in a matter of minutes, Miss?"

"Angelique. I am Angelique Huffer, Mister Fowler."

"You most certainly are," said Fowler, straight faced, and taking her hand, he raised it to his lips; a compliment which, despite everything, Angelique permitted this overgrown schoolboy to pay. Walking between Dolly and Marge at the head of her team, the worn-out child followed the caravan of horses, wagons, agricultural contraptions and laborers, down a lane which lay just a field's width from the brothers' tall, handsome home; glimpses of which were available to her between familial crowds of oaks; deaf to Fowler's inanities as he growled away happily beside her. At a considerable distance from the tall snow-house, Angelique soon found herself entering a large stable enclosure, which was even more extensive than Andrew's own, and tremendously well appointed. There were rows of looseboxes with covered walkways between them, a smithy, huge grain stores and holy of holies, troughs everywhere which seemed to fill by magic. Water from an iron pipe refilled the troughs as the horses drank.

The open space had been paved in granite cobbles eliminating the dust, mud, manure and flies that these places generally suffered and despite the strongly agricultural nature of the place, burgundy Bougainvillea softened the rust and grey of both the brick walls and slate rooves, causing Angelique to wonder vaguely whom it was that had nurtured those glorious blooms; certainly not these rather wild Fowler brothers who, despite their obvious advantages in life, insisted on laboring alongside their farmhands building muscles which moved and changed shape beneath skin as dark as that of those poor men. All in all, the brothers seemed more like the males in her own life than gentlemen farmers; Andrew Carnegie, Philip Bowman, Trewin and Uncle Lliam.

Willing grooms, in trousers tied below the knee, strode out and took charge of the score or so of horses, calling to their favorites by name, while the field hands, exhausted by twelve endless hours of labor under the eye of their masters, turned without ceremony for home, shouting their names into a little window as they passed-by a building of red brick beyond the smithy.

In that moment, Angelique's heart, broken already by her loss and by her animals' distress, bled for those men, whom she knew from bitter experience would trudge several miles home to their rotting cottages and comfortless rest. There they would sup on thin gruel in the unspoken resentment of hungry families, and rise before dawn, returning on foot in darkness and all weathers to this yard. For those poor souls working cheek by jowl with the very masters who kept them in penury would be the ultimate indignity. The practice robbed them of any vestiges of pride which they might take in their work, the meagre comfort of comradeship and much else. "Purgatory," she whispered sadly. To be an English agricultural worker was to be a slave by another name. Andrew had freed her from just such a life and now he was lost, while she, to her shame, was consorting with the enemy.

The grooms made no distinction at all between the Fowler teams and her own, and as she began the task of taking water to her horses the heavy wooden bucket was eased gently from her fingers with the assurance that,

ing332

''We will look arter they like a muvver, miss.'' Angelique was greatly relieved to see that the lads recognized her animals' distress, and gave them only short measure accordingly, it being foolhardy to let a thirsty animal drink its fill. It was so comforting to know that Belle and the others would be safe in the hands of these kind youngsters.

"I've told the grooms to feed them well and give them each a loosebox," Fowler had appeared at her shoulder clearly now tied to her by invisible bonds.

"You must be as exhausted and famished as they are, Ange… Miss Huffer. Won't you come up to the house and have a morsel to eat? I'd very much like you to meet mother, and rest until you feel quite restored."

"Thank you kindly, but I'm content to rest in my wagon. All I can accept from you Mister Fowler is water for my horses."

"Mater would cast us out into the cold world without a farthing if we allowed such a thing." The words tripped thoughtlessly from the young fool's tongue. Clearly, a spoonful of sincerity would kill this man stone dead. Even so, Angelique began to waiver, wondering what the inside of such a home would be like and additionally, whether the revered and seemingly all-powerful Mrs. Fowler, ate babies. Abstemious Fowler approached, enveloping her as he did so in the most loving and patently sincere smile imaginable, which altered his haughty demeanor no end, then taking her hand, bent over it; at which compliment she relaxed slightly for the first time that day. Despite the rather irritating immaturity of these two vagabonds, it was so reassuring to be in unthreatening company again.

"Won't you please change your mind? Come and meet mother and have tea Miss Huffer" Vouchsafe begged.

"Yes, please do," implored his partner in flattery, as though her presence at tea were the most important consideration inhabiting his carefree little world. The beauty laughed sadly at their imperfect flirtation. Both were, after all charming, well-meaning, open-faced young men, they were simply oblivious to the suffering of others; those who were denied the privileges which they themselves enjoyed; their field-hands being a case in point. In addition to which, she was starving. The acquiescence implied by the alluring one's slight hesitation was seized upon instantly by the impetuous youths as though they were two dogs and Angelique was a particularly tasty bone; they laid claim to one arm each and set sail for home with their captive almost airborne between them.

In a perfumed bower, close to a conservatory which sat like an afterthought at the end of the tall and imposing pile, a beautiful; once angelic woman, was cutting flowers. The lady moved with effortless grace, sailing in her lavender gown and milkmaid's bonnet from one herbaceous border to another, her wicker flower-basket with its palette of blooms which would have been utilitarian on anyone else, adding to her undeniable charm. Both boys bent to kiss their mother.

"How delightful, odor of horse, my favorite, second only to 'tobacco.' Did you wear it just for me?" The voice was appealingly well modulated. In reprimanding her wayward sons, the greatly revered Mrs. Fowler never once took the black pearls of her intelligent eyes from Angelique's sorrowful expression.

"Who is this young blossom?" the lady inquired with a smile; relegating her huge sons and approaching to take Angelique by the shoulders and buzz her on both cheeks.

"You look tired, and you have been crying, child," she went on, and placed the flowers which she had selected into her visitor's hands in a gesture so naturally welcoming, that Angelique found herself warming instantly to this woman.

"Come and have some refreshments and tell me what has made you so sad. Don't concern yourself with my sons. They are merely boys in men's bodies; 'full of sound and fury'… and all of that."

Tea was taken at a snow-white table on the lawn, and as Angelique consumed a complete larder of pork pie, cucumber sandwiches, pears with custard, then muffins with fresh cream and strawberry jam, all washed down with two pots of tea, her life-story and her recent catastrophe were all laid bare, with not so much as a whimper of protest or of reluctance from her.

It was decided by public outcry no less that Angelique was in no state to travel any further; neither were her team, who would require several days of rest in order to regain condition. Nor would she be allowed to sleep under her wagon when there were half a dozen empty rooms about the place crying out for occupancy, and how could Angelique think of denying Adelle her company, when Mister Fowler was from home on business, and all she had for conversation was that pair of giant oafs. Abstemious and Vouchsafe seemed happily unconcerned at being relegated to the third person, but the change which came over them when they heard of the incident that had befallen their heart's desire on the road, was extraordinary. Both men became intensely quiet and withdrawn, and their habitually euphoric expressions took on aspects of a rocky outcrop, with an edge of gladius.

Tired to the marrow of her bones, the traveler begged-off early that evening and having no inkling of just how far the generosity of this interesting family might spread she supposed that she would be sleeping in the servants' quarters, or perhaps a barn or shed. Of the two, she would have preferred the barn, for the privacy of it. As she mounted a wide and deeply carpeted staircase with Rose, 'her maid for the duration of her sojourn at the Furrow', she smiled inwardly at the memory of how, as a girl at home she had imagined the great houses to be merely larger versions of the family's cottage, with bare stone walls and dirt floor. 'The Furrow,' as the Fowler's home was known, had already disabused her of such simple, unimaginative notions.

The building itself was a work of art, with every room and every space, conforming in its dimensions to the exactitudes of the 'Divine Proportion' which Mister Fowler had naughtily claimed as his own. Without exception, the walls, floors and even the ceilings were formed of molded plaster, gleaming timber, polished marble and even hand-painted linen, while each room was an Aladdin's cave of breathtakingly extravagant furniture complemented by exquisite ornaments, paintings and statuary. With the air of a magician's assistant revealing a brilliant outcome, Rose paused at one of several identical doors atop the first flight of stairs and turning the shining brass handle pushed open the glistening oak edifice, standing aside for Angelique to enter. What was revealed was a bedroom the likes of which the young traveler could never have imagined in her most romantic dreams. The finery of the room was sublime, and yet rose, who busied herself turning down the bed and adjusting the drapes, seemed to take it all in her stride. At home in the two-roomed cottage, Angelique's bed had been a few sacks of horsehair thrown down in a corner, and even Andrew's lovely home provided only grey blankets while her narrow bed there boasted an unobstructed view of the rafters replete with their menagerie of winged and four-footed residents. In this home beds consisted of endless flower gardens of silk in positively edible shades of peach, while clouds of soft whiteness formed little couches on which she could rest her head. There were rose-perfumed quilts of extraordinary colors and designs should the night turn cool, while the wooden floor, where it was not ankle deep in wonderfully colourful rugs, was burnished to an amber translucence so that it reflected the ethereal scenes of bucolic Chinese life depicted on the walls. Angelique recognized that it was the existence of all of this that her intuition had foretold when she had decided to leave home in search of the finer things in life.

"Your bath be ready ahind the screen, Angie," said Rose, with a complete absence of ceremony as Angelique had requested of her.

"Let me 'elp you put your 'air up and get undressed, an' then I'll do yer back fer you."

The young trader soon overcame her initial consternation at this elevated level of personal attention, realizing that in this household, such things were merely the norm and was soon up to her armpits in warm, delightfully perfumed water; her hair piled on top of her head, with Rose washing her back. She could have dallied there forever.

"I'll fetch your nightdress," suggested Rose, at the first sign that the bathwater was beginning to cool. Disappearing momentarily, the girl returned a minute later holding up a white creation in silk and lace, which was no larger than a kerchief, and no more substantial than a dusting of snowflakes captured by a spider's web. Angelique had not known that such beauty existed in the world.

"Oh, Rose," she exclaimed in delighted disbelief,

"is that for me?"

"Miss Angie," Rose declared, "it be fit for a angel, and you be bootful as one of they. Let's get you dry and bring down your 'air."

The silk slipped seductively over Angelique's shoulders, caressing her flanks as sensuously as a lover's hands might do as it fell to mid-thigh and Angelique, inexplicably aroused tripped hastily to the mirror to see how she looked. One glance told all. As Rose had promised, she was exquisitely beautiful, but shockingly, every part and shade of her body was as clearly visible through the sinful creation as if she was wearing nothing at all. Angelique's thoughts turned to the effect that this apparition might have on a certain Andrew Carnegie who it seemed had supplanted Philip Bowman in her thoughts.

She was drifting happily into the world of dreams in that gentleman's arms, when she heard again Mrs. Fowler's words of warning,

"Be sure to lock your door, my dear. Those rogues of mine have scant regard for the conventions or for the laws of the land, for that matter. Mister Fowler and I sent them off to Rugby for their education, two little angels, and they returned eight years later, steeped in sin. Lock your door." Sprinting across the room she turned the key while listening assiduously for the reassuring action of the mechanism, then hurried back and jumped into the glorious bed. As she covered herself with the sheet, she saw with eyes growing as big as new moons, the large brass orb of the handle turning slowly to the full extent of its travel; pressure was applied to the door; the door resisted; the handle returned silently to its starting point. Though exhausted by the troubling day it was midnight before sleep eventually claimed her.

In the perfumed dawn, this 'explorer-in-strange-lands,' hurried to the windows to look out, full of curiosity about her surroundings. Beyond the formal gardens which abounded in flowers, hugging themselves against the dawn cold were mature trees which had been planted with great attention to the resulting views from the house. Further still, beyond those wonderfully reassuring sentinels, lay a riding which seemed prosaic, and strangely at odds with the artistry of the cultivated places; the still darkness of the fishponds, the fragile elegance of the Japanese-style bridges, birdbaths, graveled paths and walls of rust-colored brick with espaliered apple trees manacled in lime-green against them.

Straight as a die, the riding stood to green attention for miles to where, in the very far distance could be discerned the roofs of a smoky village. Further still, an impossible plane of azure blue rose high above those roofs, to meet the sky in a horizontal line. Angelique was perplexed; what she was looking at was impossible to fathom.

"Oh. It's the sea," she cried, the energy of her ejaculation indicative of her disbelief that any body of water could be so vast or impossibly elevated, without emptying towards her. Suddenly determined, she crossed the room, changed into her dungarees and duchess-like descended to the foyer only to castigate herself for this betrayal of her roots. 'I've done the meaningless things which I wanted so badly; and none of the worthwhile. I've had tea at a white table, spent the night in a house which has an upstairs; two of them for that matter, and countless rooms; and I've seen the ocean. I've been waited on by a servant and I've worn silk fit for a princess. I've even slept between fields of silk. All of which I wanted, I confess, yet I'd pass it all up just to see Andrew, my sisters and my brother back home again, safe and sound.'

Departing the slumbering house before dawn positive that her hosts would understand her desertion she hurried resolutely to the stables where she found the working day to be well advanced. The smiths were beating red-hot iron into submission with hammers which rivalled that of Vulcan; saddlehorses were being exercised and curried till they glowed, and the contraptions which Abstemious and Vouchsafe found so fascinating, were hitched up ready for the fields. She saw with surprise that one of these was a plough; or rather five ploughs in one, while the other was a harrow of rotating circular blades, which would make short work of the largest sods, dozens at a time. What took her an hour armed with a hoe would be the work of a minute with that invention. Additionally, an ancient seed drill bearing the name 'Tull' in wrought iron was being filled, ready for planting. Of the brothers however, there was no sign. She had arrived just in time to forestall her own beauties being loosed into a paddock by their stable lads.

"Good morning," she called, including everyone present in her greeting.

"Help me hitch them to my wagon instead please. I'll be leaving right-away." There was a chorus of compliance and disappointment from the grooms, at which Angelique was about to set to work alongside them when she noticed something which had intrigued her on the previous evening. Each of the numerous troughs around the place was serviced by an iron pipe supplied with a stick on the end of which was a large brass ball which floated on the water. Angelique pushed the ball downwards as would occur when an animal took a drink and sure enough water gushed instantly from the pipe to refill the trough.

"Clever, eh Miss? Mister Fowler, e's always doin' stuff like that." A brace of grooms had come to stand beside her, their young faces beaming with proprietary enthusiasm and pride.

"It is clever," she agreed.

"Yea, he gets the water off the roofs in that there resir… ressor… that fing, and the 'osses, them can drink when they wants."

"Sharp as a tack," said Angelique sincerely.

"Oh, Angie, fank goodness I caught you." It was Rose, breathless, having run from the house carrying a cloth bundle.

"They tolt me above that you'd gone off all determined like." The two girls fell into each other's arms and hugged in the sweet sorrow of parting.

"I've brought you some brekkie," Rose stepped back thrusting the bundle awkwardly at Angelique, as though the spectre of station had suddenly manifested itself between them.

"We'll have none of that," said Angelique, noticing Rose's hesitation, and hugged her new friend fiercely again.

"Tell Mrs. Fowler thanks for everything from me, Rosie, but I've got to go. Got to."

"I know," sobbed Rose. "If ony I could go too," turning her back she ran off so that no one would see her tears. The boys watched Rose go without a word. They regretted the beautiful young traveler leaving so soon and obviously cared deeply for Rose.

"Why is it called, The Fur--row?" asked the confident; the inquisitive young woman having noticed the word on a plaque, high up on a gable end and deciphering it letter by letter.

"Why Miss, it be to remind a body not to plough 'is own trench and rest in it. The master, when 'e were younger were just like us'n see. Poor as a church mouse, an' 'e 'as ris in the world by pullin' on 'is own bootstraps."

"I'll remember that" Angelique kissed both boys on the cheek almost causing them to faint, then climbing into her seat, spoke to her team and went on her lonely way, waving sadly.

Since glimpsing the ocean's serene majesty from her bedroom window, the lure of that miracle had to be satisfied so that the first crossroads she encountered that morning posed no problem to the young trader; on her right hand she surmised lay a long return home to the cottage and the love of her mother, which at this moment, she needed desperately; to her left lay the ocean, a sense of excitement and adventure, and even the possibility of finding Andrew, her brother and her sisters.

"Come away my beauties," she called and turned left leaving a quadrant twenty yards in diameter in the soft pasture.

At mid-morning passing through a bower where the woods formed a delightful tunnel of mint green, she emerged surprisingly within the walls of a conurbation, the existence of which she would never have suspected. There were many more houses than she had ever seen in one place previously, all of them two stories high and five times the size of any cottage. Indeed, these homes were so grand that the Penny's vicarage would be a poor cousin here. Many of the dwellings had roofs of flat grey stones, they sat in manicured gardens and owned carriage houses of all things. Glory of glories; emporiums; the high street was full of them, their frontages protected from the sun by canvas blinds, and people were going to, and coming from, them carrying bulging bags in which they held their purchases. It was all a heaven which she had to explore right away.

Proceeding towards the heart of this wonderful trove of fashion and necessity the ingenue found the road clogged with pedestrians, horses, carriages and wagons, between which, pigs and chickens risked serious injury while bucolic types in white smocks insisted on driving flocks of sheep through the melee, their dogs, driven frantic by it all, snapping at little boys larking around.

Incredibly, nobody seemed to be working. The womenfolk floated as though becalmed in their colorful dresses with pretty bonnets to match and stood talking to each other as though they had nothing better to do. This was all so very odd. The young trader's entrepreneurial instincts woke from their slumber. So as not to miss any opportunity to detect business and make some profit, she slowed her team to and began to search for a horse-trough. She would let her girls rest and drink while she explored this oasis of plenty on foot. Even the road, which beyond the town had been a mere dust track one wagon wide, was exceptional. It now trebled its girth like a snake which has swallowed a ferret and was paved with little square stones, obviously at enormous expense. How could this possibly be?

The aspiring businesswoman's attention was soon taken by a tall, unattractively thin individual who stood out like a roach-in-flour, mincing along with girly steps at a rate which declared his deep irritation with the world as clearly as if it were written across his forehead in letters of fire. Throwing open the gate of a very substantial two-story home and retrieving the key from its novel hiding place under a flowerpot, this repository of short temper unlocked and went inside only to reappear a moment or two later to stand like an angry pedagogue, his white hands on his non-existent hips as he scanned the street for something as-yet unidentified. Angelique sensed opportunity. Just ahead of her a bridge had been built where previously a ford had sufficed so without hesitation, she turned on to the ancient track and drove into the river where she drew rein and applied the brake so that everyone could rest and drink.

The pipe-cleaner stared directly at her for a suspicious moment or two, then seemed to shake his head as though rejecting an idea or questioning the evidence of his own eyes. Yanking a saucer of a fob-watch from his waistcoat by its gold chain, he flicked open its shining lid, acquainted himself with the time of day, then with one deft swirl returned the instrument to its home. As though this exercise had resolved every problem which beset him, he strode down the garden path and advanced rapidly along the high road toward the wagon where the amused Angelique reclined. Reaching the central arch of the span, he halted Horatius-like, staring imperiously at Angelique, and for reasons best known to himself, displayed one soft, white palm for her consideration

"I'm obviously cognizant of the fact that you are at this time, heavily laden," the castrato sang," but of necessity, must ask you to transport some furniture to my auctioneers at Poole. I'll have someone unload that stuff for you, naturally," he nodded at the huge collection of trade goods at Angelique's back. The notion that his instructions might be rebuffed never entered his custard bowl head, Angelique noted.

"I have a yard not half a mile from here where you can leave it under cover. Just drive straight on until you get to Saint Anne's cross."

"Turn right and it's a stone's throw on the left. Bolger's. Big sign above the entrance."

The choirboy described an arc above his head, employing both of his virginal palms in a gesture as unmanly as any Angelique had ever witnessed. She held her tongue, seeking advantage in the fledgling negotiations; a tactic which forced Bolger to introduce the second half of the equation; the half which he was desperate to avoid; namely the clearly nauseating topic of the carter's remuneration. The light-hearted tone in which he had expounded on the work to be done, was now supplanted by a sneering sibilance, which implied that Angelique had a damned cheek expecting to be paid for the work at all, particularly as it was himself, a person of substance, who was asking and she, a mere worker, who was being tasked. The bitter resentment suffered by the well-to-do when compelled to pay for honest work to be done dripped like bile from his tongue.

"Good morning to you, too." Angelique bestowed her most ravishing smile on this odious excuse for a man.

"I am Angelique Huffer. Carter and dealer in general goods."

"It says 'Andrew Carnegie' on the wagon."

"Do you think me a man?" Angelique disliked this irritable individual more with every second that passed.

"It's me that you are speaking to. It is I who will decide whether or not to undertake your contract, and it is I who will tender the price." Angelique's verbosity during these opening exchanges provided time for her to appraise this 'holier than thou' individual in the shiny black shoes, clothes the color of algae and a hat too small for his too large head. Additionally, the tactic reversed their social status dramatically. As she had displayed exemplary manners from the outset whilst Bolger had acted the boor, the female of the species now held the moral high ground whilst this 'runt of the litter laboured in the mire, where he undoubtedly found that suit. She was the one who now looked down from morally unassailable heights. More importantly, she had already gained a distinct advantage in the commercial joust which was to come. Bringing up the big guns in order to press-home her advantage, the beauty removed her leather hat with a flourish, allowing her hair to cascade around her shoulders, transforming herself instantly from unconscionably lovely youth to stunning womanhood. She watched coolly as the corruption-colored suit felt the planet shudder beneath his feet.

"Well. Umm. Bless me. Right, yes, I… I… I…"

She now repaid the pipe cleaner's insulting behaviour displaying her palm for his inspection.

"Stop!" she scolded.

"You may begin by introducing yourself. That is the accepted form in decent society. You do have a name, don't you?"

"Er, why yes, it's… I say, I do apologize. No idea…"

"Clearly. However, as you cannot recall it, I shall have to be on my way. The proprieties have to be observed." She made to whip up her team.

"Bolger. Fredric Bolger. Pleased to meet you, I'm sure, Miss er, Huffer." He was hyperventilating.

"So, you are capable of speech, for a while I thought that I was being accosted by the village…" She had no need to complete the sentence. Bolger understood her meaning and he had suffered enough.

"Where is this furniture? Perhaps we can do some business," asserted the now combative young woman and with those few words wrested control of the negotiations out of Bolger's boney claws. Pulling-on the brake a notch further the confident one climbed down into the ford and waded to the bank, carrying her boots under her arm. The interior of the house, at which Bolger had called moments earlier, was even more attractive than its façade when seen from the roadway. It couldn't compare with The Furrow, naturally, but to the unschooled young woman it was divine, and what was more; ownership of such a home seemed to the aspiring Angelique to be within the bounds of her hopes and dreams. Each room was as large as her cottage and bright as day due to the many large windows. Everything was as clean as a frosty morning and smelt of soap, polish and flowers. On all sides the furniture shone, brassware pulsed with life, and floral prints in the curtains and cushions filled the space with color. Angelique was enchanted. When she eventually purchased a home of her own, she vowed, it would contain many of the charming elements that she saw about her here.

"What 'exactly' would you like me to contract to, Mister Bolger?" she asked bluntly, standing in the large hallway which provided views of the 'through and through' parlor, as was the local expression for a room which extended from the front of the house to the rear. She had been forced to interrupt the unpleasant martinet in order to make the enquiry, because he seemed quite unable to rest his mouth; jabbering incessantly while managing to say nothing at all. This one clearly fancied himself to be a sharp operator.

"Oh, yes. Right. Well," he began, "it's the contents of the place, Miss."

"Huffer," Miss Huffer suggested pointedly.

'"Quite!' Of course, yes. It's the contents, Miss Huffer; all of it. I want you to take it to my auctioneer's place in Poole."

"You wish to hire wagon and driver for cash payment," Angelique corrected the irritant again, as bluntly and as rudely as she knew how.

"As you say," he murmured, addressing the carpet, and still as non-committal as the oracle of Delphos.

'How the mighty are fallen,' the whip-hand gloated. 'I do believe I detect an attitude improvement on friend Bolger's part. It's time to take control.'

"All of the loading and unloading will of course be done by your people at your expense," she instructed, "including that of my present load, which you say will be quite safe if I leave it at your local property." She wanted no grey areas or misunderstandings where this individual was concerned the man being as flaky as a Cornish pasty. These laborious operations seemed to have conveniently slipped Bolger's mind, but he could wriggle as much as he liked, he was trapped, and the cruel one knew it. The now angry operator, his face tied in a knot, sucked in a great draught of air, and took to wagging his head around like a horse troubled by flies.

"Come now, you don't expect me to carry this lot out to my wagon on my back, do you? The man seemed not to hear. His recent interactions with the carpet had been replaced by a great and abiding interest in the wonderfully bland ceiling.

"Don't make me repeat myself, Mister Bolger," the genuinely angry Angelique warned,

"or you can whistle for a carrier."

"Very well. Agreed," he snapped. Rather too loudly for Angelique's liking.

"I shall require twenty minutes to consider it all and tot up if it'll all go in one trip. Naturally if it requires two journeys, it'll be twice the price." Not waiting for further protestations from the cheapskate, Angelique turned her back on the irritant and trotted to the top of the richly carpeted stairs. She went straight along the landing to the back of the house, surmising that the master-bedroom would be at the rear overlooking the countryside. What she was looking for was the real wealth of the collection which would lie in the dressing table of the lady of the house.

Her surmise, 'courtesy of Andrew.' was correct. The master-bedroom was a large light-filled haven with pale walls and shining floors in which the double bed had only one pillow in its very middle. There was something very sad about that. Peering out of a window, she could see the enemy standing in the back garden, kicking irritably at bits and pieces like a well-thrashed schoolboy, and attempting to reassert his manliness by puffing on a cigar. Trotting to the front bedroom she flung open the window and leaned out, looking back towards the river and the ford. Her team were resting contentedly in the water, but oddly enough, there were now saddle-horses tethered to the tailgate. She was not overly concerned about theft of her purchases in such a well-to-do and public place, but if she did not get back soon, there remained the possibility that she could lose a sale. She would, she resolved, get shut of the nuisance at the earliest possible moment and hurry to her travelling home.

From the window of the master bedroom the view over the fields and woods was delightful, and she flung it open to let in some fresh country air.

"I haven't got all day," Bolger called up rudely. The man now seemed quite impervious to her charms. The thought irritated Angelique more than his foul manners. She closed the window in reply without so much as looking his way. There was no dressing table. Where one might have stood, there was instead to her delight, a writing desk by none other than Chippendale himself. It was one of the Chinese design; identical to the example that Andrew had once so admired; she decided there and then to obtain the piece and surprise her lovely man with it when he managed to get home as she knew in her heart that he would. She would place it near the fire-nook in the lounge so that whenever he might be at home, he would have everything needful for business right at hand. She held back the sudden tears which assailed her at the thought of him and approached the edifice; so tall that it almost touched the ceiling. Mahogany was such a lustrous timber, and she shared the furniture manufacturer's affection for it. She drew her hand across its lustrous surface in appreciation. Opening the desk by extending the writing tablet, she tried each of the twelve compartments thus revealed, but found them all locked, about which there was nothing surprising of course. Drawing up a chair on which to stand she reached up at the side and felt around behind the wonderfully sculpted upper facade. Sure enough; she had the key. People could be so predictable. Happily, the very first compartment that the now energized businesswoman unlocked contained what she was looking for; the departed householder's jewelry. Strangely enough there was a wedding band, the ring which most women would never remove even on their deathbeds; the piece was wide and plain and very much to

Angelique's taste. In addition, there was an engagement ring with three diamonds set very prettily in flowers of white gold, and lastly a pearl necklace with matching earrings and bracelet which Angelique believed, after giving them a close inspection, to be 'the genuine article,' and by far the most valuable pieces in the little collection. She was not one hundred percent sure of their provenance but was sufficiently convinced to allow herself an excursion on a limb. At the very back of the drawer she discovered a diamond ring of one wonderfully clear stone which was almost half the size of the nail on her little finger. Clearly, the late mistress of the house had been the apple of her husband's eye.

''So, friend Bludger,''' Angelique mused, 'you have a very poor understanding of your own business and no understanding whatsoever of women and their ways. No surprise there.' For the first time, she felt a modicum of pity for the irritable string bean. She returned the valuables to their home, replaced the key and went on with her inspection of the contents of the house; already certain that she could make a healthy profit no matter how hard the bargaining might be, due solely to the presence of the tasteful little collection. The irritant was still in the garden when she finished her appraisal and went gunning for him.

"My fee will be twelve shillings." Angelique quite enjoyed making her pronouncement. The poor thespian gasped audibly.

"Twelve shillings!" he mocked. "I want to 'hire' your damn wagon, not 'buy' it, woman. I want to speak to Carnegie."

"You are speaking to Me,'' Angelique insisted warmly,

''and rudely too," looking the boor straight in the eyes as she did so and experiencing immense satisfaction as he broke off the contact.

"I'm wondering whether you would speak to Mister Andrew Carnegie, face to face, in that fashion," she informed him. The thinly veiled threat was all that it took to knock the bombast out of the coward. Bolger's thin lipped little mouth opened and closed like that of a trout in the bottom of a boat but no sound came out. Angelique had prepared her case.

"Mister Bolger," she explained, curbing her ire,

"I shall have to stand idly-by until you arrange the unloading of my stock, then the loading of this house-lot, likewise in Poole. Then I shall have to make the return journey from Poole to your yard down there and wait yet again for your people to reload my goods. Unless, of course, you have thought ahead and arranged a return consignment for me, in which case, the fee will be twenty-two shillings." The young businesswoman paused in order to reinforce her case.

"It's a huge undertaking and it must be paid for."

"You'll leave me no profit at all," Bolger wailed, resorting to playing the sympathy card as his attempt to bully her had failed, his reticence miraculously cured by his full purse of greed.

"Then I'll bid you good day." Angelique turned with finality and proceeded as far as the rear-porch of the property where she halted in apparent indecision, as though something or other had just crossed her mind. Turning to face the furious, indecisive irritant, she proclaimed,

"There is one other way, however. What if I were to buy the lot, every stick of it? Name your price."

"I've been offered fifteen pounds," Bolger snapped injudiciously.

"As is. Where is."

"I'll pay you ten... Cash... Now," said Angelique.

"Twelve. I won't accept a penny less."

"Eleven."

"Done."

"Good. We will go inside and you can write me out a manifest. I take cash only.

"What! You don't trust me?" Bolger was all indignation.

"No! I don't. I don't know you from a sack of. Where 'money,' is concerned? My money? I trust no one, Mister Bolger.'' With Bolger's string-thin form navigating the front garden path, and the key to the house nestling safely with the receipt in her dungarees, Angelique returned to the master bedroom to secure the jewelry. She was wrapping the pearls safely in a kerchief, while humming happily to herself in the glow of her remarkable business coup, when she became aware of a revolting odor.

"And what might the likes of you be doing in 'my' 'ouse? Thievin, I'll be bound." Wheezing like a worn-out old bellows, the voice was far too close. Angelique whirled in fright to discover an enormous, shockingly misshapen, obscenely ugly individual filling the doorway. The beast was so impossibly bloated that his vast girth could not pass through the space, and he was gripping the jambs and wrestling his obesity, piecemeal into the room through main strength; all the while, dripping sweat and gasping with the effort that the task required. His belly was an extension of his sweat-dripping elephant seal chins and hung in a dewlap to his knees like dough in a bakery, beneath which the lower legs were swathed in reeking bandages through which custard-yellow pus was oozing. The room filled with the appalling stink of carrion flesh. In order to haul his gigantic bulk up the stairs without alerting her, this repulsive sack of stench must have crept up them like a predatory animal. Even so, his egg-stained clothes were quality; those of a gentleman-farmer in fact, so perhaps there was nothing to fear after all, and it was just his eye-searing appearance and revolting odor that were unnerving her.

"I'll thank you to keep a civil tongue in your head," the shuddering girl declared, with a bravado which she did not feel.

"I am here on business, as Mister Bolger will confirm when he returns. He will be back in a moment." She was lying; saying whatever came into her mind, and mortally fearful. Trembling.

"Bolger! That little weasel… He'd confirm… 'isself… a Hindu… for a quid. Now what's that, in't cloth?" The hill of blubber squelched painfully closer, cornering her. On the verge of screaming the trapped child gabbled authoritatively as she could manage while stuffing the cloth into a pocket and taking the receipt from another.

"It's a bill of sale for the furniture in this house. Every stick of it." she intentionally misunderstood the question in the bleak hope of side-tracking the beast. The obscenity shunted her, disgusting and assaulting her at once. The wet, yellow-rimmed eyes, with the living gobs of pus in the corners, merely flicked momentarily at the receipt which she held out like a shield in front of her then resumed their revolting contemplation of what might lie under her dungarees.

"That's a lie… my niece is… avin' this 'ouse… an' she wants t'… furniture int' bargain… an' I've telt Bolger. I'll 'ave it all for her… Twelve quid."

"You failed to keep your appointment with him though, didn't you? Bolger sold it to me." Angelique was guessing, rambling, grasping at straws, anything to postpone what she dreaded happening,

"Your daughter can still have it, but now it's me you must pay. Twenty pounds and it's yours… 'cept this writing desk." The elephantine pile of flesh seeped forward inexorably his disgusting head at arm's length from her but his swaying, stinking, obesity fondling her body trapping her in the corner of the room. He was laboring to breathe through his open mouth and his rancid breath was sickening. Soon she would vomit.

"An' what if I just 'ave that bit of paper? Then I'll bag the 'ole lot for free." An inarticulate hand, misshapen by suppurating sores, suddenly whipped out with surprising speed, grabbed Angelique by the hair and forced her agonizingly, humiliatingly, to her knees where she was pinioned beneath the folds of his enormous swinging sacks of lard, her struggles rendered futile. She could not breathe; she was drowning in human fat and running sweat.

"Now… what if… you just… suck my… friend… down there… int' bargain." The obscenity let go of her hair and wrapping his arms around as many of his bellies as he could gather, strained to lift the escaping folds of it above his tumescent member, as he took to thrusting his stinking crotch into Angelique's face snorting like a boar on heat.

"Suck it bitch," he gasped, "suck the fucker." The blade was in Angelique's fist. She stabbed deeply into running white fat; and again and again now in a rage. Arterial blood sprayed into her eyes. The beast shuddered soundlessly, tipping away from her, toppling backwards, collapsing under the strenuous assistance of two enraged men who were lashing at the hill of festering blubber with their fists and boots. The obesity settled rather than fell; his increasing momentum like that of a waterlogged mountainside as it succumbs to gravity, meeting the floor softly yet with an impetus that tested the oak beams of the house to their limit. His corpulence spread across the floorboards like hot offal from the slit bellies of an abattoir, restrained only by the limitations of his clothing. Angelique, almost blinded, pulled herself to her feet, trying to clear her eyes of blood, leaning against the wall and fastening on to the writing desk for support.

The Fowler brothers were taking to the monster's head now with their boots. Blood. There was blood everywhere. She ran. Suddenly vomiting painfully as she went. Choking now on her own regurgitation. Holding tightly to the banisters on the landing. Retching. Gasping for breath. Descending the stairs like a deer, six steps at a time, her contaminated hands sliding down the polished keyway of the banister she staggered out into the safety of the high road where people stared and followed, calling out to her in their concern while men raced into the house to avenge her for whatever had occurred. Not stopping until she was aboard her wagon; she sat trembling, gripping the great whip, white knuckles showing through the blood in the horror of it all. Tortured in mind she was oblivious to the attentions and proffered succor of a score of citizens who had pursued her there in a common desire to help.

The distraught child remained unaware of everyone and everything in the breathing world, as eons of carnage and its stench dragged past until at last, she thought she recognized in the far distances of another life, a comforting sound.

It was a peel of bells.

Numerous clocks offered their unique and therefore overlapping approximations of the hour of three and among their chimes came also a voice which she had heard before; an 'oh so welcome,' voice.

"Miss Huffer. Are you hurt?" Angelique looked up momentarily; she focused; and found the Fowler lads pushing their way to her through a crowd. She was safe. Without a word she relinquished the fight to those more capable of promoting it and collapsed unconscious into the brothers' arms.

Her hands had been tied cruelly behind her back, so tightly that the twine cut agonizingly into the flesh of her wrists causing blood to run so freely that it dripped from her fingertips as she stumbled up the steep and narrow steps of the gallows, shoved forward and assaulted most foully by the cruel, lecherous, insulting hands of her captors, and beaten at every step with sticks and fists.

"Murderer!" The crimson-robed judge had flung his accusing finger at her as a dualist would his epee.

"Give that awful thing to me," said Dora, reaching for the blade, "it can only bring you trouble, darling girl mine."

Angelique's dear mother had appeared beside her in the dock, but to the prisoner's consternation, her parent too was bound.

"Silence, murderous witch!" roared the judge, glaring at Dora with sufficient loathing for both mother and daughter, and to spare.

"You are the diseased tree from which this rotten apple fell. The gentlefolk gathered here today, do not wish their ears filled with the blasphemies of your coven."

At this mention of themselves, the dog skinners, grave robbers, cesspit miners, pimps, hores, and other assorted scum gathered in the body of the court, murmured as one in assent; a vile misshapen monster to which a bone had been thrown.

"Hore. Slut. Murderous bitch. You did foully end the life of a great friend and cousin of this court. A public figure of great standing. Landowner, agriculturalist, benefactor of the poor, employer of thousands, one Stanley Soothsayer Hightower, by use of a concealed blade. A hore's trick if ever there was one. And this, only days after intentionally driving a wheeled vehicle and six, over the bodies of no less than seven innocents as they begged for food. Three of your young victims being mere children."

"Get up horse," Angelique cried, mercilessly lashing a beast that would willingly work its own great heart to death for her. Rolling now with the schooner's tilt as human flesh was minced beneath its wheels.

"I sentence you to the morass," the judge cackled with satisfaction,

"to drift in the slime and corruption of your own ungodly hell for an eternity. That should provide you sufficient time to reflect on the heinous deeds for which you are guilty and clearly unrepentant. Then, at the very last, you will hang by the neck until dead at a place indicated by..."

The thunderous roar caused by the inward collapse of the court's doors, drowned out Longdrop's vituperative onslaught, and sent scrambling, the bovine masses who clogged the public space in their frantic efforts to save themselves at the expense of everyone else.

Andrew Carnegie had driven his wagon and six into the building.

"Whoa," Carnegie commanded, and standing tall in his footwell, he reached out

with his terrible whip and tilted back the judge's spittle-wet chins.

"If my heart's darling is to be hanged; why then the pool?" he demanded.

"Because the incestuous hore fucked her own father, as did her sisters before her. It is common knowledge," screeched the guardian of the law.

"She did for a member of the landed class. She keeps a blade about her person like any slut.''

The masses vomited their disgust, reveling in every word that the crimson uttered.

"Hang the bitch, she's a witch, and she fucked her father.

Hang the bitch, she's a witch, and she fu…"

"Silence!" Judge Longdrop was apoplectic.

"I shall clear this cour…" He made to pound the anvil with his gavel, but the carter's whip raced across the heads of the mob and wrenched that phallic symbol from the pilgrim's wrinkled little fist.

Unabashed and transported to a celestial plane by the good work he was doing, Longdrop turned on the upstart with alacrity.

"We never stop," he screeched, quoting Carnegie verbatim.

"Is that not what you advised this murderous slut, this incestuous slut? You are as guilty as she; I therefore concede her the doubtful pleasure of your company in the swamp. Give my regards to Huffer and Hightower. Take them down."

The rotting, waterlogged tree trunk which Andrew found floating just below the surface of the slime would bear-up only one so that he was required to swim alongside through malodorous muck as the condemned friends struggled from one sulfurous everglade of stench and corruption to another in their endless search for fast land. As the years of *purgatory dragged past, he clung steadfastly to life uncomplaining throughout; but no man can swim forever, and despite Angelique's heroic efforts to aid him, the sand of his strength ceased to flow, and he slipped soundlessly away his lips having never once voiced the love of which his grey eyes spoke so gently. Without a second thought, Angelique abandoned her poor refuge and followed her love into the deep.*

Though she longed desperately to join her man in death she would not fill her lungs with the putrid muck.

BREATHE OR DIE... ANDREW IS ALIVE... BREATHE OR DIE.

A cool sea-breeze; the warmth of the sun filtered through a divine parasol in the Japanese style. She was awake

''Back wiv us are ya.'' The question was imbued with kindness no matter how crudely put.

''Wot's ya name then? You fainted ya dizzy cow. Wot about them two fellas of yourn eh? The tall one can do me anytime.

Angelique sat up, deeply relieved to have escaped nightmare, and discovered that her wheeled couch was on a lawn by the sea, and the inquisitor was a maid if her uniform of black and white signified.

''Hello. Angelique.''

''Posh name. You don't 'look' posh. I'm susan.''

''I'm not, I'm a trader,'' Angelique could not help but smile at the no-nonsense girl's uninhibited manner.

''Oh yeah? I'm meant to go tell his knibs the bleedin butler when you wake up. Stuff im, I'm out of it.'' Susan stared with loathing at the castle of a house.

''Slave from morning till night for sod-all. Stuff em. This is me skin an' blister,

Christine. We're boaf out of it. Wanna come? Town first, then ome.''

Angelique stood up somewhat unsteadily.

''Yes; I will come. Can you wait while I tell them 'thanks?'''

''They aint 'ere. She's in Veneece? And he's down the prison.''

''Prison? I thought only poor people.''

''E' ain't 'in,' prison. E just goes down there all the time to shag the crims. Likes a bit of rough-as-guts he does. The dirty bastard.'' Cristine was not one to hide her feelings.

''That's awful.'' Angelique was sickened.

''I've got to find Andrew.''

She had not meant to make that remark and was glad when neither sister seemed to have heard it. Arm in arm with the strapping girls she went down to the sea and started along that enchanting and everlasting love affair of cool sea and warm sands towards a logjam of ships which crouched beneath a jungle of tall straight trees smothered by vines. She could not easily grasp the frantic reality of modern commerce. Even here on the open ocean where the work was immeasurably more difficult than at a wharf, hundreds of wagons, their loads so tall as to make capsize a real concern, were driving axle deep into the surf to be emptied into longboats which ferried their goods to the ocean-going adventurers and returned with whatever was contained in the ships' holds. The wagons then labored out of the surf and made their way back to the gluttonous warehouses of the port.

''I've got to pee.'' Angelique ran for the bush-covered sand dunes only to hear while she retired there that within that jungle were rough people who clearly drank to excess and swore in the most horrible fashion. Running back to the waterside she hurried to catch up. Better time could be made on the wet sand at the water's edge than ever it could in the fluffy white stuff further from the water so that the district of fine homes where 'The Hawthornes' stood was soon far behind her replaced by these mountainous, scrub-covered dunes from which the smoke of occasional campfires emanated. On each occasion that she heard voices, the lone girl would be goaded into walking faster and to comforting herself with the feel of her blade and the hope that she would come up with the sisters sooner rather than later. Though Poole Harbor had been described to her in some detail by Abstemious, her first sight of it was a revelation. It pronounced unequivocally that she understood nothing at all about this world. At an enormous gap in the sand dunes through which the ocean seemed to inundate half of England, the vast expanse of blinding silver lay calm and still, populated in the distance by tiny islands while white sails flew across the mirrored surface like crazed water-boatmen. Closer at hand, but magnified by a factor of a hundred, was a repetition of what was happening out on the ocean proper. A thousand ships lay at anchor, cheek by jowl, crawled over by a million ant-like men, all busily loading and unloading in a frenzy of activity. Everything that was being done was undertaken with an incredible sense of urgency which left her to wonder how men could work like that all day long without collapsing. Farm workers, without exception, moved at only one speed which was 'comfortable,' to say the least. Beyond the midwinter forest of masts and rigging, lay mile on mile of gigantic open-fronted warehouses, and it was to and from their cavernous maws that the endless wagon-trains came and went. 'All this,' the seeker despaired, 'and not a soldier in sight.'

"Yoo-hoo. Angie." At the very crest of an immensely tall dune stood Susan, now imitating a crazed windmill. But she and Cristine were with someone. A man. Already the rather wild girls had struck up an acquaintance with a stranger. Angelique began to reconsider Susan's suitability as a travelling companion. Clearly, all three persons on the summit wanted her to climb up and join them, but the very last thing she wanted to do was to waste time making the acquaintance of strangers. She had this endless lakeside to search, and she had to do it soon in case Andrew was forced onto one of these ships and lost to her forever. Embarrassment, of all things, won the day. Angelique simply could not turn her back on so generous a spirit as Susan had shown herself to be it was simply too rude, and so she capitulated and began the climb; resolving to make her apologies and keep the meeting short.

"There's a Cornish pasty and beer in the basket for ya," were the first words Susan spoke, and Angelique was so hungry, that the arduous climb seemed well worth the effort. After all, she reasoned, justifying her dalliance; she would have needed to stop for food had she simply walked straight on into the docks. Wearing a sly grin, in which there was nothing whatsoever malicious, Susan's sister introduced the stranger.

"Wodger, this is…? Wodger's a painter."

"Angelique Huffer. How do you do?" Angelique extended her hand. The stranger was not nearly so threatening as she had imagined him to be at a distance. She had taken it for granted that he would have to be an unemployed lay-about in order to be frequenting these sand dunes in the middle of the working day, but in fact he was well-dressed and seemed perfectly respectable, and as clean as a whistle.

"It's wuvley to meet you, Angewique," smiled Wodger, doffing his charming straw hat replete with purple silk band; with bow.

"I'm Wodger Wobinson."

Angelique allowed her relief at the man's easy, non-threatening manner to disguise her amusement at the girl's naughty jest and laughed aloud as she retrieved her poor fingertips from Wodger's pusillanimous touch. She was beginning to like the irreverent tomboys. The pasty and beer were a joy, and she ate ravenously as she joined her new friends in admiring Wodger Wobinson's watercowors which, to their inexperienced and untutored eyes, were weally wewy good. Wodger busied himself at his easel but could not refrain from making suggestive remarks about the difficulty of finding suitable nude models and lamenting his lonely evenings in his huge empty room at the Ship Hotel. This oblique invitation to promiscuity was a source of great amusement to the sisters, and behind Wodger's back, they would catch Angelique's eye and pull ridiculous faces, accompanied by lewd gestures some of them so disgusting as to be unfathomable. Cwistine took the sport to new depths;

rolling on to her back in the warm sand, drawing up her knees and shuddering in mock ecstasy moaning,

"Oh, Wodger." Despite the deep sense of outrage at this disgusting behavior, which Angelique wore like a cloak; she could not prevent herself laughing like a gypsy woman along with the girls. No harm had been done after all, she told herself, as she shook with amusement at the utterly unbelievable depths of it. The Furrow, home of her lovely wildlings, had been stuffed to the gunnels with pictures of fruit, flowers and ladies in diaphanous; not to say scandalous, gowns, and muscular men, who had contrived to shed their clothes while fighting snakes which had lots of heads. It had never occurred to the unschooled one however, to wonder how these miraculously realistic images came about, and now here she was, watching the miracle take place. How her life had changed since leaving her home and her dear, dear mother. These were different pictures to those she had seen before; there was not the intensity or range of color, nor anywhere near as much detail, and yet, with his watery paint, this unmanly man had contrived with just a score or so of brushstrokes to summon up the most lifelike and appealing images of farmhands making hay, wagons being driven into the surf, ships clogging the harbor, and soldiers in single file, wading up to their hips in to the sea.

"Soldiers!"

Angelique gasped choking momentarily on pasty. The subject of one of Wodger's paintings was what looked like a file of uniformed soldiers carrying on their shoulders, barrels of gunpowder, bundles of muskets and obviously heavy boxes; but strangely, the men's lower halves were distorted as though seen through old glass or water.

"Wodger," she choked. "Where did you do this one?" Rodger Robinson misinterpreting Angelique's interest completely, and delighted that his work would engender such excitement, turned from his easel and minced splay-footed towards his admirers, his brush held delicately high as though he thought it a magic wand. Even upside down, the painter could easily recognize the subject that had excited such admiration in the young lovelies.

To Angelique's delight, the artist turned and pointed inland across the calm waters.

"Just… there! my daawing," he declared. Angelique leapt to her feet, and shading her eyes, peered in the direction indicated. In grand isolation, at a far remove from the great mass of shipping and only a couple of hours walk away at most, lay three huge ships which positively bristled with militarism; all served by faint lines of men, who appeared to be soldiers. These were supplemented by an armada of little boats, loaded with what could be soldiery things that made their slow way to and from the sides of those floating fortresses.

"Moath of it is onwy a yard or two deep," smiled Rodger, "cumth juth up to your… dewiere." he studied the lovelies' hips assiduously in a fashion which had little to do with portraiture.

"The shipth have to stay in the deeper chann… channels." Rodger discovered to his disappointment, that he was talking to himself; the most beautiful by far of the three totties was charging in breakneck fashion downhill.

"Bugger," he breathed. "Never mind; these two have got the most gorgeous bodies for miles around." He turned and smiled at the sisters' hips, in a fashion that would leave the girls in no doubt as to what naughty thoughts were going through his mind. Their figures, as they watched their friend running along the shore, left him quite short of breath.

CHAPTER 21: Revenge Is A Dish Best Eaten Cold

Franklin and Macbeth appraised the disguise now worn by the *Glorious*. Her sides between sea and sky were solid black where they had previously been black and white. She had been renamed *Liberty*, and the vulgar attention-seeking figurehead with its fortune in gold leaf had been jettisoned. The most significant changes however were those to her rigging. The bowsprit had been extended to an extraordinary degree and now displayed the essence of the hermaphrodite system; the three huge triangular sails which could be relied upon to utilize even the lightest of airs and impart the exceptional speed with which she had just now closed on the English. Clearly, Hooligan and Teach had kept their men busy as they stood guard beyond the horizon over their shipmates marooned on the beach below him.

"What you have just witnessed Mister Macbeth, was not simply an attack by a ship of war on a merchantman it was in all probability the first naval engagement in these waters of what will come to be known as the 'Continental War.' Alternatively, the 'American War of Independence.'" There was an incredibly deep sense of satisfaction about Franklin as he spoke. It was as though he considered the prospect of a few homespun farmers and fishermen taking-on the most destructive naval and military power ever known, to be the finest idea imaginable.

"I want to put your mind at rest Sir as to my recent history, and how I came to be a prisoner," declared Franklin, "as it is a matter on which you must surely be deeply concerned from the standpoint of security." Macbeth digested in silence this further evidence of the polymath's virtual omniscience and the politician; not expecting of a reply continued with his clarification.

"It is a simple mischance. I had been home for a brief spell on matters of State. I sailed from New York on the *Carolina*, bound for Marseille. Three days after leaving port we ran into a most terrifying storm which drove us southward for three weeks or more, threatening to sink us every minute of each day. The vessel was so badly damaged that we had to put in at the Bahamas for repair, and to replace the stores spoiled in the gale. The delay was to be measured in weeks rather than days. The *Bird*, on the other hand, was about to weigh anchor and sail for France, en-route to the Fever Coast. The intention being to grapple with slavers in those waters and free the prisoners within sight of their homeland. Naturally, I jumped ship." When the Scotsman turned to appraise him; clearly thinking of anything but Franklin's interrupted journey, the diplomat went on; with the insight for which he was renowned among his fellow politicians,

"Yes, Mister Macbeth, hostilities are at a critical stage in the colonies and as we are so few, comparatively speaking, in the Army of the Continent, we are already desperately in need of good friends. I am working towards, hoping and praying, that France will be one of that number and am returning to continue my work of persuading my French friends to come to our aid. So, will you stay true to your word and transport me to Nantes?"

"Mister Franklin," elucidated Macbeth, taking a deep breath,

"We champion freedom fer ev'rybuddy, nae just the black yins. We'll see ye safely to Nantes and to Paris itsel,' if ye feel the need."

"Sir, you are a man after my own heart, and I consider it a privilege to have met you." Franklin offered his hand. Macbeth shook the hand and the man in his energetic fashion.

"The honor and privilege are mine, sur," he replied.

"How else can we help ye? It'll be a sore fight fer you colonists against Georgie boy's redcoats and they German mercenaries o' his."

"You have the advantage of me, Macbeth," replied Franklin.

"Surely you cannot be considering turning traitor to your king and country."

"Georgie boy is nae king o' mine, sur." Macbeth was short to the point of insult.

"The English are a bloody lamentable crowd," he said disgustedly.

"They've been pissed on so long by kings and knights and lords and dukes, and any other sod who's stolen a bit o' land or a few guineas, that they think it's raining. You see sur, there are 'two,' Englands and two races o' Englishmen. One is called the 'haves,' they're a wee clan; there's only a handful o' the bastarts, and the others are the 'have-nots.' There's millions o' they. This is not America, ye know. The 'haves' own everything; the land, the rivers, the trees, the fish in the rivers, the burrds in the trees. They even own the deer and the rabbits, and wurrst of all; they own the law, and as long as they own that, there'll be nae revolt here. Englishmen get strung up daily fer snaring a pheasant tae feed their starvin' bairns. Think of it. How can the bastards lay claim to a burrd? An' how can ye justify hanging a man fer eatin' one? The people here are nae maire free than slaves. They're ''worse,'' than slaves. Ye dinnae have tae go far tae see wee children wurrking fourteen hours a day fer sod-all." Franklin considered the giant student of men speculatively.

"And yet, you say they won't fight back?"

"Benjamin," said Macbeth; not bothering to conceal his anger and frustration,

"if them landed gentry bastarts are canny enough tae let the hoi polloi have just the scraps from their table an' a wee bittie thatch tae sleep uner; and they arr, the English will 'never.' rebel." Franklin did not reply, because none of what Macbeth had said was new to him. He had lived in England for many years, travelling widely throughout the country, and well knew how the rich rode on the shoulders of the people whom they shackled with the chains of poverty, tied cottages Conspiracy and Trespass hanging judges, mantraps and indentured servitude. Furthermore, he was acquainted with how the English aristocracy cultivated the notion of their 'blue blood' and their God-given right to rule, and how they went to such great lengths to widen the chasm which they had excavated between themselves and the rest of humanity. They controlled the vote; only landowners enjoying that privilege; education, the church, the government and the military, and perpetuated

ing364

Conspiracy laws, the notion of poaching, armed gamekeepers, pressgangs, and pillories and the rest of the divide-and-conquer devices so dear to their hearts. It would not have surprised him to discover 'Prima Nocta,' flourishing in certain remote places. Far below on the glistening beach, Franklin noted, in and around the village of tents, and the fires over which fish and beef now cooked, Americans and Englishmen were cohabiting in the easy friendship born of the absence of a 'landed' class.

That evening, Macbeth dismissed those of his local men who wished to go home to their families, rather than sail for Scotland. They were, after all, surplus to requirements; the *Bird*'s crew being sufficiently large to sail all five of his ships to Perth, that beautiful town of golden stone, in the Firth of Tay. Speaking sternly to his departing warriors he insisted that they should simply go on with their work around their villages as though nothing had happened and as always, keep their traps shut to everyone, including women and priests; 'particularly women and priests,' on the pain of 'very severe repercussions.'

The men departed during the night, silently and with a deep sense of achievement walking off into the darkness with the good wishes of the Americans, and the stentorian instructions of their leader ringing in their ears. Namely, to separate, find their own way home and say nothing to their wives or ''any other bastart.'' Macbeth never failed to make a point strongly by saying it often and with increased volume each time. They went happily enough none of them being sailors, and in any event, they were aware that they had already achieved great things and would be well rewarded for the considerable risks which they had taken. Some of these men were already owners of two, three or more acres of valuable productive land due to the dangerous work which they had undertaken in the fight against slavery and the newer men wanted desperately to join their comrades' exclusive gang. Trewin Copplestone was last to exit the maw of that suicidal track and step into the relative safety of the steeply sloping sward at the top of the cliff. The others, eager to get back to their families, had already been claimed by the night. Choosing a comfortable spot, he dropped his knapsack and lay down in the grass to rest while he watched the dark shapes of the little flotilla depart this bay which had been such a blessing for the ailing sailors of the bird. How things had changed, both for himself and for Lliam Hooligan since the occasion of their first meeting, a meeting that had proven so rewarding but which could so easily have gone badly awry; both being such fractious individuals, to say the least. Incredibly, Lliam, a drunken violent, illiterate tramp, was now the owner of four superb sea-going vessels, each of them worth a fortune, and was presently conducting a minister of the United States of America no less, to the French city of Nantes. For his own part, on that fateful day he had been penniless, hungry, and about to sell his only friend; his horse; Bengal. Now he had a home, good friends, and more money than he knew what to do with, his new friend having been so incredibly, insanely generous with his distribution of the enormous wealth from the *Justice*. It had seemed quite likely on parting ways, that the madman would throw in his lot with the anti-slavery movement and even become involved in the savage war between England and the emerging nation of America.

He wanted none of that. Though he was steadfast in his opposition to slavery in all of its forms, tyranny, injustice and the rest; he had seen enough of war and killing, blood and death and much more besides during his time in the East and in Africa. Now he wanted something else; he was not exactly sure of the form which the 'something else' would take, but time would tell. He would go home to Thorpe and weigh up his options from there. With Angelique now being absent for long stretches at a time, and Dora's estranged husband being neither use nor ornament, he felt sure that he could make himself helpful by doing the heavy work around the place and be some sort of company to that good woman, while he got on with establishing himself in some interesting line of business. Dora was an exceptional woman, blessed with love and compassion aplenty and a dozen other splendid qualities. Qualities which he had long ago concluded, were in short supply among the masses of mankind. He would never forget her generosity to him when they first met. She had not known him from a radish, yet she had welcomed him into her home with a smile and open arms, simply because of his friendship with her brother, and thereafter behaved like both sister and mother to him. There were few finer.

The re-named *Liberty* was the last of the five ships to make her offing, for the huge twenty-gunner had clearly been shepherding the other vessels to the relative safety of the open ocean, and now with that task successfully completed, she turned to the South and the distant city of Nantes. As she held course astride the horizon, a great cloud of blue smoke issued from her cannon, and a moment later, the clatter of the explosions reached his ears. His crazy Irish friend was farewelling him in the most extraordinary fashion. Copplestone leapt to his feet, waving his invisible hat wildly.

"Lliam you lunatic," he yelled, "I bloody love you," paraphrasing, of all people, the despised Macbeth.

As he meandered in the general direction of Thorpe, the miles passing comfortably by in the leisurely amble of a field hand which compared so well with the forced marches of a soldier, he had the real sense that he had arrived at a watershed moment in his life. His existence up until; yes; his meeting with Lliam had merely been the two sides of the same coin; the two were one, and the *one* had been unsound.

If he were able live his life over again, he would reject both with venom. There was, 'The Army' and there was, 'Before the Army.' Prior to 'taking the shilling,' he had, so far as he knew, always been a foundling; a homeless, orphaned, unwashed skeleton in bits of rags who ran with a score or more of the same. He could not recall ever having known any parents, and his earliest clear memories were those of being a pack animal, an individual part of a very much bigger creature, a stronger, faster, more cunning creature, capable of identifying the weakest member of a herd; of isolating it from its kind, and then bringing it down. Just as a pride of lions or a pack of wild dogs work together to make a kill, so every member of the gang would do his part according to his abilities, and thusly they survived and even, on occasion, thrived. Then came the army which he had joined young; even before he grew his moustache. He could not have expressed his belief in words, but at that moment of attaching his mark, the juvenile Trewin Copplestone, 'a name with which the army had burdened him,' had the vague notion that what he was joining was a brave legion who would defend England against all-comers. A select few who dripped selflessness, chivalry, comradeship and the likes. He had been naive. In the extreme.

The Honorable East India Company had been established in the sixteenth century under a charter of Elizabeth I for the express purpose of promoting trade between England and India. However, as the English government paid scant attention to the company's dealings thereafter, the worthies who held the shares in the business felt free to do just as they liked. And did. The aristocratic English soon discovered that silk could be bought 'at cost' in Jamshedpur if only one turned up at the merchant's place of business at the head of fifty infantrymen; bayonets fixed. Miraculously, the price of a cargo of salt fell by half as your squadron of lancers surrounded the evaporation pans, its operators and owners, and best of all, if some minor prince refused to grow cotton as you had instructed him to do, and insisted on planting wheat; the simple device of shooting the fool and every one of his relatives made the problem disappear into the furnace-blast of air above the inferno of his looted palace. Year after year, decade after decade, century on century the East India Company grew in infamy, power and riches. Its army grew in numbers, ruthlessness and ferocity and eventually ruled by outrageous force, guile and blackmail over vast swathes of the Indian sub-continent. It was this hoard of rapists, murderers, thieves, blackmailers, opium traders, land grabbers, and backstabbers that he joined. His reasons for doing so were few but compelling. He was starving and they gave him food. He wore nothing but lice-crawling rags and they gave him a uniform just like their own, with shiny boots of real leather; he would never go cold, hungry or penniless again. His soul cried out for family and friends. They offered him the brotherhood of the regiment. He took to the business of killing readily enough as young men do, particularly when confronted by the hard Pashtoon tribesmen of the Hindu Kush and became adept with flintlock, bayonet, saber, lance and fists. More importantly still, he could quickly turn almost any object into a weapon, a facility which made the difference between living and dying. 'A handful of sand in a man's eyes; the boiling water from your campfire, your webbing belt with brass buckle was a lash of 'blinding' efficacy.' In the 'Kush,' one lived in expectation of attack through every minute of every day. Everything became your weapon. Every individual, your enemy. His enthusiasm for the sport waned rapidly when his regiment, having suffered ten years of almost continuous hostilities were considered 'broken in' sufficiently to undertake the 'pacification 'of innocent clans of unarmed farmers; men, women and children. He and the others who refused to do the murdering were whipped, drummed out of the regiment and thrown ignominiously aboard a clipper bound for Blighty. Their month's pay was withheld. With the scales lifted from his eyes he was ashamed to have served with the infamous East India Company and outraged by their treachery. Trewin returned to his native land with a new awareness of the ways of the world, best summarized by one of his contemporaries; a Scottish ploughman and poet by the name of Robert Burns, with whose work he was acquainted. The ploughman had written, *'Man's inhumanity to man makes countless thousands *morn!'*   mourn

It all went wrong for him on the fifth day of his long trek home. Crossing an open glade in a forest which, he was reasonably sure, was the property of an enemy, the infamous Michael Astor, Trewin caught on the wind fragments of conversation, and moments later, two men appeared coming towards him with a mantrap slung between them. Neither of the gamekeepers; 'they had muskets slung on their backs,' saw him as they set down their load and went about separating the murderous jaws. With an image in his mind of the young Derwent, trapped and blood-soaked in one of those things, the soldier approached quietly.

"What the devil do you think you are doing?" he snarled. The laughter ceased abruptly as the stinking men looked up, reaching for their muskets in fear.

"Who you?" one asked cautiously, having obviously noticed the clipped accent and note of authority.

"Never mind about that. Are you prepared to smash a man's legs with that thing for the sake of a rabbit?" The chastened gamekeepers had no time to fashion a reply before a group of riders entered the clearing and spurred up to the developing altercation. The cavalry's leader dispensed with the civilities and got right to the point. Ignoring Copplestone he spoke to the older of the two keepers.

"What?"

The disgustingly filthy individual gestured in Trewin's direction with an impossibly thin arm.

"Say no," he mumbled, clearly more afraid of the horseman than ever he was of Copplestone.

"Does he, indeed?" The leader could not have been a more rounded individual, whose voice was even louder than his bilious waistcoat. Birds lifted from their nests in the trees as he bellowed.

"Bring him along, we'll hang the insolent bastard." Ropes were thrown smartly around Trewin's fighting chest, and he was dragged off his feet to bounce, whirl and drag across the clearing like a leaf caught in the wind, providing a spectacle which the riders found amusing. At the first possible moment, by judging his speed and the force of the ropes to perfection, the prisoner was able to rebound off a bank in such a fashion as to regain his feet, and break into a succession of ridiculously long leaps, the forward momentum of which was supplied by the cantering horses, so that he 'pronked' the rest of the journey in the fashion of an African springbuck utterly desperate to stay on his feet. Another hundred yards of being dragged along the ground and there would have been no need for a hanging; he was painfully ripped and bruised in every part of his body. Mercifully, his trial concluded before his stamina gave way, adjacent to a forbidding looking barn.

"Throw him in there for tonight and we'll take care of him in the morning. You two, will stay here tonight. One of you will be on the door at all times. If the little sod gets away from you, I'll skin you alive. By which, I mean that I will peel off every bit of your filthy skin while you still breath." The fact that they threw him inside the building without binding him was an ominous sign; it signified that they knew the place to be escape proof; even so the prisoner listened hopefully for loose talk with his ear pressed to the narrow gap between the lofty doors. Not only was there no loose talk; there was no talk at all. The bilious waistcoat wasn't the sort to waste his breath on a couple of morons. The facts that a thick beam at shoulder height was all that held those doors closed, coupled with the chink in the keepers' armour which was suggested by their silent fury, was all that he had going for him. Knowing that he had to get out before darkness fell, or have his neck stretched in the morning, the soldier began his search at the instant in which his eyes had adjusted to the dim light. He then advanced head-first into something which was very hard. Standing quite still, with a hand to his pained forehead he was trying to locate whatever it was whose acquaintance he had made when, annoyingly, he was struck again. Thankfully the blow was not nearly as painful as the first. Something cold and heavy was resting against his temple; a massive steel hook was hanging from the ridge-beam by a chain. Up above, the gloom was less dense due to a row of small windows. An upper floor extended from the rear wall, to about the mid-point of the building's length. He supposed that wagons would be driven inside the place and the hook and pulley would be employed to lift off fresh supplies of mantraps. A complete tour of the lower floor's perimeter confirmed that there were no doors, windows or other weak spots, and the walls were solid stone throughout. If he was going to get out of here, it would have to be by the way he came in; 'through those wagon doors.' There was no shortage of weapons, a contingency that the fat loudmouthed plunger would have been well-aware of. There were pitchforks, scythes, and even a selection of hammers at a forge by the wall that was replete with everything needed for shoeing horses, wagon repairs and the like. It would be easy to call a guard to the door and stab him in the eye with a pitchfork, but that would not get him out of here. 'Poor Angelique,' he reflected, 'she sends me off to bring her uncle safely home and I can't even bring myself home.' Realizing that such maudlin thoughts were the thin edge of surrender he castigated himself.

"Get on with it or die, Copplestone." He intensified his desperate search. Stone steps built into the wall gave access to the upper floor. Ascending quickly he established that there was little of any help to be found; the windows were too small to get through, but the drop would kill him in any event. Hanging on the walls were several mantraps. He put them out of his mind; wasn't he already in a mantrap of his own? Turning away from the disgusting things he came within a foot of stepping over the edge of the boards; directly below him was the huge anvil at the forge. Had he fallen from this height on to that thing, he would have cheated the hangman for sure. For a moment, he considered the massive object; not fully understanding why, but with the worm of an idea rapidly evolving. With hope growing like bamboo in the wet season he raced down the steps and stood there staring at the thing, his mind whirling and demanding answers.

''Yes,'' he declared, almost crying out with the beauty of it. He was getting out of this place. 'Tonight.'

''Gob, Shut." A gypo was sitting near the narrow gap between the doors. This was good, he would need to account for at least one of the verminous twins as he broke out, or he would be shot down by the other. He needed to keep them close to the doors. Very close.

"Your wife, she good," he informed the guard helpfully. For a while, it seemed as though the gypos had not heard or understood the compliment because the expected explosion never occurred; it transpired however that the master of witty repartee beyond the door must have simply needed time in which to compose his brilliantly imaginative and amusing response.

"Fuck basta. You." The poor fellow's agonized tone made it abundantly clear that he was not at all confident on the question of his wife's fidelity. The tactician had struck a chord.

"Ah, that's better.'' The battle was joined. Quickly back to the implements stacked against the wall where he selected a pitchfork and placed it at the foot of the steps, it was the best weapon available to him; with a shaft of oak, well thick, and two yards long. Its needle-sharp tines shone alluringly. Perfect for skewering nasty people. Back to the anvil. Standing hard-up against the cold monster, he measured its height against his leg, and using a file from the forge he approached the hook, whose acquaintance he had made earlier, where he found to his immeasurable disappointment that the anchor point above was fixed or rusted solid. Onward to plan B. Passing the chains freely through his hands, the inventor lowered the hook to the critical height, namely a few inches above the height of the anvil. Taking the file from his belt he worked the chain where it passed through the pulley-block so that the blaze was clearly visible in the growing gloom. When he attached the anvil to the chain, this mark would be vitally important. A matter of life and death. His own life and the gypsies' deaths.

"Rope. I must have rope." He recalled with relief having noticed plenty of rope, new rope, when he was exploring earlier and was able to go almost directly to it. He dragged a suitable length back with him and gathering it together, threw it to the floor near the hook. He was in superb condition and immensely strong, but what he now had to do would, he was sure, test that strength to the limit for the anvil was as heavy as he. Borrowing a pair of the blacksmith's leather gauntlets, he approached the beast with the same determined belief that Macbeth had shown when lifting a boulder that outweighed him. Through trial and error, he found the perfect grip, and taking a deep breath, dragged the thing in one supreme effort, all the way from the forge to the foot of the steps. The task left him gasping at the center of a constellation of little white stars. The prospect of manhandling that huge weight to the upper floor was daunting but it was merely a challenge, not a problem.

"What yous? Cut owt. Else."

"Do her from behind. She likes that.''

''I kill to def."

Well pleased with himself, the sergeant hurried back to the anvil to do the impossible. To get an object which outweighed him to the floor above. Positioning his hands and feet with care, he sucked in a great lung-full of air and strained upwards. His chest bursting and tendons stretching, two of the beast's feet rose from the floor; another great heave and the third foot lifted. Twisting now till one end was above the first tread he lowered gratefully, emptying his lungs in a great rush.

"One down, or 'up' in this case; eighteen more to go." Night had chased away the day by the time the escapee's association with the death-dealer was through and he was ready to put his sole chance at life into action, and that was all to the good because in order to shoot him, the enemy would need to see him. Lashed securely to the great hook the anvil now teetered on the edge of the upper floor directly in line with the gap between the doors; it just needed a good heave to send it on its way, but first he must make sure that he eliminated at least one of the unwashed. It would best if the victim was standing very close of course, so that he could benefit fully from receipt of the surprise parcel. Down the stairs he raced for the tenth time, to peek through the gap and ginger-up his captors.

"I'm dry as a bone, my friends, would you have a drop of the hard stuff about you?" he began politely.

"Ha dog go fuck. Hunny tunk.''

"Ha. Your wife say, '''honey tongue.'''

"Basti!" There was a flurry of action outside, and a moment later a musket was discharged. The ball splintered its way at head height into the barn admitting a narrow shaft of light in which blue smoke raced in pursuit of the lead ball. Sergeant Copplestone was no longer there, he was racing up the stairs, a pitchfork in his grip. Closing with his surprise parcel he hurled his javelin at the doors where it stuck fast and swung 'metronome like,' creaking loudly.

''Cut out.'' The gypo was at the gap between the doors; a gap which would shortly be very much enlarged. Copplestone heaved his tame rhinoceros over the edge. It plunged vertically in unimpeded malevolence its acceleration and momentum incalculable. The chain snatched up straight and rigid as a rod of iron, the roof-beam yelped in surprise under the massive strain that it was suddenly expected to support, and the destroyer's vertical course became a smooth, and perfect arc. It hurtled across the barn coming within inches of the stone-flagged floor, curving upwards once again to smash through the doors where the infuriated guard was peering inside.

"You is pig face bast." The massive impact put an end to the gypsy's jeering, and to him. Copplstone's speed of descent almost equalled that of his plaything. He was already crossing the flags towards freedom when the pendulum returned. Cutting things as close as he dared; so close that he felt the breeze of its passing he raced through the dim wreckage with his pitchfork at the ready and smashed painfully into someone coming the other way; the impact of the collision so great that both men lost their weapons as they rebounded like a couple of rutting rams and crashed to the ground. Both were up in an instant, snarling like pit-bull dogs and grappling for the killer hold, intent on finishing it quickly. Now, the advantage lay with the soldier; war and training for war, had been his daily bread for almost a decade, he had killed men with the musket, the bayonet, the sabre, the lance, and on occasion, with his bare hands. He had striven in barbaric hand-to-hand fighting against wiry tribesmen of the Afghanistan and had survived. He would survive this. Using both his opponent's bodyweight and his own in a wrestling move practiced year-in and year-out in the regiment, the soldier spun on his heel and hurled the enemy away from him, hooking the man's ankle as he released him. The unfortunate individual was sufficiently aware of his surroundings to understand that his death was imminent and was screaming even before the anvil skewered him. The horn of the steel rhinoceros, thick as a man's thigh at its base, plunged through his ribs below his right arm, destroying his lungs and exiting through his left shoulder. Snatched into the air the instantly dead victim flown to the extremity of the pendulum's range where his torso halted abruptly while his arms reached out piteously to the trees across the way. His appeal was ignored, and he was carried unceremoniously back through the barn, his dead hands clutching at straws. Utterly detached, the dragoon snatched up the enemy's musket and rushed to take stock of his position. He had noticed earlier that the barn seemed to be in an isolated spot, but he was taking no chances because the sound of musket fire would have carried for miles. Running quickly to the nearest highpoint, he confirmed that fortune favored him. He probably had a little time to play with for the nearest lights were mere candles in the far distance. Stripping off his bloodied clothes, he flung them into a horse trough and stepped in on top of them stamping the claret out of them as he washed himself. He could not rejoin the world wearing the gory color of war.

Copplestone's only wound as he departed the field was a considerable gash to his forehead which was of little moment as it was no longer bleeding. He was naked and carried a loaded flintlock over which hung his damp clothing. This had been a poor start to the life of peaceful endeavor which he had envisioned when he farewelled fleet Hooligan. 'Perhaps,' he mused, 'I should have stayed aboard the *Liberty*. A gundeck would be a safer place than this.'

By sun-up, the latter-day Adam had put a considerable distance between himself and the escape-proof prison, much of that journey along hard tracks where any gypsy trackers would be denied sign of him. Exhausted but confident that no one was on his tail, he found a suitable lookout in a copse and rested while he struggled in to his cold and horribly uncomfortable clothes. Pleasingly, through the surrounding foliage he could now glimpse what he imagined to be Alsop, its chimneys smoking as one above the forest. He walked into that pleasant little town along a field track, wishing a good morning to passing maids and field hands; eager to find breakfast and wondering the while whether the old witch who dealt in clothing and lewd observations still turned the air blue at the high street market. If the crone was still above ground, he would have a selection of corduroy trousers and flannel shirts to bolster his suffering wardrobe; and doubtless, an abundance of impertinent observations. Rather than eat inferior food at some less-appealing establishment Copplestone sat outside in the cool morning air, contemplating the events of the previous day, as he waited for the doors of The George to be opened for business. For the second time in a week, he had seen evidence of the landed class riding 'rough-shod,' over the population at large, employing barbaric machines designed to maim and kill anyone, man, woman or child; or 'horse.' Their fallback position being to hang anyone who found fault with this behavior. Even in India it was generally recognized that a human being was worth rather more than a rabbit. It was all too disgusting to be tolerated. Had Bengal jumped that hedge when put to it by the deceased Derwent, his friend might have been the one to suffer the appalling agony which ended the life of the thief. The thought was unsupportable. He twitched in revulsion, as the thought horrified him. His mood, usually so optimistic deteriorated severely, he barely tasted his breakfast and was short with the staff. Departing the town, he noticed that the old woman's stall was still thriving, but he barely glanced her way as he passed. The lunatic once again outwitted him tactically by offering loudly to perform a disgusting act upon him free of charge.

The soldier's mood hardened as the hours and the miles passed. That swine in the cowshit-green waistcoat had planned to hang him for the crime of arguing with a couple of gamekeepers and for that affront to his person and to Natural Justice. He intended extracting a heavy price. There would be blood.

'Clearly in the mind of that singularly unbalanced individual Lord Michael Astor; death in the jaws of a medieval instrument of torture, or by hanging, bestowed some sort of legality on the crime of murder.'

The strip of industrial land known as 'North Bank,' in the city of Birmingham, was so-called because many of the filthy, stinking sweatshops and repositories of human misery there, were being erected on land which formed the northern bank of what had been a minor fresh-water spring. A reliable and safe water-source which bubbled out of the ground summer and winter, even in times of drought. In earlier times there were pleasant fields where cows grazed, regiments of cabbage paraded in their number-ones and birds nested, singing in the hedgerows. Villagers who had suffered peremptory eviction from their tied cottages because their labour was no longer required due to large increases in yield per acre, drifted by the thousands and the tens of thousands into the new town, seeking work and lodging in these seething 'above ground' graves. The pleasant gulley where the reliable, clean, cold and refreshing water flowed generously became a depository for the hundreds of tons of human waste that would accumulate in the streets and alleys and courts hard by. In sheer frustration and disgust at the conditions of their lives, the populace would, on occasion, rise-up and barrow the filth downhill to the gulley in which the clear stream issued from the perpetual spring.

It was the nearest open space.

As the years passed, and the filth of dozens of small factories was added to that of the ever-multiplying courts and alleyways, the rate of degradation accelerated tremendously so that eventually, the little valley was no more. Filled to the brim with human waste, it soon transformed into a rise, then a hill, and eventually a mountain. A mountain of human filth, as high as a house and two hundred yards long. With the evidence of the sanitation problem all around them, up their noses, and sticking to their shoes; the industrialists, who were throwing up mile after mile of terraced, *jerry-built sanitation-free housing, in which to cram their workers, 'five families to a terraced dwelling' while making obscene fortunes in the process; concluded that the solution lay in incorporating cesspits in their hovels by utilizing the space under the floorboards.

*Jerry built. Poorly constructed as in Jericho whose walls fell at the sound of trumpets.

The result of this genius being that thereafter, the most recent migrants from the villages ate, slept, and copulated, with the thickness of a bit of floorboard between them and the pulsing reservoirs of their own, and others' waste. Only the most abject sort of workers; the most desperate of men; the incontinent, the insane, the alcoholics, the retarded, and those who were so deformed that their very appearance scared the populace at large, and who could find no other work would accept employment in the emptying of these hellish places.

Such was the stench when these unfortunates broke into the receptacles that legislation was passed, prohibiting this work being done during the day. Thereafter, to the odious health and soul-destroying horror of the task itself, was added the further curse of performing the work in darkness. Boards were laid on North Bank's shame; an innovation of which the aldermen were justly proud, enabling an endless line of barrows full of the most repellent substance known to man, to be wheeled nightly to the top and tipped down its ever-widening sides; not its ends, for the borough councilors were determined to keep the mountain's shape regular.

"It would not do," the city's unelected leaders proclaimed,

"To have shit dumped just anywhere."

There were perennial vacancies in the council's night shift sanitary gang for to step accidentally off the mountain's planks as inebriated souls did, was invariably fatal. As often as not, the unfortunate's hat was the only sign of his 'passing,' a remark which was made ad nauseam, brown humour being all the rage. Over the years, the firm of Wurm and Son prospered mightily through its policies of paying starvation wages, maintaining their presence at North Bank where the rents were the lowest in the country, and by cleverly and illegally expanding their rented property upwards in the most dangerous manner imaginable.

With their wrought-iron products in ever-greater demand among the burgeoning middle class, mantraps for the estates of the incalculably wealthy going out of the doors daily, and the three-bladed Rotherham plough selling like hot cakes to the new breed of gentlemen farmers, more space had to be found for increased production, at the lowest possible cost; or less. By raising their present walls upwards by a further two floors, despite the warnings of the concerned bricklayers employed for the task, they increased their available space by two hundred percent, and the ire of their fellow industrialists similarly, as those personages wanted to do likewise but lacked the necessary intestinal fortitude. So weak and unstable was the finished edifice that Wurm's long-suffering employees wielding sledgehammers on the third floor, would feel the building vibrate at every blow. The ever-present miasma of this hell on earth, and the resultant difficulty in retaining tradesmen, were not the only problems that Wurm and Son faced in clinging tenaciously to their low-rent hovel. Eventually, the filth which for years had crept irresistibly towards the track along which their materials were delivered sullied the track itself and the carters quite naturally refused to deliver. Ever resourceful, the Wurms responded by bricking up the polluted entranceway, and reinforcing the wall with step-buttresses against the ever-increasing pressure of the popular 'movement.' They then demolished a section of the wall at the rear of the premises and transplanted the front gate. Deliveries resumed.

At approximately two o-clock in the morning the cracked bells of the town-hall aided by those of a dozen churches declared the hour of twenty three as a ragged drunk, hugging his cask to his chest, careened downhill from wall to wall of a stinking alley known locally as the *Nail*; this public toilet, whore's boudoir, and lair of violent thugs who beat and robbed anyone foolish enough to walk there, existed primarily to channel filth towards the hill of shit during wet weather. The turds washed across its cobbles as though the place had been designed and built, not as a conduit for human beings, but as an open sewer. Its secondary purpose was to link Leak Hill with an insanitary sanitary lane which serviced a hundred or more of the outposts of purgatory.

Here worked reticent men, hunched-over men, men whose pores and creases were black with ingrained dirt as was their clothing, men whose right hands were invariably much larger than their left, and who, without exception, worked with vinegar-soaked cloths covering their noses. These were tanners, slaughterers, dog-skinners, iron workers, foundry men, and workers in copper, bronze, and granite. Here were abattoirs, glue makers, rope makers and dealers in bricks, wrought-iron, sand, cement, lime, glass, coal, and a myriad of other materials required by the city.

The Nail disgorged the nocturnal drunk directly into the unprepossessing rear entrance of Wurm and Son thereby causing a small, almost inaudible metallic sound, at which the legless gent fell through the gate. Sobering up remarkably quickly once inside the yard. Sergeant Trewin Copplestone closed the gate quietly behind him, and with his back to the wall and the jemmy-bar in his hand, waited expectantly for the scraping rush which always presages an attack by mastiffs. None came. Crossing the yard to a filthy door soiled by a hundred thousand grey hands, he rammed the bar home close to the lock and turned the knob, pulling back simultaneously on the steel. The wood split, surrendering with a squeal, and he was inside. Remembering how he had almost brained himself recently by walking into a lifting hook in the dark he let his eyes adjust fully and searched the gloom assiduously for objects that might injure or even blind him as he went about his business. Only when he was certain that he would not be the author of his own demise, did he get started, moving cautiously even then. Making his way across the ankle-breaking boulder-field of the shop floor, past the furnace, the Newcomen pumps and a fortune in sand-moulds for iron castings, he arrived at what would sensibly be the goods-inwards area at the back of the building where the materials required in the manufacturing processes would be delivered and signed for against later payment. Almost immediately he found what he was looking for; the very distinctive barrel of grease with the splashes of red paint on its sides; the same barrel of grease which he had caused to be delivered eight hours earlier, only moments before the end of the working day. Turning it on to its side, he rolled the thing through the gloomy warren with its thousand pitfalls, sharp obstacles, and other assorted dangers until he was roughly in the center of the building where he was equidistant from many of the vital targets of his operation. Breaking the barrel open and taking out several packets of explosives, he located these where they would do most damage. The furnace, the pumps, the stores of expensive materials and the inflammables all got his attention, while the bulk of his firepower he positioned against a structural pillar which stood roughly central to a fabrication area where mantraps were being carefully assembled. He packed the things tightly with sacks of casting-sand and lumps of metal. With the loose powder and slow match which he had purchased in Bristol, he lay trails sufficiently long to guarantee him time to get well clear; located his escape door, lit the powder, then walked slowly and carefully to the exit. With his rum-cloth over his face and his bar in his sleeve, he made his way across the yard; passed through the gate and climbed the Nail to Leak Street. Strolling uphill to a predetermined vantage point, the soldier arrived there surprisingly without incident. Despite the lateness of the hour, fleeting shadows were a common occurrence and one which he had predicted and made allowances for by having two dueling pistols about his person, in addition to the concealed iron bar. Arriving at his pre-selected observation post, he hid in the deepest shadows with his back to a damp and mossy wall, searching the gloom for the slightest movement until he was certain that there was no one around, ready to strike.

Though he was expecting it; when the explosion occurred, he almost jumped out of his boots. The outlines of that ugly cube of a building were suddenly illuminated by flames bursting through every shattering window. Then, wonderfully, the whole pack of cards jumped upwards a couple of yards into the air, collapsing in on itself, slowly at first, but with increasing momentum. The result was a bonfire of massive size and heat whose glow lit up the adjacent mountain and the struggling barrow-encumbered mountaineers.

Turning his back on Wurm and Son, the little soldier in the cause of revenge began the long journey home. 'So much for the money-grubbing devils who were prepared to manufacture such obscenities as mantraps. Now for the devils who used them.'

.

CHAPTER 22: When We Practice To Deceive

A ragged chevron of reapers advanced at the slow waltz across the hillside, followed by a scattering of gleaners, all of them weary beyond misery. It was a scene replicated at several other sites across the endless prairie of a field. The villagers of Cleave had arrived at this mild limbo in the half-darkness of dawn, when its vastness was a vaguely threatening ocean of swaying wheat. Now, with evening donning its cloak they peered bleary-eyed over a wasteland of stubble that was populated by outcrops of stooks; each one of which was protected by its own icon of straw. A hard-seeming individual with scars in his brows, ceased with his repetitive dance, rested his scythe on the ground then his aching body on the scythe. It was the unquestioned custom of ages that they were to reap the whole field, no matter the extent of it before quitting, but several acres of wheat still mocked the exhausted, miserable slaves.

"Damn his eyes," he snarled, and the curse carried to where the ancients and the nippers crouched by the hedges.

"We've done enough for the bible-bashing bastard this day. We're goin' 'ome." Well-acquainted with the custom, and with the wide spectrum of calamity that might befall them for noncompliance not a single voice was raised in objection; man, woman and child alike were beyond exhaustion, and beyond any consideration of the consequences of their actions. From all-over the rolling acres, people waded toward the homeward track as though through tar.

Little ones were lifted on to aching shoulders. Adult men took a couple of scythes each, their terrible blades safe in leather sheaths, while the women carried the babies and the youths pushed and pulled carts piled high with the reed baskets, the beer jugs, and the old timers. Their day was not yet over for they were a two-mile purgatory from rest. Before they had dragged themselves a fraction of that endless journey, the slight lift in their spirits engendered by the end of day had evaporated, and the bit of banter that always occurred at home time was exhausted. The youngsters were first to come in sight of home. One by one they gathered in a silent litter; but went no further, they who always ran the last bit. Many began to cry while the seriously concerned adults wondered vaguely what the matter could be. The 'matter' was, that the village of Cleve no longer existed. Their homes were now a scattering of stone, wood and straw. Where the hamlet of Cleve had stood that morning there was now an ugly scree of what was once cottage walls, a scattering of thatch, and smouldering fires. Not one stone stood on top of another. Even the henhouses, pigsties and fences had been wrecked; the kitchen-orchards ripped out of the ground. Thatch was burning everywhere. Worst of all the vegetable gardens had been trampled so that such remains as might be edible were mixed with soil.

"Look!" someone pointed into the far distance of the valley floor where warlike machines of destruction, drawn by unnaturally huge horses were moving in the direction of Tollpuddle on the Hill.

"Mayhap them poor devils will be next," a young man cried sorrowfully. For as long as their nemesis remained visible, the people of Cleve stood among the ruins of their poor abodes watching those base creatures who for the reward of a shilling or two were prepared to do such as this to their fellow man.

"This is *your* fault, you mouthy shits," Solomon Daybreak, an ancient blessed with one protruding tooth waved a stringy old arm as though to capture the gang of youths who were responsible for this calamity.

"You lot wot give lip to that bloody bigwig thonder, di'nt ya. Oh aye, ten agin one, so ye thought yersels so 'ard. Christ awmighty; in my day I woulda thrashed all on ye with one 'and. Well, now zee wot." Daybreak's harangue was truncated by a piercing shriek which saw misery and anger metamorphose into frantic concern which flowed in a torrent towards the cause. Daybreak hobbled in the rear of his fleeing audience; catching them only when they stopped. Shoving his way ruthlessly through to the front of the crowd to discover if there was a bone needing to be set, he discovered a sight which made him glad that he had already overstayed his welcome in this world.

Blind from birth, the Fairweather girls, twins they were, in their old age now, who would spend their days around the village turning over dirt for vegetable plots and the like, or earning a crust by peeling potatoes, apples, carrots, and sometimes doing a bit of weaving for which people would give them an apple, though the outcome be worse than useless, had been nailed to trees. They and the old people, too far advanced with the ague to go to the fields, they had all of them been crucified. Susannah Wedgewood did not require to set eyes on the atrocity to know what she must do, the horrified sobbing of those who discovered it was enough. Momentarily reinvigorated by her neighbours' need of her she turned for the undergrowth and dragged herself away to gather the necessary herbs, bark, and moss which give ease to pain and cleaned wounds against infection. Though her search required a considerable time in the failing light, some of the crucified had yet to be freed when she returned for the men could not at first find their few tools which had been scattered or stolen. Aware that Susannah was a healer of unprecedented ability, other women, disregarding the beauty's internal exile as a witch, flocked to her aid, quickly getting water on to boil, and pounding the bunches of roots and leaves which she had gathered in order to release their healing juices. With such willing help, the girl was in time to apply pain-killing poultices to the hands of the last to be freed of the great thick nails, which were so deeply driven that it required a long crowbar to wrench the hateful things out of the cambium.

Though she worked conscientiously till long into the night, with a heart that bled for the poor, poor innocents, Susannah was distracted and torn. She knew without a shadow of doubt that it was 'He' who was responsible for this barbarism, this transgression against all that is acceptable in humanity 'He who rode a black charger and whose very touch would set her on fire.'

With her keen instinct for such things, Susannah had known from the day on which she had met him that the aristocratic whoremaster who had controlled his rage so ruthlessly, and lied about the name of his horse, would take a terrible revenge on the people of this village. He was not the sort to let himself be mocked. This, she feared, was merely the first insult; gob of spit; tug of hair, gouge of eye. To knock over a few piles of roughly cut stone overlaid with straw was not a revenge, nor was it a hardship; to these capable people, it was merely an inconvenience; an annoyance. It would be the work of mere months for these country folk to rebuild, better than ever.

That terrible yet irresistible creature had something in store for those fools who had forgotten their place; and because he was a sadist, he would not differentiate between one villager and another, he would slaughter everyone. Everyone except herself.

Susannah knew with certainty that she was safe from him. She was safe because she was a delight to behold. No man she had ever met could take his eyes from her face and her figure, or was immune to her charms, and he was no exception. The arrogant whoremaster, 'she had smelt it on him, witnessed it in his manner, heard it in his voice, and suffered it in his treatment of her. He was probably planning at this moment to add her to his kennel of sluts, but he would find himself thwarted in that. Woman she was, peasant she was, slut she was not.

"Ye gods and little fishes, but she's beautiful." Three fields of daffodil-yellow rape seed distant from the drama being played out amid the devastation of the village of Cleve, Hastings lowered his telescope fondling his crotch affectionately, as he did so. Turning around he watched as Michael Astor approached and dismounted.

"Leave it alone Hastings, you'll go blind," Astor snatched the telescope from his friend's hands.

"They've left a calling card of sorts Mikey. Have a butcher's down by the spring." Hastings pushed the end of the telescope to his master's right side with the ease of familiarity.

"Jesus, bleeding Christ!" trumpeted Astor. "What the hell have they done to the poor bastards?"

"Looks to me like they crucified one or two of the walking wounded."

"Bugger me nightly Hasty," Astor was mildly amused,

"that's a bit imaginative, wouldn't you say?" Dismissive of the crucifixions he searched assiduously until he located the sole individual that he had come here to see. The Wild Rose.

"There she is," he exclaimed. "Have you seen her, Hasty?"

"Seen her!" I've shagged her six times just standin here.''

"Philistine! She is the most incredible… Look at her." Michael thrust the instrument back into his servant's hands.

"I'll stuff her till she bursts into flame.'"

"The nation expects it of you, my son."

Once-again all business, Michael Astor turned to his man and retrieved the instrument.

"Get her tonight."

Hastings tapped the dent in his forehead with his stick.

"It's all arranged Mikey."

"And keep her at The Granary, then in a few weeks, when she's been 'civilised,' shall we say, I can ride up on a white horse and rescue her. By the time the last of her mutilated patients fell into some sort of troubled, whimpering sleep, and in several deeply concerning cases, lost consciousness, Susannah had been on her feet for twenty-two hours and was tired beyond torture. Her neighbours had gone off separately to find their rest on the hard-packed dirt that had been the floor of their own homes, even though there was no home there; some of them crying pitifully. Looking around at their shadowy forms for what she knew intuitively would be the last time, she struggled to accommodate the knowledge that not one of them would be spared.

Plucking the withered flower from her hair and throwing it carelessly into the tiny belly fire which she nurtured between her crossed legs, she took from beneath her skirt a small doll-like figure, fashioned from a bit of a wooden spoon, The toy was distinctly male and dyed in the colours worn by Michael Astor on the occasion that he had lifted her from the ground and violated her private places as though she were a slut. Susannah held the tiny berries that were the figure's testicles between her thumb nails and squeezed until the soft green centres of the organisms oozed out. With great care she fed the oily stuff to the fire as she whispered an ancient incantation

Having no relatives or acknowledged friends, she would not be sorry to leave this place, after all, one was much like another. She replaced the mangled doll in its hiding place and as certain that his people would come for her as she was that the sun would rise in the morning, she went to stand beyond the pale perimeter of the desolation.

Despite her intuition, she was shocked, scared beyond toleration and about to scream for help when she heard her expected abductors approaching. Turning as swiftly and gracefully as a startled doe she saw two shapes treading softly towards her through the trampled grass, their fingers to their lips. She did not scream, she stepped towards them, peering keenly into their dim faces in order to determine their intentions. Their master's wishes were written clearly in their expressions, in every movement, and in their measured approach, so that she knew herself to be safe. Without so much as a word the immaculate, sweet-smelling men led her respectfully and considerately away with whispered compliments.

As the bright mist was shredded by the gusting wind; three schooners drawn by massive cobs sailed slowly through the unfenced meads of the valley floor, watched with interest by the people of the dead village of Cleave who breakfasted on cold-comfort or whatever scraps they could find to eat. The wagons circled and came to a halt. A fire was lit, proclaiming to the Cleavers that unlike themselves, the teamsters had something to cook. Hunger filled the villagers' existence. Those with a morsel of stale bread were eyed jealously and even angrily. Arguments were common; so that friendships and even family loyalties were tested sorely. Young men went off quietly to chase the pigs now running freely or to steal and butcher a sheep. Conversations were numberless and hopeless; for no one had any answers to the present predicament. The only real grist in the mill was that the Fairweather sisters had died in the night, as had old Henry Horton. The torture that had been inflicted upon them had been too much for their worn-out old frames. Predictably, said some, the witch; the beautiful Susannah Wedgwood, had flown the coop.

"I telt yees she were a witch, an' she'd as like to cut an' run when things got eavy," pronounced Daybreak, who was just not himself without a cup of mead in the morning.

"And them nippers hain't come back yet neither."

"What nippers would that be then, Sol?" he was asked.

"Why, them as gernt below to git news of the world at large from them teamers, a sittin' down there in the meads," bawled Daybreak, revelling in the possession of knowledge which others lacked.

"What are we goin' to do then, Sol?" mocked David Jones,

"Fall on our swords or what?"

"Does you got a sword then, David Jones?" snarled Daybreak nastily,

"that un in your breeches be too blunt to be effrycashu… to work, so I'm telt."

This observation cut far too close to the bone for David Jones, who had been married for three years come Christmas, with no sign of any little Joneses at all. David Jones jumped to his feet and walked quickly away, while the rest of the group smiled with varying degrees of sympathy at his receding back.

"Give us a shout if you need any help, Jonesy," bawled Fred Hotspur, who disliked Jones thoroughly.

"What will *you* do, Sol? Will you stack up youm old bits of stones agen?" asked Hotspur, "and fling a bit o' thatch on? Them might come back an' knock us down all over agen."

"O' course they bloody will. Like I told you young buggers, it ain't the bible-basher as did this to usun. That barefaced bastard Montague would o' did it while us was a sleepin' inside. No; it were that bloody snott-nosed dandy as is shaggin' his young Ruth. He's got bugger-all to do all day but think up ways to crucify such as usun."

"So we's buggered all ways round. Montague will drive us off hisself if it comes out that usun mouthed off at the gentry." Norman Oxford summed up their predicament with his usual economy of words.

There was silence for a while because everyone knew that Daybreak was correct. They had 'shit in their own nest,' as he had so succinctly summed things up.

"Here's the nippers back from… Hello, they's got a body with 'em."

The group of young men who had brought down this plague of torture and death, homelessness and hunger, on their own families, went hurriedly to discover what was in the wind; keen to hear any news of the outside world for strangers were a six-month novelty in these parts.

"Good day, neighbours." The whip hand was a round-faced, pleasant looking soul, who was particularly well-nourished if his chins and his enormous girth were anything to go by, with a bit of a dent in his wide forehead.

"Usun down below coon't credit wot the nippers telt us, but now I sees it with me own heyes. How did such a thing come to pass?" the carter asked generally, turning on his heels to survey the devastation anew; his thumbs thrust into the pockets of his waistcoat, which was a frantic shade of purple. Solomon Daybreak sucked in sufficient breath to allow the telling of the whole story in one gasp.

"These stoopid arseholes," he began.

"No man knows the truth of it, friend," Norman Oxford said loudly, more in the direction of Daybreak, than the teamster.

"We hear tell that England is full up to the back teeth of such injustice at this time."

"There speaks a wise man," declared the stranger, indicating Oxford with a flick of the long-stemmed clay pipe which he was enjoying.

"Why, we; that's my men and me, myself personal like, are at this same, exact and present moment of time on our way to Bath and beyond, and further, to comfort those who have been displaced, put out and victed, in the same, sim'lar and exact natur' as youm poor selves. They houses destroyed afore they very heyes and they haminals driven hoff away and stole. A Henglishman's 'ouse be 'is castle lessun the landlord, curse him, don't have to carst his eye upon em an' spoil his day by seein' 'em when 'e looks out from 'is mansion, and p'raps spies grandma takin' a shit in the bushes."

"What comfort is this that ye speak of Mister…?" asked several very interested parties.

"Franks, Ernest Franks be the name. Why souls, the jest be on the cruel tyrants; cos they fortunate fieldhands, wimble makers, thatchers ploughmen, reapers an shearers will soon be spirited away to Ta Haiti on the good ship *Porpoise*, as luxury a vessel as ever sailed the sea. Free of charge. To a life of ease and warmfulness all year long. Fruit a growin' on every tree, and a ocean so full of fish that they jump out at a man, into 'is net."

"Free of charge?" Solomon Daybreak mocked.

"Oi aint as green as Oi be cabbage-lookin,' Ernie Franks."

"I be most pleased to hear it, friend," said Franks, with such deep sincerity in both voice and expression that nobody laughed.

"Howm'soever the govmint of Ta Haiti is not payin' me to stand here walkin' about, talkin', coversin' and such, they be a wantin' honest folk to build up the nation on they free farms, what they is givin' for nothin', so as food will be growd for the towns. That's what Ernest Franks be about. I'll bid you good day, neighbours, and better fortune." Ernest Franks turned and was gone for all money.

"Free farms? You woon't know truth if bugger crep up behind an' bit your fat arse, Franks." Earnest Franks seemed suddenly turned to stone, and even from a distance, when seen from the rear, the enormous individual seemed suddenly ferocious as his good humour fled from him. He turned, and mounting the slope again, came to stand with his great girth shoving up against the man whom he rightly guessed was the source of the insult, and whom he outweighed by a bullock or two if a pound. A hard looking character with scars in his brows.

"Why friend," he growled, looking down straight into the eyes of the man whom he dwarfed, and sounding anything but friendly,

"I may ave my faults, as all men do, but waitin' for me below," he indicated his camp with a quarter rotation of his planet-like dome,

"is three Gainsborough-built schooners, a score of cobs and clydesdales, and three paid men. All mine. They is gold in my purse from the govmint of Ta Haiti for bringin' them misfortunates from up Bath way, an' I ain't brung 'em yet. I ain't the man oos fambly sleeps in the rain an eats grass." As this forthright approach elicited no response other than a malicious smirk from the unimpressed knuckler; Franks went on.

"Should it be as you wish to take this matter personal like; I shall be residin and restin below for a hour or twain, while us breaks our fast and be kindly to the 'osses. Me own preference be for bare knuckles, but you will find me most hobliging if a clog *dance

ing392

be more your thing."

Earnest Franks turned and stomped quickly away downhill, the steepness of the slope causing him to dig in his heels. He paused for a while, just a little way off, to re-light his pipe of the finest Virginia; the fragrance of which wafted over his tortured listeners who could not dream of such luxury.

"If you was to tookun us in their stead, it would save you a long march and pay just the same," observed Oxford loudly.

"Why, bless him. How often do I hear that call? 'Tis tempting friend, but I could not disappoint them poor souls wot await our comin' wiv bated breath." Franks walked on.

"You'd be home drinking ale in next to no time, and no one any the wiser," said Oxford glibly. Ernest Franks removed his pipe from his mouth and studied it intently for several minutes, while his audience studied him with equal ferocity.

*Clog dance. Protagonists fight naked; tethered one to the other by a cloth gripped in the teeth. The only weapons are wooden clogs with brass talons for breaking bones and ripping flesh respectively.

"Alas. It cannot be," he called at last.

"them poor folk up by Bath and beyond. Hunnered-acre plots of choice soil be awaiting of them; how can I…?" The new Messiah was shouted down by the protracted arguments and increasing volume of the men, and the weeping of the women and children.

"Very well. Very well," the waistcoat succumbed at last, his huge hands held aloft, as he begged for the understanding and patience of his new flock.

"Brung such bits and pieces as you 'ave down to the wagons and we shall spake to my men, cos it be they as is takin' the riks, hadditional to, as well as meself personal like." A susurration of optimism raced through the ranks of his supplicants for in their view, this new messiah had, with that bland statement, acquiesced to their wishes. The thing was cut and dried. They were leaving this place and this life of penurious drudgery, for a warm land where farms of one hundred acres awaited them. Free of charge. It was too good to be true. With muted celebration, irrepressible excitement, and many a fleeting smile, they snatched up what few objects they considered worth carrying and trooped down to the valley floor in the footsteps of the messiah, where within no time at all, they had persuaded the kind and considerate teamsters of the rightness of their cause.

How generous was the government of Ta Haiti. No sooner had the helpful men handed the women into the enormously high wagons, and then lifted the little ones into the waiting arms of their mothers than there was a distribution of water, bread, cheese and apples. What a novel experience this was for everyone, to sit in relaxation and be driven through countryside which, five miles from home, few had ever set eyes on previously. On the second day, as their euphoria lessened, and was replaced by restful monotony, their free food was eaten in the salt-air of the distant ocean so that the finality of what they were about to do, settled on them like a mantle. Some gave a thought to Solomon Daybreak, who had chosen to remain behind to bury the dead.

''And dig ole for meself,'' as he had remarked, while every man present, married or single, young or old, longed to look again upon the incomparable, unattainable, Susannah Wedgewood, to hear her voice and imagine holding her perfection in his arms. At this all-too-safe distance, the languid beauty seemed less like a witch than ever.

Their ship was magnificent. As their wagons negotiated the last corner on to the quay, with the sea air in their lungs, the gulls crying above them, the strangeness of it all in their eyes, and hope in their hearts, they were enchanted. 'Porpoise' was the biggest, most perfect, beautiful, single structure, the people of Cleve had ever seen. It was as high as three cottages stacked one on top of another, with masts that were twice as tall as any tree that ever grew, served by spider's webs of ropes so numerous that a body could barely see through them, and there were sailors leaping about up there in the branches as confidently as if they stood on Mother Earth.

Longer than the church of the Apostles at Stanyon, the glorious vessel glistened in a new coat of black paint with a single white stripe along her side. She had great sticks poking out front and back, the one at the back having a giant flag of red, blue and white shapes hanging there like at a fair at some big town. What larks. Incredibly, guarding the ship, at the water's edge, an army of soldiers in uniforms of red and black stood in a long row. As the three crowded wagons of refugees, and the menfolk trudging alongside all brim-full of every hopeful human emotion, drew to a halt the marines slammed to attention and became as stiff as frozen rhubarb in what was the most unbelievable, unexpected and gloriously uplifting salute. With that small ceremonial, the very last vestiges of the hopeful migrants' concern fell away behind them. Truly the government of Ta Haiti were treating them like kings and queens. The rush to get aboard almost descended into friction, as fear of being left behind played unsettlingly on the minds of the migrants, but happily, due to the assurances shouted out by the sailors, everyone calmed down and eventually got on to the deck without descent into actual unpleasantness. The unpleasantness began at the very moment when the soldiers, now with fixed bayonets doubled aboard turning right and left alternately at the top of the gangplank to deploy again in a long line before charging across the deck roaring their battle cries and driving the villagers back against the seaward bulwarks. From either end of the ship, wild, terrifying seamen armed with knotted ropes, raced out across the deck and laid into the men of Cleve with bestial ferocity, thrashing them into bloody submission on the deck as others fixed shackles on the ankles of the agonised and bleeding victims.

"Stand them up, sergeant." Michael Astor bawled the order over the screaming of the women and shrieking of the terrified children.

"I won't have these dogs relax in my presence." At the sound of the unmistakeably aristocratic accents, the villagers still capable of doing so turned and looked towards the back of the boat where there was a higher place with a fence. Surrounded by a coterie of uniforms and grandeur of a dozen sorts, the speaker stood a head taller than the biggest of his admirers. A handsome, young man in colourful, military-style attire. Barely a dozen of the hundreds of terrified villagers recognised the youth. He was the big wig that they had mocked in that two acres of turnips where he had left his hoss. Now they were for it. They were 'all' for it.

"Remember me?" It was a rhetorical question. Michael Astor couldn't care a tinker's toss whether this scum remembered him or not. They were all off to Haiti for a brief stay. Probably twelve months tops. 'All but 'one,' actually. The niggers lasted only a year in that hell on earth, so these dungeaters would die like flies, and serve them right.'

"For the benefit of the uninitiated," Astor declared happily, shouting above the screaming of the children, the crying of the women and the shrieks and groans of the sorely hurt,

"A baker's dozen or so of your friends and neighbours have brought this upon you. You'll know them. Your husbands, brothers, sons perhaps. Have a word do. They took it upon themselves to mock the very… Ah, here we have one of them now." There had been a small movement in the miserable, terrified and confused crowd, and a short, nasty-looking devil pushed to the front where a bayonet poked him in the chest, drawing blood and stopping him on a farthing.

"Your ringleader," declared the toff loudly, as though introducing a circus act, greatly to the amusement of his friends, and the dismay of the bovine masses. He pulled a ridiculous face, pointing with his scabbard at the thug, then cupped one ear with his palm.

"Speak up," he begged in a falsetto which pleased his hangers-on no end. The ringleader spoke,   .

"It were usun. They aint no need to…"

"Shut it you dog!" Astor was apoplectic and screeching.

"Smash him. Smash him."

The words were barely out of Astor's mouth, but the soldier had reversed his weapon and struck the little tough from ear to chin with bone-shattering force. Sailors leapt in and were thrashing the injured man with monkey-fists before he hit the deck, aiming particularly for his face and his crotch.

"Stand him up. Stand him up." Astor was once again the precocious child.

"You've no need to concern yourself about your little playmates," he assured the screeching, broken thing,

''because *you* will be dead. Do you know what we're going to do to you? No, of course you don't." Michael turned to his friends.

"Silly me," he lisped, and the delighted audience fell about laughing.

"We're going to keel-haul you."

The crawling victim was unaware of anything but pain. Agonised, the mangled, broken man cupped his smashed testicles in his hands to no avail. His nose had been destroyed and he had lost an eye. He keened as though crushed by a large gin.

"Let me explain… Shut those brats up before I chuck them over the side." Children, utterly distraught at what they had seen happen to their fathers and older brothers, continued to scream in terror, causing their desperate mothers to smother their inconsolable darlings in their skirts, folding them in their arms and 'cooing' to them to save them from that inhuman threat, which they knew for certain had not been issued lightly.

"Once you're out at sea," Astor resumed,

"it's all that churning through the waves, don'tcha know, it'll crumple your bones to shards. We'll tie ropes to various bits of you, and throw you over the side, then pull you underneath from port to starboard, or vice versa. Your choice." This throw-away line got a round of appreciative applause, in addition to hysterical, falling-down laughter.

"As you'll be naked as… Anyway, they assure me that the barnacles down there will rip every bit of flesh, penis, testicles, face from your rickety bones. Broken or not." Astor was enjoying himself immensely as his revenge began to unfold in this wonderfully theatrical way. Having friends in attendance, enjoying the show, added cream to this already delicious cake. Even he had not foreseen such a wickedly pleasurable outcome. He paused to rest in his oratory and accept a glass of champagne from Delavier who whispered helpfully in his master's ear.

"Earnest Franks and company are waiting in the wings, should you wish to present those gentlemen to your audience, sir,"

"Of course!" exclaimed the delighted thespian and slugging back his refreshment he called Mister Franks and his collaborators to the front of the 'stage.' Hastings and his henchmen could not wait to display themselves to the poor fools who bad begged them; 'actually begged them,' to be taken to Haiti, a sink of depravity, where sadists, sexual perverts and drug addicted, alcoholic madmen had free reign over what they did to the shivering slaves in their murderous charge. The group of assassins who had perpetrated the killing ruse on the village of Cleve had been concealing themselves for this very moment, and they came gleefully to Michael's side where they pretended that they were Roman Senators at the games, accepting the plaudits of the masses. Their master's joy was limitless; capering in the manner of an excited child, he dropped suede purses heavy with silver coins into the hands of three out of the four men responsible for the wickedly amusing deception which had achieved such success. Into Hastings' waistcoat pocket he thrust a gold timepiece, a superb example of the watchmaker's art, which he had selected personally for this rising star in his service. The instrument was a 'Montre a Secousses' by

Perrelet, which by some unimaginable genius remained perpetually wound up. Into the steadfast fellow's hands, he pressed a purse of purple silk; the symbolism being utterly irresistible. On an impulse, he was about to buzz Hastings on both cheeks in the French fashion, but saved himself just in time, as he noticed the sudden naked revulsion in his shipmate's face, and the slight flinch with which the attempt was met.

"Well done, well done. Well done, gentlemen," he cackled, disguising his intention, as the lowered heads of the Cleavers declared their misery and despair, not only at this irrefutable proof of their own bottomless gullibility, but also at their hateful defencelessness. As Lord Michael Astor's aristocratic entourage of bewigged, rouged and perfumed wastrels rejoiced their way ashore in anticipation of whatever further wonderful amusements their lovely Mikey had in store for them that day, they had already forgotten the hundreds of smelly untouchables about to suffer a drawn-out horrific death simply because one of their number had the utter gall to insult a member of England's 'Murderous,' class.

CHAPTER 23: Cometh The Hour

The Representative of the thirteen United States of America to the government of King Louis 16th of France, and an illiterate violent tramp, would by any measure seem strange bedfellows, but during the maiden voyage of the *Liberty* from the south coast of England to Nantes in France, a relationship developed between Benjamin Franklin and Liam Hooligan that was a source of immense satisfaction to both men. Franklin, who had been injuriously delayed in his return journey to Europe, had nothing to do all day but stand in the bows and attempt to hasten his arrival in France by force of will, while Hooligan was an empty and very noisy vessel, craving to be filled with the science, knowledge, skill and magic which now surrounded him. Franklin was a noted polymath to whom teaching, experimentation, invention and observation were the vital ingredients of life, while Hooligan was the ideal student; a man desperate for knowledge, having no preconceived notions and less conceit. On that very first day out of England, the diplomat came across the Irishman, bent over the steersman's compass, glowering at the superb instrument with obviously evil intent. It seemed quite apparent to the mature student of men, that the giant could not fathom the relationships which married the ship's officers' occasional references to the baffling lump of brass and glass with their instructions to the helmsman. Nor was he inclined to display his ignorance by asking the needful questions. Franklin's kind heart almost broke for the perennially generous; frighteningly volatile and temporarily baffled man.

"It's confusing when you're new to it, is it not, sir?" he murmured sincerely, and saw the relief spread across Hooligan's awful face as the Irishman realized that help was at hand.

"Sure, Oi don't have a clue. Lliam's the name. Lliam Hooligan." The answer was accompanied by a smile so gruesome that it scared Franklin, who well remembered being lifted bodily out of his seat by just one of this man's Herculean arms. The badly used pirate was no oil painting. If only he would wear a patch over the mutilated eye socket, it would be easier to look him straight in the… eye.

"In that case, perhaps I can be of some help."

The Irishman almost melted with gratitude.

"What's the fucker do?" he grunted, indicating the offending instrument. That innocent question opened the door of the lecture hall and Franklin, genius that he was, tripped happily inside. The pupil was delighted to discover what a simple instrument the compass was, and rightly concluded that when far out at sea, with water all around, the thing was useless, other than to tell you what you already knew, which is to say; the direction in which you were sailing. It was time for Franklin to bring compass, chart, sextant and chronometer together in one place. Such were the rewards which the new friends gained from their association that for the next several days they prowled the length and breadth of the vessel together, talking and gesturing, pointing and waving in the most animated fashion. They took their meals together and continued to work as they consumed their cold viands, trotting quickly here and there, peering in to this and under that, all in order to throw a light on 'the principle of moments, the Plimsoll line, acceleration due to gravity, latitude and the vexed question of longitude, sailing under various wind conditions, sailing into the wind, the mechanism by which the little wheel turned the huge rudder which in turn steered the gigantic ship, bifocals, telescopes, leverage and much more.' Franklin's bifocals were the topic of the second, truly successful lesson. In response to the blunt inquiry,

"What do they do?" the rotund burger removed his spectacles and standing on tip toe, reached up and placed them on his student's face.

"Look at the chart," he advised.

"Put me in a dress! That's magic, so it is." The student was delighted, not only by the effectiveness of the lenses, but for a second time that day, the sheer joy of the learning process.

"How does it work?" he demanded. Franklin was ready with the only answer which would suffice for this student.

"They bend light, in the same way that water does. When you spear a salmon, you aim closer than the fish that you are after, do you not?"

"So you do," breathed Hooligan, in a beautiful eureka moment of intuitive understanding. Franklin gently removed the spectacles from Hooligan's awed face and held them directly between the lamp and the chart which the pair were using. Each of the double lenses showed one very bright light pattern, and one that was less so.

"This is how a telescope works," said the student forcefully, as though challenging Franklin to deny it.

"Dey bend the loight an' make a little ting big."

"Absolutely, Mister Hooligan," smiled Franklin. "Absolutely."

"You tink me stupid, I suppose," said the student, his mood altering radically and sadly. Franklin replaced his spectacles on his nose, and reaching out, he held his pupil by both arms.

"I think nothing of the sort, friend Hooligan," he said.

"You are an excellent student with a quick mind and had you the advantage of education in your youth and I not, our positions could well be reversed."

Lliam Hooligan did not reply. He took one of Franklin's hands and held it for a moment in his own.

"Oim sorry for bein' a bit of a prick to ye before," he said.

"Oi had ye all wrong."

As Liberty approached St Nazaire and the narrows which would bring them to Nantes,

Franklin thought it prudent to have a word with his pupil about France and the French. He was, after all, on a mission of vital importance to his nation in the business of freeing themselves from the English yoke. It would not do for anyone aboard the *Liberty*, no matter how distant from himself that person may be, to come to the attention of the French authorities for anything other than a completely innocent reason. He had already decided to discuss with Captain Teach the matter of the crews' behaviour during shore leave.

"The French,'' he informed his pupil, "are a refined people, a hardworking law-abiding people who appreciate earnest conversation, good food and excellent wine enjoyed in convivial company and do not as a rule allow themselves to drink to excess." He was warming to his theme when the Irishman laid a hand as big and as heavy as a Clydesdale's hoof on his shoulder and said,

"Don't you worry your wee head about it, Benjamin son; Oi'll be so pissed they'll get no sense out of me atall, atall." It was all over so quickly. The partnership dissolved. The university abandoned. *Liberty* was no sooner tied up at the dock in Nantes, than a carriage had been procured and Franklin was whisked away to fight the good fight farewelled by a crew some of whom had seen through his playacting and guessed that the old man would probably be undertaking tasks inseparable from their country's health. No sooner had his old teacher disappeared into the ancient, narrow and crowded streets, than Hooligan surprised his friend and Captain by handing Teach a sizeable lump of gold retrieved from the ship's massive figurehead; an obstacle to shipping which now floated somewhere off the south coast of England.

"Martin, my child," pronounced the Admiral,

"this here is fer good tucker for the men. Sure, oi never want to see any o' that scurvy ting on me boats. Disgustin' it is. No need fer it." He then handed the captain a second lump of the gold leaf which had been melted down in the recovery process then bashed crudely together to form one homogenous whole several times larger than the first.

"What could we get here dat we could sell in Scotland?" he asked. "Where *is* Scotland, by the way?"

Despite well organised and protracted searches of the town of Nantes, as the time came to set sail for and Perth, Macbeth's home port; Hooligan was nowhere to be found. Adding delay to dismay, the man contrived to elude detection until the afternoon of the following day, when a French-speaking crewman had a chance meeting with the driver of a pony and trap. It seemed that the poor fellow had been refused payment by a monstrous Russian having carryied the beast all over the city. The cyclops had exhibited no understanding whatsoever of where it was that he wanted to go and being unable to speak a word of French had resorted, after protracted and unsuccessful searches to shouting at the mystified and very fearful driver.

Hooligan was lying on his back in a four-poster bed, snoring fit to wake the neighbors, in a brothel located within extensive grounds in one of the city's fanciest suburbs. Teach and his rowdy gang had barged into his room in the understandable hope of finding the big fellow 'up to his balls in some tasty slut,' and were not in the least disappointed. Though the exhausted Irishman was dead to the world, due undoubtedly to his heroic exertions and several vats of the local vino, he was still fully tumescent; a fact which could be ascertained from as far-afield as the door. A harlot wearing next to nothing was astride the Admiral taking full advantage of the great one's erection by pleasuring herself with astounding energy. Being gentlemen to a man, the sailors crowded into the room and watched in noisy admiration, cheering the girl on to even greater efforts as she turned to them half smiling, half swooning in her mounting ecstasy, and when the voluble lady finally shrieked her delirium for the neighborhood to hear, gave her a generous round of applause.

The Admiral had clearly endeared himself to every girl in the establishment with his unbelievable vigor and tremendous girth, and they giggled joyfully and waxed lyrical about the 'eaven,' to which he had transported every one of them; often. As the seamen dragged their friend's unresponsive bulk none too gently down the thickly carpeted stairways, and manhandled him into a waiting cart, it was not supposed that the enchanted girls were referring to Hooligan's torso when they jabbered longingly about the man's girth. Nor was it surprising to any member of the shore party that despite this obvious affection, the great horizontal warrior's pockets had been picked clean as a whistle. Not one sou remaining upon his person. Nor could any of the girls throw any light on the mystery.

That same day, with her stores full of fresh food and her holds reeking gloriously and temptingly of their cargo of excellent French cognac, the *Liberty* set free the squadron of small boats that had towed her into mid-channel, and with many a 'bonne chance,' and 'bon voyage,' set sail for Scotland and the Firth of Tay, home of Macbeth's ultimate employer the laird Monteith. Admiral Hooligan was not privy to any of this and would not see the ocean for another thirty hours.

 Autumn assaulted the *Liberty* with cold winds, sleet and intermittent fog, as though seeking retribution for the long hot summer, so that the sailors from Boston suffered terribly; their English captors having robbed them of their coats in addition to everything else.

Admiral Hooligan once again among the ranks of the living took Captain Teach energetically to task on this issue blaming the mystified then furious seaman for this complete lack of consideration of the men. More than a little indignant about such an unsound verdict Teach thanked Hooligan unstintingly for his perspicacity, and also for joining the crew; albeit a day or two late, then pointed out that the thieving Brits had stolen everything on the *Bird* that was not nailed down, a situation which was impossible to rectify while standing on station offshore as he was obliged to do, though weak from hunger, in order to guard Fleet Hooligan. "And while you're about it; pull in your stupid ignorant Irish head."

Awakened to the awful truth that he had been horribly unjust, and filthily bloody-minded due solely to his shattering case of the gueule de bois but lacking the grace and the maturity to apologize which would have been the manly thing to do Hooligan retreated in fury and moped around the ship like the overgrown child that he was until the incident was forgotten by both men.

That night, he requested that Captain Teach make for Cherbourg, a request which the touchy American obviously felt was reasonable because the following day, completely recovered from his attempt to drink Nantes dry, Hooligan found himself in the best of form being rowed ashore in that historic port. Charmed to bits by the ancient town he strode in determined fashion through the maze of narrow alleys, crowded warehouses and taverns, with his handful of men trotting to keep up, and soon discovered that which he had come ashore to find; a vast emporium stuffed to the gunnels with everything for the seaman and ships. The place was called a 'chandelier,' and Hooligan, positively transported by his brilliant discovery, could not wait to get back on board and tell Teach all about it.

By dint of heated and voluble negotiations, not to say stand-over tactics, and the wherewithal to buy in bulk, he was able to procure one hundred pea-jackets at just a smidgeon over half price, double-breasted against the wind, with two layers of waterproofing in the shoulders, and horn toggles for easy use once a man's fingers had become icicles. The bails of garments were so voluminous that they filled the longboat to the point where there was insufficient room for the whole gang, so Hooligan and two others volunteered to wait behind and be picked up later; a ruse which enabled the whoremaster to find another brothel; an invention which he considered to be first class.

To the astonishment and deep pleasure of the crew, when the Irishman eventually climbed back on board, he personally gifted a warm blue coat to every man. He had just spent the last of Macbeth's silver, in the best way possible and couldn't wait to arrive in Perth and give a coat to each of the freezing men up there too.

The Straits of Dover were as busy as any brothel. Hooligan declaring that you could walk from one side to the other without getting your feet wet; an observation which he thought novel; his own brilliance pleasing him mightily. There were ships of twenty nations ploughing north and south, while daring types raced west to east between Dover and Calais.

Playing amongst this traffic was a shoal of tiny fishing boats whose happy crews were taking their lives in their hands daily. As he handed Martin Teach his blue jacket personally, the shipowner surprised his captain by announcing,

"London, sunshoine. Set a course for London, if you please." Teach guffawed in Hooligan's face; fit to burst at the outrageous nerve of the lunatic.

"You crazy son of a," he gargled, "half of my crew, and the parents of the other half, were transported from that muck hole for stealing a loaf, or some other crime just as meritorious, would you believe. Do you want to get us all hung?" And with the subject dismissed, took to admiring himself in his new jacket. The captain's disclosure clearly meant nothing at all to Admiral Hooligan who displayed his disappointment shamelessly and volubly. Waiting patiently for the Irish donkey to run out of breath, then articulating each word clearly Teach repeated his sermon in stentorian tones.

"Once transported, you may not come back to England on pain of death." Incredibly, the bemusement and stubborn, mule-headed, single-mindedness remained; forcing Teach to master his temper with grim determination as he explained for the tenth time, in words of few syllables, that every man aboard, would be hung by the neck, until dead, if the Brits should discover that they were returned indentured servants. He was utterly dumbfounded when Hooligan, unmoved, persisted. The now irate captain surrendered all restraint unashamed in the face of insanity and informed the Admiral that, he could sail his own fornicating ship into the Houses of Parliament should he wish, but he would do so on his fornicating own, for no American would be aboard. Furthermore, in order to make port in London, he, Hooligan,' would have to sail *Liberty* back from Perth single-handed, because that was where this ship was fornicating going now so that he, 'Teach,' and his fellow abolitionists could be reunited with their ship, the *Bird*.' At which time he, his men and the Bird would sail for Boston their home port which now lay in the newest country of the world, the United States of America. The good captain concluded his diatribe with the instruction that Hooligan should embark on a long journey of a sexually perverted nature.

Realising somewhat late in the day just what a touchy subject this was, Hooligan suggested that if Teach would kindly get off his high horse, and please, please, please take him to London, only *he* Hooligan should go ashore and then only for an hour or two. He would complete his business then dash back to the ship as fast as his little legs would carry him, sure, at which point they would up-anchor, set every yard of sail in their locker and bugger off to Scotland and a reunion with The Bird.

Sacrificing his critical faculties for no good reason Teach pondered this plan for a long moment, then announced emphatically that, were he fool enough to concur, the ship would remain in midstream with cannon primed, and would not tie up at the dock on any pretext whatsoever. Additionally, every man would be armed to the teeth with cutlass and musket; furthermore, if Hooligan was not back aboard within two hours exactly from disembarking, the *Liberty* would sail for Perth without him. Teach further declared that he was giving his approval only provisionally, until such times as he had put this ludicrous fornicating proposal to the men, and the view of the majority was established, his crew being unpaid volunteer abolitionists to a man. At this point, the captain marched off as full of indignation as Hooligan had ever seen him, leaving the bemused Irishman to ponder the omnipresent curse of responsibility, which was clearly getting the better of poor Teach.

'What dat boy needs,' the philosopher concluded, 'is a damn good bender, and a woman, or two. Or three.'

The stench was first noticed as Liberty negotiated the bends of the loewer Thames at the once pleasant village of Greenwich. It was disgusting, a mixture of dead rats and vomit. Many complained loudly, and the crew covered their faces with cloth and hoped that whatever it was that stank so badly, would soon be left far behind them. As the hours passed, the repulsive reek which draped the back of the throat like cold lard, intensified to the point of being nauseating, and many a sailor emptied his belly over the side.

"It's the river," someone cursed, and with the cloths tied around their faces now wetted with cognac, courtesy of the ever-generous Hooligan, the men crowded to the ship's sides to confirm the diagnosis. To their communal astonishment and revulsion, the river was more corruption than water, a living slush of brownish-yellow puss intermixed with every form of festering filth imaginable.

"Fire on the bow," came the call from the masthead, and all eyes were turned upstream where London lay under a pall of grey smoke tinged with a sulphorous yellow gas that besmirched the sky. Those men who had lived in London prior to their transportation knew better.

"Nah," they declared, "they ain't no fiyah, Landun always bladdy looks like that." The open sewer was becoming more congested with shipping in every mile closer to the capital city, and when *Liberty* passed within a stone's throw of three British warships with almost two hundred guns between them, Hooligan belatedly became sensible of the terrible risk which he had asked his crew to take. One of the many sailors aboard the sixty-gun *Battleaxe* who had paused in his work to admire the stately *Liberty* as she approached, called out,

"Wot pow't you out of ven?" and a quick-witted Irish American replied,

"Belfast. Top o' the mornin' to ya."

Close enough for conversations to erupt, the Americans who had called London home in a previous life; feeling that things were a little too close for comfort, scuttled below decks, just in case they should be recognized, and their unlawful return reported to the authorities. On that day of ill memory, the condition of the Thames grew more disgusting hourly, so that by the time *Liberty* hove-to opposite the Tower of London, she was swimming through a lake of human and animal excreta, the offal from a thousand butcher shops, fishmongers and abattoirs; and the rotting remains of dogs, cats, rats and the occasional horse, her once lovely sides now smeared with the stuff. The crew said nothing to each other or to Hooligan. They had agreed without question, to undertake this foolhardy escapade because of their deep and abiding gratitude to the big man, for saving them from the hangman, from incarceration, for the coats, the money, their food and all the rest, but every soul aboard was disgusted by a race of people who would abuse a waterway so, and allow this obscenity to flow through a city, and they regretted their decision deeply.

"Drop anchor and get that mealy-mouthed Plumly bastard up here," roared Hooligan, and putting two fingers to the corners of his mouth, whistled up a boat from among those waiting for business at the shore. As the friends parted Teach shook Hooligan's hand with the firmness associated with despair and wished the idiot a safe and speedy return from whatever insanity he was undertaking.

"You have two hours, Lliam," he concluded,

"I can't risk all of these men further."

It was typical of the loon to respond to such an ultimatum as though it had not been issued.

"What color is your flag, the Merican one? What color is it?" he asked. Martin Teach was in the act of making a familiar reply when he clearly recalled something which he had recently discovered, and with a sudden smile announced,

"Red, white and blue, Lliam. Thirteen stars and thirteen stripes." Twenty minutes later, Hooligan and Captain Plumly-Horton were being ferried ashore by a toothless octogenarian, so decrepit that it seemed he might expire at every stroke. The old chap was in such a poor state of repair that he showed no interest whatsoever in where the boat and its occupants were heading so that the admiral was obliged to grab an oar from beneath his seat and using it as a rudder steer the water-logged hulk to the doubtful safety of the excrement-larded steps. In his cloak of royal-blue and three-cornered hat of a Captain of the Royal Navy, Plumly-Horton seemed as out of place in the rotting wreck; more water than wood, as a horse in a bedroom, and the attention that he garnered from the many layabouts and street urchins was heightened to amused fascination by growing crowds when he seemed to experience the greatest difficulty in stepping on to the shore, despite which the snot stubbornly refused to use his hands.

"Looka' this, he's drunk as a lawd," his audience cackled.

By the time the captain had mounted to the vile, vegetable strewn cobbles of the street, a large crowd of mocking, jeering, ne'er-do-wells had surrounded the 'toffee-nosed git' and his captor; a gruesome one-eyed giant who unbelievably, led the bleeder by a white lanyard tied around his neck.

'Clearly,' they rejoiced, 'this big beast who showed such scant regard for the well-to-do, would soon be wearing a much more businesslike rope around his own neck.' It was a walk of mere minutes to the middle of Iron Bridge but in that short time, the animal trainer had attracted such a vast crowd of voluble, taunting spectators that traffic across London's only avenue to the south bank was brought to a riotous halt.

'What,' the people wondered, 'was the big fellow going to do with his prisoner? And would he do it before he was arrested, treated to a show-trial and hung; his various quarters displayed in irons from this very bridge?' Hooligan did not keep his rowdy audience waiting long. Arriving at the midpoint of the ugly structure, he used the lanyard to tether Plumly-Horton to the rails, tying him up like a dog, then with a salute to the ecstatic rabble and a theatrical flourish, he whipped off the captain's cloak and strode away, contemptuously shoving vicious jabbering gin-soaked jackals out of his path as he exited stage left. The crowd erupted in delight. Plumly-Horton, whose wrists were securely bound, was wearing his splendid Captain's uniform of white shirt and cream waistcoat beneath his royal blue jacket, black shoes and white stockings, but *no* trousers or long johns. Best of all, the man was crying like a baby with fury at what was being done to him. As Hooligan distanced himself hastily from the riot that he had caused he was well satisfied to pass several Bow Street Runners and shortly afterwards, a detachment of redcoats who were doubling towards the scene of the crime.

'Within an hour or so,' he figured, 'Plumly-Horton would be in custody in the bowels of the Admiralty, answering some very awkward questions; not the least of which would be his reason for being out of uniform.'

This business was no laughing matter on Lliam Hooligan's part. It was not merely a cruel jest; it was designed in the hope of significant political ramifications. In his view, Plumly-Horton was among the worst of his kind, which made him worse than popery. The mongrel was responsible for the death of Harry the cook, and a score of others on both sides, yet the barbarian didn't give a damn, because the rest of humanity was dispensable to him in his single-minded quest for personal glory. For certain, Horton could have been kept as a prisoner aboard *Liberty* forever and a day, but fitting as that fate would be, the amateur philosopher had concluded that there existed a still worse sentence which he could bring down on the insufferable swine, one that owned the further advantage of striking at the reputation of the sadistic service that the man so venerated. For Plumly-Horton to be disgraced, ridiculed, demoted and imprisoned by those whose approval he so desperately sought; to be vilified, mocked, and found repulsive by his superiors, and reduced to less than the lowest cabin boy in the service that he cherished; that was where real pain lay for the likes of the self-obsessed swine. Let his own sort imprison the man.

Not only would they sentence him to a life of incarceration for losing his ship and fifty sons of the nobility in all probability they would turn-up to applaud his departure. This was a blow against the British Admiralty in total, as well as against the odious seaman. The publicity would crucify them. The conspirator broke into his famous lumbering run as he had little time to spare and people of several occupations to speak to; hopefully before the origins of the entertainment on the bridge were traced back to his ship.

"You've got foive minutes to make a flag." Admiral Liam Shaun Hooligan happy and proud was all business as he landed on the deck of the *Liberty* where twenty men were already breaking their backs at the capstan. He tossed a huge package to one of the sailmakers as he spoke.

"Up anchor, Captain Teach, and head downstream a couple of miles, we're looking for a warehouse called Van Rijn. It's on the north bank. We're about to make a fortune on that cognac you advoised me to buy."

"Yous fellas," he hollered to the sailmakers who had their parcel open on the deck,

"the 'merican one. Get it done and get it up the pole." As the sublime vessel made her cautious way towards the open countryside, Lliam explained to his Captain that he was about to sell his cargo of cognac to Mister Van Rijn, whom he had run into ashore and he wanted Teach to take care of the negotiations, the captain being better equipped than most for such a task. The asking price was to be five times that which Lliam had paid in France.

"Watch yourself," he advised.

"If Oi'm any judge, that Van Rijn fella hangs lower than the pope's piles. As Hooligan could neither read nor write nor cipher, he felt it quite natural that Martin would want to take charge and treated these situations as fait accompli.

"One more ting, Martin," he warned in conclusion.

"They must hand you cash money every time a net of barrels comes out of the hold. We don't want to be chasin' a wagon of drink down the road to get our pay, do we now?"

"We do not, dear child," replied Teach, who was now mastering his concern for his men's safety as not one incident of recognition or the likes had occurred in the whole two hours that *Liberty* was at anchor.

"But how do you expect me to get five times what you paid for it, you idiot? That's nearly seven hundred English pounds!"

"Tink about it, dear boy," the Admiral enthused.

"It took this great big ship and all these good men, Christ-knows how long to cart dat rubbish all the way here from froggy land. Dat has to be paid for. I'm relyin' on you, an' so are dese fellas if they're to get a coin or two for their labors."

Teach knew that he was being put upon, but damn it all; what his friend said was true, a real businessman would not hesitate to set a price that was out and out extortion, so why wouldn't he? Business was war too. With his river frontage hard-stand fully occupied Van Rijn came out on a flat barge almost as wide as it was long to greet the Liberty as the tall ship dropped anchor. He wore a scarlet coat, voluminous as a girl's dress trimmed with mink, as was his shining black hat with the ostrich feathers. For the benefit of watching river men and his intended dupes aboard *Liberty,* he struck an extravagant pose with the aid of a five-foot long walking stick of glistening silver.

"Goot. Fair goot," Van Rijn declared as the two vessels collided, and throwing off his coat, he dashed aboard the ship more like a monkey than a middle-aged merchant, so keen was he to exercise perfidy in the pursuit of obscene profit. Below decks captain Teach, Van Rijn and the Dutchman's wizened little creature of a wine-taster squeezed around between row upon row of oaken barrels stacked five high, to the location of one cask in particular; the one which Lliam Hooligan had broached in order to provide the frozen crew a bit of a warmer. Pulling the plug, the seller decanted a fair measure of the stuff into a battered pewter jug which he thrust unceremoniously at the watching buyer. Somewhat irked by the complete absence of ceremony in this philistine's way of doing business, Van Rijn consoled himself with the knowledge that he was here to rob the fool, and recovering his equanimity passed the container to his servant who took to sniffing at the vessel in the manner of a dog at the entrance of a burrow into which a rabbit has run. Breathing ever-more deeply the little charlatan wafted the scent of the liquor into the cavernous nostrils of his aquiline proboscis, becoming first concerned, then deflated, disgusted, and finally insulted, as he did so. Appalled by the odoriferous evidence the dissembler brought the jug trepidatiously to his lips and at serious risk to his life, took a thimble-full of the liquid into his mouth thereby sacrificing his refined tastebuds on the altar of business. Van Rijn watched his fellow thief in complete absorption, while Teach watched Van Rijn. For the greater part of fifteen years, the captain had dealt with larcenous, unprincipled, avaricious criminals of this thief's constitution all over the world and was confident that he knew every trick in their thick volume of duplicity, but these two mating-snakes added page after page to the chapter entitled 'Insidious.' Welcoming this cheesehead aboard Liberty, Teach had searched the man's eyes in order to evaluate the fellow's character and concluded that this one would steal from the collection plate, his own mother, the blind, and the dead. Van Rijn's obsequious little wine-taster; revolted by the poisonous draught, recoiled in utter revulsion, spitting the filthy muck onto the deck in disgust, tying his face in a knot meanwhile as though he had sampled piss.

"Is not goot, yes?" asked Van Rijn, maintaining the expression of innocence, while the servant gagged as though on the point of vomiting and declared,

"That Satan brew not cognac iss. Brandy she iss not by Gaa. She vinegar iss." Van Rijn snatched the container contemptuously from his servant with every show of playing fair with the American and nosed the beast with the utmost caution as though concerned that the creature within might leap out and sink its teeth into the blue-veined gorgonzola of his nose, the pores of which were visible at fifteen feet, in poor light. Obviously disgusted by the stink of the vinegar alone, he dutifully put the jug to his mouth, made the sign of the cross, and martyred himself in the cause of fair play. Clearly the great man was prepared to go to any lengths to do the right thing by this poor, ignorant, deckhand who had been so cruelly duped and swindled by the frog criminals. Being a gentleman, the Cheese turned his back on his host most graciously before pursing his lips and hosing the foul brew as far from his person as was humanly possible; then clearing his throat vigorously and noisily of the remnants, he expectorated that also.

"It iss mortinkfied, am I," the dissembler mumbled, kissing his kerchief; his mouth obviously seared, and looking as unhappy as a man who has just soiled his pants.

"Vinegar, she iss. I can buy, but for vinegar only price."

Teach was overcome by this verdict and clearly moved to relinquish his hold on sanity; his expression becoming a map of all the ills that beset mankind. His head began to wag in desolation at Van Rijn's condemnation, and throwing his arms wide, he addressed the heavens beyond the deck above and bawled obscurely,

"Mother of God, no. He will destroy Cherbourg for this." In his stew of concern for the good folk of that town Teach took to stumbling out and back in the canyons between the wooden mountains.

"You don't know what he is like," he wailed to no one in particular.

"He will kill the frog and start a war."

Poor Teach had staggered barely ten paces in this demented state before he felt the smaller of the rats plucking at his sleeve.

"Break pleess this one," the rodent squeaked, clearly unmoved by the captain's histrionics and choosing a barrel at random.

"So! You like vinegar, do you?" breathed the captain and snatching his knife, he whipped out the bung, sploshed liquid into the jug, then rammed the cork home, seating it with the heel of his boot. Further theatrics followed that had the same sad end. The Dutchies were desolate, but poor Mister Teach had been cheated by those frog-scoffing scoundrels who had sold him cognac of such poor quality that it barely deserved the appellation 'brandy,' charging him outrageously for the vomitous filth. It was all vinegar, but how much did he want for the lot. The whole cargo? There was a market for vinegar as for anything else, after all, and a man had to buy in order to sell; was that not so? It was the American's turn to look distraught; and he complied. His handsome though injured countenance becoming a picture of abject misery as he stated a price equal to five times what Hooligan had paid. Van Rijn's bloodless jewel-encrusted hand flew to his heart as he gasped for air and seemed to become quite light-headed.' *Had all this theatre meant nothing to this philistine?'* He was bemused, aggrieved and deeply suspicious.

Right on cue, a rowdy herd of ruffians with Hooligan among them came bullocking along the deck in the fashion of their Pamplona relatives.

"What's the holdup Captain Teach?" demanded the Irishman above the animal utterances of the herd.

"No man waits for the toide." He had memorised his lines perfectly.

"Tempers fidget."

"It's vinegar admiral." wailed Teach, clearly very afraid of what this knowledge might do to the Admiral's composure.

"*What!*" Hooligan swelled before their eyes to twice his normal hugeness.

"They have you cheated. You for cognac pay. They to you they vinegar give. 'Escargot cargo' she is," Van Rijn quipped ill-advisedly. Hooligan glowered murderously at Van Rijn, much as an executioner would consider a bare neck on a block.

"That's very funny," he said, looking anything but amused.

"Vinegar, is it?" he demanded viciously, as though daring the dutchman to restate his diagnosis.

"So souary I am, but yaa vinegar she iss." The merchant was clearly beside himself with pity at the thing's catastrophic misfortune; an emotion liberally tainted with fear for his own safety.

"Oi paid a whole bucket of silver for this muck." The giant's pagan eye flicked from side to side, seeking out someone to blame for what had been his own failing, causing Van Rijn to quake in his mink-topped boots. Shooting the messenger was not by any means an unusual response to ill-tidings in these parts.

"Roight." The troglodyte's grappling iron of a hand demolished the Dutchman's shoulder, the steel fingers penetrating to the bones.

"You; are coming wit me; tae fookin Cherbuggery. You can tell that motherless fuck that he's a no-good swindlin' son of a bitch before I shoot him in the dick and blow his importium into next week. Up anchor, Captain Teach, we're off to froggy." Throwing a lascivious arm around Van Rijn and fondling the man's buttocks lovingly Hooligan announced,

"You can bunk up wit me, Van Rijn; sure I'll keep you nice an' warm, all da way dere an all da way back."

The Dutch thief, horrified by the thought of being buggered brutally, and often, by this gigantic psoglav, clung on tenaciously to his composure in the face of this sickening threat, but the cracks, so to speak, were there for everyone to see. His piles were a bunch of grapes which bled profusely on every occasion that he visited the outhouse and caused him more grief than red ink on a balance sheet. He would not survive such a trial.

"Much haste, the broth she spoilink iss," he croaked, grasping at a straw while mixing his metaphors wonderfully well in his misery, disgust, and revulsion. Making a great show of choosing yet another barrel as though guided by some instinctive brilliance he announced.

"This one we tasting should, to wery certain being." The chosen one was duly tapped and decanted in a breathless silence which was broken only by someone's very loud fart. The servant brought the poisoned chalice to his angst ridden countenance and the fraught charade began all over again. Nosing the contents mouse-like, the fool rushed in, and with an exclamation of delight, declared

"Goot! She is goot!" All was well; this one contained elixir. A palpable atmosphere of relief swept through the surrounding herd of ruffians who sighed as one as the tension drained from them, their great white smiles appearing in the lamplight like those of hyenas circling in the veldt. He drank. Deeply. A groundswell of approbation filling the darkness.

"She wunderbar iss," he declared, more overcome than he had words to express.

Delighted by this unforeseen improvement in Hooligan's fortunes, Van Rijn grabbed the pot, sipped carefully, smiled with all of the sincerity of an ancient hore then drank blissfully.

"Ya, Got in heben, she wunderbar iss," he confirmed; utterly sickened at the prospect of being forced to pay a businesslike price. The *Liberty*'s crew took great care with the unloading of the cargo making sure that five casks and five only, were lifted out of the holds in each net. For his part, Hooligan sat comfortably at his ship's side throughout the process, graciously nodding as Teach accepted a healthy profit in silver for every barrel as it left the ship. That night, Van Rijn beat his wife for the first time in more than ten years. Unforgivably, he rebuffed her short-haired schnauzer.

"Sink the *Battleaxe* Captain Teach, and if you get a chance, bugger-up them other two what were hoidin behoind her skirts. We'll start as we mean to. To."

The ignorant drunk known as Hooligan simply could not remember the rest of the expression which Admiral Lliam Shaun Hooligan had begun to quote. With the Battleaxe and her sisters only a mile distant, the revenge-hungry sailors charged to their stations before Teach could bawl at his splendid new boatswain; gun ports clattered open, and gunners levered-around their massive engines of war, in order to get the earliest shot possible as they took the fight to the filthy Brits.

"Warship approaching! Starboard side!"

With a mile still to travel before they would have their opportunity to blunt the *Battleaxe,* the call was heard from the masthead.

"It's 'your,' bollox, Captain," rasped Hooligan, and Teach understood the implication readily. If he chose to sink the approaching man of war, the cacophony of the *Liberty*'s broadside might result in a thirty-gun welcome from Battleaxe. Teach barely hesitated.

"Enemy warship starboard side!" He roared gleefully,

"Fire at will! Sink her! Break out our colors!" It was with huge satisfaction and breathless pride that he watched the stars and stripes, thirteen of each, unfurl at the masthead; the one-legged sailmaker, Thom and his gang, having performed miracles. Today, the men of the *Bird* would strike two telling blows for their nation's freedom from Georgie boy's tyranny. By allowing his gunners to fire at will Teach knew that those ministers of mayhem would break their backs gentling their gigantic pets in to angles of fire which would enable the earliest possible shot, followed by a second shot, before the pass was complete. It would mean a total of twenty shattering blows rather than the ten balls of the broadside and would almost certainly sink the hopefully unsuspecting man of war.

Aboard the Englishman the captain and crew of the approaching *Intrepid* had lowered their guard as England enfolded the returning warriors to her bosom. With her gun ports closed and only a kerchief of sail unfurled, she passed through gentle fields of golden wheat and lush pastures with nary a care in the world, other than the appalling and shameful stench of their home. As the two huge vessels closed, the Englishman's approach placed her on the *Liberty*'s starboard bow, from where some of her seamen peered up questioningly at the masthead of the *Liberty* and were exchanging opinions on the implications of the flag which flew there, when the first of Liberty's guns ripped the calm of day in a shattering, metallic clatter of sound. The huge iron ball larger than a Maryland water melon smashed through her bows, shaking her mortally. Sailors stumbled on her decks such was the impact of that dreadful strike. Instantly, a second report shattered the air, then a third and a fourth in an incessant wave of destruction. Beyond the smoke of *Liberty*'s guns, the *Intrepid* staggered. Men screamed in excruciating agony. The masts of the now invisible ship of the line, pitched over. She was sinking rapidly by the bow.

No sooner than the target of opportunity was hammered, than Hooligan's gunners threw themselves into the task of shifting three of her weapons from the starboard side to the vacant stations opposite, bringing her complement up to the full ten. 'It wouldn't do to short-change the Brits' they laughed.

"She's turning over. The *Intrepid.* Sinking by the bow." The call from the masthead barely caused a ripple among the tense fighters aboard *Liberty*. The *Intrepid* was astern of them. The *Battleaxe* lay ahead.

"Enemy on the port bow, three hundred yards and closing!" On the gundeck Teach studied the final adjustments which would certainly facilitate two shots from each of his death dealers, the first of which would strike *Battleaxe* at the waterline, smashing through her innards. The second would send grape and chain hurtling across the three Admiralty vessels moored side-by-side, hopefully bringing down their masts and their rigging, and doing untold damage. With only seconds to spare, the preparations were complete; the ten warriors hovered over their charges with the slow match in hand.

"At will. Fire at will!" roared Teach.

Behind the bulwarks, Hooligan waited on deck with his skirmishers for the clamor that would herald the commencement of hostilities, and the possibility that the *Battleaxe* might be the first to fire. The British would have spotted the American flag only seconds after the *Intrepid* was struck. A great deal depended on the qualities of her Captain, and whether he was one who could react instantly to an emergency. A thirty-gun broadside from *the Brit* he believed, would blow *Liberty* into the riverside cow pastures. Unable to contain himself a second longer or to hide in this undignified manner he stood up to his full height at the instant in which *Liberty*'s first gun roared and witnessed the enemy's rudder being torn to shreds. Something tugged at his sleeve leaving him dimly aware of wet- warmth beneath his shirt. On the riverside track adjacent to the enemy squadron, an open carriage drawn by six black stallions with scarlet feather headdresses was racing towards the English warships, the driver whipping the horses savagely as the passenger, dressed in the uniform of a commander of the British Navy, shook his girly fist at the American raider.

"The carriage, boys," yelled Hooligan.

"Shoot shit out of it," but the oblivious skirmishers were already blasting away at any target that they could find. As Admiral Hooligan raised his musket, the coach driver dropped both his whip and the reins and clutching at his side toppled beneath the cruel wheels. Hooligan never got a shot off, the *enemy* and the fast-closing coach, which was now heading straight for the river, disappeared in the thick grey smoke, as the *Liberty* shook violently beneath him. Even as the fog thickened, his guns continued to roar with stunning effect. The masts of all three battleships groaned loudly, leaned over suicidally and finally sagged in defeat; held partially aloft merely by the intermixed knitting of their devastated rigging.

"Keep her in midstream," yelled Hooligan and raced below to ascertain how badly they had been hit, charging like a wounded bull into the pall of smoke billowing up the gangways and colliding with blood-smeared men; all of them going down in a kindling of arms and legs. Smoke was concealing everything. He advanced with his hands out in front, his footing treacherous with blood. Putting his hands in the stuff as he steadied himself against the woodwork, he slipped on boards treacherous with it, and almost fell on his head as he edged forward. The guns had stopped firing. It was over. Someone close by was screaming. Crawling forward he located a prostrate seaman. Staying down on the deck from where he could see further, he attended to the injured man. An upturned hand, the arm. The face was one that he had laughed with. What was the boyo's name? For the life of him, he could not remember. 'Why was everybody bawling like cattle for chrissake? Sure a man couldn't hear himself tink.' He searched for the lad's wounds by touch, the gunner being insensible. The man finished at his middle in a mess of mincemeat and guts. There were no legs! Back to the arm he went to try for a pulse at the wrist.

"What are you doing you eedjit?" he demanded. "Sure, the poor bastard has no legs, so how would he have a pulse?" Men staggered past in the fog. Three or four maybe, with one being dragged, 'loik a sack of spuds,' He was kicked in the face and blood flowed into his mouth. A screaming thing in red and white was being dragged topside. There was a great splinter of timber in someone's smashed leg. It went in white on one side and came out of the other as red as a cherry. Lliam followed on his knees to see if he could help, but slowly; he did not want to be the one to wrench out that devil's spear.

"Open the hatches. Get the smoke out of here. Where are we hurt?"

Hooligan stilled as he heard Teach, taking control a long way off.

"Number ten copped it, Captain, tree or fower men hurt oi tink." The voice came from only yards away from where the injured Admiral lay.

"Any more?" Several gunners answered in the negative. Could it really be, Hooligan wondered, that only three or four men had been injured by that cataclysmic strike? He crawled on to where the smoke thinned out, then got to his feet and went to confront the horror of which he was the cause.

Topside, men were crowded around two casualties; more, it seemed to Hooligan, in ghoulish fascination, than with any intention of helping.

"Boatswain, do your job," he roared, "get them fellas back to work."

"Aye aye, sir." The boatswain was as guilty as any of the crew, and he knew it.

"You heard mister Hooligan get to yer battle stations. Masthead, sing out if you sight any more limeys, and we'll have a go at them too!" The few men who remained with the wounded were not sawbones, but they were doing what they could to make the injured lads comfortable though the screams of these men were unnerving to hear; their devilish agonized faces, terrible to witness. 'Opium!' Grabbing the arm of a sailor kneeling next to him, Hooligan stared into the man's eyes, demanding his concentration.

"Get below and tap a barrel of cognac. You'll be needin' your knife. Bring a good jug of it up here, and a mug or two. Go."

"Yes, sir." As the sailor's bare feet slapped away across the deck, Hooligan rushed to his cabin, remembering with affection the ease that the opium had brought him from his own little knocks. In a few long strides he crossed the small space which he shared with teach and a couple of crew members, climbed-up on to his bunk, shoved aside his haversack and thrust his arm deeply into a cavity between the massive beams supporting the deck above. 'Nothing.' The elixir had gone.

"Oi'll kill some bitch when I get… No! Oi moved it. Oi'm losin' me moind, sure." In plain sight on a washstand, was a large water jug. Lliam stuck his fist into it and brought out the full bottle of the magic potion. Racing topside, he thrust the precious liquid into the hands of those same men who had done such selfless and successful work on shore, caring for the dying and the sick and were now with the injured men on deck preparing to carry out amputations, sew the worst wounds closed, and bandage others. They knew how to use the elixir wisely, and they understood that it was the only pain-numbing medicine aboard. When the bottle was emptied; there was no more. Admiral Lliam Hooligan resolved there and then, to keep a capable surgeon and a barrel of opium aboard every ship that he took to war. If there were medicines available in this world which dulled a man's pain, then to his way of thinking it would be criminal not to have the stuff at hand.

For two whole days, the time it took *Liberty* to clear Canvey and the Thames Estuary and get well out to sea, the three bodies lay on her deck, sewn into canvas shrouds with cannonballs at their feet. Two had died as their shipmates attempted to save them by sawing off their shattered limbs with a carpenters' ripsaw. Weston Fuller, who could read, and played the fiddle like the devil himself had been struck by a cannonball and torn in two, and James Tobin had bled to death. Men spoke in whispers and walked softly, making great detours around their fallen comrades. Incredibly, there was no damage to the *Liberty*. None! When the Admiral had demanded an explanation from Teach, the distracted sailor had replied,

"Ironside," without stopping to speak.

Unwilling to let the matter drop Hooligan questioned his gunners and discovered that by sheer chance a ball had hurtled straight through one of the gunports and hit poor Weston. He would have known nothing of it.

At dawn on the third day, the men lost in battle were buried in the manner of the sea. Such words of farewell as their mortified friends could cobble together were spoken, the plank on which the departed lay was elevated at the crown and the bodies slipped quietly into the tide from beneath the flag of their new nation; the nation for which they had given their lives. With sufficient time available to them on this occasion, the sailmakers had outdone themselves and created a masterpiece of the new symbol, specifically for the ceremony, a masterpiece which was better by far than their first hurried attempt, which to their endless chagrin still flew at the masthead. A barrel of cognac was brought topside for the wake; the one which had been savagely broached for the sake of the wounded, and the cooks did miracles with hot food against the ever-worsening weather. Men began to reminisce about the good times which they had enjoyed alongside their absent friends, and many a secret tear was shed.

CHAPTER 24: Scotland

How beautiful was the wide Firth of Tay, its gentle banks of wheat and oats swaying, 'fawn and doe,' in the sunrise; particularly to those whose affections responded readily to this ancient home. At the *Liberty*'s bulwarks men who still spoke with a Scottish lilt, after years in the fields and towns of the American eastern seaboard stood deeply moved; their gentle progress towards the town of Perth something of a homecoming, though these men knew from their parents' lips that the crofts from which they had been evicted so long ago had been reduced to rubble and their lands populated by the genocidal aristocracy's sheep.

"Ships on the port bow." The masthead's observation was lost in the resounding echoes of cannon fire as men raced to their battle stations. The massive bronze snouts, restrained mastiffs along the Liberty's flanks.

"It's our fleet at anchor in line astern," the masthead bawled.

"Battle stations." Their Captain's warning was redundant; not a man aboard was taking any chances, English trickery being what it was.

"Steersman, we will cross their T." With the boatswain roaring orders that he had been given sotto voce by Teach, and men racing into the rigging ready to change course, the massively armed vessel descended on the *Liverpool*, the *Boston*, and the *Justice,* and in pride of place, their very own, *Bird.* Their home-away-from-home.

"Come about," bawled the boatswain and at the very last second the great ship turned hard across the *Bird*'s bows bringing to bear her harbingers of death. Aboard both ships men recognized their friends and comrades, and resounding cheers broke out aboard all five vessels.

''Hang fire.'' The call echoed down the mile-long line of ships.

Intent on rediscovering the happy times which he had passed in 'Nonty Ponty' Lliam Hooligan was the first of the *Liberty*'s men to step ashore in Scotland. But only after being rowed from ship to ship, gifting a new blue coat to every suffering sailor. Among the coral necklace of brilliantly white crofts scattered haphazardly along the shoreline was an inn, and it was to that; his natural home, that he was headed when he was accosted by the strangest men imaginable. Four of them seemed to have stepped out of the past. They were outfitted in tartan kilts, predominantly of a purple and cow-pat-brown hue with what appeared to be a dead animal hanging in front, supplemented by hose which came up almost to the knee and held a knife which aspired to be a claymore. Above their dirty, once white smocks, each man had an acre or so of tartan over one shoulder, and on their heads were French berets adorned with eagle feathers. Despite this antediluvian approach to matters sartorial, it was their weaponry that held the attention of the new arrival's.

Each of the fighters was burdened by a targe* and a sword so thick, heavy and clumsy that you'd just wait till the fools got tired then stab them in the face.

"Do I have the honor of addressing Mister Lliam Hooligan?'' The speaker was the *body* that was being guarded and was a different kettle of tripe altogether. He had about him the look of a country parson, dressed as he was, all in black, other than his stockings and the profusion of girly lace things at his throat and wrists, which were as white as snow on a Scottish hilltop. The buckles of his bright black shoes were clearly silver.

"Who wants to know?" Hooligan's tone was not one of amity. A trifle late in the proceedings he began to wonder whether his flintlock was loaded, because he was certain that he did not stand a chance with a sword. The four swordsmen obviously got plenty of practice because there were great lumps missing from all four blades, and the leather of the shields was hanging in tatters.

"My name is immaterial," declared the parson with evident sincerity. "Mister Macbeth; with the Laird's leave, has instructed me to conduct Misters Hooligan and Teach to Castle Huntingmill, if they would be so kind as to grace him with their presence."

Teach and a score of others from the whaleboat had arrived and surrounded the swordsmen menacingly.

"Is all well, Lliam?" they asked, staring threateningly at the unconcerned Scots.

"Couldn't be better my sons, the captain an me is away to have the crack with Macbeth." Glancing around at his sailor friends, Hooligan inquired pathetically.

"Would ye be pals yous fellas and look after me bloody boats till we get back, sure. We're off to Castle Muntinghill." The horrified parson filled his inefficient lungs preparatory to correcting this malediction, but on reflection, saw no profit in this course of action. It was quite clear that the bog trotter was beyond help, ship owner or not.

"I have a coach waiting at the inn," he declared, opening his soft white palm in the direction of the nearby hostelry.

"We have anticipated your arrival for a week or more."

This back-handed parting shot did not go unnoticed or unrecognized for what it was by the recipients, hence it did little to improve the sailors' poor opinion of this 'jumped-up perfumed, dick-licker;' but for Macbeth's sake, they decided to let it pass. Hooligan 'did' however, promise himself that before ever he departed the Firth of Tay, he would take this little weasel by the throat and slap him silly.

The journey to Castle Huntingmill was long, silent, and uncomfortable; the discomfort being caused by the road which was a depression into which someone had thrown stones while the silence was due to the ill-feeling which lay like a pool of cold puke between the adventurers and the Laird's emissary. The vehicle had barely bounced and rattled its way out of the western suburbs of Perth, when a castle came into view; the first that the sailors had seen if their brief glimpse of the Tower of London was discounted which, when compared to the magnificence of this upward extension of the cliff upon which it sat, was no castle at all. The thing was a granite edifice, so extensive that you could put Perth inside it with room to spare, and higher than it had a right to be, because if a man stood on the top of it, he would have to hold on with both hands, sure, and how would he fight then?"

"That's a darlin' castle yer Laird fella has, sure," the Admiral enthused, forgetting his feud.

"That is not Huntingmill Castle," the parson retorted, sniffily.

"Indeed, it is no castle at all when once you have feasted your eyes on the Laird's eyrie. That is the home of Frazer's Highlanders."

"And who might Frazer and his Highlanders be, when they're at home?" asked Teach with an edge.

"It is a regiment of Scottish soldiers," declared the parson thoughtfully.

"Extraordinary soldiers," the compliment was added grudgingly.

Fast as the strike of an adder Teach backhanded the parson ferociously across the face and grabbed him by throat preparatory to strangling the man in the fury of the betrayed when Hooligan got quickly between him and his victim, determined to get some answers from the creature prior to murdering him.

''Whose idea was it to bring me to Perth?'' He bawled. Nose to nose with the injured bleeding and badly shaken individual.

''Your Laird's?"

By risking his neck in ways that had on occasion made his hair stand on end, Hooligan had gone from penniless tramp to owner of four seagoing vessels, and now before he had so much as got used to the idea; treachery might reduce him to penury once again.

"Be, at ease, sir, I, beg you." Groaned the quivering emissary, realizing that he had overplayed his hand grotesquely and hastening to diffuse a situation which would certainly have serious repercussions for himself if these smelly oafs were to mention the subject to his master. He struggled to articulate his excuses.

"Mister Macbeth is a gentleman who makes precious, few false steps; indeed, he is a rising star in the Laird's constellation. There is no risk whatsoever to yourself or your ships through your presence in Perth and Kinross. The castle lies empty other than for a small detachment of guards. To the very best of my knowledge, the regiment is disembarking as we speak in Maryland which is on the other side of the globe.'' Managing it all while drying his eyes and the trail or two of blood from his swelling lips. Silence resumed, heavy and hateful, filling the vehicle with a powerful almost tangible atmosphere.

''We have arrived."

To the sailors' astonishment the coach was now 'inside' charging up the cobbled slope of a road wide enough for ten horsemen to ride side by side, over which an impossible arch of immeasurable radius leapt a hundred feet in a single bound. Such things were not possible. Reaching the summit, the coach dipped and swayed to a halt 'inside,' a foyer of glistening timber and stained glass.

Descending in the manner of a timorous girl, the out of sorts parson made slow, hard work of leading his savage through a herd of impossibly long beards, loud Gaelic utterances, autumn's-tartans, tobacco smoke, whisky breath, sweat and glistening steel, to heroic doors of oak construction, iron hinges and brass studs. Several echoing corridors later the party decanted into a room as warm as mead and colorful as Vermeer. It was built of books.

With his devout hope of a pleasant stay in Huntingmill Castle, an assurance that he would inform the Laird of their presence, and an air of relief unmistakably tainted by loathing, the parson excused himself and left the jolly tars to their own devices. Both men headed directly to the nearest of three blazes which maintained an atmosphere complimentary to the room's purpose and had been warming their respective backsides there for several minutes when a huge spider clinging near the ceiling metamorphosed into a tiny man who moved effortlessly sideways a yard or two, clearly untroubled by gravity. The fellow's white gloves selected a particular volume from the wall, and with infinite care he descended by virtue of his rolling ladder. Once safe on terra firmer he greeted the visitors, bowing courteously.

"Guid efternoon, gentlemen, 'Harris,' is the name. Keeper O' The Books ferr the Laird. There arr sum wee bits foods and drink." When the quaint little elf spoke, he went *up* at the end. He had to indicate these 'foods' and 'drink' with a nod of his head for the volume which he was carrying tasked his strength to its limit, bending his worn-out old frame pitilessly. Harris was wearing an apron and a pair of spectacles which boasted two lenses for each eye.

"Where did you get those tings?" blurted Hooligan, astonished by this occurrence and therefore rather more loudly than he intended, causing the old man to quiver slightly as he and the tome collapsed over a table.

"They what, sur?" enquired Harris, perplexed, and not a little unnerved by the accusation in Hooligan's tone.

"Those bifocals," Hooligan blurted, revelling in his use of the correct term, and exigent for the man's reply.

"These sur?" Harris removed his spectacles and stared at them myopically, as though he had never seen them before.

"A gift from God, sur." Harris was clearly in awe of the brilliant invention and his possession of it.

"Yes," persisted Lliam more considerately.

"But where did you get them?"

"The Laird brung untold o' these frae across the watter. He gave furrst pick tae masel.' I can see like I wus a wee laddie wi' these on."

"Would ye know a wee laddie by the name o' Franklin? Benjamin Franklin?" asked Hooligan with no hope whatsoever of an answer in the affirmative.

"O' coorse Sur. Who dusnae? A brilliant man and a bonnie printer tae. It's that great man's intention tae bring books and reading tae the peepul sur, wance the warr is wun."

Incredulous at this pronouncement, Lliam Shaun Hooligan, student of everything, Admiral, ship owner, leader of men and spearpoint of the abolitionist effort did not know which question to ask first.

"And how would he do that?" He did not have a clue and he very much wanted to know the answer.

"Why, wi' libraries, sur, the likes o' this." The little fellow's gloved hand waved with the pride of vicarious ownership at the thousands of volumes that lined the walls.

"Public libraries, where the people, rich and poor can gae tae read and learn fer free. Is that nae the idea of a genius? Dae ye read, gentlemen?" The keeper of the books cast a questioning eye at Hooligan's unusual, not to say, working man's clothes.

"No!"

"Yes, Harris, I do." Matter of fact from Teach.

The delicate librarian's concerned glance never strayed from Hooligan's face.

"Then that is something tae which we must address oorsels, sur. The knowledge of the wuruld is contained in books, and the man who cannae read is at a great disadvantage in life tae he that can.'' Hooligan was not convinced. This all sounded like mumbo jumbo. He grabbed a handful of pies and retrieved a mug of warm mead from the fireplace.

"Bollocks," he scoffed, as he returned with a smile which displayed his mouthful of foods and drink, as gravy ran down into the depths of his beard.

"Name sumthin' that ye'd like tae unnerstond, sur." The little man was eager to display the voracity of his claim and awaited the giant's answer, keen as a water dog for the hunt. Hooligan considered the bifocals sitting astride that narrow, haphazard nose and chose a subject about which he was positive that he knew everything that there was to know, and which would win his point for him.

"Telescopes.'' He snorted. ''How does a telescope wurrk?"

With only the slightest hesitation, the intense little librarian turned to the very wall of books which he had so recently summited. It benefited from a walkway of delicate wrought-iron, twenty feet above the carpeted floor which along its considerable length, accessed a thousand or more volumes bound in scarlet leather each with its title in gold on the spine. Muttering quietly to himself, he ascended as joyfully as a martyr approaching paradise, and proceeded confidently to the furthest extent of the platform. At that moment, the library doors were opened by a brace of footmen in extravagant uniforms, and in walked a tall, well-set-up man whose open expression and the keen eye of a falcon, declared him to be the repository of vast knowledge, intelligence, and animal savagery.

"Mister Hooligan," the newcomer began confidently, obviously recalling the descriptions he had received of the Irishman's 'interesting' appearance,

"Thank you so much for coming so far to see me. And this must be Captain Teach of the *Burrd*. I hope that I can return such generosity in my modest way." As he offered his hand, the Laird's green eyes glanced over Hooligan's shoulder to where his bookkeeper was selecting a scientific volume.

"I am Monteith, Laird of… well, quite a lot of Scotland, actually. You must be famished; shall we eat while we talk?"

"I thought I was coming here tae meet my old chum, Fartinhay.'' Monteith considered this declaration briefly.

"How quaint; and you still came. Above and beyond the call of duty I call that. Fotheringhay is an acquaintance of mine, and a trusted one. I understand that your introduction tae him occurred under less than optimum circumstances, Mister Hooligan. I want you to know that I greatly regret that. However, it's clear that you have been able tae rise above those unfortunate events and apply yourself to the work which I hired you tae do." The Laird sauntered towards the door.

"Shall we eat?"

Lliam Shaun Hooligan, ship owner, leader of men, associate of eminent statesmen remained rooted to the floor.

"Your man here has something to show me," he brayed, deeply irritated by the reference to his 'hiring,' and the barely disguised command in that 'shall we eat.' He considered himself a visitor here; a man of means; not a bloody serf to be ordered around. He turned his back on the cheeky bastard and went to where Harris had his selected volume open and was waiting for him.

Harris stood aside with quiet satisfaction.

Teach noted the ready fury behind the Laird's outwardly calm expression, which was exacerbated by Lliam's deliberately casual perusal of the book.

To the Irishman's stupefaction, there on the pages were diagrams of ocular devices, telescopes, and over the page, telescopes cut in half in order to show the arrangement of the lenses with arrows through them, indicating the passage of light. There were lenses with fat bellies and there were others with no belly at all just as Benjamin had explained. CONCAVE and CONVEX the note said.

''The 'cave,' job is the bugger wit the dent in it he declared confidently.'' Hooligan loved this learning stuff. With that disclosure, a light passed through the lens of his own ocular organ raced along the single optic nerve and entered his brain. He resolved then and there that he would redouble his efforts to learn to read and to write; he would master both, and then he would read and learn everything that there was to learn. He would question and get to the truth of every damn thing that he did not understand. Of all his recent adventures he realized; the discovery of knowledge was the one most exciting and satisfying to him.

"Thank you, my friend,'' Hooligan placed a hand on Harris' shoulder, almost causing structural collapse while slipping the gentle little man a small gold coin with the other.

In the dining hall, Macbeth was savouring his whisky, looking flushed, wind burnished and dishevelled, as though he had been out walking and had just now come inside. The Scot bowed formally to his Laird then hastened to shake Hooligan's hand enthusiastically.

"So, you got here safely Mister Hooligan. Well done and thank you for coming." Macbeth was clearly giving public recognition to Hooligan's changed status in life. It was a refinement which the reborn one appreciated enormously. A footman in burgundy and blue, topped-off by a wig of white, sat Hooligan at the head of a table which, in his estimation was ten yards long. Facing him was the Laird, and in the middle, facing each other, were Macbeth and Teach who sat in the glow of a fireplace, hot as Vulcan's forge, in which the lunatic Scots were burning trees rather than bits of wood, and above which hung a shield and crossed battleaxes fit for the gods of war.

 A covered dish was placed in front of the guest of honor, whilst the host and his friends looked-on happily. With his single eye, he questioned the Laird who had been presented no such dish. Receiving a nod in return he was about to serve himself when his waiter lifted the silver dome disclosing a roll of parchment tied with a silk bow. Hooligan loosed the bow and the document sprang open. It was all words, and fancy shields. With a grace which he would never have suspected, Macbeth appeared at his side and easing the document gently from his fingers, read every word aloud. Then turning to address his protégée declared,

"The Laird rewards those who serve him well. You now own a substantial home in Kinross. Congratulations." Dinner was immensely enjoyable to Lliam Hooligan, owner of a country house on twenty-five acres in Kinross and to Teach who due largely to the bravery of the men present would soon be sailing home to Boston and not residing in a paupers' grave. The salmon, the venison and the beef were all exquisite, as was the wine. Hooligan imbibed handsomely, and by the time a dram of the *water of life* was poured, he would not have known it from cold tea.

What was inexplicable to the now-affable Irishman, and astounding into the bargain, was the pleasure and knowledge that he derived from his conversation with these men, with whom he had not a thing in common, and this without a single dirty joke, filthy word or rude remark.

To Macbeth's chagrin, at an appropriate moment in review of recent events, the Laird apologized formerly for the unconscionable attacks on Hooligan's person by rough men who would never serve the cause again and were clearly not being disciplined severely enough. 'There was nothing to be gained by murdering one's greatest assets, was there?'

Macbeth wanted to know everything that Hooligan had done since parting from him at the riverside; particularly the events that took place inside the shipyard and he and the Laird listened fascinated to the story which was ably augmented by Teach who interrupted now and then in order to ask insightful questions, the answers to which, would, he knew, be utterly fascinating to the entranced audience as was his intention. It was getting late, and all four men were somewhat under the weather before the business of slavery was mentioned and the question asked as to whether the admiral would be happy to serve the Laird further in the eradication of this obscenity. With maturity beyond his limited education in these matters and his state of insobriety Hooligan demurred; claiming that he was 'as pissed as a newt,' and unable to make decisions of such a serious nature until he had sobered up and on that note the party broke up, for Captain's Teach and Hooligan had every intention of returning to the Firth of Tay directly; Teach to oversee the last minute preparations aboard the *Bird* for the voyage home to America, and Hooligan to arrange the repairs to the *Liberty,* and start the search for crews with which to replace his Americans who were desperate to get home after such a protracted absence. The walking wounded were being manhandled into their coach for the return journey to the anchorage when the Laird mentioned something of an interesting notion. As a mere throwaway remark, he advised Hooligan that, as the *Liberty*, the *Boston*, the *Liverpool* and the *Justice* were captured while Hooligan was in his; 'the Laird's,' employ, naturally, all four ships would revert to himself, and he would be sending crews along to take them over as soon as was possible. After all; what would Hooligan, a landsman, be doing with four ships? Ships were nothing but a hole in the water into which one threw money, were they not?

Hooligan had been ambushed drunk, mellow and completely off guard by this astounding betrayal as he was intended to be, but even so, he displayed remarkable presence of mind. He barely hesitated before, acquiescing almost instinctively with the Laird's wishes, as a good peasant must. He gave a quick nod of the head and a meek, 'Yes sir,' as though the thought of protesting this crime would not enter his head.

'This one.' he resolved, 'is worth the expenditure of a lead ball.' Macbeth's sudden rage at this treachery boiled much closer to the surface than did that of the departing seafarers. It strangled him. Eviscerated him. It ripped out his tongue, leaving him speechless. Hooligan, that good man, that simple, unworldly fellow had taken 'Macbeth's word; his and Fotheringhay's both, and acted accordingly, risking his life in a hundred ways in the belief that he was among friends and would be well rewarded. And now? Betrayal! Betrayal for which Hooligan would naturally blame himself, Macbeth. It was intolerable.

No sooner had the over-sprung carriage braved the razed axe of the portcullis and oscillated across the timber drawbridge than two angry passengers climbed out and relieved the astonished driver of the reins and his whip.

"We'll have them," they announced as they sandwiched the coachman and enquired of the team whether this gentle trot was the very best that they could manage. Despite almost constant appeals by the poor driver to 'nae turn ower' his vehicle, the seafarers shaved an hour off the journey's projected duration; Lliam Hooligan employing the reins, and Martin Teach cracking the whip ever nearer to the ears of the lead pair. Halting at the door of the waterside tavern, the highwaymen sent the driver home on foot and Hooligan charged into the gloom of the crowded, smoke-filled pot-room to bellow at the congregation,

"Get aboard, we sail bloody now," and dashed outside to where Teach was already at the water's edge bawling for a boat having fired both pistols and was waving his hat to attract attention from the fleet. The inn had been cleared and searched thoroughly for any comatose individuals who may be lying under tables or in the surrounding heather by the time the first of the longboats departed the pebbled beach laden with drunks bawling.

''Whas goin on? Wee're on hore leeve.'' The dead and dying were thrown like so much cargo into the bottom of the lighters, and the men at the oars pulled for their ships.

"Break your backs boys," urged the boatswains, "or be beached here," and the men lengthened their stroke willingly. They were fairly skipping along, fully two hundred yards offshore, when a drunken sailor vomiting considerately over the side, observed.

"Holy fwuck. Look! Heesh drowning."

Several boat-lengths away on the port side, an exhausted swimmer was desperately trying to stay on the surface, his strength having deserted him well short of the ships. As the drunks watched in concern the poor man succumbed to exhaustion and cold and disappeared below the surface of the Firth with barely a ripple. The quickly naked Gulley was first into that malignant world and was making rapid progress toward the drowning man even before the lighter had changed course; the drunks doing their part by watching in fascination and providing poor advice. The remarkably capable swimmer soon reached the spot where the poor fellow had disappeared, and with a quick flash of his bum, was lost to sight.

"Pull you bastards," bellowed Hooligan, from the following boat, "that's our mates out there," and shoving a man away from his oar, grabbed the thing, and rowed as though trying to snap it in two. They hove-to at the approximate spot where the swimmers had sunk and several already naked men entered the water vertically, going deep to search desperately for sign of the two men in the clear, deathly-cold depths. Futility prevailed. There was a commotion as an oar was jerked from its owner's grasp. The swimmers surfaced one by one, and the gasping, hypothermic individuals were dragged aboard. A dozen drunks all-but murdered the poor patient in their attempts to pump water from his apparently dead skeleton but soon became bored and lay down beside him. It was not until much later as the longboat neared the great cliff of *Liberty*'s side that the first sign occurred that the man might live; the collection of skin and bone vomited copiously in the bottom of the boat.

"Christ awmoighty. Looka that," men chorused, "he's bin eatin' grass." Sure enough, the swimmer had vomited a great wad of slimy, undigested green stuff that slithered across the timbers underfoot. In the warmth of the galley the Scot was wrapped in a blanket and had hot soup and rum placed before him. Not a scrap of fat was there on the man's white body, and he shivered uncontrollably for a long time, so that sailors had to spoon his soup into his mouth and hold his cup of rum to his lips. Hooligan and Teach, had no time to spare wet-nursing mad Scottish swimmers; they had to ensure that every man was aboard and get underway, guns run out, before an army of Monteith's boys appeared, and claimed all five ships for the thieving son of a bitch. Both men rushed off to complete the preparations for sea but not before balling at the seamen who were milling around the Scot 'like a gaggle of women,' to get back to their posts before they found themselves going for a swim of their own.

Much later when the skeleton had recovered sufficiently to stand on his feet, he staggered on deck wearing clothes which drowned him a second time and found Teach with the signallers who were passing the captain's instructions down the line. The great concern being not to leave any of the crew behind.

"Good day to ye, sur," he said, and used the last of his strength to hold out his hand.

"I am Angus Stewart." Teach held that hand but briefly.

"Teach is the name," he replied quietly.

"What can I do for you, Mister Stewart?"

"Food, sur. Can ye spare any food? We are dying."

"We?" inquired Teach, turning automatically to scan the shore.

"Mahap ye could take us away frae heer sum place. He will kill us all if we 'bide."

Teach was at a loss.

"Who is, 'we'?" And who will kill ye… you?"

"The Laird." Unable to stand any longer, Stewart allowed himself the luxury of a controlled collapse.

"Monteith?" ventured Teach, easily persuaded; squatting down beside the heroic individual.

"Aye, the very man."

"What has occurred? Why?" Teach could not fathom just what Stewart was talking about.

"He wants all of Scotland for hisself. We were burnet oot; wi' many killed. Our hooses raised. They took wur cattle. They've been on wur heels since."

"Put me in a dress." Martin Teach could barely believe his ears. Was this the same Monteith, he wondered, who fought slavery, tooth and claw?

"I'd be happy to help … but it's not me that you must ask, Stewart; it's that man over there. I am Captain of the *Bird* only, and I carry a large crew, I can take perhaps a dozen. Lliam, a moment of your time," Teach beckoned his friend.

"How many are there of you, Stewart?"

''Hunnerds. The clan. What's left o us.

"Lliam Hooligan. Are ye a wee bit better, Mister?" Hooligan spoke considerately.

"Stewart. Angus Stewart," volunteered Teach.

Hooligan squatted down next to the other two but thought it unwise to shake Stewart's hand in case the man's arm came off.

"Take us wi' ye when ye sail sur," the man begged.

"We are starvin' and we'll aul be deed afore the wintur gets tae kill us."

"Jesus, Joseph and Mary." Hooligan was mortified.

"Why would that be? Where are you?"

"Do you have disease among you?" demanded the ever practical Teach, staring deeply into Stewart's eyes as though to divine the truth.

"We do not sur. We're starved and weak fit tae drap. We cough blood and we've got the skitters wi' eatin' the grass, but nae disease."

"How many?" asked Hooligan.

"The clan. Hunnerds.''

Hooligan never so much as blinked.

"Signaller, to all ships," he bellowed.

"Prepare to repel boarders. Run out the guns. Load with grape. Lower yer boats and follow me. Bring yer guns anshit." It would not do to be caught ashore by Monteith's kilted furies, but with his gunners at the ready and a skirmish line of twenty muskets established, the business of taking off the starving people could proceed with a degree of security.

"Where away?" asked Hooligan again, and Angus Stewart motioned to be helped up.

"There." He indicated an area of broken ground, not that far from the cottages and the inn.

"We are hiding there," he said.

Lliam's longboat was the first to crunch the shells of the beach with the others not far behind. He had brought only one other crewman with him, in order to carry off as many poor souls as possible but was soon to regret that decision. Beyond the shells and pebbles of the beach lay a stretch of sand dunes which made for heavy going, and the Admiral was puffing hugely by the time he reached firm ground. Surprisingly, there was no one to be seen in the deep and narrow gulley that lay before him, and turning towards the *Liberty* he checked his bearings

"Oh, for the love of. Would you look at that?" The blue jacket next to him advanced several paces in wonderment but Hooligan still could not see what bothered the man till the sailor pointed down at several seemingly meaningless places. Far below him in the gut of the ravine, something moved momentarily, a flash of what could have been skin appeared, then vanished. Small movements and sounds were everywhere. For a moment, it seemed that his eyes must be playing him false, but as he saw a hand here and heard a cough there, he realised that the near bank of the narrow declivity was strewn with humanity for as far as he could see. Camouflaged by their plaid and by their stillness, the people were almost invisible among the ferns and heather and huge boulders. Whenever the breeze relented, a terrible keening could be heard; it was a sound which tortured him still, it was the misery of starving children and their pitiful mothers. Hundreds of people were breathing their last in this awful place.

"Signal Francis" he ordered his seaman.

"We need a shore party of fifty men, well-armed mind you, to help these people to the boats. Get the galleys making hot food, aye, and we'll need boatswains' chairs to get them aboard; they can barely stand, I'll bet my arse."

"Aye aye, sir." The sailor, happy to obey his hero and saviour put two fingers to his forehead and was gone. Ever since the escape from the shipyard, then the astounding generosity of the blue jackets and the gift of cash, he, like his shipmates, had been Hooligan's convert. To action a direct order from the famous man was an opportunity to repay something.

Seamen were descending the slope to the streamside at great risk to their legs amid the loose boulders, some dropping from one outcrop to a lower one in their haste. There were highlanders everywhere, listless, barefoot, wet and shivering. The nearest of them to the spot where Hooligan emerged from the obstruction of bracken and boulders were curled together on the damp ground; a family by the looks of it, the mother too weak to turn and look at him, a dead boy child, its clothes taken for the other two little ones who would soon join their pathetic little brother. The father, desperate, unmanned and deeply ashamed.

"Save your family, Sir," Hooligan said quietly. Choosing his words carefully.

"Get them to the waterside. We have food for everyone." At hearing those words, a fire lit behind the Scot's eyes.

"I am yoor man, sur," he responded simply. Lliam helped the young husband to get his wife to her feet, then stood up the children.

"Take your son aboard the ship," he murmured, and picking up the poor cold body, he placed it against its father's chest. A small army of blue jackets appeared over the lip of the gulley, and seeing the prospect of salvation, hope sprung once again in the great hearts of the clansmen. People began to stir, while all along the valley many of the stronger ones got laboriously to their feet. Advancing ahead of his men he fell into a pattern of repeating what was to become his mantra on that awful, yet wonderful day.

"If you can walk, make yer way to the water, there are boats there to take you aboard ship. We have food for everyone." Those within earshot of him heard the incredible news and began to move, helping one another towards deliverance. Realising early that to spread the word was the best possible thing that he could do, he stumbled on through the defile and its endless stream of human misery.

"If you can walk, make your way to the water. Boats will meet you there and take you out to the ships. Men will be here to carry those who can't walk. Keep aholt o' yer children. We have food for everyone." Through the endless file of human misery he went, helping people to stand up, lifting children on to their father's backs and comforting distraught youngsters who could not find their parents, telling them to walk with the others so that they would soon be together again. On he went routinely lifting bundles of rag and bone whose every shallow breath might be their last; convincing them that they could get to the water where help awaited, until, at a long stretch from the shore, he came to the very last. Curled up and shivering among the boulders was a young woman with her two near-death little children under her plaid, and not a man of any class whatever to look after her. The children were beyond whimpering for food, they had cried for days but it had done them no good. Tears filled the woman's large, soft eyes as she answered the beautiful, heaven-sent giant,

"Your father sees you." She spoke the words, but not a sound issued from her frosted lips.

"Can you stand?" he asked. "And walk?" at which the young mother tried to get to her feet. Lifting her weightless form he then picked up the children and cradled them in his arms.

"Hang on to my belt." Sobbing now the girl did as he asked, and the little party began the slow, arduous and seemingly endless journey to the water. As they crept along, Lliam encouraged others whom the blue jackets had not yet reached, to follow him and promised those who lacked the strength that no one would be left behind.

"No one will be left behind. Put your mind at rest, sure. We have food for everyone. We have food for everyone." It was the comportment, ingenuity and the kindness of his rough sailor's that day, which convinced Hooligan that they would be the victors in their war, 'and his,' against the bloody British with their ridiculous 'kings,' and their 'divine rights' and all the rest of their filth.

When the admiral next saw his ships; they had been brought together and bound side by side in a solid phalanx, with the tall *Liberty* furthest offshore, and the sleek *Bird* nearest. Now the full complement of lighters pulled straight for the *Bird*, where the boatswain's chairs had been marshalled and were now able to be kept busy instead of standing idle between arrivals. Once aboard the *Bird*, the poor people could be moved easily from ship to ship. Broken families could be reunited, and space could be better allocated. At the very last shot of the battle, the aching and desperately tired admiral gathered a party of five young men bristling with weapons and sent them inland along the gulley with instructions to go a full hour's march inland in search of any living soul who might have been left for dead, and to fire off a shot if help was needed. The thought of leaving some poor starving woman or child to die alone was unbearable to him. What concerned him most since hearing Stewart's disastrous news, and his postponement of the fleet's escape from the Tay, was that an army of the Laird's boys might turn up to steal his ships. If they attacked in great numbers while some of the starving Scots were still ashore, his position would be damn near indefensible. Sorely distracted by the plight of the clansmen, he had worried the threat the way a terrier shakes a rat, but for the life of him could not conceive of a solution. Crossing paths with Longbottom, one of his captains who was struggling through the dunes with a child in his arms, the answer was suddenly obvious. 'Delegation.'

A couple of hours later, as Admiral Hooligan lay exhausted on that same dune watching the sailors as they went about their work, the world suddenly shook beneath him, a thousand broadsides rent the air as one and he leapt to his feet in consternation as an unnatural breeze passed briefly by. Beyond the cottages where the road to Perth crossed the torrent of the River Earn, ten million granite starlings raced into the sky pursued by a shape so regular, that it could only be an arch of the bridge which had straddled the turbulent Earn.

The awful thing turned slowly over, reached the apex of its flight and stooped, ever more steeply. Like a monstrous cormorant, it smashed into the Tay, creating a depression in the water deeper than a ship is tall. The tide raced to fill the void and the resulting waves pranced out across the Firth to spend themselves gentling the ships. He had begun to run, then realised that they were not under attack. Longbottom, good soldier that he was, had decided to waylay any threat from the west by destroying the bridge over the River Earn. All along the straggling line of humanity, his 'blue jackets' as he liked to think of them, had unslung their muskets and prepared for battle.

"It's alright," he bawled then struggling to the top of the dune, he took to waving his arms and hollering at everyone that all was well. Very soon his men understood his less than perfect signalling skills as being the all-clear, and stood down, allowing the migration to begin again. Teach plodded by, rubbing at the irritating scabs around his eye, as he made for 'Golgotha' as the gulley had become known, and seeing Hooligan, the Captain flung himself down for a rest.

"Lliam," he said, fiddling with the hilt of his sword, which was a certain precursor to an important announcement.

"Yes, my child?" mocked Hooligan, thinking himself very clever. Martin Teach was all business.

"Have you thought about what you're going to do with them?"

"Fillem full o porridge and take them for a wee sail on the boats," the words tripped off the tongue of he who still would not see, despite the subtle prompting of his friend.

"Yes, but where to? They can't stay in Scotland. Anywhere in Scotland. They have tried a dozen times and as many places and been caught every time." Hooligan could not respond because he had never given a thought to what he would do with these people, other than feed the poor devils.

"They walked here all the way from the kelp beds on the west coast Lliam where they thought they'd be safe, but that Monteith fella has a long reach; his killers found them, murdered them and only these got out. They haven't eaten in all the time that it took them to get here." Hooligan drew breath, and was about to suggest France, which he had liked enormously, when his friend declared,

"Lliam, we have to resolve this matter. You own… you have captured a fortune in ships. Several fortunes. You've also got hundreds of displaced Scottish cattle herders, but you have no crews."

"Bollox!''

"We are for home, Lliam, you know that, so don't look so damned shocked. Me and my men. We miss our families sorely. They must think us dead by now. Not only that, your country; 'this' country, is at war with ours. We must run or be hung."

"What will you do with *yours* then?" enquired the now deeply concerned philanthropist seeking comfort in the majority and receiving a vacant stare in response.

"With *your* people! He expostulated, you've some on the *Bird*.''

"I'll take them back home to Boston," Teach smiled, happy at the thought of doing such a great service for those poor people.

"They'll have a far better time of it there than ever they did in this place." In the light of this announcement, Hooligan could not for the life of him see what Teach had been bleating about.

"We'll 'all,'' come to Boston, Martin," he gargled as though this was the most obvious course of action of the thousand or so possibilities.

"Americy? And it's a good place to live?"

"It is, Lliam. It's magnificent. Unequalled anywhere I've been," said Teach emotionally,

"but it's on the other side of the Atlantic, a couple of months away, maybe."

"Show me on the chart, moi child," breezed the ebullient one to whom the simple imperative of feeding hungry people was providing a deep joy, intensified in the extreme in all manner of ways by his induction into the hallowed halls of knowledge. The two friends descended once more into the valley of death, and returned an hour later, supporting between them a big, barely clothed man who had not the strength to stand up. Once again aboard Liberty Teacher and pupil strode directly to the great cabin, and while Hooligan retrieved a cask of rum the captain drew open a shallow charts drawer and selected the one that would be required for the next instalment of his student's edification. With concealed amusement he slid the work of art and science in front of his now joyous adventurer friend.

"This is the beast," he declared.

"Right.'' Hooligan positively launched himself at the chart almost as though cerebral cogitations were a physical labour; the only sort he knew. Scanning the fascinating source of information, he was deeply disappointed on finding that the thing was all water with just skinny margins of land around the edges.

"Fuck!'' The Admiral was baffled. ''Where's Scotland." It was an accusation of incompetence. Teach indicated that country and took a large draught of rum in preparation for what was coming.

"And Americy. Show me your house." Jabbing at Scotland again in order to reinforce his message the mentor then stepped around to the other end of the chart where he picked out Boston with a pair of compasses. "America." He then stood silent and watched gleefully his friend's awakening to the vast wastes of the North Atlantic which lay between the two. The Irishman's deflation was clearly visible even in his posture.

"Jasus, holy suffering Christ an' all the saints," he bawled "It's round the other fookin soide, you bloody eedjit?"

"It gets worse," laughed the captain. "We are here." Teach put his index finger on the Firth of Tay, "on Scotland's east coast. We have England, Scotland, Ireland and Wales, as well as the North Atlantic between us and home and we have the whole British Navy out lookin' for us."

Lliam Hooligan, student of marine science was stunned. He had nurtured the idea that a body was seldom out of sight of land when at sea, having nothing but his recent excursion to France to go by.

"A couple of months, you say?" His devil-may-care mood fast receding into the background. "And just that cum-piss ting to get us there?"

"Ships do the crossing every day, my son, so don't be afraid, cos your old mammy here will be holding yer wee hand. You'd be taking them penniless to a country that is foreign to them, of course." Teach had become thoughtful.

"Have you any idea what it would cost to feed four hundred people for three months, or maybe more?"

"NO! And I don't give a toss. Feed them we will; by hookety crookety. The sea is full o' fish.

"And when we get there?"

Hooligan quoted Macbeth. 'Oh, ye of little faith.' He laughed as he threw an arm around his friend's shoulders.

"You boys need sojers, don't ye, cattle herders, spinners, fishermen, I've got hundreds of them? These people are as tough as ma granma's tits. Skinny or not." Lliam deposited his sticky mug well away from the treasured chart and studied the problem with his single eye close to the colourful surface.

"Will it be nort or sout we go?" he asked, looking askance at the coasts of Scotland which were pitted and torn in a way which other lands were not.

"It's six of one and half a dozen of the other." Teach drew his finger southward, never quite touching the surface of the chart, from the Firth of Tay to the twenty-mile-wide narrows of the Strait of Dover, the trickle of ocean between England and Normandy.

"If the Brits were to recognise us here, we would have no option but to turn and run," he observed gloomily, "there being no room to manoeuvre. If we go north… look at this, Lliam," he jabbed an accusing digit at the freezing Orkney Islands well north of Scotland. "There will be no English ships up here to contend with, but the seas are as bad as any in the world, and I have never sailed them, nor have our Captains. More ships have been lost to this archipelago," he lumped the Shetland Isles and Orkney together in his condemnation, "than to any other. Also, such a passage would take a terrible toll on our crews and our passengers; ill as we are."

"You're not askin' *me* for a decision here I hope, Captain Teach," Lliam mocked. "Sailing this boat is *your* business my boy, but if it *was* moi bollox, it would be sout, widout a shadow of a doubt. Sout witout a shadow o doubt.'' Hooligan repeated himself like a child well pleased with his own immensely clever poetry.

ing453

"And why is that?" Teach was not the least bit miffed at the implied encroachment on his sphere of expertise by his ship-owning friend.

"You're forgettin' one ting, Captain. At the bottom of this boat…"

"Ship."

"At the bottom of this ship; we've got them lovely boys whose daddies own the British Navy. If the buggers so much as sneeze in our…"

"Lliam Hooligan, I bloody love you." Martin's delight was immeasurable.

"South, it is. We go south." Hooligan had seldom seen Teach smile quite so broadly.

"Boatswain." The boatswain was taking a break from his rescue work; sitting on the floor eating chops, and working with a marlinspike on a lanyard, which was part and parcel of the most recently completed flag of the thirteen states and had just completed a Flemish Eye.

"Sir?" he said, looking up with a tired expression.

"Message to all ships. 'South to Nantes. Bound for boston.'"

With every ten degrees of latitude crossed as Fleet Hooligan charged southward, the weather improved, and with it, the condition of the starvelings. The flotilla had barely reached the Wash; that great bight in England's side, but what Scots began to appear on her decks, scrubbed raw, draped in freshly washed and immaculate tartan, with their long, red hair combed out and shining in the sunlight. Aboard *Liberty*, the highland menfolk were well-pleased to discover that the ship carried enormous power in her guns, and that they were to be issued small arms which were abundant, the proviso being that any man taking up the arms was of course, expected to protect the ship, just as the ship protected him and his family. Below decks, the fascinated clansmen watched the gunners practising until they could barely stand, loading and aiming their cannon, while others gawped at the naval cutlass drills which proceeded at great risks to themselves, passing seamen, wild children and excited maidens, until the weapon became an extension of American arms. The clansmen clearly longed to regain their strength so that they too, could become proficient with every weapon aboard the ship, and their poor weakened bodies would make imperfect approximations of the fighters' thrusts and cuts as they watched in warlike fascination. Never again, they swore, would any man, Scottish, English or other, ever be permitted to hurt their families, as one had so recently done.

Then a sailor went overboard. One of the many wild Scottish children, leaping into the rigging in imitation of the seamen, closed his hand on fresh air instead of hemp and dropped thirty feet into the ocean. Peter Westcliffe, a native of Long Island who happened to be climbing ten feet above where the lad was playing at the time, followed the miscreant in an instant, and the two were left struggling in the ocean by the flying hull. A boat was launched, even as the sails were being emptied and sea anchors dropped, a dozen men putting their lives at risk in the process and getting away from *Liberty*'s awful sides by the skin of their teeth, but at the cost of injuries to several men. Despite their wounds, those same men broke their backs at the oars, desperate to reach their friend of years, before he went under. Exhausted by holding up the coughing, spluttering, struggling child in the turbulent ocean, Peter Westcliffe was drowning by the time his shipmates reached him. Abandoning their oars, men leap overboard and grabbed the poor fellow. Semi-conscious, Peter was committed to holding the boy and would not let him go, making the task of getting him and the now half-drowned child into the prancing longboat all but impossible. Ill-prepared to allow his brother to die, Paul Westcliffe dropped over the side of the cutter, and clamped his hands over Peter's nose and mouth; Peter's grip relented and the child was ripped into the boat, followed a while later by his now unconscious saviour. Admiral Hooligan was seething. Once he was certain-sure that Peter Westcliffe would live, and Paulus Yohansensen's injured hand was not going to be amputated he left the anaesthetised youths' sides and went on deck where he ordered that every male child be instantly paraded before him. There was a heard of the little brutes and they all arrived, driven by their compliant yet concerned parents, fighting and yelling, and as wild as the devil.

"Shut yer gobs ya wee bastarts!" bawled the enraged Admiral so loudly that the order was heard on passing ships.

"Get in front of me, here," he raged, pointing at the space between himself and the forecastle.

"Now!" It took the tribe of fighting, screaming, racing frenzies three seconds to become a flock of sheep cornered by a bear.

"This is my ship," he roared; as though he were about to condemn them all to the mercies of the ocean, that had almost claimed one of their demented chums.

"What I say is law… One of you… eedjits has just been fer a swim." Instantly bored to distraction, the lads stared back at the creature. They were all well-aware of the fact. They had watched it happen. It was in the past. The Bauchan was wasting their time.

"See this hand?" Hooligan held out the blunt weapon towards his captivated audience, palm showing and taking a threatening step forward. The thing was bigger than a skillet.

"If I see any one of you God-cursed midgets with so much as one foot off the deck of this ship, I will skin your stinking arse with it. And don't go runnin' to your father tellin' tales neither, because I'll skin his arse, too. You see these?" Lliam deflected the gaze of the audience to three bandaged sailors behind him. "This is the price we've paid because o' you wee bastarts." Hooligan was now well into his stride, and he concluded his remarks with a gem of English prose,

"The next one of youse tae cross me will get his guts pulled out." That was it. The lesson was done, apart from an afterthought.

''You'll stay below for a week. If I see any one of you on this deck. I will throw you over the fuckin side. Get below. Bloddy 'NOW''''

Enormously pleased with his burgeoning teaching skills, the professor turned his back on the damned pygmies and went below to confront Westcliffe and shout at him too, at a range of four feet, on the matter of his foolish ways. Meanwhile the boys who had reacted like rabbits to Mother Superior's threats, were claiming that they had not been at all terrified by 'the *seonaidh*,' and bragged that their fathers could thrash the *troll* with just one hand, while he tossed himself off with the other.

Despite the captain's bold insistence that the fleet's new flag of the thirteen United States be flown at the masthead of all ships, the little flotilla negotiated the crowded waters of Dover Strait with nothing more threatening than a few strange looks from officers of Admiralty vessels, bristling with cannon, to whom the new flag and the names *Liberty, Boston, Liverpool* and *Justice* happily meant nothing at all. One week later, Admiral Lliam Hooligan's fleet entered the inland port of Nantes within a day of each other, in the fine weather of early autumn.

Admiral Hooligan and his men watched in satisfaction as the Scots disembarked in that strange new world to which he had brought them, all of them looking forward to standing on firm ground again which did not rise and fall beneath their feet, and curious about France and the French. As he watched them like a doting father, the generous adventurer was very much aware of feelings of comradeship and respect for his 'Gaels,' as he called them. During the voyage from the cold, hungry shores of the Tay to this warm, colourful, fruit bowl of French commerce, they had exhibited a resilience which, he concluded, would be found in only the noblest of people.

The feeble and dying humanity who, too weak to stand, had been lifted aboard his ships by strangers, were already on their feet, and not only taking care of themselves and their families, but were dispensing unending kindness to those who were still recovering, and to sailors who had suffered injuries or sickness as they went about their duties. They were also throwing their increasing energies into the working of the ship, no matter how unappetising some of the necessary but gruelling tasks happened to be.

The highlander's great sadness was still with them of course; and would remain for years to come, many of the families having lost those persons who were dearest to them in the terrible events of the evictions and during their route from their homeland; pursued doggedly as they were, by Monteith's murdering savages. It was the fashion in which these noble people contained that grief which marked them as a race apart. Their pain was a private thing, and not something to be put on vulgar display like washing on a bush, as certain others were wont to do. The pipes, he recalled, had lamented, as the flotilla; its new flags at half mast, had eased through the Firth of Tay towards the North Sea, for the Gaels were leaving behind them, unburied, the gashed and burned bodies of fathers, mothers, brothers and sisters. They were parting forever from their crofts and glens, their mountains and lochs, and the cattle which had been their life. Everything, in fact, which they had ever known and loved.

In those first days, their newly dead lay in dignified repose on the deck, and men made long detours around them speaking in whispers as they passed. The cold, white bodies of several tiny children had been carried aboard the ships by distraught parents who could not so much as contemplate parting so soon from their tiny blessings and in those first hours and days more of the very young and the very old had succumbed. The unending hunger, the rigours of the march, and the brutalities they had suffered, had been too much for them to bear.

At the outset, the sailmakers had been kept busy sewing canvas shrouds for these unfortunates as a matter of course, whilst the row of bodies lying on the deck grew longer daily aboard four of the five ships. The *Bird* being the exception having only a dozen or so Scots on her decks. Compounding the grief of the bereaved; whatever little canvas that could be allotted to the task was soon used up, and thereafter the dear-departed lay for all to see with just a bit of tartan to hide their poor white faces. The burials had been held-over until the fleet was well offshore, and there, on the North Sea; out of sight of Scotland, but within sight of each other, the ships hove-to, and on each of them there were unashamed tears of grief, as the bodies were committed to the deep, sliding from beneath a single flag. At the Admiral's insistence, it was a flag composed of stars and stripes, thirteen of each, which had to make do for all. To Hooligan's way of thinking, Scotland had denied his Gaels the right to life and to the security that should be taken for granted within the walls of a man's home. He would not employ for such a task, the flag of the country that had so betrayed them.

The nets were constantly full of people at that time, as he recalled, suffering from liquid bowels due to eating grass, and the good food which the fleet had been able to provide them was no help at all, as it was too rich for their scalded stomachs. Only when the cooks thought to serve watery gruel and porridge instead, did the sick begin to recover their strength. Three days out of Perth and the number of deaths had become noticeably fewer. Within a week, they had thankfully ceased altogether.

As the fleet ran south for Nantes, the early-autumn weather had improved greatly, and the warm breeze and salt air combined to spread comfort among people who had known precious little of that commodity. The morale and the energy of the clansmen positively burgeoned then, so that the women were able to relieve the worn-out cooks in the constantly working galleys. The children played on the decks, and scots began to relieve exhausted sailors of their watches and the less-strenuous tasks involved in navigating a giant merchantman through a congested seaway. He too had changed. A month earlier, and Hooligan would have been the first to disembark as the ship docked, running like a headless chicken to his well-remembered playpen, where the girls and the wine were delectable, and there he would have remained until the very moment that the last of his coins was spent or had been pilfered. That thought struck a chord as he recalled that his crews did not have a sou to bless themselves with, and after all that they had been through would be unable to sample the wonders of France. Hailing a cabin boy, he told the lad,

"Run quickly to all the ships and tell them, 'Captains to the *Liberty*. Now.'"

He had made a king's ransom in his sale of the cognac, but every penny of that was accounted for. He would need to make three times as much if he was to do more for his Gaels, than simply make them exchange one frozen shore for another. What was needed was a cargo that would sell in Boston for five times what he paid for it here. He had learned a hell of a lot from his first sally into the world of commerce and could not wait to repeat the experience.

"Martin!" he roared, cupping his hands to his mouth and leaning backwards in order to find the boyo, who was busy with his deck hands in the rigging, one hundred and fifty feet above the water. Even from where he stood, the Admiral could make out his foreshortened friend, rolling his eyes exaggeratedly, conveying the enquiry.

'What next you madman? Can't you see that I'm holdin' on by my teeth up here?'

"What the hell is it now, bog-trotter?" demanded Teach, as he exploded into the grand cabin, grinning like a hyena and tugging his forelock in mock servility.

"Some of us poor sailors have work to do."

"Sit on yer arse, shut yer gob and listen to your old mother for once in yer loife, sprat catcher," Hooligan met Teach's histrionics line for line, shoving an uncorked bottle of Bordeaux across the table.

"It's youse poor sailor boys that we're here to have the crack about," he announced tantalisingly putting his own bottle to his scarred lips as Longbottom, Belcher, Holdsworth and the recently promoted Rutland, attempted to come through the doors all at the same time. Each man blaming the others for the resulting melee and resorting to mild violence as a sure remedy.

"Come in boys, come in and welcome," Hooligan leapt to his feet, crushing the hand of each of his captains as the man extricated himself from the scuffle. He began with the serious stuff of the meeting as soon as the ruck was concluded, and everyone had a cigar, a bottle of wine, and a seat.

"Boys," he began, "our men are skint. The filty English robbed them bloind … as you know. The first ting we must do is to put that to roights, so that they can get legless and foind a decent roid in town, as is every Christian man's duty. And believe me; in dis town der are some very decent roids." This announcement met with great acclaim and lots of back-slapping and laughter, confirming the schemer's notion that he was on the right track.

"What I tawt was dis." Releasing his delectable wine for a moment he placed a very large leather bag in the centre of the table.

"This here is silver; help yourselves to one lump for each of your men; two for your boatswain, and tree for yer man himself. That should keep youse all in drink from now till we bugger off home." The mood metamorphosed in to one of quiet and genuine gratitude at this inexplicable, unheard-of generosity, and there was a rush to shake Hooligan's hand a second time despite the attendant discomfort for the man gripped like a carpenter's G clamp. Enormously encouraged by such an effusive response to such a nothing of a gesture, and keen to get on to the next item on his agenda, the Admiral had to bite his tongue for what seemed like a month or more, until the captains had counted out their largess amid much banter and laughter and guzzling of wine.

"Do you tink your boys would sail 'moi' ships to '*your*' place? Boston?" Hooligan asked at last; with the reticence of one who was asking them whether they would mind opening a vein.

"I want to take moi Gaels over there, and seein' as how you're goin' home now?" He left the sentence unfinished in his uncertainty. Captain Martin Teach, his long legs crossed in his first moment of genuine relaxation in an age leaned back luxuriously in his chair, responding.

"I believe that I can speak for the men of the *Bird* when I say that we would sail your ships full circle if you wished it, my child. Certainly, we would all be home in half the time if we abandoned you and sailed off in the *Bird*, but every man jack of us owes you his life, and we don't forget such details. We'll ferry them across the pond, no bother at all; for America's sake, as well as their own." Teach was setting the standard early, because although every man held his mad Irish saviour in the highest esteem the men of the *Bird* had been at sea for two years; some even longer now and were desperate to get home and see their people. It would take only a dribbling idiot like Gulley to remind everyone that this business could add a month to the crossing for everything to go belly up.

"I'd beat the tar outta any man who sayd diffrint," Holdsworth announced offhandedly, blowing a blue smoke ring which, from Lliam's perspective formed a halo around the giant's head transforming the black devil into an angel, and causing Lliam a moment of long-neglected religious superstition. Putting his bottle to his wide, purple lips, the Negro drank the remaining half pint of first-rate wine as though it were beer, belched long and loudly, then replacing the bottle with his cigar, blew not one but two concentric rings. There was no need for discussion.

"Tank you all, boys." The Irishman's quiet and unsophisticated gratitude was the genuine article and pathetic to see.

"Boi the boi; while dat cash money is still on the table boys," the schemer went on, as though with an afterthought,

"I was just now a watching the kilties at the market out there, and they were 'lookin' but none was 'buyin' cos they's in the same boat as yous fellas. Grab some coin for your famblies. That would be a good ting to do, don't you tink? Give it to the wifey, so that the little ones get somethin' out of it. Sure, we don't want the old man pissin' it up the wall, atall atall." Much subdued; words being quite inappropriate in the presence of the generosity of this enigma of a man, the captains quietly counted out the handful or so of coins which they each estimated to be enough for their needs.

Right on time a posy of Hooligan's girls slipped through the double doors and hid the table beneath a truly wonderful array of French foods, just as the fast-developing diplomat had arranged, and his preparations for the next set of negotiations were underway. Men are at their most malleable when full of good food and wine, and this was the case when, in the afterglow of dinner, Admiral Hooligan announced that due solely to the forbearance of the captain and crew of the *Liberty*, he had been able to make a king's ransom in the trading of his cargo of cognac in London. With the proceeds of that venture, he wanted to take on a second cargo, one which would be greatly in demand in America, would assist the war effort immeasurably, and thereby provide funds to give the penniless Scots a good start in their new home. To this end, he declared, somewhat unsteady on his feet; that he would be most grateful if they could scour France itself, between drinks, and identify such objects as would sell hand over fist in their homeland. And would they be so kind as to bring back their ideas for discussion by the captains with Teach their elected leader making the final decisions as to what to buy, and how many of each. Additionally, as a small recognition of everything that he had put the men of the *Bird* through, since their brilliant performance in escaping their confinement, he would be selling the *Justice* on arrival on the American continent and the proceeds would be distributed equally between all of them not forgetting for a moment those who had given their lives to strike a blow at the filthy Brits or had died of the scurvy. The families of those men would receive two shares. Naturally, he would be purloining that ship's seven guns before getting rid of the thing, in order to bring the *Liberty*'s broadside back up to scratch.

It had also crossed his mind he declared, to auction off the 'soft English penises' to their ever-loving mummies and daddies who would pay whatever the admiral stipulated or see their little ones sold into slavery in north Afrika.

"But we'll build that bloody bridge once we've crossed the damn ting." Lastly, he ordered that only skeleton crews should remain aboard ship while in Nontees, sufficient to take them to sea, if the need arose, and that every man enjoy equal time ashore in this most pleasant of locations. At this point, he found the comfort of the rug to be unequalled anywhere, and the water's reflections dancing on the ceiling, utterly fascinating.

The Americans of course, already had a very good idea of what was needed at home and could have written a comprehensive list without stirring; it would be comprised of tools of every imaginable description; be they the finely worked instruments of the surgeon or the more robust objects required by the blacksmith, and every trade and profession in between, carpenter, bricklayer, wheelwright, dentist, gunsmith, seamstress, cooper cook and a hundred others. Second on the list would be military equipment in all its inglorious profusion. Their real difficulty of course, lay in discovering the whereabouts of the manufacturers of these myriad items. This seemingly insurmountable problem was resolved by the French-speaking members of the crew, who had only to put the word about, that there was business to be done by those who could deliver the goods to the *Liberty* in Nantes, at the right price and within a very limited time.

Within a week, the ships had settled almost a yard deeper with hundreds of tons of cannon, mortars, lead, salt, tools of every possible description and 'as they weighed nothing at all;' the cabins were crammed with the dress patterns, cloth and the little fashion dolls which would assure the women of America that they were dressed in the most recent of styles as worn in Paris itself.

CHAPTER

Hooligan and Holdsworth were stacking the last of one hundred and eighteen inordinatelyexpensive sets of surgeons' instruments safely into the crockery cupboards of the great cabin of the *Liberty* when there came a gentle tapping at the open doors, and Holdsworth emerged from the gloom to find himself pierced by the glittering scrutiny of an officer of French cavalry.

"Good morning gentlemen. I do hope that I have not contravened your naval traditions by coming aboard your vessel unannounced," the visitor began, doing so in remarkably good English.

"The likes to you, fella. How didya get on dis here ship? demanded Holdsworth, glancing at the door to discover if the man was accompanied by a sailor. He was not.

"Naturally your guards performed their duties well," the quick-thinking stranger replied diplomatically, not wanting anyone to be flogged unnecessarily.

"I was able to assure them that I came in peace."

"'Peace' is it? Wit a blody great canon and dat knoife." Hooligan, emerged from the cupboard like a grizzly from hibernation, making a great show of locking the doors on his valuables in case the frog stole anything. The Irishman glowered at the frog's resplendent uniform which along with the rest of the snail-eater's appearance, made himself feel like a tramp again. He was dying of the dry horrors and working bent over in that cupboard had destroyed his poor head.

"Allow me to introduce myself, gentlemen," said the cavalryman, irked but otherwise unconcerned by this typical English incivility.

"I am Armand Sartine, of the Volontaires Etrangers de la Marine."

"Come again." Lliam Hooligan, having been demoted to beggar and tramp in self-comparison with the cavalryman, was both of those things once again as he eyed the man's perfect physique and colourful, immaculate uniform, his smooth-shaven skin, browned by the sun, his waxed moustaches and flowing locks, and he loathed the frog in spades. Holdsworth poured the wine and hoped that Armand Sartine did not understand the depth of Hooligan's insults. Even if he did not; the Irish battler's feelings were written in his face for the visitor to see.

'Green boots; who ever heard of a man wit ''green boots?'' Red pants and a tight blue jacket to make his girly shoulders look woide, and his belly tin. Sure, Oi'm destroyed by it all. And he has a spare jacket hanging there, wit fur round the edges, and a sword that's bent. What use is a sword that's bent?'

"I'm Capn Holdsworth o' du Boston," said the temporarily elevated boatswain with a large helping of pride, and thrust out his hand, thereby bringing the short but poisonous hiatus to an end. "And this genman, is Lliam Hooligan. This is his ship."

"Mister 'ooligan." Armand Sartine, who had returned Holdsworth's show of civility and open hand with every indication of easy acceptance and friendship, stared balefully into Hooligan's single eye and pointedly refrained from any gesture of amity, no matter how small. The lack spoke volumes.

"It is *you* that I have been sent to *collect*." Sartine was capable of exquisite diplomacy, even in English, but his choice of words and the manner of their utterance, made Hooligan feel like a hamper full of shitty laundry. As was the speaker's intention, naturally.

"Oh, it's *collect* me, is it? slurred the laundry querulously, his volume increasing noticeably;

"And just who is it that has sent *you* to collect *me*?"

"Why, the Leader of the Representatives of the United States of America to the Government of His Majesty Louis the Sixteenth of France; Mister Benjamin Franklin." Sartine thoroughly enjoyed the mystification that this proclamation caused on the butcher's block countenance of this soft penis. He drank it in as he would a good wine, then announced in a mocking tone,

"*You* may know him as, 'Mister Ben.' The honourable gentleman would be delighted also to renew his acquaintance with Captain Teach." It was not lost on the drunk that whereas *he* was to be *collected*, the anticipated company of Martin Teach was a *delight*. Hooligan had spent some of his most fascinating, enjoyable and informative hours in the company of Benjamin Franklin and would do anything for the man, but his skull was crushing him as was the throbbing drum which had migrated from the top of his head to a spot just behind his eye, hence the nature of his response was utterly predictable.

"And what if Oi'm not in the mood to be, *collected*?" The word 'collected' was heavily accented with insult. Sartine positively bristled with anticipation as he perceived an end to his unusual and detestable role of 'peace at any price' diplomacy, which the charming Mister Franklin had begged of him.

"Then I shall ave to 'insist,' monsieur," he declared gleefully. Armand Sartine had risen from the very dust in the streets of Marseille to his present exalted position, because of his iron-hard disposition, his fast fists, and his genius with the knife and the sword. He could drag this piece of corruption out of here by its misshapen nostril if he wished. 'What possible business,' he wondered, 'could the knowledgeable and intelligent Franklin, representative of a great new nation, have with this… mole?' Just as Sartine hoped it would; the Irishman's dirty paw found the hilt of his scabbard and in that same instant, the cavalryman snatched a brass-edged rule from the map-table and rapped the impertinent fool's knuckles. Hooligan bellowed at the sudden horrible pain and went stamping around the cabin, shaking his tortured hand and blowing on the raised weal that was getting bigger by the moment.

"Jasus!" He wailed. "Oi wasn't going to pull the damn ting." Sartine tossed the straightedge back onto the table and crooking his little finger; 'the ultimate insult;' made a metronome of it under what was once the Irishman's nose.

"We must not touch a sword which we do not intend to use, nor should we take the name of the Lord in vain, Mister 'ooligan," he declared, enunciating the lecture in time with his finger's reprimand.

"Your coach is waiting."

"How long will you be gone?" asked Holdsworth of both men; throwing oil on the water and hoping that "ooligan' would take the hint, while thrusting flutes of champagne at them. He was incredulous that the clever old man whom he had known as Mister Ben, was in truth, an important member of his new nation's government on what was clearly a mission of secrecy in which he, Freedman Holdsworth, a black man, had played his small part, albeit unwittingly.

"Mister Franklin and his associates are awaiting this one and Captain Martin Teach at Chateaubriant. It is not far. One night; maybe two." The soldier accompanied his answer with a Gallic shrug, which implied; 'What's the difference?' Unfortunately, the delightful Martin Teach was ashore and could not be found.

When the English build a castle, they invariably incorporate the purpose for which it is intended in its design. War. The result as often as not is a pile of inconceivable ugliness, strong, useful and fit for purpose, but sinfully unappealing, nevertheless. The Europeans on the other hand, the French, the Germans and the Italians, build just as strongly, if not more so, then they make the thing beautiful. The towers of Chateaubriant had exchanged battlements for tall conical hats, beneath which, smiling eyes had replaced arrow slits. The utilitarian boredom of the grey British wall was replaced by many a dip, curve and decorative architectural device, so that the overall relationship between breadth and height, when observed from any vantage point whatsoever, made a glorious wedding cake of 'her.' All such beauty being feminine, naturally.

"Congratulations Mister Hooligan, your heroic actions have proven you to be a loyal citizen of the United States of America, and I am at liberty to declare the matter which caused me to bring you out of your way." Franklin was delighted to put behind him the trial by fire of leading Hooligan through a declaration of loyalty to the new United States.

With the rest of his delegation looking on; every member mentally ticking off every statement; crossing every 'T,' and dotting every 'I', Franklin got straight down to business. He explained to the tramp turned ship owner, in the simplest of terms, that they; 'the delegation,' had watched his short, profitable and wonderfully promising career with growing interest. The fashion in which he had closed the trap on the British Captain Plumly-Horton had been inspired, and his dealings with Carstairs of evil memory and the other captives; firm and resolute; and not one whit short of what was expected of an American officer.

"Sure, oi had no idea oi was so foockin' clever," the one so addressed chortled. It was an observation which made Franklin pray devoutly, that the chapel enjoyed the provision of one of his recent inventions; the 'lightning rod.' To clothe the *Bird*'s suffering seamen at his own expense had been an act of unequalled generosity; munificence of a kind which the delegation hoped would flourish within the hearts of their new nation.

"And how in the name of Beezlybubzy do yous fellas know all this shit?" the model citizen enquired. Not liking one bit the thought that they had someone who was following along at his arse watching every damn thing that he did.

"Please put your mind at rest friend," said Laurens, "this is war, and we have informants everywhere. You damn near killed our man watching the *Battleaxe* when you sank her."

"We have a man spyin on the *Battleaxe*?" The idea filled Lliam with conspiratorial glee. 'He had thrown a grenade in to Whitehall with his Plumly-Horton escapade,' noted Burns, 'and sunk one hundred and sixty guns; disabling many more as he escaped down the Thames.' In short, Lliam Shaun Hooligan was the very man the delegation required; and ideally placed for a task of monumental importance to the advancement of the war effort.

"You have very sensibly filled the *Liberty*, how I applaud that name, with materials required in America showing the same good judgement as you displayed with your cargo of cognac. We too, have been busy, Mister Hooligan," Franklin included his collaborators with a gallic gesture which had become a physical addition to his vocabulary.

"We have obtained gifts from the French Government to the value of tens of millions of pounds, in the shape of all possible materials required to fight the British Army to a standstill."

"And oi have four more ships sittin' here in Nantes about to cross the watter," intruded the New American, shipowner, merchant and philanthropist.

"Sure, I'll carry your stuff boys, and no charge," the patriot had anticipated the delegation's request.

"Enormously generous as that offer is; regrettably, we cannot accept it," countered Franklin.

"Without payment, you will have nothing to feed and pay your sailors, or to repair your ships and a myriad of other expenses. You must accept the going rate, and a fine rate it is. In the course of the years to come, we will need you, and men like you, to undertake many a dangerous voyage on behalf of our nation, and if we reward you suitably on each occasion, we know that you won't refuse us."

"Done," said Lliam, with a simplicity from which the members of the delegation knew they would have to protect their protégé.

Hooligan was preparing for bed that evening by dropping his clothes on the treacherously shiny parquet floor, in the impossible splendour of his quarters, when there was a thump at his door and the now drunk delegation piled into his room and headed straight for the wine cabinets.

"Do yous buggers never sleep?" he bleated, tired after the long ride and the endless talking. He continued to undress and crawled naked into the heavenly bed, hoping that the fools would get the hint.

"Good news, Mister Hooligan. Great news, in fact," chortled Adams, spilling champagne everywhere he turned.

"Captain Hopkins has struck again." Laurens had abandoned the frosty dignity of his daytime persona and was fit to burst.

"It has been a marvellous week for our naval men," bawled Burns, handing the horizontal Hooligan a flute of champagne, and disappearing into a sofa which was upholstered in the same colour as his coat, so that thereafter his interlocutors found themselves addressing a disembodied head.

"Indeed, it has," chirped Fieldsend, stealing Burns' thunder, "one of our Captains; chap by the name of…"

"Hopkins," bawled Franklin. "Not only battered a couple of English sixty-gunners but…"

"Made them surrender, then sailed them into Bordeaux as prizes. Which means, that alongside your own endeavours Mister Hooligan, we have taken six of their battle ships out of contention and increased our fleet by two in the matter of a week or so." The door opened during this unwarranted display of glee and into Lliam's bedroom swept four beautiful and supremely elegant women, all a-twitter and smiles and fluttering fans. Lliam hid beneath his sheets. Thinking that he had better not postpone his most pressing business longer, Franklin came quickly to his favourite's side and deposited his expansive backside on the bed, causing it, and its occupant, to list considerably to starboard.

"Now, Mister Hooligan," he said portentously, addressing his remarks to the sheet which covered the Irishman's shame,

"I have here several documents of immeasurable importance to the progress of the war." He held a sealed package at Hooligan's line of sight, only to have it snatched rudely from his hand.

"There are five. Each is an inventory. They are for the *Liverpool*, the *Boston*, the *Bird*, the *Justice*, and even one for the *Liberty*. Now listen most carefully, Mister Hooligan. You must check with the greatest care that everything listed here actually comes aboard your ships and stays there till you tie up in Boston. If you sign the merchant's docket for five thousand muskets and you receive only four thousand…" He let the thought hang in the air.

"Roight," said Lliam.

"No sir," said Franklin with an edge.

"We of the delegation are trusting you, an American citizen, with millions of pounds worth of materials that are needed desperately by men who are bleeding and dying in pursuit of our freedom." The chosen one sat up at that and listened attentively, despite the shrieking of the females and the suggestive grumblings of the men.

"If you should accept sand for gunpowder, second-rate muskets without flints, string for slow match and rags concealed within bales of supposed broadcloth, you will have failed the union badly. We charge you. Put your best men to the task of inspecting everything that we send you. 'In detail.' Is that understood?"

"It is Benjamin, honest." Hooligan was by this point deeply concerned yet elated by the confidence that the universally admired polymath was showing in him. 'Millions of pounds? He didn't have a clue what just one million was, but it sounded like a boat load of coin.' He stuffed the package beneath his ever so sweetly scented pillow, drew the covers over his head and closed his eye, but soon gave up all thoughts of sleep due to the riotous celebrations.

Within the hour, he was mounted on one of Sartine's wonderful stallions, with his documents under his shirt, and was trotting westward at the head of a squadron of French cavalry.

In varying states of insobriety, the crew of the *Bird* were gathered on the deck of the *Liberty*; some were draped over the sides, feeding the fish; others lay spread-eagled on the planks, snoring loudly, while still others were heard to declare their deep and abiding love for their shipmate, while clinging to inanimate objects which in no way resembled an American sailor. The similarly wine-affected Captains and boatswains of Hooligan's five vessels stumbled around on the poop deck, miserable as recently castrated bulls. After much mumbling, drooling and nodding of heads Teach stepped forward, and a little sideways; he cleared his throat, and from the centre of the deck, spat over the side with commendable range and accuracy.

"Men," he began, addressing the assemblage of horizontal, recumbent and tortured humanity, many of whom were now praying fervently for death,

"Your nation has chosen *you* to signic-ficant oppration, quipment to our soldiers athome." Teach stumbled suddenly to the side and vomited into the wind with predictable consequences.

"You will member," he claimed preposterously on his return clinging for support to the woodwork and wiping his soiled face with his forearm. Becoming unbalanced; the leader of men tipped forward; see-sawed precariously atop the rails and was about to fall painfully onto his nearest audience members ten feet below, when he was rescued by the seat of his pants; Holdsworth being conveniently close by; and dragging him back.

''Member Mishter Benny," the leader of men commanded obliquely, when once again in an upright posture, "Good old. Sail wiv suffered with us, uncom----plaining, ----some o youssons o' bischis." The crew were prepared to excuse this unfortunate lapse; their beloved Captain not being a seasoned drinker, as were they.

"Turns out. Turns out, the merschant, wasn't old Benny a merchant, anhe washn't Misher Ben, goodolbenny.

By this point in his oratory Teach had the undivided attention of a good one-fifth of his audience which in the circumstances was utterly astonishing.

"Mishter fact wash in Frank. Mishter Frank Benja…, the leader of our nation's govmint of Franche, our great aa..."

"Gaaaawd." On the deck below, Gulley vomited copiously, noisily and painfully in the face of Taylor who was lying unconscious, starfish-like on the deck, breathing through his mouth. At this stage, the 'brass' staggered away with Teach in their arms, confined everyone to their ships till nightfall and imposed a ship-wide liquor ban other than in the hallowed precincts of the grand cabin of course; where, it was generally accepted that men could imbibe sensibly, and not behave like pigs at the trough.

It is invariably the case in large organisations such as an army, a navy and even the crew of a ship, that within its ranks are to be found talents, experience, knowledge and abilities in a whole world of human endeavours, and such was the case with the crew of the *Bird*. With little or no direction from their well-meaning but inexperienced officers, the men organised themselves, once sober, so that every man was doing what he knew best in the task of ensuring that America received every item that the French government had so very generously paid for. Each of the five vessels was served by several 'goods inwards' functionaries, two armourers, one jeweller, 'for the inspection of medical instruments, chronometers and other technical bits of kit required by the corps of engineers,' and a gang of men who, having no particular skills applicable to the task at hand, took it upon themselves to try on every pair of boots, which they tested by jumping on top of a single pebble in them, in order to discover if the soles were suitably robust for soldiers who might march a thousand miles before this war was over. Muskets and gunpowder were tested in unison by emptying each barrel of powder into a second barrel and firing off a shot from every shovel-full; each time with a different musket. Every bale of cloth was broken open and spread across the decks, carefully inspected, then re-folded, squashed tight by the combined weight of six crewmen, and bound up once again. A whole encampment of tents was laboriously erected, and the poles, pegs and lanyards checked for numbers and quality, and so it went for six full, exhausting and satisfying days, until at last, every item on each of the manifests was confirmed safely aboard, accurate in volume or weight, perfect in operation, and complete in every way.

Those persons who thought to swindle the poor ignorant sailors with fakes and 'shoddy' had their rubbish burned before their eyes and were then tossed into the harbour in order to teach them their manners. On the morning of departure for Boston, a large group of seadogs had come together in the grand cabin of the *Liverpool*. Present were every man who could boast considerable experience, either as Captain or boatswain of a sea-going vessel. There being insufficient maps available they had formed tight little groups at the tables while two others had to resort to the deck and were referring to the charts as Lliam Hooligan was speaking. As the gigantic toddler was the undisputed owner of four of the vessels and the very best man ever to set foot on a ship, the congregation were happy to wink at this break with protocol. The real work would come when their captain had the helm.

"Thank you, Mister Hooligan," said Teach at last, when the seductive charms of being listened to no matter what you said, eventually palled for the big man.

"Gentlemen, we have only a couple of hours before the tide, so don't make me repeat myself. Our cargoes, as you will have gathered, are of immense value and of dire necessity to our armies. We must get safely to Boston, and to that end as Mister Hooligan mentioned, we will have to forgo the trade-winds and avoid the sea lanes, because they will be crawling with Brits who would be overjoyed to take us back to London. We all know what captivity is like, so; from here in Nantes, the *Liverpool*, the *Boston*, the *Bird*, and the *Justice*, will travel west southwest till they skirt Spain, then head due south to Portugal and Lisbon in convoy.

"Then we go south to Madeira," the captain stabbed a finger at the spoonful of soil which lay a thousand miles west of the North African country of Morocco.

"Hopefully we will then get turtles, fresh fish, fruit, and certainly plenty of wine. Down here, we should be well out of the range of the British squadrons who, it stands to reason, will be disrupting our trade with Europe, also as you will see from your charts, we will then be on the same latitudes as Spanish Florida, well to the south hopefully of the Brits once again. Having crossed the pond we will put in at the first American-held port and make plans according to the state of the war as we find it.

The *Liberty* will not be with you; she will return to England, where Mister Hooligan has family business, then join you in Madeira. Until that time, you will have only stern chasers for protection," Teach recognised Hooligan, "for which we are grateful Lliam, while the *Justice* carries seven guns. In the absence of the *Liberty*, she is your best protection; stay in sight of her, where possible. Just one more thing. You all have prisoners below decks who are worth their weight in gold. Don't hesitate to buy clear passage by showing them to the enemy. None of us wants to spend another day in the bilges. Bring the little sods up for fresh air now and then and feed them properly. There is no need for us to do to them what they did to us." With that, the meeting broke up, and lunch was served with omelettes and coffee, crusty bread and golden butter in vast quantities.

It was not until an hour or so after the little flotilla entered the Atlantic proper that two of Sartine's dispatch riders rode into the docks on horses that were all but finished. They carried the news that Boston was full to the brim with English and Hessians.

CHAPTER 26: Blood Is Thicker Than Water

Within hours of Plumly-Horton's screaming outrage of embarrassment on London's Iron Bridge, the broadsheets of that city were trumpeting the story to the heavens, for on the faint chance that the news hounds might miss the event, the perpetrator had barked the salient points at several establishments as he rushed back to his ship. Within two days of the Admiralty's fall from grace every broadsheet in the Home Counties carried tales of ships which had been misplaced, and nautical calamities such as the theft of a certain Captain's trousers. Within a week, the story had reached its port of origin where cartoons bearing a very distinct likeness to Lord Michael Astor viewed in profile, were to be bought, with the naked lord bent over a bath in which reclined a naked lady.

"Are you sitting on it?" he asked. Through a window in the background could be seen the *Glorious*, sailing away under an oversized American flag. One of the famous, or more truthfully, 'infamous' London hacks had lamented at length on how a big-wig and captain of the Admiralty ship *Justice*, had contrived to lose his trousers in public and; by the by, had lost his ship, and his crew of half a hundred young good-for-nothing lordlings to boot; not, it had to be said, to a noble and chivalrous enemy, perfumed, powdered and articulate as the navy gangs tend to be, but to a motley crew of 'Americans' of all people. Civilians at that. It was widely known, even in Admiralty circles, that the poor colonials owned no navy and manned *both* of their warships-come-oyster boats, with men who could neither read nor write nor cipher. There were those writers, satirists and cartoonists, who had long memories and possibly an axe or two to grind, and these kind souls recalled the first occasion on which Plumly-Horton had lost a ship. Incredibly, he had lost his crew on that occasion also. Caricatures were soon published of the good Captain with his many chins his slow eye and ample belly to the fore, leading his officer cadre homeward through the snows of Canada, while in the background, his last surviving crewman roasted over a Blackfoot fire.

Incandescent with anger at the damage done to the Navy's reputation, and the mockery heaped upon the service; and worse still, upon himself, by the doings of the vainglorious Captain Plumly-Horton, the Lord Lieutenant of the Navy, raged at his appalled underlings for almost a quarter of an hour. The usually sanguine old man had good reason for his pique. Every broadsheet in the country carried the story of how a handful of American prisoners of war had broken the accepted conventions of modern hostilities and exhibited the utter gall of escaping from lawful captivity in the middle of England. Not only that; the unlettered had destroyed a shipyard in which, on that very evening, He personally, and the Prime Minister of England himself, the Honourable Fredrick North, were being wined and dined by the infamous Lords Astor, filthy slave-traders both. Incredibly, a coterie of Lords of the Admiralty; Cornwallis; Field Marshal of land forces in the Americas, and a gaggle of generals, were all aboard the ship as she was being stolen from under them.

'Naturally enough,' the broadsheets hollered, 'the Admiralty were not about to take this slap in the face in their normally recumbent posture and sent their very best man in pursuit of the naughty colonials, only to have that worthy; one Bartholomew Plumly-Horton, his crew, and his ship, all captured in ignominious defeat by the barefoot illiterate unwashed squirrel shooters.'

'N.B.' the story chortled. 'The captured crew were the wonderfully well-educated naval officers of tomorrow; being to a man, the sons of high-ranking Admiralty personages.

It went on. ''Despite every ship of the British Navy, the most powerful military force ever to exist, now searching manically for the FIVE (5) ships; purloined by the American farmers, bakers, street sweepers AND it is believed, 'buffalo hunters,' only a week or three later, the twenty-gun leader of this wonderfully capable flotilla sailed boldly up the Thames to The Iron Bridge, where it sat unmolested at anchor for a couple of hours in that sea of faeces, according to the most reliable of sources, while its giant, one-eyed Argonaut tethered the forgetful, and semi naked, Plumly-Horton like a dog to that symbol of Britain's genius.'' The Lord High Admiral had wiped his brow of cold sweat at this point, tossed off a flute of champagne, and continued with his reading of what was old news to every man present.

"Escape; Mark Two," the apoplectic one enunciated.

'Clearly, the dog skinners and bakers were feathers for every wind which blew, and one particularly advantageous gust must have blown them purely by chance, into a port in France where they availed themselves of a cargo of cognac, which, by the by, they had time to sell *lock, stock and barrels,* as they returned to sea after their day trip to town. London town.

Coming across half of the British Navy reclining in holiday mode, they simply could not refrain from sinking the sixty-gun *Intrepid* at Greenwich, and the one hundred-gun *Battleaxe*, kindly mauling *Revenge* and *Serpent* as they were about it. Having several strings to their bow, the naughty American skirmishers also shot the coach and horses out from under Captain Goldsmith of the *Battleaxe*, causing him to drive into the river and drown in the diarrhoea for which that waterway is famous.' The aspect of the disgusting publication, which the old man did 'not' bring to the attention of his listeners, was the caricature which accompanied the verbiage. The obscenity was a large line-drawing of himself seated in his bath with his nose lodged in the arse crack of the naked Plumly-Horton, who was bent double, searching the murky depths. The caption read, "I've found it. Oh! Sorry, sir."

"How was it possible," he ranted, in the faint hope that if he were to repeat himself, these limp-wristed, aristocratic sodomites who blighted his life, might take action independent of himself, "for a hundred New Haven plebs being held in the middle of England, to escape from, burn down, and utterly destroy one of the largest ship-building facilities in the country; then make off with three brand new vessels; in addition to their own; cheating the hangman at Bristol of his salary by a whisker? How is that possible?" Pausing for breath in the stunned silence which accompanied version two of his tirade, the great one continued,

"One of which ships, gentlemen, is a twenty-gun behemoth, capable of wreaking havoc among the thousands of our unarmed merchantmen around the globe. Which! Which, I say, at the time of its disappearance, sat in a dry dock of all things, and; and I say; was hosting the Prime Minister and a hundred of his close friends, to dinner, alfresco on her decks. How? I say how, did they do that, if you please? Then. Then I say, they thrashed the evil genius Plumly-Horton when he attacked them, 'contrary to orders, by the by,' stole 'his' ship in addition; making five in all and killed or captured the cretin's crew; all of them the sons of England's finest naval personages. Then they had the gall, the gall I say, to navigate the Thames. The Thames, gentlemen, as far as it is possible, and tie a half-naked, self-obsessed madman, wearing the jacket of an English naval officer, to a Bridge. A bridge of all things, and not content with all of that; destroyed four Admiralty vessels as they returned to the sea. Without suffering any real damage to their ship, apparently." The last remark was an afterthought. The supreme commander was not a happy man.

"I want that Plumly imbecile court-martialled," he concluded. "I want him persecuted to the… prosecuted to the full extent of the law," and sank into his plush scarlet chair; quite spent.

"And" he was on his feet again, "I want this matter investigated thoroughly. Thoroughly, I say."

The members of the review board in the court-martial of the now infamous Bartholomew Plumly-Horton came together initially, and by mutual agreement, at the sublime, Savoy Hotel in London. 'After all, if one was going up to town, one may as well make the stay an enjoyable and comfortable one.' The board was composed of five of the Admiralty's most senior officers; all of whom happened to be acquainted with the events surrounding the previous occasion on which the solipsist in question had misplaced a ship. Three of these exalted personages, had served on the board which examined the man on that earlier occasion, and they still trembled at the memory of the murderous, bloody-minded, sanctimonious gall of the swine in sacrificing every member of his crew, in order to preserve his officer cadre. In which endeavour, the loon had been successful, every one of the commissioned officers serving on that ill-fated voyage having returned safely to England. Rumours still abounded however, of cannibalism, and the selling of innocent crewmen as slaves or food to the tribesmen of the Inuit, Blackfoot and Crow persuasion in exchange for furs and guidance across the limitless wastelands of snow and unbearable cold that was Canada.

The Presiding Officer, one Admiral Lord Beattie of Devon, was to be assisted in his inquiries by the Commanders Tennyson and Edmonds, and the Rear Admirals Goforth and Carstairs. Without exception, these gentlemen were Lords of the land, each with a seat in the House of Lords and more pertinently, each had a son or close relative aboard the ill-fated *Justice*, the second ship which Bartholomew Plumly-Horton had somehow contrived to lose. None, however, felt that this tenuous connection to the case in any way proscribed his involvement, for each considered himself to be of sufficiently robust character to resist any temptation to deal unfairly with the toadying imbecile. It was the accepted norm in these matters that the court-martial should take place as closely as possible to the root-cause of the inquiry, as this made available to the inquisitors, persons and places which might impinge on the case; on this occasion however, the colleagues chose Admiralty House, Whitehall, London, ostensibly because its acoustics were so very good, but in fact, because it was so close to Barratts, their club; because its rooms enjoyed the most sublime frescoes, and its Chippendale chairs were the very last word in comfort.

Quite naturally and correctly, it was considered bad-form for the members of any tribunal to discuss a case prior to questioning its subject in court, but on this occasion, the chosen ones were comrades who had given their lives to the service of the nation; had fought side by side at great cost to their health and were proud that their male heirs had found their example meritorious; to the extent that the sons had followed the fathers into the Senior Service. As a result of these tenuous justifications, rather more than the usual amount of champagne was consumed, tongues were loosened, and before long, rumour and innuendo had replaced fact, innuendo was replaced by gossip, and gossip by malicious out-and-out lies. It thus became common knowledge, that this odious Horton fellow had sacrificed their much-loved offspring to his limitless and ridiculously unrealistic ambitions. Clearly, he was not fit to captain a toy boat on the Serpentine. Sufficiently anaesthetised to cope with the delivery of justice, the five took their seats. Admiral Lord Beattie made eye contact with each of his friends, cleared his throat and articulated his absence of bias with his opening salvo,

"Wheel it in, Sergeant-at-Arms." For some thirty years, since the statute was enacted, it had been the right of any officer being interrogated, to be escorted into the lion's den by men of equal rank to himself. Only one had so opted. The rest had abjured on the grounds that, for what was a mere matter of ceremony, the escorts would be required to travel to London from far flung ports all over the country, wherever their ship was docked. For the second time, Bartholomew Plumly-Hardon exercised his right, and was escorted into the Rose Room by a brace of Captains of twenty years' service. For the sake of this ceremonial of thirty seconds duration, one had travelled to London from Glasgow and the other from Hull.

The escorts came to attention with a slight click of the heels, recognised the authority of the board with the hint of a bow, and left. Marooned on an imaginary island whose co-ordinates lay ten paces directly in front of the inquisitors' steely visage, the accused removed his hat, putting it under his arm and stood erect but at ease; much as though he had been invited to tea. He had the composure, it was noticed, and the filthy cheek, to remain silent, thereby requiring Admiral Beattie to introduce himself and the members of the board to Plumly-Horton, instead of the reverse. Beattie, much put out, then went on to outline the business of the inquiry. His opening remark was not encouraging for the sack of conceit standing in front of him.

"I perceive that you are in uniform today, Captain." Plumly-Horton's huge contempt was inviolate. The civilities dispensed with; Beattie began the questioning.

"Where is His Majesty's Ship, *Justice,* which you took to sea, sailing from Poole, on the first day of last month?"

"I do not know. She was crimina…"

"If you would limit yourself to simply answering my questions, we shall more rapidly get to the bottom of this shambles," Beattie observed dryly.

"Where are the forty-eight junior officers of this service, who formed the crew of the said, *Justice*?" As he put the question, Beattie could see in his mind's eye, his dear grandson Malcolm, accepting the sword of rank, from his very own hands, only a few months earlier.

"A handful died in battle. The remainder bar one, were to be held as prisoners of.

"Handful?" raged Goforth, whose eighteen-year-old son was aboard the *Justice.*

"They are young men. The nation's finest young men; not pastries; you idolatrous vagabond. I'll give you 'handful,' sir." Goforth's soul was blistered by Plumly-Horton's totally unsupportable, cavalier attitude, and crucified by the knowledge that his lovely son might be among the 'handful' of dead.

"Did you not make it your business to…?"

"I was rendered unconscious during the action. The crew surrendered and are now held prisoner aboard enemy vessels." Apoplectic with rage, Goforth was on his feet, having knocked his chair over backwards and spilled his champagne.

"Never interrupt me again, sir, if you value your skin," he screeched his fleshy face the colour of a black-dorris plum.

"Thank you, Commander," intoned Beattie gently, with real sympathy and understanding for the poor fellow's tragic state of mind. A steel-shod marine clattered forward and restored Goforth's chair and his wig, which had dropped to the floor, and received a smart buffet around the head for the clumsy fashion in which he performed the operation.

"Why?" It was Beattie again.

"Why what?" asked Plumly-Horton tartly, trampling once again on the very toes of insubordination.

"Why did they spread our men between the five ships?" mused Beattie almost to himself.

"Bargaining purposes, 'obviously.' If any one of the five ships is seriously threatened by one of ours, they can simply march their prisoners on-deck and we would be obliged to 'hang fire.'" The frowns behind the table grew more pronounced at the swine's criminal detachment from the fate of his crew, for whose welfare he was solely responsible. Beattie was already smarting from Horton's, 'obviously.'

"'All but one?' What does that imply?" he asked, trying manfully to contain his anger, and his agonising concern.

"It was not an implication; Plumly-Horton does not imply. It is a fact to which I can testify, as I saw it with my own eyes, that one of the crew was hung by the pirates." The man's tone dripped malice. This statement hushed the room as no other could. In the horrified silence which followed it, pigeons could be heard cooing in the gutters outside, and a stupefied marine breathed,

"Fawkin'ell," a lapse which would later cost a perfectly innocent soldier the flesh of his back. The massively ugly Louis XIV clock at the far end of the room, ticked away sixty-two seconds before Beattie could bring himself to ask the question.

"Whom did they hang, Captain?" Men held their breath and prayed.

"It was Carstairs."

The witness blurted the poisonous intelligence without so much as a shred of compassion for Rear Admiral Carstairs, the dead boy's father, who was sitting directly opposite him. In point-of-fact, the prisoner's tone was so laden with derision that the naked statement carried the venom of a curse, and implied that the event had been utterly predictable, due to the plainly observable lack of moral fibre in the deceased. Carstairs slumped in his seat as though shot in the chest, his arms fell to his sides, dragging his notes, inkwell and blotter, on to the floor. White as death and trembling visibly the Rear Admiral got to his feet, attended by Goforth, and pulling himself together to stand erect and proud, asked of Beattie,

"I wonder whether I might be excused, sir?" He received the nod and walked away. Rising as one, the board paused in the business at hand until their friend had left the room and the doors had been closed behind him. Drawing himself up to his full height, the tall Scot tugged at his uniform, picked up his gloves, and stepping down from the low platform on which the board were seated, approached the prisoner, coming to a halt inside the man's personal space.

"In forty years at sea," he declared, "I have never been so disgusted by the behaviour of a Captain of this service." With that, he struck the source of his discomfiture viciously across the face with his gloves; aggrieved that they were chamois and not chain mail, in desperate hope of a challenge. None was forthcoming, though Horton's fury was barely supportable, his slow eye almost doubling in size.

"So," Beattie resumed, "the people we are dealing with are out-and-out murderers, gentlemen." He addressed this remark to his remaining colleagues.

"The war with these 'Americans,' as they choose to call themselves, will clearly scrape the bottom of the barrel when push comes to shove.

"Not at all." The accused could barely wait to deliver his news.

"While I was uncon… indisposed, my crew saw fit to surrender. To surrender themselves, and my ship, to a gang of ragamuffins. Illiterate, unwashed ragamuffins. Having thus saved themselves, Carstairs then dishonoured us all by gutting an enemy who had spared his life. It was for that craven act that they hung him." Goforth, Tennyson and Edmonds exchanged ambiguous glances which contained the common dread that their sons and nephews might be among those killed in action; their sorrow for poor Carstairs senior; but mostly their loathing of this reptile that hissed its vituperation at them. The board had arrived at a point where they could barely look at this worthless, inhuman ball of self-obsessed conceit. Because of this individual's naked lust for fame, their sons were either dead in an unnecessary conflict, or imprisoned in the bowels of an unidentifiable ship for as long as the continental war might last. Always supposing that they could survive such a hellish travail.

"So you blame your crew for this catastrophe, Horton?" Goforth was livid.

"Naturally." The man's shadow of a smile asked, "Wouldn't you?"

"You feel strongly that your men did wrong in surrendering?" the Scotsman proposed.

"It is not the plumly-Horton way."

"Captain" Beattie's tone dripped loathing.

"I have the manifest here." The Admiral referred to the document as he spoke.

"Three of these trainee officers were fifteen years of age, eight were seventeen, one was eighteen and the remainder were no older than twenty-two. As recent entrants to the service, they were virtual strangers to the naval cutlass, many could not so much as lift that weapon, and yet you expected them to fight hardened seamen who had been tearing up the slave trade for many years."

"They were trainee officers of His Majesty's Royal Navy." The captain straightened his back.

"Is that your considered response?"

"It is."

Beattie took a deep breath, staring hard meanwhile, at a point in the middle of the reptile's forehead, into which he was confident that he could put a lead ball at thirty paces.

"Be so kind as to accord me my title, Captain." There was acid in Beattie's quiet rejoinder.

"As you wish… Sir." The cool one made it abundantly clear that he considered himself the equal, or better, of his tormentors in everything but rank.

Equidistant between the board and the source of their ire stood a glass-topped table, on which lay a length of pure-white lanyard and several flat-bottomed model ships. The bench exchanged a few words and having decided that it was time to discover in detail how the fatal events and the loss of *Justice* had proceeded, they rose and approached their recent innovation, taking up stations exclusively on the opposite side to that occupied by Horton, as though fearful of contagion, or of seeming to display the smallest degree of sympathy with the man.

"Approach the table if you please, Captain," said Tennyson, and when the accused obliged, he said,

"Use the lanyard to define the coastline where the action took place, then locate the pirated ships as you remember them lying at anchor." Happy to oblige the old buffers in their most recent nonsense, Plumly-Horton did as he was requested and positioned the three pirated vessels accurately, and even demonstrated the approach of his own vessel from the west of the bay in question. Tennyson meanwhile watched the man rather than the model ships and recognised the self-congratulatory conceit that directed the criminal's actions on that damnable occasion.

"Bearing in mind Admiral Harding's admonition that you should not under any circumstances engage the enemy; would you be so kind as to elaborate on what it was that convinced you that there was no other option for you but to attack. Commence at the point at which you came in sight of the enemy."

Horton took to their game as a masochistic monk would take to a rusting cilice. At long last, he had the opportunity to display his brilliance to the very dullards who had the power to promote him to master of a one- hundred-gun ship of the line. This was an opportunity of which he would take full advantage. He grasped the toy ship *Justice* with vast enthusiasm and 'sailed' it along the imaginary coastline to where he had first seen the enemy sitting at anchor, 'like fish in a barrel.'

"The criminals were all ashore having left only a couple of men aboard each vessel," he gloated.

"What was it that convinced you captain that this competent and destructive enemy were all ashore?" Commander Edmonds was riveted.

"They were visible on the sands, seventy perhaps eighty of them, perhaps more. They had built themselves a perfect village of tents in which to live." Horton spoke slowly so that Edmonds would understand.

"Only skeleton crews remained aboard their three vessels. The situation called for an instant response. Naturally, I perceived that a daring Captain could dash in and kill three 'birds' with one stone."

"Naturally," drawled Goforth, sickened by the man's introduction of humour to the telling of this most shameful episode in the history of the British Navy.

"Clearly, you were unaware that being an abolitionist vessel the *Bird* alone carried an army of almost one hundred fighting men?'' 'Castrated, garrotted, broken-on-the-wheel,' by this input Plumly-Horton in a panic and desperate to deflect attention from it steered 'Justice' to a point between two of the enemy vessels.

"Perfectly positioned thusly; I sent raiders to board both. Everything was going according to my plan when I was rendered unconscious. I know nothing more."

"Yes! You declared earlier that you were beaten into unconsciousness. As you had not quit your own ship, it stands to reason that you had been boarded." Beattie shouted as the trap closed.

"These ships," Beattie jabbed a blue-nailed finger at the toy boats anchored in the supposed bay.

"were unarmed merchantmen, were they not, and you with only seven guns at your disposal, chose, contrary to orders, to take the bait and attack them. Did you never wonder where the twenty-gun *Glorious* was, man?"

"Had I not been rendered unconscious I would have taken all three and delivered them to Lord Ast..."

"To whom? To that wastrel, Michael Astor," bellowed Beattie.

"Where is it written that a Captain of the British Navy receives his instruction, and reports to, a self-confessed slave dealer and not to his own commanding officer? It was in hope of reward from that sump of perfidy that you acted so was it not?''

"Did the enemy do the right thing by the prisoners who died in the battle?" Edmonds asked, deeply upset, only to be ignored.

"I would never have surrendered," yelled Horton.

"Oh, we're back to that are we?" snarled Beattie as his self-control fled him.

"Those little boys let you down, it was all their fault. I Sir. Never yet. Never yet Sir, met a fifteen-year-old who could 'wield' a naval cutlass, let alone use one.''

Edmonds tried again.

"Were the dead properly farewelled?" he asked, and desperate to escape Beattie's wrath, Horton 'took the gap' and answered the less vituperative officer.

"Strangely enough for such heathens; they were. The enemy awarded full honours off Brest as they went south. I was brought on deck as a witness to the fact."

"Brest! Are you seriously telling this board that the escapees discussed their position with you?" Edmonds again.

"I know that coastline well."

"But you were beached in London," Beattie countered.

"Yes, they drove south possibly as far as Nantes, where they took aboard a cargo of cognac, then sailed for London."

"Cognac? London?"

"The ship was full of the smell of it, naturally."

"Is it not true," shouted Beattie, getting back to business, and thrusting an accusing finger at the model of *Justice*,

"that the twenty-gun *Glorious*, the most dangerous of those vessels pirated from Minster, rammed you, boarded you, and took our lads and our ship? I say again, sir. You fell into the simplest of traps, did you not; a trap set by those oyster dredgers, and mule skinners whom you so disdain? Did it not occur to you that the *Glorious*; all twenty guns of her, was hiding behind the horizon waiting for a fool such as you to disobey a direct order from the most respected Admiral in the Service?"

"I never once saw a vessel of that name during the action. Her name was '*Liberty*,'" raged Horton; letting slip his true self, and the crucial truth that he had been boarded. He was aghast. This was not the way it was meant to go at all. About to protest, he was silenced by Beattie.

"Be so kind as to wait outside, Captain." The doomed one recognised that seemingly harmless request for what it was. His death-knell. The board watched in loathing as the accused removed himself, escorted closely by marines. The case against the man was so clear-cut, that Admiral Beattie felt that he need only get the nod from his associates, in order to make a ruling, and this he duly did.

"Sergeant-at-Arms?"

When Plumly-Horton once again stood before him; the tall, severe, professional seaman got to his feet and came around the bench to deliver his verdict. He did so in order to look down on the man physically as well as morally.

"Plumly-Horton;" Beattie intoned,

"You are found guilty of all charges against you. You are hereby reduced to the rank of 'ordinary seaman prisoner and condemned to life in prison."

''Damn your fuckin eye,'' the interjection was halted by a marine's full-bloodied slap in the face which would have dropped an ox. It dropped the good captain.

''Get him up. Get him up.'' Beattie could not wait to continue.

"You will be incarcerated for life, at his Majesty's naval station on the Falkland Islands in the south Atlantic, where you will undertake hard labour in the sanitation of Admiralty vessels, under conditions of leg-irons, half-rations, and solitary confinement. That is all." With a nod to the Sergeant-at-Arms Beattie turned his back on the walking gusunder and resumed his seat. The ferocious marine crashed to attention; clattered across the floor of brilliant teak and attempted to drive his steel-shod foot through the glistening boards as he rooted himself, face to face, with the prisoner.

"Arrest this man," he bawled addressing a perfectly innocent cherub floating high above Horton's head and two rankers crashing to attention in their leader's image, marched briskly to the prisoner's sides, gripping his arms so tightly that the man winced. Snatching the hat from the criminal's head; 'the fool having had the temerity to replace it,' the Sergeant-At-Arms drew back, and with the power of a haymaker, hit Horton across his red and swelling face with his open hand. It had begun. Such was the force of the blow that the sound generated caused the pigeons on the ledge outside to take to the air. The various cloth indications of rank were ripped from the prisoner's jacket; 'the stitching having been razored beforehand for this very purpose,' and the all-but-unconscious man, bleeding at nose and mouth was dragged out by his guards.

The board members watched Plumly-Horton's retreat to an existence which he would suffer in bitter cold, constant hunger, endless fourteen- hour days of hard labour at the most disgusting of tasks that the service could devise, for the remainder of his life, and all of this to be endured in the complete and utter exclusion from the society of his fellow men; yet still they wished devoutly that they could hurt him more. He had sacrificed their sons on the altar of his ambition.

CHAPTER 27: Macbeth

In the shade of a spreading oak Macbeth had dug only one grave, and in it he had reverently placed a simple jar bearing the ashes of his darlings so that they would be together for eternity. Oblivious to time, hunger, thirst and all else, he had sat in the grass by their side through the night, tortured by the loss of them. He would never again know the exquisite joy of holding his little one in his arms while she deposited her big wet kisses on his face, or creep into her room, hand in hand with his adored wife, to watch the child sleeping. His wife, Tamsin, how he worshipped her; and always would. A philistine the likes of himself had no right to so much as contemplate the love of such a wonderful woman as she; and yet that unimaginable blessing had been bestowed. The beauty had returned his love and more. She had rescued him; made him whole. And now this. As the God-cursed sun came up; christening him anew as 'Murdering Thief,' he was so reduced, so abject; that to retain his sanity he strove for only one objective; to be able to whisper their names without greeting like a big lassie. That was his only thought.

In the dawn, he said his farewells.

"I cannea stay," he told them. "I am a fugitive the now. A murderer. Some men shouldnae be allowed tae draw breath, and I killed one such; tae keep my honour intact, ye ken. I shall have tae run, but I will come back to see ye whenever I can." He knelt to kiss the unadorned stone which marked their home. The unresponsive thing was rough, cold and lifeless, as his existence now was, and always would be, until death permitted him to join his sweethearts again.

On that loathsome day of ill-memory, Macbeth had paused till Hooligan's coach had finally passed beneath the portcullis of Huntingmill, then hurried inside in pursuit of Monteith whom he had discovered in the great hall.

"What did ye mean, 'keep his ships?'" he demanded of the astounded Laird.

"Hooligan widnae have sailed a thousand miles out of his way if he."

"You forget yourself Macbeth," snarled Monteith. "Lower your voice, you dog. It is not for you…"

"It is not for *you* sur," raged Macbeth, "tae play the devil wi' *my* honour." Macbeth was furious as he approached Monteith, who moved closer to the fire to enjoy his brandy in comfort.

"Your honour!" expostulated Monteith.

"Gillies don't have hon…" Macbeth's fist destroyed Monteith's face, driving the man's wine glass into his eyes. Blinded, the Laird collapsed into the blaze screaming in agony. Beyond reason, now that his good name had been made ordure in the minds of such worthwhile men as Hooligan and Teach whose good opinion was as gold to him, the berserker grabbed a battle-axe from the chimney breast, and flinging it high above his head, brought it down with the fury of the betrayed. The great curved blade struck Monteith in the chest splitting him from his Adam's apple to the point where the lower ribs met, turning to jelly the organs, arteries and muscle with which it came in contact, crashing through the ribs at the backbone and deflecting against the irons and the granite flags. He released the weapon

"*Nemo Me Impune Lacessit,*" he growled, well pleased with his blow.

"I'll be needing this." Cold as ice now, he cut the thongs of the thief's sporran and poured its stream of gold into his own. Raking his throat severely he spat with satisfying accuracy into the trench wound and left; taking with him the twin of the axe that protruded from monteith's corpse.

As he reached the doors, he turned and addressed the dead man, mocking him formally in his outrage.

"Ye can play fast and loose with yer own honour, but not wi' Macbeth's." With vast disdain for the horrified footmen who now congregated there, hesitating to approach the awful scene he barged through the whey-faced individuals and made for the stables. Aware that the guard's outside would be quick to investigate how it was that he was spattered with blood he tapped his forehead with the axe opening-up a trench wound and allowed his blood to run freely down his face on to his smock to join the laird's own. His condition was enjoyed greatly by the crowd of guards outside who were well acquainted with their laird's predilection for violence.

''Annoy the big man did ye?'' Macbeth fained fury at this insolence.

''Have a care Connolly, he advised halting momentarily, glowering threateningly into the soldier's eyes until the fellow lowered his gaze.''

It would have been far too obvious a ploy to gallop straight to the Firth; the Laird's dogs might catch him as he waited to be lifted from the beach. He cut across country instead, turning down a narrow lane in Perth where the road was moss covered and he would leave good sign. His evolving plan was to approach the shore of the Tay some twenty miles further east than where the ships now lay at anchor, and hail them as they passed by on their way to the sea, as they would undoubtedly do very soon. Martin Teach and Lliam Hooligan being men who would not relinquish their ships simply because some Laird or other had snapped his fingers. 'Bowing the knee wasn't much to their taste either. Not to anyone.'

Needing to cross the raging current of the river he rode to the nearest point at which this was possible; creating a detour which would cost Monteith's people half a day or more.

Ten miles nearer to the sea than the place where the little fleet lay at anchor, he dismounted and relaxed while he waited for them but as the hours crawled passed taking with them his elation and with darkness fast approaching he concluded that he had been too late; the little fleet was already at sea. Without so much as an exclamation of disappointment he saddled up and went on his way.

''It's no use cryin' over spilt milk," he informed his horse, and rode south-west for the historic town of Stirling. His darling girls waited beyond untold horizons. He had to get home and carry them away to safety before Monteith's scum came looking for him. Many hours later the five ships now with hundreds of his countrymen aboard sailed passed the place where Macbeth had waited en-route to Nantes in France.

Copplestone allowed himself a full day's rest then packed a bag and departed telling Barabus that he would return in a day or two.

"I don't suppose there be any point in a man arksin' where you's goin' then?"

"I don't believe there is."

"'Tween you an' Mister Mucbeff, you two 'ave cornered the market in secret fings, I reckon," the boy moaned, only to be roundly and imperiously ignored for his trouble. Copplestone came home on the second day. Again, he rested for a day then packed a bag with supplies, secured a shovel behind his saddle and rode off in the direction of Barabas' concealed caravan, only to return minutes later with the arcane machine of death lashed behind his saddle.

"You telt me that you weren't a goin' ter set that damnt thing," the boy snorted bravely. Bengal seemed to halt unbidden.

"Men are hung, not for stealing horses, but that horses might not be stolen," said Copplestone obscurely. Bengal walked on.

In the light of a quarter moon, the soldier cut the track rather further south than he had judged would be the case, at around two o'clock in the morning; so far south in fact, that he would of necessity pass one of the gatehouses of Jamaica Place as he rectified his error, but that was a matter of no real concern. Keeping to the dark strip of grass in the centre of the track he rode quietly past the enormous wrought-iron gates behind which the miniature castle of the gatehouse was in darkness, travelling on until he located the flash where he had de-barked a tree. This spot was concealed from the big house, and sufficiently far away from it for any noise he made to go unheard, though the constantly patrolling roughnecks were a serious concern. Hefting the mantrap over the vaulted top of the wall, he lowered it quietly to the ground on its bit of rope, then tossed the shovel over, blade first, so that it would pierce the dirt like a Fuzzy-Wuzzy's pigsticker. Standing in his saddle, he summited the wall, selected a landing spot and dropped.

 The 'mark,' was very much a creature of habit, albeit a mentally unbalanced creature of habit. For all six of the days that Copplestone had observed the man, Astor had risen early in his favourite suite, his bedroom and dressing rooms being located above the library on the south-east corner of the stupefyingly large home. Within an hour or so of rising, he would proceed, candle lit, to his breakfast in a basement kitchen in the far-distant west wing, whose many denizens had been hard at it since four o'clock. From there, he would emerge an hour or so later; usually at well before seven o'clock. Without exception he would be smoking a cigar and would meander across the lawns and under the trees; several of whom he would converse with in the friendliest fashion, until he came to the west wing, where he liked to drop quickly, stiff legged, down to the formal garden with a rapid percussion of his boot-heels on the wide stone steps. He would select a blossom for his lapel, talking to himself as he strode along the manicured path, gesturing angrily on occasion, and even striking out at imaginary irritants. When this mood passed, he would look guiltily around. Once satisfied that he had not been observed in his aberrant behaviour, he would take the narrow; rose-bordered 'perfumed-path,' to the waterfall thing known as *The Jacob's Ladder.

*Water was caused to flow down a mountain of steps designed to agitate the flow creating liquid silver which was a delight to behold.

'The perfumed path.' It had been designed and constructed for Copplestone's purposes alone.

Astor arrived early. Had he known what awaited him he would have remained in bed. He appeared from beyond the western wing of the house well before seven o'clock, seeming immensely self-satisfied. His breakfast; or last night's conquest; or both, must have been magnificent. True to form, he drum-rolled his descent to the formal garden and sure enough he selected a buttonhole for the day as the soldier eased back further into cover to watch.

''Damn him to hell!'' The swine had turned around. He was going back toward the house. Snapping a slim branch with a clap like a pistol-shot Copplestone broke cover, striding out into the clear as though lost, risking it all on one throw of the dice. 'Would the man whistle up dogs to rip him, or call for some bruisers to beat him to a pulp?'

"Son of a bitch." Astor glanced around obviously in hope of a roughneck or two. There were none but he strode confidently towards the smaller man in the manner evinced by all school-yard bullies as they approach their victims, absolutely convinced that the victim would put up no resistance whatsoever. Playing the devil's advocate, Copplestone took several quick steps towards the misanthrope and noted with satisfaction the brief slowing that this caused. Astor kept coming but exhibited noticeably less bluster. He entered the narrow rose-perfumed pathway. Should he ever reach its end, he would be only five yards from where his nemesis waited with clenched fists. Half of the path's width had been blocked by a gardener's barrow and adjacent to that obstruction one of Astor's own playthings lay deeply buried in the pebbles, dirt, leaves and bits of moss.

Michael Astor did not emerge from that pathway. Faster than the strike of a cobra, that moss, those leaves, pebbles, and dirt, suddenly flew skyward around the stricken individual, as though swept up by a cyclone, the terrible jaws slamming shut in the flesh and bone of his lower leg. The sadist's handsome face contorting instantly in a rictus of unbearable agony, and he screamed in a fashion which Copplestone had hoped never to hear again. Michael Astor no longer existed. His corporeal being, his sadism, his grisly memories, secret knowledge, demented plans and obscene lusts, his wealth, land, houses and treasures, were all incinerated in an ever-expanding universe of pain. Notwithstanding the metamorphosis which he had wrought, Copplestone's loathing was by no means quenched. It had only just been birthed. He charged, blade in hand, at that spawn of the devil who was now in a purgatory of his own making, roasting over a raging fire on a spit thrust up his anus, ripping through his entrails and exiting his gargoyle mouth. Grabbing the obscenity by the hair, Copplestone was yelling in manic ferocity into that twisted visage.

"See what it's like, you Quran-spouting chundi?"

He was raging insanely, his blood-thirsty blade desperate to drink; and he was suddenly and painfully aware of the fact. Aware and horrified by his own state of mind. Justice had been done, had it not? He relented.

"Death's too good for scum like you." He flung the tormented caricature away in revulsion, not at what he had done to it, but at its perverted nature. Servants were mincing from the house, stampeding from the stables, and wading from the lakeside, unable to locate the source of the screaming. He was surrounded. Reluctant to abandon the evidence of his righteous handiwork Copplestone backed into the trees, soaking up every delicious second of his revenge on that sadistic piece of ordure. 'Better to let him live like this than to kill him.' He ran hard for the perimeter wall with not so much as a sound of anyone in close pursuit, but breathless at the thought of being shot in the back, that worst of all sins. At last the boundry's impossibly great height manifested itself and leaping desperately up the face in a much practiced style he got his elbows over the top at the first attempt and swung a leg up and over to sit astride it. Bengal came at the trot to his whistle, but as the horse drew close, his trailing boot was grasped from below. He was tipping. Inexorably. Being dragged back off his perch. Clinging desperately to the brickwork, he wrenched his foot savagely upwards, and felt the spurs cutting deeply through someone's hands.

"Bengal." he grasped the saddle-horn and urged his mount away causing himself to be dragged painfully and requiring him to mount in the style of a circus act while leaving Astor's dog behind him, to bleed and lick his wounds.

He was bored, a condition 0worse than physical injury. Contrary to his initial notion that he could find contentment in the English shires through a life of earnest endeavour and empire building Copplestone had discovered during the first act that the sedate life was not for him. Nor ever could be. Walking your horse, in no way compared with galloping. The indoors was a poor substitute for fresh air, and familiar scenes could not hold a candle to the endless vistas to be enjoyed beyond every hill. With Dora having passed on, and Angelique it seemed, never to return, life was flavourless, but then, it had occurred to him that even if both women were present, he would need more. Much more. At mid-morning of one particularly aimless day, he was unearthing a root of potatoes for dinner, a meal which as often as not would be taken with the ever-loquacious Barabas, when his need for action became so strong that he was choked by it.

Abandoning all thoughts of food and the agrarian idle, he speared the soil with the spade, saddled Bengal and rode off directly for the home of the ghastly Macbeth for if anyone knew of Lliam's whereabouts it would be he. Disdaining the beaten tracks he went cross country, leaping hedges and walls, laughing for the sheer joy of it, scattering livestock, and being cheered on by thickets of labourers wherever he went. The unnatural silence of Macbeth's home was that of the Hindu Kush. Dismounting at the entrance to the property he proceeded on foot through the pasture to the garden gate which strangely, lay open. Parents of little children always ensure that the garden gate is tightly shut. The curtains were not drawn, and the brass doorknocker wore the patina of neglect. Weeds choked the flowers beds and the vegetables.

"I think they're dead. The Mrs, and the little one. Everyone else is dead. The master's away still." The soldier whirled quickly; startled by the voice, and aghast at the declaration.

ing503

Beyond a wall on the outbuilding side of the house, where stood the barns and the servant's quarters, a young man whom he recognised only vaguely swayed like a reed in the breeze as he supported himself with a hoe. The young fellow had clearly been very ill. He was as pale as a distant memory, but his bloodshot eyes were sunk in great pools of corruption. His poor hair had fallen out leaving patches of pale skin, though he seemed barely out of his teens. He coughed painfully and spat bloody mucus.

"I din't dare to go inside."

Unable to support his weight any longer, the lad stepped forward in order to lean against the wall. Copplestone nodded his understanding; the awful news sickening him. Returning to his mount he took a shirt from his saddle bag, wet it with rum, secured it around his face then strode to the rear of the property where he found the scullery door unlocked. It was Gujranwala all over again. Ice cold sweat cut slices from his ribs

"Is anyone home?" he called and repeated the question as he explored the several rooms on the ground floor, uncomfortably cognisant that he was merely delaying the inevitable. Predictably, there was a sweet and terribly unpleasant smell, despite the rum. Mounting the stairs, he postponed the inevitable further by glancing in to the three smaller rooms, deeply disturbed by the thought of what he would likely find in the master bedroom. He was well acquainted with death and corruption, his nostrils having many times filled with the reek of rotting flesh, yet this was different. Beyond this door, Macbeth's beautiful wife and adorable child would now be reduced to reeking masses of putrefaction. He turned the handle and entered.

Two sightless skulls, mocked by their lovely hair, stared back at him from the marriage bed. Mother and daughter bound together in death, as they were in life. The stench was terrible. Something was dripping onto the floor. Trewin closed the door behind him, charged downstairs and ran outside into the fresh air.

"Stay there," the boy called as he was about to vault the garden wall.

"Maybe I still have it."

"Where's Macbeth?" The soldier inquired, remembering all too late that Macbeth and Hooligan might be somewhere between Nantes and Perth by now, if all had gone to plan.

"No idea. Gone fer days on end sometimes."

"I shall have to cremate them where they lay. His family. They are too far gone for a husband and father to look at." The boy nodded his understanding.

"I'll do the same wi' the lads. Theys straw in't barn."

"Tell Macbeth that I could not allow him to find them as they were." The boy nodded again as his blanket fell to the ground, his condition eliciting a comradely intake of breath on his interlocutor's part. No meat clung to the lad's ribs while the sagging skin was all purple blotches and weeping sores. As he mounted Bengal at the top of the drive, the cleansing flames burst with a roar through the thatch of the once love-filled home.

The unsettled but determined Angelique ignored the rowdy business that was being done ashore and concentrated on the military ships; thinking it unlikely that a man so recently pressed into service would be free to watch the entertainment or whatever it was that was causing such a noise. Terrified of being shot by those soldiers whom she had discovered prowling through the woods with muskets at the ready, she made her stealthy way forward and came to a place which afforded a distant view of the gigantic vessels whose massive bulk appalled her but transported her also by the power and majesty that they projected. In their martial malevolence, they seemed to be a castle, an army and a navy in themselves. How on earth did they stay afloat, she wondered? It seemed to her that anything so huge must go straight to the bottom.

"Andrew!" She saw him immediately, and delirious with joy waved her hat to him before she could restrain herself. Terrified, she hid away again hastily yet in that same instant she felt that Andrew had noticed her. He was standing with two other men who were probably prisoners also for all three of them were out of uniform. A seaman in a black hat and a stupidly short jacket shouted something into the face of one of those unfortunates. As the poor man hurried to obey, the black hat dealt him such a vicious blow that he cried out in pain but barely broke step, so scared was he. Andrew did not wait for some of the same he grabbed the bully by the throat, put him to the deck and was lost to sight; but no, he was sprinting to an open port, passed thickets of gawping soldiers hurtling through the space, head-first and plummeting to the water twenty feet below, entering it like an arrow. Angelique was galvanised, never had she seen anyone leap head-first into water, and from such a height! She held her breath as she waited expectantly for him to surface, her eyes locked on the place where she thought he might reappear. He did not. The seconds became minutes and the minutes a trial as she hung on desperately with still no sign. She gasped strenuously for air realising that she had been holding her breath for the sake of her love. 'Her love.' How wonderful a thought. If only she could swim, she would throw herself in and save him. Ages dragged by in hope, fear, and desperation for much longer than a man could stay underwater and yet; she still believed; she believed because she could not bear to lose him. Soldiers had run to the ship's sides and presented their muskets, waiting gleefully for the deserter to surface but even they lost interest so tardy was the inconsiderate swimmer in presenting a target.

"Angie." It was less than a whisper, just a vibration amid the incessant roar of the cicadas. She turned, searching the long grasses, reeds, and bullrushes and there, in deep cover was his beautiful face, wearing that loveable smile. Andrew, her dearly loved Andrew, put a finger to his lips for silence, and beckoned her to him.

"God, but you're beautiful," he declared, as though men with guns were not queuing up to shoot him and crushing her to him kissed her with such passion that despite her recent fear, her body stirred as never before. ''Yes darling,'' she told him. ''Please.''

Several days later, tired by the long trek but happy, Angelique walked hand in hand with Andrew to the door of The Furrow which was flung open while they were still at the foot of the steps to reveal a smiling Adelle. Descending with that wonderful grace which Angelique loved so much the handsome woman grasped her visitor oh so gently by the shoulders and kissed her on both cheeks.

"So, you found him, Angelique. I never doubted you for a moment," she declared, looking lovingly into the girl's shining eyes.

"You must be Andrew." Tripping up to the grinning youth, Adelle extended her hand, palm downwards, at which he surprised and delighted both women by gently taking Adelle's fingertips in his own and bending over her hand in the most courteous fashion. It was unsurprising but very disappointing for Angelique, that Abstemious and Vouchsafe were not at home, for she wanted so much to thank them for all they had done for her; for saving her from that vile beast and for their assistance in finding Andrew. This however was a small fly in her ointment of happiness as with evening approaching the lovers departed The Furrow, waving happily to everyone as they went.

He had sat so long near the ruins of his home that his arse was flat, but he had mastered his grief and had to leave. If he delayed much longer, he would find himself decorating the gallows out there at Golgotha. For a moment or two, he considered riding to Stranraer House and killing its occupant before fleeing the country. The swine was as guilty as sin. It was Fotheringhay that had ordered the ships to Perth. After serious consideration, he rejected the notion because the risks were far too great for such small reward; that man kept more guards around him than Balhousie. With any luck he would meet the man again some day. He went to lean against a wall beyond which his sole surviving fieldhand had been ploughing since well before dawn and when the team drew level with him, he called out.

"James. A minute of yer time, if ye please."

"Whooaaa there, hoss," croaked the youth, and taking the reins from around his shoulders, attaching them to the handles of the plough.

"Yes, Master how can I help you?" The youngster came to lean against the wall, a fresh-faced, obliging sort of a lad with a bit of black cloth tied about his arm. Almost fully recovered from his brush with death, he smiled easily.

"I'm leaving, James. As you are the only survivor in my employ, and a good man in tae the bargain, I'm giein the place tae you, land, livestock, buildings, the lot. Who knows, ye may fancy building up the hoose again, there's plenty timber aboot the place and the walls stand as firm as ever, it's just the timber and thatch ye'll need tae replace." The boy had pushed-off from the wall and stood up straight but had not said a word.

"You know its boundaries well enough. There's eighteen acres. Let no man take it from ye.'' James Ford said not one word.

"I have a condition." The young man nodded almost imperceptibly.

"Take guid care o' the grave. Bid them 'good morning,' now and again perhaps. I'll be back tae see ma lassies whenever I can."

James Byrn nodded again in sympathetic understanding.

"I'll dae it legal. You'll be gettin' papers."

Without shaking the hand of the newly rich James Byrn Macbeth mounted and rode away, only to pause briefly,

"If anybuddy comes askin'; ye dinnae ken where I am. You've nae seen me. Dinnae let them see the grave."

The young ploughman had not uttered a word yet returned to his work with a sense of urgency which was an unwelcome stranger to him. Dead inside, Macbeth rode to the village of Thorpe, where Lliam Hooligan and Trewin Copplestone had stayed recently. He had little enough time to spare; assassins would be on his tail like bloodhounds when word of the Laird's demise reached them, but he needed to thank Copplestone for what he had done to save him from discovering his wife and wee angel in death.

'He was a good wee man; a hard wee bastart right enough, that soldier,' Macbeth knew no higher compliment. Copplestone and Hooligan together; Macbeth loved them like brothers in arms and grimaced sadly at the very thought of the two madmen who would now be cursing him as a traitor. There being very little to the village of Thorpe he rode through its length barely meeting anyone, then took the lane to where he remembered that beautiful young lassie, Angelique something or other, used tae live. 'She was well named, that one.' Noticing the new slate roof, and as he drew closer, the carpenter-built gate, he knew with certainty that he had the right place. There was only one man connected with the penurious hovels of Thorpe who had silver enough in his purse for such extravagance. Barabbas met him at the gate.

"Mister Macbeff. Good day, your majesty." The lad grinned like a gin.

"Barabbas; what are ye doin' here, laddie?"

"I live 'ere now Sir.''

''Do ye? What about the fambly?''

''Well to tell the.''

''Macbeth!'' It was an overjoyed Lliam Hooligan who had emerged from behind the house with every display of friendship. Such was the Scot's relief at this totally unexpected outcome that he experienced a moment or two of light-headedness. 'So, the Irishman had not blamed him for the betrayal at Balhousie and his terrible concerns had been for nought.' Dismounting he hurried to embrace his comrade in the abolitionists' struggle, but Hooligan was having none of it and kept him at bay with a very sincere handshake. Copplestone was there too and the beautiful Angelique who was holding the arm of a tall young man, well put together.

''You're just in time Macbeth.'' declared the Irishman obscurely,

''We're off to the coast in the morning, to meet the Liberty. Come and eat.'' That evening Hooligan gifted Dora's cottage which he had built from scratch with his own hands so long ago, the land the milk cow the chickens and the strips, to an ecstatic family with seven children and in the morning he and his friends set out for their rendezvous with the Liberty.

CHAPTER 28: Pearl of The Atlantic

The fine weather which had blessed the flying hermaphrodite almost continuously since her remarkable maiden voyage forsook the *Liberty* as she came in sight of Madeira, that colourful pebble lost in a world of water. The playful immature waves, their white tops taunted by a cool bracing wind, quixotically matured into darkly scowling adults whose cruel merciless faces roared southward whipped onward by a malevolent, shrieking harpy of a gale. The sky also proved unfaithful; discarding her pleasant smile in favour of a black countenance of implacable fury she fell on the *Liberty* as though to crush and drive her under.

"Shorten sail. Batten down!" roared the new boatswain greatly to the ire of the disbelieving Scots, who had already been required to reduce their darling's canvas by half and could perceive no good reason for such timidity. Storms were a regular occurrence in the highlands and did no harm to anyone, other than to get them wet. Even so, they raced their shipmates into the sky, only to be mocked for their tardiness on arrival in the shrouds. Thus it was, that with everything lashed down as tight as English hemp could make them, with sail shortened to the expanse of three large kerchiefs and the crew clinging to anything within reach the Scots' first sight of the archipelago was taken through tortured eyes, squinting into liquid birdshot.

As the *Liberty* approached her, the wondrously colourful territory of Porto Santo, the nearest island of the archipelago metamorphosed into a jagged outcrop of iron-hard featureless coral, crouching in ambush amid the wet equivalent of hell; a harbinger of death, intent on ripping out the belly of any ship unfortunate enough to be driven her way. It was then, a mere prayer short of the invisible town of the same name that the racing cliffs of water caught the great ship, grasping her as cruelly as lionesses clawing at the flanks of a doomed kudu. Mountains of a far more threatening nature than those of the islands overhauled the fleeing vessel, driving her forward at impossible speed, hoisting her stern so high that her bows plunged Javelin-like into troughs from which it seemed on each successive occasion that she could not possibly emerge. Sail was shortened desperately again, with every available man forced into the rigging where they strained shoulder to shoulder, agonised by the ice-cold rain while hanging on grimly for their very lives as the wind grasped at them, intent on tearing loose the weak and the unskilled and flinging them into the louring wastes, never to be seen again, their last cries unheard. As the tortured ship shuddered under the weight of water charging chest-deep across her decks, and the masts bent to the point where only the rigging averted disaster by straining in reserve, everyone aboard quailed with horror in their hearts. At the worst of times a great lurch to starboard confirmed that the ship was beyond the control of its masters, for no captain who retained his sanity in this horrid asylum would alter course in such a fashion and expose his ship's flanks to that implacable enemy. Now they were all finished. It was merely a matter of a moment or two. The black cliffs of water presently smashing her stern would strike her sides, roll her over on her beam and drive her under. Above decks and below they tensed; waiting; each man, woman and child reduced to an exiled and solitary repository of fear.

When he realised that the ship and everyone aboard her was lost, and that his attempts to save two youngsters frozen in the rigging were futile; Trewin Copplestone, debilitated, his frozen limbs refusing to comply with his instructions and his conscience on the rack, close to death with cold and exhaustion, descended trepidatiously to the deck. Wedging himself between the arms of a capstan, he hung on there, struggling to fill his lungs in an atmosphere which was more water than air. A torturous eternity dragged passed as the very dregs of his will to fight-back drained from him until at last in his despair he surrendered to fate and allowed himself to be swum across the deck to smash against the stable doors. Head-first he kicked his way under one of them only to add the threat of being stamped to death by the hooves of a terrified Clydesdale to the myriad of his horrors. As the tortured ship heaved over on her side yet again, he slithered downhill beneath the partitions, with only a faint notion of which stall was Bengal's. Dying, he clambered to his feet and there, almost as scared as himself, was his friend.

"Don't worry old chum," he gasped, "we'll go together if we must." The devilish attacks persisted, crucifying him in every suffering part of his being with nails of ice until he had long since passed the point at which surrender was inevitable. He could take no more of the painful cold and the incessant battering as he was thrown first against this wall, then the other by the shuddering of the doomed vessel; but he would not leave his friend's side. Watery blood ran from a deep wound in his scalp where his head had come into violent contact with Bengal's bared teeth but thankfully the wound was sluiced by regular torrents so that his friend did not have the scent of blood to contend with. Driven to the very edge of despair, he crammed his feet against the base of the walls, and with the last of his energy, wrapped his arms around Bengal's thick neck.

"Hold up, my beauty," he groaned, and hung on semi-conscious and welcoming death. He was startled from his lethargy by a sound which he had been dreading to hear; the splintering of timber smashed by the hooves of a crazed animal. For a sickening moment, he believed that it was his own Bengal who had destroyed his flimsy stable door, but it was not. The animal in the adjacent stall, emerged chest deep, its legs slipping from under it. Crazed with terror the doomed beast was seized by the flood and rushed over the side to its death; lost to sight in an instant. There was an equine shriek, crueller still than that of the wind, then nothing more. The dying soldier's grip was failing him though he tried desperately to hold tighter to his saviour. During the testing time, he lost consciousness again and fell to the floor to be washed about mercilessly, like so much flotsam between his mount's stamping hooves. Yet another horror struck like the hammer of Thor itself; throwing mere mortals about violently like discarded dolls, as their floating coffin rolled clumsily sideways down into the slavering maw of death. Beyond the frail bit of timber bulkhead, the wind screeched its glee at the demise of these creatures who dared to venture out on Neptune's glory.

Slowly, very slowly, the *Liberty* braced herself; her bones creaked, her knees of English oak returned the gale's screams, fought back, shrugged off the mountains of water that doubled her weight and began to recover. Her last shreds of canvas snatched and snapped like mastiffs at the wind and dragged her upright by main force easing her forward, imperceptibly at first, incrementally, she adjusted to the unprecedented attacks on her flanks. Human hearts beat again; breath that was held, was then released, for she lived still. *Liberty* was again forging ahead, repelling Poseidon's desperate flailing, leaning so far yet again that she must never come back, and yet, still fighting for her very life.

In the fevered imaginings and prayers of men; the wind began to lessen, and the seas to relent if immeasurably so as the horizontal rain changed its point of attack, impossible volumes falling vertically as though a river debouched from a cliff high above intent on a drowning. Understanding what was happening, the experienced sailors breathed more easily, 'Teach must have risked it all to turn the great ship into the protection of the invisible island of Madeira itself. With only his vaunted navigational skills and self-belief to guide his hand,' he had done the unthinkable; but saved them.

The assault still raged, but there ahead of them lay a tiny refuge; a league or two of calm in an ocean of calamity. They had won through. Not for nothing had they unanimously voted Teach their Captain. Frozen to the very marrow of their bones and so weakened that they could barely cling to the greasy, waterlogged ropes, men descended unbidden from their tortured existence to huddle together in such corners as seemed less exposed to the biting wind. There they clung on to timber and to life until the ever-vigilant boatswain was able to organise their replacement, and with approbation, free them to go below. Despite her dishevelled state, *Liberty* made measurable headway for the remainder of the night, creeping forward through the labyrinthine darkness populated by vivid fears, until at last, her weary master gave the much-awaited order, and she dropped anchor off the invisible Funchal, capital town of Madeira.

By morning, the malevolent allies of wind, water, darkness and bitter cold had become bored, just as the accents of Boston, Providence and New Haven had predicted in the darkest hours; much to the scorn and disbelief of those more often heard in Stirling and Argyll.

The new day which greeted the survivors aboard *Liberty* as they at last ventured on deck, was sublime. They would live on. Terror was supplanted by limitless joy, bitter cold by pleasant warmth, darkness was now sunlight with colours so brilliant as to confound the eye. Not so, that which greeted Lliam Hooligan who despite having scared himself half to death all night, hanging on to a spar and being waved about like a child's flag a hundred feet above the deck, found the strength to descend with a youth hanging inert over his shoulder. Both men collapsed there on the deck and lay still.

In these latitudes, the sun burned off the mist of the worst of storms even before it showed its face to the solitary figure in the nets, so that when the seasick, bruised, and in some cases injured, highlanders began to emerge, the day was bright, and the rugged beauty of Madeira lay before them. The hills were clothed in every shade of green, marked here and there by cliffs of red and gold with occasional volcanic outcrops of cinder grey.

At the foot of those ramparts, nestling so very comfortably between them and the ocean, lay the town of Funchal; stone-built in the Portuguese style in order to take full advantage of the splendid climate. Elegant homes and businesses were crowding timidly around its ancient Catholic cathedral, like sheep around a shepherd, while further off, the slave-shacks declared such evidence to be a vulgar untruth. Those Scots who were of a homesick disposition, were reminded by this place of the well-to-do neighbourhoods of Oban or Aberfeldy, uprooted and transplanted in a warmer, more colourful clime; its outlook, a strip of pale sand and a bay which; dissatisfied with its own extraordinary palette; borrowed from the colours of the mountains, boasting French Marine, azure, beryl and teal, but also turquoise, shamrock, privet and olive-green. All of this and the ever-present sprinklings of blossoms of a thousand hues made this haven a delight to behold.

Captivated by such a profusion of colour, warmth and charm, the immigrants drifted to the ship's sides, and lifting their little ones, gazed in wonder that the world which had dealt with them so harshly thus far, could contain such gems, such sanctuaries, such beauty. There was no sign of the *Justice*, although the *Bird*, the *Liverpool* and the *Boston* had all arrived safely and lay at anchor among many others inside the harbour formed by the curve of Funchal's shore.

'What had he done?' Lliam Hooligan was torn. The missing Justice held hundreds of people for whose lives he was responsible, to say nothing of all the stuff for the war.' A grey cloud of concern descended upon him which would discolour his conscience until he hopefully saw her again, safe and whole.

There being many advantages in contiguity Teach brought the *Liberty* deeper into the harbour during the mid-watch and anchored her within a few hundred yards of the others, a couple of leagues offshore. He too, wondered about the fate of the *Justice*. He had good friends aboard and a cargo much needed by his country. His new country. A country that would soon be free of British tyranny. He liked the sound of that and rolled it around on his tongue once or twice.

Lliam Hooligan breakfasted on a mountain of grilled oatcakes spread with a concoction of fish with eggs, complimented by mashed potato fried till it was crispy and roasting hot; all of it wonderfully flavoured with some of the spices which his adoring Scottish girls had purchased in Nantes and redolent of the eating establishments of that distant well-loved town. His magnificence had not so much as considered complaining, when the gorgeous creatures had expected him to accompany his meal with nothing stronger than coffee but could not consider himself properly set up for the day until an hour later, when he served himself a few pints of particularly good ale, during his tour of inspection. Deep in the holds of the ship, three levels of which lay beneath the gun deck, he was greatly relieved to discover that despite considerable injury having been inflicted on two of the five hatches, his cargo remained undamaged due mainly to the exercise of a bit of forethought, a field or two of canvas, and a mile of good English hemp. It was all as dry as summer in the infernal regions. Satisfied that nothing had been damaged or soaked or shifted dangerously by the storm, he was squeezing between boxes of muskets and pallets of tents as he searched for a way out of this endless cave when he met several men clearly infected by an unspoken misery. The group could not and did not try to conceal the dismal frame of mind that had beset them having served food and water to the English prisoners held in the unendurable captivity that only a ship can inflict. These men understood better than most, what it was like to live in complete darkness. It reduced a man's body, but worse and more painful still, it reduced his mind.

"What sort of state are they weasels in?"

"We feed and water them well, Lliam, as you ordered," said one, "but even if you gave them hammocks, it would still be prison in the dark, below the waterline, standing in filth. Rats. The dark." The others nodded in agreement.

"What do ye reckon?"

"They ain't no easy damn answer, Lliam," confessed a sailor, who like himself wore a patch over one eye and had rope-burn around his throat. Lliam liked the man immediately for his evident masculinity.

"If you give 'em light, they might set fire…"

"That's bollocks." The slack mouth was the fool called Gulley. The eye patch ignored the fool.

"If they timed it right and lit the back of their cave, we'd have to get 'em out just to save the ship. Quick. And that might be all the chance they would need. If there was any space above the waterline; why, my vote would be to build a pen like them bitches do wit' the niggers, or even chain 'em an' let 'em on deck ever so often." This considerate, though impossible sort of regime seemed more to the gang's liking; there was a lot of head-nodding going on.

"So, they's on deck them Brits, an' one of 'em grabs a shipmate and knifes him…"

snorted Gulley. The prospect was so very likely that nobody contradicted the loud-mouth know-all.

"Look what they done to 'Arry. Arry was my mate" The afterthought all but unmanned poor Gulley.

"What would you say to throwing them over the side for an hour to wash the muck off? Feel the sun on their backs. You could all carry muskets."

This idea was given a cautious welcome by the men.

"Right! Speak to the captain and see what he says." Hooligan hurried on ahead; there were three more ships to inspect and time was wasting; he would waste none of it caring for rats. When he at last got topside, desperate to wet his throat, he found that all three longboats and both knockdowns were busy ferrying people to and from the shore, so he had no choice but to stand and wait at the ship's side. Many of the Scottish maidens thought the world of the gentle giant, unconcerned by his looks and deeply impressed by the fine qualities of the man. They came to hang around his neck like fragrant rosaries as he waited; pressing their well-developed bodies against him while he nursed a semi in his pantaloons as, he felt sure, they were all well-aware. The Admiral had seen these maidens dancing one of their stunning spectacles called the 'sword dance,' watching unblinking as they skipped around on a cross formed of two razor-sharp blades at the risk of cutting off their feet, and he knew damn well that they wore not a thing beneath those tartan kilts. Making his escape which was the last thing he wanted to do the frustrated leader of men eventually squeezed into an already overloaded boat and made the steersman divert to the *Bird* on his way to the beach. When he looked up in farewell at the *Liberty*, the beautiful Flora something-or-other, was leaning suggestively over the side, gazing lovingly at him. Smiling knowingly, the raven-haired beauty moistened a finger at her full, wide mouth and trailed it down the pale skin of her slender throat to the deep shadows between her heavy breasts. Had he been standing Hooligan would have toppled into the sea. 'The filty bitch.' Shocked he was. Shocked by this public display of filt, forgetting meanwhile that "filty bitches," were very

ing518

much a preoccupation of his. Despite his public hauteur he looked back long and often to where the girl watched him still, and those aboard who noticed, smiled sympathetically in their happiness for the insanely generous, frighteningly grotesque madman.

It was clear from the incessant comings and goings of the ship's boats, that the crews and passengers of the *Bird*, the *Liverpool* and the *Boston*, were taking full advantage of their presence at such an oasis of beauty and promise, and the leader of men could readily understand why, but with three more cargoes to inspect, he knew that for his own part, it was his God-cursed luck never to see the inside of any class of a tavern this day. 'Sure, this being an Admiral bollox was a royal pain in the arse.'

Finding that the *Bird* was being guarded by only a handful of men, he set aside the formalities, climbed aboard, returned the young guard's adulatory handshake, and went straight below decks, where he found Holdsworth bent over a chart of the islands. The big Negro had not heard his approach.

"Sure, this Captaining malarkey has made a boring son of a bitch out of a big black boring son of a bitch," he observed.

"Lliam, you old tup," grinned Holdsworth, his shining handsome face splitting in two with pleasure at seeing his friend safe and sound.

"You look like shit. Rum or Madeira?"

"I'll have madeeryo. Where is she?"

Holdsworth grabbed a couple of pewter tankards and filled them from a jug with what looked to the Irishman like the blood and milk of a goat; freshly sourced.

"Saude," grinned Holdsworth, and touched Hooligan's cup with his own.

"Slowly Lliam, it's not beer, it's wine," he advised, and watched in amusement as the Hooligan swallowed 'like a two-bit hoar.' Perennially on the lookout for profitable cargoes, the born-again Admiral swilled the liver-coloured liquid noisily around his palette, and instantly became a convert. He resolved right away that he had just found the stuff with which to fill up any empty spaces on his boats, 'and the *Bird's* as well,' if the Americans were of a mind to make a quid. He would run the idea past Teach, naturally; Martin being the anointed one in such matters as buying and selling.

He conceded in the dusk and deeply frustrated by his inability to find fault aboard his ships he paddled himself ashore in the warm darkness; a lone drunk, bawling obscene sea shanties in a boat built for thirty. Steering by the oil lights which lined the thoroughfare behind the beach he aimed for the cathedral whose tumescence was clearly visible in the night sky, but the god cursed Cat'lics kept moving the damn thing and he was obliged to tack all over the ocean on his way in. The locals, who were indulging in the 'passeggiata,' the pleasant continental custom of strolling to-and-fro, seeing and being seen, were appalled. The emergence from the ocean of a drunken horror, loudly mouthing obscenities, sent them home early, cursing the uncivilised protestant pigs from the frozen north who insisted on inflicting their poisonous presence on a refined God-fearing society. Many of them, in their well warranted Christian irritation, to apply the thumbscrews to their house slaves; or to rape a pretty one; or two. Weary, but well pleased with the way his enterprise was pulling together, Hooligan dragged the prow of the huge boat as far as he could on to the sand and lay down to rest for a moment, until he got his breath back. He was asleep at the instant in which his drunken head touched the warm sand, and hence oblivious to the water filling his boots as it crept up the beach. Lifting the stern of the cutter, the tide swung the two-tonne boat around and placed its prow gently on the drunk's heaving chest.

Those cursed creepy-crawlies were making enough racket to wake an innocent citizen who needed his rest. A tribe of ankle-biters were screaming like eedjits running wild through this forest and not a soul would bother his bone-idle arse to take the belt to the little bastards at all. Men were bawling, women were jabbering, and the beef was roasting. He could smell it. Beef was roasting close by, or he was a bloody Dutchie, but for the life of him he couldn't get up off his arse. Something was holding him down on the ground. Worst of all; some demented Scottish murderer was strangling the damned pipes. Was there no peace? And him with a head like 'a fookin stamp mill.'

"Mister Hooligan. A hair of the dog that bit ye." He was being raised up to the vertical, by persons unknown; whether-or-not he wanted to stand mind you, so he protested in the abstract at this foul intrusion to his off-duty time, but no one was up for a fight and anyway a pot was being thrust into his hand by a half-naked bag of startlingly white bones in a kilt.

"Slanje var, friend Hooligan," said the bones. A herd of grinning idiots there was, surrounding himself and the bare-naked slanje variest, all of them raising their jugs and drinking like priests who had found the key to the communion wine. His legs wouldn't work. If these eedjits let-go-of him; he was done for. He took a swig and tasting only his own disgusting mouth spat in the dirt, but mostly down his front, then tried again with similar results.

"Where the fuck am I?" he asked very quietly, vaguely remembering something about having a boat on top of him, and drowning. There was no class of a boat here at all. Nor even a sea. This place was a jungle.

"It's our wee hame frae hame, Mister Hooligan sur, and welcome. We call it Ballachulish. Welcome frae all of us, tae our wee town. What we have is yoors, ye ken.* We'd naer had a chance tae thank ye for all that ye've done fer us, and all that, us being on the *Liverpool*. Stay with us a while, eat, drink. The Admiral didn't have a clue what the naked loon was talking about. What was more; he couldn't care less, so he took refuge in reticence. Tottering into the highlander's arms, he grasped the man's hand, mainly in order to remain upright, and crushed the thing, wordlessly while staring ferociously into the stranger's blue, warlike eyes. The Scot was clearly transported by this manly stuff, so, to the surprise and delight of the whole clan, he gave every one of them a dose of the same, then without a word, staggered off to find that roast beef and madeerio, watched all the way in worshipful silence. Beyond the shade of the trees, he staggered into a cauldron of blinding light and heat such as he had never known. It was terrifying, unbearable. Tearing off his clothing and dropping it behind him as he went, he piled his stinking shirt on top of his head for protection; all the while being drawn along by the aroma of roast beef. 'Jasus, Oive got to have some of that stuff.' He was in an encampment that much was clear. A whole village of shacks there was consisting of legs and roofs but no walls. There were hundreds of Scots and sailors and women and ankle-biters around, all as happy as monks with a new flagellum; the sea was flopping onto the sand and themselves were flopping into the sea.

"This is the life," he bawled at no one at all and squeezed his poor head in his hands in the torment of all the saints themselves. His Gaels were living on the beach. The sailors too. 'Who would've tawt of it?' Half-naked people were milling around all over the shop, stuffing their faces, guzzling booze and flinging themselves headfirst into the water. He would bloody well join 'em, that's what he would do. They could sail those damned ships up their arse, for as long as they were on this island, he Lliam Shaun Hooligan, would be livin' right here in the hot, fresh air. He struggled on like the saint he was through the burning sand, barely aware that he was being followed by a growing crowd of his disciples, all happy just to be near their saviour for a while. 'Where was that beef? That was the ting.'

By the time he discovered the fire-pit, over which a whole carcass, ten feet long was sizzling he was sizzling himself sure with the sun hammering his head flat. He had discarded most of his clothes on the way only to have half of Scotland pick the damn things up and trail along in his wake, as if he was Jesus Christ All fookin moighty hisself. This had to stop. Now! Before some bastard got a fat lip. His appearance at the kitchen caused another riot. Every lassie within a hundred miles ran up squealing like banshees, fit to tear his poor brain from his skull as he shoved through the crowd of them to get at the sizzling grub. Untold numbers of young women draped themselves around his neck, while another dozen or two attached themselves to his poor arms and pulled till they were wrenched clean off. Unable to suffer any more of this bollix with the brain too big for the 'crameul cavorty,' he was about to explode and make them all cry when he remembered Macbeth and heard the omniscient fucker whispering in his ear.   *Ken   Know

''You saved their lives, man. It's purfecly natural that they'd want tae show their gratitude. They think you're a hero, so gie them just a wee bittie hero.'' Armed with a couple of pounds weight of the most delicious beef ever cooked, wrapped in bread that was as flat as an Arab's sandal, and tasted like the bastard's feet, the persecuted one shook off his worshippers and staggered away westward, intent on mounting a high outcrop of rock; one obviously deposited there a million years ago for no other reason than to free a man from unwanted gratitude, which was a great big fat pain in the arse. By the time he had staggered up to the summit, careful not to spill his drink or drop his sandal, the whole clan had congregated below him. They were silent; waiting; and for a moment, he was seduced by power. He couldn't do it. He couldn't tell them lovely colleens to leave him and his dick alone. 'He didn't 'want' them to leave his dick alone.'

"I bloody love you," he bawled, and almost fell off.

"Friends," he said, starting from scratch, his voice carrying all the way to the far end of the beach, where lads were leaping into the sea from a rock like his own, and echoing back to him.

"You're bloody good folk... none like ye." He raised aloft his drink and his hot beef sandal and was applauded madly.

"The beef's great.   The bread's shoite."

The boys who had been going around in circles, leaping into the sea, splashing to the shore, climbing up and leaping into the water again, had stopped; mesmerised. Something had occurred, a skinny youth about to jump, halted his frantic rush at the last moment and stepped back, transfixed. There was an upheaval in the water as something huge... black like an upturned boat… something so big as to be instantly appalling. Lliam Shaun

Hooligan of the County Mayo Hooligans stepped off his own lofty perch, dropped twenty feet to the sand, rolled, and was up, painfully sober and charging in one fluid movement. The children were screaming again, but the sound had a different meaning to it now. Terror. The hard, wet sand at the water's edge gave good footing and he went like a hare with a greyhound up its arse, being overtaken by other frantic men. In his desperation to get to the child lying in the water he seemed to be running in glue. A black shape. A fin a yard high. What had he heard about this? 'Like a mantrap,' Macbeth had said. The fastest way was straight up the sloping rock, just like the leprechauns had been doing. The climb bled the speed off him. Hitting the edge, he leapt out as far as he could, and glimpsed something huge, grey and circling; then the child below as he fell, still on the surface but face down, his fan of black hair like the pistil of a huge scarlet poppy of undulating water.

'Mother of Christ!

The water!

It was red!'

He struck and went under, into liquid flesh; warm and red, kicking furiously for the surface, came up gasping, sucked in air and water grabbed the child's dead-still arm all in the same instant and churned for the sand, kicking hard and pulling in a frenzy of terror with his one free arm, dragging the boy who weighed nothing at all; driven by fear of the teeth as big as his willie and the mouth loik a fookin mantrap. Being clutched now by a crowd of desperate, shouting men that he couldn't hear. Their eyes wide and white. He staggered and collapsed in the shallow water, releasing the boy to them. The red boy, the boy with no legs.

"Christ, save us."

The child's legs were gone. Ripped in half, he was.

"Jesus, Joseph and Mary. The horror of it."

Hooligan got to his knees, crawling in terror out of the beast's filthy water. There was crying and wailing. The poor demented mother shrieking now in her own agony. He was on his feet and staggering away from the awful thing falling but still crawling through the hellish heat toward the jungle.

The mother's agony which would tear at her poor heart for ever. The others keening also. His memories were too terrible to admit. He could not be around it, this agony of women. He could not bear to hear the women cry. He covered his ear with his hand got back on his feet and fled, staggering along the beach, oblivious to the concern of the crowds. Into the forests at last, and the blessed heaven-sent roar of the cicadas. Himself was crying. Bawling like a baby and not knowing why. He rubbed angrily at his treacherous eye until the cursed thing stopped its leaking.

''Thank Chroist.'' He cursed. He was sucking-in air like a bellows.

"You care too much, Lliam Hooligan." The voice was more loving than any he had ever known. He sensed that it was Flora, even before he turned around. The beauty took his ruined head in her gentle hands, reached up; kissed him on his scarred mouth and led him to her home in the forest.

"You're talkin' shoite," he snorted at Teach, and watched Angelique lift yet another long-legged child into the saddle for a pony-ride along the sand; a child much like the one that they had laid to rest only days earlier. Andrew Carnegie would be back from Funchal town soon, with his team which he had swum ashore; the lad was making good money carting stuff around the island, just as he had predicted he would. It would make sense to get a ride into town wit' the boy when he went back there. Teach was still laughing at him, damn his hide, which was a sure sign that the bugger was correct, again, and himself as wrong as popery. Hooligan hated being wrong.

"I'll prove it to you. We'll go down to town and I'll show you," Teach chortled. Ignoring his friend's mockery Hooligan turned to face the assembled Captains and changed the subject.

"Right, we're agreed then," he pontificated. "One. The prisoners will be banged up in sheds on the decks, in leg-irons. Two. Everyone must clean demselves with paper and wash their stinkin' arse after being in the nets. The jocks and us included. Every bastard." The captains nodded. Smirking.

"Tree. Every time a horse is exorcoised, it will be moored to a mast, 'before,' it gets outa the stall. Now, dere's just one more ting; scurvy." Eyes rolled exaggeratedly to a general chorus of amusement as Lliam climbed into the saddle of his hobby horse.

"You fellers can do what you damned well like on the *Bird* but listen to this." He motioned at the half naked crowds in straw hats who populated the beach outside the hut.

"Did you ever see anytin so unskurvyish? An' a month or two back, dey were bangin' on death's door trying to get in."

"Christ Lliam, you been force feedin' 'em like a French goose," Longbottom observed.

"Yea, but it's not just dat, is it?" frustrated that he could not make his lieutenants understand him the admiral was instantly angry with them and himself. He didn't yet have the words.

"Think about dis," he suggested.

''The only place you get scurvy, is on a boat. You don't get scurvy on land." There was no reply.

"Sailors who get heaps of biscuit, still get scurvy, and it ain't just because they're on a boat. Fishermen who go out at sun up an come home at noight for din dins don't get it. I'm tellin' you boys, if we do like the filty Limeys does… Dere you go; dats why they call them 'limeys,' and take lemons and limes and oranges and anytin what grows, we will get across that 'Lantic, no bother. Oi don't loik givin' orders; but I want me boats crammed full of that stuff. You should see the oranges going onto that *Poseidon* down there," he nodded at a distant English ship.

"They ain't got no scurvy."

"We know you're right, Lliam," someone drawled.

"No one wants to see any more of it. We'll do as you say, and gladly." Hooligan knew that he was right too. Knew it in his bones. 'Look at this place. A man would never see scurvy on this beach in a hundred years.' As he glanced around the idyllic scene, he saw that the Scots and the sailors living here understood right enough, because the important stuff had been well taken care of. Three barrels provided beer, rum, and Madeira, for the taking, and there was fresh clean drinking water which ran from a stone channel that came from some-place-else. There were open-sided little 'but and bens,*' thrown up to provide shade from the sun. Racks of fish were hanging up to dry, alongside a whole beef, from which people could carve slices and make their own beef sandal. But there was also watermelon, oranges, limes, peppers, fresh bread, onions, corn, potatoes and five sorts of cheese. The answer was 'good food,' not just 'plenty of ship's biscuit,' and he knew it. If the sailors did what he bloody-well told them; then these four of his five ships would make the journey in good health. It was a crying shame, he concluded, that the *Justice* was not here to benefit from his wisdom. When he caught up with it at Tenerife, he would impart his higher knowledge to those buggers too. If she had got there.

On the forest track beyond the beach, Carnegie had returned and was standing beside his cart; spooning with Angelique who now wore a kilt. That vehicle was the clumsiest, ugliest conveyance that you could ever wish to see. A two-wheeled thing carved out of a whole tree and weighing a damn sight more than the load it carried. 'Them Portageezers wouldn't know what day it was.'

He wondered momentarily what the hell the locals had done about shifting all manner of rubbish before *Liberty* and Andrew Carnegie had pulled into port.

"Macbeth, Levi, Trewin come wit me boys, and we'll show this smart-assed colonial prick a ting or two," declared the Admiral, indicating his smug captain.

"And we'll roide into town in style." The anointed ones shared a conspiratorial laugh and followed their unbelievably, but amusingly, ignorant friend towards Carnegie's monstrosity of a cart with wheels taller than a man. Those Captains and boatswains who were remaining behind watched the gang depart, chuckling sympathetically at the poor devils who were now responsible for a twenty-two-stone four-year-old, who stood six-foot-six on his bare feet, and was blessed with the temperament of a demented mule.

The business property of Diogo Vaz Teixeira would have put many a French chateau or English country-house to shame. Situated above and to the west of Funchal, the romantic estate boasted superb southerly views across the forests to the quiet suburbs of the town and the limitless ocean beyond, and gloried in an atmosphere redolent of forest flowers, seasoned with salt and pepper. Formerly cloaked in woods, the hills inland of the sprawling property now lay in the ordered tranquillity of vineyards where colourful workers slaved fearfully in the green geometrical expanse. Only the twenty acres or so immediately around the house were walled, and within that secure bastion, the building itself was further served by a moat which was kept clear and fresh by virtue of one of the channels which brought water from the ravines in the hills above. Towers with steeples abounded, and leaded windows, some tall and narrow in design as though for use by archers, lent a warlike note which was complimented by the drawbridge and portcullis, both features of the divine baroque entranceway. Glorious summer being the sole nature of the weather hereabouts, the rooms had been arranged around a wonderfully large and cool atrium, where much of the day-to-day business of the remarkably successful vintner, Tiexiera was conducted beneath exquisite sunshades of Polish lace. The four desperados were impressed. They stood on the drawbridge taking it all in, just as poor students absorb anything that their tutors tell them, while considering the highly decorative architectural devices and artistic stonework of the veritable palace.

"So, you're sure that this madeerio will sell at your place?" asked the nuisance for the tenth time. "I'm not wantin' to spend a bloody fortune and have to drink the stuff meself."

''You'd like nothing better,'' was the general sentiment of the meeting.

"Would I put you crook?" inquired Teach. "Did you make some coin when we off-loaded the cognac on that Dutchie, or did you not? I'm telling you with my hand on my heart,'' he patted his arse,

''Madeira is a very big seller back home. It's highly sought-after and gets top prices.'' Not wanting to be overheard by the locals, the friends turned their backs for a moment on the home of the opposition and walked away as they put the final touches to their strategy.

"How many casks do you think we can take?" Hooligan was keen to fill his holds to the gunnels.

"Well now, this is what I was trying to tell you back there in Ballachulish," Teach stipulated, as though talking to a child, trying enthusiastically to cause an Irish explosion which, to his disappointment, did not eventuate.

"But would you listen? Of course not, you know-all son of a bitch. There's plenty of space left in the holds, and the ships are all still riding a bit high in the water, but I couldn't even guess at what sort of numbers it would take to fill them. What I 'do' know is this. If we buy the stuff in those little casks that they use here, we will be carrying as much air as wine." Hooligan stared thoughtfully into his friend's handsome face, scarred courtesy of Michael Astor's red-hot poker and considered calling him a stupid bastard or better still a 'stupid American bastard.'

"So, what do we do then?" he asked. Bland as he knew how.

"It's your gold Lliam, but my advice would be to insist that we buy it in tuns. Huge bloody barrels as big as a haystack. They mature the stuff in tuns and then they sell it to small people in barrels and in small casks. We are not small people; we will buy it in tuns and carry less air and less wood to Boston. Less barrel, less air, more profit."

"What a load of bollocks. You sir, are so tick, I don't know how you get dressed in the mornin.'" Hooligan shook his head in pity.

"Less wood."

Teach was unmoved, shading his eyes, he was peering at an open-fronted barn in which resided two-wheeled carts, pallets of brand-new casks, and young vines, ready for planting.

"Come with me child," he said, dripping condescension, and stalked off in the direction of those hogsheads. In the comparative cool of the lean-to he approached a truncated barrel which conveniently sat empty next to thousands of casks.

"This is a barrel.''

"Roight. I know what a bloody barrel is, you wee snot."

Teach ignored the petulant child and placed five of the small casks inside around the circumference and then placed three more in the middle; an arrangement that necessarily left gaps between the casks which he pointed to enthusiastically. He then stood aside in order to display the day's lesson.

"Less wood, less air," he bragged, supercilious as he knew how.

The dawn broke.

"Well, bugger me nightly," the undeniable proof right there at the gang's knees.

"No thanks. Not while there's dogs in the street." It was the traditional reply. Noticing the smiles which now surrounded him the overgrown child deduced a great deal.

"You!" he shot. "You knew dis all along and din't say a bloind word to stop me makin' a narse of meself, you malfeasant little pricks." Macbeth's charming smile may have broadened.

"There is one present," the scot chided, "who was so sure of his ground that he told his gainsayers that they were, 'talking drivle.' I didn't feel particularly inclined to project myself intae such a conversation."

"'Partly inclined to perfect meself,'" mocked the deflated one, wearing a schoolyard expression.

"Stuff you then, the lot of yous." Their squabble thusly resolved, the gang passed happily once again, across the drawbridge and as no one was around to serve them, strolled into the moderately busy atrium where they sat down at a table to await service, surrounded by sea captains from all over the world, all wonderfully relaxed and groaning away to each other in well-oiled stupefaction. A selection of hard liquors was soon brought to their table by a servant whose hands were purple, the timid individual placed the silver tray on their table then left without eye contact or conversation. Admiral Hooligan watched the silent one as he departed and reached for a drink.

"Sure, you'd think he'd had his tongue cut out," he selected a tumbler and reached for the whiskey.

"He has," brayed Macbeth. Andrew slapped Hooligan's hand loudly.

''We don't drink before doing business. He's a slave. I bet they had his balls off too. The Portuguese are a cruel bunch.''

"The dirty bastards." Hooligan was incredulous and dismayed.

Being a wily old crook of many years' experience Teixeira made the revolting customers wait precisely the correct length of time that good business ordained; enough to let the

God-cursed unbelievers know that he was a very busy man and in no need of their patronage, but not so long as to infer that their business was not appreciated. They would by that time have drunk half a bottle of hard-liquor apiece and be as easy to strangle as a kitten. When he made his entry to the atrium through a far grander doorway than the one from which his eunuch had emerged, he was wearing a fez, and an ankle-long, flowing garment of cream-coloured Egyptian cotton, embroidered in rust and tan, in whose folds his hands were properly concealed because a personage exalted as he, resides in the intellect alone.

"I am Diogo Vaz Teixeira." he boasted modestly, in heavily accented English,

"May I be of assistance gentlemen?" His black, murderously cruel eyes noted that these pagan buyers of dregs and horse piss just so long as it was cheap, had not availed themselves of his hospitality. 'Strange. As a rule, their type drank like camels, but with less grace.'

"I am Martin Teach," said the captain standing but not offering his hand and thus relieving Teixeira of the need to bathe a second time that morning, "and this is Mister Hooligan." Lliam Hooligan, millionaire, remained seated, his long legs crossed. He glowered insultingly at the merchant and made no attempt at a greeting.

"Mister Hooligan has come to taste your most exquisite Madeira and possibly make a purchase." With that simple statement Teach inverted the order of seniority which Teixeira had imposed by his tardiness.

"Of course." Smarting at the foreign dog's implications and tone, Teixeira snapped his fingers within their cosy retreat, and almost immediately an individual in garishly colourful working clothes exited a small door like a cuckoo exiting a clock, he bowed to the group. The newcomer wore knee-length umber trousers and a belted woollen jacket in stripes of a dozen colours. On his feet were the clumsiest shoes ever made which in Hooligan's considered opinion had been carved out of the local stone. The man's greasy black hair was parted precisely down the middle of his head, causing the visitors to wonder why he did not wash the stuff if he was going to bother parting it. Purple hands were a common affliction in this place clearly.

"Salem will attend to your needs, gentlemen, I pray Allah some of our poor produce meets your exacting standards." With that mild insult the proprietor was gone.

"What a prick," observed Hooligan loudly enough for Teixeira to hear. Gesturing for the rabble to please follow him, Salem set off along an endless cloister whose vaulted roof made a cavalry charge of his footfalls. Entering an incredibly wide and lofty interior which might once have been a church, the irreverent mob crossed its cavernous spaces with no appreciable reduction in the volume of their blasphemies, and dropped down several flights of wide stone steps, eroded ankle deep by a hundred million footfalls. The pilgrimage was then stalled by arching doors, more iron than wood with the story of creation carved in deep relief into their surface.

'Stone Feet,' as Hooligan had christened their uncommunicative guide, then drew the mother of all keys, which was fully a foot long, from the interior of his coat of many colours, and ceremonially unlocked the holy-of-holies with a revealing flourish. He then clog-danced to one side in order to afford the ignoramuses unobstructed access to the sanctuary, and to distance himself from any bolt of lightning with which his God might murder the irreligious pagans. The vast chamber was well-lit. Numberless torches seated in iron brackets on the walls illuminated an endless succession of arches, beneath which resided a hundred tuns each as big as a cottage, and a thousand majestic vats, tens of thousands of barrels, likewise with the smaller, portable casks, and millions it seemed, of dusty bottles lying on their sides in racks, which extended a far distance.

Surprisingly, the vault was not cold as the intrepid buyers had expected it to be.

"It's not cold down here," blurted Hooligan; giving voice to what all four Europeans were thinking.

"Madeira wines perform best when warm, that's the secret of the vats" volunteered Teach, who laid a finger alongside his nose as he spoke.

"This must be the fookin vatacombs then." Hooligan announced; 'humorously' he thought, but no bastard laughed.

''Sod the lot of you then,'' he grunted. Bloody annoyed.

"Here is Madeira," Salem signed, implying it seemed to the customers that the latter day Joseph had other vaults like this tucked away somewhere, full of yet to be sampled delights. Totally accepting of his master's implied opinion of these timewasters, Salem took the bit between his teeth and cantered towards the deeper recesses of the vaults, where the poorer years were stored for easy access by Protestants and other riffraff only to find that he was not being followed. To his consternation, the benighted philistines were heading for the tuns of what was 'the finest elixir' ever conjured by the partnership of mortal man and God. He bridled and galloped in pursuit.

"I'll give this one the taste test, Salem, ma boy." The moving mountain was as loud as he was repellent. He was leaning irreverently against the belly of a tun of the unequalled Forty-two, as though it was his fat, undoubted hoar of a wife; not intimidated at all by his surroundings and the presence of perfection. By means of facial expressions and hand gestures poor Salem indicated that this would not be possible. Why, the vat of heaven's own ambrosia had not yet been decanted. Lovingly he brought the cyclops' attention to the scarlet wax seal around the tap, cupping it in his purple hands as though it were his new - born son.

"Gimme some then man; I haven't got all day," Hooligan smiled wickedly, frightening poor Salem who had turned a deathly ivory tone beneath his oaken skin even in the golden light of the torches; he grasped his prayer beads beginning to hyperventilate as he did so.

''I'll do it chum.'' Andrew reached helpfully for the holy-of-holies sympathetically, letting the poor fellow off the hook.

"That will all being Salem, you may going."

Very similar in shape to a tun, and almost as large; a christian monk had appeared at Salem's elbow, having deserted a gang of English captains who were haggling even over the dirt-cheap camel pee. Without a word, Salem turned and escaped thankfully; his hooves clattering across the flags.

"I other hear your speech word with that," said the newcomer.

"I am Diogo Cao, at service. We a impasse; no?" Hooligan considered the pompous ass who of necessity, held his arms out at his sides.

"No, we don't," he replied objectionably.

"I want to try dis stuff. Now." He indicated the Forty-two with a jerk of his head. Patting its underbelly affectionately, as though he already owned it.

"Desole, me he not poseebla be," intoned Cao, delighted to thwart the wishes of this ugly, foul-mouthed peasant.

"She be not decant."

"Mister Hooligan does not require you to decant it," Teach snorted down his nose.

"If the stuff meets his exacting standards, he will buy it. All of it. And more besides." At a loss for an answer to such a barefaced lie, and now at an impasse of his own, Cao began to sweat profusely and as the interlopers let the silence draw out to the 'embarrassing' stage while fingering the arsenal of weapons under whose significant burden each of them laboured, said.

"Mighty I sugges?"

"No. You moighty not. Gimme some of this stuff and stop fucking about or oill get that Dago Max Teararse down here."

"My friend here is of an unpredictable and I might say, utterly objectionable turn of mind," Teach was all sympathy.

"Perhaps it would be better."

Tears of fear and self-pity left trails down Cao's fat mixed-race faces.

"Moment," he sobbed and waddled away deeper into his underground principality.

"You bastard," hissed Copplestone grinning.

"Give the man a chance. You've had your fun."

"Yeah, alright. Don't you start as well," said the unrepentant Hooligan,

"there's nothin' worse in dis world than a big, fat spoilsport."

"I'm not fat," observed Trewin

"Or big," noted Macbeth.

Cao reappeared in a matter of minutes, bearing a silver tray forward of his gently-swaying, monumental, puff-making obesity. On the tray rested glistening wine glasses, a crystal decanter and several kerchiefs of virginal whiteness. He was breathing hard as though he had been running.

"Thank you, Mister Cao," said Copplestone expansively.

"My friend, Mister Hooligan here, has something to show you." Whatever that 'something' was, Hooligan didn't have a clue, until the soldier made a filthy gesture, staring intently meanwhile at the Irishman's crotch, where the madman kept his purse.

"Oh yea, so I do." The customer retrieved the chamois leather sack from within his drawers with much unnecessary fondling of the contents thereof and drew the strings.

"Will these fellas do ye?" he inquired pouring a minor avalanche of gold coins into his paw. The effect of this display on poor Cao was wondrous to see. His expression became that of a major fellon reprieved in the moment when the noose went around his neck and his bitter tears of despair were succeeded by an oily seepage of relief and joy. The mating-worms of his wet lips positively drooled.

Placing the silver tray on a tasting table of glimmering juniper, he wrung his soft, white hands in ecstasy, his eyes tightly closed, and face turned upward towards an invisible heaven.

Protruding from the wax seal of the 'Dog's Silly Farty Two,' as Hooligan christened the elixir, were short lengths of twine which terminated in small wooden toggles. Taking these expertly between his fingers, Cao tugged gently with the confidence of long practice, and the binding sliced effortlessly through the scarlet wax allowing it to fall free.

"Senor." Cao proffered the tray and each of the peasants selected a glass. Positioning himself well, as was his habit of years, the winemaker ensured that the ceremony could be enjoyed by all of those present; always supposing that any one of them was capable of such a level of understanding and appreciation; and holding the decanter beneath the tap with the care that he would expend holding the new-born christ, drew off a small quantity of the elixir, sufficient only for modest drinks. Pushing the wooden tap back into its home, he thumped it apologetically with what reminded Hooligan painfully of a judge's gavel, then poured for his guests and himself. Cao sipped reverentially becoming one with the wine while surreptitiously watching the savages, who drank like sand but with less appreciation and had the gall to declare the ambrosia, 'better than angels piss.' A compliment of which he was unable to clear his troubled mind until the moment of his death a month later, when his mistreated heart gave up the ghost and refused to tap even one more vat. His passing would be long remembered in the dark hearts of the family Teixeira because, at the precise moment of his departure, Cao had tapped a vat of the De Gama Seventy-one in order to adjudge its progress towards perfection, and the delectable contents had washed the floor of the vault. On occasion, Teixeira would visit the grave of his former employee, and when no one was looking, curse the fellow roundly and urinate on his christian stone.

"We'll take that one then," rejoiced Hooligan slapping the oak loudly as though it was his horse and beginning to enjoy himself.

"Get some seats and some eats down here, can't ye?"

"And get a messenger too. I'm going to need every one of my men here, pronto." Teach had the bit between his teeth. "We'll try that one now."

Two score and more of the crofters remained on the beach from where they waved a sad farewell to Fleet Hooligan, as the heavily laden ships departed Madeira for the Canaries, a second archipelago which lay hundreds of miles to the south. The parents of the poor child killed by the enormous shark could not so much as think of sailing away and leaving their recently departed son alone on a strange island, and so they stayed. The dead child's adult brothers and sisters and their families, quite naturally, had also decided to stay behind. When all was considered and weighed in the balance of life, there were many far worse places to live, they had remarked, than the idyllic Pearl of the Atlantic. The four ships had been at anchor there much longer than the Americans would have liked. Homesick, and desperate to see their families once again, and to bring help to their countrymen in the war, they would have happily sailed straight passed The Pearl but for the necessities of repairs, water, fresh food and the last stages of their recuperation, and that of the Scots. As they waved farewell to their bereaved Scottish friends, the sailors were looking forward confidently to seeing Boston again soon. The captains and the boatswains of all four ships had proven their worth and more; the ships were in good condition, the English had been housed in their new humane jails, and everyone aboard was in good spirits.

"Boston, here we come," they shouted the sentiment gleefully from mast to mast, at each other, at the sea, and at the sky. Not for them, the end of a rope in some limey prison.

"I love ya, Lliam," they would bawl aboard the *Liberty*; should they glance down from the gods and see the monumental rogue on the deck below, all fitted out in his brand-new pea jacket of blue, as were they. Witnessing the sailors' joy in the thought of going home, the Scots were enthused also, and threw themselves into the work of sailing the vessels with the high spirits and energy with which they had endeared themselves to the Americans, with the result that the ships were sailed as close to the wind as ever they were, and good time was made, though they did not catch *Justice* before the Canaries.

Despite all that the Brits had done to them; the months of incarceration on the *Bird*, the theft of all their belongings, the death and wounding in combat of a dozen of their shipmates, and the cowardly murder of Harry the Cook, there wasn't a man among the abolitionists who was sorry to see the mean-minded. holier-than-thou misanthropes brought up out of their black hell and caged on the deck. Prisoners or not; they were to some acute degree, men after all, not rats and having them on deck somehow lifted a burden from the shoulders of sailors who had no wish to be gaolers. Lowering themselves to the levels of an inhuman enemy was not to the taste of Liberty's people.

The new cargo was incredibly heavy; so heavy that each vat had been dispatched to the ships in strict rotation in case any one of the vessels became accidentally overloaded. Captains and boatswains had worked their men to a standstill emptying the holds so that the monstrous tuns could be safely secured, directly on top of the keels as deep in the bowels of the ships as could be. This had been a worthwhile and critical task, one which resulted as the knowledgeable seamen expected, in the fully laden ships sitting deeper, safer, and more comfortably in the water, and responding in a more agile fashion to both rudder and sail. Confidence burgeoned.

On the decks of the three largest vessels were extra tuns destined for the holds of the absent *Justice*; Hooligan having overlooked nothing in his gamble on making a huge profit on his investment. He had risked it all on the promise of a killer increase and saw no point in hedging his bet. He could always blame his long-suffering pal Teach and curse him for a 'son of a bitch' if it didn't work out.

CHAPTER 29: The Obscenity

"Run out the guns. Load with grape. Women and children to safety. Signal the fleet to close on *Liberty*. Skirmishers aloft. Target her officers." The boredom which always plagued Teach and his crew on these long runs, died in an instant. Others in Fleet Hooligan had spotted the approaching danger simultaneously, and their course alterations were followed in turn by the backmarkers, so that by the time the stranger was in long cannon range, they had gained the protection of the gun platforms, *Justice* and *Liberty*.

"She's flying our colours." The call came from the foremast and was confirmed shortly afterwards by the other lookouts. Suspicious of a ruse de guerre Teach could not afford to let anybody relax.

"Prepare to fire," he ordered in his measured fashion and his boatswain roared the order. Still the stranger came on with no lessening of speed, her bows crashing into successive hillsides of immeasurable power to send mists of white water across her decks; her flanks now visible and her sixty-gun armament a terrible reality.

"Her guns are not run out." Despite the reassuring call, the tension aboard *Liberty* was palpable as the combined speeds of the vessels flung them within cannon range and then broadside, in moments measured in heartbeats.

"Her guns are not out." It was the foremast.

"She's shorting sail." The huge stranger was close enough now for the keenest eyes to ascertain that the observation was accurate; she had not run out that terrible armament and clearly intended to 'come about.' Relief swept through the ships' companies. The *Spartan* was a friend.

"She's American," the call came redundantly an instant after the sublime vessel unfurled the thirteen stars and stripes, a bright barn door on her jack staff.

"Hang fire," bawled the boatswain, but the order was lost amid the celebrations and the shrieking of the excited children who had scrambled up on deck, their distraught mothers unable to restrain them. What a sight the great warship was as she turned in a vast arc, her splendid sails glowing in the sunlight, coming about to sail alongside *Liberty*, leaving only a narrow chasm of surging ocean between them.

Ill-prepared to tolerate the frustrations of communicating through speaking trumpets, the *Spartan*'s Captain indicated that he wanted to send an officer aboard *Liberty*. Without delay, a belaying pin was slung bolus fashion across the intervening torrent, barely missing a racing child, and clattering across the deck bringing with it a fishing line, which enabled a thicker cord and finally a substantial hemp rope, to be hauled from the warship to the deck of the Liberty. Expecting this operation to be repeated in preparation for the boatswain's chair to be rigged, sailors snapped up the umbilical and took it one and one-half turns round the mainmast for the advantage of its friction; signalling that at this end, all was ready. Displaying less concern for his personal safety than would a wild boy when climbing a garden fence, a uniformed officer threw himself over the side of the American vessel and grasping hold of the seemingly animate hemp dropped into the chasm to hang by his hands, spider-like above the racing maelstrom. Every man, woman and child aboard *Liberty* flocked to the side in admiring fascination and concern at what the tiny figure was doing.

"Lower a boat!" barked Teach, having never seen anything like this, then had to repeat himself in a rage as fascinated sailors were slow to respond. Hooking one knee over the heaving lifeline and locking his ankle in place with the other leg, the figure began to drag himself hand over hand towards *Liberty*, a torturous trial, thirty yards long, ahead of him.

''Belay that.'' Teach was instantly convinced of this man's capabilities. Aware that a rogue wave might snatch away the intrepid sailor at any moment, and ready to take corrective action on the instant; the supportive team did the unbelievable and paid the rope out two yards or more, so that the fearless visitor would have the advantage of travelling downhill as far as the midway point. It was a tactic which paid dividends immediately though it threw the acrobat dangerously close to the malevolent grasping of the breakers. The improvement in his condition was such that he made astounding progress, advancing almost at walking speed. Working well together, the fast-tiring wranglers were soon compensating for the height of successive waves, as well as the ever-changing distance between the charging leviathans. At the halfway point, the relentless peaks being forced between the hulls were clutching at the madman's coat tails, despite the gut-tearing efforts aboard Liberty's decks.

"He'll never make it," English malice raised its shrill voice as the now tiring hero began the uphill stretch, the maladjusted youths chanted in hateful unison.

"Drown. Drown. Drown. Drown." Hooligan, and a gang of sailors who had been chased from the galley for filching, were devouring haggis while thoroughly appreciating the American's display of manliness when the English broke the spell. The marauders hurled the remnants of their meal at the spoilsports from short range, so that it splattered off the bars into the eyes of the charmless drones, silencing them momentarily.

"If ye don't have nuthin' noice to say, don't say nuthin' atall, me ma used to say."

Cognisant of their and their countryman's flagging strength, the rope-men called desperately for reinforcements, and with two dozen Scots flinging themselves into the task, the rope was hauled all but rigid. The uphill struggle instantly became the relative ease of the flat, and the acrobat's progress resumed reassuringly, as everyone aboard Liberty held their breath. The closer the tiring sailor came to the leviathan's side; the less the rope bucked in its efforts to dislodge him, and with five more torturous yards left to the safety of waiting arms, the hero did the unbelievable and caused every enchanted woman aboard to gasp in terror for the young god's safety. With his tortured muscles shrieking for relief and cramp threatening to dislodge him, he summoned up every ounce of energy remaining in him and launched himself up and over so that he lay chest-down on the rope with one ankle hooked over it and the other leg hanging as a counterweight. Incredibly, as the American covered those last yards, pushing with one leg and dragging himself with arms of fire; he was smiling. Many other arms almost exclusively female welcomed the stranger aboard, the Scottish lassies being thoroughly discomfited by this display of naked masculinity. Balancing easily at last on the Liberty's heaving bulwarks, seemingly unaware of the threat of death racing passed at his back, the gutsy officer beamed broadly at his admirers as though he had just entered a drawing-room, and declared

"I certainly hope that you are bound for the States, ladies, you're all so beautiful." The crowd was suddenly lit up by the smiles of the enchanted lassies, many of whom found it necessary to kiss him on both cheeks when he alighted as the American was remarkably handsome, in addition to having nerves of steel and muscles of iron. Swamped by the deluge of questions shouted at him, and the affectionate embrace of the women, the visitor found it necessary to seek refuge atop a hatch, on to which he leapt with agility.

"First things first," he bawled, begging for silence with upraised hands. When at last he could make himself heard, he began.

"I am Levi Nasser of the *Spartan*, that little ship over there. Thank you for your welcome, and your assistance in the crossing. I hope to get to know you all, but firstly I would welcome a word with your Captain." As Teach emerged from the crowd, Nasser invited him aloft; clearly intent on having his 'word' in public. This unassuming behaviour endeared him even more to his admirers; the females among the crowd looking forward very much to Levi's, 'getting to know them.'

"Where are you headed?" he asked, speaking not to Teach, but to the crowd.

"Boston," they chorused. "Via Hispaniola with the trade winds."

"What are you carrying?"

From the melange of answers proffered, it became clear to the very pretty Levi Nasser, that below decks, the *Liberty* had vast quantities of Madeira, an invaluable arsenal destined for the Continental Army of the United States, high-value English prisoners, hundreds of Scottish immigrants bound for America, and a dozen horses.

When Levi repeated that the Scottish girls whom he beheld were the most beautiful addition to American society ever known, they almost swooned as one and positively surged forward while their reticent menfolk were not swooning at all and were beginning to wish that they had dropped the rope, and 'pretty-boy' with it. Suddenly serious, Nasser announced.

"Boston… unfortunately… is overrun by the English."

Waiting unconcerned until the howl of disappointment had ceased, he continued,

"As is New York, Philadelphia, Charleston and Savannah." There was silence. The immigrants had suddenly found their hopes dashed, and themselves lost in a vacuum of ignorance and uncertainty. Hooligan had hoped to land his Gaels at a major port; a city where they could find work, and housing while they got back on their feet in the New World. It sounded to him now, as though America was suddenly a British outpost. Aware of the consternation that his words had generated in the hearts of the tartan crowd, Levi resumed.

"They hold our cities, but they cannot move out of them because we hold the land; three thousand miles of it. The Minutemen have them cowering in their forts. We hurl mortars at them every day. Spain and France have declared for us. We 'will' win our freedom. With your Captain's forbearance, I suggest the following. Firstly, we sail to Sint Eustatius in the Dutch Antilles. It is not one whit out of your way; where you can sell your wine at the very best price; get fresh food and clean water. With the major cities either under siege or in enemy hands, you will have the devil of a time selling it otherwise. Then, we sail north to the United States and put ashore all those who want to land, as near to Boston as is possible, or indeed, anywhere else that takes your fancy. We can get you ashore in a thousand places; then we will get the weapons to our army, the one proviso being the attentions of the English ships of the line. There are swarms of them in the north." A storm of raucous cheering and mockery greeted this last remark liberally seeded with barbed and hateful insults aimed at Nasser personally. Pleasingly to Nasser's countrymen and the clansmen, their new comrade showed himself sublimely unperturbed by the insulting English assessment of his character, his parenthood, the number of his fleas, and his habit of bathing but once a year. He was even tolerant of their suggestion that he, an officer of an American ship, could not so much as conjugate his Latin verbs. He waited patiently, even attentively, until the youths emptied their jugs of putrid invective thus revealing their utter lack of imagination as their bitter ejaculations petered out miserably. Nasser then agreed wholeheartedly with his gainsayers confessing that his Latin was non-existent; his French execrable, and his command of English, questionable; but as a seaman, he was top of his class. It was not *he* who had been taken prisoner of war by an unarmed merchantman and now hooted like a monkey in a cage. His allies were delighted and roared in approbation while the English fumed and scowled and spat in impotent fury. He was not finished with them. Deadly serious and seemingly deeply concerned he asked generally,

''How could anyone so young become so bitter and hateful of his fellow man?'' His was an inquiry which clearly struck home, for the youths so addressed found themselves unsure for the first time in their cosseted lives and incapable of reasoned argument. Throwing an arm around the shoulders of the taller Captain Teach, Levi turned his back on the vanquished English and once again addressed his admirers.

"If you will allow me to speak privately with your Captain, he and I will make plans for getting your cargo and yourselves safely ashore; thank you all for bringing it. In the meantime, *Spartan* will range ahead of you and provide some protection for your fleet until we get you landed in the States." This message was particularly well received by the highlanders, so after a quiet word or two with Teach, Nasser addressed Spartan through a speaking trumpet,

"Sint Eustatius." Canvas unfurled immediately aboard the warship causing *Spartan* to surge gratefully forward like a racehorse given its freedom to run. A score of interested observers joined Levi and Captain Teach in the grand cabin for their proposed tete a tete on strategy which became instead an inspection of the cargo so kindly donated by the French. This number included Lliam Hooligan, Trewin Copplestone, the *Liberty*'s shiny new boatswain, Angus Stewart that same brave individual who had all but drowned in the service of his clan,' off-duty sailors and fascinated highlanders. 'The crew of the *Bird* were unpaid volunteers to a man, and democracy was their watchword. The business of the ship, was their business.' It was during this inspection that Teach confirmed the oft-repeated rumour that as soon as she was re-provisioned in Sint Eustatius, the *Bird* would be departing for its home port of Boston where the crew would take their chances with the English. They would do so without concern for the fate of the Liberty because the Scots were now tremendous seamen and could crew the ships as well as any man. The declaration, though not unexpected, caused heads to hang in a reflective silence for a while, and the few Americans who would be staying on with Hooligan as they had no family or home other than a ship regretfully shook the hands of those dear friends who would be leaving. The men of the *Bird* had been through much together in the previous couple of years and parting would be easy for no one.

Hooligan had been shaken by the news that there was no major town in which he could disembark his Scots, in addition; the loss of his great friend Martin and the men of the *Bird* added considerably to the weight which he now felt settling once again on his shoulders. Winter was coming, and he had to find food and housing for hundreds of people, while at the same time getting the news of his vast quantities of munitions to an army lost in a million square miles of wilderness.

The first of the bodies was noticed on Levi Nasser's ninth day aboard the *Liberty*; it floated mournfully across her path, black, bloated and mutilated by fish or by its murderers. An hour or so later, two more were spied. The unwelcome word spread quickly among the migrants and soon, curious people hung over the ship's sides to verify for themselves this unlikely occurrence, only to be appalled by what they saw, the memories of the torn remains of loved ones deserted unburied on the slopes of Ben Cruachan being cruelly fresh in Scottish hearts. Men climbed into the rigging searching the horizon assiduously for the floating obscenity responsible, which by their calculations had to be a few hours ahead and two or three degrees south, while pledging bloody revenge on the inhuman creatures who had inflicted such a fate on those innocent people. Sundown approached all too soon for there was still no sign of the slaver, but what 'was' discernible, flouting an otherwise clear sky were the far-distant banners of an approaching storm, waving high and arrogant as lions-rampant in the darker shades of blue on a ground of black. Those clouds were an ominous sight to any sailor who had sailed these latitudes before.

"All hands; shorten sail. Lash everything down. Women and children below decks," the officer of the watch knew what terrible thing was approaching. Martin Teach found Hooligan in the grand cabin, struggling through his reading lesson with Abraham Abrahamson, a student of law who had abandoned his studies in favour of the life of a fighter in the abolitionist cause. The captain paused sympathetically until his friend had halted like the verbal cripple he was, to the end of a sentence of his lesson and declared,

"There is a slaver just a few hours ahead of us, Lliam. We are going after her."

"Oh are we now?" Deeply irritated by his own pedestrian progress in the business of reading, Hooligan was at his most objectionable.

"Have you forgott dat we have a million pound of stuff under our arses to get to your fookin army; an oi don't have a clue where dey are. Dis is no time to be puttin' the world to roights boyo," Abraham sucked in his breath in disbelief that any man in his right mind would address the iron hard Teach that way. Martin Teach absorbed his friend's blatant mutiny with apparent equanimity, but there was a dangerous edge to him as he replied,

"Mister Hooligan. Friend. Lliam. I have informed you of my intentions simply as a matter of common courtesy. We are going after that floating sump, and we are going after her *now,* there is no *wrong* time for putting an end to slavery." With that the Captain turned his back on the infuriating Irishman and left; wondering if the man would ever mature sufficiently to stop his mouth flapping in every breeze. He was in full flow, giving his instructions for the necessary course alterations, the make-up of the boarding party, the eradication of the slaver's murderous crew, and the transportation of the poor Africans to the Virgin Islands, only a day's sail ahead, where they would be freed to fend for themselves, when Hooligan, accompanied by Copplestone whom the Irishman had recruited to his cause, pushed his way through the crowd.

"Captain Teach, will you not reconsider this distraction from our much more important…" Copplestone the dragoon, who was clearly mortified with concern for the poor soldiers awaiting the *Liberty*'s weaponry was delivering his opening salvo at a distance measured in yards and within the hearing of dozens of the passengers.

"Enough," shouted the instantly furious captain, halting this insolence effectively as a ball of lead to the frontal lobe.

"The working of this ship is none of your business Copplestone, so remember where you are; and stay the hell out of it." Copplestone was silenced. The soldier understood very clearly what Teach was inferring and was acquainted with the punishment for mutiny. Not so, the belligerent idiot at his side; Hooligan had learned nothing from the captain's warning or from his ally's sudden and extraordinary capitulation.

"We've got to be getting the stuff to the Army, Martin. Not go floatin' round the bloody world playin fairy godmother to a bunch of blacks dat you've never met."

"Shut your mouth sir." The captain's handsome features had become a mask of fury.

"One more word out of you Admiral and I shall clap you in irons. I am the captain of this vessel, and it would behove you to remember it."

"Irons? Irons is it? And me on me own fookin boat?" mocked Hooligan, glancing at the women in his audience for support but when none materialised lapsing into a foolish stuttering silence as he had shot his only bolt and lacked the mental acuity required to formulate another.

Wallowing infuriatingly in his own ineptitude while everyone was witness to it, the Irishman reverted to making pathetic, childish and completely unwarranted accusations of ingratitude on the part of Captain Teach, who had forgotten that it was Hooligan's boat that he was playing with but was shouted down by the seaman who was not prepared to tolerate his friend's drivel in public.

"You sir," Teach launched his hand almost into Hooligan's face.

"Are the most stubborn, donkey-headed, one-eyed son of a bitch that I ever met. You have been an American for six weeks and you feel that you can give me lessons on patriotism. You can't tell port from starboard, yet you know with certainty what is best for this ship, this fleet and the people aboard. Let me remind you, Mister Hooligan that it was to the captain and crew of the *Bird* that Mister Franklin and his associates entrusted their cargo, not to an ignorant, illiterate landlubber who happens to have stolen a few ships. Without us, you would still be in England with your thumb up your arse." This unexpected vulgarity on the part of their very proper Captain caused an uproar of laughter as the tension broke, and it became happily apparent that their mad saviour was not going to talk himself into a spell in the pokey or worse; be thrashed insensible by the champion pugilist Teach. The undeniable truth of his friend's words crushed Hooligan as no rockfall could. Bitterly, he recalled the exquisite Armand Sartine and heard the frog banging on about what a big fat 'delight' it would be for Franklin and his mates to see Captain Teach again; while himself; Lliam Shaun Hooligan, was to be 'collected' like a sack of stinking laundry. Painfully and publicly deflated, he reverted to type. Every instinct, every nerve, every natural response in his body urged Hooligan to batter his friend's face flat, then and there, and the great muscles of his chest and arms twitched beneath his shirt in anticipation of action but he could not do it. Something stickier than the glorious red haze of violence was holding him back. Without a word he turned aside and pushing his way through the captivated crowd, went below.

It was Angus Stewart who saved the lost soul from both himself, and yet another monumental bender. The little leader of men found the gigantic baby skulking in his cabin, taking refuge in a bottle.

"Mister Hooligan," he began formally,

"I must speak my mind to ye."

"Go ahead. Sure, it's the day for it," Hooligan was savage.

"Your behaviour does ye no credit, sir," Stewart stated candidly.

"You must very soon learn to know your worth among men, and tae recognise the worth of others or perish."

"And what do ye mean by that? 'Perish' is it? And whose goin tae 'perish,' me?" Sensing a threat, the brawler shaped enthusiastically to meet it.

"What I mean by it is that, without Martin Teach; me and my clan; all o' us aboard this ship, would be lyin' dead in the Firth of Tay. They telt me that it was he that drug me oot of the watter tae tell ma story. They say that it was Captain Teach as trapped some English Captain and gave you the *Justice* as a prize and lost old friends doin' it."

"They tell you a whole mountain of shoite for a man who eats at my table," Hooligan snarled nastily in as foul a non sequitur as was ever issued. Incensed by the revolting thought process that would contaminate the mouth of a grown man with such injustice, the little scot raised his voice accordingly as he fired back.

"What they did *not* need to tell me, is what I know for myself, Lliam Hooligan. This ship and its people would be at the bottom of the sea wur it not for your friend and ours; Captain Martin Teach. Have you forgotten the calamity off Madeira? You owe your ship, your cargo, and your life to that man, sur, as all o' us do. We've depended on him alone, every hour of every day since we met him. Do you not unnerstand that it's yersel you should be looking at wi' a keen eye sur; not Captain Teach."

"Is that your lot?" snorted Hooligan, utterly incapable of gracious behaviour at that moment; drowning as he was in a stew of powerful emotions that he was unable to master. Stewart's expression altered significantly at this insulting reply, and he took an involuntary and threatening pace towards the bigger man. Mastering his rage, and composing himself only by dint of ruthless effort, the peacemaker continued with what he had come to say.

"Friend Hooligan. Lliam. We are all deeply in your debt, and we love you for all your generosity. But you anger people beyond what they can bear. Every man has his pride, just as you do, but you rob them of theirs to preserve your own.

Remember this though, Lliam Hooligan, in your future dealings with Angus McFarlane Stewart. No man offends me with impunity. To save his interlocutor the indignity of weighing the lightly veiled threat in the presence of the man who issued it Stewart withdrew immediately; leaving the criminally generous, utterly immature and often objectionable Irishman to hopefully grow up before he brought disaster upon himself and everyone else.

Dinner was magnificent. Hooligan had not imagined that food could be so various and so delicious. It was better than the stuff at Chateaubriant and even Huntingmill. Best of all, his waitress was his glorious Flora, whom he suspected, was in league with the little people and was putting spells on him, which left him tongue-tied when he was near her, while

Martin Teach was served by Salome, the poor girl who had been held prisoner by the English aboard the *Bird*. Martin and the girl were seldom seen apart of late. Having scrubbed mightily under the pump, and with his beard and his flowing locks trimmed by the adoring Flora, Hooligan the Repentant, 'a role in which he was fast becoming word perfect,' dressed himself in his very best, and declared himself completely ready to deliver his abject apology to Teach for his outrageous interference with the working of the ship. He need not have bothered. The incident had come and gone in the good Captain's eyes and having once delivered his opening gambit; that constant friend would not let the repentant one refer to the matter, nor did he do so himself, during what transpired to be a most enjoyable evening, in so far as it could be recalled.

In full regalia and holding his invitation in his hand, Martin Teach had entered the admiral's lair at precisely seven o'clock and inquired,

"What's for dinner Irish; Humble pie?"

The anticipated squall struck during the baked fish; its initial assault so violent and sudden that the inebriated Hooligan, who was pouring yet another cup of wine for the legless Teach, found himself pouring the stuff into the man's lap, an accident which pleased and amused the participants so greatly that Lliam poured, and Martin bathed, until the bottle was quite empty. Flora and Salome exchanging bemused, disbelieving looks shook their lovely heads as their heart's desires descended into drunken, uproarious stupidity; 'And the evening has barely begun,' their expressions said.

The men aboard *Liberty* that night would thereafter declare that the storm off the Virgin Islands was, equal to if not worse than, the one which had so threatened the ship off Funchal. Driven by shrieking winds, gigantic mountains of water fell upon the vessel hour after terrifying hour. The black faces of those malignant walls of water smashed into her sides and raced across her decks as deep as a man is tall. Their irresistible force swept away everything that was not securely tied down, and much that was, and made movement about the decks impossible so that those poor souls in the rigging were marooned until such times as the seas relented or drove her under. She should have been crushed in a matter of hours, but she was no ordinary ship. She twisted and turned, dived and climbed; running before her tormentors only to turn and defy them, and then run again. At the darkest time, with all four of the capable masters aboard *Liberty* either injured, exhausted or drunk, Levi Nasser himself took responsibility for the ship, and every living soul aboard her into his own hands. He had poor Gulley freed from the wheel where the man had been secured with rope for two full hours, and had the unconscious hero carried below with orders not to return. He replaced the steersman with not one but two muscular Scots who seemed impervious to wind, water and much else; then went below and released the exhausted teams at the pumps; replacing them with a posse of willing Scottish lassies who were used to strenuous work and more than glad to lend a hand. The charming wildlings had taken over the duty in as energetic a fashion as any Captain could wish. With the incoming water being equalled by that pumped out, and the vessel being steered as well as the seas allowed, he then went topside to attempt the impossible. Negotiating the minor waterfall of the gangway to the upper deck, the new broom then set about organising a task that was imperative to the survival of the ship and everyone aboard, but as it would probably cost someone his life, he could not ask one of the men to perform it, he would have to do it himself. With her decks now a millrace of tremendous power it was impossible for men to undertake critical duties, or to relieve the poor devils who clung, trapped, exhausted and near death of cold. His intention was to establish a network of safety lines from stem to stern to which men could attach themselves and move about the decks with a degree of security. He had seen this done once before during a typhoon in the China Sea, and he hoped that he would never be required to replicate the feat. Naked, wet as a herring and bitterly cold Levi Nasser took the first steps of the longest journey of his life. Tethered by a rope which he had passed twice around his middle and tied in front and dismissive of protestations, and predictions of annihilation, he began his journey from the stern while his objective was the bow itself. As he staggered in the grip of the tide, his invisible prize seemed as unattainable as the moon, but his duty was clear, and he would not deny it. With his lifeline being paid out by crewmen each of them lashed to timbers he took his first turn around the massive stanchion of the steering mechanism, and a second around the uprights of the poop deck rail. That was the easy part and now the worst of it began. Flung around and thrashed like the flags at the masthead, he was lowered into the waist-deep maelstrom midships, and struggled into a torrential hell; bitterly cold, battered, and blinded.

Following him, sailors worked their way forward along his line and secured themselves and his cable to each of the strongpoints that he made from where they would free more hemp, paying out the rope to Nasser as he fought his way along the torrent of the deck. On numerous occasions, the naked and bleeding man was swept back to and beyond his last strong-point, and at others he was smashed into painful collision with the ship's timbers. Twice he was carried in terror over the side, and twice he was recovered by his team's and his own strenuous efforts. At the relative safety of each of the three masts his torments were such that having attached to the supremely strong monument he could not bear to go on and had loitered for endless intervals, ashamed and afraid. Cursing himself foully he once more forged a path into the darkness, the horror and the merciless assaults of the sea.

It was with the last dregs of his vast stores of energy and nerve that he untied himself and secured the rope to the bowsprit. It was done. Exhausted in mind and body he severed the umbilical before anchoring himself. It was a mistake that a cabin boy would not commit. He was in the act of re-attaching himself to it with a running loop, when the bows dove into yet another hill of menace, and he was ripped away as though he were a leaf in a mountain torrent and carried over the side. Invisible to his shipmates his helpless drowning form raced the length of the vessel, crossed the bulwark a second time and hammered into agonising contact with the smashed watertight doors.

When the poor man regained consciousness, drunken idiots were for reasons unknown throwing water in his face and demanding to know why it was that Levi was out of uniform and had dyed his hair white.

Nasser's herculean work bore fruit. Men who had been trapped and freezing in the rigging descended thankfully to the decks where they attached themselves by running loops to the ropeway and made the still perilous journey to safety. Their replacements then risked-all to add a network of necessary spurs to Nasser's central highway.

Nature relented with a suddenness equal to that with which she had attacked. The wind abandoned its murderous work, leaving in its wake a mocking zephyr, while the seas called a temporary truce; discoloured and muddy brown with branches and the occasional tree afloat in them, but playful and unthreatening. The prisoners were brought up one at a time from their dungeon for with the storm at its height, *Liberty* had struck some unknown object and the planking had been sprung below the water line. Terrified of drowning like rats, the cosseted English lords had laboured long and enthusiastically at the pumps which was a feature of their prison while the lassies had looked on in a certain ironic amusement.

She had lost much of her canvas, and in places even the furled sails were shredded and ripped away. One of them had taken with it the Harris twins, orphaned children who had remained aloft, determined to behave like men, even though ordered below for their own safety; the boys had given their lives for very little for when at last it was possible to take a reading it was discovered that the *Liberty* had fought all night simply to remain where she was; not a yard of progress had she accomplished. Of the slaver, the *Spartan*, and the rest of Fleet Hooligan, there was no sign. Unconcerned and full of Dutch courage the drunken fools in the grand cabin had laughed their way through the evening until they had collapsed; all the while oblivious to torrents of seawater that smashed through the splintered doors above and swamped the galley, extinguishing the fire and caused Flora, Salome and Angelique, who was their cook for the evening, to wade to the salon. There the girls perched with their feet on their seats as the water beneath them swilled the drunks around like hops in the dregs of a barrel of beer.

"Mark Twain."

Two full days of searching the island's coast were rewarded by the discovery of a suitable river in which they could hide the gigantic ship while the necessary repairs were made. With men deployed to swing the lead, and canvas reduced to a small kerchief while another dozen individuals clung in the rigging searching for possibly fatal sandbars, Liberty crept inland. 'It would not do to run-aground unintentionally and in full view from the ocean, after all.' What her people were seeking on this uncharted island was a spot in which to beach the *Liberty* and lay her over on her side so that the carpenters could access the sprung planking. It would be a place far enough inland to be hidden from prying English eyes yet still tidal so that she could be floated-off after the repairs were affected. The proximity of large trees was also essential as these would be critical in facilitating the work. They would act as anchor points so that the immeasurable traction of the capstans could be brought into play.

Gloriously colourful parrots were conversing raucously in the rigging when the famous drunks eventually emerged unsteadily onto a deck which leaned steeply. Both men glowered impotently at the infuriatingly noisy birds for an extended moment but unable to halt the cacophony sloped away, balling for a boat to take them ashore. Here the loud privet-green jungle crept down to overhang the silver sand, its deep shade giving way before the tyranny of the sun.

Their responsibilities apparently a thing of the past the careless commanders collapsed beneath the palms and promptly fell asleep, waking occasionally only to be violently ill before lapsing once again into unconsciousness.

The sole discordant note in this pleasant anchorage was voiced predictably by the imprisoned lordlings who found themselves crammed like cordwood on top of each other due to the ship's unusual attitude. They had cursed volubly at the two drunks who had the confounded insolence to ignore their betters and gone on their way with not so much as a 'by your leave.'

"Like shit in a bottle," Hooligan remarked at the time; succinct as always.

Nasser of the white hair had beached her at low tide, out of sight of the ocean; anchored her firmly in place and taking hawsers five turns around each of the masts, secured her to the trees beyond the beach. With thirty men at each capstan and a dozen in reserve the great hawsers came up so tight that moisture hissed from them accompanied by sounds suggestive of severe indigestion. Under such stress those same hawsers became deadly dangerous should they part, but as slowly as sap oozing from a newly cut plank, the great vessel had heeled over, exposing a single section of sprung planking. It was time for the carpenters to go to work.

It was noted in the log that a further four men had been lost during the night. The voyage was taking a terrible toll, and though the journey was far from over the rollcall was becoming noticeably shorter as time went by.

Barely an hour or so out from the ship, the soaking army of gasping volunteers were wishing that they had not bothered coming on this horrid jaunt, one pair of eyes being quite sufficient to discover any Brits creeping around these seas. The top of the cursedly steep mountain was still nowhere in sight, in fact nothing was in sight; nothing but twisted trees draped with tough black vines as strong as hemp ropes which when cut delivered rivers of the coolest sweetest water ever tasted. The hill which the explorers were climbing was almost as steep as a wall so that they advanced with their faces in the undergrowth while underfoot the detritus was so treacherous that with every step upwards, a man would slip and slide three back down taking with him the unfortunates following in his footprints. In addition to which, everybody had the runs through eating heaps of the delicious and oh so plentiful fruit with which the canopy was laden. The unimaginable beauty and colour of the birds and the furious protestations of the monkeys on the other hand were experiences which enthralled and amused everyone.

"Sky!" That simple observation altered everything. Smiles replaced scowls, jests replaced moans, and weary men and women were instantly invigorated. The party virtually ran the last mile or so to the summit where on arrival everyone inexplicably became a child again, pointing out to others the magnificent sights which he or she could see and demanding that everybody look at them also. It was immediately clear that they were now standing on an island of possibly ten miles in length by six at its widest in the shape of a teardrop. All-around them the seas were innocent of ships and the party rejoiced in the knowledge for to be trapped ashore in such an indefensible situation would mean a hanging for sure. One individual was not at all enthused, the seaman stood as still as laboured breathing allows for a protracted interval staring as though he could not understand what he was studying then approached Levi Nasser, who was the nearest of the brass and was equipped with a glass.

"Mister Levi." He began and speaking very quietly pointed out something in the far distance. Nasser threw up his telescope and quickly located the object of interest.

"Put me in a frock and call me Angela, well spotted Walters. Copplestone," he called,

"It's that damned slaver." This announcement caused a fever of activity as glasses were aimed and studied and passed from hand to hand so that within minutes everyone had sighted the wreck. It was broken in two, high on a reef and while her forequarters stood still the remainder seemed in danger of imminent sinking.

"Ten o'clock," Copplestone, employed the military terminology, and the telescopes were again centred on the wreck which would serve as 'twelve' and then swung sixty degrees to the left where they soon located a large crowd of people hurrying along the sand. A small number of whites were driving away four-score of naked African women in the manner of drovers shifting cattle which is to say with many harsh orders backed up by slashing canes.

"Christ. They must have left the rest to drown." The men were incensed but by no means surprised.

"The dirty bastards," Carnegie voiced their thoughts

''Battle stations boys,'' Everyone raced downhill to emerge from the jungle three hours later near a field of broken coral only yards from the wreck due to some excellent compass work by the officers. The *Doughty* had parted midships; her back broken on the rocks. Her after-half was about to break loose and sink as it was being worked like a *shaduf by the ocean, alternately hoist then dropped by successive rollers, filling and emptying her smashed guts which were a whirlpool of terrified drowning human beings.

"Oh, my word; they's men in there. I can see them." Gulley threw caution to the wind.

"Come on boys," he hollered, and in his distress raced into the waves and dived through the first of them emerging on its seaward side swimming strongly for the distant wreck. He was followed enthusiastically by four more confident swimmers, two girls and two young men who stripped as they charged into the water only yards behind him. The remainder of the party knew full-well that their own swimming ability was so poor, that they would never make it to the wreck, let alone be of any assistance to the poor devils trapped inside.

''Five men, with me shouted Carnegie and departed at a measured run with the intention of joining up with the pursuit group sent out earlier to chase down the captive women. As the impatient and deeply concerned non-swimmers waited there in the shallows, willing their comrades on and hoping that they would not lose their lives in what appeared to be a suicidal undertaking, one of Carnegie's men returned, exhausted by running through sand. The trail of the poor African women he gasped, was clearly written in the sand and punctuated liberally by blood, occasional manacles, one corpse and two exhausted girls, all but finished, who were being cared for at the forest edge by people who knew nothing of such matters and needed help to carry the poor creatures to safety. The unfortunate prisoners had been tracked by to an extensive tobacco plantation that was being worked by hundreds of slaves.

*Shaduf . A seesaw device for lifting water from the Nile. 'Theory of moments.'

There was an enormous European style house and even an extensive loading dock stretching out into deep water where large vessels were capable of being loaded. By the scout's estimation, the odds were, about twenty enemy overseers to the fifteen men of the *Liberty* who would hopefully be assisted by the slave population once liberated.

The uninitiated could never have replicated what Gulley and his friends achieved that day. To allow one's-self to be swept into the giant meat grinder which was the separating and crushing together of two murderous phalanxes with their splintered timbers eager to shred man or girl into an unrecognisable stew was an act of true heroism. To look upon the scene of carnage within, was nothing less. Mutilated bodies and savagely injured victims of the wreck littered the forward section many screaming in the unsupportable torments of desperate injuries. Trapped behind a palisade of vertical timbers aft, clung a mass of struggling, drowning humanity.

Gulley was the first into that carnal house. Watching intently from several yards distant, he soon understood the action of the swell and the response of the wreck to each awful surge. Bawling at his followers to do as he was about to do, he positioned himself as closely as he dared to the meat grinder that the *Doughty* had been reduced to and at the instant in which the jaws parted, he fed his body to it. Dragged in and swallowed at tremendous speed by the flood he grabbed hold of whatever was available to him and climbed with the energy of terror between the spears. As the others followed his example Gulley stood astride the shattered timbers, ready to grab their wrists and drag them to relative safety.

Behind a palisade of vertical timbers aft, dozens of men were suffering continuous assault by the ocean which surged in voraciously through gaping wounds, dragging away with it the exhausted and those with nothing on which to cling. The two races considered each other speculatively, while the wailing among the tortured blacks lessened as they sensed that this group of whites were somehow unlike the last, and that rescue might be at hand. John Glasgow a crippled lad, bawled above the crashing of the water and the tortured screaming of the timbers,

"Snap the bars at their mid-point. Levers. This thick. Long." He held up his hand showing a space of about four inches between thumb and fingers, which equated with the space between the offending bars. The team scrambled quickly away, searching in the semi-darkness of the wreck's mid and forward sections for a lever which was both long and strong enough to defeat those iron-hard pillars; pillars of teak which had withstood the wreck and everything that the African prisoners could devise to throw against them. Gulley alone approached the bars and shoving his hands bravely between them made every sign of friendship. The news raced through the Africans and immediately there was a visible determination to assist the whites in whatever they were doing. The searchers soon emerged from the depths of the lower hold struggling beneath the weight of a spar, which at its thinner end would pass through the gaps. Working together with the understanding of long practice Liberty's people eased the awkwardly long timber which they knew to have the tensile strength of steel, through a gap at hip height, the height at which they could exert most leverage as the blacks edged aside to admit the thing. When it came up tight, the whites hurriedly regrouped hurling their weight at the lever with the effort of desperation. The studs bent a little; groaned a lot; but held. Behind that implacable barrier, the blacks were conferring urgently, initiating a great upheaval of movement as men sacrificed their relative safety for the good of all, and slithered backwards, deeper into the sea of death. Now there was the combined weight of a score of men behind the effort, as every prisoner who could get near the huge lever added his strength to that of the whites. The first pillar splintered with a gunshot as both black and white tribes crashed down in a tangle of limbs like an upset chess game

A hugely muscled black tore the two bits of the broken stanchion out of his way and squeezing through the lifesaving space took Gulley's hands in both of his own with every expression of friendship thereby confirming a truce between black and white.

"Anders.'' Bawled Gulley, ''Take this man and some of his mates an' get that bloody boat launched and keep the damn thing off them rocks."

"Aye aye, sir," responded Anders, though Gulley was simply an ordinary seaman as was he. Laying claim to the first gang of Africans he indicated through sign language that they had to climb to the deck above then confused them by heading off through the belly of the ship. Once out of the water and standing on timber which did not rise and fall beneath them, his gang found the going easier, and coming across an open gun port they were able to climb out and get up on to the upper deck and comparative safety. The huge longboat which Anders had noticed earlier was out of its cradle and lay wedged against the bulwark on the seaward side, having obviously suffered an abortive launch. He and the blacks were checking her seaworthiness when the deck on which they stood shot backwards several yards hurling everyone down like skittles. A terrifying cacophony of metre-thick timbers being twisted and torn like straw rope occurred and the rear half of the broken vessel tore free of the rocks sinking by the stern in moments, her masts snapping like twigs and thrashing the sea as they toppled. Black men and white filled the resultant whirlpool, a struggling terrified melange of self-preservation and selflessness, bravery and terror. At great peril to themselves those who could swim seized the drowning and the unconscious and began to drag them to the distant beach, while the few poor devils who could not swim grasped wide-eyed at anything and anyone in reach as they struggled for life. Gulley's major concern was proven groundless for being men of the Niger River many of the blacks were powerful swimmers.

Eighty-one men escaped death that day; an event of such moment that there followed an outbreak of hand shaking, fist touching, clapping and chest pressing, as the men of half a dozen black tribes, and two white, declared their friendship and gratitude, and their recognition of each other as warriors of considerable worth. Parched and ravenous, the Africans hurried into the bush where they soon found both water and fruit, then returned to the sand laden with food for their rescuers, but rather than display the good-will which was evident previously they gathered now in exclusively tribal groups. In mere moments the prevailing ethos of shared-humanity and common-good had fled leaving six nations glaring at each other in the mutual distrust and dislike of centuries. Some went so far as to retrieve lumps of corral and thus armed adopted a certain swagger and threatening attitude which was not evident previously.

Yet again it was Gulley who, instantly outraged by this tribalism reacted to the emerging threat. Bellowing loudly and furiously and waving a huge blade threateningly as he advanced on the men he had saved, he had everyone's undivided attention immediately. By crazed histrionics and sign language accompanied by awful noises he insisted that all men of all tribes and all colours were one; except the crew of the Doughty many of whom were lying dead in the waves. Dashing in his rage to one of the white corpses, he grabbed the thing by the hair, hacked-off the head and holding high his gruesome lesson turned incandescent to the Africans who surrounded him as he mandated that 'this,'and only 'this.' was the enemy, and that others of the breed were at this moment driving the wives and daughters of the Bambara, and the Djerma into slavery and worse. He completed his pantomime with a performance which his much-impressed shipmates understood to mean,

''We wouldn't have risked our fucking necks out there had we known that you stupid bastards would turn on each other when your women were being driven away by the white men who enslaved you.

As a direct result of this uninhibited lecture on the theme of, 'my enemy's enemy is my friend,' it was as one army, African, American and Scottish that the considerable force began to run in the traces of the stolen women.

Obviously enamoured of the arm-long knives with which the whites were armed the avengers had not travelled far before the covetous glances of the unarmed Africans were

ing563

rewarded with gifts of dirks and naval boarding axes, gifts which to these men who were innocent of steelmaking were of immeasurable worth and inexpressible beauty. Now they were men again, men who chanted their battle songs as they ate up the miles in a loping run which the Europeans found difficulty in emulating. The singing stopped abruptly at that time of day when the apparently horizontal transit of the sun begins an obvious decline and as the men of the liberty watched intently the warriors spread out wordlessly across the sand in a deployment which gave every man room to use his weapon freely.

Whatever it was that had alarmed the Africans had caused them to infiltrate the jungle darkness with the utmost caution; they were followed by the sailors who very late in proceeding became aware of the awful contrast to the pleasing sounds of birds and waves which was the flesh-shrivelling crack of whips.

Light soon showed beyond the sudden cool darkness and the avengers paused unbidden many meters into deep cover at the edge of an endless field of tall leafy plants in which hundreds of slaves were working in mute resignation. Bringing the whites together the acknowledged leaders among the blacks signed that the pale-skins were not expected to risk their lives further in the coming battle and that they should remain in reserve while the men of the Niger took the necessary steps to free their countrymen from this nest of vipers. Trewin Copplestone was having none of it and advanced, quickly asserting his military prowess on the impatient killers. He wanted to be certain that every one of the black soldiers was armed and as his audience watched in happy fascination, he selected a bamboo of suitable diameter and with a mere four cuts of a sword manufactured a lethal stabbing spear in a matter of seconds. The tribesmen loved it and those with blades set to work rapidly so that very soon every man owned a lethal weapon while those with knives owned two and they went forth armed particularly well and very capable of taking revenge. Creeping forward in cover to the very edge of the wide expanse of plantation-land the Africans spoke quietly to the men working the crop and told them that they would soon be free. Nervous energy crackled across the landscape as the news was disseminated in a fierce longing for action. Soon, it began. Seeing a mounted overseer approaching their position the blacks spoke quietly again to the nearest slaves.

"Do not turn around brothers we will be kindly with this one." The joke was enjoyed immensely. Five men armed with European weapons went quickly into the field and put themselves in the way of the rider, a white whose face was as ugly as his character. Drink and drug-affected the sot turned his bleary gaze and addled mind on the nearest of them; closed on him at the walk and dismounted. Foolishly he did so on the blind side. In the same instant that the overseer's view of him was obstructed by the horse, the tribesman struck. The villager of Djerma leapt forward and sliced almost through the white's leg at the back of the thigh.

Screaming in a crescendo of agony the man collapsed as the four other warriors joined in his demise slashing and stabbing him until he no longer resembled a human being. Slaves snatched up the dead man's small armoury of weapons, two pistols, his whip, the panga, and his musket, and were off and running; joined by their brothers as they went. His handsome face a mask of blood and hatred, the tall individual who bore the awful tribal scars of the Djerma called to his troops. Followed by his similarly gruesome friends, he retraced his steps to the forest and entered the gloom desperately slowly thus allowing his eyes to adjust to the new reality. Searching the white faces which stared back in silence at him he moved along the skirmish line until, with a cry, he shouted, "Geel." and grasping the hand of the gratified Gulley, pressing it to his chest for a long moment. One by one, the others did likewise, and then with every intimation of gratitude and respect for fellow warriors, went to war. Gulley being quite overcome by emotion collapsed; still conscious but greatly depleted.

At a distant fold in the land, the freemen of no less than four warring tribes of the Niger River, the Bambara, Matinki, and Djerma among them paused and with a last expression of friendship and a salute of steel made their farewells as one army of vengeance.

"Back to the ship," roared Nasser, "when they realize they're free, they'll kill anything white." With the shore presenting the easiest running by far, the *Liberty*'s men retraced their steps to the water's edge and ran till exhaustion overtook them. As they rested breathless someone called out from his place at rear-guard.

"Son of hore; look at that." A few surviving Europeans were now trapped at the end of the plantation's pier which was crowded with black men intent on revenge. A last couple of shots were fired, the sound of them arriving after the appearance of the smoke, and then there was the slaughter.

"Let's go lads," bawled Nasser, as he and Copplestone formed a new and very alert rearguard. They had set free a tiger which would kill indiscriminately.

Landfall was the Caribbean island of Sint Eustatius a fast-developing centre of Dutch commerce; an invaluable entrepot in the Antilles, a mere speck of jungle and rock lost in a world of water. Interestingly it was the smallest stone in a necklace of emeralds which graces the smooth blue throat of that warm sea.

Prior to the war, this tip of a sunken volcano was a sparsely populated delight, but with the French, the English, the Spanish, and the Americans, all being on a war-footing, the canny Dutch quickly made the place the centre of all trade between Europe and the Americas, and while the other nations did the fighting; the Dutch made the money. Levi Nasser was as good as his word; the flotilla, which continued to sail in a tight formation, made good progress and in eleven more days made safe harbour in that tropical paradise become enormous drunken brothel. Vessels of twenty nations, jostled at the hardstands and the shores teemed with sailors, slaves, soldiers, merchants, and brazen, colourfully dressed women.

Cavernous warehouses now lined the white sand shores, behind which the jungle-draped mountains rose almost vertically, and where there had once been rocky outcrops in the water, these had been tamed, flattened, walled and cobbled, and turned into very serviceable quays where ships moored in an unbroken line a mile long, to load and unload.

Promising to personally supervise the re-provisioning of the *Bird,* in order to ensure her earliest possible departure, Lliam Hooligan browbeat the long-suffering Martin Teach, his master salesman, into taking charge of negotiations where his huge cargoes of Madeira wine were concerned. His single proviso being that his much put-upon friend should obtain a price that was five times what he had paid for the stuff in The Pearl.

This seemingly extravagant demand transpired to be a business decision of sheer brilliance. Though he had to hold out for three days of unremitting pressure; through bargaining skills based primarily on intransigence, belligerence, and bloody-mindedness, Martin Teach eventually got his price, and even succeeded in bettering it. He perceived early in the struggle that as often as not, the crafty merchants of Sint Eustatius had sold-on Lliam's wine; even before they had completed its purchase. In anticipation of getting their hands on the ambrosia at an acceptable price, they would have their customers tie up alongside Fleet Hooligan, so that the wine could be winched out of one ship and deposited straight into the other. In this way, the merchants made their profit without so much as touching or even seeing the goods. Thereafter, Teach and his team of emissaries went back to sea, boarded each of the unending queue of ships arriving at the island, and offered the Madeira at a slightly higher price than the Dutch were prepared to pay, but less than that at which the cheese heads would on-sell it. In this way Teach turned what would have been a startling profit into a positive gold mine.

Having thus made a second fortune for his friend, the captain was assured by Hooligan that, 'for an American, he wasn't a bad sort of a bitch, atall, atall.'

Hooligan, Copplestone, the Captains and boatswains were busy also, supervising the unloading of the huge tuns of Madeira wine from all five ships and cramming the resultant hold-space with military hardware, off-loaded from the *Bird* and the *Justice*. Lliam Hooligan the businessman had plans for the *Justice*. When the English officer-training vessel had been emptied of weaponry, including her personal armament of seven guns, he had the unlucky ship towed into the middle of the lagoon and anchored there, much to the bemusement of the Scots who had to break their backs doing the towing in the now certain belief that on this occasion their crazy Irish saviour really had lost his mind.

With the echoingly empty *Justice* anchored in what Hooligan considered to be a prime site for the sale of sea-going vessels, he climbed to the top of the mainmast and retrieved his home-made flag of the thirteen states which he dropped to the deck with the instruction,

"Fold it toidy boys, it's goin' on me wall."

It was pleasing to him in the extreme that the whole outlandish exercise, as was his intention, had drawn a great deal of interest from the milling throng who swarmed both the hardstand and the hundred ships tied up there, because he then put a speaking trumpet to his lips and hollered in the most ungentlemanly fashion,

''Dis ship will go to the first bastard that puts the bargain price of a thousand English pounds in moi fair hand.''

Several merchants of the middle eastern persuasion incensed by the fashion in which the cyclops and his filthy collaborator, were robbing them of business, flung up their muskets and took pot-shots at him from the water's edge, but to their mortification they did not have the range. Unperturbed; Hooligan promised these ruffians loudly, on their sister's virginity, no less, that,

''If we have any more of them shenanigans, oi'll swing that *Liberty* around in a troice, and give youse Arab bastards a broadside, sure.''

Within two hours of his voluble assault on the peace of the neighbourhood, he had sold the

Justice for what he knew was a give-away price of precisely one thousand English pounds to a Portuguese gent, whose ship had turned turtle as it was about to make its overloaded offing from the island.

Three days later, the *Bird* sailed for Boston, once again under the old firm of Teach and Holdsworth, with seventy or so of her crew intent on getting home without losing their ship to the English. Between them, they carried the thousand pounds received for the *Justice,* equally shared, with two shares set aside for the families of those men who had given their lives in the cause of freedom, just as their friend had promised.

Before they cast off, many of the *Bird*'s men had found an opportunity to shake Lliam by the hand and have a private word or two about this and previous extraordinary acts of generosity, and noticing this behaviour, the highlanders wondered what titanic service he must have done for those sailors, as he had for themselves. As the departing ship caught the breeze, her crew appeared in the rigging, every man dressed in his blue jacket; her stern chaser firing a five-gun salute.

"You're mad, you bastards," their benefactor bawled after them, delighted by it all, but mystified as to the reasons for this overt display of affection. His mystification was intensified when his Gaels joined the adulation and going down on one knee around him, took to babbling some Gaelic rubbish at him; mortifying him until he was 'destroyed with it.' With the departure of the *Bird*, and more particularly of Martin Teach, Hooligan's concern for his Gaels returned full force. He could not rescue them from the horrors of one starving coast, simply to abandon them on another, but what to do in order to secure their future was beyond him. He well recalled Martin's now tantalising question in the Firth of Tay.

"But what will you do with them?" the American had asked, and his own irresponsible, childishly stupid reply.

"Fill them full o' porridge and take them for a roide on the boats."

The burdensome responsibility which had been growing steadily as they neared their journey's end, had been strangling him ever since Levi Nasser had enumerated the difficulties ashore.

A week or so after his great loss the troubled gent was leaning over the side of the *Liverpool*, watching, fascinated by the way the girls' kilts swayed as they hauled carts of food to the quayside, when he realised that the answer was all around him. His highlanders were the most independent and capable of people. They made their own clothes; shoes, kilts, plaids and 'bunnets,' as they called their hats. They built their own houses, fed themselves, herded cattle, and fished the lochs. If there were no towns in which they could find refuge, they would have to build one of their own.

"Angus," he bawled, and a moment later, the round, ginger countenance of Angus Stewart appeared at the mouth of a gangway.

"Aye Lliam, what is it?"

"Are you married, Angus?"

"He most certainly is," came the reply in the most pleasantly modulated of voices; an attractive woman appearing from below to stand proud and beautiful at Stewart's side.

"Mrs Stewart," he began ominously.

"Iona," the charming lady smiled, as though mildly amused.

"How can we help ye, Lliam?"

"You spin yer own tartan, do ye not?"

"No Lliam," Iona responded gently.

"We shear our own sheep, then we wash and dye the wool. From the wool we spin our own yarn, and then we weave our own cloth from that yarn, and from the cloth we make our clothes. Why don't ye tell me what bothers ye, Lliam, mayhap we can help?" Iona approached, took hold of the giant's hand as though he were a troubled little boy and in a gesture of such innate kindness that it almost unmanned him.

"The English have got the towns," He blustered.

"What I was tinkin; if I get all the axes an stuff, youse could build your own town. You'll have to build yer own houses and fend for yerselves. I've got to take the guns to…"

"Of course, we will, Lliam." The kindly woman crooned,

"We never expected anything else." The concept was so grand, so imaginative, and so very much to their way of thinking and doing, that the Stewarts were overcome. For his part, Lliam Hooligan's relief was so great that he gathered up man and wife in his arms and would have danced a jig, but for Iona's patent embarrassment. He released husband and wife immediately, much chastened.

"You're goin' to need some stuff." he announced, happily returning to his badly flawed theme,

''Come with me and we'll buy a ton of it.'' Iona reached up, placing her hand gently over the big child's terribly scarred mouth to put an end to his babbling.

"The clan wurrks together, and decides what is best together, Lliam. It would be best if we talked aboot this as a clan." Thus it was, that the highlanders met early in the following dawn to hear Lliam's proposals for their fresh start in a new world. They gathered thoughtfully expectant on the sand with the ocean flopping ashore behind them and gave an ear to Trewin Copplestone, who had been roped-in to present Admiral Hooligan's master plan. The soldier mounted to the higher ground beneath the palms in order to see and be seen, while Hooligan tried to hide behind the rest of the Brass and one of the tall trees.

"Good morning, everyone," Copplestone began.

"Doubtless you are concerned by the question of what will become of you, now that our new nation's enemies hold all of the major ports on the Atlantic coast." There was not so much as an inference of concern among his listeners.

"Mister Hooligan has a plan, which he believes will calm your fears." Not a sound or a facial expression revealed any fears.

"Mister Hooligan has two major objectives. One is the expedient delivery of the military hardware below, to the Continental Army of the United States. The other is your safe establishment in terms of housing and a sustainable food supply. Winter will come soon enough. Mister Hooligan believes that his proposal will achieve both ends; always supposing that it is acceptable to you all. Just a week or two north of where we now stand lies an inland waterway which itself is a hundred and fifty miles long, and in places, as wide as thirty to fifty miles. Its shores are a succession of beautiful inlets, each more beautiful than the one before; or so I'm assured;'' he shared a smile with Levi Nasser, ''where there is unending land to be settled and farmed." The crowd moved slightly.

"The waters of the bay itself and of the inlets, many of which are as big as Lomond, are full of fish, oysters, crabs of both soft and hard shells, and ducks and geese in season." The people murmured.

"The soil is unequalled for arable farming and livestock, both." The gathering had a life of its own becoming a single giant creature.

"There are a million acres of tall straight trees ideal for the building of what are called log cabins, as houses, fencing, boats, firewood, furniture, shingles; that's slabs of wood for your roofs. There are deer, bears, wolves and other animals which you can shoot for food, leather, and warm clothing." Copplestone glanced at Nasser, who stood at his elbow.

"There are Indians. That is what the local people are called. Some are friendly. Some are not." The highlanders now broke into animated conversation but hushed as soon as they realised that the little soldier had more to say.

"Now for Mister Hooligan's proposal. In order to take advantage of this bounty that nature has provided, you would of course require saws and axes to cut down trees, ploughs and horses to break the ground, and sheep and cattle from which to breed your herds. Pigs and chickens; muskets, powder and ball; fishing nets, carpenters' tools for your furniture and boats; pots, pans and every other necessity; tinderboxes, surgeon's instruments, lasts for shoemaking, the list is long. Mister Hooligan's intention is to provide this material in sufficient quantities for you to not only survive, but to prosper." Trewin was at this point, drowned out by the deluge of cheering and irrepressible happiness, and the chanting of Lliam's name. Hooligan refused doggedly to present himself.

"Some sharing will be inescapable, obviously." Trewin resumed, "Not every man can have his own plough, nor every woman her own loom. Some sharing and working together for the general good will be required. I'm told that you are well acquainted with that way of doing. Given the tools, you can manufacture these larger items such as ploughs, identical to the originals or even better. He intends to do this for you free of charge. He has one proviso. When the opportunity first arises, he wishes that you will declare yourselves citizens of this country in the presence of a justice of the peace as he himself has done, and when required to do so, defend your new nation against the English. Again, that's something that you are used to."

"We've only a few hunnerd years at it but," yelled a wit to general acclaim.

"Lastly; we are reliably informed, that the further north we travel in the Chesapeake Bay, the nearer we can get to the Army of the Continent, who are at a place which lies further north still and is called Valley Forge. Mister Hooligan will, on arrival in the north of Chesapeake Bay, at the confluence of the Susquehanna River, journey overland in order to find our Army. He would welcome the company of a few more young men who are not troubled by sleeping rough, or the odd skirmish. At this moment, we already have a party of seven, including Lliam and myself.

You will of course have the advantage of living aboard the ships during the coming winter should your houses not be complete. Obviously, these will be excellent protection against the weather and against any warlike persons. Mister Hooligan has been advised that everyone, men and women alike must carry weaponry and that you should never let-down your guard by so much as one inch. Thank you."

Angus Stewart emerged from the crowd at this point and mounting to where Lliam was still rooted backstage muscled the Irishman forward, presenting him to the huge crowd he called to his people,

"Give Lliam yer answer."

The clan positively rioted in joyful disbelief that such generosity could exist in this world. They threw their bonnets into the air and laughed delightedly in each other's faces with the excitement of it all; after all; they didn't have a pot to piss in.

CHAPTER 30: Hastings

Hastings was at home with his new love, proudly acclimatising to his new dwelling while revelling in counting his loose cash. He was experiencing an entirely novel mood; one of domestic peace, ease and general goodwill for humanity at large and therefore made no effort to understand the importunate braying from outside. Only when the astoundingly satisfactory count was recorded, and the sack returned to its home in the stones of the chimneybreast did he saunter to the door and step outside.

''Its'is lordship Sor. E's in a mantrap.'' Hastings ran. He ran hard and the gardener fellow ran with him guiding him to where a noisy bloody crowd were milling around like so many cattle. Labouring for breath, the big man entered the perfumed path which and drove mercilessly through the mass of hateful revellers in his urgency to get to his friend.

''Get out of my fucking way,'' he balled, shoving yet more bloody-minded voyeurs viciously into the thorns.

'Screaming humanity,' was nothing new to him, it was his stock in trade and the source of the cash which he revelled in, but this was Mikey his lifelong friend doing the screaming. Laying about him with the back of his hands he cleared the last of the sodding sightseers out of his way and discovered the obscenity. The leg had been smashed in half at

ing575

the knee so that the shin twitched at an impossible angle while the huge muscles of the thigh, now unrestrained by tendons leapt around with astounding vigour as though animals were fighting in the bloody trousers. On the ground in the gore and the dirt was a Mameluke servant of all things who incredibly was working at the injured man's side trying desperately to defeat the device.

'This was not an attempt at murder. If it was, then Michael Astor would be dead.' This was simply a revenge of some sort. A very cool, well-planned revenge and Hastings knew there and then with utter certainty the identity of the perpetrator. He also understood why the rebellious little swine was so intent on that revenge and just what the bastard had in mind for himself. He recalled the muscular little hardcase who had abused those two disgusting gypos for laying traps. 'That little grunt really does have an axe to grind,' he mused; remembering how the man had cheated the noose by smashing his way out of the stone barn above the Oakley Meads. One gypo, skewered by the bloody awful anvil, and the brother lying dead with his bones smashed-in beneath the splintered doors. 'Brilliant, it was, bloody brilliant.' Surely, all of that would have been revenge enough. No this was personal. Political. That little battler understood how many beans made five.

"Get that bloody alchemist Reynolds here smartly and a cart to carry the master on,'' he yelled.

''Do something bloody useful for once in your life," and dropping to the ground he shoved his arm beneath the iron and yanked hard on the release pin, feeling the tension ease. Instead of jerking free and tearing out a pound or two of minced beef, as was the norm with these beasts, the jaws held on like a mamba. The teeth had probably lodged fast in the bones below the knee for they stubbornly remained where they were; deep in those shattered remnants and the mess of jelly to which they had reduced the calf. This was going to be nasty.

Struggling out of his coat, he nodded to his brother in arms to do likewise and between them they cushioned those razor-sharp teeth and heaved the filthy invention open against the will of the spring-steel, sweating the cold sweat of fear that the other might leave go and let the jaws slam shut again guillotining fingers. The beast's surrender was accompanied by a revolting sucking-sound while Mikey screeched like a harpy as a hosing of his arterial blood sprayed the front ranks of pressing ghouls. Closer than most like the alpha bitch in a pack of hyenas, that little slug Delavier took his fair share of the warm-stuff full in the face and immediately returned the compliment by vomiting on the object of his veneration and on the rescuers around him.

"You gutless bastard," Hastings raged. Drown yourself.

Astor and his rescuers were not the only recipients of Delavier's largess. Mortified by his involuntary and unfortunate ejaculation, he shared the remainder of his puke equably among the ghouls as he whirled away; so that between blood and vomit; most paid a high price for their voyeurism.

"I'd pay good money to watch this stuff," growled the mameluke, grinning and Hastings; temporarily vulnerable, allowed himself a nod of the head. Even as he spoke the ballsy servant had whipped off his belt and was fashioning a tourniquet to stop the haemorrhage.

''Gimme your cigarrellos.'' the man demanded, and initially at a loss, Hastings retrieved his silver case and having pocketed its contents, rammed in the slim silver container beneath the belt, trapping the artery against the bone. With each twisting of the leather the blood-flow lessened then finally stopped.

"If this thing bites again, we're history. It's not locked open." It was true; Astor's huge, immovable bulk still lay within the jaws and every move could cost his rescuers a limb; if not their lives. The Mameluke snapped the handle of a yard-brush and used a piece of it for leverage. Wedging the bit of wood securely with infinite care, he let go. It held. Hastings cleared his eyes of blood and puke with his shirt sleeve and glowered at the army of servants who had been gathering at the end of the path. There were enough of the ninnies there to eat the man, let alone lift him.

"Get a holt of him anywhere you can and don't leave go no matter what," bawled the Mamaluke, taking charge as though born to it even before Hastings could so much as arrange his own thoughts. Some among the crowd rushed to obey.

"And watch out where you put your sodding feet, or you'll be screamin' too. 'The man was a wolf in mamaluke's clothing.'

Several interminable minutes passed as the confused, scared and nauseated volunteers who had come just to gawk; not to risk their own skin, sorted themselves out, all of them struggling to get a satisfactory grip on the patient without suffering a similar fate.

"Are you right?" grunted Hastings, and being answered several times in the affirmative, said,

"One, two, three lift." The dozen men involved hoisted the twisting, shrieking victim to hip height, and stumbling and cursing as they tripped over their own feet, the feet of others, and the cursed thorny rose bushes, somehow got their awful burden and their own legs out of the reach of the deathly contraption and along the path to clear ground. A handcart had materialised on which the bloodied and horrified bearers attempted to place their red and slippery patient, an operation during which they twice dropped the man causing agonised shrieks, curses, accusations of blame and copious quantities of sick.

Hastings and his fellow slaughterman meanwhile got well clear of the cursed machine and ripping up a kerb stone smashed it down on the release plate causing the jaws to slam shut like the doors to the ovens of hell.

Shaking bloody hands in mutual respect the brothers-in-arms-and-legs retired to a bench built for midgets, from where they gathered their thoughts and watched the awful procession as it arrived at the portico.

''You just never bloody know what's round the next corner, eh?''

"You never spoke a truer word," the servant laughed without so much as a pretence of sympathy or loyalty; showing strong white teeth, now pink. The man had impressed Hastings to the point where he was moved to take a couple of surviving cigarillos from his ruined coat and give one to this singular individual, he lit his own then loaned his bloodied tinder box.

"How much do ye earn in the big house?" he asked without preamble.

"Coupla bob less than bugger all. But I won't be 'ere long." The reply was candid and refreshingly free of servility.

"Wi' our Betty doin' a bit in the kitchens, we get by for now. Just takin' a bit of a rest on our travels like."

"How'd you like to work with my people, up at the sharp end? You'll make ten times what you make indoors." Hastings never took his eyes off Michael Astor's progress as he questioned the man. That soft penis Delavier was skipping alongside the master, holding Mikey's hand in the fashion of a mother trying to comfort a sick child. He wondered seriously just how suspicious of him, if at all, that little weasel was. If the obsequious bastard suspected disloyalty in anyone; absolutely anyone at all, there was no force on earth that would prevent him from relaying his concerns to his beloved master. It would need only a drop of poison in Mikes ear for his employer and great friend to turn on him like a ravenous dog, and send him down the road, barefoot, bleeding, and penniless, and goodbye to this best of all billets. He had been stupid enough to drop his guard when he had found Mikey in that trap, flapping around like salmon in a net with the butler watching him like a hawk. The decision was made. He would draw a blade through the man's throat. Returning to the present, Hastings found his fellow rescuer scrutinising him candidly.

"I knows you; you're that fella what does the dirty work for our pal over there." The servant nodded at the recumbent Astor's courtage. Hastings was not used to being addressed in such an offhand fashion but decided that this was not the moment in which to discipline his potential protege.

"Can you ride?" he asked and received a simple nod in reply.

"Shoot?" Another nod.

"Are you up to squeezing answers out of a body?"

Without saying a word, the blood-soaked stranger blew a long plume of smoky affirmation, with as little concern as if he had been asked whether he would like a drink. The man's confidence and self-assurance were cornerstone solid. In this character, there was a complete absence of the overt bravado and extravagant claims that were the hallmark of lesser men.

"What's your name?" Hastings made no attempt to shake hands.

"Seed. Kane Seed." The man spat-out Astor's blood that had run down on to his lips.

"Get cleaned up and come to my cottage, Seed. We're going for a ride."

He would, he decided, ride to Windward Palace and inform Bismark of the tragedy that had overtaken his son; that would be the right thing to do. The journey would kill two birds with one stone by also allowing him to discover whether Seed's cock-sure opinion of himself was merited. He always had a place in Mike's regiment of retainers for a good man who was as cool under fire as this one promised to be.

Lord Bismark Astor was, 'Not at home. Due to the disappointment to which he had subjected Field Marshal Cornwallis by allowing the *Glorious* to be purloined from under his nose the supreme commander and his regiment had been required to travel on to Weymouth, where other ships were available for the Atlantic crossing. In the light of this, Bismark Astor had not only voted Charles Cornwallis the luxury of one of his new covered carriages he had accompanied the Field Marshall on his journey, in the hope that he might be of some assistance to those risking their lives for king and country. They were revolting, you know. Those Americans.'

Hastings had never heard such a wagonload of horse shit. Bismark loathed Cornwallis like the plague.

"We're going to Weymouth," he informed Seed as he remounted, and the two men rode on to that busy port, arriving in the early evening to discover Astor at the Bull, the only building with soldiers on guard outside. To the annoyance of its regulars and its guests who had been unceremoniously ejected, the old boy had commandeered the inn exclusively for himself, Cornwallis and the High Command. Hastings relayed the news of the awful fate that had overtaken Michael as considerately as he knew how, fully expecting the father to rush home to the son's side, but the man barely reacted. He was more interested in the advantage which accrued to himself through Hastings' availability during the period of his son's infirmity. Clearly Michael's insane outburst at the scene of the arson had driven a very deep wedge between father and son. With a modicum of manipulation, that wedge could be put to good use in the service of himself. It was a rare breeze that blew no one some good, after all.

"You must come with me to Boston," Bismark announced peremptorily," your master will have no need of you in his present circumstances but I shall. I have business to attend to beyond the puddle. We shall stay for a six month," he added reassuringly, as though Hastings had a choice in the matter.

"In the light of the troubles over there, I shall require a good man. We sail in the morning. Bring one or two stalwarts, if there are any with you." As he talked, Astor scribbled out a note which he sealed with wax and imprinted with a ring.

"Make yourself comfortable aboard the *Bellerophon*." He pressed a gold coin and the note into Hastings' waistcoat pocket and dismissed him with a flick of his manicured fingers.

Emerging from the inn Hastings discovered that Seed and the enormously valuable horses were gone. Not that he gave a damn. Astor was robbing him of his woman.

Bismark had spent a very pleasant evening in the company of his military acquaintances and retired feeling particularly smug. He had not intended travelling to America within the foreseeable future, let alone on the following morning. A bit of ingratiating was as far as ever he meant to go; but the talk at dinner had been all about the construction of a deep-water port at Yorktown in the colonies, which would facilitate the re-supply of British troops from the sea. The development was to be so deep and so wide, that one-hundred-gun, ships of the line would be able to bring in and take out, thousands of soldiers and hundreds of tons of stores according to the needs of the garrisons. A secondary advantage, but no less important was that the gun platforms could, by their ability to approach so close to the town, lend their massive firepower to that of the army, should the place ever be under attack, or even siege, by the great unwashed. Ever the businessman attuned to the opportunity to make a profit; Bismark had declared his intense interest in the project. 'As everyone was probably aware, he was at that very moment, advancing the science of deep-water ports only fifty miles distant at Minster. Father, son and their engineers had already accumulated a wealth of knowledge in respect of the problems which these vast undertakings presented; and in their resolution.'

Quite naturally, Cornwallis and his chums, who knew nothing of such things, had seized upon this opportunity to avail themselves of his expertise in such matters, and after much persuasion, Astor had graciously acceded to the militaries' wishes and joined the expedition. He had been at pains to point out, that such knowledge did not come cheaply, and he would require evidence in writing of the British government's willingness to meet his fees.

CHAPTER 31: The Wild Rose

"I shall have to cut just below the knee; tib and fib are both shattered, as you can see. It will require some nice, clean cuts in order to tidy things up a bit old chap, so be ready with the clamps, what? This loose flesh too; beyond repair, full of bone fragments.'' Surgeon Reynolds shoved around a handful of Michael Astor's minced calf as though it were tripe on a butcher's block. Doctor Hall, a similarly eminent surgeon who was assisting for the day, nodded his large red dome knowledgeably, and excavated his left nostril of some dry snot which had been irritating him.

"Were he mine, I would follow exactly the same course of action," he concurred, while examining the filth which had stuck beneath his fingernail.

"When the time comes for the wooden leg, the bounder will have the advantage of a freely moving knee joint; it'll make stamping on people so much easier for him. What?" Hall had repeated Reynolds,' 'What?' affectation, 'one of the King's own,' simply to alienate the senior man.

Aiming for the patient, Hall flicked his snot across the room. He had no need to conceal his loathing of the troll on the table, Astor was oblivious to everything due to the stuff that Reynolds had poured into him; in addition to which; he, Hall, had personally exhibited the foresight to banish that obsequious tittle-tattle of a manservant Delavier, to the gardens. If the fawning little spy was going to puke, he could bloody well do it elsewhere. Bad enough to save the life of a murderous, sadistic snake in the grass, but to sniff puke while he was about it was beyond the Pale, 'wherever that might be.' Hall considered old Reynolds surreptitiously as the surgeon busied himself tidying-up the mess and tossing little portions of 'ravioli' on to the floor, where his cats leapt upon them.

The old alchemist had made some very significant advancement or other with the poppy; the 'ever-generous 'Papaver Somniferum,' and the resultant liquid was as effective as a kick in the cranium from a clydesdale. He would have to get the secret out of the old boy, one way or t'other. Hall shoved his crotch hard up against the table in order to get some leverage and pulled back the jerking flesh just below the knee so that the splintered bones protruded.

"There you go, old chap," he panted with the effort, "I'd use a… rip saw… if I were… you." He released his grip in order to shove a cat off the patient's chest.

"Perhaps it's just as well, in that case, that you are not me," responded Reynolds; quite miffed that Hall had rushed in where fools would fear to tread and taking up his favourite saw which famously boasted thirty teeth to the inch, rather than the rip saw's ten, sawed off neatly, the remnants of Michael Astor's lower leg bones. Reynolds' fastidious approach did not extend so far as to necessitate the cleaning of his instruments between operations. All of those thirty-teeth-to-the-inch were encrusted with the dried blood of Lord Lambeth who in a drunken stupor had collapsed on his own driveway one night and had his legs minced by a coach and six.

"Big stitches for the officers," laughed Hall, as the tying-off of the blood vessels was accomplished and proceeded to close as though it were the parson's nose of a Sunday turkey on which he was operating. Reynolds resolved to never again work with the unrepentant charlatan.

Michael Astor struggled desperately through the sulphurous, ever-hotter oil of the

Styx, shoving similarly damned and drowning criminals beneath the bubbling surface as they clutched at him, wild-eyed and ferocious in their terror.

On the distant bank, for which he strove so determinedly, black cloaked spectres of bone and rotting flesh wielded their scarlet scythes among the evidence of their industry; so numerous now that the shore was composed not of rock, but of corpses stacked so high, that their blood ran in streams to stain the seas incarnadine.

And yet he struggled on; biting and gouging; rabid in the service of self-preservation, till at last, his feet and knees came into blistering contact with the lava-hot rock of the shore, still he persevered, for the land meant breath and life, while the sea meant certain death and therefore Hell.

His feet first seared, proceeded to smoulder, then burst into flame; he was cooking alive even as he struggled to mount the rose-red banks of volcanic lava atop of which were the waiting slaves of Satan.

He woke.

A coach! He had sent a coach for her; could it be true? Was it a cruel jest? Susannah Wedgewood hesitated, though the door of the marvellous vehicle was held open obviously for herself by a smiling man in pink and blue, who had just now placed on the ground a divine Pekingese of a stool, to boost her up to the steps.

"Allow me, ma'am," the perfectly exquisite servant begged, and offered to assist her. Susannah could not help but notice that the hand which he extended to her was held at shoulder height, and in such a configuration that she had no recourse but to place her fingertips daintily, within the circle of his white glove, thus avoiding the need to hold a servant's hand.

Only when Susannah was seated comfortably did the man's complete attention remove from her. He kennelled the Pekingese under the seat and with a bow of the head, closed the door securely. Eight colourfully uniformed men, a magnificent coach, and ten horses; it was all too wonderful and unimaginable to be true. Her lover-to-be had sent eight men, a coach and ten horses, to bring her to him. Even so, she would have preferred by far, to have been met by him alone. He had preserved her, while condemning the rest, yet he was not here to meet her. She was torn.

Her poor neighbours. Goodness knew what would become of them; never-the-less it was all so very new, grand and exciting, so utterly delightful, for herself.

Somewhere along the course of her journey to the new world, she became aware that her surroundings had changed; the patchwork of dark cow pastures, and fields of mud with their regiments of vegetables drawn up in serried ranks, interspersed with those scruffy places left to lie fallow, had somewhere given way to a rolling ocean of grass populated by regal oaks, under whose dark, spreading sails amorphous herds of deer floated, resting vigilantly. Fences gave way to berms which no animal could negotiate, while tracks consisting of a series of puddles became smooth paths of pebbles, autumnal in the moonlight. Wonderfully contrived vistas lay on every hand with unsuspected lakes glimmering amid the trees and the improbable rise and fall of the land, incongruous temples, follies and statues kept her in awe.

 A brilliant confection illuminated from within filled her avid vision. Could that spreading grandeur be a single house, and was this unimaginable magnificence the home where she was to be installed? A million candles must have been lit to welcome her, for the divine residence disputed with the heavenly bodies so bright was she, brighter by far than the mellow light of the moon.

The coach drew up adjacent to the wide steps of the main entrance. The carriage door was opened, the Pekingese was positioned, and she was handed down by an enormous man who was nothing if not round. His startling marigold waistcoat adorned with buttons of mother-of-pearl.

"Good evening, Miss Wedgwood." The muscular individual displayed a warm smile which was genuine and welcoming.

"I do hope that our somewhat unorthodox behaviour did not upset you," he rumbled. Susannah now understood the meaning of the word, 'unorthodox.'

"My name is 'Hastings' and this is The Granary, a property of my master Mister Michael Astor, whom I understand you have met. He is detained by business but will join you as soon as is possible. Won't you come inside your new home?"

"Thank you, Hastings.'' she responded regally but ascending the wide and numerous steps which formed the foothills of that sculptured mountain she was surprised to learn that Hastings was master of her private bodyguard. Was her association with Michael Astor somehow a threat to her personal safety?

It did not concern her, that she was dressed in boots, dungarees, a man's jacket and a coat of dirt. She was a stunningly beautiful woman; and as she well knew; in this world, nothing else mattered. The lofty doors; several times taller than she; opened simultaneously as though by magic at her approach emitting a golden glow lately escaped from a foyer which had much in common with the inside of a lantern. The place shone with the light of innumerable flames, reflected endlessly by chandeliers of myriad crystal prisms. Pink-clad footmen bowed her inside where she was greeted by a handsome woman who received her seamlessly from Hasting's tender care, commiserating with her for being driven around the countryside at such an hour.

She was introduced to a dozen of her staff with whom she was expected neither to shake hands nor converse, before being whisked off upstairs to the Azure suite, where a relaxing bath and supper awaited. After all; 'she must be ravenous and exhausted.'

Susannah had never bathed anywhere other than in a river or under a pump, breaking the ice in winter, and certainly never in the presence of other people. At The Granary, she was to be spared such hardships. Clearly, she could not possibly cope with the demands of washing herself and naturally two maids had been appointed to help her. Giggling excitedly, the prettily uniformed friends bowed their charge into the magnificent bathroom, which was as warm as a summer glade, having a fire at either end while candles glowed all around. There the happy lasses proceeded to undress her as though this was the most natural thing in the world. How delightful was her honeyed skin in this light; she would be sure to accidentally let Michael Astor glimpse her like this. Despite her initial misgivings, Susannah suspected that there would be something wonderfully seductive about being pampered all over, and she yielded to it blissfully and completely, with a suddenness which surprised her. Her body was a thing of great beauty, and she was unashamed.

All reluctance dispelled, she could not wait to be immersed to her chin in that welcoming lake of fragrant white lilies, rose petals and bubbles hence at her new friends' urging, the ingénue stepped over the broad, tiled wall of the bath and sank down into the luxury of warm, deep heaven. Millie concentrated on washing and drying her hair, while Susannah, her eyes closing in bliss, surrendered as Jenny caressed her all over with some delectably sensuous thing known as a sponge, which the girls claimed had once been alive and lived in the sea.

Supper followed at a small table, perfectly positioned at one of several French doors open to the pre-dawn starlit sky. There was warm bread with butter and mutton, golden mustard, tomatoes, grapes, cheese and wine; after which there was coffee in a cup so delicate that she hardly dared to lift it, and all of this served by a pleasant young man who stood somehow inconspicuously across the room from her while she ate; never once, she noticed, looking directly at her.

Her bed, when at last she fell into it, was a soft, white cloud to which a sack full of straw could not hold a candle.

When her lover to be did not appear on the first day, Susannah's disappointment was intense, and in her womanly conceit, deeply annoying. Initially she blamed herself imagining that reports of her unsuitability had reached him, and he had thus forsaken her and would never come. Soon she would be deposited on the open road beyond The Granary's gates. The following day she woke in the early afternoon reinvigorated, renewed in spirit and able to accept that Michael would come to her as soon as he could, just as Hastings had informed her initially.

He did not appear on the second day, or the third, with the result that she allowed herself to be absorbed by many of the new things to which she was being exposed, simply by living in these wonderful circumstances. It was then that it occurred to her that his absence was nothing to do with business, he was merely allowing his underlings time in which to groom her. The man was the very devil.

She was not offended. She was an unlettered country girl, utterly devoid of education; probably lacking everything which made a lady, and yet Michael Astor, Lord Michael Astor, was so smitten by her beauty, that he was prepared to go to these lengths to smooth her path into his world. As things stood, she was unable to go riding with him, to take tea, or hold a conversation, and she accepted all of this as the unvarnished truth. Instead of a disappointed Michael Astor, there was a small army of men and women, every one of whom deferred to her, yet had something to teach her, some knowledge or other to impart which would make her more acceptable to her ruthless saviour.

She recalled the footman who had handed her in to the coach which Michael had sent for her and understood that her education had begun at the very moment in which she had dipped her fingertips in the well of the man's white gloves. It soon became abundantly clear that Mister Michael preferred his women to be spotlessly, glowingly clean; with particular attention to those 'important little places' as Jenny had referred to them, as she lingered rather longer than was 'absolutely necessary,' knowledgeable in the use of cutlery, table manners, deportment, riding, singing, small talk, flower arrangements, the arts of being a good hostess, and a dozen other abilities and charms. When a woman rode with Michael Astor, she had to be as brave as a lion, as alluring as the Queen of Sheba, sweet smelling, and side-saddle; there was to be none of this culottes-wearing, straddling of a horse like some loosely educated trollop from one of society's lesser houses.

Susannah resisted not at all; she loved every moment of it. She had always known that she was made for better things than hopping clods but just as she had no idea about her parentage or her early years neither could she imagine by what good fortune the change would come. Her existence to this point had been endured behind a veil of fog, devoid of expectations.

Despite the incalculable; the utterly impossible odds; it had happened; just as she had prayed; the spirits had hurled her into the orbit of her wishing star and his heart had been ravaged by her. If she was assiduous, she told herself, in absorbing all that a lady would know, she might well live for ever in this privileged and so very comfortable fashion. The rogue might even fall in love with her without she threw the bones, or even her use of charms. Would that not be divine?

Men; all of them; thought with their dicks. They were not capable of seeing a well-turned ankle without wanting to fuck its owner, whomever she was. Such was their preoccupation with sex that it was written into the language in such worn-out old notions as 'an angel on his arm and a hore in his bed.' A formula guaranteed to bore both parties into stalagmite inertia. The answer lay in never letting a man see you in any state other than your ravishing best. Never letting him take you for granted, while conversely; never refusing him, an objective which could be achieved by allowing him to believe that such were his skills and subtleties as a lover, that he had seduced you when in fact, you were desperate for him all the while. Your modesty overcome, he would be enabled to have you in the lewdest fashions, in the kitchens, the stables, on the lawn, or in the bath, and think himself the clever one. One had only to accidentally touch a man, anywhere between his feet and his sex-obsessed head for him to drag you into any available refuge and take you in the most delicious fashion before the pair of you hurried back to your guests. With her at his side, Michael Astor's life would become the sexual wonderland that every man on earth lusts after. Only as a sequel to his placing of a ring on her finger.

'Injured and dying?' the knowledge trampled roughshod on her soul. Her heart yearned painfully for him. In her concern, she had threatened her keepers with dismissal if they did not take her to him without delay. It was a power which she wielded only intuitively, but the cruelty worked, and worked well. Within a few hours of issuing the command, she had alighted from her carriage, at the home where her lover lay.

As she mounted the steps of the sublime mansion Susannah reflected on the potency of her spells. The riddle she had cast was intended merely to unhorse Astor, to sap a little of his overflowing arrogance. To gentle the man and leave him more disposed to her womanly wiles. It had worked all too well. Beyond belief. She began to wonder about the nature and extent of Michael's injuries, and to what degree she could benefit by being at his side in his hour of need.

CHAPTER 32: Chesapeake

The strategy of avoiding the sea lanes despite the less favourable winds, had served the little fleet well; so well that they had sailed three thousand miles without so much as a sighting of a British ship of the line, or even an armed merchantman capable of their capture. The Admiral could see no advantage in deviating from that policy for the last leg of the journey, and accordingly agreed with his new Captains that on making their offing from Sint Eustatius they would set a course due north; a course which would keep his ships a full thousand miles off the Georgia coast, a margin that would have shrunk to a mere hundred by the time they reached Virginia and the mouth of the blockaded Chesapeake Bay.

The hair shirt, which is the responsibility for the lives of others, and in which Hooligan had unwittingly dressed himself by rescuing his Gaels, had not inflicted its refined torture on the unschooled Irish marauder until that awful time off Madeira when it seemed that the Scots would all drown. Now however it pinched, bit, scratched and clawed at him minute by minute leaving him no peace and he began to long for a life of ease. He would; he resolved carry his people to safety and then get to Valley Forge. If he survived that little trip he would then give some thought to his gorgeous woman's needs and how he would make a life with her.

Levi Nasser had now made it very clear that the mouth of the Chesapeake and indeed the entire eastern seaboard of America was presently patrolled by Admiralty ships while the bay itself was an English lake with as many as a thousand ships regularly visiting its vast expanse. Soon his vitally important undertaking would undoubtedly be threatened by the limitless power of the British navy. That confrontation occurred much earlier than the inexperienced Hooligan could ever have foretold. Only six days out of Eustatius, with

Spartan far ahead on one of her many destructive scouting runs, and himself cursing Longbottom and Belcher for falling far behind; the safety-spell broke.

"Sail to the nor-east." The call from the masthead woke the men of the Liberty to the reality that they were not the only tricky fellows on the ocean.

"She's English and she's coming around."

This announcement brought loud and sustained rejoicing from the English lordlings and many predictions that it would soon be the unlettered, unwashed uncivilised unappetising Americans who rotted in a cage

"Steady as you go' please boatswain. Gun ports closed. Prisoners, women and children below." Levi Nasser was imperturbable. He turned smiling to his comrade and shouted,

"I do believe that we can capture that little boat Lliam."

The animal trainer left off his pastime feeding volleys of apples to the English and joined the men at the bulwark all of whom were studying that distant enemy very closely indeed.

"Capture the bastards, is it?" he rejoiced, and slapped his new friend on the back with such force that Nasser dropped his superb telescope. It struck the planking once and leapt into the tide.

"Well thank you very much Lliam." Levi stamped away in righteous anger at the needless loss of the superb instrument, watched by the bemused Hooligan who was saddened by the continuing deterioration in that upright gentleman's condition for which he could discern no good reason atall atall. In an effort at restoring relations by obeying orders he straightway grabbed by the neck the first of the prisoners to exit the cage and dragged the squealing piglet none too gently below decks, effectively pulling his chained nancy-boy chums behind him.

With the prisoners safely secured below where they could in no way warn the approaching English of what awaited them, he rushed back on deck and made the arduous climb to the lookouts' eerie.

"Thet fool's goana board us Mr. Lliam," the watchman predicted.

"Look! She's run out her starboards. Sure enough, as Lliam squinted into the distance, he could discern that the English ship had in fact run out only her starboard-side guns. Hanging precariously over the edge of the platform he roared at the tiny, foreshortened figures far below,

"Make yersels scarce, they're away tae board us."

He was of course far too late with his warning; everyone was already in ambush. Following the business with the *Battleaxe* and the discovery that his ship was impervious even to a full broadside, he had sneakily altered Liberty's appearance by having the carpenters strip away the decorative timber around her gun ports, remaking her as an unarmed merchantman.

Obviously confident of meeting no resistance whatsoever from a mere tradesman the captain of the much smaller English patrol-boat approached as though about to tie up in the Pool of London and a mere couple of hours after being sighted, she came alongside.

"Pwepare to be boarded," the order was piped, in the shrill tones of an adolescent, and the accents of England's aristocracy. As the vessels kissed, a dozen grapples were thrown from twenty feet below, binding them; the English *Implacable* with her five small guns run out, and the gigantic *Liberty* with none. Hooligan positioned himself midships next to the barrel of apples in which, he had placed his greenstone club. His breathing had quickened, and his muscles jumped and quivered uncontrollably in anticipation of action. The posey of blue-uniformed officers who preened pretentiously around *Implacable*'s steersman; now did so twenty feet below Hooligan's decks; a contingency which did little for their air of superiority. Hanging like a wart where a chin should reside on this pile of self-importance and privilege was an enforcer who clearly enjoyed his work. The mongrel carried a wooden baton tied to his wrist and the broad welts in the flesh of the English deckhands was proof enough that he liked to use it. The walking corpse owned a fleshy face which was too red, knitted brows that were too dark and slack lips which were too wet. Worse still in the opinion of the men aboard Liberty; he was too 'alive.' Liberty's sailors, who knew his sort well, watched him with loathing.

A child in the uniform of a full Captain of a British man of war, detached itself and proceeded forrard, followed by a couple of officers and the bully boy.

"I am Captain Lieutenant Sebastian Fwobisher Moowhead, of His Majesty's Ship *Impwacable*. You are my pwisoner, sir." This surprising claim by the mezzo soprano, interrupted Hooligan's cogitations. Fwobisher Moowhead had to be at least fifteen years old and weigh-in at not an ounce under six stone, wet through. The delicate eunuch shrieked his pronouncement as though no man in his right mind would object to having his ship commandeered by a precocious child and a coven of pretty uniforms. 'Sure, they were as mad as snakes, these English.' When the grapples were thrown, the cowed English seamen had broken their backs hauling on the lines, until the two ships were locked together in unlovely union; an operation which met with not so much as a peep of protest out of the seven visible seamen on board *Liberty*, all of whom had descended from the rigging, and were now apparently absorbed in checking this, and tightening that. Fifty more crouched in hiding. Uninvited, the cream-faced captain made the long climb to come aboard the American ship, followed by two of his officers and the brass-knuckles.

"I'll take the nasty bastard Angus, then off we go." This stuff came as easily to Hooligan as the guzzling of hard liquor.

"I want that fwag wemoved dyweckly," announced the delicate one, as he descended trepidatiously in his high-heeled shoes on to *Liberty*'s deck, assisted by his second in command.

"What are you cawying?"

"Roight you are, sir," replied Hooligan, obviously more than happy to please.

Putting two fingers to his forehead, he announced ridiculously,

"We're cawying a fookin great heap of artiwawy, powder and shot for the Army of the Continent; so dat dey can shoot the shit outa the loikes o' you." Fwobisher Moorehead looked as though he had been stabbed with a hot bayonet in his yet-to-descend testicles. He drew himself up to his full four-feet-seven and hissing vitriol announced castrato like,

"Tho, twying to widicule your betterth hey." A nasty snarl had twisted the child's milky face.

"Thith, gentleman, ith Mithta Twubshaw, my dithipwinawian," as though every individual within hearing had not figured that one out for himself.

"Mithta Twubshaw doth not like to heaw the Bwitish Admiwalty mocked. Have a care, or I might athk him to dithipwin *you*." Intent on impressing his now smirking masters, Twubshaw closed threateningly to within arm's length of Lliam Shaun Hooligan of County Mayo, grinning through teeth which would grace a graveyard, clearly believing that mere contiguity would have the Irishman shaking in his shoes. When Hooligan displayed not one sign of a quiver and instead, stared down threateningly with unblinking loathing into the boatswain's gin blurred eyes, the sadist's grin faltered, and he left-off his display abruptly.

"We will inthpect your cargo," announced the songbird. Hearing this, boatswain Stewart leapt with alacrity to fling open the door to the gangway so that the victorious British could go below where a traditional Scottish welcome awaited them.

''This way Sur,'' he carolled; saluting smartly as the gentry went through the door, stepping elegantly over its tall threshold. Twubshaw was about to follow his masters when Stewart slammed the door shut and put his back to it as he drew his pistol. The boatswain growled in panic and was raising his weapon when Hooligan said,

''Hey Lavender suck this.''

Slow-witted as he was sadistic 'Twubshaw' turned just in time to glimpse death approaching. The heavy greenstone club-and-axe combined smashed horizontally through the man's face mincing bone, flesh and brains to jelly.

"All hands," yelled Stewart, and instantly the deck was crowded with screaming Scots, who dropped from *Liberty*'s side on to the English deck below, and laid about them with their swords, going first for the officers, and any seaman who put up a fight. There were surprisingly few. Swinging aboard the enemy Hooligan raced below. There would be gunners waiting there to let rip, and he wanted no unnecessary damage to either ship. If the English fired so much as one cannon, his own men would blow *Impwacable* out of the water, and that was a contingency which had to be avoided at all costs. Lliam wanted to add Impwacable to his collection of boats.

The dark and cramped British gun deck was alive with humanity and stank with the sweat of fear. A score of men were serving her guns while waiting expectantly for the order to fire. Powder-monkeys were scuttling about everywhere, some with buckets of gunpowder, some with water but all crying in abject terror of what they knew was coming.

"Hang fire!" he bellowed, not knowing what else to do, and was attacked before the words were out of his mouth. The half-naked Englishman who offered a two-fisted welcome was hard as iron and battered Lliam's torso with punishing blows some of which the brawler managed to absorb on his arms and shoulders. Then something struck him full in the face and he went down on his back like a sack of spuds. As the English pugilist crabbed in with the boot, a flying apparition in tartan hurtled head-first and javelin-like into that warrior's face with a sickening impact and both men dropped to the deck, slithered across its heart of oak and lay still. Trampled by the hooves of a gang of tartan berserkers Lliam was content to lay where he was and let the Scots ran amuck subduing whatever resistance they could find, real or imagined. There being rather more of the latter. It was all over in minutes.

With *Implacable*'s officers caged, alongside those of the *Justice*, and the unlamented Trubshaw absent without leave, Levi Nasser, pertinent as ever, took it upon himself to explain to the subdued English sailors what was happening.

"We are the United States ship, *Liberty*," he began, indicating the huge vessel behind him with a jerk of his head.

"I intend to keep your officers prisoner but put you lot ashore, or at least into your boat in sight of shore. We are off the coast of the Carolinas." The gunners stared back at him in bovine silence. Their expressions habitually inscrutable for reasons of their own safety from the attentions of their sadistic little Captain and the unlamented Twubshaw. Weighing up the rabble carefully, Levi took a gamble and said,

"If any of you are pressed men, and you want yer freedom, you're more than welcome to join us in our fight against The English King, lords, dukes, hanging-judges indentured-servitude and slavery." He could all but hear the thinking going on behind those bland expressions. Sidling forward from the herd, careful to make no quick moves which would get him shot or hammered, one brave and bleeding young man broke out his colours.

"I'm wiv you, mishter," he said extracting a loose tooth with filthy finger and thumb. His boldness opened the flood gates as all but three of the deckhands, perceiving an end to their miserable penal servitude declared themselves for America. The powder monkeys had no reservations whatsoever, they had already run to stand behind the 'people in dresses' of whom they had the vaguest of memories; people who smiled down affectionately and patted the heads of the poor, miserable little creatures.

"We're all pressed men," someone bawled. "A pox on the bastards." As the three remaining obdurate types were hustled away to prison, Nasser made a couple of things clear to the rest.

"Don't think that you can just take the easy way out, yous fellas," he warned them.

"If you side with us in our fight for freedom from Georgie boy and his redcoats, you must stay faithful, if you don't you'll wish you'd gone with those fools. That thwine

Twubthwaw,'' the gale of sudden laughter lightened the mood, ''is dead.'' He was drowned out by the uproar of approbation which this statement engendered.

''And the toffs are my prisoners, so you have nothing to fear from them, but we will still put you ashore if you wish it. You can maybe find loyalists and make your way back to England if that's what you want. It's your choice."

"To the devil with England! Bugger-all but hard graft and empty bellies. I'm with you," said the lad who had made the first move, and his example was followed in ones and twos by his more cautious shipmates. Deeply concerned that this behaviour could conceal the possibility of treachery, Nasser had the English seamen herded aboard Liberty under heavy guard and bunched them up midships where he then displayed their ex-captain Frobisher-Morehead and his chums chained hand and foot for their inspection, at which the badly treated men most of whom had been ripped from their families by press-gangs realised that they 'really were free' and attacked their tormentors with fists and boots intent on getting revenge while they could. It was all that the crew of liberty could do to keep the English 'brass' alive; all of them suffering severe life-threatening injury in the revenge attack.

The confluence of the Atlantic Ocean and the Chesapeake Bay where a billion gallons of pure fresh water dilute daily the brine of the limitless ocean, is a vast area. An expanse which would have required at least a dozen fast men-of-war to blockade effectively; men-of-war which the Admiral-Presiding, was not prepared to commit to that task, as already in place was a seven-thousand-strong British Army stationed on the James River, a tributary of the Bay, who owned an attachment of six cruisers of the Fleet Class. Such a combined force was more than sufficient to take good care of any eventuality on land or sea in this theatre of war Cochrane had declared.

The intelligent and much-decorated Admiral, Inglis Alexander Cochrane, resorted instead to anchoring three gun-platforms equidistant across the bay's entrance along the line seventy-six degrees west of longitude, supported by land-based observation points and long-range guns on both northern and southern spits, a stratagem which offered surveillance of the deeper channels and the ability to 'chase and destroy' across the remainder. The strategy had proven sufficient to deter all but the bravest and most desperate of blockade runners.

With sea-anchors deployed, the massive vessels armed with sixty guns apiece merely held station facing west; thusly relieved of the need to turn and chase their prey. It was an effective ploy and one with which the captains of Fleet Hooligan were well acquainted, having been thoroughly briefed by the admirably fast and ever-busy Spartan who ran the blockade at will.

 Accordingly, for three seemingly endless days and nights Levi Nasser's mastheads spied from behind the horizon on the English sixty-gun Nile, the leviathan which sat at the centre of the English line. The result of which caution was a plan that was nothing short of desperation and should therefore been rejected out of hand.

Visibility in Liberty's grand cabin was rather less than that in heavy fog because while on Sint Eustatius the score of young Scots present had discovered tobacco and insisted on smoking the stuff continuously. Their mood was jovial as friends from the five ships renewed their acquaintance. The entrance of Levi Nasser instantly recognisable due to his white hair changed the mood and there was silence by time the naval officer had climbed onto a chair to address the war-party.

''Gentlemen.'' He began, his voice well-modulated and authoritative,

''On behalf of your clan and of the United States of America I want to thank you for volunteering to undertake this onerous task. This night will be as dark as any this month and so you will go. As you are well-aware gentlemen, between you and your new country lies that British sixty gunner Nile whose arse you can see from the crow's nest.'' The laughter was tainted by introspection.

She weighs possibly two hundred tons and will have a crew in excess of two hundred and sixty men in addition to a company of very hard marines. You in your rowing boat are going to sink her.'' The American had played for a laugh and duly got it.

"Liberty will attempt to run the blockade, but at a league or so short of the enemy she will suffer a change of heart and divert. Behind her she will leave two lighters. Yours and the explosives. With utter silence and extreme caution, you will approach Nile's stern where you will position your little gift close to the rudder under her overhang where any stray sparks will not be seen. The fuses as you know are all under the canvas coverings so there is 'no' possibility of that occurring. Light the fuses and depart eastward to be picked up later. Get blacked up and be ready; we will arrive at the drop point in a couple of hours. That's all.''

This was more like it; the volunteers laughed and joked in their youthful impetuosity punching each other playfully at the promise of striking the unsuspecting brits. The three endless days spent spying from behind the horizon had lasted aeons in their fevered, action-starved minds.

Two murderous hours of intense darkness on a boisterous sea made memorable by sinew-stretching muscle-burning torture at the oars disabused the youths of the notion that this was something of a jaunt. At every stroke the slackening tow rope would come up tight, almost jerking shoulders from their sockets causing each desperate man to pray silently that he would not be the one to fail his shipmates by throwing in the towel. The mountainous stern of the 'Nile,' awash with dark malevolence and incalculable power was quite suddenly an overwhelming presence causing the commandos to register their own heartbeats as the beating of drums, the drip of water from the oars as the crashing of breakers on a rocky shore. Complete silence was an imperative. Nile remained dark and somnolent though vigilant sentries, lookouts and marines certainly hung in her rigging and patrolled her decks all of them terrified of falling asleep on duty; not for nothing did the abbreviation HMS mean 'his majesty's sadists.' Ten strokes of the cat-of-nine tails; a typical reward for such a crime was a death sentence far worse than the instant nature of the rope. At ten yards from the barn door that was Nile's gigantic two-foot-thick rudder the oars were shipped without a sound and the two open boats glided in under the cliff-face of the enemy. Reassured by the loud slapping of the water against the overpowering majesty of the hull the six anointed swimmers slipped over the side into the dark ocean to prevent noisy contact between their little boats and that malevolent beast.

In the human being, cerebral reaction waits upon the senses and even, on occasion, the emotions, thus it was that when Satan the malicious chose to rip away the blue cloak of night in whose comforting folds the bulk of Scottish hopes reposed, the doomed youths stared upwards in awe at the beauty of a false dawn in which unnaturally large diamond stars shone on a ground composed of pastels of pink through the blues of old bruises. They heard all-too-late the shrieking agony of the dragons which raced from the Nile's deck into the pitiless sky to paint the night so; and watched appalled and mesmerised as a cauldron of liquid fire poured down on them; beautiful and murderous. Twenty young men instantly became tormented human torches, their screams curtailed agonisingly by inhaled tongues of flame.

John Glasgow, a crippled youth who had deemed his contribution thus far in the fight for freedom to be inadequate had volunteered for this jaunt accordingly. Aflame, shrieking and dying in an agony which was incomprehensible this side of the grave he leapt overboard and into the explosives. His detonation of the mountain of combustibles caused a cataclysm of magma-hot expansion in which the surface of the ocean boiled instantly. Nile's stern was smashed inward, howling in splinters through the great-cabins and officers' quarters as far as the gun-decks, and the flames which were dragged searingly through those spaces engulfed everything and everyone in their horrid grasp, incinerating hundreds of men in an instant.

Liberty and Justice arrived directly to pour cannon fire into the floating pyre, staying on station suicidally late, then fleeing under full sale only to have those sails shredded by the power of the explosion which sank Nile with all hands when the conflagration found her powder store.

This culling of the very flower of the clan's manhood was a scourge which ripped open the crusting scars of Ballachulish, dragging the bereaved clan beneath the surface of the Acheron so that they still moved, breathed conversed; and yet were drowned by such a loss. Thus it was that the immigrants displayed a dearth of interest or enthusiasm for their arrival in the new lands, considering the rising sun to be an intrusion on their grief, the happy breeze disrespectful, and the uncaring hills of Virginia, heartless.

The vast Chesapeake was cluttered with innumerable craft, their owners going about their business utterly oblivious it seemed to the war which was raging around them. It was all too painful to bear. There were fishing boats with the sails of a dhow, dredgers distinctive due to their enormously extended beams and triangular sails, coasters laden with bricks and timber, the snows of private owners travelling around the country on business, and brigs laden with timber tobacco, cattle, leather, and manufactures of every denomination. Veritable regattas of boats of the home-made variety were being sailed at breakneck speeds between the hulls of death, their owners laughing in delight at their own mastery of wind and wave; many of these proudly and inexplicably displaying the deeply loathed flag of union.

Nasser was unconcerned, for none of these civilian vessels presented an imminent threat other than that of reporting his fleet's position to the British military, an operation which would consume days. Even so, he planned to transit the waterway by finding sanctuary during daylight in one or other of the numberless inlets or rivers which formed Chesapeake's convoluted coastline and to race north during the hours of darkness for it would not do to fall at the last hurdle. Only two hundred nautical miles now separated the fleet from its destination. About to give the order to tack to the north in search of such an inlet a call had him peering upwards to where the lookout pointed to the north.

''Enemy ships.''

A breathless child approached.

''Mr Levi, three gunships heading this way.

Ignoring Hooligan's advice to, 'shoot shit out of them, Nasser thanked his friend sincerely for his valuable input and climbed to the masthead.

''What have we got Luke?'' he enquired and was handed a superb telescope of French manufacture and a nod to the north in reply. At a very long distance three gigantic men-of-war were wallowing southwards directly towards his present position. Were he to head north he would confront the hostiles within hours and to detour around them would add a full day to the journey.

To the east lay the wide mouth of the James River on whose banks he knew, a British army of seven thousand men supported by a squadron of Admiralty frigates lay just thirty miles upstream.

'Should he race north and perhaps be spotted by those destroyers or continue on his easterly course and hide in the James River with all of the risks which that course of action entailed.' Neither option being particularly attractive he held his easterly bearing but beat 'to quarters' even so.

Macbeth, and a gang of off-duty sailors deeply asleep in coils of rope were awoken by a clamour of infuriated protest from the throats of crowds of people who now vented their horror and anger at the ships side. Liverpool was at anchor, long musket-shot from an extensive raft on which.

''Astor!'' Aboard that raft Bismark Astor much to the amusement of his cronies was thrashing a blood painted servant with the edge of an epee, each scarlet-spraying brush stroke opening a great gash in the man's ploughed flesh and eliciting screams of hellish agony.

"Bastart! A boat! Lower a fucking boat!" Clambering over the side the Scot dropped fifteen feet into a lighter already overloaded with incandescent seekers after revenge who 'got away,' with precision and pulled fit to break the oars. But they were too late. Driven overboard the tortured black was drowning; his persecutors throwing little bits of wood for him to clutch and falling-abought laughing as the poor, hopeless slave obliged.

An eon of almost silent frustration dragged passed in the concentrated effort of advancing the attack causing the lighter to smash into heavy contact with the enemy; a collision which flung the men at the bows aboard the raft amid a sudden cacophony of hate. Silk clad effeminates were grabbed by balls and hair, raised aloft and hurled into the tide while the remainder of the flock fled in terror intent on extending by a few seconds their sojourn in this world; there being no place of safety in which they could hide. Some in their terror committed suicide by leaping into the ocean. The remainder should have followed that example. The Scots cut, stabbed, strangled, booted, slashed and garrotted their way through the flock until nothing but blood-soaked death lay at their feet.

Standing at the stern of the lighter the frustrated Macbeth arrived late at the festivities and had to rip Astor from the clutches of a comrade's strangle hold. Dragging the filthy sadistic bastard back to the lighter he flung it headlong aboard, happily causing serious injury if the swine's screeching was to signify

"Oh my Sainted!"

Whatever it was that the raiders saw through the now redundant theodolites it caused them to charge back to the lighter and pull upstream to where fleet Hooligan now lay anchored in line astern.

Row-upon-row of shivering, terrified slaves half-standing, half-drowning, out of their depth and clutching at life, were holding as vertically as possible tall poles of red and white.

Fleet Hooligan's boats were already in action ripping the tortured souls from the water and ferrying them to the motherships despite volley-fire from the banks where the water-shy overseers raged.

Summoning up what little courage they possessed three of the misanthropes put to sea in the smallest imaginable rowing boat in a desperate effort to avenge this daylight robbery and thereby keep their jobs. Clearly devoid of the skills involved in rowing their own boat these terrified throwbacks to a time even darker than their own existence, approached the offending vessels by a serpentine course which saw them tack in almost every direction made available to them by a compass. By sheer trial, much error and the passage of an hour they closed eventually on a large lighter already half full of their slaves and the thieves who were stealing them.

The culprits, both male and female were wearing dresses! Unhappily for the weaponised trio of seated citizens whose trade lay in refined cruelty, torture, maiming, branding and rape they had approached the boat in which Trewin Copplestone was a member of the crew. The evangelists for righteousness voiced their threats and curses while gripping on tightly with every terrifying lilt, dip and sway that their tiny craft subjected them to; behaviour which said much about their characters. Copplestone, his boys and girls were led to believe that if they did not want to be shot where they sat they must follow the intrepid trio to the banks where they would be jailed, then provided a fair trial before being hung.

Clearly concerned for the safety of his visitors the soldier relinquished his oar and standing not-at-all tall enquired solicitously as to whether the charming rogues could swim. Caring insufficiently to wait for their reply he then swung up his sporting shotgun and blasted the hull and various body parts out of the boat. The fear crazed Neanderthals drowned as they had lived, each one trying to extend his own disgusting existence incrementally by climbing on to and murdering his erstwhile colleagues. It was all very ugly and thankfully brief.

Heartened by this evidence of a better sort of white man the poor slaves still in the water more-readily accepted the proffered help and dragged themselves energetically over the gunnels of the rescue boats and the operation continued to completion leaving not one soul behind despite the uproar of enraged whites and volley-fire still emanating from the shore.

As night imposed its presence the fleet was preparing to weigh anchor when several of the men who had been pulled from the water asked to be rowed back to land; they had wives and children whom they would not leave. It was a sad time for all involved but the respect which those men were accorded due to their devotion and commitment to their families was immeasurable. Those brave, loyal and loving men returned to a purgatory, from which, only death would liberate them.

That night, aboard the fleet, the four score of rescued men enjoyed warm delicious and sufficient food, compassion and equality, possibly for the very first time in their tragic lives.

Two days of unseasonal fog followed during which the Africans moved in limitless fascination around the vessels, intrigued by every aspect of their design and workings. Being fieldhands most of them knew not one word of English, but with sign language, rapid sketches and facial expression the divide was bridged to everyone's reasonable satisfaction. With willing help from the Scottish women, the newcomers made kilts and jerkins of their blankets and wore these garments with great pride while letting themselves be led around the decks by children who had discovered the novelty of adults who were prepared to engage with them; in addition to which, the blacks refrained from smacking them around the head in the manner of the whites.

Dawn of the prophesized and long-awaited day found the fleet at anchor in an inlet of truly stunning beauty many miles from the main body of water and hence discovery, amid the rolling grassland, forests and hills of the promised land. Stepping ashore the excited immigrants were amused at the sight of the English prisoners being exercised by the stick-wielding Africans. Cooking fires were being lit parallel to the mile-long cordon of ships and the morning air was redolent of all manner of food for which queues of hungry, happy adventurers were already beginning to form. Hooligan watched all of this from the cross-trees of the liberty one hundred and fifty feet above the water. He was planning a monument for those poor souls who had been lost since leaving Scotland; a burden which weighed heavily on him.

Deeply satisfied at having delivered his people to a new life in this beautiful place he was already preparing to embark on his next expedition; the vital task of finding the Army of the Continent at Valley Forge and bringing them the news of the vast amounts of war materials that reposed in his ships. His understanding was that the place sat hundreds of miles northwards, lost in a wilderness populated by scalp hunters, redcoats, wolves and grizzly bears. He would have to leave his adored woman in the safety provided by the clan and the thought that this day might be his last with her weighed heavily on him. 'Life was easier sleeping under a bush sure.'

FIN

This Septic Isle

Natural justice asserts that Britain; all of it, should belong to the British; but the ravenous three headed dog Cerberus, which has ever savaged the flesh of the people, long ago extinguished that delightful condition.

The drooling creatures three identities; Royalty, Religion and Democracy swallowed that tasty morsel many years ago.